Smiler

BOOKS BY

VICTOR CANNING

Mr. Finchley Discovers His England
Mr. Finchley Goes to Paris
Mr. Finchley Takes the Road
Polycarp's Progress
Fly Away Paul
Matthew Silverman
Fountain Inn
Everyman's England (travel)
Green Battlefield
Panthers' Moon
The Chasm
The Golden Salamander
A Forest of Eyes
The House of the Seven Flies
Venetian Bird
The Man from the "Turkish Slave"
Castle Minerva
His Bones Are Coral
The Hidden Face
The Manasco Road
The Dragon Tree
Young Man on a Bicycle (and other stories)
The Burning Eye
A Delivery of Furies
Black Flamingo
Delay on Turtle (and other stories)
The Limbo Line
The Scorpio Letters
The Whip Hand
Doubled in Diamonds
The Python Project
The Melting Man
Queen's Pawn
The Great Affair
Firecrest
The Rainbird Pattern
The Finger of Saturn
The Runaways
Flight of the Grey Goose
The Painted Tent
The Mask of Memory

VICTOR CANNING

Smiler

A trilogy

The Runaways

Flight of the Grey Goose

The Painted Tent

HEINEMANN : LONDON

William Heinemann Ltd
15 Queen Street, Mayfair, London W1X 8BE

LONDON   MELBOURNE   TORONTO
JOHANNESBURG   AUCKLAND

The Runaways first published in Great Britain 1972
© Copyright by Victor Canning 1971

Flight of the Grey Goose first published 1973
© Victor Canning 1973

The Painted Tent first published 1974
© Victor Canning 1974

Smiler trilogy first published in one volume 1975
© Victor Canning 1971, 1973, 1974

SBN: 434 10787 5

Text set in 11/11½pt Photon Imprint, printed by photolithography,
and bound in Great Britain at The Pitman Press, Bath

Contents

The Runaways

1

Lightning Strikes Twice

It had been raining all night, and all the morning; raining hard all over Dorset, Wiltshire and Hampshire. It was a cold February rain, filling the ditches, swelling the rivers, and stripping the few dead leaves that still clung to the trees. It made quagmires of the cow treads at field gates, spouted over blocked gutters, and flooded the low-lying roads so that passing cars sent up bow waves of spray and soaked unlucky passers-by. Now, at half-past eleven precisely, as Smiler was being driven in a police car under the escort of two burly patrol men, the father and mother of a thunder and lightning storm was brewing overhead. At first it was a few little murmurs, slowly rising to a full-scale roll and rumble of heavy thunder. Suddenly there came a great stabbing, downward sword thrust of lightning that turned the whole world into a blue and yellow dazzle of light.

Smiler jumped in his seat and cried, "Blimey!"

The policeman alongside him smiled. He said, "Nothing to be scared of, son. Just think – if we hadn't picked you up, you'd be out in it soaked even more." He glanced at Smiler's pile of wet clothes on the floor of the car and then at the blanket-wrapped figure.

It was a red, yellow and green striped blanket and all that could be seen of Smiler was his head sticking out of the top, his fair hair still wet. Smiler – real name Samuel Miles – was fifteen years and five months old. He had escaped two weeks before from an approved school, and had been picked up that morning by the police. He had been caught because of a tip from a farmer in whose barn he had been hiding (and whose hens' eggs he had been eating, sucking them raw).

Smiler wasn't scared. The lighting had just made him jump, that was all. It took quite a lot to make Smiler scared. Smiler could look after himself. He was tallish and well-built with a friendly, squarish face, a pressed-in smudge of a nose, and a pair of angelic blue eyes that, when he put on his special smile, made him look as though butter wouldn't melt in his mouth. But if Smiler didn't scare easily there were also a lot of things Smiler didn't like.

Smiler didn't like school, for instance. Particularly he didn't like ap-

proved school and he had run away from it after exactly thirteen days'
and four hours' residence. Smiler didn't care for the country either – not
because it scared him or he felt out of place there (Smiler could always
make himself at home in new surroundings). He just preferred towns
and cities where there were more opportunities for picking up the odds
and ends of things that made living tolerable.

After all, when you were mostly on your own, you had to eat and
drink, have a bit of money in your pocket and be able to go to the cinema
now and then and treat yourself to a Coke in a café when you felt like
company.

Most of all, he didn't like the long periods when his father went off to
sea. Then, instead of living in lodgings with his father and having a
wonderful time, he was always dumped with Sister Ethel and her husband, Albert. Smiler didn't like living with his married sister and her
husband. Not because he didn't like them. They were all right except
when they were fussy about their house and their furniture and
grumbled because his hands always marked the paintwork. Also, Smiler
didn't like being idle. He liked doing things. He liked to be busy. The
trouble was that people made such a fuss about some of the things he
did. . . . Well, like pinching a bottle of milk from a doorstep if he was
thirsty, or nicking a comic book from a shop if he felt like reading.

The driver, eyeing Smiler's reflection in the interior mirror, grinned
and said, "You look like a red Indian in that blanket. Little Chief Sitting
Bull."

At that moment, two hundred yards ahead of the car, a streak of lightning flared earthwards. It seared itself into the top branches of a tree at
the roadside, wreathed its way down the trunk and hit the ground with a
crack that made the whole earth shake. A great branch was split from
the top of the tree and crashed across the road, blocking it. The police
car braked and skidded to a halt twenty yards from the obstruction. A
small car coming in the opposite direction was not so lucky. The branch
fell a few yards in front of the car. The driver braked hard and the car
slewed sideways into the block.

The two policemen, alert as all good policemen should be in an
emergency, jumped out of the patrol car and dashed through the rain to
give assistance to the driver of the other car who, as a matter of fact, was
more shaken and shocked than injured. It took the two policemen a good
three or four minutes to climb over the obstruction and to assure
themselves that the driver was in no great distress. It took the driver of
the patrol car another few minutes to get back to the car so that he could
send out a call to headquarters reporting the road blockage and sum-
moning assistance.

As he sent out the radio call, he knew that the moment he had finished he would have to add another — reporting the escape again from custody of one Samuel Miles. In the car mirror as he sent his report the policeman could see the back seat. The only evidence that Smiler had ever sat there was a damp patch on the leather. Smiler had gone, his pile of clothes had gone, and so had the blanket!

Smiler at that moment was three hundred yards away running barefooted along the side of a ploughed field, pelting up the slight slope to a crest of woodland which he could just glimpse through the driving sheets of rain. He ran holding his hands round the tucked up edges of the blanket, his naked legs and thighs mud and rain splattered. All his clothes and his shoes were gathered in front of him in the blanket.

As Smiler kept running he was smiling to himself because he was free. This time — because there were some lessons he only had to be given once to remember — he meant to stay free. Just what he would do with his freedom he didn't know — except that he was going to enjoy it until his father got back from sea. When his father returned he knew he would quickly clear up the whole mess and misunderstanding that had sent him off to reform school. And heaven alone knew where his father was at this moment, somewhere on the high seas, cooking away for the crew or maybe giving them a tune from his mouth-organ on the after-deck.

As Smiler disappeared into the rain-shrouded countryside, the second policeman returned to the car, took one look at the back seat and said, "He's hopped it!"

"Gone," said the other. "With our blanket. Do we go after him?"

"In this weather? And with this mess on the road? Not likely. Anyway, he won't get far when the call goes out for him." The policeman grinned and said jokingly, "Wanted, Little Chief Sitting Bull. Height five feet two inches, fair-haired, blue-eyed, age fifteen plus, wearing a red, green and yellow blanket — or wet blue jeans, grey shirt and brown jacket. Approach with caution. This man is dangerous." He paused, thought for a moment, and added, "I forgot. Addition to description. Wanted person's face is heavily freckled."

"Funny thing," said the other, "you don't often see boys with such freckled faces these days, do you? They seem to have gone out of fashion or something."

As the two policemen went back to the road block to try and clear it, Smiler reached the cover of the woods at the top of the hill. He crashed into the undergrowth like a rocket and put up a couple of pheasants that flew away, honking and screeching with alarm. The noise so startled Smiler that he slipped and fell flat on his face. Because of the effort of his clumsy running and the loss of the little wind he had left from the fall, he lay there panting like a stranded fish. For the few moments while he rested, getting his breath back, Smiler gave himself a talking-to. He was a great one for talking to himself in moments of crisis. He lectured himself now, face close to the wet, leaf-littered ground.

"Samuel M.," he said (Smiler was other people's name for him and he didn't care much for it. It was a silly kind of punning joke on his name. He preferred Samuel M. because that was what his father called him), "you got to think this out. You're wet and muddy and half naked. Your clothes is all soaked and your belly's rumbling a bit now and then because all you've had in the last two days is them eggs just raw and nothing to write home about. You are wanted by the police. Like a real criminal, which you aren't. It was never you that took the old lady's handbag. Thing Number One, then. Them cops down there won't follow you, not in this weather with that accident to look after. Good. Thing Number Two. You got to get warmed up, fed, and into hiding. You got to look for a safe and sheltered anchorage where you can get everything stowed shipshape and work out a new course. And, Thing Number Three is, you'd better get them wet clothes on. Just wearing a coloured blanket is going to make you stand out like a catherine wheel against a tarred fence."

So Smiler got to his feet. Stark naked under the leaden, rain-deluging sky, he began to pull on his wet blue jeans. As he struggled with them, hissing with effort through his teeth at their awkwardness, there was a massive bellow of thunder from away to the west and the whole sky was lit with another blaze of lightning, slashing earthwards. This time, though Smiler could not know it, the lightning was doing exactly the same for another prisoner as the previous bolt from the blue had done for him.

*   *   *

Ten miles away, northwest of the wood in which Smiler was dressing and about four miles a little southwest of the Wiltshire town of Warminster, was the large country estate and ancestral home of the Marquis of Bath. The mansion was called Longleat House and the estates around it Longleat Park. Part of the park had been turned into a wild animal reserve. Every day of the year cars rolled into Longleat Park bringing tourists to see the treasures of the beautiful Longleat House and also to see the Lions of Longleat and the other animals which were kept in huge, penned-in stretches of the parkland. Every day cars moved around the road which twisted and twined through the high-fenced animal enclosures.

The road ran first through the East African section which held giraffes, zebras, ostriches, and antelopes; and then on through the monkey jungle with its baboons that often cadged free rides on top of the cars; and so into the lion reserve where the kings of beasts sometimes lay lazily across the roadway refusing to move out of the path of the cars until the mood took them. Finally the car procession entered the cheetah area.

Today because it was February, and a storm- and rain-filled day, there were no more than three or four cars in the whole animal reserve. At this moment there was none in the cheetah section. In fact, there were few animals out in the enclosures either. They no more liked the rain and the storm than human beings. The baboons were in their dugouts and the lions in their wooden pens or stretched out on the sheltered verandahs of their huts. In the cheetah reserve all the cheetahs were under shelter in their huts – all, except one.

This cheetah was a female. Her name was Yarra. All the cheetahs in the enclosures had names . . . Apollo, Chester, Lotus, Suki, Tina and Schultz. Yarra was a full grown female. She weighed a hundred and thirty pounds. She stood nearly three feet high to her narrow, raking shoulders and from the point of her black nose to the tip of her long tufted tail she measured seven feet and one inch. Yarra was a good-tempered animal. She had been captured as a cub in Africa, brought to Germany and from there to Longleat Park.

She was a magnificent animal. Under the rain the spots on her tawny orange coat were as black as small wet coals. The dark lines of her face maskings, running from inside the eyes down around her muzzle, were boldly drawn charcoal lines. Her throat and underbelly were creamy white, and her eyes tawny gold. As she moved she swung her long tail from side to side, flicking little sprays of rain from the tuft at its end.

When the Cheetah Warden came into the enclosure in his Land-Rover and Yarra felt in the mood she could jump in one easy long-flowing movement to the top of the driving cab. Sometimes, to give the cheetahs exercise, the warden towed a trail rope from the back of the Land-Rover with a piece of meat tied to it for the cheetahs to chase. Even though he accelerated to forty miles an hour Yarra could easily keep up. If he had gone at sixty miles an hour she could have held pace with the car for a while.

Today Yarra was strangely restless. The rain and the thunder and lightning had increased her restlessness. It was not the restlessness that overcame her and the other cheetahs when, from time to time, they marked with their keen sight the movement of guinea fowl, partridge, pheasant or young deer moving on the free slopes of the parkland outside the enclosure. At those times they raced to the wire fence, longing for the freedom of the hunt and the chase, only to turn back and stalk the length of the wire, stubby ears alert, the desire for complete liberty moving hot and strong through their powerful bodies.

Now, something else had made Yarra restless and she did not know what it was. All she knew was that where normally she would have taken shelter from the rain, she now wanted to remain outside, moving up and down the long line of the boundary fence. Up and down, up and down she stalked. The fence was strong and made of two-inch iron mesh. It was over twelve feet high with an inwards overhang at the top, and it was supported on strong wooden poles with here and there a large concrete support to give added strength. Inside the outer fence, a few feet from it, was another fence, about four feet high. Yarra and any of the other cheetahs could have jumped this inner fence easily, but they never did. What was the point of jumping this fence when it was clear that the outer one was a barrier that could never be overleaped?

There was a low rumble of thunder from above and a stronger burst of rain that slashed into Yarra's face. She sat down on her haunches close to the inner fence, shook her head and blinked her eyes against the rain scud. She remained there, sitting upright like a sphinx, her eyes on the long grass slope outside the high fence, marking the low flight across it of a bedraggled rook. The slope ran upwards to a patch of ploughed land and then on to a wood that marked its crest. Here and there a fir tree stood out stark, glossy green against the February blackness of the other trees.

Another rumble of thunder broke out above and Yarra moved on, her restlessness eating into her. She lowered her fore quarters almost to the ground. Raking with her hind legs at the wet and muddy grass, she sent little clods of earth flying into the air. She turned her head sideways, seeing the cheetah hut at the bottom of the enclosure. Closer was a great fallen oak tree which the cheetahs used as their playground. She opened her jaws, flexing the skin back over her teeth and gums, and gave a long half-snarling, half-hissing sound that ended in a short, snapping spit.

It was at this moment, as Smiler was pulling up his wet jeans over a wet shirt ten miles away, that the sky above burst with an earth-shaking roar of thunder. A great bolt of lightning was loosed through the low-hanging clouds, setting the grey day ablaze with vivid light.

The lightning hit the outer fence of the cheetah enclosure ten yards below Yarra. It ran in an exploding aura of blue fire the length of the wire mesh. It found the metal bolts in a concrete support and ripped fence and support from the ground as though a great hand had smashed and flung them down. The falling top half of the support flattened the low inner fence a yard from Yarra. She leapt, snarling with fright, into the air. Her nostrils were charged with the smell of burning from the lightning strike. She came down from her panic bound on top of the collapsed outer section of the boundary fence. As thunder rolled angrily again she was gone, her whole body, every nerve in her, impelled by fear and shock. She streaked away up the grassy slope towards the wood in a wild, fast-leaping run, moving like a tawny-gold streak at top speed.

Within thirty seconds of leaving the cheetah enclosure she was in the wood on the hill crest, the first burst of fierce speed dead in her. She found a small path and moved along it, trotting now. Fear and panic were easing from her. With her fright and shock gone, she now found the strange restlessness she had known all day still with her. She gave herself over to it in a way she could never have done in the enclosure because she was at liberty.

It was less than twenty minutes before the Cheetah Warden in his Land-Rover discovered that Yarra was gone. Over his walkie-talkie set he sent out a message to his headquarters and arrangements were immediately put in hand to organize a search party. By then Yarra was well away, beyond the wood, moving slowly down the lee of a small orchard of bare apple trees. The land dropped steeply below her. A mile away she could see the line of a road with cars speeding along it.

Yarra stopped, watched the road for a while, and then turned and began to work a line across country parallel to the road below.

2

Shelter for Two

If there was an instinct in Yarra to keep away from human beings and roads, there was the same instinct in Smiler. Dressed now in his own clothes, the blanket abandoned under a bush, since he knew it was too distinguishing a mark if he should be sighted with it, he half-walked, half-trotted along the downlands that ran away from the wood. He kept just below the crest of all ridges because he knew, without having to think about it, that if he walked the crestlines he would be too easily seen. He had no idea where he was, not even the name of the county, nor of the nearest town. All he had known was that the policemen had been taking him to Salisbury. Salisbury meant nothing to him except that he vaguely remembered that there was a cathedral there.

His wet jeans, although they were warming up a bit with his body heat, rubbed him on the inside of his thighs. His wet shirt clung to him under the heavy, sodden weight of his jacket like a tight top skin. He was hungry and he kept thinking of all the second helpings he had refused in his life. Beautiful pictures of steaming sausages and beans, hamburgers and packets of golden potato crisps floated before his eyes until he sternly gave himself a smart talking-to and said, "Samuel M., keep your eyes open for danger not for food."

He travelled for two hours across country and not for a single second did it stop raining. The thunder and lightning went gradually, sliding away into the east and finally dying out with a few muffled grumbles and a pale, distant streak of blue fire. The rain soaked into his thick tweed jacket so that it grew heavier and heavier on him. The water ran down his fair hair, plastering it to his head like thickly spread butter. It seeped down between his shirt collar and his neck and trickled over his naked body cooling down any heat his exercise was giving him. He shivered now and then. He began to feel miserable, too, but he told himself that misery was to be expected in the circumstances and the best way to beat it was to find shelter for the coming night.

He crossed three roads, one of them a main highway, hiding first in the hedges until the coast was clear and then darting across. The policemen, he knew, would have sent out a pickup call for him. The last thing he was going to have happen was to be picked up and taken back to the reform school.

Now and again he would sing quietly to cheer himself up. The songs were always ones his father had taught him, ones he had sung while his father played his mouth-organ. Sometimes when his father was home from sea they would go out on borrowed bicycles – Sister Ethel's for him and her husband's for his father – and they would freewheel down hills both of them singing madly. Once or twice his father had hired a car and taken them out. Each time, when they were on some quiet road, his father had let him drive and he had soon picked up the knack.

He was trotting up a river valley, following a small partly overgrown path, the stream heavy with flood water to his right, when he saw ahead of him a low greystone bridge. Smiler came cautiously out on to the bridge and looked up and down the road. There was no one in sight. On the far side of the bridge, set a little back from the water's edge, was a long, low, thatched cottage. A board on the garden gate read – Ford Cottage. Farther up the road was a yard entrance. Rising above the thatch of the cottage he could see the corrugated iron roof of a barn that stood behind it.

Smiler eyed the cottage for some time. There was no smoke coming out of any of the chimneys. The curtains at all the windows were drawn. He whistled quietly, speculatively to himself for a moment and then trotted up the road to the yard entrance.

The big gate was shut and there was a padlock and chain on it. Beyond the gate was a courtyard with a well in the middle and beyond that the barn with an open bay at one end which clearly served as a garage. The back of the house showed no sign of life. For a moment or two he stood there as the rain poured down on him. He slowly licked his wet, cold lips as though the cottage were something to eat.

But Smiler was not going to be caught a second time. Things were not always as they seemed. Take that old farmer who had turned him over to the police – he could have sworn that the old man had never suspected that he had laid up each night in the warm hay of his barn – but he had known and had not let Smiler suspect it until the police car had swept into the farmyard just as he was coming out of the hen house with eggs in his hands.

So Smiler made a reconnaissance, right around the house and barn, peering through the chinks in the drawn curtains and going right into the barn and up the wooden ladder to the hay-filled loft. He noticed, too, that there were no recent car tracks on the soft mud at the entrance to the car bay. At the back of the car bay, covered by a groundsheet, was an old bicycle.

A few minutes later Smiler was in the house. It wasn't a difficult procedure. Back in his home town there were certain boys he had mixed with who had a considerable knowledge of the ways of householders with their keys when they went away. Nearly everyone locked the front door and took the key with them, and nearly everyone locked the back door and hid the key somewhere handy where the woman or friend who came to keep an eye on things could find it. The back door key of Ford Cottage was tucked away on a low rafter that formed part of the support for the porch over the door.

The back door opened directly into a large kitchen. Smiler went in and locked the door behind him. It was a nice kitchen, though now a bit gloomy with the yellow and red curtains drawn. It had all the modern appliances, including a deep-freezer, and on one of the walls was a big picture of a group of pink flamingoes standing in shallow water.

Smiler put out a hand and flicked the light switch by the door. The centre light came on. Smiler flicked the light off. He went to the sink and turned the cold tap. Water ran from it. He turned the hot tap. No water came from it. Smiler decided that if it became necessary he would puzzle that one out later. The most pressing need at the moment was to find some food and something warm to wear.

Five minutes later Smiler was out of the cottage (the back door locked and the key returned to its place) and up in the hayloft of the barn. He had with him — found in the kitchen sideboard — two tins of sardines with keys sellotaped to them for opening, a big, unopened packet of slightly salty biscuits and a large bottle of hard cider. The whole lot he carried in a thick car rug which he had found in the little hall outside the kitchen.

Smiler picked himself a spot on the hay bales where he could lie and watch the yard through a dusty, cobwebbed little window. Methodically he stripped off his clothes, wrung them out as best he could and then spread them over the bales to dry. The red dye of his socks had run and given his feet a rosy pink hue. He wrapped himself in the thick, warm car rug. It was made of a furry sort of nylon stuff and tickled his bare skin in a pleasant kind of way.

All his dispositions made, Smiler sat down and began to attend to the inner man. Within fifteen minutes he had eaten all the sardines, and drunk the oil they were preserved in. He had worked his way through two-thirds of the packet of biscuits and had considerably punished the contents of the bottle of cider. Almost immediately he began to regret the cider because it started to make his head spin a little. He had to keep flicking his eyelids up and down to clear his vision so that he could watch the yard outside. But it was no good. Flick as he might, he could not keep his eyes from wanting to shut. There were moments, too, when his head seemed to be spinning so fast that it threatened to take off like a helicopter. The last thing Smiler remembered before slumping into sleep was giving himself a good talking-to, saying, "Samuel M., my lad, you wolfed your food and swigged your cider like a glutton. If you don't end up by being sick, it'll be a miracle."

* * *

While Smiler was sleeping flat out on his hay bales in the loft, and snoring so loudly that anyone who had come by the barn would have heard him, Yarra was about a mile and a half away from him on the far side of the valley through which the river by Ford Cottage ran. The rain had slackened to a thin drizzle now. Some time before, following the line of the road she had first seen, Yarra had found herself coming into an area with more and more cottages and houses. Instinctively she had turned away southwards to avoid, although she didn't know it, what were the outskirts of the town of Warminster. Her restlessness was still with her and with it now there was also another feeling. Yarra was hungry. It was between five and six o'clock in the afternoon which was past the time at which the cheetahs were normally fed. More significantly, this day was a Tuesday which meant that Yarra was hungrier than usual because in the Longleat animal reserve Monday was a fast day for all the big cats. They were given no food on that day for health reasons. In their wild state the big cats hunted and then ate, and then only hunted for food again when hunger returned. To feed them regularly every day would in the end have dulled their appetites and injured their health. So, each Monday, they were starved. Yarra now had her eyes open for the chance to find something to eat.

Moving along the grass headland at the side of a field of young winter wheat, which was bounded by a post and wire fence, Yarra caught the quick movement of something white to her left. Immediately she froze in her tracks. She remained statuesquely still, her right foreleg poised immobile in mid-air. Beyond the low fence was a small run of pasture that sloped up to a line of tall elms. Through the trees showed a glimpse of a red-roofed house with a wisp of smoke coming from its chimneys. At the foot of the elms was a large wooden chicken-house, perched up on iron wheels so that it could be moved from one field to another. Scattered around the henhouse and out across the field was a flock of White Leghorn fowls.

Yarra watched them and rich saliva rose swiftly to her mouth. She stretched her jaws silently and then dropped low to the ground. For all

her bulk Yarra moved under the bottom strand of the fence wire like a
silent flow of undulating, molten, tawny gold, shadowed by the fast ripple of her markings. Once through the fence she remained for a while flat
to the ground. Fifty yards away she marked the nearest straggler from
the flock, a cock bird with fine rain-washed comb and wattles of shining
vermilion. The great arch of its white, cockaded tail was ruffled now and
again by the wind which was rising, coming in from the west to sweep
away the last of the rain.

With a slow deliberate movement Yarra rose to her feet. Her eyes on
the cock, she moved forward. Her body was charged with the controlled
intensity of her stalking and the sharp lust for food inside her. Every
movement she made came from instinct and from hereditary memory.
Although she had been captured as a well-grown cub, and had never
done much hunting for herself, she moved now as surely and
knowledgeably as though she had spent all her time in the wilds where
she had been born.

She was twenty yards from the bird when it saw her. Its head turned
with a jerk that flicked wide its cape feathers and tumbled its bold crest.
At these movements Yarra streaked into action. She went fast across
the winter-pale grass in two running leaps. The cock bird screamed in
alarm and jumped high, wings slashing the air. Yarra took the bird three
feet from the ground, her jaws closing over its lower neck, crushing and
breaking the vertebrae. A great white explosion of feathers sprayed into
the drizzle-soft wind. Farther across the pasture there was a noisy gust
of alarm calls from the other fowls as they scooted across the grass with
flapping wings for the shelter of the henhouse.

Yarra, holding her prey high, raced back to the wire fence and cleared
it with an easy spring. She loped away down the far side of the field and
then turned through an open gateway out on to the hummocky, steep
sides of a sweep of bracken- and gorse-covered downland.

She found a hollow, ringed by gorse and broom bushes and, couching
down, the cock between her outstretched paws, began to eat it. She tore
and gnawed at the carcase, relishing the warm savour of its entrails and
stringy flesh. She ate like a cat, seldom holding the food with her paws,
but jerking, chewing and tearing at it with her strong teeth. When she
had finished there were left only the wings, the once boldly arched tail
and the stout yellow legs of the proud cock.

Her meal finished, Yarra groomed and cleaned herself, licking the
margins of her great jaws, and carefully combing with her rasping
tongue her creamy chest mantle. She lay for a while on her side, contented, her head twisted back on one shoulder, and grunted once or
twice with the pleasure of the food inside her.

The rain stopped and the wind, swinging from the west to the south, strengthened and began to clear the clouds from the evening sky so that a few early stars showed thinly. Yarra rose, her old, unnameable restlessness back with her. But this time there was habit with it, too. Each night in the cheetah reserve Yarra with all the others — Lotus, Apollo, Schultz, Suki and the rest — was herded by the warden in his Land-Rover into the night pen at the bottom of the enclosure where they were shut in. In fact it was seldom necessary for them to be herded in by the warden. As darkness came habit activated them and they sought the cover of the warm, straw-floored hut of their own accord. Night was coming fast now and Yarra moved on to find a place to shelter herself.

Half an hour later, the dusk thickening, she came down a valley side and up on to a high bank above a main road. A car went by quickly with its sidelights on. Its movement did not alarm Yarra. She was used to cars and to the smell of exhaust fumes. The small lights on the car puzzled her a little but with the passing of the car her curiosity went. She dropped down the bank side on bunched feet and was across the main road like a shadow. On the far side a minor road, stone-walled and thorn- and hazel-topped, ran down towards the river. Something white in the hedge attracted Yarra's attention. It was no living thing but she padded towards it with caution, sniffed it and then passed on down the side road. The white thing was a small direction board with the words — Ford Cottage — on it, followed by a black arrow pointing down the road. Three-quarters of a mile away at that moment Smiler was sitting up in the gloom on his hay bale, groaning and holding his head, knowing that within the next few minutes he was going to be violently sick.

Yarra padded down the road, flicking a front paw now and then with irritation because the ground was running with water from the overflow of a small ditch at one side. Although it was almost dark now she could see well enough to mark the stir of a blackbird settling to roost in the mid branches of one of the hazel growths on the bank. As she neared the bottom of the lane she heard the sound of the river running in high spate. She crossed over a stone bridge, the noise of flood water loud below her. She stopped just short of the white padlocked gate which was the barn entrance to Ford Cottage.

Her eyes went over the house, cream-plastered, the old thatch grey in the dying light. Then she saw the barn across the yard with its garage bay and to the right of that an open doorway cut in the lower weather-boarding of the barn side. The doorway reminded her of the doorway at the side of her sleeping hut at Longleat. For shelter and warmth at night she knew you went through such a door. She took one long leap, went high over the five-barred gate, landed silently in the yard and then padded forward towards the barn.

She was almost at the old wellhead in the centre of the courtyard when a figure came through the open barn door. Yarra froze. With immobility she became part of the gloom, her spotted pelt merging into the night shadows, her bulk blurring against the grey and indigo courtyard surface and the hedges and walls of her background.

The figure turned along the side of the barn with a curious stumbling and flapping movement and disappeared. Yarra knew it was a human being, the scent told her that, though it was the first time she had seen one who walked with this curious flapping movement. It was a tallish human being. The large human beings, Yarra knew, had to be treated with respect. It was the very small ones that roused her and all her kind, the children who looked through the windows of the cars going round the park. To her they were small game to be hunted, like young deer; the right size to be stalked and killed. Sometimes in the park Yarra and the other cheetahs would be suddenly and unpredictably aroused by the sight of a child and would lope alongside the car and chase it for a while. But this figure was too big to rouse any killing instinct in her.

She waited for a while to see if the figure would return. After a time, she unfroze slowly and padded across to the barn door.

*   *   *

Smiler, bare-footed, wrapped in the car rug which flapped about his body in the strong night wind, had been sick in the little orchard that lay behind the barn. He felt better but his head still ached and his stomach was queasy and tender. Despite the blanket, he was cold, but for the moment he wasn't sure about going back to the barn. He had a feeling he might be sick again. The dizziness in his head was still there, too. That came from the cider. He'd swilled it down as though he'd been parched from thirst in a desert for weeks. He had had the same experience once before when he had gone for a day's fishing with his father. He remembered now how his father had grinned at him and said, "Samuel M., never drink too much cider under a hot sun and on an empty stomach." His father had given him black coffee from the thermos and put him to sleep in the back of the borrowed car.

Smiler walked down a small path to the edge of the river. He knelt down and splashed water over his face and head.

Five minutes later, he went back to the barn. The ladder that led to the top loft was just inside the door. Beyond the ladder the bottom floor of the barn ran back in darkness for about thirty feet. His head still dizzy and throbbing, Smiler turned through the door and groped for the ladder rungs. He was busy giving himself a good talking-to about eating and drinking like a pig. He was so busy doing this, in fact, and so full of self-pity for his queasy stomach and pounding head, that he did not hear the sudden movement of an alarmed Yarra rising to her feet on a patch of straw litter. She came up fast, dropping her shoulders, sphinx-like head thrust out, jaws open, her face-mask wrinkled with a mixture of fear and anger. She gave one sharp, spitting hiss of warning — which went unheard by Smiler as he climbed his way up the steps, grumbling aloud at the awkwardness of his blanket.

Yarra, silent now, holding her warning position, watched him go. He disappeared. There was a thump as the trapdoor at the head of the ladder was dropped.

Yarra heard noises from above. Then there was silence and she slowly relaxed. She settled again in the straw litter, flat on her side, her head thrown back at an angle from her shoulders. She was tired and she was disturbed by the restlessness in her. She could sense a slight irritation in the line of dugs along her belly. Her belly, itself, felt strange and, as she lay stretched out on her side, showed that it was slightly swollen. What Yarra didn't know, and what her Cheetah Warden at Longleat would have been delighted to know, was that she was going to have cubs. The father had been Apollo and the mating had taken place thirty days previously. In sixty days' time Yarra was due to litter. Cheetahs seldom breed in captivity and those at Longleat had never shown any signs of doing so — which was perhaps the reason why Yarra's condition, for she showed but little, had gone unnoticed.

Slowly, her restlessness fading, Yarra dropped away into sleep.

Above her, rug-wrapped in a nest of hay, Smiler slept, too, and dreamt that his father had got a job for him in his company. They had shipped to sea together and here they all were; deep in the dazzling blue of the South Seas, sitting on the foredeck, sun streaming down, and albatrosses, frigate birds and gulls thick in the sky. The off-duty crew were gathered about them as his father gave out on the mouth-organ and Smiler, strong-lunged and musical, accompanied him in their favourite song:

"The gallant frigate Amphitrite, *she lay in Plymouth Sound,*
Blue Peter at the fore-mast head, for she was outward bound.
We were waiting there for orders to send us far from home,
Our orders came for Rio, and then around Cape Horn . . ."

Smiler snored gently in his sleep. A barn owl looked down on him from a dark roof recess at the end of the loft and then took off through an eave opening on silent wing to forage. Down below Yarra slept, jerking her head now and then as a stiff stem of straw tickled her muzzle.

3

A Door Is Closed

Just before first light Yarra woke and left the barn. She went through the orchard and down to the river where she crouched at the stream-side and drank. Flicking water from her muzzle, she turned away and moved slowly up the narrow footpath that fishermen used in the trout season. A hundred yards from Ford Cottage an unwary moorhen got up from a dead patch of reeds almost under Yarra's nose. She took it with one swift pounce. She carried it to the cover of a thicket of briars and ate it.

It was over an hour later when Smiler woke. He was warm and dry and he felt better. He lay back on the hay looking out of the dusty window. Over the top of the cottage he could see the tips of a tall row of poplars on the far side of the river. Two starlings sat on the television aerial fixed to the chimney of the cottage. Through a broken pane of the window came the sound of sparrows quarrelling under the barn eaves, the belling of tits from the stark apple trees in the orchard and the distant drone of an airplane. From its dark perch right up in the angle of the rooftree of the barn, the owl opened one eye briefly to observe Smiler and then closed it again.

Smiler lay thinking. The first half hour of waking in the morning was his best time for thought. It was a time of day when things seemed to present themselves fresh and clear. At the moment it was impossible for him to work out any grand plan of campaign for the future. He had to be content with a short-term view, and his short-term view was that he had to keep out of sight of people as much as possible and have a base which would give him shelter, warmth, and food and drink. Ford Cottage seemed a good base if it were empty and going to be empty for some time. That was something he had got to find out if he could. The deep-freezer and the food cupboards were well stocked as he knew. The question of making use of someone else's house and supplies didn't worry him very much. After all, he told himself, if things were the other way round and he was the bloke that owned the house and there was a young chap like himself on the run — because everyone had just got everything wrong — he wouldn't have minded a bit if that young chap had helped himself. His father often said — didn't he? — that God helped those who helped themselves but God helped those most who helped others. There was no questioning that. Thing Number One, then, was to find out if the cottage was really unoccupied and, if possible, for how long it might stay that way.

Now Smiler, when he had put his mind to it, could be extraordinarily patient and industrious about any job he undertook. If you're going to do something, then make a proper job of it, his father was always saying, because, if you don't, you'll founder in the first stiff breeze that comes along.

So, from his barn window Smiler watched the cottage all that morning. The only person who came to the house was a postman who appeared at mid-morning and pushed some letters through the back door slot. Twice a red tractor came down and back the side road, moving over the bridge and up the steep wooded rise beyond. For lunch Smiler ate all the salt biscuits that remained and drank the little cider that was left.

An hour later he had a shock. From the window he saw an elderly man come walking down the road. He wore a tweed coat and a checked cap and he stopped at the courtyard gate and looked across to the barn. Smiler saw him shake his head and then come through the wicket gate at the side of the large gate and cross to the barn. Down below Smiler heard the open barn door being banged-to on its catch. His heart beating fast, he saw with relief the man moving back across the yard to the lane. When the man was gone Smiler gave himself a black mark for carelessness. The door had originally been closed on the catch and he had left it open. The elderly man was probably some neighbour who could have fancied it had blown open in the night's wind and had taken the trouble to close it. But if he had, Smiler argued, then it probably meant that the neighbour knew there was no one in the cottage. After all, you didn't go around shutting a friend's barn door if you knew the friend would be back soon, say like that evening, or the next day.

An hour after the man had gone Smiler went out of the barn – closing the door after him. Keeping his eyes smartly open, he slipped across to the back door. He took the key and opened it. The lock was a Yale. Smiler put the key back on the porch rafter and, once in the cottage, closed the door on the free catch. He could get out from the inside by turning the latch. He went through the hall to the front door and found that the lock there was a Yale too. That was fine, because if he heard anyone coming in the back he could slip out of the front unseen.

In the kitchen he picked the mail from a wire basket that hung under the letter flap. There were two letters in white envelopes addressed to a Major H. E. Collingwood, Ford Cottage, Crockerton, Near Warminster,

Wiltshire, and a picture postcard adressed to Mrs. B. Bagnall at the cottage. The picture on the card was a view of Mont Blanc across the Lake of Geneva and the message on it cheered Smiler up a lot. It read:

Dear Mrs. B.

Mrs. Collingwood and I send our regards and I am happy to say she is much improved in health though it will be a good month yet before the medico will be able — we hope — to give her a clean bill of health.

When you next come in and find this will you please check the level of the central heating oil tank as I don't trust that oil fellow to call regularly to top it up.

Kind regards to you, Mr. B., and family.

Sincerely,

H. B. Collingwood.

So, thought Smiler, the Major is away with his wife for quite a time and Mrs. Bagnall, whoever she was, came in now and then to keep an eye on things. Well, all he had to do was to keep a weather-eye open for Mrs. Bagnall. Considerably perked up, whistling gently to himself, he gave himself a good wash at the kitchen sink. He dried himself on a roller towel fixed to the back of a door next to the washing machine. Opening the door, he discovered that it held a small central heating plant. Now from Sister Ethel's Albert — who was a plumber and electrical engineer — Smiler knew quite a lot about heating plants. Albert had often taken him on jobs and was, anyway, forever talking about his work. This plant was set at 60 degrees Fahrenheit, and the time clock was adjusted so that it came on at nine o'clock at night and went off at eight in the morning . . . enough, Smiler knew, to keep the cottage warm and damp free and to avoid any danger of pipes freezing up.

Smiler put the letters and the postcard back in the mail basket and tidied up the sink from his washing. As a precaution he pulled the roller towel up so that no one could see that he had used it. He then made a quick tour of the cottage, promising himself a more detailed one later. This done, he slipped out of the back door and over to his barn, closing the door after him.

He took with him — strictly on loan — a small portable transistor set which he had found in the Major's study. The inside of his shirt was pouched with a can of corned beef, key attached for opening, a packet of Ryvita biscuits, and a bottle of orange juice. He ate and drank unhurriedly, although he was considerably sharp-set with hunger. While he ate he turned the radio on very softly.

Some time before it got really dark Smiler gathered up his empty sardine tins and the corned-beef can and the now empty packet of salt

biscuits and the cider bottle. Holding the rubbish clasped to his breast
he went down the ladder frontwards, without the use of his hands,
bumping his bottom from rung to rung to keep his balance. At the
door he jerked up the catch with one shoulder and hooked the door
open with his foot. The dusk was thickening. There was no one about.
He slipped out. Because he was only going to go a few yards to the
river to dump his rubbish he left the door open. To close it would have
meant the nuisance of putting all the tins on the ground and using his
hands.

     He went quickly round the corner of the barn and through the garden
to the river which was still running high with the previous day's rains.
He threw his load into the flood water and then bent down to wash his
hands which had become sticky with sardine oil.

                              *   *   *

Yarra came wraith-like through the gloom at the top of the garden. She
saw Smiler by the river, her head turning at the movement of his arm as
he tossed his rubbish into the water, her nostrils catching his scent
almost at the same time. She moved on without pausing and without
any great interest in him. The scent was the same as she had caught the
previous night, though the shape was leaner and no flapping came from
it. Had she been hungry and in a bad temper just the sight of him might
have stirred resentment. But she was well-fed and wanted only the comfort of her hut and the litter of warm straw. That morning she had
worked her way upstream on the right bank of the river through steep
plantation slopes of young firs and old woods of bare trees. She had
taken a grey squirrel — tempted out by the sunshine — as it had scurried
for the trunk of a tall beech, jumping and pawing it down from the
smooth grey bark when it was six feet from the ground. Full of her
waterhen meal, she had done no more than take a bite from its soft belly
and leave it. Most of the day she had passed in the river woods, moving
away whenever she had heard voices or sounds that disturbed her.
During the late afternoon she had come out of the woods at the top of
the river slope. Here, on a long, rolling down, she had put up a hare from
a clump of dead bracken. Yarra had seen hares before moving across the
parkland pasture outside her Longleat enclosure. They had always
excited her just as did the young deer that also moved beyond the wire in
freedom. She had gone after the hare, hearing the thump of its feet as it
raced away. The hare had had a fifteen-yard start on her but, although it
had twisted, zig-zagged and doubled at top speed, she had moved like an

orange-gold blur and taken it within a hundred yards easily. She had eaten it, relishing the meat which was strange to her.

Now, full of food, wanting only her resting place, she passed around the barn and through the open door to find her litter of straw. In the darkness she pawed with her claws at the flattened straw to shape and bulk it. Satisfied after a while, she dropped flat on it. She stretched her legs stiffly, tightened her shoulder muscles, and then relaxed, her head cocked over one shoulder watching the open doorway.

A few moments later Smiler came through the door, humming softly to himself. Momentarily Yarra's mask wrinkled and she opened her jaws, half-threatening, but making no sound. There was no real malice in her.

Smiler closed the door on the latch, felt for the ladder rungs in the darkness and went up to his loft and dropped the trapdoor quietly.

* * *

That evening before going to sleep Smiler listened to the radio for two or three hours. He had the set turned down very low and tucked into the hay close to his head. When the news came on he was interested to hear whether there would be anything about his escape on it. But he was disappointed. It would have been quite something to have had his own name broadcast.

However, there was something about another escaper. A cheetah (Smiler tried to picture what a cheetah was like and fancied it was something like a panther or leopard) which had escaped from the Longleat wild life reserve the day before had not so far been found. Smiler – whose home was at Fishponds on the outskirts of Bristol – had heard of Longleat and its lions though he had never been there. No one had yet reported seeing the animal but the Longleat authorities had said that it was not likely to travel far. It was probably still quite close to the park or somewhere in the large tract of country in the triangle made by the towns of Frome, Warminster and Mere. Anyone seeing the animal was asked to keep well away from it and to inform the police or the Longleat Park authorities. At the end of the news there was a short interview with a man from Longleat Park who gave some general information about cheetahs. In the course of it he said that the name of the escaped cheetah was Yarra and that it was a female.

Before sleeping Smiler lay comfortably in the hay thinking about the cheetah. He'd often gone to the Bristol Zoo but he couldn't remember whether he had ever seen a cheetah there. Actually he didn't care much for zoos. Having animals in big parks like Longleat was much better.

Pacing up and down a cage was no way to live. Being at a reform school — although he hadn't stayed there long — was a bit like that. Do this, do that, and being watched all the time, feeling and knowing every moment that you were a prisoner. Even having a big enclosure to live in wasn't really good enough, he felt. Not if you were a wild animal. All right for cows and sheep. But not for a leopard or a lion or a cheetah. Yarra . . . that was a nice name . . . same sort of name in a way as Tarzan. Yarra and Tarzan. He saw himself in a loin cloth swinging through the jungle trees. His faithful cheetah, Yarra, followed him far below, looking up when he gave his jungle cry. He liked animals, though he had never had many. The best had been a mongrel dog, black with white patches and a head that had a bit of Alsatian in it, called Tessa. His father had brought it home for him one day. Tessa would do anything for him. When he went to stay with Sister Ethel, while his father was at sea, she had made a terrible fuss. Tessa's hairs got all over the furniture and carpets. In the end, he was sure, Tessa had got fed-up with all the fuss, too, because one day while he was walking her on the downs she had gone off and never come back . . . Tessa . . . Yarra . . . and Tarzan. He yawned, switched the radio off and stretched out to go to sleep.

* * *

So far Smiler and Yarra had been lucky. No one had sighted either of them. Two of the wardens from Longleat had tried to follow Yarra's spoor marks from the point of her breakout. After a time they had to give it up because the rain had washed them away. Nobody had tried to follow Smiler's tracks. The police had sent out their signals and had alerted all patrol cars and the local constabulary with a description of Smiler. Now they were pretty confident that the need for food or shelter would make Smiler show up somewhere pretty soon. It was no time of the year for living rough, particularly as Smiler was far from being a country boy. The police had, of course, got in touch with Sister Ethel, giving her the news, and telling her that if Smiler appeared she must report him at once.

Ethel and her husband, Albert, were at this moment in the sitting room of their little villa in Fishponds having cocoa before going to bed. It was a small neat room, everything shining and brushed, and polished and dusted. Albert had his slippers on. He was never allowed in the room without them. Albert was much easier going than Ethel, though he would never have dared to break any of her rules in the house. He was master only in his own workshop.

Ethel said, "That boy's always been a trouble and always will be. He's got a wild, stubborn streak in him – and I wouldn't know where it came from."

Albert knew that everybody had streaks of some kind in them. You just had to make the most of the streak you were handed out with, as – he had no doubt – Smiler would do with his one day. He liked Smiler.

He said, "My opinion is he run away from that place because he knew he didn't ought to have been there in the first instance."

Ethel put her cocoa mug down precisely in the middle of a little table mat and said, "He went there because he was a bad one. Knocking an old lady over and taking her bag. And before that always lifting and taking things. Bad company makes bad habits."

Albert sighed gently. "He was light-fingered, yes. But I'm not sure he was any more than that. Not violent. Not Smiler. He wouldn't harm a fly, let alone an old lady. All right, at the time it looked black against him and I thought he had done it. But now, on due and full consideration, I don't think he did. Not Smiler."

"He was always nicking things and getting into scrapes. The way you start is the way you go on, and you go on nicking bigger things and getting into bigger scrapes. And that's what happened. Although he's my own brother, I have to say it."

Albert put his mug down on the polished table top, discovered his mistake and moved it to his little table mat, and said reflectively, "It's all a matter of what they call psychology."

"Whatever are you talking about?"

"Psychology. How the mind works. Smiler was what they call compensating for his home life – or rather for the home life he wasn't getting. No mother and his dad off to sea nine months out of twelve and only us to come to when he was on his own –"

"And what's wrong with us? We give him as good a home as anyone could."

"That's just it. As good as we could. But it weren't good enough, Ethel. He never knew his Mum and he missed his Dad. We couldn't do anything about that. But he, unconsciously, you understand, tried to. That's why he went out and about nicking things and getting into scrapes. He was what they call making his protest against what society was doing to him."

Ethel sniffed loudly. "Well, I must say, that's the fanciest notion I've ever heard. And anyway, conscious or unconscious, he did that old lady and she stood right up in the juvenile court and identified him."

Albert rose. His cocoa was finished and now he meant to go out to his workshop and smoke his goodnight cigarette. He liked to sit on his bench and puff away while he dreamed impossible dreams – sometimes like being able to smoke in the parlour and the bedroom, to flick ash on the floor, to put his feet up on anything he chose and, perhaps now and then, to have a bottle of beer instead of cocoa for a bedtime drink.

He said pungently: "That old lady was as blind as a bat! She couldn't have recognized her own reflection in a mirror! And I don't believe she ever had twenty pounds in her handbag. Smiler had only ten on him when they nabbed him five minutes later." He moved to the door and added, "Well, I hope the lad's found a fair billet for tonight. It's freezing out."

"That poor boy," said Ethel. "His father'll raise the roof when he comes home."

"When," said Albert and went out.

*　　*　　*

Albert was right. It was freezing. It froze hard all night. When the first light began to come up over the easterly ridge of the river valley it was to reveal a world laced and festooned with a delicate tracery of frost. The frost ribboned the bare trees and hung from the thin branches in loops and spangles. It had carpeted the grass with a crisp layer of brittle icing, and had frozen the water splashings under the old stone bridge so that they hung in fanglike stalactites, and had coated the small pools and puddles with a black sheeting of ice. It was a rime- and hoar- and ice-covered world made suddenly dazzlingly beautiful as the first lip of the sun showed to strike gleams of white, gold and blue fire from every branch and twig and every hanging icicle.

The brightening crack of light under the barn door woke Yarra. She rolled over and sat up on her haunches. She tightened the muscles of her long forelegs to ease the night's laziness from them. She sat, sphinx-fashion in the gloom like an ancient Egyptian cat goddess, her liquid amber eyes watching the light under the door. Although the door was closed, and had not been the previous night, it did not seem strange to her. The door of her hut at Longleat was always closed during the night and the warden opened it early in the morning. She sat waiting for the sound of his feet outside. Sometimes he was early and sometimes late.

Half an hour passed and the warden did not come. Yarra rose to her four feet, walked to the door and sniffed at it. Then she turned back along the far wall. Her restlessness was coming back fast. She walked back to her straw, scraped at it, working her shoulder muscles, and then went to the door again. She wanted to be outside, where the world was full of sounds, blackbirds and sparrows calling, the beat of a car's engine passing down the narrow road and the low, mocking caws of rooks moving from their night roosts to forage on the iron-hard field furrows.

Annoyed now, she raised herself on her hind feet and scraped against the shut door, rattling and banging it impatiently.

The scraping, rattling and banging from down below eventually woke Smiler. He lay on his hay bed, still a little muzzy with sleep, listening to it. It took him a minute or two to remember where he was. When he did, he jumped quickly to his feet and stood above the trapdoor. Somebody was down below! With the thought his heart began to thump with alarm. He knelt down and cautiously lifted the lid of the loft trap an inch and peered through. His eyes, dazed from the sunlight which was streaming in through his loft window, could make out nothing in the gloom below. Then, as his eyes slowly adjusted themselves, he saw the movement at the barn door. For a moment or two he watched, his mouth open in amazement. Then – with a swift, panic reaction – he dropped the trapdoor and shot across the holding bolt which was fastened to the top of it. He dropped back to a sitting position on the hay, clapped a hand to his forehead, and said out loud, "Blimey O'Bloody Reilly!"

4

A Door Is Opened

As Smiler sat there considering the situation the skin of his scalp crept with a slow shiver of fear as he realized what a narrow escape he had had. Not this morning – but last night! When he had come back from throwing the rubbish away he had closed the barn door and *that thing* had already been in the barn! He had closed the door and climbed the ladder and *that thing* must have been watching him! And now *that thing* was down there and he was up here!

What on earth was he going to do? To help his thoughts he swigged off what remained of the orange juice. Then, because no helpful thoughts came, he drew back the bolt of the loft trap and raised it a few inches cautiously. Down below Yarra was padding restlessly up and down. She caught the slight movement of the loft trap out of the corner of her eye and swung round. She backed away a little, raised her head, and made an angry movement of her jaws.

Smiler could see her clearly now. He saw the wrinkling of her face mask, the white shine of her teeth, the restless switching of the long tail, the tensing of the high powerful shoulders, and the long, lean length of her forelegs and body. He dropped the loft trap back into place and bolted it.

Smiler was no fool. He could put two and two together faster than many young lads. "Samuel M.," he said to himself, the problem on his hands now overcoming his shock and fright, "what you have got down there is that escaped cheetah! Yarra. That's right. And what you are stuck with right now is that you can't get out until you get her out. That's Thing Number One without any question."

He got up and went to the barn window, scratching his head. He looked out. It was still very early in the morning. The sun was only just half clear of the valley ridge. He took a good look at the window for the first time, and he saw that it was not fixed in its frame. There was a hook catch at one side. He pushed this up, opened the window and looked out. Six feet below him and a little to his left was the top of the barn door. Two-thirds of the way up the door and on the side closest to him was the door latch. It was a curved handgrip with a thumb press latch above it that had to be pushed down to lift the small cross lever on the inside of the door free from its notch so that the door would swing open. The door, he remembered, was awkwardly hung. Once the catch was free the door would swing inwards of its own weight.

With his head stuck out of the window he considered his plan of campaign. The window was big enough for him to get through. He could hang on to the sill and drop to the ground. It was a fair drop but not so far that it worried him. Once in the yard all he had to do was. . . . Well, what? Press the thumb latch down, give the door a push and then run for his life while that animal came through the opening after him like a streak of gold light? Not so-and-so likely he told himself. All right then, what? Just drop to the ground, and then go off and tell the police or someone that he had found the cheetah and it was shut up in the barn? Not so-and-so likely! He'd never get away with that one. It would be giving himself up and they'd have him back in reform school before you could say knife. No — there was only one way. He had to get the door open from up here and let Yarra go off on her own. Then, when she was well away, he could go down himself.

He turned back into the loft. What he wanted was a long stick with which to reach down and press the thumb catch. The loft ran well back beyond the bales of hay he had been using for a bed. When he had first come up he had made a careful inspection of the place. At the back of the loft he found a long-handled hayfork with the head broken off. It was about four feet long and would not reach the door. But in one of the corners of the loft he found a disused hutch for hens. The floor was made of long narrow strips of wood. Smiler pulled one of the slats free. Because he enjoyed problems like this, he was soon all set to try to open the door. The hay bales were all bound by lengths of binder twine. He took a couple of lengths of twine from the hay bales and lashed the hutch slat to the end of the broken hayfork. He had no trouble with making a proper lashing. His father, though a ship's cook, was also a seaman and Smiler had had a thorough grounding in tying knots. He spliced the two lengths of wood together, finishing off the whip-binding, neat and tight, so that he had a firm join. The rest was easy.

He took another look down through the loft trap at Yarra just in time to see her raise herself against the door and begin to tear at it with her forepaws. She saw his face through the hatch and turned at once and came in a swift bound to the foot of the ladder.

Smiler dropped the hatch with a bang and shot the bolt across. He went to the window quickly. Yarra was getting angry at being shut in. He pushed his home-made pole through the window and after a couple of attempts managed to bang down the thumb catch. The door slowly began to swing open.

Before he could get his pole back through the window Yarra was out.
She came out slowly, stopped a yard from the open door, and then
looked up at Smiler. She gave him a quick snapping hiss and then loped
away around the corner of the barn. Seeing her only for a few moments
in the full sunlight, Smiler was awed by her beauty. Her picture
remained in his mind long after she was gone. He only had to shut his
eyes and he could see the tawny gold pelt with its close-spaced black
spots, the blunt, short-eared head with the long bracketing black face
markings, the amber eyes and the graceful droop and upturned tuft of
her tail and, most of all, the slow muscle flow of shoulders and haunches
as she moved away.

*   *   *

Yarra passed that day in the same area. The restlessness in her she was
used to now and, since she had her freedom, the habit was strong in her
to want to come back to her barn shelter at night.

She went up the river and stopped to drink just above the barn where
a small carrier stream came into the main stream over a low waterfall. In
the woods higher up the river she marked the movement of a cock pheasant foraging among the dead leaves. She covered twenty yards of
ground before the bird saw her. It took off too late and was brought
down in a burst of feathers by one sweep of her taloned right forepaw.
She ate. While she did so she heard the sound of children laughing and
playing away across the river, heard the whine of cars on the not too distant main road running from Warminster down to Mere. She was outside, by at least a mile, of the triangle of roads joining Frome, Warminster and Mere. That afternoon, late, she ran down another hare on
the downland above the river woods.

The frost had held all day and as the winter sun began to drop and the
air turned even colder Yarra came off the downland. She was passing
through a thicket of trees, studded here and there by tall, rank growths
of wild rhododendrons, when a keeper, shotgun under his arm, stepped
out on to the path ten yards ahead. Man and beast saw each other at the
same time. Startled, Yarra backed away, lowering head and shoulders
threateningly, and gave a slow snarl. The keeper, seeing her threatening
stance, acted instinctively. He swung his shotgun to his shoulder and
fired.

The swift movement of the gun, although she had never been fired at
before, was warning enough for Yarra. Sudden movement marked
something you either hunted or avoided. This was a large human, not
something she hunted. She leaped sidewards into the cover of a patch of

young birch. The keeper fired, first one barrel and then the other as
Yarra disappeared into the gloom of the birches. The gunshots echoed
through the wood. A few pellets from the spread of shot that rattled
against tree trunks and the hard ground caught Yarra on the left flank,
stinging and biting into her. Then she was gone at top speed through the
woods.

The keeper stood in the centre of the path trembling with shock. No
fool, he began to move quickly back up the path towards the open fields
at the top of the wood. The wood was no place to stay in with an animal
like a cheetah about. Recognition had come to him only after he had impulsively fired. Ten minutes later he was telephoning from his cottage to
the Warminster police station.

*   *   *

That morning, after Yarra had gone, Smiler stayed in the loft. He
waited patiently to see if the postman was going to call or perhaps Mrs.
Bagnall, come to do some morning housework in the cottage. Eventually
he saw the postman ride by the cottage on his bicycle, but he did not
deliver any letters.

An hour later Smiler was in the cottage, the back door locked with the
key on the outside so that he would have warning if anyone came. He
had a drink of water from the tap, sluiced himself for toilet over head
and neck, and then opened a tin of baked beans and ate them with a
spoon from the can. He tidied up meticulously and then started another
inspection of the house.

The hallway running to the front door was red carpeted and hung
with small, coloured pictures of birds and flowers. There was a big oak
chest in it with a wide shallow glass bowl on top. The bowl was full of
odds and ends. On either side of the hall were a dining-room and a large
sitting-room, one wall of which was covered entirely with bookshelves.
In the window stood a flat-topped desk. Its surface was inlaid with red
morocco leather and tooled around the edges in gold-leafed designs. It
was as nice a room as Smiler had ever been in in his life. The chairs and
settees were comfortable and well-worn. He was sure there would be no
fuss if you put your feet up on them.

On the top floor, which you went up to by way of an open staircase
with roughly carved bannisters and supports, were three bedrooms. One
was large with two beds in it. The others had a single bed each. Leading
off the big bedroom was a bathroom. The bathroom, wide and spacious,
had a long window that looked out over the well-yard at the back. The
bath was blue and tiled on two sides. Each tile had a picture of a fish on

it. Smiler had never seen a bathroom like it, and it had a nice scented smell which he liked. If it had been his Sister Ethel's, he thought, no one would have been allowed in it without having a bath first. He poked about in it for a while and opened a mirror-fronted cabinet that hung on the wall. There were lots of bottles, tubes, toothbrushes, packets and sprays and pill boxes in the cabinet. When Smiler closed the cabinet his reflection confronted him in the mirror, snub-nosed, blue-eyed, freckles all over his face like the markings on a skylark's egg, and his blond hair tousled all over his head. He took a comb from the shelf under the cabinet, wetted it under the cold tap, and tidied his hair.

Then he went down to the sitting-room and looked at the books on the shelves. Smiler liked books. Although he preferred adventure stories, strip comics and do-it-yourself books, he would read anything even if he didn't understand half of it. At Fishponds, if it were raining or he felt bored or he didn't want for a while to be with the other lads, he would often go into the Public Library and sit over a book in the Reading Room. The woman who ran the place was a bit sniffy with him at first but she had got to know him and, providing his hands were clean, she let him stay as long as he liked.

There were hundreds of books on the cottage shelves, a lot of them about fishing and hunting, rows of novels, a pile of Ordnance Survey maps at the end of one shelf, and on the bottom shelf a row of the Encyclopaedia Britannica. Smiler knew all about the encyclopaedia. His father had once told him that you could find out about everything in it. And it was true, as Smiler had more than once proved in the Reading Room.

For two hours Smiler sat on the floor enjoying himself. Although the curtains were drawn plenty of sunlight filtered through. Because of the central heating which had been on all night, it was not cold. He looked up all about cheetahs in the encyclopaedia. Not that there was much about them, just twenty lines or so. Smiler was interested to read that, for centuries in Persia and India, cheetahs had been used for hunting small game and antelopes. They were hooded, then taken out, and, when the hood was slipped, away they went after whatever it was. He remembered Yarra coming out of the barn. Yarra and Tarzan. Yarra and Samuel M. . . . He lay back on the floor, saw himself with a cheetah on the leash, the cheetah hooded, and the two of them moving along a great hillside then . . . Wheeeh! Off came the hood, the leash was slipped, and Yarra was away after a deer!

He sat up and grinned to himself. Some hope, Samuel M., he thought. Anyway that cheetah was miles away by now if it had any sense. He pushed the book back on to the lower shelf. As he did so he saw that at the end of the shelf, wedged between the last volume and the wooden upright, was a large glass bottle. Smiler recognized it at once. His Dad liked his whisky at night and had had bottles like this. It was a dimple-sided whisky bottle. In the top was a home-made cork with a slit cut in it that you could drop money through. The bottle was three-quarters full of sixpenny pieces. Smiler picked it up. It weighed like a bomb. He shook it, and then wondered how much there would be in it. . . . Pounds and pounds. Ten at least.

As he put the bottle back he suddenly heard a key scraping at the back door lock. Smiler was up and into the hall and out of the front door like a shot. He ran across the garden away from the road and bridge. He raced up the hillside and turned into a small clump of stunted yews. From here he could look down on the cottage and barn.

Although he couldn't see all the courtyard at the back, he could see the big white gate at the entrance. While he watched he was pleased to think that he had not left any tell-tale traces in the house. He was on the run and could not afford to give himself away. The whisky bottle was back in its place, and all the books. And he had tidied up the kitchen, wiping the sink fairly dry from his washing, putting the spoon away in its drawer, and dropping the empty baked-bean tin in the waste bin. If his Sister Ethel could have known how tidy he had been she would have thought he was sickening for something or working up to some out-rageous request to be allowed to do something she would normally have refused. Then he began to worry about the baked-bean tin. Whoever had gone in might look in the bin and see it. That would give the game away. Or say they knew exactly what had been in the cupboards and spotted how he had helped himself? Well, there was nothing he could do about it now.

After about five minutes Smiler saw a woman come across the little bit of the yard he could see. She had a blue woollen hat on and a thick brown coat, and she wheeled a bicycle with a black shopping bag hanging from the handlebars. She was dumpy-looking and oldish. She pushed her bicycle through the side wicket gate and then rode away over the river bridge and up the slope beyond.

Smiler gave her a few minutes to get clear and then he began to move back. But he did not go to the cottage. He went along the hillside through the trees and dropped down into the side road. He walked down the hill, looking as though he were out for a stroll, past the big white gate and on to the bridge. Here he leaned over the parapet and pretended to be looking at the river. But his eyes were on the house and the front door, and the curtained windows. For all he knew more than one person might have gone into the house and only the woman had come out. It proved a very wise precaution. He had hardly been there a few minutes when the front door opened and a girl came out. She slammed the door to lock behind her, and then came across the lawn, out on to the road, and towards Smiler who was still hanging over the bridge parapet.

She was a nice-looking girl – with a tanned complexion and shoulder-length black hair – wearing a shiny red plastic coat and high black boots. Back in Fishponds there had been plenty of girls who hung about with Smiler's friends. Smiler didn't dislike girls, but he hadn't got a lot of time for most of them. They never seemed to say or do anything that was particularly interesting. Just laughed and giggled most of the time, or talked about clothes and a lot of nonsense.

As the girl came on to the bridge she saw Smiler. Smiler stared down at the river and hoped she would pass on. She didn't. She stopped behind him and said, "Hullo."

Smiler half-turned. "Hullo," he said.

"What are you doing here?"

"Just looking at the river," said Smiler. She seemed all right. She had a friendly smile and it suddenly occurred to him that he might get some useful information from her. He nodded his head at the cottage. "You live there?"

"No. My mum does for them. Once a week. I just come down with her."

"She the one that went up on the bike?"

"'Sright."

"Whyn't you go back with her?"

The girl laughed. It was a nice laugh and her teeth showed very white against her tanned face. "You're a one for questions, aren't you?"

"Sorry. I was just asking."

"Well, I comes down with her on the back of her bike. But as it's all uphill going back . . . well, I walk. She came down to pick up the letters, but I stopped to dust the dining-room."

"Don't nobody live there, then?"

"They're away. I haven't seen you around before, have I?" The girl leaned over the parapet a yard from him.

"No."

"Where you from, then?"

For a moment Smiler hesitated and then he said, "Oh, over War-minster way." To forestall further questions along that line, he went on, "Where do you live?"

"Up the hill. 'Bout a mile. Lodge Cottage. You know it?"

"No."

The girl, who clearly had time on her hands and, like all girls, welcomed a chat — which didn't surprise Smiler — picked a lump of moss from one of the bridge stones and dropped it into the river, saying, "She's going down fast."

Puzzled, Smiler said, "Who is?"

"The river, of course. After all that rain. She's going down."

"Plenty of fish in there. I suppose?"

"Trout and grayling. My father's the water keeper. There's big trout under this bridge. Over three pound some. What's your name?"

Feeling easier in himself and now alert to gain any advantage that would help him, Smiler said, "Johnny. Johnny Pickering." Johnny Pickering was a boy that Smiler knew but didn't like. "What's yours?"

"Ivy, but I don't like it much. All my friends call me Pat."

"I like Pat best, too. How often do you and your mother come down here?"

"Once a week. Every Wednesday, mostly. But I don't always come. See that —" She suddenly nodded downstream.

Smiler followed her indication just in time to see a blue streak of fire flash across the water and disappear round a bend lower down. He said, "That's a kingfisher. I know that. Seen them when I been fishing with my Dad."

"My Dad don't like 'em. They eat the young trout." She straightened up and gave him a bright smile. "Well, I got to go. But if you live in Warminster I might see you sometime. I'm starting a job there next week. In Woolworth's. Bye."

"Bye."

She walked away up the hillroad and just before she turned a corner she looked back and gave him a wave of her arm. As girls went, Smiler thought, she wasn't too bad, and she hadn't got her face all plastered with lipstick and eyeshadow and stuff.

He waited another ten minutes and then slipped into the courtyard to the back door. Mrs. Bagnall, for he had no doubt about that now, had left the key on the rafter. He went in, leaving the key outside as usual.

The letters had gone from the basket behind the door. His baked-bean tin was still in the waste bin under the sink. He put it in his pocket. Then he took another tin of sardines from the cupboard, some frozen bread rolls from the deep-freezer and went back into the barn loft, carefully shutting the barn door after him.

He put the rolls in the sunshine on the window sill to thaw out, and then lay back on his hay and decided that he had to do some serious thinking. It was now very clear to him that his plan of campaign was not good enough.

No, Samuel M., he told himself, it just was not good enough. What he was doing was living from day to day and from hand to mouth. Also, he was living in dangerous territory where he could easily make some silly slip-up that would give him away . . . like that baked-bean tin, for instance. Mrs. Bagnall could easily have looked in the waste bin and found it. Then the fat would have been in the fire. Or she might just as easily have spotted that the sink, although he'd wiped it over with a dishcloth, wasn't really dry. Or even that the dishcloth – which ought to have been dry – wasn't. And all this food that he was nicking! . . . Mrs. Bagnall might spot things gone. . . . No, he had to make himself really safe. Not just for a few days. That was no good. He had to keep away from trouble until his father got back and sorted things out. Nobody else could, because nobody else was going to believe him about that old lady's handbag. . . . That old geezer in the juvenile court, when he'd tried to tell the truth, had just looked over his glasses, made a sour face, and grunted.

He lay back and stared at the barn rafters and began to think it out. It was hard work because almost at once problems began to come up. By the time he had worried *them* out they had given birth to other problems. It was nine months before his father would be back, maybe a year, and he had to keep from being caught all that time. . . . And, what's more – he was going to keep from being caught!

Sustained thought was hard, fatiguing work. The hay was warm and soft. After about two hours – with a break to eat sardines and half-thawed bread rolls – Smiler dropped off to sleep.

*　　*　　*

After being shot at by the keeper, Yarra kept moving fast. She was angry and disturbed; but the few small shot which had caught her left flank had caused no real harm to her. Her pelt was rough and wiry, without the natural sleekness of most felines, and not more than two or three pellets had penetrated her skin. The line she took across country was along the valley side, well above the river. At one place she dropped down the ivy-coated bank of the small road that led down to Ford Cottage and crossed into a plantation of young conifers. She moved diagonally down through the young trees until she reached their boundary. Below her the ground fell sharply away to the river.

She sat on her haunches looking down into the valley. It was growing darker every moment now. Up the river, away to her left, was the bridge and the grey roof thatch and white-plastered end-wall of Ford Cottage. Beyond it the bulk of the barn roof showed against the darkening sky. Away to her right, farther downstream and towards the north and Warminster, she could see the lights of houses and cottages. Sometimes the movement of car headlights swept along the main road.

After a time she dropped down to the river, found the fishing path and walked slowly upstream toward the stone bridge. She came out on to the road at the bridge side, crossed, and leapt the big white gate. She moved like a shadow close to the cottage and then across to the barn door. It was shut.

She sniffed around its lower edges for a moment. Then she leaned against it with the left side of her body, not to try to open it, but to rub her flank against it and ease the slight irritation of the gun shots in her skin. That the door should be shut she could not understand. Always the hut door was open at night in Longleat Park for the entry of the cheetahs. This was now her hut. The door should be open. She lazily stretched her jaws and gave a low, protesting rumble from her throat. Then she padded the length of the barn and moved around the open car bay. It smelled of oil and petrol and she wrinkled her nostrils in displeasure. She knew the smell and did not like it. Sometimes in high summer, when the cheetah enclosure was packed with parked and slowly moving cars, the same smell got so strong that she with the other cheetahs would move away upwind in the enclosure to avoid it.

She moved back to the barn door and raised herself against it, drawing the talons of her left forepaw in a great rasp down the rough wood surface. The movement shook the door and made it rattle on its hinges.

Up above in the loft the noise came faintly through to the sleeping Smiler.

Yarra rasped at the door again, more vigorously, rattling and shaking it. When it did not open she snarled and spat angrily.

The noise this time came clearly through to Smiler. He came out of sleep with a start just in time to hear Yarra rattle the door again.

Heart thumping, sure that someone was coming to take him, his brain still fuddled with sleep, he was on his feet quickly and at the window. At that moment Yarra moved back, squatted on the ground, and sat staring at the door. Smiler saw her clearly.

His eyes wide with surprise, for in mulling over his plan of campaign all thought of Yarra had gone from him, he clapped his hand to his forehead and cried, "Cor, Blimey O'Bloody Reilly – she's back again!"

5

A Change of Colour and Name

There was no doubt in Smiler's mind of what he must do. Although he hadn't thought about Yarra much in the course of the day, he instinctively accepted that, since she was a fugitive like himself, he could not refuse her shelter. They were both in the same boat.

He got his home-made pole and opened the barn window. It was getting darker every minute now. Yarra heard him and saw the movement of the window. She backed away a few yards and raised her blunt head, stretching her jaws wide, and giving a low rumble. She knew this human being now and so far he had presented no threat.

Smiler, pushing the pole through the window, murmured, "All right, old girl. Won't take a moment."

He jabbed down in the gloom at the barn door latch. After a few tries, he hit the thumb press and the door swung back slowly. He pulled the pole back through the window and watched Yarra. The tension went from her. She padded in a small semi-circle around the open door, looked up at him once, and then moved slowly into the barn.

Smiler closed the window and then went to the trap in the loft floor and listened. He could hear the restless movements of Yarra scraping and shaping her straw and then a heavy thump as she dropped to her bed.

Well, that was all right, thought Smiler. She was all comfy for the night. She would be gone just after first light in the morning and he could go down and close the door. However, right now, he took the precaution of shooting the bolt across the trap door.

He went back to his own bed and turned the radio on softly. An hour later the news came on. The local news was given before the national news. The local, South of England news made no mention of one Samuel Miles, but it had plenty to say about Yarra, the cheetah, who was sleeping a few feet below him. The public were warned that she had been sighted that day a couple of miles from the village of Crockerton in the valley of the River Wylye. It was felt that she was still in the area and people were warned to watch out for her. She would be dangerous only if cornered or suddenly surprised. She was most likely to be dangerous

to young children and parents were warned not to let them move about
unaccompanied. Everyone was warned that it was unwise to walk alone
in lonely woods and remote areas. A cordon was being thrown around
the area of the river valley where Yarra had been sighted. It was confidently expected that she would soon be captured. Then there was an
interview with the Cheetah Warden from Longleat Park, who was
asked some questions about cheetahs, their habits and what they ate,
and how dangerous they really were, and so on. Smiler chuckled to
himself through all this. Yarra was in the news, and she was just below
him.

But after the news was over, Smiler got a bit worried. Yarra was no
trouble to him, and it didn't worry him that she might go about taking a
few chickens . . . but she was dangerous to small children! Well,
oughtn't he to do something about it? Oughtn't he to drop out of the
barn window now and go and find the nearest policeman so that Yarra
could be caught?

And if he did?

Well, Samuel M., he told himself, that would be the end of you. They
would all think you were a good lad and had done the right thing.
They'd probably interview you on television and radio – but in the end
you'd be shipped back to that school.

It was a difficult problem. Yarra would go off tomorrow and almost
certainly she would be caught – and he would still be free. Anyway, he
wasn't too keen about dropping out of that window right now, landing
with a thump on the gravel, and having Yarra, maybe, come out after
him like a streak of greased lightning. That wouldn't do anyone any
good, particularly Samuel M. But if Yarra weren't caught tomorrow?
Then she would come padding back here to her shelter. Well, that one
wasn't difficult to work out. Tomorrow evening he would leave the barn
door open and he would stay in the cottage. He could watch the barn
from the bathroom window. The moment he saw Yarra come back he
would go out through the front door and up to the village of Crockerton.
Bound to be a public telephone box there. He could call the police, say
where Yarra was, refuse to say who he was – and then he would have to
take off smartly.

Down below him, he heard Yarra stir on her straw, and he said aloud,
"Old girl – if you got any sense you won't come back tomorrow. And I
hope you don't, because I don't want to lose a soft billet."

He dropped off to sleep, thinking that it was hard that on top of his
own problems he had the problem of the right thing to do about Yarra.

●   ●   ●

The sun was well up over the valley ridge when Smiler woke. The owl was back on its king post roost after a night's hunting. On the floor below the post were two or three fresh pellets which the bird had spewed up, little wet balls of fragile mouse and shrew bones, fur, and feathers from a wren that it had taken at the first paling of morning light. Smiler stretched and yawned. He had a busy day ahead of him, and maybe a dangerous one. He had his own problem to deal with and he meant to tackle it properly. No half measures. He lay for a moment, going over it in his mind, and then suddenly remembered Yarra.

He got up, unbolted the trap and looked down. The lower part of the barn was empty. Yarra had gone.

Smiler went down, peered cautiously around the corner of the open barn door to make sure that the coast was clear and then, closing the barn door, he went across to the cottage.

He went into the kitchen, had a drink of water and some biscuits and then washed his hands. There was no point in having a good wash yet, he thought.

Although he had bad habits – like smoking an occasional cigarette – and was no respecter of small items of other people's property when he was bored and idle and needed some excitement to make the day shine a little, Smiler was fundamentally a good sort. When he wished, he could be methodical, industrious and reasonably honest. In addition he was intelligent and a quick learner. He was also shrewd and far-thinking in an emergency; and he was in an emergency now. The emergency of keeping Samuel M. out of the hands of the police and all the other busybodies who wanted him to go back to that school. No thank you. Not for Samuel M. He was going to stay free until his father came back and sorted things out. . . .

After giving *his* problem much thought the previous day he had come to the following very clear conclusions:

1. He couldn't hang around Ford Cottage and the barn for nine months, cadging food and shelter.

2. So long as Major Collingwood was away, however, he could just use the barn for a sleeping place.

3. He had to find out exactly where he was (somewhere near Warminster was all he knew), and he had to go out and get a job so that he would have money for food and other things.

4. But to get a job wasn't all that easy, because the moment he showed his face anywhere some policeman with a long memory would recognize his fair hair and freckled face. He had, therefore, to disguise himself somehow – though there wasn't anything he could

do about the freckles! But he could do something about his hair and about his clothes.

5. As for the job, well, he was strong and handy and people were always advertising for help around the place. He would have to get a newspaper and see what was going.

6. And, to do all this — because people were always full of questions — he had to have answers as to who he was, where he lived, and so on and so on. For public purposes Samuel M. would have to go and a new lad take his place.

7. And if he stuck it out and wasn't caught, then some time he would have to telephone the shipping company offices in Bristol and find out what date his father was due back so that he could meet him.

It was a long list but Smiler felt that he had worked out the answers to most of the immediate problems, and he now set about them with a will. If there was something to be done he liked to get on with it.

He went first into the sitting-room and from the dimpled whisky bottle he shook out two pounds' worth of sixpenny pieces and wrapped them in his handkerchief. Then he went through the pile of Ordnance Survey maps and, after some time, found the one he wanted. It was Sheet 166 and on the red cover the town of Warminster was marked with a lot of others. Smiler liked and knew about maps. When he and his father had gone off on their trips they always used a map.

Smiler spread the map on the floor and he soon found Warminster. A mile and a half south of it was the village of Crockerton in the valley of the River Wylye. Smiler picked out the side road running down to the river bridge at Ford Cottage. He decided to take the map with him. Mrs. Bagnall was not likely to miss it on her weekly visit.

Next, Smiler went up to the bathroom. In ferreting through the bathroom cabinet he had seen two things which he had remembered when he was tussling with his problem.

One was a bottle of tanning lotion and the other was a tube, in a packet, of hair colouring. Dark Brown, the label said. There was a leaflet of instructions with the tube. Smiler read them carefully. One, wet your hair and apply half the cream as you would a shampoo. Two, lather it up and then rinse it off and squeeze surplus water from the hair. Three, apply the rest of the cream and lather well. Now leave the foam on for five, ten or twenty minutes according to how dark you want the hair to go. Four, rinse until the water runs clear. Then set your hair in your favourite style. Smiler grinned. His favourite style!

He stripped off his shirt, ran some water into the basin and set to work. It wasn't as easy as the instructions made it sound. He got the stuff over his face, neck and hands. It was a chocolate brown colour but when he tried to wash it off his hands and face it paled to a sort of sunburnt red. But – after twenty minutes – it looked all right on his hair. He wouldn't have called it dark brown, but it was brown enough — though there was a slight greenness about it. He then took the tanning stuff and worked it into his face and hands and around the back of his neck. It didn't cover the freckles by any means but it looked all right. Quite good, really, Samuel M., he told himself. After that it took him some time to clean up the basin using an old nail brush and a piece of soap from the bath holder. He combed his hair in his natural style, which was straight back without a parting, admired himself, and then began to explore the house for clothes. He was going to keep his own jeans, but he wanted some shirts and socks and something to replace his brown tweed jacket. The clothes he had been wearing at his escape he knew would have been listed in his description by the police.

Major Collingwood was a small man, Smiler soon realized. He found two old blue flannel shirts that would be a fair fit, three pairs of thick woollen socks, a thick grey pullover with a hole in the elbow and a well-worn green anorak with a penknife in one of the pockets. In a cupboard under the stairs he found, too, a pair of Wellington boots that fitted him. As his own shoes were the worse for wear he took them.

Conscious of the liberties he was taking and not overlooking the fact that the moment he went out into civilization he *might* be unlucky and be picked up, Smiler felt he had to try and put himself square with Major Collingwood. He went to the desk in the sitting-room and found a pencil and some sheets of notepaper. It took him some time to get the letter the way he wanted it and he screwed up the spoilt sheets of paper and put them in his pocket.

His letter read:

Dear Major Collingwood, I hope you find this and will understand that I am really only borrowing and will make it alright when my Dad comes back, like paying for the food, and so on, and making up the bottle sixpences if I don't get to do it myself — the sixpences, I mean – when I get the job I hope to get. I have tried not to make a mess except for some hair dye on the corner of the bathroom curtains. It is a nice house and I hope your wife gets much better.

Signed, Hunted. (P.S. I can't give my right name right now, for reasons.)

Also the bike, and some other odds and ends, which maybe I will have returned.
Signed, H.

He took the letter to a corner wall cupboard which he had previously looked into. It held bottles of drink and glasses and also a half-empty box of cigars. Smiler reckoned that Mrs. Bagnall was not likely to open the cigar box, but the Major would when he returned . . . perhaps the first evening. He put the letter in the box.

A few minutes later, the cottage locked, Smiler was back in the barn. He stowed all his loose stuff away out of sight under a hay bale. Dressed in a clean shirt and socks, his own jeans, the grey pullover and the anorak and the Wellington boots, he was ready to tackle Warminster.

Shutting the barn door after him, he wheeled the bicycle from the car bay around the back of the barn. A small path led around it and out through a field gate a little above the main gate entrance to the cottage courtyard.

Smiler freewheeled down past the cottage over the grey-stoned river bridge and began to pedal up the slope to the main road. He had already memorized his route from the map which he carried in his anorak pocket along with the handkerchief full of sixpences.

The side road met the main road just above the village of Crockerton – which Smiler later found out was little more than a handful of houses with a post office and general store. He turned right on the main road and twenty minutes later was in Warminster. He had already given himself a lecture on how he was to behave once he had left his shelter. The thing to do was to act naturally and as though you had a perfect right to be doing whatever you were doing. People only noticed you if you let your worry about being noticed show. So Smiler rode into Warminster whistling to himself. He parked his bike against a wall in the High Street and went into a newsagent and bought a copy of the local newspaper. It was called *The Warminster Journal and Wilts County Advertiser,* and it cost him fivepence. He was rather pleased with himself that he had already taken out a few sixpences from his handkerchief, so that he didn't have to haul his bundle out in the shop to get at his money. He put the newspaper in his pocket and then cycled around the town a bit to get the lie of the land. Although he was acting naturally, he knew that any moment something could go wrong. That being so, he knew it was wise to have some idea of his bearings and possible escape routes.

He ended up in the free cark park near the railway station, rested his bike against a wall and went into the cafeteria. Once inside, the warmth and smell of food made him realize that he was very hungry. He got himself a plate of sausage rolls, two slabs of fruit cake and a cup of coffee and then sat in the window where he could keep an eye on his parked bicycle.

He drank and ate with relish. He decided that it might be going to turn out his lucky day. He'd got fresh clothes, a fresh appearance, a bike to get about on, and money in his pocket. So far, no one had so much as given him a curious glance, not even a policeman who had walked past him on the pavement as he came out from buying the newspaper.

On the inside of the very first page of the newspaper, under the *Situations Vacant* column — sandwiched between *Experienced Sales Woman wanted to take charge of boutique* (*outer wear and underwear departments*) and (believe it or not and Smiler had to chuckle) *Male Cleaner, full or part-time, required at Warminster Police Station* — was a job going that sounded right up his street. It read:

STRONG LAD wanted, kennel work, experience not necessary, good wages, free lunch. — Mrs. Angela Lakey, Danebury Kennels, Heytesbury.

Well, Samuel M., he thought, that sounded all right, particularly the free lunch. For a moment he remembered longingly Sister Ethel's Irish stews. Whatever else she was not, she was a jolly good cook. Kennels, eh? Well, he liked dogs and he supposed he could be called strong. But where was Heytesbury? He didn't want to be too far from his barn if he could help it. Always supposing he got the job, of course. He took out his map and consulted it. It didn't take him long to find Heytesbury, which was just inside the right-hand edge of the map. It was about three miles south-east of Warminster. He saw that he could take a back road from Heytesbury, through a place called Sutton Veny, and, by another side road, come down to the river below Crockerton without having to go into Warminster at all. He worked out that by this route — if he got the job — he would only have about three or four miles to go.

A few minutes later Smiler was cycling east from Warminster towards Heytesbury along the main road, wondering what Mrs. Angela Lakey would be like.

*　　*　　*

Yarra, when she left the barn that morning, followed her usual route up the river, keeping just inside the fringe of the woods, but she was unlucky with her hunting. Half a mile from the cottage she put up a drake mallard from the edge of a swampy hollow just inside the wood. The drake went up like a rocket and with him, unexpected by Yarra, went his mate. For a moment the choice of two targets made Yarra hesitate. When she leapt for the female mallard she missed it by a foot. Farther on in the woods she put up a wily old buck hare.

The hare raced away down the wooded slope, twisting and turning. Yarra went after him, but his twists and turns in and out of the trees balked her of a clear, fast run. At the bottom of the slope Yarra expected the hare to turn up or down the river bank. The hare, however, which had lived a long time and knew when something faster than he was on his tail, took off from the bank in a long leap. He splashed into the water and swam across. Yarra pulled up on her haunches and watched him go. Only if she were absolutely forced to it would she take to the water. She watched the hare go caterwise down the river with the strong current and then pull himself out on the other side and disappear. She wrinkled her mask in disgust. She was hungry now and even more restless than she had been on any other day. Because of this she was in a bad temper. She raked the ground with her back legs, her talons sending a shower of dead leaves and twigs and earth flying. An hour later, she was almost at the end of the wooded valley slope where the trees gave way to rough pasture. Fifty yards ahead she saw a lean grey shape at the edge of the water. Yarra froze and watched.

It was a heron standing in two inches of water where the flooded river lapped just over the bank. Below the heron a back eddy had cut a deep pool close in under the bank. It was a favourite fishing place of the heron. When the water was high he knew that the trout and grayling liked to get out of the main current and seek the shelter of the slower pools and back eddies near the bank. Here, too, in winter there was more food than in mid-stream for often the floods washed fat worms, grubs, and insects out of the eroding banks and floated them down for the taking.

Yarra watched the heron for a while and then lowered her body close to the ground and began to stalk him. She kept close to the cover of the winter dry clumps of flags and reeds and the high tufts of dead nettle stems. She had never seen a heron before. The bird moved once, sliding its head an inch lower, dagger-like beak a foot from the stream.

The heron, the wisest and most cautious of birds and possessed of infinite patience, was well aware of Yarra. When she was thirty yards away he had caught, from the corner of his eye, the slight sideways flick of her tufted tail. There were times in Yarra's mounting excitement when she could not stop that momentary flick. But the heron – hungry like Yarra, hungry as all wild birds and beasts are during the lean months of winter – meant to have his meal. He had fished all morning without success. Now, riding in the back eddy, not three feet below him was a good-sized grayling, moving up and down on the alert for food, but so far not rising high enough for the heron to risk a thrust of his beak.

Yarra worked her way forward five yards more and knew that she needed another two yards before she could risk her forward spring and leap. Some instinct in the old heron, who still held Yarra in the corner of his eye as he watched the grayling, told him exactly when he could risk himself no more. Flat to the ground Yarra inched herself forward. She was bunching her muscles for her leap when the grayling below the heron came surfacewards like a slim airship rising. The heron's beak rapiered downwards and took the fish. With the movement Yarra sprang and the heron rose, great grey-pearl wings spreading wide, his long legs tucking up behind him. He planed away and flipped the grayling round in his beak to hold it sideways across the body. Behind him there was a splash. He drifted down river and climbed leisurely into the wind.

Yarra's slashing right forepaw had missed the heron by a foot. Unable to stop her forward progress entirely the front part of her long body came down in the water. For a moment, until her strong haunches could hold and then haul her back, her forepaws and head and shoulders went under.

She pulled herself back on to the bank and shook her head to free her eyes of water. More bad-tempered than ever, she sat on her haunches and licked at her shoulders and neck mantle, grumbling angrily to herself. It was at this moment that she heard down river the sound of men's voices and the bang and rattle of sticks against the trees.

Yarra, disturbed by the noise, headed away up river at a lope. At the edge of the wood she turned uphill, making for the high ground and the wide stretches of pasture, downland and young plantations which she had visited on previous days.

Behind her moved the hunt. It had been well organized by the Cheetah Warden. Making up the hunt were local farmers, gamekeepers and other volunteers. There were also several policemen on foot with walkie-talkie sets to keep in touch with four patrol cars. These cars were set out along the main roads that, with Warminster as its apex, formed a triangle marked at the extremities of its base by Longbridge Deverill (a mile on from Crockerton) to the south and Heytesbury to the southeast. In the middle of the base road joining Longbridge Deverill and Heytesbury was the village of Sutton Veny.

A long line of beaters had been formed early that morning on the southern outskirts of Warminster. Now, spread wide across the valley, the line was moving up river. Beyond Crockerton the line had swept round, formed up along the right bank of the river and was beating its way uphill through a wide stretch of trees and plantations known as Southleigh Woods. At this very moment the Cheetah Warden was stan-

ding on the river bank where the hare had leaped into the river, bending
over the spoor marks Yarra had left in a soft patch of mud.

* * *

It was two o'clock in the afternoon when Smiler found his way to
Danebury Kennels. At the far end of Heytesbury a small road ran off to
the left, up a narrow valley that sloped down into the main valley of the
River Wylye. Danebury House was a mile up this road, approached by a
short drive. It was a large red-bricked house with an untidy lawn in
front of it and stable and kennel blocks at the rear. A narrow strip of
vegetable garden ran up the hill at the back of the house. On the far side
of the house was a thick standing of beech and birch trees.

Smiler rang the front door bell and waited. Nothing happened. A cold
wind was sweeping up the hillside and he was glad of his pullover and
anorak. He rang the door bell again. A few minutes later he heard a soft
shuffling noise inside. The door was opened. Standing before him was a
very tall, very large woman of about forty. She had a big, squarish, red
face and an untidy mop of short black hair. She wore a green sweater
tucked into the top of riding breeches. On her feet were long, thick, red
woollen stockings one of which had a hole in it through which part of a
big toe showed. She was holding a leg of cold chicken in her hand. As she
chewed on a mouthful she surveyed Smiler as though he were
something that the dog had brought home. She finished her chewing
and then said brusquely, "Well, boy?"

Smiler, not sure of his ground, pulled the newspaper from his pocket
and said, "Please, Ma'am, I've come about the job."

She eyed him for a moment, then looked at the chicken bone, which
was now gnawed clean, and tossed it away out to the lawn over his head.

"Oh, you have, have you? Well, let's have a look at you. Turn round."
Her voice was brisk, but not unkind, and there was a small twinkle in
her dark eyes.

Smiler obediently turned round, facing the lawn. A small Jack Russell
terrier came out of the beech coppice, trotted across the grass, picked up
the chicken leg and went back into the trees with it. Somewhere at the
back of the house what seemed like a pack of a hundred dogs all began to
bark and howl together.

From behind him the woman – who was Mrs. Angela Lakey – said
briskly, "Right. Nothing wrong with rear view. Turn round."

Obediently Smiler turned about. Mrs. Lakey reached out and took the
top of his right arm in a firm grasp and felt his muscles.

"Strong boy wanted," she said. "How strong are you, boy?"

"I'm strong enough, I think, Ma'am."

"Time will show." Mrs. Lakey bent forward a little, peered at his face and said, "You're very sunburnt for this time of the year, aren't you?"

Smiler said quickly, "My skin's always like that, Ma'am."

"Don't call me Ma'am – call me Mrs. Lakey. What I'll call you from time to time – if you get the job – is nobody's business. All right, come in and let's have your particulars." She turned away down the hall. As Smiler followed, she called over her shoulder, "Shut the door. Fresh air's for outside houses, not inside."

She led the way down the hall and into a side room. It was a large, bright room, very lofty, and looked out over the lawn. And it was like no room Smiler had ever seen before. Around the walls were hung fox masks and brushes, glass cases with stuffed fish and birds in them, and a thick patchwork of framed photographs of horses and dogs. Over the big open fireplace, in which burnt a pile of great three-foot length logs, was a large oil painting of a fresh-faced, grey-haired man dressed in white breeches and hunting pink. He sat in a highbacked chair and held a riding crop in one hand and a large, full brandy glass in the other. (Later, Smiler learnt that this was Mrs. Lakey's dead father who had been a Colonel of the Hussars.) Before the fire, between two shabby leather armchairs, was a round table which held a tray of cold food and a full glass with a thick white froth on it which Smiler – because of his father – immediately recognized as a glass of stout. On the back wall of the room were rows of rod-rests with fishing rods stretched across them. Below these was a long low book-case full of volumes packed into it in an untidy jumble. There was a large rolltop desk just inside the door, open, and crammed to bursting with papers and all sorts of odds and ends, including a very old typewriter.

Mrs. Lakey told Smiler to sit by the fire. She went to the desk, rummaged in it, and found a pencil and a piece of very creased paper and came back and sat down opposite him.

She put the paper and pencil on the table, took a tomato from the tray, bit into it, and said, "Cold snack, today. Milly's away shopping. I've got a lot to do this afternoon so, with your permission, boy – " She gave him a smile which suddenly took all the sterness out of her face. "I'll victual up while I take your particulars. Name?"

In the barn the day before Smiler had gone over in his mind – when he had decided he must go for a job – the answers to all the awkward questions he knew he would be asked, and he had his replies ready.

"Pickering," he said without hesitation. "Johnny Pickering."

Mrs. Lakey wrote it down, and said, "Age?"

"Fifteen and a half."

"Address?"

"I live with my aunt, Mrs. Brown, At Hillside Bungalow, Crockerton. My mother and father . . . Well, they're dead. They was killed in a car accident three years ago."

"Sorry to hear it. Damn cars. They're just murder on the roads. Horse and trap — you got a tumble and a bruising and that was that. Never mind. Times move. Can't alter that. Any previous job? References?"

"No, Ma'am — I mean Mrs. Lakey. I left school Christmas."

"Any experience with animals?"

"No, Mrs. Lakey. But I like 'em. And I had a dog once."

"Willing?" Mrs. Lakey raised the glass of stout to her lips and watched him over the top as she drank.

Puzzled, Smiler said, "I don't really know what you —" Then understanding dawning, he went on quickly, "Oh, yes, I'm willing to take the job. I'd like it."

"No, boy. I mean are you willing to work hard? Sober, industrious, clean and tidy? Always cheerful and no clock watching? Can't have you if you're not all that — and cheerful. Milly hates a gloomy face around the place. Likes boys that whistle and sing and look like the whole day is just one glorious top of the morning to you. And you've got to have a good appetite. Milly can't bear cooking for those who pick and scratch and don't enjoy their victuals. So what do you say?"

A little out of his depth, Smiler said, "I think so, Mrs. Lakey."

"Good." Mrs. Lakey finished her stout. "You seem a likely number to me. Anyway, the advertisement's been in for two weeks and you're the first. Wages — three pounds a week. Free lunch. Sundays off. Half days to be arranged as work permits. Start at seven-thirty. Finish at five this time of the year. Later, as the sun god stays with us longer. Five shillings an hour overtime. Working overalls provided. Anything in that frighten you?"

"No, Mrs. Lakey."

"Well, it would most of the young lay-abouts these days who want a four-hour day, meals off golden plates, two months' paid holiday a year, and then wonder why the country's going to the dogs. Which is the biggest slander on dogs ever uttered. And talking of dogs, let me tell you, my bark is not worse than my bite. My bite is terrible!" She winked at him suddenly.

Smiler, who it must be confessed, was a bit confused and uncertain about her, was warmed by the wink. He said, smiling — and Smiler's smile, Sister Ethel had always said, could charm the birds from the trees — "You seem very nice to me, Mrs. Lakey."

Mrs. Lakey looked at him, slowly grinned and then cried heartily,

smacking her thigh, "Well now, it's a compliment I'm getting! The first
for ten years. Right now, run along with you. Let yourself out. Be here at
half-seven tomorrow and we'll see how you shape up."

"Yes, thank you, Mrs. Lakey. I'll do my best."

"You'd better. No less is accepted."

Smiler let himself out and was chased all the way down the drive by
the Jack Russell snapping at his back wheel. But Smiler didn't mind.

Going down the valley road to Heytesbury he began to whistle to
himself. Everything had gone perfectly. Samuel M., he thought, you
carried it off like a hero. You've got a job, as easy as kissing your hand.
Milly? Who was Milly, who didn't like gloomy people, only big and
cheerful eaters? Well, he'd soon know. And soon know, too, what he had
to do. Crikey! — seven-thirty! That meant he would have to be up by
six-thirty. Ought he to buy himself an alarm clock in Warminster? Yes,
he'd certainly have to do that. If he turned up late, he knew he'd have
Mrs. Lakey on his tail, biting worse than her bark. In high spirits he
began to swerve from one side of the road to the other. Free lunches and
three pounds a week. He was in clover.

* * *

In the rough pasture on the plateau at the valley top, Yarra put up a rabbit and killed it within three yards. She carried it into a clump of wind-
dwarfed thorn trees and ate it. It was a small, winter-lean rabbit and
nowhere near satisfied her hunger.

She moved out of the trees and began to quarter the ground
eastwards across the rough amber-coloured grasslands. A hundred
yards from the edge of a Forestry Commission plantation of young,
waist-high firs she put up a hare. The hare laid its ears back and went
like the wind. Yarra raced after it, the memory of the hare she had lost
by the river giving her a fierce determination to catch this one. The hare
reached the edge of the plantation and found its way blocked by a three-
foot high, small-meshed wire fence. It turned right along the fence ten
yards ahead of Yarra. She swung across the angle at top speed and leapt
for it. Her forepaws smashed down on its back, talons gripping into the
fur, and her hindquarters skidded round to crash into the fence. She bit
clean through neck and vertebrae, and lay where she had made her kill to
eat.

As she began to worry and chew at the soft belly of the hare, a black
and white striped Land-Rover came over the ridge of downland away to
her right. Yarra heard and saw it simultaneously. She looked up from
her meal and watched it. The Land-Rover was moving towards the top

end of the fence which ran down the plantation side. Two hundred yards away it turned and began to bump and sway slowly along the fence. Her strong jaws clamped across the belly of the hare, Yarra stopped eating and watched the Land-Rover. For the moment there was no fear in her. The Land-Rover was exactly the same as many she had seen in Longleat Park. She had chased meat trailing on a rope from behind one of them. She had jumped to the cab roof, and even gone to the open cab door of the Cheetah Warden's car when he tossed her a lump of meat which hid worming or other medicines.

She lay watching the Land-Rover come down towards her. As it neared her she let go of the hare, opened her jaws, and gave a slow, warning spit and hiss. She wanted to eat undisturbed.

When the Land-Rover was within forty yards of her, the driver and the man beside him saw her. The driver stopped the car. The man beside him began to speak into his walkie-talkie set. Over the air the news of Yarra's discovery and her location went out to the police cars on the roads and to the policemen who were with the line of beaters now moving slowly up through Southleigh Wood.

The top boundary of the wood lay a few hundred yards down the slope from Yarra. She watched the Land-Rover for a while and, when it did not move, she began to eat. Almost immediately, from behind her, Yarra's quick ears caught the growing sounds of men moving up through the wood. A few of them — who had not yet received the warning of Yarra's discovery —were still beating and rattling their sticks against tree trunks and thickets. The noise disturbed Yarra. She was hungry still and she wanted peace and quiet in which to eat. She stood up, gripped the big hare in her jaws, and leapt over the wire fence into the plantation of young firs. She began to trot fast across the plantation, northwards towards the road that ran from Crockerton, down across the River Wylye and on to Sutton Veny. The noise of men and rattling sticks followed her faintly, so she decided to keep going until she was free of it altogether.

Five minutes later she was across the Crockerton–Sutton Veny road. The noise died away and she padded into a tall clump of wild rhododendrons and couched down to eat her hare. As she did so, from the leaden sky above, the first fat flakes of snow began to drift down, slanting a little in a cold wind that was rising fast.

*   *   *

Smiler did not go back to Ford Cottage along the Heytesbury–Sutton Veny road. His anxiety not to be late for work in the morning decided him to return to Warminster and buy a cheap alarm clock in Woolworth's. The girl assistant at the counter was a bit amused when he paid for it all in sixpenny pieces.

"I been saving up," said Smiler.

"Just for an old clock?"

"Present for me mum," he said.

Riding away down the Crockerton road, Smiler thought that it would be nice if it had really been a present for his Mum. He had never known her because she had died a year after his birth. But he knew a lot about her from his father who worshipped her memory.

Before he reached the cottage it began to snow and blow hard. Large, heavy flakes filled the air, whirling and spinning in the wind, and he was glad to pull up the hood of his anorak for protection. Now, as he neared the cottage, he began to think of Yarra. He had to leave the barn door open and, if she came back, he had to do something about her. Yarra, it seemed, was his last problem to tackle before he could start at Danebury Kennels and begin to work his passage for the next nine months.

He hid his bicycle in the orchard at the back of the barn and then slipped round, keeping his eyes open in case Yarra was about already, and opened the barn door. The courtyard had an inch covering of snow. The fast falling flakes rapidly obliterated the footprints he made in crossing to the back door. He shut himself in, leaving the key outside, and then went upstairs to the bathroom to keep vigil on the barn door. He took up with him a packet of biscuits and a pork pie which he had bought in Warminster for his supper. He washed them down with drinks of cold water from the basin tap while he sat on the broad window ledge, one curtain drawn partly back so that he could watch the door.

He kept his fingers crossed that Yarra would not come back. For two reasons he wished this: one, because giving her away when she was on the run like him seemed the act of a traitor, though he knew he had to do it for the safety of other people, especially small children; and two, because it was going to give him a lot of trouble. He didn't want to have to turn out and cycle somewhere to find a telephone because he knew it would mean that he wouldn't be able to come back safely to the cottage until Yarra had been taken. The thought of a night out in the cold made him far from happy. However, Samuel M., he told himself, if she ever comes you have just got to do it.

But Yarra did not come. Smiler watched the barn door until it got dark. There was no sign of Yarra. Some time after nightfall the snow stopped as suddenly as it had begun and the sky cleared. With the reflection from the snow on the ground and the clear starlit sky, it was quite bright outside. Smiler could easily have seen Yarra if she had come round the barn to gain her shelter. He waited dutifully until the eight-day clock in the hall struck nine (Mrs. Bagnall wound it up once a week when she came). Then he gave up his vigil. He found himself a couple of blankets in one of the spare bedrooms, rolled himself up and went to sleep. He had set the alarm clock for six o'clock in the morning.

6

Yarra Moves On

The snow saved Yarra from being caught. While she was eating her hare, the beaters came out on to the pasture behind the plantation and met up with the Land-Rover. Messages were sent to the police patrol cars. The hunting line was reformed and swept forward through the young firs as the snow began to thicken.

Yarra was disturbed by the sound of the men crossing the Crockerton–Sutton Veny road fifty yards behind her. She was sighted as she left the cover of her clump of rhododendrons. A couple of the men – unwisely – gave loud shouts that alarmed Yarra even more. She went away at a gallop northwards. She cleared a hedge into a field of young winter wheat, and followed the line of the hedge. The snow falling on her coat melted fast and made her uncomfortable. She hated the wet. As long as she could hear the noises of men behind her she kept going steadily. When the noises died she slackened her pace, but still kept going.

She was in strange country now and her movement was dictated by the lie of the land. She kept close to the hedges and over open ground trotted fast from the cover of bush clump to bush clump. When she met a small wood or coppice she went through it just inside the boundary so that she could break to open ground if danger threatened. Always, when she had the choice, she kept to the high ground rather than the low. Before she crossed any road she waited and watched for the sign of humans before passing over. The snow was so thick now that she could only see about ten yards ahead. The darkness was deepening every minute. The snow and the approach of night were her allies. The snow rapidly filled the tracks she left and made fast going hard work for the men who followed. After an hour they had lost all contact with her. When darkness finally came, with the snow still whirling and beating down, the hunt was called off except for the police patrol cars on the triangulation of roads. If the patrol car men could have known it, they were wasting their time. Yarra had long crossed the side of the triangle which was formed by the Longbridge Deverill–Sutton Veny–Heytesbury roads. She had crossed it a few yards short of the point where a road bridge spanned the River Wylye.

Yarra had found the river by hearing the noise of a small waterfall above the bridge. After crossing the road she followed the river downstream. Since missing the heron it was the first time that day that she had seen the river. The river reminded her of her barn shelter. Half a mile down the bank a black shape loomed up out of the darkness and the now thinning snow. It was a dilapidated fishing hut with a large plank seat inside for fishermen to rest on and have their lunch. Drifting snow had melted on the earth floor and formed a shallow puddle of mud and water. Yarra turned into the hut, sniffed around at its smells, and then leapt on to the broad seat. She sat on her haunches, facing the narrow open doorway. She began to groom and clean herself, licking at the inside of her muddy, wet thighs and nibbling at her swelling dugs where the restlessness inside her seemed to be lodged. She had no hunger, but she was tired and bad-tempered. Once, for relief, she uttered an angry, snarling rumble, jaws wide, her face crinkled and her eyes blazing. If anyone had come to the door of the hut at that moment they would not have had a very warm welcome.

Outside the snow stopped and the sky began to clear. Yarra went to bed, on the hard board, twisting and scraping restlessly until she was settled. The river ran by, murmuring quietly to itself. A water vole made a plop as it dropped into the stream and began a night forage down the bankside. A barn owl sailed low on silent wings over the water meadow, quartering the grass and reed tufts for mouse or shrew movement. A fox coming up the river, flicking his pads fastidiously against the thawing snow, caught Yarra's scent from the hut. He decided to have nothing to do with whatever made it, and trotted a wide half circle away from the hut to the river path above it. In an old wren's nest in the roof of the hut a sleepy dormouse burrowed its snout into its fur for warmth and gave a sharp *bleep*. In her light sleep Yarra heard the noise and flicked one stubby ear momentarily. Beyond the river and the railway, cars moved along the Warminster–Heytesbury road, their headlamps washing cottages, hedges and trees with gold light.

The low depression system which had brought the snow up from the west against a strong east wind now moved away east itself. The high pressure area that followed it swung the wind gently into the west and the temperature rose. The snow melted fast and in a couple of hours was gone from all but the sheltered dips and north slopes of the high ground.

At three o'clock in the morning Yarra, stiff and uncomfortable from sleeping on the board seat, woke and left the hut. She went down river and over the railway line. On the southern outskirts of Heytesbury she struck a side road into the village. The night was still, and deserted of all humans. She crossed the river by the road bridge and padded into the

village. Her scent roused two dogs in near-by yards to a frenzy of
barking. She came out on to the main road at the side of the Angel Inn.
She paused for a moment, looked about her, and then crossed the main
road and went north up another side road. A few yards up the road on
the left-hand side was a large red notice board with a white-painted in-
scription which read:

IMBER ARMY RANGE
ROAD CLOSED 1 MILE AHEAD

Yarra padded up the tree-bordered road leisurely. The road
steepened, mounting the higher contours of a narrow combe running up
to the far-stretching plateau of the easterly part of Salisbury Plain. As
Yarra passed the drive entrance to Danesbury House the Jack Russell
terrier saw her. The terrier slept on a rug in the window bay of his mistress's bedroom where the curtains were always drawn back at night.
The movement of Yarra on the road caught the alert eye of the un-
sleeping terrier. He jumped up, body and tail quivering with aggression,
and began to bark his head off. From her bed, half in sleep, Mrs. Angela
Lakey reached over to the floor — where she kept a small pile of hassock-
like cushions for the purpose — and hurled one at the terrier, hitting him
amidships as she muttered, "Go to sleep, you old fool!"

Above the house the road cleared the tree line. Where it ran on to the
first of the open downland and the wide sweeps of the plain which the
Army used for artillery, tank and infantry training, there was a small hut
at the side of the road. The road itself was barred with a red-and-white
painted drop-post. The hut was not manned at night. Yarra went under
the drop-post, and then left the road for the easier going of the rough,
wild grassland. She went across the country for half a mile, veering
away from the road. Ten minutes later, on the side of one of the
downland slopes she came across an old, rusted Sherman tank which
was used as a target for practice shoots. The turret had been blown
askew. The tracks lay collapsed and wrecked on the ground, and there
was a large gap in the side of the empty hull. Yarra walked around it,
sniffed at the cold metal work, and then looked through into the hull.
Somebody had long ago dumped a load of cut bracken inside and
covered it with a couple of sacks to make a resting place. To one side of
the rough couch were some empty beer bottles and a litter of old
cigarette packets and newspapers.

Yarra jumped inside, sniffed around the small interior, and then
began to tread the sacks and bracken to make a bed for herself. When

she was satisfied she flopped down and stretched out her forelegs, easing her muscles. In a few minutes she was sleeping.

Above her on the inside plates of the tank someone had written in white chalk – *Bombardier Andy Goran, only 5 yrs and 13 days to serve.* Under that, in another hand, was – *Please leave this hotel as you would wish to find it.*

*   *   *

The alarm bell brought Smiler out of bed with a jerk. Outside it was still dark. He had a quick wash in the kitchen, ate some of the biscuits he had left, and then tided everything up in case Mrs. Bagnall made a surprise visit.

When he went out it was to find that the snow had all gone and there was a fresh wind blowing. Seeing the bulk of the barn against the sky, he tiptoed over to it. He didn't want to leave the door open all day, but he wasn't overlooking the fact that Yarra might have come back at some time during the night. He crept down the side of the barn. When he came to the door he reached quickly for the handle and pulled it shut with a slam, dropping the catch. He stood outside listening. If Yarra were in there, the noise would have wakened her and he would hear her movements. No sound came from inside the barn.

A few moments later Smiler was pushing his bicycle up the hill away from Ford Cottage. At the top of the hill he began to ride and soon passed the spot where Yarra had crossed the road with her hare. But Smiler was not thinking about Yarra. He was giving himself a talking-to for not having thought of buying a bicycle lamp in Warminster. Although it was light enough for him to ride without danger, it was still officially dark enough for him to be showing a light. The last thing he wanted was to be stopped by some patrolling local policeman and have to answer awkward questions.

Warm and snug in his pullover and anorak, he turned left at the crossroads in Sutton Veny. He had a good memory for maps, a "bump of locality" as Sister Ethel's Albert used to say. Thinking of Sister Ethel and her Albert, Smiler decided that some time soon he would have to get a message to them that he was all right. He didn't want them going about thinking that maybe he was dead, or anything like that, and then writing off to his Dad and putting the wind up him. The problem of how he could send a message, without giving himself away, occupied him as he rode.

Some time later, the light in the easterly sky brightening fast now, he passed over the Wylye river bridge at the point where Yarra had crossed

the road on her way downstream. To his left he could hear the sound of
the little waterfall. From the river bridge it was not far to the main road
that led to Heytesbury.

Smiler arrived at Danebury House at twenty minutes past seven. He
was met at the drive gate by the Jack Russell whose name, he later
learned, was Tonks when he was not in disgrace, and Mister Tonks
when he was, which was pretty often. Tonks gave him a yapping
welcome and then trotted up the drive alongside him.

Smiler was met at the back door by Mrs. Angela Lakey. She was
dressed as he had seen her the day before, except that she now wore gum
boots and a red beret.

She greeted him heartily, smacking him on the back, and said,
"Morning, Boy. Punctual. That's what I like to see. Begin as you mean
to go on." The whole time he was to be at Danebury House she never
called him anything else but "Boy".

She gave him a cup of hot coffee in the ketchen, and instructed him in
his duties. She then took him outside and "showed him the ropes" as
she called it.

At Danebury House, Mrs. Lakey – and her sister, Miss Milly Finn –
ran breeding kennels for English and Gordon setters. They also had
boarding kennels where people going on holiday, or Army folk going off
on a tour of duty abroad, could leave their dogs. There was a small section, too, which held room for about eight cats. Mrs. Lakey would have
nothing to do with these. She didn't rate cats very high in the animal
creation. But Miss Milly did and they were her responsibility, though
Smiler had to look after them most of the time. Miss Milly ran the
house, did the cooking, and kept the books without any outside help.

In addition to these animals, there were also two hunters in a stable
near the beech copse. These Mrs. Lakey hired out to people who wanted
to ride or hunt – but she took very good care that they were the kind of
people who understood and could handle horses. There was a chestnut
mare, Penny, and a bay gelding called – for some reason Smiler never
discovered – Bacon. Bacon, he soon found, liked to give you a quick nip
if you didn't watch him. Penny was very even-tempered except that now
and then she would see things under her nose that no one else could see –
invisible fairies or dwarfs or snakes. Then, she would leap sideways or
pirouette like a ballet dancer on her hind legs – and off you would come
unless you were wise to her weakness. Over the stable loft there was a
pigeon cote full of white fantail doves. In a run at the bottom of the
vegetable garden lived twelve white Leghorn hens – known as the
Apostles. At the back of the kennel runs was a storehouse where all the
hound meal and dog-and-cat meat was kept and cooked in a big boiler.

Although Smiler had nothing to do with the horses to begin with, he had plenty on his hands. It was, he soon learned, his job to cut up and cook the dog meat, weigh up the hound meal, feed all the dogs and cats and keep their water bowls full. He had to clean out the kennels twice a week and lay new bedding, feed and water the hens and collect the eggs, and exercise the setters, in the five-acre paddock beyond the beech copse. He had to groom and brush all dogs twice a week, fetch in the logs for the house from the wood stack, wash down the horse-box, and dig the vegetable garden when he had any spare time. Also it was his duty to keep an eye on Tonks who was at perpetual war with the fantails and the Twelve Apostles.

On the first morning, as Mrs Lakey rattled off all this to him and "showed him the ropes", his head spun and he felt that he would never be able to manage. After a few days, however, he was managing easily, though – since he hated digging– he made sure that he didn't often have spare time for that. His free "working overalls" turned out to be ex-Army stock, green, and covered all over with brown, yellow and black camouflage markings.

Overwhelmed a bit by all this on the first day, the most cheering thing for Smiler was Miss Milly, who was younger than Mrs. Lakey. She was short and plump, fair-haired and fresh-faced, and jolly and kind. Her kitchen was spotless and smelled always of baking and cooking. She never called him "Boy". Right from the first it was "Johnny" which was a bit awkward, now and then, when she called him because he forgot that he was Johnny and didn't answer.

Smiler's first free lunch was a revelation that banished from his mind any culinary prowess that his Sister Ethel could show.

When he was called for lunch, Miss Milly said, "Gum boots outside the door, overalls off, face and hands washed, and then to table, Johnny." She talked a bit like Mrs. Lakey but there was always laughter and kindness in her voice.

Johnny ate in the kitchen by himself. After he was served lunch, the two sisters would have theirs together in the dining-room. That first day he was served steak-and-kidney pie, Brussels sprouts, and butter-creamed mashed potatoes. He had a glass of milk to drink with it and fresh-baked bread. For "afters" he had a great slab of treacle tart with custard and could have finished up with Cheddar cheese and home-made bread if he had had room for it. Later, when he really got into his working stride, he never missed the cheese and bread.

That first day there was only one personally awkward moment for Smiler.

At the end of the day he came into the scullery next to the kitchen where he had been instructed to hang his working overalls each night. Miss Milly was there, polishing a pair of tall, black riding boots belonging to Mrs. Lakey.

"How long does it take you to get home, Johnny?" asked Miss Milly.

"Oh, not long, Miss Milly." He had been instructed to call her that.

Miss Milly nodded and then stared thoughtfully at the sheen she had worked on one of the boots and said, "I know Crockerton well. Hillside Bungalow? Can't recall that, Johnny. Where is it?"

Smiler hadn't the faintest idea where it was because he had just made up the name without giving it a location. But he gathered his wits and said, "Well . . . it's sort of . . . Well, you know, not in the village and not exactly outside of it."

Miss Milly grinned. "That's a good description for finding a place on a dark night. New, is it? One of the new bungalows?"

Smiler wasn't going to be pinned down, so he said, "Well . . . it's not really new. Nor old either. It's sort of past the post office and then down a little sidepath towards the river."

"Near the old millhouse, you mean?"

"That's right, Miss Milly."

"Well, ride home carefully."

From Mrs. Lakey he got a different farewell for the day. As he wheeled his bicycle out of the yard, Mrs. Lakey came round the corner on Penny which she had been exercising in the paddock. She pulled up, looked at her wrist-watch, and said, "Finished for the day, Boy?"

"Yes, Ma'am . . . I mean, Mrs. Lakey."

"Shut the hens up?"

"Yes, Mrs. Lakey."

"Good. Well, Boy, we'll make something of you. You move well. Should stay the course if your wind holds. Right, cut along, Boy. Get a good night's rest and come back fighting fit in the morning."

She moved off on Penny and Smiler rode down the drive, accompanied by Tonks as far as the gate.

In Heytesbury he stopped at a garage and bought himself a bicycle lamp with the last of his hoard of sixpenny pieces. The garage assistant looked at the money, looked at Smiler, winked and said, "Been robbing the poor box, then?"

*   *   *

Yarra left her tank shelter not long after first light. Outside she stretched herself and then spent some minutes giving herself a good grooming. It was a clear, almost cloudless day with a brisk wind blowing across the plain from the south-west. A solitary lark, emboldened by the bright sun, climbed aloft and held a short song practice for the promised coming of Spring.

Her grooming finished, Yarra loped away down hill from the tank. At the bottom of the dip she found a pool of rain water and drank. For the next two hours she circled wide over the plain and saw many other old tank targets dotted along the down sides and hill crests. She was on the eastern portion of Salisbury Plain, an area about six miles long and five miles deep. The whole plain was about twenty to thirty miles long, a vast expanse of rolling, dun-coloured grass and downland, broken here and there by smooth, shallow valleys and combes and an occasional isolated clump of trees on a ridge. In some of the deeper valleys were scrub and thorn areas. Over the whole stretch there was not a plough-patch to be seen, not a domestic animal to be found grazing. The land all belonged to the Ministry of Defence and the public for the most part was excluded. When people were admitted on special days or at the week-ends they had to keep to the rough tracks and roads which criss-crossed the plain and which were marked at frequent intervals with notices that read:

DANGER – UNEXPLODED MISSILES
DO NOT LEAVE THE CARRIAGEWAYS
YOU HAVE BEEN WARNED

When the red flags were flying at the Army entrance points to the plain, known as Vedettes, nobody was allowed entry except the military personnel engaged in training or manoeuvres. For the whole of the great expanse of the plain there were five Land Wardens who patrolled the roads and tracks in Land-Rovers to see that no unauthorized persons came into the area. For the eastern portion of the plain, where Yarra was, there were two Land Wardens.

Great tank tracks scored the slopes and plateaux of the plain. Where the tanks had permanent road crossings these were marked with black-and-yellow-topped posts to warn car drivers of the thick mud they might expect to find on the road.

It was a wide, desolate area given over by day to the troops, though even they were lost in its vastness. Also, it was the home of many wild creatures – the hare, the fox, the stoat and weasel, the wild deer, the rat and the rabbit and a few families of feral cats – household pets that had wandered into the wilderness and reverted to their ancestors' old way of life. Sometimes a sheep-killing rogue dog found sanctuary on the barren terrain and made forays at night down into the farmlands that bordered it. In the air above the plain flew the buzzard, the kestrel and the sparrow hawk, all of them ever alert for the movement below of pheasant, partridge, and the small birds that lived in the tall grasses, the thickets and patches of wood. In fact, although the plain looked barren, it teemed with life – raven, rook, and wood pigeon, all the mice and shrews, and the gentle slow-worm, the inoffensive grass snake, and the swift adder. At one time, unhappily extinct now and commemorated by the name of an inn on the western part of the plain, one could have seen the great bustard.

This then was the area into which Yarra had moved and close to which Smiler had found a job. Just as Smiler on his first day of work had eaten well, so did Yarra as she roamed the plain.

Walking away from the rainwater pool, she saw the movement of a field mouse in the grass and caught it in a single bound. Like an ordinary cat, she played with it for a while, throwing it around her, bounding and leaping about it as though it were still alive and trying to escape her. Then she carried it in her mouth for a little while, became bored with it, and dropped it for a scavenging crow to find an hour later.

She put up a rabbit from behind a boulder and raced, doubled and twisted with it at her leisure and finally killed and ate it. Half an hour later she flushed one of the feral cats from a clump of gorse. It was a three-year-old tabby tom. He streaked to a nearby solitary dead pine and found sanctuary on a branch eight feet above Yarra. He arched his back, lofted his tail stiffly, and spat and swore down at her. Yarra sat back on her haunches, eyed him, and spat and hissed back. But she had no desire to leap or climb after him. Maybe, deep within her, was some feeling that made her content with a brief passage of family formalities.

At mid-day, she lay in the sun just below a ridge top, her orange and black pelt merging into her background so that from fifty yards she was practically invisible. A mile away, on a distant slope, sat an old Churchill tank. As Yarra blinked her golden-amber eyes against the sun, watching the tank, there was a loud crack of noise away to her right. Almost immediately, alongside the tank, the earth fountained upwards in a plume of mud, grass tufts and black smoke. Yarra flinched at the sight, and gave a silent gape of her jaws to show her displeasure.

There was another crumping, cracking noise from the left. This time an anti-tank shell hit the Churchill in the fore part of its hull. A large piece of plating flew up into the air, spinning like an ungainly black butterfly, the whirr of its clumsy wings coming distinctly across the valley to Yarra's keen ears.

Yarra got up and moved away, going over the downland ridge behind

her and seeking another resting place. She was at the start of learning
many lessons. She was to come to know the sound of guns firing, the
crack of a rifle, the mad chatter of automatic weapons, the whip-crack of
artillery and the slow, heavy thump of large calibre shells exploding —
and to move away from all such sounds. She was to come to recognise
the deployed line of battle-dressed infantrymen moving up to a crest, the
rattle of an approaching tank or troop carrier, the movement of Army
jeeps on road and grassland, the monstrous gnat-song of helicopters in
the air above — and to move away from them all. But on most days the
plain was free to her and the other animals and birds during the early
morning hours and again in the slow-stretching evening hours, from five
or six o'clock onwards, when the Army packed up its warlike gear and
went back to barracks and billets at the sprawling garrisons and en-
campments of Larkhill, Bulford, Tidworth and Warminster. All this
Yarra was to learn, but not without danger and many a sharp lesson,
given once and not forgotten.

On this, her first day, she moved and hunted in comparative peace.
She killed two hares in the afternoon and ate them both. Since she only
needed about three pounds of meat a day to keep her satisfied, and had
now had far more than this, she hunted no more. It was this that saved
the life of a young deer that, hidden in a stretch of bracken, scented her
as she approached downwind. The deer broke cover and went away in a
long, leaping, bounding run. Momentarily Yarra moved in pursuit, impelled by a natural reflex action. But after a few yards, she broke off the
chase and stalked into the bracken from which the hind had broken. She
found the deer's couching place, sniffed around it and then lay down and
rolled and scrubbed her back on it, taking pleasure from the deer's scent
just as a dog rolls in ecstasy over the long dead body of rabbit or rat.

As the light began to go from the sky, and great banks of high-
towering, dark rain-clouds slowly formed in the west and began a
ponderous sweep across the plain, Yarra went back to her tank. She
found her way easily for at no time during the day had she been more
than a couple of miles from it. She slipped into the hull as darkness came
and sniffed around. She played for a moment with an empty beer bottle
and then stopped because she disliked the noise it made on the steel
flooring. She arranged her bed, dropped to it, stretched herself, shook
her head and settled to sleep.

*　　*　　*

Seven or eight miles away Smiler was settling down for the night in the
barn. He had arrived home at last light. The door had been shut all day

so that he knew Yarra could not be in the barn. In fact, the garage assistant (all the local inhabitants were full of gossip about the escaped cheetah) from whom he had bought his bicycle lamp had told him that the radio had reported that it was thought that the cheetah had gone down river towards Wilton and Salisbury. Anyway, she hadn't been sighted by anyone that day.

With Ford Cottage itself all neat and tidy, and no obvious signs in it of Smiler's brief occupation, Smiler now took up permanent quarters in the barn. He had everything there he needed. He had his clothes, the borrowed radio, two borrowed blankets from the spare bedroom, a small store of food he had bought in a Sutton Veny grocer's on the way back, and drinking and washing water in a bucket he had found in the lower part of the barn. He had his bicycle lamp for light should he need it, hay to sleep on, the alarm clock to wake him in the morning, and the bolt across the trapdoor so that no one could take him by surprise during the night. The first day of a new regime was almost over. He had got himself fixed up. He had got himself a job that paid well and gave him one square meal a day. Samuel M., he told himself, you are in clover. He switched on the radio very low and lay back for some pleasant listening before he drifted off to sleep.

Back at Danebury House in the large, untidy sitting-room Mrs. Angela Lakey was sitting in one of the leather armchairs before the fire, smoking a cigar and sipping now and then at a glass of whisky. Tonks was asleep before the fire. Miss Milly was sitting in the other chair, writing out the monthly bills for the kennel boarders. She sipped now and then at a glass of sweet marsala wine of which she was very fond, although it tended to give her indigestion.

Mrs. Lakey said, "Well, what do you think of the boy, Milly?"

"He's a good boy, Jelly." Jelly was her nickname for her sister and Mrs. Lakey had learned to put up with it over the years, though she didn't like it.

"Could be," announced Mrs. Lakey slowly. "Tonks has taken to him. That's a good sign."

"I've taken to him, too," said Miss Milly, and added, "The next time I'm over Crockerton way I think I'll call in and have a word with his aunt." Then, after sipping at her glass of marsala again, she went on, "And Jelly – you were doing your mean act with him. For all the work that Johnny has to do three pounds a week is not enough. He should have four."

"Nonsense, Milly. Three's ample. Boys should work for the love of a job. All they want is a little pocket money to keep them happy."

"Four," said Miss Milly. "He's got to pay his way with his aunt."

"Three, Milly."

"Four, Jelly."

Mrs. Lakey sighed and said, "Toss you for it."

"Right," said Miss Milly and she produced a well-worn double-headed shilling from her handbag. She spun it on the table and, as it revolved on the polished surface, said, "Heads four, tails three."

The coin settled down and showed a head.

"I win," said Miss Milly, smiling.

Grinning, Mrs. Lakey said, "You always do."

"Only when right is on my side. Anyway, I'm glad for Johnny. He's got a nice smile."

"And you've got a soft heart, Milly."

"And so have you, Jelly. Only you don't show it often. Yes, as soon as I get a chance I'll go and see his aunt. Poor Johnny, how awful losing his mother and father like that."

The Lost Village

When Smiler arrived at work the next morning he was greeted first by Tonks, and then by Mrs. Lakey at the back door and invited in for a cup of coffee. This, he discovered, was to be the usual custom. Over the coffee Mrs. Lakey told him he was such a likely-looking lad and showed such signs of being a good worker that she had decided to up his wages to four pounds a week. However, he would have to take on cleaning out the stables and feeding Penny and Bacon. Later, if he showed any signs of taking to it, she would teach him how to ride. "Though," she said, "you're going to be too big, Boy, ever to make a jockey. But you look as though you may have a good seat and a fair pair of hands."

During the following days Smiler buckled down to his job with cheerfulness and a good will, and soon knew his way around the place. Among the animals some soon became great favourites with him.

Of the setters he particularly liked two. One was a yellow and white English setter dog called — though not on his Kennel Club pedigree — Lemon Drop. The other was a black and tan Gordon setter bitch. Although called Fairy, she was just the opposite, being big, heavy and clumsy, but with a fair turn of speed whenever she put up a rabbit. When he took the dogs for the afternoon walk around the paddock and up the little valley beyond it, he always had to keep an eye on Lemon Drop because the dog had a habit of wandering. Wherever Smiler went Tonks would go with him — unless he was away with Mrs. Lakey somewhere.

There was plenty of coming and going at Danebury House. People came to look over puppies they were thinking of buying, people brought and fetched cats and dogs from the boarding kennels, and once the Hunt met there before going off one Saturday. It was on that day that Smiler saw Mrs. Lakey in all her glory. She was mounted on Bacon, wearing a black top hat, a creamy white cravat at her throat, black hunting boots on which Miss Milly had put a shine that, she said, "would wipe the eye of the sun itself".

Smiler got to know all the calling tradesmen: the butcher, the baker, the milkman and the dogs' meat man who called twice a week. And

everyone got to know Smiler (Johnny) and to accept him. Miss Milly
fussed over him like a mother hen and he fed like royalty. Outside, Mrs.
Lakey kept him hard at work. He grew stronger and harder, and could
hump a hundred-weight sack without trouble, and wheel twelve loads of
stable and kennel litter in an hour without being troubled for breath.
After two weeks Mrs. Lakey put him up on Penny and gave him his first
riding lesson. It ended with him being thrown into a quaggy, watercress
pool in the middle of the paddock when Penny saw one of her private
fairies. But at the end of the first week Mrs. Lakey said, "Good, Boy.
You look less like a sack of hay on a seesaw than you did."

On the road between Crockerton and Heytesbury people got to know
Smiler on his morning and evening passage and waved to him. At Ford
Cottage he had fallen into an easy routine. He slept in the barn and
before he left hid all his belongings away under the hay. He went into
the cottage every night when he got back and checked the mail which
had been delivered in case there was a postcard from Major
Collingwood to Mrs. Bagnall saying that he was coming back. He saw
Mrs. Bagnall once or twice as he passed Lodge Cottage on the Sutton
Veny road. On Sunday – which was usually his day off unless Miss Milly or Mrs. Lakey wanted him to do something special for overtime work
– he would get on his bike and explore the country and then go into
Warminster to the cinema in the evening. He earned four pounds a week
and saved the best part of it, slowly amassing a small hoard of pound
notes which he kept in a tin box behind a loose board in the barn loft.

Before the first month was out he found a way to write to his brother-
in-law, Albert, and his sister, Ethel. One day the dogs' meat man (who
had taken a liking to Smiler) said he was going down to Southampton on
a Saturday to see a football match. He asked Smiler if he would like to
come along. So, Smiler took a Saturday off and worked the Sunday and
went with him. In Southampton he posted a letter to Albert and Ethel.
It read:

Dear Sis and Albert, Don't worry about me I am doing fine and am
shipping to sea for six months. Can't tell you the name natcheraly.
Not to worry I am in the pink.

Samuel M.

Albert – against his will, but forced by Ethel – took the letter to the
Bristol police. They passed the information on to the Southampton
police, and the Southampton police made a few enquiries around the
docks and shipping companies but "natcheraly" got nowhere!

So there was Smiler, nicely settled between Danebury House and

Ford Cottage. The weeks went by. February, which was a real fill-the-dyke month that year, passed. March came with its high winds and occasional days which were hot enough to make one think of summer. The hazel and willow catkins bloomed and the snowdrops gave way to daffodils and crocuses. The drab, flat winter grasses began to show a faint new green. In the gardens there was early almond and cherry blossom. Once or twice smart snowstorms returned to remind everyone that winter wasn't going to pass without a few last skirmishes.

Every fortnight Smiler went into Warminster and bought himself a tube of dye and some tanning lotion from Woolworth's to give his hair and face a new dressing. Every time he did so Mrs. Lakey would look at him the next morning oddly. Miss Milly would smile over the kitchen table at lunchtime and think how brown and healthy Johnny was from all the outdoor work.

Once when Smiler was in Woolworth's buying his dye and sun-tan, he also went on to the electrical counter to get a battery for the transistor set from the cottage which he still used at night.

As he was looking over the display, a voice said, "Hullo, you."

Smiler looked up to find himself meeting the dark eyes of Ivy (who liked to be called Pat) Bagnall.

"Hullo," said Smiler.

"You're Johnny Pickering, aren't you? Remember me?"

Smiler said, "Course I do. Pat Bagnall."

"How you been then?" asked Pat.

"Not bad."

"You still living in Warminster?"

"Yes, sort of. Just outside."

"Ever go to the Youth Club?"

"No. I don't go for that scene."

"You ought to try it. Like to come one night with me?" She said it with a smile and a little toss of her head which Smiler liked. At the same time he knew that the last place he wanted to visit was a Youth Club. People who ran Youth Clubs asked questions and took an interest in you.

"Can't really," he said. "I work most nights."

"Where?"

Smiler did some quick thinking and replied, "Oh, a garage down Heytesbury way. On the pumps."

"Every night?"

"Well, most." To change the subject, he went on quickly, "You like it here?"

"So-so. But I'm thinking of getting another job."

Smiler, not wishing to be further involved, and giving up the idea of buying a battery from her, said, "Well, see you around some time."

He moved down the crowded length of the shop. The girl at the cosmetics counter had seen him talking to Pat. After work she said to Pat, "Who's that chap I saw you talking to? One with a green anorak."

"Oh, him. He's just a chap I know."

"Dyes his hair, don't he? And uses suntan stuff?"

"Course not."

"Does you know. Comes in regular once a fortnight." The girl giggled. "And they say us girls is the vain ones."

That night, as Mrs. Lakey and Miss Milly sipped at their after dinner whisky and marsala, Mrs. Lakey said out of the blue, "That Boy."

"What boy?" asked Miss Milly.

"Johnny."

"What about him?"

"He's good with animals. Got Captain Black's brute of an Alsatian right under his thumb. Dog would lick his boots if he said so."

"Animals are good judges," said Miss Milly.

"So would people be if they used their ears and eyes. Anything about him ever worry you, Milly?"

"No, Jelly. He does his work and he's got a good appetite. Polite, cheerful, and clean — for a lad. Why?"

"I just wondered, Milly. Just wondered. Did you ever get to see his aunt?"

"Not yet. I haven't been over that way."

"Well, don't bother about it. I met old Judge Renton in Warminster yesterday. He lives Crockerton way. Asked him about the boy and his aunt. Said she was a good, solid body. Spoke well of the boy, too. So don't bother, Milly. You've got enough on your hands already without going parish visiting."

Mrs. Lakey picked up a newspaper and hid behind it.

*   *   *

While Smiler was settling in at Danebury House, Yarra was settling on the plain. By the beginning of April she was very close to her cubbing time and had grown heavy and full in the belly. She could still lope and trot tirelessly. But now, when she hunted a hare or rabbit, she killed her quarry quickly because she did not like to keep at top speed for long.

She found food easy to come by and knew a dozen places where she could always get water to drink. She lived mostly in the tank she had first picked for her sleeping quarters, but if she roamed far she had five other sleeping places, two of them nature-made lairs and three in abandoned tanks and lorries.

At Longleat Park there had been no news of her since they had lost her in the snowstorm. This worried the Cheetah Warden because he felt that she might have had some accident and been killed. She could easily have fallen down an old well or been shot by some farmer or keeper by mistake and then buried to avoid awkwardness over her death. Or she could have been swept away in a river flood. Or she could have caught some disease which had killed her. Her carcase might be quietly rotting in some lonely spinney or gully. But in his own mind the Cheetah Warden did not really believe any of these possibilities. On the other hand he could not understand why she had not been sighted. He had not overlooked the possibility that she might have found her way up on to the plain. As the Army authorities would not give permission for a full-scale drive across it unless there was a definite sighting, the Cheetah Warden had asked the Land Wardens who ranged the plain to keep an eye out for Yarra.

So far none of them had sighted her, but two of them had passed quite close to her in the course of the passing weeks. They missed seeing her when she was in the open at a distance because her coating merged into the background in perfect camouflage. Chiefly, however, they missed her because she moved about during the early morning and late evening. During the day, if she heard the sound of a car or tank engine, the crackle of firing or the shouting of the soldiers, she went into hiding at once. The nearer her time came, the more cautious she grew.

But this did not mean that Yarra had not been seen. Many of the birds and animals knew her. A carrion crow marked her morning and evening rounds. When she killed he would wait, circling aloft until she had eaten, and then move down for his pickings. The deer knew her and her scent and moved fast the moment it came on the wind to them. One or two lucky hares, who had escaped her, knew her.

The only human who saw Yarra during this period was Smiler. It was on an April day when the fat leaf buds were shedding their wrappings and beginning to green the trees, when the sheltered banks held the pale full glow of primroses, and some of the early blackbirds and thrushes had begun to lay. Smiler lost Lemon Drop on a walk up the coppice-studded valley. He only kept on leads the boarding dogs who were allowed out. Lemon Drop and Fairy and the resident setters were allowed free. Mostly they were obedient to him and came when he called. But Lemon Drop was a wanderer. When Smiler got back to the kennels he missed him. It was four o'clock and both Miss Milly and Mrs. Lakey were out. He knew he would be in trouble if they came back and he had to report Lemon Drop missing. He put the other dogs in their kennels and went away in search of him. He knew exactly where he would most likely be. Right at the top of the valley there was a small wood of lofty, smooth-barked beech trees. Lemon Drop had a passion for squirrel hunting there, and the squirrels now were out and about from their semi-hibernation.

Smiler went up the valley path at a steady trot towards the beeches. When he was fifty yards from the trees he heard Lemon Drop barking. He called and went in after him. From the sound of the barking he could tell that he was at the top end of the wood which was bounded with a wire-netting fence to prevent cattle straying through to the plain.

He found Lemon Drop at the foot of a tall beech tree. The tree grew right alongside the fence and some of its branches hung over it. Lemon Drop was looking upwards and barking furiously. He took no notice of Smiler as he approached. He ran round the tree, whining and barking, and then raised himself against the smooth bark of the great bole, looking upwards.

Smiler looked upwards, too, and immediately stood transfixed. Lying along a thick branch that ran outwards from the tree was Yarra. She was looking down at the dog from a height of about fourteen feet. Although Yarra was not unduly disturbed, she now and again gave a threatening hiss and spit and switched her long tail to and fro irritably. The perch on the branch was a favourite resting place of hers when she found herself in this part of the plain. She liked to lie up there, catching the warmth of the westering sun.

For a few moments Smiler saw her clearly, the sunlight catching her orange-and-black-spotted pelt, one foreleg dangling over the bough. Then she scented him, turned her head, and saw him. He was a big human being and she knew better than to stay where she was. She rose and moved quickly outwards along the branch. She jumped from it in a great leap that took her clear over the boundary fence, and went across the grass in a long, fast gallop.

Lemon Drop rushed to the fence, barking and growling. Smiler went after the dog and caught him. He slipped the lead on to his collar and held him. Away in the distance Yarra was soon lost over a rise in the ground.

Smiler walked away, dragging Lemon Drop after him, protesting and whining for a while. Smiler knew all about the plain now and how it was used by the Army. It was a wild place and, he argued with himself, soldiers could well look after themselves. So, why shouldn't Yarra be left to her freedom there? In a way he was glad to have seen her. Locally there were all sorts of rumours about her. That she had been killed, that she'd been seen well south of Salisbury in the New Forest, and that she'd gone back to Longleat and was hanging around in the woods there. Joe Ringer – the dogs' meat man who had become very friendly with Smiler – said that he knew for certain she'd been shot by a farmer, skinned, and her pelt turned into a rug for the front parlour, But Joe always had a different story from anyone else. In fact Joe was full of stories and most of them came from his own imagination.

Smiler decided that the best thing he could do was to forget that he had ever seen Yarra and to keep the dogs away from the plain. If he reported Yarra to Mrs. Lakey it would only bring the police and other people around and he would have to tell his story and attract too much attention to himself. Reporters would want to know who he was and where he lived, and might even want to ask questions of his non-existent aunt at Hillside Bungalow! That would put the fat in the fire. No, Samuel M., he told himself – just pretend you never saw her.

When Smiler got back to Danebury House Mrs. Lakey and Miss Milly still had not returned, but Joe Ringer was there. His little green van was in the yard and he was off-loading the dogs' meat into the store house.

"Where've you been then, Johnny? All the dogs back and you not here. I could have pinched the silver from the house and helped myself to a dozen eggs."

"Lemon Drop went on the loose," said Smiler. "Had to go and get him."

"Itchy feet and a sharp nose he's got. But too big for delicate work like . . . well, let's leave it at that." Joe winked.

Smiler knew exactly what he meant, because everyone knew that Joe was a poacher in his spare time. Joe was a small, wiry middle-aged man, with very dark hair and a dark complexion. He had gypsy blood in him. He had worked around Warminster and Heytesbury for fifteen years earning a living trading, knackering and poaching. He lived in a small cottage in a side lane running off the Heytesbury–Warminster road.

The cottage was close to the river. There was an untidy sprawl of tin sheds and huts behind it which were filled with all sorts of junk. Joe lived alone and did for himself. And he lived like a king. One way and another, whether in season or out, Joe fed himself and his friends on the fat of the land – trout, pheasant, partridge, jugged hare, delicious rabbit stews, baked grayling and – come Christmas time – turkey, duck, and stuffed pork. Eating was Joe's joy – though he never put on weight. Also, there was always a large cask of cider just inside his kitchen door. When Joe had taken Smiler to the Southampton football match, he had given Smiler supper afterwards. Smiler had been so full of food and cider going home that he could hardly cycle straight. Smiler liked Joe, and Joe liked Smiler. Sometimes Joe let Smiler drive the old green van up and down the road between Danebury House and Heytesbury.

And Joe knew perfectly well that Smiler (Johnny to him) didn't have an aunt living at Crockerton. Joe, who was curious about everyone and everything, had made a few careful enquiries. Joe was always on the look-out for bits of useful information that he could turn into an honest shilling or two. But Joe had a mystery in his own life, too. He guessed that Smiler had also. And because Joe liked Smiler – he kept what he knew to himself and asked no questions.

Joe now said, "What you doing Sunday next?"

"Nothing," said Smiler.

"Well then, I got an order for some early peewees' eggs. Like to help me collect 'em?"

"Peewees?"

"Peewits, Johnny. Lapwings. Them birds what nest up on the downs. Could be some laying already. Ten bob a dozen I can get. Give you a quarter of what we make? All right?"

"Yes. I'd like that, Mr. Ringer."

"Right then. My place. Eight o'clock. And don't blab it around. The eggs is protected."

"Protected?"

"By law. Shouldn't take 'em. But if nobody did the things they shouldn't the world would stop going round. While we're out I'll show you somethin' too. Place where my old Daddy used to live."

*　　*　　*

While Joe was talking to Smiler, Yarra was making her way northwards across the plain to her sleeping place. The evenings were much longer now. After the soldiers had gone there was still a good two hours of daylight. It was a time when Yarra liked to be abroad and hunting.

Because of the cubs she carried there were days when she was full of hunger and would eat three hares and any odd partridges or birds she could flush up. There were other days when the hunger forsook her altogether, and she just liked to roam to ease her restlessness. This was one of those days.

Above her in the evening sky as she moved the lapwings – whose eggs Joe was going after – were flying. Now and again when Yarra, un-suspecting, passed close to a nest a bird would come tumbling and diving down at her with a fierce, rushing sound of wings. Yarra ignored them.

Yarra went north for about three miles, then dropped to a shallow valley which had a road running through it. She crossed a small brook bordered with watercress patches. As she jumped it a snipe went up from a clump of marsh grass by the water and zig-zagged away down the valley in a swift, clipping flight.

Yarra crossed the road and went up a long barren slope, studded here and there with turf-topped weapon pits. She went right to the top of the long slope and came out on its ridge.

Below her was a long, narrow combe running away to her right towards the far stretches of the plain. From where she stood the hillside dropped very sharply to the valley bottom. For a quarter of a mile either side of her the hillside was too steep for the passage of tanks or troop carriers so that its peace was never disturbed. Tank tracks ran up the bed of the valley. On the far side, and lower down, there was a group of tall trees. Beyond them showed a narrow piece of road and a collection of village houses, roofs and windows shattered, gardens wild and overgrown, and not a soul to be seen moving. Beyond the houses on a rising slope, partly seen through bushes and trees, was a grey-stoned church. Its tower reached up to the sky and was ornamented with five tall stone pinnacles.

During the day, as Yarra knew, the village was often busy with soldiers and their vehicles. But at night it was always deserted. It was a village lost and isolated in the miles and miles of the plain, and it was a village which held no human life except when the soldiers came.

Yarra dropped down the valley side. Fifteen feet below the ridge grew four or five mixed ash and alder trees, their bases screened with blackberry and thorn growths. Behind them was a chalky patch of loose ground outside an opening just big enough to take Yarra's body. Inside, a narrow passage-way curved back a couple of yards and then opened out into a small, circular den about five feet in diameter. Years and years before, the entrance had been no more than a rabbit hole in the valley side. Generations of rabbits had tunnelled and warrened the chalky soil. Parts of it had collapsed and become enlarged. A pair of badgers, years before this moment, had taken it over and made it bigger. In the loose soil of the earth, thrown and eroded out of it, seeds had been dropped by birds, or had fallen from the coats of rabbit, badger and fox. Many vixens had cubbed there after the badgers left. Trees had sprouted and grown, and briars and thorns had seeded and flourished to make a screen that hid it. In all the years that the soldiers had used the plain, not one had ever found it. Yarra had found it when rabbit hunting along the ridge. Inside it was dry and warm, and Yarra meant to have her cubs there.

She had used it now for more than a week. During the day, when the soldiers were about in the village below, she liked to lie just outside the entrance, sleeping or dozing, and sometimes watching the far movements of men and vehicles.

She went into it now. In the half gloom she scraped at the loose chalk floor, then dropped to it and made herself comfortable. She lay, stretched flat out, her legs thrust away from her body, her head turned back on one shoulder. It was the way she liked to lie before sleeping.

Suddenly she twitched and stirred and gave a little growl. Inside her one of the cubs had kicked and moved. Yarra's head dropped. She licked at the line of her swollen dugs. The movement came again from inside her. She opened her great jaws in a yawning, silent unmasking of her fangs.

Within the next forty-eight hours Yarra was due to cub. That day was a Thursday.

*   *   *

When Smiler got back to Ford Cottage that evening, he made his usual cautious approach. It was a well-worn routine with him now. He first rode by the cottage on to the bridge to check for signs of life. Then he hid his bicycle in the copse behind the barn. From the kitchen garden he made a closer inspection of the house before slipping into the barn. When the light began to go, he always made a visit to the house to look at the letters which had been delivered while he was away. He left long before the postman called. He knew something of Mrs. Bagnall's habits now, too. She always came on a Wednesday morning. But sometimes if she was passing the cottage of an evening she would just look in to collect any mail for forwarding to Major Collingwood abroad. Smiler's chief concern was that there should come a day when the Major would send Mrs. Bagnall a postcard saying he was coming back. He knew, of course, that he might miss such a card when Mrs. Bagnall collected mail while he was away. But that was a chance he had to take.

What Smiler didn't know was that the Major was a man of uncertain routine. Sometimes he wrote to Mrs. Bagnall at the cottage, and sometimes he wrote to her at her own house. And what Smiler would have been very concerned to know on this evening was that Mrs. Bagnall that morning had received a card at her own house from the Major. It said that he and his wife – who was now in good health – were coming back on Sunday afternoon.

8

A Happy Event – and Others

Yarra had her cubs at six o'clock on Saturday evening. It had been a beautiful, warm April day. She lay most of the time on the patch of chalk just outside the cave entrance, blinking her eyes in the sun and watching the valley and the deserted village. Chiff-chaffs were calling in the tall trees. There was a bright sparkle of water by the road, where a spring rose to feed the little brook that ran through the village and away down the far valley. Two cuckoos exchanged their call signs most of the morning. Once a jay flighted up the valley side and sat in an ash above Yarra and scolded and shrieked at her. The movement in her belly went through her in slow waves and she changed her position frequently to find ease. She saw a Land Warden's patrol car move through the village twice during the day.

As the afternoon finally wore away Yarra got up and went into the gloom of the cave. Within an hour two cubs were born. They were little larger than kittens. Their eyes were shut and there was only the faintest shadow of marking on their grey bodies. Yarra cleaned herself, nuzzled the cubs close to her and licked and groomed them. They made pathetic mewing noises, their wet pelts starred with white chalk dust. After an hour they found her dugs. They butted and chewed at them for a while, finally found the coming milk, and began to suck. One cub was slightly larger than the other. This was a male. The other was a female.

Yarra lay happily with them, her head facing the cave entrance, her ears alert for any sound. When darkness came the cubs slept, cradled into the warm fur of her belly. Yarra caressed them with her muzzle and now and then licked at them. The restlessness had gone from her and she was at peace with the world.

With the coming of dawn light she was suddenly hungry. She stood up. The cubs sprawled away from her clumsily and then found one another. They huddled blindly together as Yarra left the cave.

She went up over the valley ridge on to the wide plain lands. Dawn was just coming up. On the wind from some distant farm came the sound of a cock crowing. A few early larks had risen and were filling the sky with song. Yarra trotted up the ridge to the higher reaches of the combe where it shallowed and finally merged with the long, undulating slopes of the high plain. Coming down wind to her Yarra suddenly caught a familiar scent. She froze and surveyed the ground. There was a slight movement in some tall grasses fifty yards ahead. Against the grass Yarra's keen eyes picked out a brown, white-mottled form, and she moved fast. Her body now was lighter than it had been, and there was a fierce joy in her that spurred her on as much as her hunger. A small fallow deer took to its feet ahead of her and went away like the wind. The deer, unlike a hare that would have twisted and doubled and tried every trick in the book, kept to a straight line, relying on speed.

Yarra ran it down within a hundred yards. She leapt and hit it at top speed, bowling it over. The two animals rolled in a flurry of bodies and flying legs. When they came to a stop, Yarra's jaws were clamped across the deer's neck, her forepaws ripping at its throat. The deer died quickly and Yarra settled to eat.

She ate first into the belly, and then the meat from one of the deer's haunches. leaving most of the hide untouched. When she had finished and was full she left the carcase and turned back down the valley.

High above her, a carrion crow, marking her early morning sortie, had seen the chase and the kill. When she had started to eat he had planed down to a rock outcrop on the far slope to wait. As Yarra left he moved in to have his breakfast. A roving pair of rooks saw him and came down to the feast. They kept some distance away and darted in only now and then to snatch a morsel.

Yarra went down the valley fast, along the tank tracks. In one place turning tanks had scoured a great depression and had broken the earth crust deep enough for a small spring to burst through. The water bubbled up cold and clear. Yarra drank and then went up the steep valley side. She did not go straight back. She climbed out of the valley over the ridge and then moved along out of sight from the valley and the deserted village. When she was directly above the cave, she came back over the ridge, her silhouette low against the skyline, and dropped the few feet down to the cave.

Inside the cubs had become separated and were mewing and shivering. Yarra gathered them into the warmth and shelter of her belly fur. They soon found her dugs and began to suck. Yarra lay back as they fed and purred softly to herself.

* * *

Smiler was up early that morning, too. He had a quick breakfast of cheese and biscuits in the barn, washed himself in his bucket and then cycled off to Joe Ringer's cottage.

Joe was waiting for him by the van. It had double doors at the back. Inside the body was boarded off from the driving seat so that Smiler could not see if there was anything in it.

To Smiler's surprise Joe drove into Heytesbury and then took the road up to the plain past Danebury House. He stopped at the post-barred entry and made Smiler get out and raise the pole for him and lower it when he was through.

Back in the car Smiler said, "Mr. Ringer, we aren't allowed up here, are we?"

"Officially, no," said Joe with a wink. "But if a man obeyed every *no* there was going, he'd grow moss on himself in a month. Nothing to worry about, Johnny. I know every inch of this place. And on a Sunday I can tell you exactly where the Land Wardens will be and when. Just leave it to your Uncle Joe."

A bit later, when Smiler saw the notices about unexploded missiles, he asked about them.

"Eyewash," said Joe. "They pinched the land from the public and now they don't want 'em a-tramping over it. But the officers and their friends shoot and hunt over it. Think they'd do that if there was land-mines and such like about? No, me lad, most you'll find is a few empty cartridge cases, some signal flare cannisters, and maybe a shell what ain't gone off when it should. You see anything you don't fancy – then leave it alone. I'll teach you all the tricks. Just leave it to your Uncle Joe."

Joe drove along the road for about a mile and then turned off down a rough track. Five hundred yards up the track was an abandoned Nissen hut with both ends missing. Joe drove the small van into the arched span of rusty corrugated iron and it was effectively hidden from sight.

A few minutes later they were moving over the long sweeps of a small plateau hunting for the lapwings' nests. Joe had a pair of field glasses and would sit for a while watching the birds in the air or for bird move-ment on the ground. The peewits nested right out in the open. When they came down from flight to their nests they always landed some way away and then moved through the long grass towards them. After watching an area for a while Joe had no trouble finding a few nests. Smiler was far from being an expert. Once he was standing looking about him for a nest when Joe said, "Go on, Johnny – you got a nest there."

"Where?" said Smiler.

"Right under yer nose," said Joe, pointing.

Smiler looked down. A yard in front of him on the almost bare ground he saw a shallow depression with three eggs in it. The eggs, green-and-brown-marked, blended perfectly against their background.

"Only one from each nest, mind," said Joe. "Mother Nature's a generous old gal – but she don't like greedy people."

They spent the whole morning looking for nests and collecting the eggs, which Joe packed into a series of small boxes that he carried in his haversack. Once, he caught Smiler by the arm and pulled him down quickly.

"Stick your head between your legs and your hands under your arms – like this. And don't move!"

Smiler crouched on the ground as he was told. Not far away he heard the sound of a passing car.

"What is it, Mr. Ringer?" he asked, head between his knees.

"Land Warden. But he won't see us. Not at this distance. White face and hands is the give-away. Particularly if he happens to use his glasses. Right now we look just like a couple of big mole hills, lad. Leave it to your Uncle Joe."

The noise of the car died away into the distance. Joe raised his head and winked at Smiler.

"What would they do if we was caught?" asked Smiler.

Joe grinned. "String us up to the nearest tree, I don't think! No – all you'd get is a good talking-to. Unless your pockets was stuffed with pheasants or hares – or maybe peewees' eggs. But you don't want to worry about them old wardens. Come up here a few times with me and I'll learn you. Fancy, all this good poaching ground just given over to a pack of mostly city-bred soldiers what don't know a bull from a cow!"

Confident under the protection of Joe, Smiler thoroughly enjoyed the morning. Because he knew that Yarra was up here somewhere, he was tempted once or twice to tell Joe about her. But in the end he decided against it. If they should come across Yarra by accident he knew there would be no danger. Joe would know how to deal with the situation.

At mid-day they went back to the van to eat. Joe had loaded aboard cold pork sausages, hard-boiled eggs, a loaf of bread, cheese, ham and pickles, and two bottles of cider. They ate like princes with the wind singing through the grasses, the larks carolling above and little clouds of black gnats hovering above their heads. Smiler ate until he was full, but he was careful with the cider. He knew what it could do to him. And Joe's cider was *extra* strong.

After they had eaten, Joe decided that they had gathered enough eggs. They left them in the van. Joe said, "Now I'll show you where me old Daddy was brought up."

He then proceeded to take Smiler on almost the same line across country as Yarra had taken a few days before. But when they came down into the valley which held the deserted village, they hit it just above the church. Joe sat down on the slope and pointed to the shattered and derelict village.

"That's Imber village, Johnny. What's left of it. Prettiest village on the whole of the plain it was till the Army folk took it. See the church? My Grand-Mammy's buried there. And my Daddy grew up in a house that ain't standing no longer."

He sat, telling Smiler all about the place: how the Army, years before, when they had bought the great stretches of the plain for training, had left the people to live there. But when the Second World War came, the people all had to leave so that the village could be used for training American and British troops in the skills of house-to-house fighting. At the present time the same training still went on.

"See that big place down there across the road? That's Imber Court. That used to be the big house. Not a door, not a pane of glass left in it. Soldiers by day, rats by night. I tell you, when the folk had to leave this place, Johnny, it broke many a heart. Course, *they* very kindly out of their big military hearts lets 'em come back once or twice a year. Special treat to have a service in the church."

Joe shook his head and puffed at his pipe. Then, his eyes running up the narrow combe beyond the village and to the sky at the far end of it, he pointed and said, "See them?"

Smiler followed his pointing finger. High in the sky two large, broad-winged birds were circling slowly. Below a smaller, blacker bird was rising towards them. Suddenly the two higher birds dropped together towards the one below. They rolled and dived and swooped close about the smaller bird.

"What are they?" asked Smiler.

"Pair of buzzards and the feller below is a carrion crow. Them is a-fighting. Reckon down below there you'd find a dead rabbit or hare and they're arguing the toss about who's goin' to feed first. You keep your eyes open up here, Johnny, and you'll see lots of things. I'll teach you."

Smiler said, "It must've been nice living up here."

"Well, that's what comes of fightin' and having wars. And people poking their noses into other people's business, and other folks likin' to dress up in uniforms and all that rigmarole." Joe lay back and laughed. "Know somethin', Johnny? A real secret? They took me for the Army a long time back. But they couldn't hold me. I upped and run, and they never caught me. Never. I'm a deserter of long standin' – and that's the way I'm going to be for the rest of me life. And you're the first one I ever told, Johnny."

"Oh, I won't tell anyone, Mr. Ringer."

"Don't suppose it would matter much after all this time if you did, Johnny. And don't keep givin' me that Mr. Ringer bit. I'm Joe to me friends."

After a while they made their way back to the van. But Joe did not drive off right away. He looked at his watch and made Smiler listen with him until they heard the sound of a Land-Rover passing on the road which they had left that morning.

"Regular as clockwork mostly they is, them Wardens," said Joe. "Time your watch to 'em."

A few minutes later they were driving back along the road and Joe was promising that he would bring Smiler up to the plain again very soon.

"We'll take the ferrets and nets up and have a go for the rabbits. Set a few traps for hares maybe – though they ain't much eatin' at this time of year. Oh, I'll show you around this place, me lad, so you'll know it like the back of your hand. Keep your ears and eyes open and not a soul will worry you. Yes, just you leave it to your Uncle Joe."

Because Joe made him stop and have supper in his cottage, Smiler was late getting back to Ford Cottage.

He cycled back through the gloaming in a very happy state of mind. At the river bridge over the Wylye he stopped and looked at the water. Joe had promised to teach him all about trout fishing – in season and out. "No findanglin' about with flies. You want a big trout – then you want a big worm on the hook." He was going to show him his way around the plain, too. The thought of the plain gave Smiler a nice, warm, excited feeling. It was so big and wild and full of life. Yarra was up there, too. He like the thought of that. At supper, in a roundabout way, he had brought up the subject of Yarra. What, he had asked Joe, would he do if he met the cheetah, say, on the plain? Joe had said, "Just stand your ground, lad. Stand your ground and stare it out. She'd go. Specially with a lad of your size. Now, if you was a little nipper . . . well, that might be different. But mostly all animals want nothing to do with humans. Give 'em the chance and they're away. You know what? I stared out a bull once. Real ugly he acted, too, for a bit, but I stared him out. Went away with his tail between his legs. It's the human eye, you see. Animals – 'ceptin' domestic ones – can't stand human eyes. Or," he laughed, draining his glass of cider, "– maybe it's just the faces they can't stand."

As Smiler came down the hill from Sutton Veny towards the river, he passed Lodge Cottage. The lights were showing behind the sitting-room curtains. Pat Bagnall was probably in there watching television. He had been into Woolworth's since he had spoken to her there, but she was not behind the electrical counter. So, he guessed, she must have got herself some new job.

Happy, though tired, Smiler free wheeled down the hill, past Ford Cottage and across the bridge, as he always did, to give it a look over before venturing in. Within a few seconds his happiness had gone.

As he drew level with the courtyard entrance he knew that his shelter had been taken from him. It was still light enough for him to see a car parked in the courtyard. The big five-barred gate was unpadlocked and open. From the kitchen window a light shone out. He rode to the bridge, propped himself on his bike against the parapet and looked at the front of the house. The dining-room window was dark, but there was a light showing through the sitting-room window, and another from the main bedroom. He guessed at once what had happened. Major and Mrs. Collingwood were back!

Smiler sat on his cycle and stared at the house. Dismay filled him and he groaned quietly to himself, "Oh. Crikey! Oh, Holy, Smoking Crikeys!"

At that moment from the dark sky above a fat drop of rain splashed on to Smiler's hand. He looked up. A quick splatter of heavy drops fell on his face as the first of a series of fierce April rainstorms swept through the river valley. In two minutes the rain was lashing down, churning up the surface of the river and sending Smiler racing for shelter – for the only shelter he knew.

He cycled back up the hill, hid his bicycle in the coppice and then hurried back around the rear of the barn. He surveyed the rain-blurred yard for a second or two and then slipped round and into the barn. Standing at the dusty window in the loft he stripped off his anorak and watched the house. For the moment all he could think of was that *they* were back. What was he going to do? WHAT WAS HE GOING TO DO? Then, pulling himself together, he began to give himself a good talking-to. Samuel M., he said, stop trembling and being scared. You've taken a little water aboard, but you aren't sunk yet by a long shot. Just think it all out! Nice and cool! No panic! NO PANIC! JUST THINK!

He sat down on a bale of hay and began to think.

*   *   *

Inside Ford Cottage Major Collingwood was in the sitting-room by himself having his coffee after a late supper. His wife was upstairs doing something in their bedroom. He got up and went to the corner cupboard where the drinks were kept. He had had a long travelling day and he felt like a glass of brandy with his coffee. As he poured himself the brandy, his eye fell on the box of cigars where Smiler had lodged his letter of apology. The sight of the box made him wonder if he would celebrate his home-coming with a cigar. He reached out for the box, touched its lid, and then changed his mind. He did not often smoke cigars, keeping them mostly for his guests. No, a little extra brandy would perhaps be a better celebration. He lifted the bottle and added more brandy to his glass.

Upstairs Mrs. Collingwood went into the bathroom to set out fresh towels which she had taken from the airing cupboard. As she drew the curtains she noticed some small brown stains and frowned to herself. They looked like rust marks, she thought. But how could curtains go rusty? She puzzled over it for a moment and then put it out of her mind. Anyway, she had long ago promised to treat herself to a new pair of curtains for the bathroom.

Downstairs Major Collingwood sat contentedly with his brandy and coffee. He was happy because he was home and even happier because his wife was fully recovered. His eye fell on the sixpenny bottle on the bookshelf. It looked just the same as when he had left it – which it should have done because Smiler had conscientiously replaced all the sixpences he had borrowed. When it was full, the Major promised himself, he would take the money and buy a present as a surprise for his wife. It was a generous decision because he had been really saving up to buy himself a new fly-fishing rod.

Hearing the rain pelting down outside he told himself that he really must go out and put the car in the barn garage. But then he felt so comfortable that he decided against it. A little rain wouldn't hurt the car for one night. In fact it would wash it clean.

* * *

While Major and Mrs. Collingwood were comfortably installed in the cottage, Smiler lay on his hay and did a lot of thinking. His first panic had long gone and he was being very practical. When Smiler wanted to he could really think a problem right through. By the time he fell asleep he knew just exactly what had to be done. It was going to take a little bit of careful handling, but he was sure that he was man enough for the task. He slept. In the hay close to his head, deeply buried, was the alarm clock which he had set for five o'clock. He had to be away in the morning long before there was any chance that the Collingwoods would be awake.

* * *

In her den, on the hillside above Imber, Yarra slept with her cubs. All night the rain-storms swept south-west across the plain. Once Yarra woke to find the cubs sucking at her. She nosed at them. Their pelts now were dry and soft and silky with a fine fuzz of hair. Outside she could hear the gurgle and splash of storm water cascading over the lip of the cave entrance to the bare chalk below. Down in the village a marauding old dog fox, hungry enough to dare the weather, turned into the deserted ground floor of Imber Court to see if he could pick up an unwary mouse or rat. In a corner of one of the bare rooms he found half a corned-beef sandwich left there two days before by a soldier. The fox ate it with relish.

9

A Change of Lodgings

The alarm clock woke Smiler. Outside the noise of the night's rain was gone. He got up and set about his plan of evacuation. He gathered all his spare clothes into a bundle and tied it with string so that he could sling it on his back. He put his tin with his money in his anorak pocket. He had saved almost twenty pounds by now. The alarm clock and a few other odds and ends he tucked inside his anorak. Keeping the light of his bicycle lamp low he tidied up the loft. There was nothing he could do about the transistor set, so he left it in full view on a hay bale. Down below he put away the bucket he had used for washing. Then, not without some sadness because he had come to think of it as home, he left the barn.

He got the bicycle and rode down to the stone bridge. He stopped for a moment and looked back at the black bulk of the cottage where Major and Mrs. Collingwood were sleeping soundly. Some time, he thought, the Major would find his letter, the transistor set, and miss the bicycle. What would he do then? Report to the police? Or just shrug his shoulders. After all, it wasn't much of a bicycle. Smiler had already had to buy two new tyres for it. Anyway, thought Smiler, there was nothing he could do about it except some day send the Major the price of a replacement bicycle. Yes, that's what he would do. He certainly didn't want to dip into his savings right now to do it. At any moment he might be in real need of money if he had to make a fast get-away to some far place.

He pushed his bicycle up the hill and began to ride slowly to work. He reached Danebury House in good time as he had intended. He knew the habits of the house well now. Mrs. Lakey never appeared out of the house before half-past seven.

Tonks met him at the gate with a welcome bark, but Smiler gave him a sharp word of warning and Tonks was obediently quiet. He rode round to the stable and put all his stuff up into the loft under a bale of straw. Then he went up to the garden and let the Twelve Apostles out into their run, picked up the eggs which had been laid overnight, and took them down to the kitchen.

While he was there Mrs. Lakey came in. She gave him an odd look and said, "You're around early this morning, Boy. Bad conscience or bad dreams, or both?"

"It was all that rain, Mrs. Lakey. I couldn't sleep."

"At your age you should sleep through a hurricane."

She gave him his coffee and then Smiler went about his morning jobs. Although he did his work well his mind wasn't really on it. Last night in making his plans he had been confident, but now as the moment for putting them into action grew nearer and nearer he wasn't so sure about them. People liked you and were friendly to you, and all that. But when it came to doing a real favour — and without asking too many questions. . . . Well, that was a horse of a different colour. However, he couldn't be gloomy for long. It was such a splendid morning after the rain. The April sun was a burnished ball in the sky. The rooks were cawing their heads off in their nesting colony at the top of the roadside elms. Blackbirds and thrushes were filling the air with riotous song and the paddock, when he exercised the dogs, was a sheet of green enamel. A wren had nested in the stable and flitted fussily around while Smiler was mucking it out. Half-way through the morning Lemon Drop and Captain Black's Alsatian had a fight and Smiler had to break it up. Outdoor work had made him strong now and he held them apart easily, giving them both a good talking-to.

At mid-day Miss Milly gave him boiled beef and carrots and his favourite jam roll with custard. When she asked him what he had done on his Sunday off he felt that it was better to say he'd gone for a bike ride, rather than tell her about Joe and the peewees' eggs. But she gave him an awkward moment when she said, "I saw you come from my bedroom window this morning, Johnny. What on earth was all that stuff on your back?"

"Stuff, Miss Milly?"

Miss Milly grinned. "Yes, stuff, Johnny. A big package on your back."

Smiler thought fast. "Oh, that, Miss Milly. That's some stuff my auntie wants me to take to the cleaners in Warminster on the way back."

"You don't leave till half-past five, Johnny. They'll be shut." Smiler's working time had been extended with the lengthening evenings.

"Not till six, Miss Milly. I can just make it."

Miss Milly shook her head. "I don't want you cycling like a mad thing up that dangerous main road." She winked at him. "Mrs. Lakey's taking Bacon to be shoed at four. You leave at five. But keep it to yourself, Johnny, or there will be considerable dissension between ever-loving sisters."

"Thank you, Miss Milly."

So Smiler left at five, laden with his household goods, to face the most testing part of the day.

He rode up the valley to Joe's cottage and left his bicycle and belongings just inside the garden gate. He went round the back of the cottage and found Joe repainting the faded sign on the side of his green van. The sign read – JOS. RINGER – DEALER – ALL GOODS HANDLED – LOWEST PRICES. Joe had got as far as the word PRICES.

He turned and saw Smiler and paint dripped off his brush to the yard floor.

He grinned and said, "Hullo, Johnny. Finished for the day?"

"Yes, Mr. Ringer."

Joe frowned. "Joe it is and Joe it must stay." He turned and pointed to the fresh white sign. "Eye-catcher, eh? Lowest Prices – know what that means? If *they* got something to sell – I pays the lowest prices. But if *they* wants something from me . . . well, then if I don't like their face *they* pays the highest prices. Economics, that is. What you hoppin' about from one leg to the other for?"

"I'm all right, Joe."

"Then why you lookin' as though you'd lost a shilling and found threepence?"

Smiler hesitated for a moment and then decided to plunge. "I got a bit of a problem, Joe."

"We all have, lad. Is it economic, personal, or religious? Help offered for all but the last. Like a glass of cider to loosen your tongue?"

"No thank you, Joe."

"Then I will – to give me strength. From the look of your face you must have murdered the Lord Mayor of London. Here, hold this brush."

Joe handed the brush to Smiler and went to the house. He returned with the cider jar and an old chipped china mug. He filled the mug and sat down on a box.

"Now then, Johnny me lad. Let's hear your problem."

Smiler hesitated for a moment and then he blurted out, "I got to find lodgings, Joe. And . . . and . . . I thought you might be able to help me."

Joe grinned. "Seeing as we're friends, and that's what friends is for, eh? Helping one another. But don't let's give the old horse a good gallop afore we knows where we're goin'. What you want lodgings for? You got a perfectly good auntie over at Crockerton. Don't tell me you've had an up-and-downer with her?"

"No, we haven't quarrelled. It just is . . . well . . ." Smiler didn't like telling a lie to Joe, but for safety's sake he had to. "Well, she's gone away. This morning. And she won't be back for a month. More maybe. And she thought it would be better if I found lodgings near the job. I could pay about two pounds a week. And if wanted give a hand around the place. And then –"

"Whoa!" cried Joe. "Rein her in a bit! Your auntie's gone off this morning?"

"That's right."

"Why, me lad?"

"Her sister's very sick. Down in . . . in Bristol."

Joe considered this and said slyly, "You sure it's Bristol and not, say, Yarmouth?"

"It's Bristol. She's very old and very sick, this sister. She's my auntie, too." Smiler was rather pleased with this last touch.

"Naturally," said Joe. "And your aunt only heard about this this morning and had to pack her gear and hump it away to Bristol?"

"Yes."

"Short notice, eh? But then sisters is always inconsiderate to one another – they tell me. Who's going to look after Hillside Bungalow?"

"The woman next door."

"As a good neighbour should. You'll go there now and then to run an eye over it, like?"

"Most week-ends, yes."

Joe finished his mug of cider and refilled it. He sat considering Smiler very closely, his face, brown as polished oak, half-thoughtful, half-smiling.

Then he said, "You want to give me a straight answer to a straight question, Johnny?"

"Of course, Mr. Ring – . . . I mean, Joe."

"Well, then Johnny, me lad, you listen carefully. I'm a man as likes to keep his own business to hisself. I make a living and the ways I do it ain't always by the book. But I haven't never done anything really bad. You know what I mean by that?"

"I think so, Joe."

"You'd better *know* so, Johnny. By really bad I means something you wake up and think about in the night – and you know it was really bad and you wish you'd never done it. You get what I mean, Johnny?"

"I think so, Joe."

"I mean like I wouldn't want to help anyone to find lodgings that had, say, pinched money out of the church box, or knocked off the till in a shop, or had been some kind of tearaway who'd think nothing, say, of bundling a poor old lady off a pavement and pinching her handbag.

Them's the kind I wouldn't help. So give me a straight answer, Johnny. You ever done anything like that?"

Smiler hesitated. He liked Joe and he wasn't going to lie to him over this – not even to get a good lodgings.

He said, "I pinched a few comic books sometimes. And, maybe, nicked a bottle of milk or a bar of chocolate that just happened to be there. But I didn't ever do anything bad like you said. Not ever. Cross me throat and hope to die!" He pulled the edge of his hand across his neck.

Joe nodded. "Just like I thought." He stood up. "Well then, about these lodgings. I got to admit that they're hard to come by. Specially at the price you're offerin'. But it just so happens that I like a bit of young company about the place. And, it just so happens that there's two bedrooms here and I only uses one. And, it just so happens, Johnny me lad, that not bein' hard up for an odd penny I ain't out to make a profit from a friend – so you can have the room for a quid a week. Make your own bed, keep your room tidy, help in the house – and the yard! And neither of us ask awkward questions of the other when we can see as how they ain't in place. Suit you?"

Delighted, Smiler cried, "Oh, thank you, Mr. Ringer!"

Joe frowned. "'Nother thing. Every time you call me Mr. Ringer you muck out the pig pen. Joe it is."

"I won't forget, Joe."

"Don't mind if you do now and then – that pig pen's an awful chore. Now then, pop out and get your bike and your stuff. I seed you comin' along the lane humped up like a bloomin' camel. And Johnny, another thing."

"Yes?"

"I don't think as I would mention your change of address to Mrs. Lakey and Miss Milly. They mightn't think I was a fit and proper person for you to lodge with."

"Of course they would. You're super."

"All the same. Don't let on. What women don't know won't worry 'em. Though I must say, they usually finds out in the end. Bring your stuff in, and then we'll go get ourselves a couple of fat trout for supper."

* * *

At the time when Smiler was taking his belongings into Joe's cottage Yarra was coming out of her den on the hillside. Imber village had been full of training soldiers all day and they had stayed rather later than they usually did. Yarra, too wise now to risk showing herself when there were human beings about, had kept in the den or at its mouth all day. When the cubs were full of milk and sleeping, she had lain half in and half out of the entrance watching the valley and the village below. All day there had been a movement of tanks and trucks through the place, the crackle of blank ammunition being fired and, now and again, a green or red flare would burst in the bright air and drift earthwards with a plume of tawny smoke rising from it. Higher up the combe a squad of soldiers had been firing two-inch mortar bombs over the ridge at an unseen target. Once a badly aimed mortar bomb had exploded on the ridge thirty yards behind the cave. It had shaken loose chalk and small stones from the roof. Yarra, touchy now that she had young to protect, had grown angry and hungry. But she would not leave the den until the men had gone from the village.

When at last the valley and the village were peaceful, Yarra left the cave. She moved swiftly up on to the ridge and then passed along it just below the skyline. The dry, tawny grasses of winter were marked now with new growths. Trefoils and small harebells showed their blossoms on the rabbit-bitten bare patches. Hungry, Yarra's keen eyes marked every movement around her: the flight of an early bee; the dance of a small hatch of flies above a rain pool; the flirt of wing and the scut of a rabbit's tail. But she wasn't interested in a rabbit. She wanted more substantial game.

High above Yarra three pairs of eyes watched her. The two circling buzzards, lazing aloft on a rising thermal current, saw her and drifted in her wake. While they mostly hunted for themselves, taking small birds, rodents and young rabbits, they were not too proud to feast at the remains of another animal's table. In the past Yarra had provided them with free hare and deer leftovers. So they followed her, spiralling round and round, waiting for her to make a kill.

The carrion crow, an ancient, weathered bird of the plains, watched Yarra too. Sliding across wind above her, but far below the buzzards, he turned a neat somersault and came down under the stiff breeze to perch on a solitary thorn that marked the valley ridge a few hundred yards from the cave. The crow knew the buzzards were watching Yarra's movements. He knew that if she made a kill they would give him no peace to take a supper from the leavings. It was not that he was afraid of them; but they were big, flappy-winged birds. They would – as they had often done – come sailing down above him, rolling and mewing a few feet above his head and upsetting him. This evening the crow felt in the mood for a more peaceful meal. And at this time of the year he knew where to find one. This was the time of the year when Nature began to spread her banquet for the predators. Nests were filling with young birds. The rabbit holes and warrens held young. The hare forms in the young bracken and tall grasses sheltered leverets, and almost every dead mole hill held a mouse's nest that could be dug out. The carrion crow knew that any hole or cranny was likely to hold something good to eat.

For many days now he had seen Yarra coming out of her cave entrance and he was curious. He watched her move away into the distant folds of the plain and then he flapped slowly down to settle on an ash outside the entrance.

He cocked his head and listened for any sound from the cave. He could hear nothing because the cubs were deep in milk-gorged sleep. He sat there for ten minutes and considered the entrance. It was bigger than most he knew. He was a wise old bird and realized that once inside a rabbit hole there was little chance of using wings for flight. All he would have was his great beak and claws to defend himself. He considered the cave entrance for a while, the westering sun striking turquoise and purple sheens from the long feathers of his great square tail. He uttered a bad-tempered *kwaarp,* and then flew down to the cave entrance. Slowly he began to stalk inside, jerking his great head about, on the alert for the slightest sound or movement. He turned the corner of the small tunnel run and was faced with the gloom of the cave itself. Although a fair amount of light seeped through into the cave, the crow stood there for a while until his eyes grew accustomed to the gloom. After a moment or two, the crow saw a slight movement at the back of the cave as one of the cubs stirred in its sleep. The crow moved forward, deliberately, cautiously, step by step, his great black beak held ready to thrust. One blow with his beak would break and pierce the skull of a young rabbit or kitten.

On the plain Yarra put up a hare from a small hollow filled with dead bracken drift. One of the buzzards high above saw the movement of the hare and the fast take-off of Yarra as she went after it. The buzzard mewed loudly, calling to its mate. The other buzzard swung downwind to close formation. The buzzards hung together, swinging round in a tight circle, watching the hunt.

Yarra closed rapidly with the hare, which was one she had chased before. It was a big, well-fleshed animal that knew its way around the plains. Before, it had escaped from Yarra by diving under a derelict tank where she could not reach it. But this time there was no such refuge in sight. The hare raced away with ears and eyes laid back. He could see Yarra following and gaining on him, no matter how much he swerved and switched, side-jumped and doubled and twisted. Yarra overhauled him fast. When she was three feet from him she went into her killing leap. The hare saw Yarra spring from the ground behind him.

Desperate, he produced the only trick he had to offer. As Yarra took off
– the hare stopped dead in his tracks. One moment he was going at top
speed and the next he was crouched motionless in the grass. Yarra sailed
right over the top of him, overshooting him by a yard.

The hare flashed round and was away. Yarra, angry and hungry,
screwed sideways as she landed, her talons tearing up grass and soil. In
fifty yards she was on his tail again – and this time she did not miss.

The buzzards above her saw her make her kill, mewed excitedly to
one another, and began to drift lower on the evening wind.

In the cave on the hillside the carrion crow was now standing two feet
from the cubs. He could see them clearly. Although he had never seen
anything like Yarra before, the cubs were no surprise to him. He had
killed many litters of wild-cat kittens. These were kittens, young and
tender.

He waddled forward, beak poised for the kill. As he did so, a stone in
the roof, loosened by the mortar bomb during the day, dropped from its
place and thudded to the ground behind him. The crow turned with a
jump and a flap of his wings. He faced the cave entrance warily. After a
while his tenseness faded. He turned and moved again towards the cubs.
They were lying a little separated and the crow instinctively chose the
larger for his kill.

He stood a foot from it, lowered his head and sharp beak and prepared
to jump in and thrust with all his power. At that instant a shadow
passed over the back wall of the cave.

The crow swung round to face Yarra as she came quickly into the
cave, carrying a large hare in her mouth.

It was the last thing the carrion crow ever saw. Yarra dropped the
hare and leapt for him. Her jaws took him under the neck as he tried to
fly up. Holding him, she killed him and then, still gripping him in her
teeth, shook and swung him about so that long black primary and small
breast feathers floated about the cave. Then she dropped him and went
to the cubs, waking them as she nosed and muzzled and licked them.
They had been saved because, as Yarra had settled on the grass to eat
her kill, a new instinct in her had suddenly been born, an instinct which
was soon to become a maternal habit – the instinct to take food back to
her lair for the cubs. She had brought the hare back to share with her
young, though it was going to be many days yet before they would be
ready for solid food.

*   *   *

At Ford Cottage Major Collingwood came into the kitchen. He had been pottering around the garden and barn. It was now time for him to tidy himself up before having dinner. He was a kind, pleasant-looking man, his dark hair well streaked with grey over the ears.

He said to his wife, who was mixing up eggs to make an omelette, "You know, love – some blighter's pinched that old bike from the barn."

Mrs. Collingwood smiled and said, "Then you should be glad. It was just a load of old junk. And you'd better get cleaned up. Omelettes won't wait for anyone – not even retired Army majors."

"It's funny," said the Major. "Not just about the bike. But I got a funny feeling in the barn."

"Indigestion?" Mrs. Collingwood smiled and cocked an eyebrow at him.

"No, my dear. But I'm pleased to see that you are now back in all your former *rude* health."

"What kind of feeling then?"

"As though something's been about."

"You mean a ghost?"

"No. Somebody. I just get that feeling."

"Well, then, perhaps it's the one who had the sardines because I'm quite sure Mrs. Bagnall would never have taken them."

"You mean you've missed sardines? From in here?"

"Either that. Or I miscounted before we went away. Six tins, I thought. Now there're only three."

"How could you possibly remember?"

"A woman does. Now go and get cleaned up. I told you –"

"That an omelette, like Time, waits for no man."

Major Collingwood went upstairs looking thoughtful and a little puzzled. And Major Collingwood, since he had done all his service in the Royal Corps of Military Police, was the kind of man who rather enjoyed a puzzle or a mystery. Since his wife had now mentioned the marks on the bathroom curtain, he studied them carefully before beginning to tidy himself up.

* * *

The cause of Major Collingwood's puzzlement was at that moment sitting with Joe in his kitchen having supper. Each of them was enjoying a grilled brown trout from the River Wylye which ran along the end of the field below Joe's cottage. Although it was a few days before the trout fishing season opened officially, it would have made no difference to Joe if there had been two months or more to go.

An hour before he had given Smiler his first experience of poaching trout. They had gone down to the river at the end of the field. Here, across the stream, was a set of hatches – like large wooden doors – that could be raised or lowered to regulate the flow of water to the weir pool below.

They sat on the hatchway run above the top of the pool and Joe tied a hook on the end of a spool of nylon line, which had a small stick through the centre of it. He showed Smiler the right knot to use. A half-blood knot, he called it. Then he threaded several worms on to the hook and clipped a heavy lead weight on to the line three feet above the hook.

They sat on the hatchway planks and Joe dropped the hooked, baited and weighted line into the water. He paid it out very gently as the bottom current took the lead weight slowly downstream along the river bed.

"You sits here like this, Johnny me lad," said Joe. "And it being still light you looks all innocent and enjoyin' the view. Then, if'n a river keeper shows up, or one of the gents what has fishin' rights, you just lets go the spool gentle. The whole lot sinks and you come back next day and fish it out. Always lookin' innocent and enjoyin' the view is important."

As he spoke he paid out line slowly, keeping a slight tension on it through his fingers.

"But if you is left in peace, you just pays away the line like this. Sooner or later one of them big trout below the hatch what the fishing gents can't ever get with their little bitty flies, will go for the worms. And, Johnny me lad, let 'em go for 'em you must. Even when you feel 'em. Let 'em take it all. No striking like the fly-fisher folk do. That old trout'll hook himself in no time. Like this one! Whoa!"

The line in Joe's hand suddenly streaked away and Joe let it run for a moment or two from the spool. Downstream a fish suddenly broke water in a great silvery jump. Joe held the line firm now, and the trout dived and darted all over the pool for a while. Then Joe began to haul the fish in without any finesse and lifted it up to the hatch on the end of the line.

"Always use a good, strong nylon line. Six or eight pounds breaking strain. The old trout won't worry about the thickness of the line if'n there's a bunch of worms on the end."

He smacked the head of the trout across a wooden post of the hatch opening, unhooked it, and dropped it into his pocket. He said, "Now then, you have a go. I've got my supper."

He made Smiler thread fresh worms on the hook. Smiler paid out the line as Joe had shown him. Within five minutes he had caught his supper. It was a beautiful brown trout, firm flanked, and flecked with lovely red and yellow spots.

"Kill 'un quick. That's a kindness some of these fancy fishers don't always bother about. That's a nice fish. Pound and half. It'll eat like nothing you've ever tasted before. Leave it to Uncle Joe. You'll see."

Later, Smiler sat with Joe in his new lodgings, the both of them eating grilled trout and drinking cider (Smiler being very careful how much he took, and Joe treating it like water). As he washed up the supper things for Joe afterwards, Smiler remembered how worried he had been that morning about how it would all turn out. And it couldn't have turned out better! It just showed that it did no good to worry too much about things that *might* happen. Though what he would have done without Joe, he just didn't know. Samuel M., he said, don't you ever forget what a good sort Joe is. . . and one day. . . . Well, one day you've got to find some way of paying Joe back. Say, for instance, you got really rich. Rolling in it, because you invented something that was bringing in thousands. . . . Well then, you could buy Joe a new van. . . . Yes, that was it. A new van.

He stood there day-dreaming over the washing up. There wasn't a cloud on his horizon. In five or six more months his father would be back.

* * *

While Smiler day-dreamed, Major Collingwood and his wife were having their after dinner coffee. The Major went to get himself a glass of brandy. His wife said she did not want one. This time, seeing the cigar box and feeling extra happy to be back and that his wife was in such *rude* health and, because, after all, there was no place quite like home – particularly when you had a wife like Mrs. Collingwood – he told himself that he jolly well would have a cigar with his brandy.

So, he opened the cigar box and found Smiler's letter. As he looked down at it, the telephone began to ring in the hallway. Mrs. Collingwood went to answer it. Major Collingwood stood there, reading Smiler's letter.

10

Enquiries Are Being Made

Major Collingwood liked the tone of the letter. Whoever "Hunted" was, he was a decent sort of chap with some kind of conscience. But if he liked the letter, he also liked mysteries even better. Being retired he had plenty of time on his hands. He had already found the transistor set in the barn, and had said nothing to his wife. The letter offered him a little detection work which he felt might fill many a long hour. However, because he knew his wife wouldn't like the idea that someone had used the house while they were away — it might make her nervous and upset — he decided for the moment to say nothing to her.

He slipped the letter into his pocket before she came back from the hall, and sat down with his brandy and cigar. He had decided that he was going to trace *Mr. Hunted,* quietly on his own. When he found him . . . well, then he would decide what to do.

When his wife came back, she said, "That was the Cokes. They want us to go to dinner next Friday."

"Splendid," the Major said. His friend Mr. Coke was a retired Chief Constable who still kept in very close touch with all police affairs and criminal incidents in the area. He could have an interesting chat with him without giving his private mystery away.

When he went up to bed that night, the Major took a closer look at the bathroom curtain, and then a closer look at the contents of the bathroom cabinet. He smiled to himself. If you used dark brown hair dye it could only be to make your hair darker, surely? But if you used sun-tan stuff before summer came. . . . Well, that was interesting now, wasn't it? He would have to think that one out.

* * *

The next morning Smiler rode to work as happy as a lark. He was so light-hearted, in fact, that he had to sing aloud to himself. Smiler had a good voice and he sang a favourite ditty of his father.

> *"Go tell Aunt Rhody,*
> *Go tell Aunt Rhody,*

Go tell Aunt Rhody,
The old grey goose is dead.

The one that she's been a-savin',
The one that she's been a-savin',
The one that she's been a-savin',
To make a feather bed."

Some days later Joe heard him singing one of his songs, and Joe joined in. At some time in his life Joe had been to America and he taught Smiler lots of new songs. Sometimes of an evening they would have a concert just for themselves, and Joe would bang away on an old piano he'd bought for five pounds and Smiler would sing his head off.

But this morning Smiler was singing just for himself because of the happiness inside him. He went about his work singing and whistling. Every time Miss Milly heard him outside she would stop what she was doing and smile and nod. Sometimes, if she knew the tune, she would go on with her work, humming it to herself. Only Mrs. Lakey said to herself, "That Boy's worse than having a canary about the place." But even she was pleased because the only thing with a long face she liked was a horse.

It was the beginning of two months of bliss for Smiler. April ran into May and early Summer smiled on the valleys and plains. Marsh marigolds, frogbit and water crowfoot flourished on the pond in the paddock. The primroses went and the bluebells came. Bryony wreathed up the hedges and the wild garlic flourished under the trees by the river. The trout and grayling grew fat on flies, nymphs and caddis grubs. The fledglings feathered up and felt an urge in their wings that made them restless in their overcrowded nests. The cuckoo pints unfurled their green sheaths and attracted small insects to crawl about over their stigmas and pollinate them. In the hedgerows, the real cuckoos had long deposited their eggs in other birds' nests.

Up on the plain Yarra looked after her cubs and hunted for them. Their eyes opened and their pelts began to take on the characteristic cheetah markings. Yarra brought them small birds, mice, shrews, once or twice a green lizard, and rabbits and hares. They grew stronger and steadier on their feet but still stayed within the cave. When they were bored they fought one another. When fighting bored them, the male would sometimes explore towards the mouth of the cave. Whenever Yarra saw him doing this she would cuff him back.

Smiler began to know the plain, too, for Joe often now took him up there poaching. Sometimes of an evening, for the evenings had now

grown long with daylight, Smiler would go up on the plain by himself.
He knew the movements of the Land Wardens' Land-Rovers now and
easily avoided them. He came to learn every dip and slope, every hollow
and valley-side for miles around the deserted village of Imber. He had,
too, his own ways of going on to the plain, avoiding the Vedette en-
trances. Since he now lived with Joe he could walk from Joe's cottage to
Imber in little over an hour.

Often when Smiler went up to the plain he took with him Joe's field
glasses. He loved to lie just below some ridge-top and watch the wild
sweeps of country. Through the glasses he came to know the
movements of many of the animals. He knew the foxes and the buzzards
and, on the fringe of the plain not far above Danebury House, he knew a
badger's set. Watching late into the dusk one day, he had seen the old
boar badger come out for his night's foraging.

But the thing that really excited Smiler — and something he had never
told Joe about — was that he had three times seen Yarra. The real reason
he had not told Joe about it was that about four times a week Joe went
down for the evening to the Angel Inn at Heytesbury. When Joe took
too much cider aboard he had a habit of slipping the guard on his
tongue. Smiler didn't want him to talk about Yarra in the Angel because
that would mean a search and hunting party going up for her. Smiler
didn't want her caught. Her freedom had somehow become linked with
his own freedom. He felt in a funny way that it would be dead unlucky
for him if he ever betrayed her.

He first saw her through his glasses on a Sunday evening. She was
some way from Imber, hunting. He picked her up as she came quickly
over the skyline. For five minutes he watched her quarter and hunt along
a slope a mile from him. She took a hare and he saw for the first time in
his life the tremendous turn of speed cheetahs can produce. The second
time she was much closer to him. He was sitting up on one of the high-
stilted observation platforms which the Army used for soldiers to watch
the fall of shot around tank targets. It was on the side of the valley that
ran eastwards from Imber. In the valley bottom was the small brook
that came down through the village. The stream had almost dried out
to a trickle now as its spring source slowly fell off. But there were still
a few pools along its length. Yarra came down to the brook to drink not
a hundred yards from him. She lapped like a cat for a while. Then she
turned and disappeared behind the trees that fringed the road leading
to Imber.

The third time he saw her was from the farm buildings at the back of
Imber Court. He was watching the pair of buzzards circling over a
narrow combe that ran up to the north from the village. One of them

suddenly mewed and planed downwards out of sight beyond the steep valley-side. The other buzzard followed. As Smiler brought his glasses down, following the birds, he saw Yarra come quickly over the ridge crest.

She came a few yards down the steep side and then disappeared behind a leafy screen of ash and alder trees. Smiler moved up the opposite side of the valley and examined the trees through his glasses. His observation being now from a different angle, he saw at once the tunnel entrance behind the trees. He watched it for an hour and there was no sign of Yarra. He guessed that it was probably her resting place or den, and made a note to himself to keep well away from it. There was plenty of room for both of them on the plain.

So the days passed for Smiler and Yarra. Smiler worked at Danebury, grew stronger and brown-tanned over his freckles so that he needed no artificial sun-tan. But every few weeks he had to dye his hair. (When it wanted cutting Joe would do it for him in the yard.) He always dyed his hair on an evening when Joe was down at the Angel, and he was very careful to clear up all signs of his operation afterwards. And he now knew where Pat Bagnall was working. He had gone into the food market in Warminster to get some supplies for Joe — and there she was sitting at a check-out point! There were a lot of people waiting to pay for their goods so he only had a brief talk with her. He met her again one Sunday morning when he was down at the river getting a couple of trout for his and Joe's evening meal. She had come down for a ride with her father, the river-keeper. He was doing something to the hatches lower down river.

Smiler was glad to hear this because he already had two fat trout hidden in the bushes not four yards from them.

Although he liked her, he didn't care for the direct way she put personal questions.

She wanted to know where he lived.

Smiler nodded his head across the fields to Joe's cottage. "Over there — with my uncle, Joe Ringer."

Pat laughed. "My dad knows him all right. Fancy you being related. Hope you don't carry on like he does sometimes. Dad says he's worse than otter or heron where fish is concerned.

"Uncle Joe's all right, believe me," said Smiler stoutly.

"Where do you work, then? Still at the garage, Heytesbury way?"

"Not now. Got a job at Danebury House. With Mrs. Lakey."

"Oh, her. My dad knows her, too." She giggled. "Lash-'em-and-Bash-'em Lakey he calls her. Says she should have been a man. But he likes her."

"So do I," said Smiler. He grinned at the description of Mrs. Lakey. It was not far off the mark.

Then, with a sly twinkle in her eye, Pat said, "Still dye your hair, then?"

Under his tan Smiler blushed. "What do you mean?"

Pat laughed. "Girl I know in Woolworth's says you used to buy hair dye there – and sun-tan stuff."

Thinking quickly, Smiler said, "What if I did? It wasn't for me."

"For who, then?"

"Well. . . . For my Uncle Joe."

"What's he want it for?"

Desperate, feeling himself led into deep waters, Smiler said, "I can't really tell you. He mixes it all together and . . . and . . ." A brainwave came to him. "Well, if I tell you, promise never to let on to anyone? You'd get Uncle Joe in trouble."

"Promise."

"Well, this mixture. He uses it on white hens' eggs. Dyes 'em brown and it don't come off when you boil 'em. People prefers brown eggs and Uncle Joe sometimes only has white ones. But don't you tell."

Pat laughed. "What a crook. But I won't tell."

It took Smiler another ten minutes to get rid of her. He went back, with his trout, feeling limp with all the effort of making up his story, and had two mugs of cider instead of one with his dinner.

* * *

When the cheetah cubs were well over a month old they no longer stayed all day in the valley-side den. Although they were growing stronger each day, they were still clumsy on their feet and were a long way from being able to hunt for themselves. A rabbit or a hare could easily outrun them. Early each morning and late in the evening Yarra would take them out on to the hillside or up over the ridge on to the pain. For their education she would stalk and catch a mouse or shrew. Without killing the animal, she would release it so that the cubs would chase it. Then they would fight and quarrel as to which one should eat it.

Yarra never took them far away. She stayed by them during the day and made sure that they never went far beyond the entrance to the den. Sometimes when they were out together she would leave them briefly to hunt down a rabbit or a hare, and then, the cubs following, trot back to the den where they would all eat. Although her milk was now drying up, the two cubs still suckled at her during the night. Feeding the cubs during the day and keeping near them often left Yarra hungry. When they were fast asleep at night, and there was no danger of their straying, Yarra would go out on her own and kill for herself.

The nights now were mostly warm and light. Her eyesight was keen and it was seldom that she failed to turn up some game. She knew now the patches of bracken and small spinneys where the deer rested. She hunted always upwind, waiting for the scent of deer, hare or pheasant and partridge to come drifting down to her.

It was towards the end of May that Smiler first saw the cubs. Always when he was Imber way in the evenings he would take up a position on the far side of the valley and spend half an hour watching the entrance to the den. One evening he saw Yarra come out of the entrance and stand sniffing the air for a while. She moved farther out and the two cubs followed her.

Smiler nearly dropped his field glasses in surprise. Although he knew from local gossip that Yarra was a female, it had never occurred to him that she would have cubs. No mention had even been made that she was carrying young when she had escaped.

Tense with excitement, he watched Yarra lead the cubs along the valley side. He saw her pouncing into the long grass after mice and grinned and chuckled to himself when the clumsy cubs imitated her example.

He went back to Joe that evening hardly able to conceal his excitement. He wanted to tell Joe all about it. In fact, he felt guilty that he couldn't share this wonderful piece of news with Joe, but he knew what Joe was like. It would make such a good story in the bar of the Angel Inn that Joe would never be able to keep it to himself.

So, Smiler kept quiet. It gave him a nice warm feeling that he was the only one who knew. It was his secret. Also, there was another feeling in him. Yarra had escaped from captivity. She had become a wild animal again and was raising a family. She was doing it, too, in a wild area of ground right in the heart of civilized England. Smiler, although town-bred, had now become a country boy. From talks with Joe and Mrs. Lakey and – most of all – with Miss Milly, he knew how the countryside was becoming spoiled and polluted and how hard it was these days for wild animals to survive. The hedgerows in which the birds nested were being pulled down and wire fences put in their place, making it harder for them to find breeding sites. He knew that mechanical reapers and binders had almost exterminated the corncrakes. He knew, too, that long ago Salisbury Plain had held the great bustard. He heard Miss Milly go on about the use of pesticides and chemical fertilizers that poisoned birds and animals and seeped into the rivers to kill fish. Sometimes he even felt bad about the poaching that he and Joe did, but as the game they took was usually rabbit, hare, pheasant or woodpigeon of which there were plenty he did not feel too guilty. That Yarra – not even a native animal – was managing to survive in the midst of all this gave him a great sympathy for her. He was determined that Samuel M. wasn't going to be the one to give her away.

* * *

Meanwhile other secrets were being kept or defended unknown to Smiler.

First of all there was Major Collingwood, who by now had discovered the loss of his old green anorak, and guessed, too, what had happened to the old bicycle. Weeks before, during his dinner with Mr. Coke, he had pretended that he wanted to be brought up to date on the local events which had occurred while he and Mrs. Collingwood had been abroad. He was told, of course, about the escaped cheetah, Yarra. He was told, also, a lot of other things which were of no great interest to him. But he *was* told that a young lad, named Samuel Miles, who had run away from a reform school only to be caught by the police, had escaped again in a storm while being taken to Salisbury. The escape had taken place some six or eight miles south of Warminster. This interested Major Collingwood very much. "Hunted's" letter, he felt, read like a young lad's letter.

Some days later, he went into the police station at Warminster. He knew the Police Inspector there and got a description of this Samuel Miles and all the facts that were known about him.

The Police Inspector, who was a friend of the Major, said, "What do you want to know all this for?"

The Major winked and said, "Sounds a very enterprising young chap – if *you* haven't picked him up yet. I thought I'd like to try my hand at it."

"Well – you'll have to go abroad again if you want him. He wrote a letter to his sister some months ago, saying he was shipping to sea."

By the time the Major left he had been given the address of Ethel and Albert. A few days later he drove to Bristol to see them. Of course, he knew by now that Samuel Miles was very fair-haired and very freckled. The question of hair dye and sun-tan stain no longer puzzled him.

When he met Ethel and Albert and talked to them there was no doubt in his mind that the person who had taken his bicycle and anorak, eaten his wife's sardines, borrowed his sixpenny pieces (and paid them back) and stained the bathroom curtain was none other than Samuel Miles, known as – Albert told him this – Smiler. Ethel, who had got it back from the police, showed him the letter which she had received from Smiler. One glance told the Major that the handwriting was the same.

The Major said, "Do you think he really went to sea?"

Albert said, "Could have done. It's in the blood. That's where his Dad is – and won't be back for another six months or more."

"There's more than the sea in his blood," said Ethel. "There's wildness. Bad company did it. Led 'im astray. Fancy – knocking an old lady down and taking her bag."

"I don't believe it!" said Albert.

"You did when it happened," said Ethel.

"Changed my mind," said Albert. "Smiler wouldn't 'ave done that. And wherever he is, Smiler won't turn up until his Dad's back. Thinks the world of him, he does. Thinks he can straighten it out. You mark my words – moment his Dad's back, he'll turn up."

"You must both be very worried about him," said the Major.

Albert grinned. "About Smiler? No. If ever there was a boy that could look after himself, it's Smiler."

When the Major left he was inclined to agree. He found himself more than ever interested in Smiler. Driving home Major Collingwood decided that if Smiler had used the cottage and the barn then someone around the place, one of his friends or Mr. and Mrs. Bagnall, or their daughter might have seem him. He decided to make a few innocent enquiries. He asked Mr. Bagnall and got no help from him. He asked Mrs. Bagnall with the same result. Then one day, meeting Pat Bagnall pushing her bicycle up the hill from the bridge, he stopped and had a chat with her. He talked about this and that for a while and then said, "While I was away did you ever see a young lad – say between fifteen and sixteen – around the place? Tallish, strong lad, he'd be. Darkish brown hair and very sun-tanned. He could have been wearing a pretty old, green anorak.

Pat thought for a moment, but not because she didn't know the answer. It was an exact description of Johnny Pickering. She knew the Major well. He was a nice man and she liked him. But she liked Johnny, too. The Major's innocent question did not fool her. He had asked it in just the same way as her mother and father did when they were trying to get something out of her, or to trick her into giving something away she didn't want to give. So she said casually, "No sir, I can't say that I did."

And that – for all his cleverness and professional training – was as far as Major Collingwood got for the moment.

* * *

It was about this time that Mrs. Lakey discovered that the Boy was living with Joe.

Mrs. Lakey was a keen fisherwoman. On two mornings while fishing the pool below the hatchway for trout she had looked across the field and seen Johnny feeding the pigs in Joe's ramshackle pen. As, on each occasion, the time was half-past seven of a Sunday morning – for Mrs. Lakey believed that it was the early fly-fisher who caught the best trout – she found it a little unusual.

A few days later when she had to call on Joe to give him some directions about dogs' meat supplies she tackled him in her usual straightforward manner.

"Joe," she said.

"Yes, Ma'am?"

"Is that Boy living with you?"

"What boy, Ma'am?"

"Don't wriggle like a worm on a hook with me, Joe. The Boy."

"Oh, you mean Johnny, Ma'am."

"You know perfectly well who I mean. He's living with you?"

"Yes, Ma'am."

"Why?"

"Well, 'cos in a way, I'm kind of his uncle. Distantly relationed, you might say, to his aunt."

"Being you, you might say anything. Why isn't he with his aunt?"

"The one at Crockerton, you mean, Ma'am?"

"I've never heard of another."

Joe smiled. "Oh, yes, Ma'am, he's got another. What lives in Bristol. And that's where 'is Crockerton auntie is right now. Lookin' after her, 'cos she's sick. Got a very bad leg. Plays her up somethin' cruel every summer. Not to mention hay fever. Martyr she is to every ache and pain goin'. I remember 'er as a small girl – always a-pickin' up somethin' or the other. A medical wonder she is, really. Once 'ad mumps three times running as a girl –"

"I don't imagine she could have had it as a boy. And I'm not in the mood for medical fairy stories. The Boy lives here with you?"

"Yes, Ma'am."

"With his aunt's permission because she's away?"

"Yes, Ma'am."

"And you're kind of distantly his uncle?"

"Yes. Ma'am."

"And no doubt you're seeing he doesn't get into bad ways?"

"Yes, Ma'am."

"Never poaches, does he?"

"Oh, no, Ma'am."

"Or worms for trout?"

"Oh, no, Ma'am. And he goes to church sometimes of a Sunday." Joe put on a very serious face. "And I really do hope, Ma'am, as how you don't think that I ain't a fit and proper person to bring up me own nephew. Ain't he given you every satisfaction at Danebury, Ma'am?"

"He has, Joe. And that's the way I want it to go on. So, you watch your step with him. He's a good boy as boys go."

"The best, Ma'am. Couldn't be in better hands than with me, Ma'am. Though I says it meself."

"And if you didn't say it yourself who else would?"

When Mrs. Lakey got back to Danebury House she told Miss Milly about the Boy's change of abode. Mrs. Lakey privately felt that Joe was as fit a person as anyone for a boy to live with, though she wouldn't have said so to his face. If fishing was dull she wasn't above putting a worm on a hook herself to get a trout. Apart from all this, Mrs. Lakey was a person who – though always ready to help if asked – was a great believer in letting other people, especially young people, work out their own problems. She didn't know what the Boy's problem was, but as far as she could see he was coping with it perfectly capably at the moment.

11

Two Mothers Meet

By the first of June the cheetah cubs were seven weeks old. They were faster and steadier on their feet and could mouse-hunt for themselves, and were sometimes quick enough to take a slow-moving young lark or green plover in the long grasses. But they were still too young to run down a rabbit or a hare. Yarra provided the bulk of their food for them. The odd small stuff they caught for themselves would by no means have kept them alive.

However, there were times now when Yarra, sensing the future when they would have to fare for themselves, would sometimes cuff them away from the game she brought back. She was deliberately making them hungry now and then to strengthen their own hunting instincts. She would eat first, spitting and mock-snapping at them if they tried to approach until she had had her fill. If she awoke in the night to find them sucking at her dugs she would roll away from them, denying them the little milk flow that remained. Also in her, though not understood by her, was now a different kind of restlessness from the one she had known when she had been carrying her young. Yarra, like all her kind, was a sociable, pack animal. She did not like to live alone. Now that the cubs were growing and her maternal instinct had been satisfied, there was a new want in her. She had a need for the company of her own kind. This restlessness made her, when she left the cubs sleeping in the den, roam wider than she had done in the past. Somewhere in the vastness of the plain there had to be others of her kind, another Apollo to mate with, and other cheetahs to pack and hunt with. It was this that one night took her quartering and hunting into the face of a stiff north wind which was blowing almost a gale across the plain.

Once or twice she put up a rabbit, began the chase and then broke off. She was hungry but there was a stronger need inside her. Within an hour she was, although still on the plain, in new country to her. The wind whipped and flattened the tall grasses, blowing out of a cloudless sky that was ablaze with stars. Now and again she heard a small brown owl call. She watched the navigation lights of an airliner wink and blink across the sky. She scented deer twice but ignored the instinct to hunt.

Eventually she came out on to a high bluff at the northern extremity of the plain. A wire fence ran along the ridge of the bluff. Below, the land fell away into a great valley, the fields seeded with corn, the long slopes broken here and there with patches of woodland. Two miles away the occasional headlights of a car moved along an unseen road.

Yarra turned left along the fence, the wind buffeting at her thick, rough coat. Once she squatted on her haunches, sphinx-like and immobile, and then raised her head and gave two or three angry, rasping calls. She moved on and put up a rabbit from the lee of a gorse bush. She leapt and caught it by the neck, clamped her jaws hard, holding it until it died of suffocation. She dropped it and passed on.

When the fence angled downwards, following the slope of a combe-side, she followed it for a hundred yards to the foot of the combe. Here the fence ran along the edge of a large grove of tall beech trees. The high wind was bending and whipping the leafy top branches of the trees, making a loud soughing and whistling noise. Yarra stopped just short of the wood. Beyond the fence was a pasture field, the grass short from cattle grazing. A new scent came downwind to her.

It was a scent she had known before, but not for a long time now. Sometimes it had come to her in the cheetah enclosure at Longleat. She had also known it now and again in her first days of escape. She lifted her muzzle into the wind and took the scent. From the side of the wood which ran down the edge of the pasture there came a low, anxious, bleating sound. With the sound came a movement which Yarra saw at once.

At the woodside in the pasture something small and white stirred. The bleating sound came again, almost drowned by the rushing noise of the wind through the beeches.

The white object moved again but stayed in the same spot. Curious, Yarra leapt the fence and began to walk slowly towards the object.

The side of the beech wood bordering the field had been fenced off with strands of barbed wire which ran on thick posts. Posts and barbed wire were old and in places had collapsed. Twenty yards from Yarra strands of wire lay coiled and twisted on the ground. Caught by the leg in one of the coils was a small calf. In its struggles to escape the coil had pulled tighter and now it was firmly trapped. It was an Ayrshire calf, white-coated with a scattering of brown markings.

As Yarra approached it made an anxious, lowing sound and then stood still. It saw Yarra. Yarra watched the calf. It was no larger than some of the deer she hunted and she waited for it to move. From its scent she knew it was good eating. The fact that it stood still made her curious. Slowly, with her high-shouldered, deliberate walk, she paced towards the calf, but made a small half-circle to come past it. This brought her slightly upwind of the calf and her scent reached it. Catching Yarra's scent, and instinctively sensing the menace in the way the cheetah walked, the calf plunged and bleated and tugged against the wire that was trapping one of its hind legs. The length of wire pulled away from a holding staple in its rotting post. The calf bounded forward about six feet and was brought up with a jerk as the wire was held by the staple fastening in the next post.

The movement excited Yarra and she raced in and leapt. She landed on the calf's back and brought it crashing to the ground. Yarra's jaws clamped across the back of the calf's neck, choking all sound from the animal.

Her weight holding the calf down, Yarra tightened her grip. The calf kicked and struggled under her as she slowly throttled it, worrying and shaking its neck. High above, the wind, funnelling up the narrow combe, roared and whistled through the tall beeches, ripping off leaves and small twigs.

From farther down the sloping pasture the calf's mother had heard the distress calls of its young. She came downwind now, along the edge of the wood, seeking her calf. The wind carried her scent to Yarra, but her nostrils were full of the same scent from the calf. Also, Yarra heard no sound of the cow's movement towards her because it was drowned by the high soughing of the gale wind blowing through the trees.

The calf died under Yarra. She opened her jaws and released it. As she did so, she saw the movement of the Ayrshire cow almost on top of her.

The Ayrshire was a big animal. She had calved more than once before. She had a sleek white hide, blotched with cherry-red and brown markings over her forequarters. Like all Ayrshires her horns were very distinctive. They were long, and curved outwards and upwards and then slightly backwards. Formidable weapons. Under any other circumstances the cow would never have approached Yarra. But now she was impelled by her maternal instincts.

She lowered her head and rushed at Yarra. Yarra turned and leapt sideways to avoid her. She was a fraction too late. As she rose into the air, the cow jerked her head with a quick sideways slash of her horns. The left-hand, long, curving horn struck Yarra in the side, daggering deep into her belly just below the bottom of her rib cage.

Yarra gave a sharp angry, spitting snarl of rage and pain as she was flung high through the air. She thudded to the ground, rolled over, found her feet and then raced away as the cow came charging after her.

Yarra leapt the boundary fence and kept moving fast. Blood dripped from her wound. She went up to the head of the combe and headed southwards, back across the plain towards her den and her cubs.

As she moved, the pain in her belly nagged her. Once she halted and sat and licked at the wound.

Behind her in the pasture field the Ayrshire cow nuzzled and sniffed at the prostrate form of the calf. No movement came from it. (The next morning when the farmer saw it, he was to think that foxes had found the trapped calf and killed it, but had been driven off by the mother before they could eat it.)

Yarra took a line straight across the plain for her den and her cubs. She had three miles to go. With every step she took her pain increased and she grew more and more exhausted, and weaker and weaker. Behind her the gale-flattened grasses and the bare tracks were spotted with the trail of her life blood.

She kept on, following her line and her instinct to return to her cubs. Now and again she stumbled, only to pick herself up and move on. She reached the top of the ridge above the den and half-rolled, half-slid down the slope to the little screen of trees in front of the cave entrance.

She stood at the entrance, exhausted, her flanks heaving with the effort of breathing, her head dropping lower and lower on her long neck. She took a step forward to the entrance, staggered and fell. As she struggled to rise again and reach her cubs, she died.

*   *   *

Yarra died on a Friday long before daybreak. As morning came the wind which had been all night in the north slewed round into the north-west and brought thick, low-flying clouds sweeping over the plain. Rain began to fall steadily, a hard, warm, persistent summer rain.

The cubs, waking from sleep at first light, came out of the den and found their mother. She lay stretched out stiffly, the rain soaking into her pelt. They sniffed around her, not understanding her immobility. The male pawed for a moment or two at her neck to wake her and butted at her with his head. Then, not liking the hard, driving rain, he shook his body free of the clinging water drops and trotted slowly back into the den. The female stayed outside longer. She was hungrier than her brother. This was the time of day when normally Yarra took them for their morning hunting. She walked around Yarra making small mewing noises and then, getting no response, bad-tempered little spitting sounds. She crouched, flicked her small tail and jumped once or twice playfully at Yarra's flank. Yarra showed no movement. The cub, hungry, nuzzled at Yarra's dugs, hoping for milk. No milk came. After a while she moved back into the cave.

Yarra lay under the rain. The water, gathering on the steep slope above the den, now began to run down through the grasses in growing trickles and rivulets.

The mate of the carrion crow which Yarra had killed came flying low along the valley ridge. It saw Yarra and wheeled and circled for a while over her. Not trusting the immobility of the body below, it slid away down the valley to forage among the Imber village ruins.

The rain lasted all day. Down at Danebury House Smiler worked wearing an old Army groundsheet tied over his shoulders. Although he wanted the rain to finish, he knew that it could well last all day. It was coming on a strong wind out of the northwest, the kind of wind his father always called a *cat's nose* wind, though his father couldn't tell him why sailors gave it that name. He wanted the rain to finish before the evening came because he had planned to go up on the plain to see if he could spot Yarra and her cubs hunting.

At six o'clock as he cycled back to Joe's cottage, it was still raining. The river was beginning to rise fast, and the road ditches and drains gurgled and spouted with torrents of frothing brown water. Smiler realized that there was no hope that it would stop that evening. He decided that after his supper he would walk from the cottage to the main road and get the bus to Warminster. There was a good film showing which he wanted to see. With luck, he thought, he might persuade Joe to come and then they would go in the old green van and Joe would let him drive. Often now, Joe would let him take the wheel. Smiler was becoming a fairly confident driver, though Joe wouldn't let him drive in Warminster itself for fear of being caught by the police. Smiler wasn't yet old enough to have a provisional driver's licence. However, along the country roads Joe didn't mind a button about Smiler driving.

Up on the plain the rain had kept the cubs to the cave all day. Now and again one or other would venture out and inspect Yarra. As there was still no movement from her they eventually gave it up and huddled together at the back of the den, growing hungrier with each passing hour.

Towards midnight the rain stopped. The sky cleared swiftly of clouds and the fresh-washed stars shone down diamond-bright. The male cub, aware of the absence of rain noises in a moment of wakefulness, got up, stretched himself, and moved towards the mouth of the den. He was hungry. The lashing rain which he disliked had gone, and he knew that on the valley slope there were mice and shrews and small roosting birds to be caught.

He was two feet from the mouth of the cave when there was a noisy, rumbling sound. The few stars on the low horizon which he could see beyond the cave entrance suddenly disappeared. Something large and heavy hit him sharply across the neck. He spat and snarled with anger and bounded back to the rear wall of the den — as the roof of the cave entrance collapsed.

Weakened and loosened by the persistent rain which had soaked all day into the ground, the ancient archway of the tunnel entrance had suddenly subsided and sealed up the entry to the den.

Outside, the ground above the cave slipped forward in a minor avalanche, sweeping turf and chalk and stones downwards in a spreading fan which half-buried Yarra's body. When the movement ended all that could be seen of Yarra was her head and shoulders and her forelegs. Behind her the mouth of the cave was blocked. Inside against the rear wall, the two cubs huddled together in fright.

Later that night a travelling fox caught Yarra's scent and came a little way down the valley side to investigate. It sat for a long time looking at Yarra and then moved on. At first light the two buzzards, spiralling hundreds of feet above, saw her. The sandmartins hawking the early morning midges and gnats low along the hillside saw her. A white-bellied mouse rummaging among the branches of the tree-screen saw her. All of them knew her and all of them still kept their distance.

In the cave behind her the two cubs mewed, growled and spat, knowing only their hunger and growing thirst. The male cub explored the blockage and found a small puddle of water trapped in a hollow of the tunnel floor. He lapped at it and was joined by the other cub. By mid-morning their water supply had been exhausted.

At noon Smiler, who had planned to go up on the plain as soon as he was free, was asked by Miss Milly if he would mind staying and working through the Saturday afternoon. She and her sister were going to Salisbury, and two different lots of people were coming to Danebury Kennels to collect their dogs.

Mrs. Lakey and Miss Milly did not return until six o'clock, but when Smiler got back to Joe's cottage, knowing he still had plenty of time to go up on the plain for a few hours, Joe said:

"You thinking of going up top for a few hours tonight, Johnny?"

"Well, I was, Joe, if it's all right."

Joe shook his head. "It's just the opposite. All left. Heard in the Angel this lunch time that the Army people is 'avin' a special all-night exercise up there. They'll be goin' in about now and won't be out until mid-day tomorrow. Thought I'd tip you off."

"But they wouldn't see me, Joe."

"Too risky, me lad. They might be up to anything tonight. Place jumpin' with troops – and helicopters, flares and Old Nick knows what up in the sky. You keep out of there until tomorrow mid-day."

"But Joe, I'd be –"

"Nothing doing, Johnny. I got a responsibility for you. Seein' that you live 'ere and, in a way, I'm sort of your uncle. No, you want to go anywheres tonight then go down to the river. This rain'll 'ave made the big trout lively and fast on the fin."

So Smiler – although he had an inward tussle with himself – went down to the river and contented himself with a brace of nice trout.

Up on the plain during the night the cubs moved restlessly and hungrily in their den, feeling the rumble through the earth of tanks passing up the valley below. They heard, too, the thudding vibrations of exercising troops moving along the ridgeway and the muted gnat-sound of helicopters that passed low over the plain. Now and again, too, came the far thumps of shells falling and exploding.

* * *

Just before twelve the next day, Smiler cycled up to the Heytesbury Vedette hut, going fast past the entrance of Danebury House in case Tonks should be about and spot him. If the Vedette hut were unmanned and the red danger flag not flying he knew that there would be no troops about. He carried his lunch and his field glasses in a haversack on his back, and he was wearing the Major's old green anorak.

The hut was empty and no flag flew. He hid his bicycle in a field down the road. In a few minutes he was heading across the plain by one of his many routes to Imber. He had no fear of Land Wardens because they never showed in their Land-Rovers an hour or so either side of mid-day on a Sunday.

He came down the valley slope past the old church into Imber. He crossed the road and circled away behind the ruined Imber Court and up the far valley side to his favourite spot for watching Yarra and the den.

It was a clear warm day. He settled himself in his grassy hollow and took out his field glasses and polished the lens and eye-pieces.

The moment he focussed on the mouth of the den he saw the half-buried Yarra. At first he thought she was just sunning herself against the cave mouth. Then he saw the scar on the slope above the cave. The glasses brought up clearly the torn turf and the bare soil and the piled debris closing the mouth of the cave. For a moment he sat there too surprised to know what to do or think. He looked at Yarra again and this time realized with a sharp pang of anguish that she *really was* half-buried.

He jumped to his feet and avoiding all cover began to run down the valley side. However, at the bottom of the valley he stopped. His heart was bumping and he was panting for breath but, over his shock and distress at the thought of Yarra being dead, good sense was suddenly taking control. Yarra *might not* be dead. She might just be trapped and unconscious. If she were still alive she could be dangerous. You've got to go cautious, Samuel M., he told himself. And what about the cubs? Where were they?

He went up the valley side at an angle that would hide him from the road through Imber and also take him clear of the cave. Reaching the ridgetop, he went over it and moved slowly back along it until he judged that he was level with the cave.

He crawled through the grass. Long ago he had learnt not to expose himself on any skyline of the plain if he could help it. He peered over the side of the steep drop and had a clear view of Yarra. From the way she lay he was certain she was dead. Her pelt was matted and dirty from the past rain and earthfalls. Her head was twisted a little upwards and her mouth gaped unnaturally, showing her teeth. As Smiler saw this there was a dead weight inside him of sadness. Hard against the back of his eyes he felt the sting of tears and fought them back. He and Yarra had, in a way, escaped together. Now, Yarra was gone. It was awful. It ought not to have happened. She should be still as he was, free and fending for herself.

Lying there, he buried his face in his arms for a while. Then he slowly got up and went to the little plateau where Yarra lay behind the screen of trees and bushes. There was absolutely no doubt in his mind now that she was dead. Even so, he approached her warily. Leave nothing to chance, his dad had always said. Better be safe than sorry.

But there was no doubt about it. Yarra was gone. He moved to her and put a hand on her neck. It was stiff and there was no warmth in the pelt. He looked round and saw the blocked mouth of the cave and guessed how the collapse had happened . . . during all that recent rain.

Then, as he looked at the jumbled pile of loose turf and soil, he heard very faintly a thin half-mewing, half-complaining noise. He went to the blockage and put his ear against it. The noise came again. This time, mixed with the mewing, was a brief, angry, spitting sound. Although he didn't know it, it came from the male cub.

Smiler sat back on his hunkers and scratched his head. For the moment Yarra was gone from his mind. The cubs were trapped inside the cave. What on earth was he to do?

Now Smiler was nothing if not practical and resourceful. Faced with a big problem he knew how to worry his way through it and sort out the right decisions to be made. And he had a big problem – and a lot of little ones – on his hands right now.

Take it slowly, Samuel M., he told himself. Sounds as though the cubs are both still alive. Thing Number One is, you've got to get them out. Thing Number Two is. . . . He began to sort his way through the situation.

As he sat there the buzzards up above saw him and swung away. All day they had watched Yarra and had been on the point of closing in for a cautious inspection. The carrion crow in a tall treetop at the valley mouth could see him. The carrion crow had become bolder during the day and had twice walked around Yarra from a safe distance but had lacked the courage to move in close. The sandmartins hunting the high-flying noon insects above him, and a hare couched farther down the valley side, had long seen him. Dozens of birds and animals were well aware of Smiler as he sat on his hunkers dealing with his problem.

A few minutes later and Smiler was making his way over the ridgetop. Not far away was one of the many firepoints which were dotted across the plain. These held beating poles for fighting the rapid fires often caused by some soldier throwing away a burning cigarette end. The one he was heading for, he knew, held an old spade.

The cubs had to be dug out. They would be hungry, thirsty, and frightened – and young animals in that state might be difficult to handle. He would have to face that one. Neither of them was big enough to do him any real harm so long as he watched himself. Then there was Yarra. He had to do something about her.

The next three hours were very busy ones for Smiler. He had to go down twice to Imber, and each time had to keep a sharp watch for any patrolling Land Warden. In those three hours there was a time of great joy for Smiler and a time of great sorrow.

12

Smiler Takes Charge

Within twenty minutes Smiler was back with the spade. He began to
dig at the blocked entrance to the cave, working hard and fast and
expertly. Fortunately the collapsed roof of the den opening was all loose
soil and turf. There were no heavy stones amongst the debris. After
about ten minutes hard going he had worked his way through the
top part of the blockage, digging slightly downwards all the time.
Suddenly his spade went through the last of the block. A small hole
about the size of a man's head opened up and the sunlight poured
through it.

He stopped digging and waited, listening. Inside the cave, the two
cubs had long heard the sound of Smiler working away with the spade.
When he finally broke through both of them were huddled together
against the back wall of the den. The sudden sunlight blinded them. The
male cub arched his back and snap-hissed, half in fear and half in
defiance. The female crouched by him, more hungry than frightened,
and gave a series of small mews.

Outside, Smiler clicked his tongue and gave a few low encouraging
cries. He reached back and got his haversack. Inside, wrapped in grease
paper for his lunch, was a small, cold, roast chicken. He broke off one of
the legs and held it just outside the hole. He couldn't see the cubs, but he
could hear them moving and crying now.

Inside the cave both cubs suddenly got the scent of the chicken. They
ceased their noise. The male cub, drawn first by the smell of food,
moved slowly forward towards the patch of daylight at the front of the
cave. Two feet from it he stopped. He could see part of Smiler's face and
the smell of the chicken was now stronger. The hunger in him overcame
this fear. He climbed up over the loose soil to the opening.

Smiler, shaking with excitement, saw the male cub's head framed just
inside the opening, saw the short stubby ears, the black lines of the face
masking and the orange-brown pelt, black-spotted, of the cub's neck.
Behind the male cub, the face of the female cub appeared. Smiler
reached forward and dropped the chicken leg just inside the opening.
The movement made both cubs jump back a little, spitting and hissing.

Smiler, holding himself very still, guessing that movement would alarm them, made soft encouraging noises.

After a moment or two the male cub came forward slowly, then suddenly pounced, grabbed the chicken leg, and disappeared back into the cave, followed by the female cub. Smiler was overcome with a great joy. Frightened they might be, but they had taken food from him.

He tore the chicken in two and threw half of it well into the cave. It landed near the female cub who was worrying around her brother to get at the leg which he was eating and guarding from her with swift strokes of his forepaws. She turned and seized it and ran into a corner of the den. As she did so, the sunlight funnelling into the cave was abruptly blocked off. Undisturbed by this the two went on with their eating.

Outside Smiler had blocked the little opening he had made by piling large turfs and clods of earth into it. It was all part of the plan he had worked out when he had faced the problem on his hands. The cubs had to be fed and watered, but for the time being he could not risk their coming out of the den and escaping from him. Yarra was dead now. They were *his* cubs and he had to look after them sensibly and see that they came to no harm until he could work out a plan for them.

While the cubs ate in darkness, Smiler dragged Yarra free from the soil that partly covered her. He knew exactly what he must do with her. Not that he liked the idea, but it seemed the only thing for him to do. If he buried her on the hillside or up on the plain he could never cover up the evidence of his digging. Some soldier might spot it, or scavenging rats or foxes might find it.

Scattered all over the plain were dozens of old wells which had been dug in the years long past when the land had not belonged to the army, and the long plain sweeps were grazed or tilled. Smiler knew such a well at the head of the valley. Hating every moment, but knowing he had to do it, he dragged Yarra a quarter of a mile up the valley to the well. It was in a little clump of thorn trees. The Army authorities had years ago capped most of the wells with concrete tops or wooden platforms so that the exercising troops should not fall down them by accident. This well had a timber top. The thick planks were loose in places. Smiler pulled a couple aside. The well was a very deep one. He dragged Yarra across the platform and let her drop through the gap he had made, As he put the heavy planks back there were now tears in his eyes. It was a moment of great sorrow.

Keeping in cover all the way, he went back to Imber village and found an old bucket which he filled with water from the spring near Imber Court. He took the bucket back to the den, left it outside, and then went back again to the village. This time he returned with three or four short lengths of plank from the broken-up floor boards of one of the cottages, and a small, battered old tin bowl.

For the next hour Smiler worked away, keeping a sharp look-out for the movement of any Land Warden. He was following the plan he had worked out.

He opened up the small entrance to the cave, made it larger, and then tossed the last half of the chicken through to the cubs. They took it and began to quarrel over it. He filled the tin basin and put that through the opening on to the floor just inside. The smell of the water brought the cubs at once to the basin. To Smiler's delight, both cubs rushed to it and began to lap thirstily, taking no notice of him. He was tempted to reach his hand through and stroke them. He decided not to do this. He was country-wise enough now to know that if you wanted to be friends with an animal you never rushed things.

While the cubs drank and then went back to their chicken, Smiler worked at making a small plank doorway for the considerably reduced mouth of the cave. He arranged it so that he had three short planks fixed vertically down across the mouth. The middle plank he organized so that he could pull it upwards at will to make an opening. The outside planks he fixed firmly top and bottom with a packing of soil and turf which he firmed down with heavy strokes of the flat spade head.

When this was done Smiler tidied up the outside of the cave as well as he could, clearing the small plateau where Yarra used to sun herself. He spread turves and old leaf mould from under the tree screen around the place to make it look less disturbed. Then, knowing that the cubs were well fed and watered for the time being, he left them.

All the way back to Joe's cottage, while he went his secret ways across the plain with the larks giving their evening chorus above him, Smiler was occupying himself with *his real problem*.

Yarra was dead and the cubs were alive. But the cubs were not old enough to look after themselves. He ought to tell someone that they were up on the plain so that they could be caught and taken back, say, to Longleat where they would be looked after properly. But if he told Joe about them, or Miss Milly or Mrs. Lakey, it would mean that a lot of public attention would be drawn to himself. Publicity would lead him back to the reform school. He could, of course, just make an anonymous telephone call to the police or one of the Land Wardens, telling about the cubs but not giving his name. But not even that would save him, because the news would become public, be in all the papers and be talked about — and then Joe would hear about it. And Joe was clever enough to put two and two together. Joe liked having secrets and could keep them. Smiler suspected, however, that Joe couldn't keep a really big secret. Not when he had been an hour or two in the Angel. "Cheetah cubs up in a little old cave in Imber valley?" Joe would say to himself. "And some unknown person – sounded like a boy's voice it's said – telephoned about 'em . . .?"

Joe would look at him, Smiler, across the supper table and say, "Wouldn't 'ave been you by any chance, would it, Johnny lad?" And that would be it. Joe had shown him all the secret ways around Imber and that part of the country. Joe knew how much time he spent up there. Joe would know that if *anyone* was ever going to spot Yarra's cave, and then find out she had cubs, and go to the trouble of digging them out and building a door. . . . Oh, Crikeys, thought Smiler. Joe would have it out of him in no time. And then the word would go round! He was pretty sure that Joe already didn't believe the story about his aunt at Crockerton. . . . Oh, Lordy. . . . There would be that reform school waiting. Once Joe knew something was bound to go wrong.

So, that evening, sitting by himself in the gloaming on the river bank – Joe was already away to the Angel – Smiler came to a big decision.

He *had* to keep free until his father returned. Also, he had to see that the cubs were properly looked after. That meant he had to telephone the police or someone. And *that* meant that the moment he did so he would have to take off. Right away from this part of the world, covering his tracks as he went. He would have to go right away and find another job somewhere. But he didn't want to move on. He liked working at Danebury House. He liked Miss Milly and Mrs. Lakey (though not quite so much), and he liked Joe (better than anyone), and, in a way, he quite liked seeing Pat Bagnall now and then and having a chat with her.

But, Samuel M., he told himself, no matter what *you* like and what *you* want to do – you've got to tell about the cubs. Samuel M., that means you *have got* to move on. Not today. Not tomorrow. But pretty soon. As soon as you've got a plan made out for yourself.

Sadly, Smiler went back to the cottage and counted his savings. He had thirty odd pounds, a few bits of clothing, a bicycle and a suitcase which he'd bought to carry his gear in. All he needed now, was a plan. It would have to be good, because when he disappeared *that* would start questions, too. . . . Crickeys, it wasn't going to be easy to work out.

* * *

However, during the next week while Smiler was worrying at his plan for disappearing, he had the cubs to look after.

This was very hard work. He was up before dawn and away from the cottage long before Joe was awake. He would ride up past Danebury House, hide his bicycle, and make his way across the plain to the cubs. Food was no problem. He packed his haversack with dog meat from Joe's store and dropped a shilling into Joe's cash box and then to pay for it. He would give the cubs their breakfast, refill their water bowl, and then shut them up and be back at Danebury in time for work. In the evening when he had finished work at Danebury, he would take some dog meat from the kennel store and go back up to the cubs and give them their evening meal.

Within three days the cubs got to know him. When he came to the cave door he would whistle to them. The moment he pulled up the plank they would be waiting for him, snapping and spitting with excitement. But he was worried about giving them exercise. Young animals could not be kept shut up all the time. Fortunately the male cub solved this problem for him.

Smiler arrived on the fourth evening to find that the middle door plank had been butted away. Both cubs were playing around by the tree screen. He saw them as he came up the steep slope and they saw him.

Smiler stood where he was, not knowing what to do. Then, to his surprise, the cubs began to move down towards him. He gave his low whistle. They broke into a fast trot through the long grasses, every high-shouldered movement and graceful stride they made reminding him of Yarra.

Smiler crouched down. The cubs came to him, but stopped a few feet short. The female squatted on her haunches. The male padded slowly about at a safe distance. Smiler pulled his haversack round and took out a piece of meat and held it up. Immediately the female came towards him.

Smiler got to his feet and, holding the piece of meat high, began to move up to the den entrance. Both cubs followed him. Just before they reached the small plateau, the male cub made a sudden leap towards the meat that nearly took Smiler by surprise. It was a higher jump than he had thought the cub could make.

After that it was easy. Smiler tossed two large lumps of meat into the den and the cubs went in after them. Smiler watered them. Before he left, he made the door much firmer so that they could not get out. On the way back to the cottage he thought about exercising the cubs and worked out a plan for the next morning.

It worked perfectly. He pulled up the plank door and held his meat-filled haversack close to the opening. Both cubs came to it. Smiler moved away and slung his haversack high on his back. He moved up the valley side for a hundred yards. The cubs followed him and the scent of

the meat in the haversack. When he turned and went back to the cave
the cubs turned with him. At the cave entrance, he threw meat inside
and the cubs went in after it. That was the beginning of their training,
and they learnt quickly.

By the week-end, so long as he had meat in his haversack and they
had not been fed, they would follow him. By the middle of the next week
Smiler could hang his haversack high on a branch of one of the screening
trees and walk off. The cubs would go with him, though the first time
the male sat obstinately under the tree for a while.

At the end of two weeks, the rule was firmly fixed. Both cubs followed
him for a walk before returning to the cave to be fed from the haversack
that hung from the tree. By this time, too, the cubs would let him handle
them, stroke them, and massage their necks which they loved. If they
strayed a little from him they would come back at the sound of his whistle. Smiler was delighted with all this.

It was nearing high summer now. The cubs were growing fast and
were well used to Smiler. So long as the weather was good and the cubs
were fed and watered, there was no hurry, Smiler told himself, about
settling their future. The days wore into July and every morning and
evening Smiler would exercise the cubs up the long narrow valley and
across a small stretch of plain at its head. Fed or not, they came with
him, answered his call, and had no fear of his touch. Though Smiler was
always careful when he did this. Twice the male cub had scratched him
inadvertently in a moment of rough play.

The buzzards knew the trio and so did the other birds and beasts. At
the valley head one evening a young rabbit got up from the grass and the
male cub went after it and caught it. For a moment or two Smiler did
not know what to do. He realized that it would be dangerous to try and
take the rabbit from the cub. So he turned and began to walk back
towards the den. The female followed him. He whistled to the male as
he walked. After moment or two the male, mouth closed over the rabbit's neck, turned and followed him, carrying his prey. The male cub
carried the rabbit back and into the den.

So, slowly, Smiler learnt how to handle the cubs in different
situations and the cubs came to know Smiler. And Smiler gave them
names. The male he called Rico and the female Afra. He didn't know
why he called them that, but he was rather pleased with his inventions.

* * *

Although by now Smiler had long made up his mind what he eventually
must do about things he kept on putting it off because he enjoyed being

with the cubs so much. Each time that he made up his mind to do something, he had changed it within a few minutes of being back with them.

During the fourth week of his taking charge of the cubs, unknown to him, a decision began to be made for him.

One Friday evening Joe said to him, "Johnny my lad, tomorrow afternoon I'm a-going to give you a treat. And don't tell me you don't want to come because you want to go up on that old plain. What you got hidden up there, anyways? A gold mine?"

"I just like being up there, Joe."

"And so do I, Johnny. But a change won't do you any harm. A treat I'm going to give you and a treat you're goin' to have. We'll be back by six so you can slip up there for an hour after, if you want."

So Smiler, who never liked disappointing Joe — and even felt a bit guilty for keeping his cheetahs secret from him — said he would like to have a treat.

Joe duly gave him his treat, the both of them driving off in the green van. By the time Smiler — who had thoroughly enjoyed himself — got back ke knew how to solve part of his remaining problem.

While Joe was giving Johnny his treat, Major Collingwood was having tea with his wife at Ford Cottage. They were having it out on the small front lawn that overlooked the river. The Major, although he still thought about it now and then, had long ago lost his interest in tracing Mr. Hunted. He had come to a dead end. The Major was the kind of man who, when he came to a dead end, didn't like to stay there long. He turned round and found something else of interest to do.

He was reading his newspaper and feeling rather sleepy from the hot sun. The sound of the river running by lulled him. Now and again he dozed off as his wife chatted to him. Sometimes he came out of his doze to catch the end of one of her sentences and to make some polite reply.

From a somewhat deeper doze-off, he surfaced briefly to hear his wife finishing a sentence.

". . . and although they work him hard enough over there, I thought now in the long evenings he could give you a hand."

"Give me a what, dear?" The Major blinked his eyes open.

"Give you a hand in the garden. He's a good worker, Angela Lakey tells me."

A little more awake, the Major said, "Who is?"

Mrs. Collingwood laughed. "Why, Johnny, of course."

"Who on earth is Johnny?" asked the Major.

His wife shook her head. "Sometimes I think your memory is going altogether. Johnny, the boy who works for Danebury House. And if you want to know where Danebury House is, it's where I go riding sometimes as you well know. I've spoken to you about him before."

"Not that I remember. Perhaps I was asleep at the time."

"Well, he's a nice boy. He lives with that awful Joe Ringer. He's a tall, strong boy with dark-brown hair and sort of freckled under his sunburn. I don't know where Angela found him. She doesn't seem keen ever to talk about him. Almost as though there was some sort of mystery about him, I feel." She laughed. "You'd think he was an escaped convict, or something. Would you like some more tea, dear?"

The Major sat forward in his chair, suddenly deep in thought. "Tea?" he questioned.

"Yes, dear. The brown liquid that comes out of a teapot and which you drink from a teacup. Really, I think this sun is too much for you!"

But it was not the sun that was too much for the Major. It was his old interest in Mr. Hunted which had suddenly revived, though he was careful not to show it.

He said casually, "Oh, yes, I think I've seen him cycling about Heytesbury. Does he wear an old green anorak sometimes? Like one I used to have?"

"I believe he does. Yes, he does sometimes. Well, anyway, I was thinking that if he had the time we might . . ."

The Major didn't hear her because he was thinking, too; thinking that he would like to have a look at this Johnny, a good look without Johnny seeing him.

This he managed to do twice during the next few days. He also met Miss Milly in Warminster shopping the following Monday and had a chat with her — among other things about Johnny. He learnt that Johnny had an aunt called Mrs. Brown who lived at Hillside Bungalow in Crockerton. She was away at the moment tending a sick sister in Bristol. Since the Major lived almost in Crockerton himself he knew perfectly well that there was no Mrs. Brown and no Hillside Bungalow there. With all this knowledge, his certainty grew that Johnny was really Samuel Miles. The Major, who was a goodhearted, conscientious, and kind man, but one used to Army discipline, found himself with a problem which he knew would take him a little while to think out. To think out, that is, for the real good of Samuel Miles, known to his friends as Smiler or Johnny.

It was more than a week before the Major, who had a few other enquiries to make, came to his decision and knew exactly where his duty lay.

13

The Sleep-walker

Smiler was never to forget the happiness of his days with Afra and Rico.
They were bright summer days and rainy summer days. They were
days when the movement of the cubs racing and hunting at the top of
the valley printed pictures in his mind which he would always
remember. They came to his whistle now and, unless they were hunting,
trotted close to him. Their pelts were taking full colour, the amber,
black-spotted coats rippling above their muscle movements. They
caught mice and rabbits, and twice they packed together and ran down a
very young hare. When they killed Smiler never attempted to take their
kill from them. If he had time he would wait until they had eaten.
Otherwise he would go back to the den and they would follow, carrying
their catch. He still regularly fed and watered them. Also, he had forever
a watchful eye for Land Wardens or late exercising troops.

Sometimes he lay in the grass and the cubs would romp over him as
they played together. The early morning and late evening air was full of
the smell of wild thyme. With the passing of the days Smiler hated the
thought of the day that was coming, the day already fixed in his mind
when they would have to part company. He would have liked to stay up
on the plain with them forever. If there had been no other people to
bother them they could have lived easily. There was water, food to be
found, and plenty of shelter. Even in the winter he reckoned they would
be able to manage. He saw himself in a commodious cave, a fire burning
at the entrance, and Afra and Rico lying together well away from the
flames, while the winter wind shrieked outside. He knew it was all a
dream. But it was a good dream to have.

One warm moonlit night, he spent the whole time on the plain with
them because Joe had gone away on business to Southampton and was
staying with a friend down there.

When Mrs. Lakey met him at the kitchen door next morning she took
one look at him and said, "Boy, you're as red-eyed as an albino. Don't
tell me you had too much of Joe Ringer's cider last night?"

"No, Mrs. Lakey, I'm always careful how much I have of that stuff."

"St. Patrick himself keep you that way, Boy. He always prescribed it

in moderation – and left each mortal to decide for himself what moderation was."

At lunchtime Miss Milly said, "That's a bad scratch on your hand,
Johnny. I'll fix it for you with a plaster."

Rico a little rough in play had bit lovingly at Smiler's hand that night
and torn the flesh. While she was attending to his hand, Miss Milly went
on, "Jelly and I are going to dinner with a Major Collingwood at
Crockerton on Friday. He asked me some time ago if you'd care to do a
little week-end gardening work for him? Shall I tell him, yes?"

Smiler's hair nearly stood on end.

He stammered, "Well . . . well, Miss Milly, I don't think. . . . Well, I
like to have a bit of time to myself at week-ends."

"And it's right you should. I'll tell him to cast his eyes elsewhere."

If he could have told her the truth Smiler would have said that the
coming week-end was going to be his last at Danebury, his last in this
part of the world. On Sunday morning he meant to be up early and away
in Joe's green van with Afra and Rico. It would mean creeping into Joe's
bedroom to get the key of the van from his jacket pocket, but Joe always
slept like a log on Saturday nights after his visit to the Angel. Smiler knew
that he would have no difficulty in getting the key. He planned to leave a
letter for Joe explaining where he could find the van. The thought of
leaving Joe was almost as bad as that of leaving the cubs.

The last few days of Smiler's time on the plain slid by. The buzzards
had brought off a young one from a pair of eggs and were teaching it
acrobatics high above. The carrion crow flew solitary about her foraging
and scavenging. Charms of goldfinches worked the tall thistles and
weeds on the plains, and the barn owls quartered silently and soft-
winged on their night hunting. Each morning and evening Smiler was
with Afra and Rico. He had put all his affairs in order ready to move off,
to stay free until his father returned. He knew his father would believe
him when he told him that he had not robbed the old lady. His father
would turn the world upside down, too, until other people believed it –
and then he wouldn't have to go back to the reform school. He hadn't
robbed the old lady and that was that!

*   *   *

On Friday evening Mrs. Lakey and Miss Milly went to dinner with the
Major and his wife. They had drinks in the evening sun on the lawn just
outside the open dining-room windows. An occasional trout rose to a fly
on the river, dimpling the surface. A kingfisher flashed downstream, and

a family of yellow wagtails bobbed and played over the gravel spits along the banks.

Mrs. Lakey and Miss Milly were very old friends of the Major and his wife so that the Major did not much relish what he was going to have to say and do. Being a military man he had decided that, if a thing were to be done, then it was better to do it quickly.

Mrs. Lakey was seated with her glass of whisky, Miss Milly with her sweet marsala, Mrs. Collingwood with a glass of dry sherry, and the Major with a slightly larger whisky than the one he had given Mrs. Lakey because he felt he was going to need it.

After a few minutes pleasant social chat, the Major cleared his throat and said to Mrs. Lakey, "Angela, there's something which I must discuss with you and Milly. It's serious and it's about your boy, Johnny. Johnny Pickering who lives with Joe Ringer."

Miss Milly said, "Johnny's a good boy, Major. But he just wants his week-ends free. So I'm afraid he doesn't want to garden for you."

"Afraid of a little extra work. Like all boys," said Mrs. Lakey. "Though the Boy is better than most. Furlongs ahead of any other I know."

"No, I don't mean about working for me," said the Major.

"Then what else could you possibly mean, dear?" asked his wife. "After all, we can just get someone else to do —"

Very firmly, the Major said, "I am not talking about gardening. And I would appreciate it if you ladies would kindly give me your attention for a few minutes without interruption."

"Very military all of a sudden, isn't he, Jelly?" said Miss Milly. "Just like father used to be when anything went wrong. Like when one of the grooms —"

"Be quiet, Milly, and drink your marsala," said Mrs. Lakey. "Though how you can like the stuff —"

"What about Johnny, dear?" asked Mrs. Collingwood. "Has he been poaching with that awful Joe Ringer?"

Even more firmly, the Major said, "Dear ladies, I would like to get this matter settled, but if you keep interrupting it will take all night —"

"And the dinner will be spoiled," said Mrs. Lakey. "But carry on, Major. I think I know what maggot has got into your apple. The Boy is Samuel Miles, isn't he?"

The Major looked at her in astonishment, and cried, "You knew?"

"Almost from the first. You don't always have to look at a horse's mouth to tell its age. Think I can't spot it when a boy's got something to hide that dyed hair can't cover?"

"*Who* is this Samuel Miles?" asked Miss Milly.

"The Boy," said her sister.

"Your Johnny," declared the Major. "He's escaped from an approved school."

"Johnny's a good, kind, honest boy," said Miss Milly stoutly. "I don't believe a word of anything you're going to say."

Mrs. Collingwood sighed. "So far as I am concerned I would just like to know what everyone is talking about."

"Then listen," declared the Major almost crossly. "His name is really Samuel Miles and he's been in this house, dyed his hair, and eaten our sardines, and taken my anorak and covered up his freckles and . . . How on earth, my dear, do you think your bathroom curtains were stained?"

Mrs. Lakey smiled and said, "It's the most lucid explanation I ever did hear, Major. Worthy of an Irishman. And what is more the Boy has no aunt called Mrs. Brown of Hillside Bungalow, Crockerton, and if he escaped from an approved school and then from the police, more power to his elbow. Any two things better escaped from I can't imagine. *But* it's not our job to do the work of approved schools or the police so —"

Pompously, the Major said, "He attacked an old lady and stole her handbag."

"Never!" said Miss Milly. "What an awful thing to say about Johnny! I think I must have some more marsala."

Mrs. Collingwood, moving to help Miss Milly to more marsala, said to her husband, "Darling, take a deep breath, count ten, and then start at the beginning. Funny, I thought it looked like your anorak. There was a splotch of red paint on it that —"

The Major snorted and cried, "Will you all listen to me!"

Mrs. Collingwood smiled, Miss Milly sipped at her marsala and Mrs. Lakey began to light a small cheroot. A blackbird sang from an ash tree. In the woods across the river a woodpecker drummed against the trunk of a beech. A pack of sparrows began quarrelling on the thatched roof, and the Major — who had used almost his parade ground voice — began to explain, telling the story of Samuel Miles as he knew it.

One afternoon in Bristol an old lady had been jostled off the pavement by a boy and her handbag stolen. A policeman, seeing the act from a distance, had gone after the thief. Around the corner he had spotted a boy running down the pavement. The policeman had caught him and found that he was holding the old lady's handbag with ten pounds in it. The boy was Samuel Miles. His father was away at sea and he was living with a married sister. Samuel Miles had denied the theft, though he *had* been in some small bits of bother with the police before.

Samuel Miles' story, however, was that he had been standing just round the corner when a boy he knew had come rushing past him and had tossed him the handbag, shouting "Hide it!" The boy was one Johnny Pickering. They were not friends. In fact they disliked one another. Samuel Miles had said that when he was caught running away he was really running after Pickering to make him take the handbag back. Both boys were about the same height, and both had fair hair. Samuel Miles had said that Pickering must have seen the policeman and, once around the corner, tossed the handbag to him and run on.

But, the Major explained, in the juvenile court the father and the mother of Pickering had both sworn that their son had been at home all afternoon. One of their neighbours had sworn the same. The court had decided that Samuel Miles — and evidence had been given to show that Samuel Miles did not like Pickering — was lying to save himself. They had found him guilty and decided that he must go to an approved school.

At this point Miss Milly said stoutly, "It's not true. Johnny would never do such a thing."

"It's the father and mother of all lies," said Mrs. Lakey.

"I think, it's a lie, too," the Major agreed. "But the point is, if Johnny is to be proved innocent, it can never happen while he's on the run. We've got to tell the police about him. Then we can have the case re-opened. We can get at the truth and have him cleared. He's worked hard and honestly for you, Angela. He paid back what he borrowed from me — except the anorak and the old bike — and what do they matter? He's shown resource and initiative in looking after himself and —"

"I think, dear," said Mrs. Collingwood, "that we all understand and agree with you. But it does seem hard to go —"

"Snivelling to the police," said Mrs. Lakey. "It's like deliberately putting a good dog down before its time. But, there's some sense in what the Major says. How can the law do anything for the Boy unless the law has got the Boy?"

Miss Milly said, "You've known all this for a long time, Jelly. If you think he ought to be given up, why didn't you do it ages ago?"

"Because, Milly, I don't jump fences until I come to 'em. And this fence is now right under the horse's nose." She looked hard at Major Collingwood. "You believe in the Boy's innocence?"

"Absolutely. I made a few enquiries about this Pickering family. They haven't a good reputation. I think they were lying to protect their son."

"And you think you can clear things for the Boy?"

The Major said importantly, "Yes. I have friends in the police in Bristol. They'll listen to me. All we have to do is tell the police where Johnny is and then I'll lay a hundred to one we can clear things up."

"I don't like it," said Miss Milly. "You mean let them know *right away*? Think of poor Johnny at home now having his supper after a hard day's work and the police walking in and taking him to spend a night in a cell. . . . Oh, no!"

The Major pondered this, then he said deliberately, "You've a soft heart, Milly – but it's got to be done."

Miss Milly stood up. "You really want to ring up the police now?"

"Yes, Milly," said the Major.

"Then," said Miss Milly firmly, "don't expect me to sit down afterwards and take dinner in your house. How could I?" She turned to her sister. "Jelly, I'm going home. If anyone thinks I could take a bite of food knowing all the time that – "

"Milly," said Mrs. Lakey, "ease back in the saddle a bit." She turned to the Major, and went on, "The Boy has been free for months. Twelve hours' delay won't do any harm, and he's not going to run away because he knows nothing of all this – "

"And," interrupted Mrs. Collingwood, "I'm not having my dinner party ruined. We've got smoked salmon and then a beautiful piece of lamb, and a sweet it's taken me all afternoon to make. Milly and Angela are staying. You can tell the police first thing in the morning."

The Major looked at each woman in turn. After a few moments he shrugged his shoulders. "Well, I suppose it won't make any difference. All right. I'll telephone them first thing in the morning."

"And glad I am to hear it," said Mrs. Lakey, "for if Milly had gone, then so would I – and there's nothing I like better than smoked salmon and a nice piece of lamb."

"Poor Johnny," said Miss Milly. She sat down and took a sip of her marsala. "Never in my life will I believe that he ever robbed an old lady."

"We'll prove he didn't," said the Major. "But until it can be done, he's got to be held in custody by the proper authorities. That's the law."

"The law," said Miss Milly vigorously, "is an ass!"

"Agreed, Milly," said her sister.

At that moment Mrs. Bagnall, who helped Mrs. Collingwood when she gave a dinner party, appeared at the front door and said, "Dinner is served, madam."

*   *   *

While Mrs. Collingwood's dinner party was in progress, Smiler was walking back down the valley with Afra and Rico towards their den. The light was fast going from the western sky. The jackdaws were returning to their roosts in the church tower at Imber. Fox and badger were beginning their night prowls. Moths blundered through the warm, still air.

When they reached the entrance to the cave, Smiler knelt down and with either hand rubbed the rough-pelted necks of Afra and Rico. Afra purred and nuzzled her head against Smiler's bent knee. Rico turned and closed his jaws gently over Smiler's hand. He knew now just how hard he could hold without harming Smiler. In the pale light the golden eyes of the two animals shone softly, their black face-markings giving them a faint, laughing look.

Smiler was aware of a lump in his throat. Samuel M., he was telling himself, tomorrow night you'll be putting them away in the cave for the last time. Sunday morning, first thing, you'll be up and away with them. They won't see this old plain again, and neither will you. No, Samuel M., you won't see Danebury again, nor Joe, nor a lot of people and places you like. . . . Not for ages and ages, anyway. . . . Not until your old Dad comes back and can clear things up.

He stood up, tossed some meat into the cave and watched the cubs enter. Then he boarded up the entrance securely and began to make his way home.

When he reached Joe's cottage, it was nearly eleven o'clock. Joe was in the kitchen having a last glass of cider before going to bed. He offered Smiler some, but Smiler had a glass of milk instead.

"Been up top again then, Johnny?" asked Joe.

"For a bit."

Joe gave him a long look and said, "Milk ain't no good for what you got by the look of your face. For a bad case of the glooms there's nothin' like cider. Anything special happened?"

"No, I'm just tired, Joe," said Smiler.

"It's honest labour what does that. Been trying to avoid it all me life — without success. What about a bit of a singsong on the pianer then?"

"No, thanks, Joe. I'm for bed." Smiler began to move.

Joe said, "Sure there's nothin' wrong? Nothin' that you'd care to tell me about?"

"No, really, Joe. I'm all right."

"All right then, me old cock," said Joe. "Up you go then, and get your head tucked under your wing."

So Smiler went to bed, and not long afterwards Joe did the same. The cubs up on the plain were already asleep. Miss Milly and Mrs. Lakey were driving home from the Collingwoods' dinner party. The Major and his wife were together in their sitting-room. The Major was having a small glass of brandy and looked very thoughtful.

After a moment, he said, "I don't suppose they would do it — but perhaps it would have been better if I'd made them promise not to."

"Promise what, dear?" asked his wife.

"Promise not to warn this Samuel Miles that the police will be coming for him early tomorrow morning."

"Really!" exclaimed Mrs. Collingwood. "I'm glad you didn't do any such thing! You would have lost two very good friends — and made me very angry. They wouldn't dream of such a thing!"

The Major said, "They're both very fond of him." He smiled suddenly. "And they're women — you never know with women. Not logical. Not when their emotions are roused."

"I think," said Mrs. Collingwood distantly, "that you'd better leave that brandy and go to bed. You must be over-tired."

*   *   *

Yet, in a way that he would never have been able to guess, the Major was quite right about women. With some it is the heart and not the head that rules.

At four o'clock the next morning Smiler woke up. It was still some way off daybreak. He lay in bed, heavy-eyed.

As he did so there was a sudden sharp splatter of gravel against his window pane. Smiler sat up, puzzled. The noise of gravel came again and he realized that it must have been such a noise in the first place which had wakened him.

He got out of bed and crossed to the window and looked down. On the narrow path below he could make out a greyish form. Smiler opened the window.

"Johnny?" A pale face was turned up to him from below.

"Who's that?" he asked.

"Keep your voice down. It's me, Pat," came the answer in a whisper.

"What on earth are you doing here?"

"Come to warn you, Johnny. Get dressed and come on down and I'll tell you. Hurry, I got to cycle back home afore they wakes and finds I've been out."

"But I don't understand."

"Course you don't, stupid, until you come down and I can tell you," said Pat. "Hurry now."

Still puzzled, Smiler dressed in a hurry and went quietly downstairs so as not to wake Joe. Pat Bagnall, in jeans and a thick jumper, was waiting for him in front of the house. She came up to him quickly and took his arm.

"Now, you listen to me, Johnny, and don't interrupt 'cos I've got a lot to say, and I've got to say it fast so's I can get back and not get into trouble."

Then she told him about the Collingwoods' dinner party and how her mother always on such occasions went down to help. Her mother, while taking things into the dining-room, had overheard the conversation about Samuel Miles, alias Johnny Pickering, through the open windows. When her mother had got back that night she had told her husband all about it, full of the gossip and excitement. Pat — who wasn't supposed to hear — had heard everything, too, because she had been up in her bedroom reading before sleep.

"When it's all quiet-like you can hear every word they say down below. So that's why I'm here. I had to wait till late to come out — and I got to get back fast before Dad starts moving."

"Crickeys!" said Smiler. "What am I going to do?"

"Don't be stupid," whispered Pat. "You got to get away. You don't want to be taken up again, do you?"

"No, of course I don't."

"Then you've got to move fast. Right now. Get your things and go."

And Smiler saw that he had to do just that. The Major might wake very early and call the police.

"It's all right," he said. "I was planning to go — tomorrow. Thanks for coming to tell me. But why ever did you?"

"What a question! Because I like you, of course. And because I don't believe that grown-ups always can do what they say they can do. I reckoned it was up to you to choose. Course, you can stay and face it out if you want to."

"Not likely. I'm off. Only my Dad can clear me up. He knows how to deal with Mr. Pickering and that lot. Gosh, it was brave of you to come."

"Course it wasn't. You got money, and things like that?"

"Yes."

"Then be on your way, Johnny. And Johnny —" She came closer to him.

"Yes?"

"When you're settled — you can write to me, if you want."

Her face came close to Smiler's.

"Course I will when it's safe."

"Promise?"

"Promise."

She reached forward suddenly and kissed him. Then, with a little bubble of laughter, she was gone, running across the garden grass.

Smiler watched her go, not knowing quite how he felt, but knowing that he was feeling like he had never felt before. Then he turned and went quietly back into the house. All his things were more or less packed already for his Sunday morning departure. Now, he had to go a day sooner and there was a big problem. He *had* to get the key of Joe's van. Without the van his plan was ruined. Joe had not been to the Angel that night. Joe might wake up. Well, he would have to risk that.

He went up to his bedroom and collected his things. He came out on tip-toes and put his stuff quietly on the floor of the little landing. In the darkness he moved stealthily towards the door of Joe's bedroom. He knew exactly where Joe's jacket would be hanging with the key in the pocket. The thought that Joe might wake brought a quick flush of sweat to his brow. Slowly he reached out his hand to the door knob.

At that moment the door of the bedroom opened and in the growing light from the bedroom window he was faced by the figure of Joe. Smiler jumped backwards, almost frightened out of his skin.

Joe said not a word. He just stood there. He wore an old woollen nightcap, and a long white nightshirt – but not so long that it hid the fact that he wore his socks in bed. Joe's eyes were shut tight.

Before Smiler could recover from his alarm, Joe began to speak in a far away voice, a kind of religious, preaching voice.

Joe said, "Done it ever since a child. Doing of it now. Walks in me sleep. No cure for it. When I wakes up I don't know what I done – could be murder. Don't know what I heard – could be where a pot of gold's buried. Don't never know what I'm doing or hearing. Like I might 'ear two people talkin' under me window. Like I might know one of them's in trouble and got to get away fast and far. And for which purpose – as all the world knows – there's nought better'n a car. Say a nice little green van what the police'll find somewheres later and return. That's always assumin' that the one what wants it 'as the key –"

His hand came out and up slowly and the palm opened. In it was the van's ignition key.

"Oh, Joe –" began Smiler, but Joe interrupted him sharply.

"Don't never talk to anyone what walks in 'is sleep. Dangerous. Could give 'em the jumps for the rest of their mortal. Here, lad."

The key was tossed to Smiler who caught it.

Joe stood there, immobile, but a smile slowly passed over his face. One eye opened and shut in a wink, and he said, "Don't ever remember anything I says or does when I walks in me sleep. Terrible affliction if you lives on a cliff. Well, God bless anyone within 'earing at this moment – and send me a postcard sometime just saying – 'The old grey goose ain't dead'."

He winked once more, with the other eye, and then turned back into the room and shut the door. With tears in his eyes and a lump in his throat, Smiler picked up his stuff and ran downstairs and out into the yard. Five minutes later he was driving towards Heytesbury on his way up to the plain. It was Saturday and too early in the morning for the Vedette hut to be manned or for any troops to be about. Smiler knew that he had a clear two or three hours before anyone would be astir to bother him. That was more than enough.

*   *   *

Tonks saw the green van go by Danebury House and barked his head off until Mrs. Lakey, half in sleep, reached for a cushion and nearly knocked him from the window seat.

Pat Bagnall was back in bed, lying awake and dreaming. Down below she could hear her father stirring in the kitchen.

At Ford Cottage the barn owl had just returned from its night duties, full of food. In the cottage Major Collingwood was lying flat on his back, mouth open and snoring loudly. Mrs. Collingwood pushed him over on to his side and said loudly, "Quiet!" The Major became silent.

In her bedroom at Danebury Miss Milly lay awake having a little cry to herself and wrestling with temptation. She wanted to get up and drive to Joe's cottage to warn Johnny. But she knew she could not do it. She was a woman of honour, and anyway in the long run it would all be for Johnny's good. After a while she started to chuckle to herself. Fancy never guessing that Johnny dyed his hair! Right under her nose, too. Perhaps she needed glasses.

And in Joe's cottage, Joe lay abed and chuckled, too. They wouldn't see Johnny for smoke. No more than they had ever seen *him* for smoke when he had run away from the Army. Some things you just had to run away from. Just as there was some things you just had to run towards. . . . Like a bit of poaching or a nice pint of cider. Good lad, Johnny was. Wonder whatever it was that made him so fond of the plain? Not a girl, that was sure, 'cos there was none up there. Animals, he'd bet. . . . Just loved animals, Johnny did. God bless him.

14

Hail and Farewell

At the Vedette hut Smiler got out of the van and lifted the road pole. He drove through and then went back and lowered the pole.

From the hut the road ran due north to drop finally into the Imber valley. By now Smiler knew all the roads and tracks like the back of his hand.

The sky was lightening fast. The pearl-gold flush in the eastern sky was beginning to strengthen with the coming of the sun. The larks were already aloft and in first song. A pair of greenfinches flirted across the road in front of the van. A kestrel hovered over the tank which Yarra had first used as a shelter, watching for the movement of mice around its rusted sides. There was a heavy dew over the grass and the spiders' webs, hung from thistle to thistle and mantling the small bushes, were beaded with glittering moisture drops. High in the morning sky a jet fighter drew a long, straight vapour trail which began to rag away at the edges into little curls of cloud.

Within ten minutes Smiler was at Imber. He drove the van under the cover of the open barn at the rear of Imber Court. Taking his old haversack in which he had brought some dogs' meat, he walked around the side of Imber Court towards the valley in which the cubs lived. Under the tall trees at the foot of the valley a grey squirrel scurried away from him and raced up one of the trunks. The pack of jackdaws from the church tower flew overhead. The lip of the rising sun broke the edge of the far plain, throwing long bush and tree shadows.

Smiler walked up the valley bottom, alongside the tank tracks. He tried not to think that it was the last time he would go up to the den. Instead, he thought of how good Pat and Joe had been to him last night. Going by Danebury and hearing Tonks bark had been a bad moment. He was leaving all the animals there. Then, as he began to climb the steep slope to the cave plateau, he could think of nothing else but Yarra. He sniffed hard. Yarra had gone for good. And now he was going . . . right away, miles away. Because he felt so miserable, he gave himself a good talking-to. It's no good, Samuel M., he said, snivelling about things. Life is always changing. Like Joe said, if it didn't, then men would grow moss on 'em – just like the rocks.

At the den mouth he pulled the planks and Afra and Rico came leaping out to him. They had heard his whistle as he came up the slope. The sight of them cheered him up at once.

They were well grown now and their tawny, spotted coats rippled and caught the day's new light as they moved. Afra had a creamy mantle showing under her neck. Rico's tail was long and drooping and could give you quite a crack if he happened to swing it across your face when you knelt to fondle him.

He dropped to his knees and played with them for a moment or two. After a while Rico, always the greedier, began to worry and paw at the haversack on Smiler's back.

"All right, my beauties," said Smiler. "A walk first and then food."

He started off down the steep slope, back towards Imber. Rico raced ahead and began mouse-hunting from tuft to tuft of grass. Afra found a tattered little white parachute from an old signal flare, picked it up and carried it for a while.

The birds and the beasts of the little valley watched them go. The three buzzards, low flying at the ridge-top, soared and hung over them. The carrion crow, dealing with a dead rabbit on the far slope, looked up and watched their movements and wondered what Afra was carrying. A deer couched in bracken followed them with large, liquid eyes. A hare got up well ahead of Rico and raced away followed by the cub. But there was no fear in the hare because it had more speed than Rico. The cub soon gave up the chase and came galloping back at the sound of Smiler's whistle. A pair of yellow hammers scolded them from an ash tree and a grass snake fifty yards ahead slid away to safety as it caught the thud, thud of Smiler's approaching footsteps.

At the small spring which was now down to a feeble trickle, Smiler let the cubs drink. When they had taken their fill, they followed him up to the van.

He opened one of the back doors of the van, took meat from his haversack and tossed it inside. Rico jumped in immediately for the food, but Afra stood her ground for a moment or two. She sniffed around the back of the van and Smiler wondered whether he was going to have trouble with her. He took another piece of meat, held it briefly under Afra's nose, and then jerked it into the van as she made a move for it. Afra leaped into the van after the meat.

Smiler closed the door and locked it. He went round and got into the driving seat. The back part of the van was boarded off from the front. At some time Joe had made a small hatchway in it so that he could reach back and take things from the interior without getting out. The hatchway was fastened with small bolts, top and bottom. Smiler made sure that they were secure and then drove off.

He went back through the shattered, derelict village. Beyond the village, instead of taking the right-hand turn which led to the Heytesbury Vedette hut, he carried straight on.

The road rose up a gentle slope and came out on to the wide, open stretches of grass land. Half a mile down the road he turned left at a crossroads and began to bump his way along a narrow, rutted track. After a while the surface of the track grew better. Some minutes later Smiler was driving down the northern scarp of the plain, not far from the spot where Yarra had been attacked by the Ayrshire cow. He passed another empty Vedette hut. A little later he was off the plain near a small village called Erlestoke through which ran a main road. Smiler turned the van left-handed, westwards along the road. A mile along the main road, he drew up. He slipped the hatch bolts and peeped through at the cubs. There was straw in the van for them to lie on. They both came to the hatchway. Smiler rubbed their masks and then pushed through some more meat from his haversack.

He bolted the hatchway and drove on. He knew exactly where he was going, and he knew all the roads from the many drives he had taken with Joe. As soon as he could he left the main road. By now the police might be at Joe's cottage. If Joe couldn't keep from them the fact that the van was missing the police would put out a call for it. Well, if they did, they did. That was a risk he had to take.

In fact, he need not have worried. When the police came to Joe's cottage, Joe had been long up. He had taken Smiler's bicycle, wheeled it to the river and thrown it in. When the police arrived Joe at once told them that Johnny and his bicycle were gone. Which he could truthfully do. The police never asked him about his van. Joe reported its loss at midday when he went to the Angel.

*   *   *

Later that morning, not long after Longleat Park had been opened to the public, Apollo, the cheetah male, who had been the mate of Yarra, lay along the bare length of a branch of the fallen tree not far from the sleeping hut.

The sky was cloudless. Now and then Apollo raised his head and blinked in the strong light. Across the road and the grass two or three other cheetahs were pacing up and down the wire enclosure, their eyes on the free parkland beyond, the parkland over which Yarra long ago had escaped.

A few early cars were beginning to trickle through the animal enclosures now. Apollo watched them come around the curve of road which held the fallen tree. They had no interest for him. Every day he saw them. They usually stopped a little higher up the road from the tree where they could get a good view of the whole enclosure.

Apollo yawned and wrinkled his mask, then snapped at a worrying blue bottle fly. One of the cheetahs by the fence flopped to the grass and began to roll on it, its long legs high in the air. A nuthatch landed on the far end of the old tree and began to work its way around and along a branch with short, jerky movements. Apollo watched it, half made to rise and then subsided. It was hot. He swung his long tail and thumped the tree trunk. The nuthatch flew off.

At that moment a small green van came around the curve of the road behind Apollo, turned up the little slope and then drew in to the side of the road. It was about twenty yards upwind of Apollo. Apollo watched it.

In the van was Smiler. He knew all about Longleat Park and its animal kingdom. This was the place that Joe had brought him to for his treat. On that day, when they had got as far as the cheetah enclosure, it was as much as Smiler could do not to tell Joe all about Yarra and her cubs. He had made Joe stay a long time in the enclosure, the other cars drawing out and passing them.

Now Smiler had returned bringing with him, safely hidden in the van, as he had long planned, Afra and Rico. They were now out of the cub stage, were young cheetahs.

Smiler looked across at Apollo, and the size and beauty of the animal made him think of Yarra. Behind him Afra and Rico moved restlessly in the van. The various animal scents that had come to them as they had passed through the other enclosures had roused them.

Smiler sat for a moment wishing he didn't have to go on with his plan, but knowing he must. It was the best thing for the cheetahs. Once it was done, he knew that he could not hang about and see how Afra and Rico would be received. He would have to move on because at the entry to the enclosure he had seen one of the black and white Land-Rovers of the Game Wardens.

Smiler turned and drew the bolts on the hatch. You've got to do it, Samuel M., he told himself. You've just got to do it.

He opened the hatch wide. Afra and Rico came to the opening. Smiler held up a piece of meat he had saved and then leaned over and quietly opened the door of the cab.

Rico slid through the hatchway and went for the meat Smiler held. Before Rico could take it, Smiler threw it out on to the grass. Rico jumped out after it.

Afra came through the hatchway after her brother and sat on the seat at his side. She looked out at Rico.

"Go on, Afra, go on!" urged Smiler. But Afra sat on her haunches, twisted her neck, and rubbed the top of her head against Smiler's shoulder.

"Afra, please," Smiler pleaded. Afra sat where she was. Desperate, Smiler eased himself sideways and pushed Afra off the seat to the floor. She turned briefly, spat-snapped nervously at him and then lifted her muzzle. A mixture of new and familiar scents came flooding through the open door. She jumped down to join Rico.

Relieved, Smiler pulled the door shut and drove off. He drove, sniffing and fighting back the tears which pressed against the back of his eyes. He went up the road as fast as he could without drawing attention to himself. As he went he watched Afra and Rico in the mudguard mirror. Rico was couched on the grass, chewing at his piece of meat. Afra was standing up, slowly swinging her blunt head and long neck as she looked around the enclosure.

A turn in the road at the top of the enclosure took them both from Smiler's sight, and he told himself, You've looked after the cubs, Samuel M. You've done the right thing. Now you start thinking about yourself.

* * *

Apollo was the first living thing in the enclosure to see the young cheetahs. Even before he saw them he had caught their scent coming downwind to him. As the van drew away they came into view. His head jerked up alertly. Slowly he raised himself to a stalking position and began to move out along the length of the fallen tree trunk. At the end he stopped, watching Afra standing and looking round, seeing Rico on the ground worrying at the meat. Their scent was strange, but it was cheetah scent. Cheetahs in captivity do not always take kindly to the introduction of new members.

Suddenly Apollo leapt from the end of the trunk in a long, curving spring. Ignoring the few cars that moved up the road, he walked slowly, deliberately across to the young cheetahs. Afra turned and faced him and then dropped her shoulders and opened her jaws in a silent gape, half-menace, half-fear. Rico looked up from his meat and rumbled a caution for Apollo to keep away.

By the fence the other cheetahs had caught the new scent. Slowly they began to move towards the young cheetahs, not directly, but in small, exploratory arcs.

Apollo moved to Rico and lowered his head. Rico — Apollo's own son

— snapped at the big male to guard his meat. Apollo's right forepaw swept out and cuffed Rico away from the meat. Rico rolled over and over for about a yard. He came to his feet, shook himself and then moved confidently back to his meat. Apollo had done to him no more than Yarra had sometimes done.

Apollo watched Rico come back and drop to the meat, almost under his muzzle. For a moment Apollo's paw rose and then the movement stopped. He let Rico take the meat, and turned. Afra was standing just behind him. Ten yards away the other cheetahs had bunched together, some standing, some squatting, all watching Apollo. All of them knew the power of Apollo and respected him.

Slowly Apollo lowered his head and sniffed at Afra, who now stood timidly still. She made a small complaining sound. Apollo squatted back on his haunches. He yawned, raising his head and blinking at the sun, and then he dropped flat to the ground, head and shoulders high, facing the other cheetahs. Afra squatted a foot from him. Rico ate behind him. The cars passed slowly along the road, and the other cheetahs, as though they had been given some command dangerous to disobey, slowly turned and moved away.

Apollo had accepted Afra and Rico. Father, son and daughter were together.

*   *   *

POSTSCRIPT: Joe's old green van was found by the police late that afternoon. It was abandoned in a lay-by on a main road twenty miles from Longleat. Lying on the driving seat was a note that read:

> *This van belongs to Joe Ringer of Heytesbury.*
> *Say to him the old grey goose is still flying.*

Flight of the Grey Goose

1

Destination Unknown

It was a fresh, sunny morning in July. Big puffballs of cloud rolled lazily across the sky from the west. In a lay-by at the side of the main road, a grey squirrel was sitting on the edge of the rubbish bin, fastidiously nibbling at a stale piece of cake which it had found.

A little farther down the road was a boy with not many months to go before he reached the age of sixteen. At his feet was a battered old suitcase. He was tallish, fair-haired, and well built with a friendly, squarish face – heavily freckled under his sun-tan – a pressed-in smudge of a nose and a pair of angelic blue eyes which, when he put on his special smile, made him look as though butter wouldn't melt in his mouth. From the cheerful grin on his face as he waved to the traffic it would have been difficult to believe that that morning early he had given the police the slip for the second time in the last six months. He was wanted by them for absconding from an approved school. Although his friends called him Smiler his real name was Samuel Miles. Actually he preferred Samuel M., because that was what his father called him. That, too, was what he called himself when he gave himself a good talking-to – which he often did when he had some problem to face. And on this sunny July morning Smiler really did have a problem to face because by now the police forces of Dorset, Wiltshire, Hampshire and a few other counties were all on the lookout for him.

"Unless, Samuel M.," he told himself, "you pick up a lift soon and get out of this area some police car is going to come along and pick you up. And then, my lad, you'll be sunk for good and all."

It was at this moment that a long, high-cabbed white lorry came down the road towards him. Smiler gave it a wave and a cheery grin automatically. To his surprise the lorry pulled up slowly just beyond him. Smiler ran down the road to it.

The driver leaned over and opened the nearside cab door. He was a round-faced man of about forty with an old white cap perched on the back of his head, the peak pushed up at a sharp angle. He wore green overalls, had a broad smile on his face, and alongside him on the bench seat sat a largish black dog with a white patch on its chest and a large grin on his face.

The driver said, "Where you headin' for, son?"

Smiler said, "I dunno, exactly."

The driver chuckled. "Destination unknown. Good as any. Hop in. You're the second this morning."

Smiler swung his case and then himself up into the cab and closed the door. The lorry moved off down the road.

Smiler, who was polite by nature and by policy, said, "Thank you very much, sir."

The driver chuckled. It was a nice, friendly, happy sound. "Strictly 'gainst company rules. But all rules is made to be broken at times. You want to sit and brood over your worries or listen to the radio or talk? Take your choice. All the same to me."

Smiler said, "I don't mind talking, sir."

"Wise choice," said the driver. "Silence is golden but weighs heavy. The radio is full of woe — or pop music which is worse. But talk is human and friendly. Also, don't call me 'sir'. I'm Bob Peach. Peachy my friends call me, but you stick to Mr. Bob till I tell you you've served your time which —" he winked "— could be anything from an hour to a hundred years 'cording to the way things go."

"Yes, Mr. Bob," said Smiler.

"Well then," said Bob Peach, "Go ahead."

"Go ahead what?" asked Smiler.

"Go ahead and talk. That's your choice. You got to start. Only fair."

Smiler, a little unsure of Bob Peach, was silent for a moment and then said, "What did you mean that I'm the second this morning?"

Bob Peach nodded towards the dog which was sitting between them. "Him. Another 'Destination unknown'. Like you. Sittin' I was, havin' a bite of breakfast by the road, when up he walks, no collar, no name, free as air and cadges a bacon sandwich from me. Bit skinny, ain't he? But he'll fatten up. Hops in the cab with me, won't take 'Go home' for an answer. Probably because he ain't got one and here he is. Sitting like a lord and not a word to be got out of him."

Smiler took a good look at the dog. He knew quite a bit about dogs and liked them. This was a biggish dog, but in no way a pedigree one. There were touches of Alsatian and sheepdog about him. He was quite pleasant to look at but definitely very much a mixture. The dog looked at Smiler, panted a little with the warmth of the cab and let a long red tongue flop over the side of his mouth. Smiler scratched him behind his ears and the dog shut his brown eyes in ecstasy.

"He ought to have a name," said Smiler.

"If he's got one he won't tell. What do you reckon we should call him?"

"Rex?" suggested Smiler.

"Too grand. He ain't no aristocrat. He's a good, common, solid, mixed up all-dog dog. What's your name?"

"Samuel," said Smiler.

"Samuel what?"

"Samuel Miles," said Smiler and wondered why, in the circumstances, he was being so truthful – except that with someone like Bob Peach it wouldn't have seemed right not to be. Then, to avoid any further questions about himself, he went on quickly, "What do you think he should be called, Mr. Bob?"

Bob Peach, his eyes on the road ahead as he drove, said, "Bacon. I been thinkin' about it coming along. Things like names must be fitting always. And that's what brought us together. The smell of that bacon sandwich. What do you think of that?"

"I don't see why not," said Smiler. "I used to know a horse called that."

"Horse or dog, no matter," said Bob Peach. "It's a good name. Comes well off the tongue either in anger or love, and not going to be answered by any other riffraff of Fidos, Tims, or Rovers or what-have-yous. All right then, that's settled. Subject number one discussed and disposed of. What's the second item on the agenda?"

Smiler said, "It's your turn, isn't it, Mr. Bob, to start something?"

"So it is. Fair's fair. Well then, let me see. What about a few personal questions? You got a father and mother?"

"No mother, Mr. Bob. She died when I was a baby. But I got a father." Smiler said it proudly for he considered he had the best father in the world. He added, "He's in the merchant navy. A cook. He's away at sea right now."

"A sea-faring man. There's a life. Here today and gone tomorrow. Just like me. Long distance driving. Always something different coming up over the horizon. A great life if you've got a touch of the gypsy in you."

"What do you carry in this truck, Mr. Bob?" asked Smiler, who was rather keen to steer away from too much personal talk.

"Marine stores and equipment. From Southampton. Going to Bristol now. Then on to Birmingham and Liverpool and then back home again. Since you don't know where you want to go you can take your choice of any of 'em or some spot along the route."

Smiler, who had been born in Bristol and had a Sister Ethel who lived there still with her husband, Albert, wasn't too keen on Bristol. When his father was at sea he lived with them. Although he liked both of them Smiler wasn't too comfortable living with them. They were very fussy

about the tidiness of their spick and span little house and grumbled
because his hands were always marking the fresh paintwork. People,
somehow, always seemed to be making a fuss about what he did. . . .
Well, of some of the things. Like pinching a bottle of milk from a
doorstep if he was thirsty, or nicking a book from a shop if he felt like
reading. Though there had never been any call to send him to approved
school because he just hadn't done what they had said he had done. The
last thing in the world he would have done would have been to pinch an
old lady's handbag with twenty pounds in it. Still, when his father got
back he would settle all that. That was why, after exactly thirteen days'
and four hours' residence in the approved school, Smiler had run away
and had been managing on his own ever since. In the last few months
Smiler had become very good at looking after himself.

He said, "I'm not keen on Bristol, Mr. Bob. Could I go to Liverpool?"

"Liverpool it is. Or any place in between that you might happen to
fancy. Shan't get there until tomorrow. But you and Bacon can kip
down in the cab tonight if that suits. All right?"

"Yes, thank you, Mr. Bob."

Bob Peach smiled to himself. He had two boys of his own, though
they were much older than Smiler, and there was not much he had to
learn about boys. He could tell a boy who was in trouble easily enough.
And he could sense very quickly whether a boy was a bad or a good apple. This Samuel Miles was in some kind of trouble, but he was prepared
to bet that he wasn't really a bad sort. But Bob Peach knew too that you
had to take your time with boys in trouble. No good pressing them. If
they wanted your help or advice they would ask for it in their own good
time. Until then you just kept things going nice and easy and didn't ask
any awkward questions.

So Bob Peach drove to Bristol and part of the time he and Smiler
talked, and part of the time they listened to the radio or were just silent
with their own thoughts. In between them sat Bacon, leaning against
Smiler and settling down happily in friendly company in the way all
dogs of good character and no fixed abode do. And every time that
Smiler saw a police car parked ahead by the road, he would bend over
and pretend to scratch his ankle, keeping his head well down until the
car had been passed.

When they reached Bristol and Bob Peach drove the lorry into a yard
to unload part of his stores, Smiler strolled out into the road and found a
telephone booth. All Smiler possessed in the world was the thirty odd
pounds he had saved up from the job he had worked at during the past
few months, his battered old suitcase with a few clothes and odds and
ends in it, and the clothes he stood up in; a rough blue shirt, a shabby

green anorak and a pair of patched blue jeans. Being at large in Bristol made him uneasy. Some of his old school friends might spot him or – if he were dead unlucky – he might run into Sister Ethel or his Brother-in-Law Albert, so he was glad that there was a telephone booth just around the corner from the yard. He looked up the number of his father's shipping company in the directory and called it. Making his voice sound as rough and grownup as he could he asked when the *Kentucky Master* was due back in the country and at what port. He was told that at the moment she was scheduled for some time at the beginning of October at Greenock. After making this call Smiler contemplated ringing his Sister Ethel to tell her he was all right and she was not to worry – which he knew she would do anyway. But he decided against it. It would be better to write her a letter in a few days' time when he was well out of the Bristol area. Then he went back to the yard and sat waiting in the cab of the truck until Mr. Bob had been unloaded and was ready to move on. There was some trouble over the load which Mr. Bob was delivering, and it was some time before they moved off.

After leaving Bristol Bob Peach drove northwards through the green English countryside with Bacon and Smiler beside him. Now and again Bob would flash his lights or blow his horn to some passing lorry driver he knew. In the fields the cows grouped themselves under the broad shade of trees. Rooks gritting on the road ahead of them flew up as they approached and, in the clear air above, the swallows and swifts performed their aerobatics. They went through small country towns and large industrial towns and past farms and cottages. Most of the time, whatever they were talking about, Smiler was thinking that it was a long time to October and that he would have to get himself settled in somewhere safe and sound and find himself a job. His thirty pounds would not last for ever.

Once he said, "Where's Greenock, Mr. Bob?"

"Greenock. That's on the Clyde. Near Glasgow. Take a load up there sometimes. Why?"

"That's where my father's ship berths."

"Oh, want to get up there, do you?"

"Well, not just yet. Not till October."

"And what you goin' to do until then?"

"Get myself a job, I suppose. I don't like doin' nothing."

"Neither do I. Takes all the sap out of you."

For a moment Bob Peach considered pursuing enquiries about Samuel Miles, but decided against it. If the boy wanted help he would ask for it soon enough. He seemed a capable sort and able to look after himself.

At seven o'clock they stopped at a transport café and had a meal and
Smiler got a plate of scraps from the kitchen for Bacon. Some time later
Bob Peach turned off the main highway on to a side road. Half a mile
down the road was a large picnic area on the edge of a wood. Bob Peach
pulled into this.

He said, "Can't take staying in transport lodgings in the summer. Kip
out in the open. Saves money and it's healthier. You and Bacon can have
the cab, I'll sleep in the back. Now then, why don't you and Bacon take a
stroll before turning in? I'm going to sit and read me paper over a bottle
of beer." He pulled from his pocket the evening paper and a bottle of
beer which he had bought at the transport café.

Smiler and Bacon jumped down from the cab and moved off into the
trees. Although Smiler had been born and lived nearly all his life in
Bristol he had in the last few months become very much of a country
boy and now knew that, next to shipping off to sea like his father, he
would prefer always to live and work in the country. He went happily
through the trees with Bacon at his heels.

Behind him Bob Peach took a swig at his bottle of beer and shook
open the evening paper. His eyes rounded with surprise. "Cor, luv a
duck!" he said.

There, staring at him from the centre of a column on the front page,
was a head and shoulders picture of Samuel Miles. Not a good
photograph and one taken eighteen months before. But it was un-
mistakably Samuel Miles. The caption at the head of the column read –
COUNTRYWIDE SEARCH FOR RUNAWAY BOY. Even as he
began to read the account the thought went swiftly through Bob Peach's
mind that half-a-dozen drivers had been reading the evening paper in
the transport café. In fact, now he thought of it, one or two had given
Samuel Miles an odd look as they had gone out. It would be a miracle if
no one had recognized that broad, snub-nosed face, the thick freckles
and the wide friendly eyes.

●   ●   ●

Some way in the wood, sitting by the side of a small lake with Bacon
close to him, Smiler was eyeing the water. There wouldn't be any trout
in it, he thought, but it looked good chub and carp water. Maybe some
tench. A mallard duck moved along the fringe of reeds and bullrushes
with a little flotilla of ducklings following in line astern. A swallow
dipped to the lake surface and made a ring like a rising fish. Life in the
streets of Bristol had made his eyes sharp, but life in the Wiltshire countryside in the past months had made them even sharper. In the country

you had to be all eyes and ears. Somewhere in the trees on the far bank a wood pigeon was cooing. A hatch of flies moved ceaselessly up and down in their mating dance over the reeds and he caught the flick of a waterhen's white scut under some overhanging branches. He thought of the times his father had taken him to places like this fishing, and also of his recent friend Joe Ringer who had taught him to poach trout and anything else that was going with the best of them. October was a long way ahead. A very long way. And Greenock was in Scotland. He knew nothing about Scotland except that up there they ate haggis and made whisky and wore kilts. His father was fond of a glass of whisky now and then. October. Scotland. He gave a sigh and shook his head. They were both a long way off. Funny look that chap in the transport kitchen had given him when he went to get the scraps for Bacon. Almost as though he knew him. Perhaps the police had put something on the radio about him. He remembered the last time he had escaped from the police when they were taking him back to approved school. Then, he had gone into hiding, kept right out of sight. "You was being hunted then, Samuel M.," he told himself, "and you acted sensible. But now . . . Blimey, you really haven't been very sensible. Staying right out in the open, riding the roads with Mr. Bob, giving everyone a chance to see you."

Bacon came back from foraging around the lakeside and thrust a wet muzzle against his ear. Smiler got up and began to go slowly back to Mr. Bob and the truck. He had made a quick decision. He would sleep the night in the truck, but early in the morning he would be up and away before Mr. Bob was awake. Mr. Bob was nice but there was nothing he could do if the police or anyone else spotted him. Yes, that's what he would do. Take off and keep clear of roads and towns until the hunt for him had cooled off a bit. After that he could look for a job of some kind. Thank goodness, too, the weather was good. He could sleep rough in the open for weeks yet if he had to.

He moved through the trees, away up the slope from the lake. A jay scolded him from the shelter of a hawthorn bush. A grey squirrel ran up the side of an oak trunk and somewhere, high up in one of the trees, a thrush began to sing. For a moment Smiler felt very sad. He liked company, and he liked Mr. Bob. He liked being settled and having a job and knowing that he only had to wait out time till his father got back and sorted out the approved school mix-up. Perhaps, he thought, he'd risk riding just a bit farther with Mr. Bob.

He reached the top of the small rise and began to move down towards the picnic area and Mr. Bob's truck, Bacon at his heels. Through the trees he could glimpse part of the white side of the truck. Then, as he drew nearer, he saw that a car was drawn up behind the truck and he

heard the sound of men's voices. At this moment a man passed by the
car, and the sight of him was enough to send Smiler diving for cover
behind a bush. It was a police patrolman.

Smiler worked his way round to the other side of the bush and got a
clearer view of the picnic area. What he saw made him give a quiet
groan and his heart thump fast.

Drawn up by the truck was a police car. The blue light on its roof was
still flashing. Standing by the car were two patrolmen and Mr. Bob had
a newspaper in his hand and one of the policemen was pointing to
something in it. The other policeman went quickly back to the police car
and Smiler saw him pick up the hand microphone and begin to speak
over the radio.

Smiler didn't wait for any more. He was bright enough to guess what
could have happened. Mr. Bob had bought the evening paper in the
transport café where the chap in the kitchen there had given him an odd
look. "Samuel M.," he told himself, "if you want to keep out of trouble,
this is no place for you."

He crouched down and moved away into the trees, taking all the
cover he could. When he reached the top of the rise above the lake and
was well out of sight, he straightened up and began to run. He found a
grass-covered ride cut through the wood and jogged down it at a steady
pace. It was then for the first time that he realized that Bacon was with
him still, keeping close to his side, loping easily along, his red tongue
flopping out of his mouth.

*   *   *

Two hours later the policemen, after having made a close search of the
nearby woods for Smiler and Bacon, returned to Bob Peach.

"He must have come back and spotted us," said one of the policemen.
"Took off again. Why won't a boy in trouble realize that you don't get
anywhere by running away?"

Bob Peach gave a small grin and said, "If you really want to know, I'll
tell you. Because he's a boy, and all boys is young animals with an instinct to keep away from you boys in blue. Here –" he reached inside the
cab and pulled out Smiler's battered case "– you'd better have this.
Stuffed full of the crown jewels it probably is."

The policeman gave him a sour look and took the case.

The other policeman said, "What was this dog like he had with
him?"

Bob Peach screwed up his face for a moment in thought and then said,

"Well, I'd say it was kind of smallish. Half-terrier, half-corgi. All white, except for one brown ear. You could recognize it a mile off 'cause it runs with a kind of limp." He paused, and then added, "The left ear — that's the brown one. I know you chaps like all details to be exact."

2

The Professor Takes a Hand
—and More

For two days Smiler and Bacon avoided civilization as much as they could. If they had to cross a road they waited until it was more or less clear and crossed quickly. When Smiler had to buy food and drink he would slip into a small village store and then be gone like a shadow. He had found an old sack and some binder twine and made himself a small haversack to carry provisions. He washed the sack and his only shirt by a stream and dried them in the sun. He bought himself a cap in a country shop which he pulled well down and he made a collar and a lead from the binder twine for Bacon. But there was little need for the lead because Bacon kept faithfully to his heels and – somebody in the past had well-trained Bacon – if Smiler told him to sit and mind his haversack, Bacon would sit and guard it until he returned.

Right from the start Smiler established what he considered was the safest routine. Once the sun was well up they stopped travelling and found a place to hide and rest. The first night they slept on piles of pulled green bracken in a little woodland dell five miles from Mr. Bob's truck. As he lay there Smiler looked up and picked out the Big Bear and then the North Star. From his father he knew most of the principal stars and he had already decided to head northwards. They were up before dawn and, steering now by the sun, kept going until almost mid-day when they found a place to rest until the afternoon was almost worn away.

The second night they found a stack of fresh cut hay, burrowed into it, and slept warm and comfortable with the sweet smell of new mown grass in their nostrils. Between them they ate meat pies, sausage rolls, corned beef, tinned sardines, biscuits, buns, apples, oranges and once – as a treat for Smiler – a small bottle of pickled onions. They drank spring and river water with now and then – for Smiler – a bottle of beer or a can of shandy or Coca-Cola. And once Smiler bought half-a-dozen brown eggs from a cottage and a new loaf from a village store. He made a fire and boiled the eggs hard in an old tin. He and Bacon finished the lot between them for supper with a can of salmon. Bacon showed no signs of distress, but Smiler was awake half the night with a violent stomach ache.

They went north steadily if slowly and erratically, and Smiler had no idea where he was. The names of the villages meant nothing to him. Sometime, he decided, he must buy a map so that he could find Greenock on it. Thinking things over he had come to the decision that if his father was going to berth at Greenock in October, then there was no reason why he shouldn't go to Scotland as soon as he could. England was all right but the police here knew all about him and had long memories and sharp eyes. Up in Scotland probably no one knew about him. He'd heard, too, that it was a wild sort of country of mountains and lochs and rivers with plenty of room for a person to find a niche for himself without risk of meeting a policeman at every turn of the road.

On their fourth day at large, as they were travelling after their afternoon rest, it began to rain in a steady downpour. They were moving across a wide stretch of orchard country, the trees globed with green, unripened apples. Within five minutes the two were as wet as fishes and far more uncomfortable. With Bacon at his heels, long bushy tail bedraggled and lowered to a half-mast position, Smiler ploughed on looking for some shelter. The trees gave no cover. They just seemed to drip more water as well as rain on them. There wasn't a tractor shed or a barn in sight without going near a farmhouse. After two hours of wet and miserable walking they came out on to a main road. In the fading light Smiler saw, stacked just off the road, a pile of large section concrete pipes which had been unloaded there in preparation for some drainage works. A few cars were zipping up and down the road, their lights on and their tires hissing on the wet surface.

Smiler surveyed the pipe sections. Bacon at his side gave himself a shake and sprayed water from his coat. "Samuel M.," said Smiler, "any port in a storm and beggars can't be choosers."

He crawled into the cover of one of the pipes. Bacon went with him and drew close to him so that Smiler could feel the dog shiver now and then. Smiler sat there and watched the occasional car go by. All the food he had left in his sodden sack was a sliced loaf and a piece of cheese. He pulled them out. The loaf slices were sodden with rain. Smiler broke the cheese in half and wrapped two limp, doughy, soggy slices of bread round each half. He gave one to Bacon who ate it ravenously. He ate the other himself and tried to pretend that it was a delicious cheese roll. A cold draught blew through the pipe and the concrete was hard on his bottom, elbows and shoulders as he tried to make himself comfortable. It was, he knew, going to be a long and uncomfortable night.

To cheer himself up, he began to think of his father. Living in Bristol with his Sister Ethel and her Albert was all right, but nothing like as good as the times when his father was ashore and they lived together in

lodgings, went on fishing expeditions and to football matches. Where
was his father now, he wondered? Berthed in some foreign port? A
warm, tropical night all around and palms rustling in the soft breeze and
fireflies flitting about their tops. Probably he'd be sitting on deck in the
cool after the heat of the galley and giving the other lads a song. A great
singer was his father and he, Smiler, knew all his songs. Perhaps, he
thought, if he gave himself a song, pretended that he was warm and
comfortable, it would help. He began to sing one of his father's
favourites —

> There were two ravens that sat on a tree
> And they were black as they could be;
> And one of them I heard him say —
> Oh where shall we go to dine today?
> Shall we go down to the salt, salt sea —
> Or shall we go dine by the green-wood tree?
> Shall we go down to the salt, salt sea —
> Or shall we go dine by the green-wood tree?

But as he finished the first verse, Bacon raised himself on his forefeet,
lifted his head up and began to howl like a wolf. He made so much noise
that Smiler had to stop singing in case someone heard them both. There
was nothing for it but to try and get some sleep, so Smiler curled himself
up and, using Bacon as a damp pillow, shut his eyes and wooed sleep. It
was a long time coming, but when it did he slept soundly.

Smiler woke the next morning just as the sun was coming up. The
rain had gone. Early morning traffic was beginning to move up and
down the road. Stiffly, he and Bacon emerged from their pipe and went
back over the hedge to get away from the road. Both of them were damp,
bedraggled and hungry. They ploughed through the wet long grass of a
meadow, the grass starred with tall ox-daisies and creamy spikes of
meadowsweet above which the bees were already long busy. The top of
the meadow was bounded by a small, fast-running stream. Smiler took a
look at the sun and saw that the stream was running from the north to
the south, so he began to move upstream with Bacon at his heels.

After about a hundred yards Smiler suddenly stopped and raised his
head and sniffed. He sniffed two or three times and slowly his mouth
began to water. He looked down at Bacon and said, "Bacon, my lad — if
there's one morning smell that you can't mistake it's eggs and bacon
frying."

Slowly the two moved cautiously upstream, following the delicious
smell. They came to a small clump of willows growing at the stream side

and went into them. The smell grew stronger. In the middle of the clump, close to the stream's edge, they saw a large sheet of black plastic material which had been tied in a canopy between four trees with the loose ends pegged down on three sides to make a snug shelter. The opening faced away from them. Over the top of the sheeting a thin, blue curl of wood smoke showed and the smell of cooking was very pungent and appetizing.

With Bacon close to his heels Smiler moved around the side of the shelter. Just in front of it was a small fire, burning in a neat fireplace made from stones taken from the stream. On the fire was a large frying-pan which held four rashers of bacon, two eggs and a sausage, all sizzling gently away. It was a sight which made Smiler's midriff ache. Sitting just outside the tent affair on a small canvas folding stool was a man with a long twig in his hand with which he was turning the sausage and bacon as they cooked.

He looked up at Smiler without surprise. Then he looked at Bacon. And then he looked back at Smiler and slowly winked.

Smiler, anxious to establish good relations, said politely, "Good morning, sir."

The man said, "Good morning, boy." He looked Smiler up and down again and it was the kind of look that missed nothing. Then he said, "A good morning after a bad night. How did you and your companion, *canis mongrelis*, make out?"

"Not very well, sir," said Smiler. "We slept in a drainpipe by the road back there."

The man nodded. "In my time I have done the same, but it is not to be recommended. Man was not framed to sleep on the arc of a circle. It is a question of the relative inflexibility of the human spine. I presume that it was the aroma of a traditional English breakfast that brought you this way?"

"We're both pretty hungry, sir. That's if you've got enough to spare. I could pay for it. I've got some money and —"

The man raised a warning hand. "Please, boy — do not mention money. Friendship and shared adversity are the only coinage recognized by true gentlemen of the road. Would I be right in putting you at two eggs and three rashers — plus a sausage? And for your faithful hound I have an old ham bone somewhere in my gear and he can have the pleasure of licking the frying-pan clean later."

"Gosh!" said Smiler. "That would be jolly super — if you can spare it."

"Say no more."

The man turned, reached back into his shelter, and dragged out a

battered old perambulator with a tatty folded hood and began to ferret
in it for provisions. In no time at all he had found eggs, bacon and
sausage and they were in the frying-pan. The ham bone was unwrapped
from an old newspaper and handed to Bacon. Then from the battered
pram the man pulled out another folding canvas stool and handed it to
Smiler saying, "Rest your juvenile posterior on that."

Smiler opened up the stool, sat down, and watched the man as he now
began to give serious application to the cooking of an extra breakfast.

He was a funny-looking old boy, thought Smiler. He had long black
hair to his shoulders and a straggling black beard. His face was brown
and furrowed with wrinkles. Above a nobly beaked nose his eyes were as
bright as a hedge-sparrow's eggs. Smiler, who wasn't much good at
guessing ages, felt he must be much older than his father. For clothes,
starting at the top, he wore a bowler hat whose blackness had a nice
green shine like verdigris on copper, and his jacket was made of green
and brown tweed and was patched and torn. His trousers were of blue
denim and tucked into a pair of green gum boots. Underneath his open
jacket he wore a red T-shirt on the front of which was a printed head of
a man with long flowing hair and the word – Beethoven – under it.

The man looked up from his cooking and asked, "And what would
your name be, boy?"

For a moment Smiler hesitated. Then he decided that this man didn't
look the kind who would read the newspapers much or listen to the
radio, so he decided to tell the truth.

"Samuel Miles, sir. Most people call me Smiler. But I don't care for it
much."

"Neither do I since I don't care for half-cooked puns anymore than I
do for half-cooked buns. I shall call you Samuel. And your four-legged
friend?"

"That's Bacon."

"A good name. Of course, after the great philosopher and not the
comestible of that ilk." Then seeing the baffled look on Smiler's face, he
went on, "Never mind. Allow me to introduce myself. I am Professor
Roscoe Bertram Crimples. That, of course, is my true name. I have
others which necessity from time to time makes it desirable to employ.
But then, as a gentleman of the road yourself, you, no doubt, understand
that perfectly well."

"Yes, of course, sir . . . I mean, Professor," said Smiler.

"Capital, Samuel. We who live outside society must be allowed our
little stratagems."

"What are you a Professor of?" asked Smiler.

The Professor reached back into the pram for two plates and cutlery and said over his shoulder, "I am a Professor of all the Ologies. You name one and I am a Professor of it." He turned and began to dish the breakfast from the frying-pan with a knife and fork. The sight and smell made Smiler's stomach feel hollow.

"Name an Ology," said the Professor severely.

A bit stumped for the moment, all his eyes and attention on the coming breakfast, Smiler searched around in his mind desperately and finally said, "What about Geology?"

"A fine subject. One of the oldest. *Granite is hard and sandstone is soft, but Time's withering hand turns all to dust.* I am, you see, also a bit of a poet – although the rhyme is bad which is due to the early hour of the day. Now let us eat while the water boils for our coffee."

He handed Smiler his plate and knife and fork, put an old tin can full of water into the embers of the fire, and then began to attack his own breakfast.

The two of them tucked into their breakfast while, a little way to the side, Bacon cracked and gnawed at the last of his bone. A bluetit came and sat on a branch above the canopy, scolded them, and then flew down to investigate a slip of bacon rind that Smiler tossed into the bushes for it. The stream ran behind them, making a pleasant musical sound, and the morning sun slid higher and bathed them with its warmth. It was one of the best breakfasts Smiler could remember and it was crowned by the Professor's coffee which was strong and laced with liberal dollops of sweet condensed milk.

Over his coffee, the Professor produced a small cheroot from the inside pocket of his jacket and lit it. He tipped his bowler hat back, blew a cloud of blue smoke, and contemplated Smiler. After a few moments he said, "Well, Samuel, state your problem."

A little guarded, Smiler said, "Problem, Professor? What problem?"

The Professor shook his head. "All mankind has problems. And that includes boys. Wandering about the country with a dog with a bit of string for a collar, carrying an old sack for luggage, spending a night in a concrete pipe – I don't have to be a Professor of Sociology to know you must have a problem. *Adrift on the troubled sea of life – victim of, who knows what strife.* The metre's bad but the rhyme is good. I'll do better later in the day. So what's your problem?"

Smiler, who liked the man, still felt that he ought to be cautious.

He said, "It's a bit private, Professor."

"All problems are, more or less. But since I'm a Professor of Problemology, too, you can tell me. Troubles dealt with in the strictest confidence. No charge. But since you're not quite sure how to go about it, let's see if we can tackle it diplomatically. You're in trouble?"

"Yes, Professor."

"On the run?"

"Yes, Professor."

"Guilty or not guilty?"

"Of what, Professor?"

"Of what you're running away from, of course."

"No, I'm not. It was all a mistake and —"

"Hold it!" The Professor cut him off. "Not so fast. No need for details. I know truth when I hear it. Running away and not guilty. Good. Running where to?"

"Scotland, Professor."

"A fine country — though I never cared for it. The cooking is terrible. And why Scotland?"

" 'Cos my father's ship berths up there in October and I got to meet him so that he can sort things out for me."

"Splendid. He sounds like a good father. But Scotland's a long way off and so is October. Walking easily you could do it in a month."

"I want to get up there as soon as I can."

"Why?"

"Because — like I said — I'm on the run and the police down here —"

"— are keeping their sharp official little eyes open for you? Is that it?"

"Yes, Professor."

"The solution is simple. You've got money?"

"Yes, Professor."

"How much?"

"Twenty odd pounds."

"Then take a train."

Smiler shook his head. "I couldn't do that, Professor. I'd have to show myself at a station in some town. There's always police at stations. And on the train, too, there'd be people and the guard and ticket collector."

"Spare me the passenger list," said the Professor. "There are different ways of taking trains. Would you consider three pounds too expensive for a place on a train with no need for stations or meeting passengers and police?"

"Could you fix that, Professor?"

"Why not? I'm also a Professor of Fixology — for them that I like."

"Would you for me, Professor?"

"*Consider it a settled deal. No need for contract or big red seal.* Better. But still not of the highest order."

The Professor stood up and put the frying-pan down in front of Bacon for the dog to lick clean.

Smiler said gratefully, "I was very lucky to meet you, Professor."

The man smiled through his beard. "You were, Samuel. You were. But do not judge the rest of the human race by me – otherwise you'll be in for disappointments. Yes, you were very lucky. Right – now we'll strike camp and go and make your travel arrangements. *Caledonia stern and wild waits to greet the runaway child.*"

"I'm not a child," said Smiler stoutly.

The Professor grinned. "For the sake of the rhyme you have to be. No offence intended. Now you take the canopy down and I'll pack up the old pram."

So the two of them set about striking camp. When it was all done, with everything stowed away in the pram, the Professor with Smiler's help cleaned up the camp site, poured water over the fire embers and finally left the place neat and tidy.

It was very soon clear to Smiler that the Professor knew every inch of the countryside in this area. Pushing the pram along small tracks and paths, and occasionally lifting it over a stile or locked gate, they went away across a long stretch of heath and woodland. Finally, after a long climb to the head of a small valley, they came out on to a wide reach of flat grasslands which was traversed by a small, high-hedged dusty road.

On the road Smiler took over the pushing of the pram while the Professor walked at his side and gave him a running commentary on everything which they passed. He knew the name of each bird, each flower, bush and tree. And Smiler, walking with him, thought what a nice but odd sort of man he was. He was the kind, he thought, that old Joe Ringer back in Wiltshire would have liked. But Joe Ringer and all his time in Wiltshire now seemed a long way behind. Ahead of him lay Scotland, October and his father. Three pounds from his twenty would leave him seventeen pounds. That would be more than enough to keep him going until he found a job.

A mile down the road they came to a level-crossing. To one side of the red and white gates stood a tall signal-box and someway beyond it Smiler saw the platform and buildings of a small station.

The Professor said, "You wait here, Samuel, while I go and have a talk with an old friend. But first the money. A little grease to oil the wheels of commerce."

From his back pocket Smiler pulled out the stout brown envelope in which he kept his money. He slipped three notes out and handed them to the Professor. Then he put the envelope back in his pocket.

Smiler and Bacon sat on the grass at the side of the road while the Professor went along to the signal-box and climbed the steps to the control room at the top. He went in and Smiler could see him talking to a man in shirtsleeves.

After a little while the Professor came back, smiling and nodding his head.

"Is it going to be all right?" asked Smiler.

"It is, Samuel. *The great iron road to Scotland lies ahead – and you will travel it on a moving bed.* Not bad. Not good. In between. That's the trouble with my poetry. Now then, we've got to wait until nine o'clock tonight. I'm going on into the village to stock up with provisions. Give me a pound and I'll bring some back for your journey."

"Would you, Professor?" Smiler fished for his brown envelope again.

"Of course. A small service gladly performed. Meanwhile you make yourself scarce around here. Keep off the road and be back just before sunset."

Smiler said, "Of course. But, Professor, while you're in the village could you get me an envelope and some paper and a stamp? I got an urgent letter to write."

The Professor's eyes twinkled. "Correspondence, eh? *Some brown-skinned, bright-eyed girlfriend – don't grieve for me, darling, we'll meet in the end?*"

Smiler chuckled and shook his head. "No – I got to write to my Sister Ethel that I'm supposed to live with while my Dad's away. I got to let her know I'm all right."

"Of course you have. Highly commendable behaviour," said the Professor and he set himself behind the pram and with a wave of his hand began to push it over the level-crossing.

Smiler watched him go. Then he turned back up the road with Bacon at his heels and went through the first gap in the hedge. Scotland, he thought. He was really going to Scotland. Things were turning out well, and the best turn-out had been meeting the Professor. That was a real stroke of luck.

At eight o'clock Smiler returned to the level-crossing. The Professor was sitting on the grass bank waiting for him. From the pram he produced a load of provisions for Smiler. As Smiler packed them into his haversack, the Professor said, "You've everything you need for a two-day journey. Got you a couple of bottles of water, but go easy on it. You might or might not get a chance to fill up along the way. The packet of dog biscuits is because I presumed your four-footed friend is going with you."

"Well, yes, of course," said Smiler. Somehow it had never occurred to him that he would do anything else but take Bacon. They were both wanderers, had both been "destination unknown" types when they had met.

When he had finished his packing, Smiler wrote his letter to his Sister Ethel which the Professor promised to post for him.

The letter read: *Dear Sis, I am O.K. and doing fine but until Dad comes back I got to keep out of the way. Don't worry for me I have a dog now who is a faythfill freind, and others what are helping me along the road. Tell Albert hello and love to you both. Samuel. I am alright for money as well. S.*

When the light began to go from the sky and the last skylark had ceased its chorusing and dropped to the ground, the Professor said, "Time to move. *The shades of night are drawing nigh – Time for friends to say goodbye.*"

The Professor pushed his pram into the cover of some bushes. Then the two of them walked down the track past the signal-box and took up position on a steep embankment outside the little railway station. Here, alongside the main tracks, was a long length of track which made a shunting bay. The Professor explained that twice a week a northbound goods train came up the line and pulled into the bay around nine o'clock. It stayed for about fifteen minutes to let main line traffic through and then drew out to continue its journey northwards. The signalman in the box, having been paid, would turn a blind eye while Smiler selected a wagon and climbed aboard. All Smiler had to watch out for was that the crew of the diesel engine and the guard did not see him.

"Which they won't," said the Professor, "because they always use this break to have their supper."

Ten minutes later, the goods train pulled in, hauling behind it a long line of open and closed wagons.

The Professor, who was clearly very knowledgeable about trains, said, "Closed wagons no good. Locked. Open ones are the ticket this time of the year. Well ventilated but protected from the weather by their tarpaulins. But you don't want coal or machinery. Makes hard lying." He eyed the long line of wagons and then nodded. "Don't worry. I've spotted one for you."

He stood up and looked up to the engine and then down to the guard's van. There was no sign of the engine crew or guard. He began to move down to the line and Smiler and Bacon followed him.

Smiler's heart was thumping a little fast now. He'd hitchhiked plenty of times, and ridden buses dodging the conductor to avoid paying a fare – but he had never jumped a train before. He had read plenty of stories of people who had. Sometimes they could only manage to get underneath the truck and then they often fell and had a leg chopped off by the wheels.

They stopped close to an open wagon which had a green canvas tarpaulin over the top. The Professor squinted at the ticket on the side.

"This will do." He reached up, a knife suddenly in his hand, and cut one of the holding ropes of the tarpaulin. "I'll give you a leg up. You wriggle under and then I'll pass the dog up. All right?"

In the growing dusk, Smiler looked up at him and said, "Yes, Professor. And thank you very much for your help."

"Nothing at all, boy. Nothing at all. Adversity brings out the common humanity in us all. Now then, up you go!"

As Smiler reached for a hold on the truck, the Professor crouched down and gave him a bunt up with his shoulder. He then steadied him with his hands as Smiler crawled in. Smiler went under the canvas like an eel and tumbled into the wagon on to a layer of smooth sacks – which he found later contained agricultural fertilizers. He crouched on the sacks and shoved his head and shoulders back through the canvas opening and reached for Bacon as the Professor held the dog up.

Smiler hauled Bacon in and then popped his head out again to say goodbye to the Professor.

The Professor stood outside in the gloaming, his bowler hat cocked to one side, his big black beard teased by the light breeze of the evening, his bright eyes twinkling. Smiler liked him so much that he half thought of suggesting that the Professor should come with him. With someone like the Professor around there wouldn't be any trouble that could not be overcome. They could camp out on the mountains of Scotland and look after themselves easily. He was about to put this to the Professor when the man said, "Goodbye, Samuel. Keep a cool head and a steady hand. And give my qualified regards to Scotland. *By brae and burn and lonely glen – Who knows when we'll meet again?* Not good. Not bad either for this time of night. God keep you, my boy."

The Professor gave something suspiciously like a sentimental sniff, doffed his bowler regally, and then turned away.

Smiled said, "Bye, Professor. Thanks for . . . for everything."

Smiler watched the Professor move up the embankment and then become lost in the shadows of the trees at its top. Smiler ducked under the canvas and in the semi-darkness began to make himself comfortable, stacking aside some of the sacks to make himself a space to lie in, settling Bacon down with a big dog biscuit, and telling himself what a bit of luck it had been meeting the Professor.

Ten minutes later the goods train pulled out of the siding and hit the main track north. And five minutes later Smiler – always methodical – in checking over his possessions discovered that the brown envelope with his money in it had disappeared from his pocket.

For a moment or two he couldn't understand it. He was always careful with his money and he knew that he always buttoned his back pocket when he put the envelope in. He sat there, listening to the *rump-bump-rump* of the wheels over the rail joints and stared at the shadowy form of Bacon, crunching away at his hard biscuit.

Suddenly he said aloud to himself, "Of course! That old Professor. He nicked it. Cool as a cucumber. He nicked it when he bunted me up. The old devil . . . !" For a moment or two he didn't know what to feel or think. Nearly twenty quids' worth up the spout. Then, suddenly, he rolled over on the sacks and began to laugh, telling himself, "Samuel M., you was done. He turned you over as neat as neat. But it don't matter, Samuel M. The only thing that matters is Scotland. You can get a job there and earn some more money."

Laughing still he rolled over and grappled with Bacon, the two of them mock fighting, as the train clattered steadily northwards.

3

Operation Grey Goose

The goods train was not a fast one. During that night it frequently drew off the main line to let passenger trains go through. Once during the night Smiler poked his head through the canopy while they were going slowly through a station and he caught the name – Penrith. It meant nothing to him except that he was pretty sure that it wasn't a Scottish one because it was too soon to be in Scotland yet.

He and Bacon slept on their smooth sacks. Now and again Smiler would wake to hear the *clackety-clack-clackety* of the wheels over the rails and to feel the wagon sway and swing below him. At first light he woke, feeling stiff and cold. He poked his head out to find a fresh dawn breeze cold on his face. There was a rose-pearl flush in the eastern sky against which was silhouetted a line of bare, grey-shadowed hills. Shivering, Smiler ducked below to escape the morning chill. He and Bacon had breakfast from the provisions which the Professor had bought. Smiler drank from one of the water bottles and he poured some of it into the inside of his cap for Bacon to drink. Luckily Bacon was very thirsty and lapped it up before much of it could soak away through the lining. Despite the breakfast, which Smiler thought would have warmed him up, he found that he was still shivering. It was so bad sometimes that his teeth rattled together and his body trembled all over as though someone were giving him a good shaking. Within the next hour things got worse. He had a bad pain in his stomach, his head began to ache, and now and then, instead of shivering, he went hot all over. In fact he felt very queer indeed. All he could do was to lie with Bacon huddled close to him and think how miserable he was.

Sometimes he found himself talking out loud to himself or to Bacon.

"Samuel M., you've ate something bad. I only hope it don't turn to a touch of the collywobbles. Not here."

He lay there, half-awake, half-asleep, his body going hot and cold, and his mind beginning to wander a little like it did just before going off to sleep so that things that started out sensibly slowly turned into nonsense. Fever, he thought. He'd had something like this once before when he was at his Sister Ethel's house. For a while he wished he were there now. Warmly tucked up in bed with Sister Ethel to look after him. "Say you was to die, Samuel M.? You might be here for weeks till they found you with the faithful hound beside you." Then the awful thought struck him that, maybe, as well as pinching his money, the Professor had poisoned his food. The Professor was a mad man, perhaps. Going about robbing and killing boys . . .

Slowly Smiler passed into an uneasy feverish half-awake half-asleep dream. He lay in the wagon while the train went steadily north through Dumfries, Kilmarnock, Motherwell and into Glasgow. Here, without Smiler knowing a thing about it, except for the bangings and shoutings that came through into his dreams, the train was broken up. The wagons were shunted and reshunted and a new train formed. At six o'clock that evening the train pulled out of Glasgow (where lower down the River Clyde lay Greenock to which his father was to return in October) and headed even farther northwards, rattling and swaying towards the highlands of Scotland.

Once, just before dark, Smiler came round, feeling a little better. He sat up and gave Bacon a drink and some dog biscuits. But he could neither eat nor drink himself. After this he lay back and dozed off. This time he dropped into a deep sleep, untroubled by dreams.

Smiler woke to hear Bacon whining gently. Then, in the darkness, the dog licked his face. He sat up and was pleased to find that, although he felt a bit as though he'd been pummelled all over, his head was clear and the hot and cold shivering fits had left him. And then he realized something else. The train was not moving and there was stillness all around.

Slowly, Smiler got to his feet and poked his head out of the wagon. It was a still clear night with a blaze of stars overhead. The truck stood in a siding with three others, but there was no sign of the rest of the train. Smiler decided that, whether he was in Scotland or not, he had had enough. He gathered up his belongings, lowered Bacon over the side, and dropped down after him.

Together they went across the waste ground at the side of the rails, climbed a fence and then dropped down a steep grass slope to find themselves on a road. Smiler looked up at the stars, found the North Star, and saw that the road ran west and east. He went westwards along it, Bacon at his heels, and after about half a mile came to a junction with a larger road. A signpost pointing south read – *Fort William 4 miles*. Smiler, having no idea what time it was, but knowing it must be very late because there was no traffic about, decided to make for Fort William.

He was feeling much better now and, as he walked, he took stock of his situation. He must have been in the truck a long time . . . a night and a day and almost another night. With luck he must be in Scotland. Sharp against the starlit sky he could see hills around him. He had a sack of provisions, the clothes he stood up in, Bacon for company and – how much money?

He turned out his pockets. There was a loose pound note in his trouser pocket and a handful of silver change among which were two fifty-pence pieces. Altogether he had nearly three pounds. Well, that wasn't too bad. He was already feeling better. It was clear to him now that after all that rain and sleeping out in that drainpipe he had caught a feverish chill. Yes, he was feeling much better and, what was more, hungry. But he wanted something better than sardines and bread. A proper breakfast, like the one the Professor (that old devil) had provided. Eggs and bacon and hot coffee! His mouth watered. There might be an all-night café in Fort William. If not, he would have to wait until morning. He moved down the road, his spirits returning. Bacon trotted at his heels and, from somewhere away to his right, came the cry of a nightbird which he recognized at once from his days with Joe Ringer. It was the whistle of a lone flying curlew.

* * *

Smiler, in fact, kept clear of Fort William until the sun came up. If he walked around the place on his own at night, he had decided, he might be spotted by some curious policeman. Breakfast would have to wait until the proper time.

When he did go into the town that morning it took him no time at all to realize, from the way the people spoke, that he was in Scotland. He knew the accent well because there was a Scottish family that lived next door to Sister Ethel. And all the things in the tourist shops told him that it was Scotland: the dolls dressed in tartan kilts and the picture postcards. The town itself stood on the side of a great loch with mountains on both sides. He found an early-opening lorry drivers' café and went in for breakfast. While he ate, he decided that he must buy a map. From his expeditions with his father he was fond of maps and could read them well. He had already seen one in the window of a newsagent's shop. The price marked on the cover was fifty pence. As he ate he debated with himself whether he would buy it or go in, say for a box of matches, and nick it. After a time he decided that, since he was in Scotland and in a way making a fresh start, he would buy it. It would make a hole in his funds, but he was sure that he would soon get a job somewhere. On a farm if he could. He didn't want any town job. No, thank you. He wanted a job where there wouldn't be too many people about to ask awkward questions.

By half past nine he was sitting on a seat on the town promenade that overlooked the loch, studying the map he had bought. He soon found Fort William and saw that it stood at the head of Loch Linnhe where the Caledonian Canal started running up through Loch Lochy and Loch Ness to Inverness. But the thing that surprised him was how far north Fort William was from Glasgow. It was miles away. Still, that was no worry. He had until October to get back to Glasgow and then Greenock.

By half past ten Smiler and Bacon had walked back through the town and northwards to where another road ran off westwards along the shores of another loch, called Loch Eil. Smiler had picked this road because eventually it reached the sea. If he couldn't get a farm job along the way, well, he might get something in a fishing village on the coast.

By eleven o'clock Smiler and Bacon had got a lift in a ramshackle farm lorry that took them well along the road and finally dropped them at a place called Glenfinnan. Smiler and Bacon walked onwards for another two hours but it was hard going because the road was narrow and full of holiday traffic. Smiler decided to turn off down a side road as soon as he could.

By six o'clock that evening Smiler and Bacon — on Smiler's own admission — were well and truly lost. They had taken a side road that led up through the lower slopes of the hills to the south. At first the rough road ran through growths of rowan and birch trees. After a time these were left behind and they were out on long stretches of grassland where small parties of sheep with grown lambs grazed. Smiler had decided to ask at the first farm he came to for work. But they passed no farm. They came to a fork in the road on a flat bluff covered with worn grey rocks. There was no signpost, so Smiler tossed up for it and took the righthand fork. It began to drop down through a narrow valley. High above it were steep heather-covered slopes with racing cloud shadows darkening their purple sweeps. The road grew rougher and narrower, dwindling now to a path more than a road, and a small burn ran alongside it. Smiler and Bacon followed this track for over an hour, sometimes going up and sometimes going down, sometimes parting with the burn but always meeting it farther on. As the track grew slimmer, the burn grew wider and became a small river. Quite a few things watched Smiler and Bacon pass by.

From a tall pine a pair of hooded crows saw them. Couched in bracken on the slopes high above, a roe deer doe with month-old twin calves saw them both, and a golden eagle, circling so high against the

sun that Smiler could never have seen him, watched the movement of
Bacon on the track and the human being with him.

An hour later when Smiler had told himself ruefully that he was getting nowhere fast, the track dropped steeply into a narrow, tree-lined
glen where the small river rushed over a rocky bed in noisy turmoil.
Smiler and Bacon came out of the trees at the foot of the glen to find
themselves on a loch shore. There was not a house or a human being in
sight, and Smiler groaned at the thought of having to go all the way back
along the track. To his right the loch ran away into the distance and disappeared into a grey haze from which rose the dark slopes of a range of
mountains. To his left the loch reached back into the hills for about a
mile and then swung away at an angle sharply so that the rest of it was
hidden from him by a steep craggy shoulder of hill. The loch itself was
so wide that the far shore, he guessed, had to be more than a mile away.

Smiler sat down in a grassy hollow above the shore and consulted his
map. Unfortunately it was a large-scale map. Although he could pick out
where he had turned off the main road he couldn't find any track marked
after the righthand fork he had taken. And as for the loch — the whole
map where he thought he might be seemed to be a blue-marked
patchwork of lochs. Stumped for the moment as to what to do, Smiler
untied his haversack and he and Bacon had a meal. After the meal they
stretched out in the sun and slept, both of them tired out from their long
walk.

*   *   *

While Smiler and Bacon slept, a little farther down the lochside an old
greylag gander was paddling quietly along the shoreline, dipping his
long head and neck below the surface from time to time to root and feed
in the thin carpet of underwater vegetation. The greylag was a prisoner
of the loch for, though it could swim and paddle quite easily and walk
when it went ashore, it could not fly. Its left wing had been broken close
to the body. When it swam or walked the wing dragged loosely and
awkwardly at the side of its body. The greylag had spent the winter on
the loch and the moorlands above it. Early in the year it had taken off
with its companions to make the long journey north to its Arctic
breeding grounds. As the small skein of birds had moved down the loch
a golden eagle, not yet a year old, had swooped at the geese.

The leader, seeing the eagle coming, had raised a quick *gang-gang-
gang* alarm call and the skein had scattered in all directions. The young
eagle diving downwards had been confused by the sudden wild
scattering of the geese and had lost sight of the goose it had marked out

for its prey. It had come out of its swoop and swung in a low curve at the nearest bird which it had hit clumsily on the left wing but failed to grasp with its talons. The injured goose had plummetted to the water and the golden eagle had soared upwards in vain pursuit of the wildly scattered skein of birds.

Unable to fly the injured greylag had been forced to stay on the loch. Over the months a great many animals, and a few people, had become aware of its presence. But none of them had ever been able to come near it. Disabled, it had learnt new cunnings and each night it roosted well out in the loch on a lonely pinnacle of a small rock island.

The greylag came now up the loch shore to the little sandy stretch of beach above which Smiler and Bacon slept in their grassy hollow. The bird knew the beach well. At the far end there was a growth of reeds and rushes where food could be found. On the shore above the reeds, too, was a wide stretch of rich grass on which it often grazed.

This day the gander paddled past the beach and foraged for a while in the rushes. Then, after taking a good look at the lochside, it went quietly ashore towards the grass, its left wing dragging awkwardly. As it did so the greylag was watched by an animal that had often seen it before, an animal that had once or twice stalked it but had never been able to get close to it.

In a wind-stunted oak close to the mouth of the river which ran into the loch, a wild cat was lying sunning itself on the crotch of a branch. The wild cat had been there a long time. It was a female with young kittens that waited for it now in their lair deep in the heart of a rocky cairn on the hillside above the river.

The wild cat had seen Smiler and Bacon pass by and disappear into the grassy hollow beyond the beach, and then had seen the greylag working its way up the shore line. Curled up in the angle of the tree trunk and the branch, its grey-brown streaky coat merged in a perfect camouflage against the weathered bark. With close-lidded amber eyes it watched the greylag finally come ashore and begin to graze on the grass ten yards from the water's edge. The wild cat watched for a time and then saw that the usually cautious greylag was slowly grazing farther and farther from the water.

The cat rose, arched its back and stretched its legs, and then dropped quietly to the ground on the far side of the tree. It was a big female, weighing over twelve pounds. Slowly it began a long stalk of the feeding greylag, keeping as close to the loch edge as it could so that it would eventually come between the water and the gander. It moved – a grey-brown shadow, short ears close to its flat skull – foot by foot closer to the greylag, taking advantage of every heather and bracken patch and inching across the more open ground pressed tightly to the thyme-studded grass. Within five minutes it was only a couple of yards from the greylag, hidden almost behind a weathered piece of old tree-trunk drift stranded on the shore by the last high water rise of the loch. It eyed the greylag, marking the dragging left wing, the flesh-coloured bill and feet, the ashy, greyish-brown plumage and the dull white belly and white tail tip as the unsuspecting bird moved a little closer to the piece of old drift wood. Suddenly the wild cat's mouth opened, moving in a silent spasm of excitement, and its hind-quarters rose slightly and waggled as the strong rear legs drove against the ground and launched it into a fast running leap. The cat landed square on the back of the bird, its claws raking at the plumage, its mouth clamping on the base of the long neck. There was a scurry of grey and brown feathers as the greylag was bowled over. The gander hissed with fear and then gave a long, panicking *gang-gang-gang* call of alarm.

The noise woke Bacon immediately. He jumped up and barked and saw at once the confusion of fur and feather on the sweep of the grass by the lochside. Catching at once the strong smell of cat, Bacon raced towards the fight, barking as he went.

His barks woke Smiler. He sat up sharply. For a moment his eyes were dazzled by the westering sun, and he wondered what on earth was happening. He was so dazed with sleep that for a moment or two he could not remember where he was. Then he saw Bacon racing towards the cat and the greylag.

Smiler jumped to his feet and went after Bacon. Long before he reached the patch of grass the fight was over. Clamped as it was to the bird's back, the wild cat had seen Bacon coming. It leaped away, turned for a second arching its back and lofting its tail as it spat defiance at Bacon, then it raced along the shoreline and reached its tree yards ahead of the dog. It went up the trunk and lodged itself in the highest branches while Bacon circled round and round below, barking and growling.

When Smiler reached the greylag it was lying on its side, its broken wing spread awkwardly out from its body, paralysed with fright. The ground around it was covered with feathers and wisps of down from the bird's breast. Smiler bent down and picked the bird up. He guessed at once that something was badly wrong with its wing. He settled the wing gently against the bird's flank and cradled it in his arms. For a moment or two the greylag struggled and hissed and then was silent, fear and shock overcoming its natural instinct to struggle for freedom.

Far up the beach Bacon was still barking and dancing around the tree. Smiler, who had seen the wild cat streaking away, shouted to Bacon. Bacon came reluctantly back, turning every now and then to eye the tree

and to growl menacingly. When Bacon reached Smiler, the greylag
struggled wildly at the sight of the dog. But Smiler held it gently, talked
to it and finally the bird settled down in his arms, giving an occasional
loud hiss if Bacon came too close.

So, there was Smiler standing on the edge of the great loch, lost, with
not a house or a human in sight, and with an injured bird in his arms, a
bird that he was pretty sure if released would not survive long. Softly he
caressed the bird's neck and back. He liked animals and the sight of one
in distress always upset him.

He stood now with the bird in his arms and said, "Samuel M., here's a
proper do. You don't know where you are and you got an invalid on your
hands." Then to the greylag, he said, "And you stop hissing at Bacon.
Weren't for him you'd be a goner."

It was at this moment that a noise came to his ears. It was a gentle
put-put-putting. He looked up and saw coming down the loch, about
two hundred yards away, a small boat with an outboard motor.

Smiler went down to the water's edge and, holding the greylag with
one firm arm and hand, took off his cap and waved it, shouting at the top
of his voice. The boat proceeded serenely up the loch. For a while Smiler
thought that he was not going to be seen. There was only one person in
the boat, sitting at the stern and steering. Then, when the boat was a
good way out and almost past him as he shouted and waved, he saw it
alter course.

The boat came slowly into the shore. As it entered the shallow water
the person at the stern cut out the motor and tipped the engine forward
so that the propeller should not foul the bottom. As the boat ran straight
into the beach the helmsman jumped overboard into a foot of water and
dragged the bows up on to the sand.

The person turned and faced Smiler. It was a girl. She was about the
same height as Smiler and, he guessed, about his own age. She wore a
floppy green beret with a yellow bobble on top and her long hair was tied
at the back of her neck with a yellow ribbon. Her smooth skin was as
brown as a berry and she wore a loose grey jersey and blue denims rolled
up to her knees to show bare legs and feet. She was a pleasant looking
girl with dark brown eyes. Bacon went up to her and sniffed at her bare
legs and she put down a hand and teased one of his ears as though she
had known him all her life.

She said, "What are you doing here?" She had a nice, soft, Scottish
accent.

"I'm lost," said Smiler. "And this here is an injured bird. Some old cat
thing went for it just now. Bacon chased it off, but I think it got its wing
broken."

The girl came up close and looked at the bird and then said, "No wild cat did that. That's Laggy. We've tried to get him often but he never lets you get near. Had that broken wing for months, poor laddie." She gently touched the white nail on the tip of the gander's pink beak and went on, "Where you from?"

"England," said Smiler.

The girl laughed. "I can tell that from your voice. But England's a big place. What's your name and how did you get here?"

"I'm Samuel Miles. But how I got here is a long story."

"Then save it for some other time. We've got to do something for poor old Laggy. Come on, we'll take him to the Laird."

"Who is the Laird?" asked Smiler.

"Who is the Laird?" The girl echoed him, and then laughed. "You are a stranger around here for certain. The Laird is the Laird. He owns this beach we're standing on, the whole loch and half the mountains around."

"Gosh, he must be a very rich man."

"Rich, aye. But not in silver. Come on, in you get. By the way —" her face went suddenly serious as though she were aware that she had been lacking in courtesy — "I'm Laura Mackay. My father farms down the far end of the loch." She reached her hand out and took Smiler's. She gave it a shake that crushed his fingers.

Laura Mackay pushed the boat back a little way into the loch and Smiler, holding the greylag, waded through the shallow water and got in. Laura slipped an arm round Bacon and lifted him aboard. Then she got aboard herself, went to the stern and lowered the outboard motor and started it. They circled away from the beach in a tight curve and began to move up the loch. In the bottom of the boat, Smiler noticed, there was a small battered suitcase and three large, bulky sacks.

From the shore the loch had looked quite smooth. As they moved out on to it Smiler found that there was quite a wind blowing and driving up a long series of choppy waves. Now and again one of these would smack against the bows and come spraying back over them. So far as Laura was concerned, Smiler noticed, she seemed unaware of the flying spray.

It was getting late now and the westering sun, although it held the southern shore of the loch in bright light still, had thrown dark shadows over the side on which Smiler had been resting with Bacon. The south shore was mountainous. Steep crags and cliffs came right down to the water's edge. As it was impossible to talk above the noise of the motor and the loud *smack-smack* of the waves against the bows, Smiler sat in silence, nursing the injured greylag, and watching the moving shores of the loch. It seemed a very long time since he had got off the train at Fort William that morning. The day had gone by like a kind of dream so that up until now it hadn't really come home to him that he was actually in Scotland. But he knew he was there now, with the fresh loch spray dewing his face, the stiff breeze flattening his anorak against his body and, everywhere he looked, rowan- and pine-marked crags and cliffs and beyond them the rising sweeps of mountains.

There was a touch on his shoulder from behind. He turned to find the girl holding a sweet bag to him. He dipped in a hand, took one, and gave her a nod of his head in thanks. It was a peppermint and he sat sucking it happily. She was a nice girl, and he liked her. Crikeys, too, she was strong. She'd gripped his fingers as though she were going to break them off. A farmer's daughter, that was why. Probably helped her father about the place. Hard work. Work – that was what he had to find. He wondered if later he should ask her about a job with her father. But soon after he had finished the peppermint he forgot about work. Suddenly his stomach had turned a little queasy and he wondered if the movement of the boat was making him feel funny . . . seasick, maybe. Indignantly he told himself, "Don't be daft, Samuel M. How can you be seasick with your father a seaman, and this not the sea even?" But there was no doubt about it that he was feeling a little odd.

To take his mind off it, he kept his eyes fixed firmly ahead. They had now turned into that part of the loch which Smiler had not been able to see from the beach. As they moved up this arm of the loch, Laura kept the boat closer to the south shore to get more protection from the wind. Smiler could see a long way ahead a big island in the centre of the loch and a little way beyond it three smaller islands. From the big island the others all seemed to go down in size so that the last one was no more than a large stump of rock sticking out of the water.

Approaching the biggest island Smiler saw that it was faced with small cliffs on top of which grew stands of pine and other trees. Over these he could just glimpse the light of the sun touching grey slate roofs of what looked like towers of some kind. As they moved farther away from the south shore and out towards the island Smiler lost sight of the roofs. A handful of terns came hovering over them, some of them diving into the water to take small fish. Seeing them, Bacon stood up and barked. The noise made the greylag struggle a little in Smiler's arm, but he held the bird firmly and tried not to take any notice of the funny feeling in his head and stomach. Even if he were a little seasick he wasn't going to show it in front of a girl.

Behind him Laura, her face wet with water, her grey jersey spangled with it, put over the tiller and ran the boat closer to the craggy shore of the island. She motored the length of the island and then rounded its far end to give Smiler a view that he would never forget.

They swept round a small cliff and before them was a wide bay biting into the island, finishing in a semi-circular sweep of sand and pebble beach. From the beach the ground ran back in a flat meadowland of grass, then rose steeply through a scrub of juniper and yellow blooming bushes of whin to a small wood of silver birch and rowan trees behind which rose the bulwark of a tall wall made out of great stone slabs. Above the wall, like an illustration from some fairy tale, stood a castle. Smiler's eyes widened at the sight. It had round towers at each corner and a larger central one and they were all capped with conical, grey-slated roofs. Some of the windows were no more than slits in the walls, others were large and three-pointed, like church windows, and the higher ones had stone balconies. From one of the towers a flag was flying, a flag with a blue ground and a white saltire cross, the flag of St. Andrew. From one corner of the castle a long flight of steps zigzagged its way down and finished in a small stone jetty that reached out into the waters of the bay.

Behind Smiler, Laura cut the motor. As the boat headed silently to the jetty steps she said, "There's the flag flying. The Laird always flies it for me when I come up. And there's himself, too, waiting on the jetty. Now don't you move until I'm alongside and she's fastened properly. We don't want to lose poor old Laggy now we've got him."

Smiler hardly heard what she said. Turning into the bay the force of the wind and waves had been cut and they moved across calm water. He stared at the castle as though he were seeing something in a dream, some place of legend. And oddly, he felt that he *might* be dreaming for his head seemed as though it had floated a little way free of his shoulders and his body felt as though at any moment it would float up and try to rejoin his head. "Samuel M.," he told himself stoutly, "take a grip. You're still, maybe, a bit churned up with that chill you got in the drain-pipe, or maybe it *is* seasickness. But whatever it is, you aren't going to show it in front of strangers. Particularly not if it *is* seasickness. What would your old man think?"

As he lectured himself, the boat drifted into the jetty. Laura held on to the rail of the bottom step, steadied the craft, and then jumped out with the stern painter and made it fast. Then she ran nimbly to the bows and grabbed the bow rope and made that fast. As she did so Smiler stared wide-eyed at the man who waited to greet them on the jetty steps.

Now, he told himself, he knew he was dreaming, knew that it wasn't just light-headedness or seasickness, but that he must be in some crazy world of fairies and magic.

The man at the top of the steps was old and he was very tall and had long spindly arms and legs. He had a crop of loose white hair and a crop of even looser white beard. Above a kilt with a silver mounted sporran he wore a small, tight, green tweed jacket. On his legs were pinky grey woollen stockings with tartan tabs at the side. Down the right stocking a skean-dhu had been thrust, its handle just showing and glinting in the sunlight. Under his jacket he wore a tight black woollen sweater with a rolled collar close up under his beard. But the really astonishing thing about him was that he was covered with animals.

Smiler couldn't believe his eyes! On his right shoulder was a jackdaw. On his left shoulder sat a small brown owl. From one of his jacket pockets poked the head of a red squirrel and two white and brown piebald mice sat in the open gape of the other pocket. A small yellowy-brown bird, which looked to Smiler like a yellow-hammer but wasn't, sat on top of the silver mount of the sporran. And while Smiler watched, mouth open, there was a clap of lazy wings from the air above and a white fantail dove made a landing on the same shoulder with the jackdaw.

Laura glanced at Smiler and grinned at his surprise. Then she said, "We'll have to put a lead on your dog until he learns manners. Stay there till I explain things to the Laird."

She turned and ran up the steps to the man who gave her a shout of welcome, "Laura, my bonnie lass!" and clapped his arms around her so that all the birds on him went up in the air in a flurry of wings and the mice and squirrel disappeared into his pockets.

Laura said something to him which Smiler couldn't hear. Then she turned and came down and reached out for the greylag, saying, "Come and meet the Laird. You got a lead for the dog?"

Smiler nodded, fished in his pocket for Bacon's twine lead, and slipped it through his collar. He and Bacon stepped ashore and followed Laura up the steps.

The Laird watched him come, blue eyes twinkling under white eyebrows in the sun-and-weather-beaten face.

When Smiler reached the top step the Laird said — and for such a thin and spindly man his voice was surprisingly robust — "Well now, what has the girl brought this time? Always some lame duck — and very pleased I am to see old Laggy. We've wanted him for a long time. And — bless my sporan — a boy and a dog. A combination as old as time. And what do they call you, laddie?"

Overawed, and still feeling very seasick, Smiler said nervously, "Please, sir . . . my name's Samuel Miles and . . . and this is my dog. He's called Bacon. Bacon because —"

But Smiler never got round to explaining why Bacon was called Bacon. At that moment everything about him began to spin as though on a merry-go-round. The Laird, Laura, the birds and animals, and then the tall pines, the steps and the high towers of the castle, swooped round and round in a mad, giddy whirl until, with a little sigh of protest, Smiler closed his eyes against it all and collapsed gently at the Laird's feet and knew no more.

4

The Laird Defers a Decision

When Smiler woke the next morning it was to find himself in a strange bed in a strange room. It was a big fourposter bed with a red velvet canopy from the edges of which hung little gold tassels. The wooden posts at each corner of the bed had been carved with birds, beasts and flowers, with here and there the gnomish faces of merry little men and women peeping out from behind a flower or a bird. Smiler was lost in the bed. It was wide enough to hold four people with ease, and took up most of the space in the room, which was not a big one. In the wall across from the foot of the bed was a tall window, pointed at the top. The sun came streaming into the room to show up a badly worn carpet and two or three pieces of heavy oak furniture. Away to the right of the bed was a narrow wooden door, its hinges and fastenings made out of wrought iron.

Smiler lay there trying to sort out where he was and what had happened. Slowly the events of the previous day came back to him. He knew that he must have been still suffering from the chill he had caught and the sickness which had been with him during the railway truck ride. He was a bit fed up with himself for passing out at the feet of the Laird the moment he had met him. That was a pretty bad start, he thought. And in front of Laura Mackay, too. Samuel M., he told himself aloud, they'll think you're a real sissy.

He pulled himself up in the bed and it was then that he discovered that he was wearing pyjamas. They had red and white stripes and were miles too big for him. Somebody had folded the sleeve cuffs back to make them more comfortable, but underneath the bed clothes he could feel that his feet were trapped and tangled in the long length of the trousers. As he was struggling to get some freedom for his feet, the door opened and the Laird came in.

He was dressed exactly as he had been the previous day, but the wild population which inhabited his clothes and body had changed. There was a jay sitting on his right shoulder and a brown bantam hen on the other. The head of a black and white kitten peeped from one pocket. The flap of the other pocket was closed but Smiler could see the outside bulge and move as something stirred about within.

The Laird came up to the bed, gave him a beaming smile and said, "Well now, how's the invalid this morning?"

Smiler said, "I'm all right, thank you, sir. But I'm not really an invalid."

"Of course not, laddie. Just a touch of the overdoing-its. We gave you a glass of hot milk with a drop of malt in it and you curled up in bed like a dormouse in a nest."

"Malt, sir?" If there was one thing Smiler hated it was the cod-liver oil and malt which his Sister Ethel — who was old fashioned in her remedies — sometimes forced on him.

"Ay, malt, laddie. Whisky — the first medicine any true Scot turns to."

Smiler's eyes widened. "You mean I had whisky, sir?"

"Aye. Just a dram to drive out the shakes."

"Gosh. . . !" said Smiler. "That's what my father drinks sometimes."

"Then he's a wise man. Now what do you feel like doing? A few more hours there or get up?"

"I'd like to get up . . . Oh, what about Bacon? I mean, sir, I hope he's been behavin' himself."

"No trouble. All animals have natural good manners. Leave 'em alone for a bit and they soon work things out for themselves. He's settling down nicely. Right then, you stay there until Laura's brought your breakfast and then you can get up. After that we'll go into a thing or two. The present is a fine and glorious thing but one must always keep a weather-eye on the future." For a moment he gave Smiler a quizzical look, his face growing serious, and then he suddenly winked and turned towards the door.

Smiler, who never had any trouble deciding quickly whether he liked people or not, knew that he liked this tall, gaunt man. He said, "Please, sir, what's in that other pocket? Not the kitten one."

The Laird turned at the door. "Ye've a quick eye. That's Meggie." He put his hand into the pocket and pulled out a long length of grass snake, the animal's sleek body twisting and coiling around his hand and wrist, the blunt head weaving so that Smiler could see its white markings.

"Blimey!" said Smiler, delighted. "She's super, isn't she?"

"Aye, laddie, she's beautiful. I can see you know more than a little about animals."

"I like them, sir. You can always get on with 'em — if you takes your time and don't rush 'em."

"No truer thing was ever said." The Laird put the grass snake back in his pocket, gave Smiler another wink and then was gone.

Smiler lay there, feeling his old self again, and thinking what a nice man the Laird was. Any man had to be nice that animals trusted like that. When he'd been in Wiltshire, before going on the run again, he had learnt that, and he'd learnt about animals too. They were all nice, really. It was just that you had to learn to handle them properly.

A little later Laura came in with his breakfast tray. Smiler did full justice to the meal. He had coffee, and porridge with cream and brown sugar on it. Then came three boiled eggs with freshly baked bread and salty, tangy butter. After that he had the same bread spread with strawberry jam – but it was a different kind of strawberry jam from any Smiler had had before. Laura, sitting on the end of the bed and watching him eat, explained that it was made from the wild strawberries that grew in the meadow and banksides below the castle.

She was dressed as Smiler had seen her yesterday and she chatted to him as though she had known him for years. She was, Smiler soon realized, a real old chatterbox. All you had to do was to ask a question and she was away. Smiler soon knew a lot about her and about the Laird and the castle.

He learned that the Laird's real name was Sir Alec Elphinstone. He owned the loch and this castle, and acres and acres of the wild mountainsides around the loch. But none of the land brought him much money. A great deal of the land was let out to tenant farmers and the rents were very low. He also let the salmon and sea-trout fishing at the lower end of the loch, but the part from where she had picked up Smiler, and right up to the far end beyond the castle, was never let because the whole of that area was kept as a wild life sanctuary. The Laird had been a surgeon in Edinburgh but had retired ten years ago when his wife had died. He had one son who was a Captain in the Royal Navy. On the island he kept all sorts of animals which had been injured and which he treated until they were well enough to go off and look after themselves.

"But the trouble is," said Laura, "lots of them don't go off. They get to like it here and just stay on. I come up once every week or so to bring him his post and supplies and usually stay a night and tidy things up. And it needs it. He's the most scattersome man I ever saw. I bring the animals up to him. The people around bring them into the farm. He doesn't like people up here. Not that he doesn't like folks. He's aye one for the ceilidh now and then –"

"A what?"

"A ceilidh. That's a party. Singing and dancing and – for some of them – a drop too much of the whisky. Like some of my brothers I could name."

And name them she did. She was the last child of five — all the rest boys. One of them worked on the farm with her father, one was a deckhand on a fishing trawler, and the other two were married, one a schoolteacher in Inverness and the other a sergeant in the Glasgow police force. (Smiler hoped that this brother would never come to hear about him!) She, herself, helped her mother in the house and also did some farm work. It was she who had baked the fresh bread that Smiler was eating. She always made a batch of loaves for the Laird when she came up.

Exhausting for the moment the subjects of the Laird, the castle and her family, she drew a quick breath, pushed the long brown hair back out of her eyes, and said, "And now what about you, Samuel Miles from England? What are you doing in Scotland? If it's no a rude question?"

For a moment Smiler was stumped. Then he said casually, "Oh, I'm kind of travelling. Seeing things until . . . well, until it's time to meet my father."

"What, all on your own? Just with a dog?"

"Why not? I can look after myself. I'm going to get a job, too. Maybe on a farm."

Laura laughed. "A lot of good you'd be if you go fainting all over the place."

"I didn't faint. I just . . . well, I'd just overdone it a bit. The Laird said so."

"Aye. He'd say anything that suited him. I'll warn you — he's got his eye on you. But maybe if it's a job you're after you won't mind."

"What do you mean?"

"You bide your time and see. But he lost Willy McAufee last week. Took off for a job in some factory in Fort William." She stood up. "Well, I can't sit here and listen to you chat all day. I've a few things more to do then I'm off back to the farm. The bathroom's just down the stairs outside and you'll find all your clothes there." She took the tray and gave him a cool, half-smiling look. "And just when and where are you meeting this father of yours?"

Smiler, after a moment's hesitation, said, "He's a cook on a cargo ship. I'm going to meet him at Greenock . . . fairly soon."

"And you've no mother or other family?"

Smiler, who was getting her measure, said with a grin, "I thought you had more things to do that listen to me chat?"

Laura grinned too. "In other words, mind me own business. And why not, too? If there's one kind of body I can't bide it's the chattery, nosy-parker sort." She went to the door with the tray and called over her shoulder as she went out, "Bye. I'll be up next week sometime so I may see you – if you haven't taken off for Greenock."

Smiler found the bathroom and his clothes. The bath itself was ancient and rust-marked and big enough for a porpoise to swim in comfortably. Over the bath was a shower head and Smiler took a cold shower. The water was so cold that it made him gasp, but afterwards the whole of his body glowed and he felt a different person.

Back in his room, dressing, he smiled to himself at the thought of Laura's curiosity. She was as bad as his Sister Ethel. Looking out of the window he realized that his room was in one of the round towers. It had a view down over the castle wall to the beach and the small jetty. As he stood there, he saw Laura with the Laird at her side go down to the small boat. Bacon he saw was trotting happily at the Laird's heels.

For a moment or two the Laird and Laura chatted as she stood in the boat preparing to start the outboard motor. Smiler would have been interested if he could have heard the Laird speaking.

He said to the girl, "Thank you, Laura, my lass. Give my regards to your mother and father – and I'll see you next week sometime."

"I'll be up, Laird."

"Oh, and Laura –" the Laird put his foot on the bow of the boat ready to ease it off – "There's just one wee favour you can do me. Until you come up again it would be a kindness to me and most perhaps to him, if you said nothing about the boy being up here. Would you do that?"

Laura smiled and nodded. "Of course, Laird. You think he's in trouble?"

The Laird chuckled. "There's not a boy alive in the world who isn't in trouble of some kind. It's the nature of the animal." He pushed the bows out and stood and watched as Laura started the motor. The boat swung in a half circle and headed out of the bay and Laura gave a wave of her hand as she went.

From his window Smiler watched her go. To his delight he saw two fantails swoop down from the castle roof and circle round the boat until it reached the craggy point at the end of the bay. Then they came flying back and settled on the ground at the Laird's feet where Bacon took no notice of them at all.

*   *   *

It was some time before Smiler could find his way down from the tower to the main hallway of Elphinstone castle. The top part of the building was a maze of narrow, twisting stairwa s and stone-slabbed passages with here and there a lance-pointed window to light the way. Finally he came out on to a top landing, floored with great oak planks and lit by a big four-paned mullion window. On the walls were time-darkened oil paintings of men and women. Most of the women wore great sweeping dresses, their powdered hair piled high, and some of them had children leaning against their knees and greyhounds lying at their feet. The men – who mostly looked like the Laird – were young and old and a few of them wore tam o'shanters and kilts and carried bucklers and claymores. The bright sunlight through the window showed a fine layer of dust on the oak planks and the balustrades of the great wooden stairway that ran down to the main hall. The hall had a large refectory table running down the middle around which fifty people could have sat, and there were more oil paintings on the walls. Near the main door, which led out on to the terrace, was an ancient suit of armour, its chain mail and breast plates finely stippled with patches of rust. The whole place, Smiler told himself, would have made Sister Ethel's fingers itch to begin spring cleaning.

A big open stone fireplace took up part of one wall of the great hall. A couple of peat slabs smouldered in it on top of a pile of grey-white ash which had accumulated over the months. Sitting by the fire in a shabby wing-backed green velvet chair was the Laird. He was reading a newspaper. At the side of his chair on the dusty floor was a pile of other newspapers and letters which Laura had brought up to him. Lying in front of the fire as though he owned the place was Bacon. He looked up and thumped his tail in greeting as he saw Smiler. As Smiler went across to the Laird a white fantail flew through the open terrace door and perched on top of the suit of armour.

The Laird looked up, peering over the top of a pair of wire-rimmed spectacles he wore for reading.

"There you are, laddie. You managed to find your way down."

"Yes, thank you sir."

"Well done. Many's the time in the past that we've had to send out search parties for guests lost somewhere between here and their bedrooms." He grinned. "A few we never found. They're maybe still wandering around somewhere in the corridors."

As Smiler chuckled, the Laird nodded to a chair on the other side of the fireplace and went on, "Sit ye down. I want to have a chat with you. A straight man-to-man talk."

Smiler sat on the chair and said, a little nervously, "Yes, sir. What about, sir?"

"About you, of course, Samuel Miles." He laid the newspaper on his lap. The bantam hen on his shoulder was sleeping cuddled against the side of the white beard. The jay on the other shoulder flew off with a flash of white and blue and disappeared through the terrace door. "This," said the Laird tapping the newspaper, "is *The Times* of London, two days old, brought up by Mistress Laura with my mail and the other back numbers of newspapers. Up here we have neither radio nor television. News comes slow but sure and I always read *The Times* diligently. Now, over my breakfast this morning, I came across a very interesting little piece in here –" he tapped the paper again "– very interesting. You'd do me a favour by reading it and then I'd appreciate your comments about its subject." He handed the newspaper over to Smiler who saw that a half-column had been ringed around with red pencil. "Take your time," said the Laird and he fished at his side for an unopened letter.

Smiler sat and read the report in the paper. As he had begun to suspect while the Laird had talked, it was about him and his exploits in Wiltshire. It told how he had been sent to approved school for stealing an old lady's handbag with twenty pounds in it at Bristol; how he had run away from the school and changed his name, dyeing his fair hair brown and hiding his freckles with dark sun-tan lotion, and had got a job as a kennel boy with two elderly Irish gentlewomen on the edge of Salisbury Plain. The article told how Smiler had lodged with a scrap-dealer and poacher called Joe Ringer and how the last thing that had been heard of Samuel Miles was that a truck driver had given him a lift northwards, and how he had disappeared one evening into the woods taking with him a stray dog, called Bacon, a small white mongrel, with a brown left ear, which walked with a limp.

Smiler finished reading the report and lowered the paper to his knees to find the Laird's bright blue eyes steadily on him.

The Laird said, "You're that Samuel Miles, laddie?"

"Yes, sir."

"Would you care to answer a few questions? Maybe one or two could be a mite personal."

"You can ask me anything you like, sir."

"Frankly answered. That's what I like. Right." The Laird reached out a foot and rubbed the recumbent Bacon on the shoulder. "How did our friend Bacon here, come to change so quickly from a brown-eared limping white mongrel?"

"That must have been Mr. Bob, sir."

"Mr. Bob?"

"The truck driver. He was a nice man. He must have told the police wrong . . . on purpose perhaps, sir."

"On purpose of course, then. And how did you get to Scotland?"

"The Professor – he's another man I met – put me on a railway truck full of fertilizer sacks. I got off at Fort William. He was a nice man, too."

The Laird reached into his pocket and pulled out a pipe, a tobacco pouch and two piebald mice. He began to fill the pipe, eyeing Smiler, and the mice clambered back into his pocket. He said, "You've the knack of falling on your feet, it seems, and the knack of looking after yourself. Have ye the knack too of dipping your hand into other people's purses?" His voice was severe as he said this.

Smiler said quickly, "Of course not, sir. I used to nick a few small things from shops once. But not any more. And I never took the old lady's handbag. Never!"

The Laird lit his pipe and puffed a great cloud of smoke into the air. Then he said, "Show me the boy who hasn't nicked a few small things in his time and I'll look for the beginning of angel's wings on his back. Now tell me about the old lady."

"Well, sir, it was like this . . ."

Smiler told the story while the Laird puffed at his pipe, listening and nodding now and then. One afternoon in Bristol an old lady had been jostled off the pavement by a boy and her handbag stolen. A policeman seeing the act had gone after the thief. Rounding a corner he had seen a boy running down the pavement. The policeman had caught him and had found that he was holding the handbag with the money in it. The boy was one Samuel Miles. His father was away at sea and he was living with a married sister. Samuel Miles had been in some small bits of bother with the police before. But Samuel Miles' story now was that he had been standing just round the corner when a boy he knew had come rushing past him and had tossed him the handbag, shouting "Hide it!" The boy was one Johnny Pickering, and no friend of Samuel Miles. In fact they disliked one another. Samuel Miles said that he was caught running away because he was running after Pickering to make him take the handbag back. Both boys were the same height and both had fair hair. Samuel Miles had said that Pickering must have seen the following policeman and, once round the corner, tossed the handbag to him and escaped. But in the juvenile court the parents of Johnny Pickering had sworn that their son had been at home all the afternoon and that Samuel Miles was lying to save himself.

Smiler finished, "But I wasn't fibbing, sir. Pickering did it. They sent me to approved school and I escaped. I been running ever since in a way – because I know nobody can sort out the Pickerings but my Dad. When he comes back, he'll soon put it all right. And, until he does, I'm keeping away from that approved school. His boat – the *Kentucky Master* – docks in Greenock the beginning of October. I got to keep out of the way until then." Smiler stood up. "You don't have to tell the police, do you, sir?"

The Laird took the pipe from his mouth and pointed to Smiler's chair. "Put your bottom down on that again, laddie, and listen to me."

"Yes, sir." Smiler sat down.

"Now then, let's get a few things straight. First, I believe you didn't steal the bag. Second, are you sure your father can sort this thing out?"

"Oh, yes, sir. He'll know how to deal with that Pickering lot."

"Aye, I can imagine that. But October's a fair stretch away yet. What will you do until then."

"I'm going to find a job. I'm not afraid of work."

"So I gather. And you've a touch with animals, too, it seems. You must tell me how you came to be so familiar with them, but that can wait for some evening over supper. Mistress Laura tells me your father's a ship's cook. What kind of cook are you?"

"Well, I'm not too bad, sir. Joe Ringer taught me a lot. Sir. . . ?" Smiler stood up, and then went on, "Was you thinking, maybe, of offering me a job here?"

The Laird shook his head. "No, lad, I wasn't thinking about it." Then, seeing the glum look on Smiler's face, he said, "I stopped thinking about it five minutes ago. You've got a job here —"

"Gosh! Holy Crikeys, sir — that's smashing!"

The Laird waved his pipe. "Sit down and stop dancing like a monkey. You've got a job here, where I can keep an eye on ye. You've got Willy McAufee's job, the daft unreliable loon who went off to Fort William a week ago. You'll get your board and lodgings. Cook as needed. Odd jobs as needed. Help look after the animals. Housework as needed — and by Saint Andrew, himself, it is needed. And anything else that is needed. By the time you've finished your day you won't want to do anything but fall into bed and sleep. And in return you get two pounds a week. And meanwhile I'll seriously consider the question of whether I should report your whereabouts to the police." His blue eyes twinkled suddenly. "At a conservative estimate I should think it will take me all of now until October to come to a decision. We Elphinstones were always long-winded ones for making up our minds. Now let's take a walk around the place and I'll show you your duties."

The Laird stood up and went to the terrace door. For a moment Smiler stared after him, hardly able to believe his luck. The Laird wasn't going to tell the police and he'd got a job! Just the kind of job he knew he would like. He jumped up from his chair and hurried after the Laird. Bacon rolled over to his feet and followed Smiler out into the sunshine of

the grey-stoned terrace with the bright water-glitter of the loch
stretching into the distance like a moving mirror.

*   *   *

For the next two hours the Laird took Smiler on a conducted tour of the
island. At the far end of the beach a large area had been penned in with
wire netting from the bed of the loch up to a height of four feet above
water. It was here that the wild fowl lived. There were two great black-
backed gulls that were recovering from the effects of oil pollution, a
family of four young merganser ducks that had been abandoned by their
parents which had either been shot or fallen prey to some marauding fox
or wild cat, a pochard duck that had lost the sight of one eye from an attack by a hooded crow, and a dozen or so other water fowl, some of
which were perfectly healthy. The Laird explained that there was no
netting over the top of the extensive pen so that the birds were free to fly
away when they were recovered or felt like it. The trouble was that a lot
of the birds preferred to stay where they were. Some flew away during
the day to feed up and down the loch and its shores and came back to
roost at night. Some even raised their families within the pen. On little
islands in the enclosure and along the reedy banks there were small
rush-thatched houses for sleeping and breeding quarters. At the back
of these were a few completely wired-in runs where new arrivals
were kept. In one of these was the greylag gander which Smiler had
brought.

"Later today," said the Laird, "We'll take him into surgery and see
what we can do. The poor lad is as thin as a rake."

In one of the other special pens was a miserable looking heron which
had broken its right leg and this was now splinted up.

"When I first started," said the Laird, "I used to treat broken legs
with plaster. But the fool beasts thought it was something good to eat
and would peck it all away till the point came when they would take a
tumble on their heads and looked surprised. Now I know better. Always
use a light wood splint."

On the far side of the castle, built up against the tall stone retaining
wall, was a large aviary, and a set of wired runs for animals. In one of the
runs was a young otter which had lost the foot from its left hind leg. In
another was a large mountain hare with a wide bandage round its neck
where it had been mauled before escaping from a fox. All these pens and
runs Smiler was told it would be his duty to keep clean and the occupants fed and watered. But the more Smiler went round with the
Laird the more he realized that there were far, far more healthy animals

about than injured ones. A young roe deer moved freely among the scrub of the sharp pine-crowded rise at the back of the castle. Red squirrels scampered without fear among the branches and pigeons and doves hovered over their heads as they walked. Some settled now and then on the Laird, waiting for him to put his hand into his pocket and bring out corn for them to eat. Halfway up the slope in a small clearing there was a pile of beaten sand at the entrance to a badger's sett.

"That's where Bill and Jennie live," said the Laird. "I've had them five years and each autumn we ferry the year's young across to the lochside and turn them free. Otherwise we'd have a population explosion. You know, sometimes the little devils swim back. Did you know a badger can swim?"

"No, sir," said Smiler.

"Well then, learn this, laddie – whatever anyone else may say to the contrary there isn't a four-legged creature in the world that can't swim when it wants to. Now come with me and I'll show you one of the best swimmers in the world."

They climbed through the rising wood until they were above the level of the topmost turrets of the castle and then plunged down a steep slope until they were standing on a sheer crag top that faced southwards across the loch. Fifty feet below them was the clear water. The water was about twenty feet deep and Smiler could see every rock on the bottom.

The Laird lay down and pushed his head out over the fall and made Smiler do the same. He pointed out a large submerged rock a little way out from the foot of the crag.

"See behind it, laddie – that long grey shape. Looks like a sunk branch. But watch and you'll just spot the little movement, the waggle of its noble tail. That's a salmon. A big chap, about twenty pounds. Came in from the sea months ago, and he's waiting there for the autumn floods. When he feels the loch rise he'll be away and up the burn he was born in to find a mate and spawn. And good luck to him if he ever makes the sea again, for to be born and to beget and then to die is the usual lot of the salmon. Though a few make the spawning journey more than once. Usually the hen fish. One night I'll tell you all about the bonnie fish. See, away to his left there, two smaller shadows? They're sea-trout. I'll show you how to catch them."

Smiler, who was fascinated by fish and fishing, and had learnt something about both from old Joe Ringer, could have rested there longer watching the fish. But the Laird, whose ample years had not impaired his activity nor dimmed his love of talk, stood up and turned back to the castle.

As they entered the pine trees, a large, slow-moving golden labrador came slowly up the path to meet them.

"That's Midas," explained the Laird. "His eyes and his nose are as sound as they ever were but he's a wee bit deaf. So, if you walk up behind him unawares he takes it as kindness if you give a loud cough to warn him. If you don't, he's apt to turn and give your leg a nip – unless his nose has warned him in time that you're a friend. He and Bacon have already met."

They went back to the castle, and at the door to the great hall the Laird said, "As for the house, you can explore it for yourself and if you get lost I'll send Midas to sniff ye out. In the closet off the kitchen – that's way down in the bowels of the place – you'll find all the hard-weather clothes, gum boots and stout shoon you need. There's an accumulation of generations of Elphinstone gear there. Enough to fit an army. But, for the moment, let's concentrate on lunch. Bread and cheese and a bottle of beer for me. For yourself there's all the milk you can drink. Which reminds me, I didn't show ye the cow. That's another job for you – the milking of her. I'll give you a lesson later today. Now, off with ye, and see what you can find in the kitchen. You've the eyes, ears and nose God gave you – they should lead you to all we want. Away with you now."

Slightly overwhelmed Smiler hesitated for a moment, then he said, "Yes, sir. I'll do my best."

"That's the spirit, laddie," said the Laird and he headed for his armchair and the remaining unopened letters and newspapers.

Smiler, with no idea where the kitchen was, went across the great hall and through the first door he saw. Overwhelmed, and a bit confused, he might be, but he remembered how in his last job in Wiltshire everything had seemed strange and a bit too much at first, yet within a few days he had everything sorted out and was feeling at home.

As he picked his way down a gloomy flight of stone stairs, hoping it would lead to the bowels of the castle and the kitchen, he said out loud, "Samuel M., just take it easy and use your loaf and things will sort themselves out." Then he chuckled, and putting on an accent added, "Ye canna do more than your best, laddie." Then the chuckle died and he groaned, "Oh, Holy Crikeys – milking a cow! How am I goin' to manage that?"

5

The Watcher from the Shore

It took Smiler some time to find the kitchen. Below the main floor of the castle there was a warren of storerooms, larders, dairy room, gun- and rod-room, old-clothes- and boot-room, and a dozen other rooms which at the moment he had no time to explore beyond opening their doors and convincing himself that they were not the kitchen. The kitchen itself, when he found it, was a pleasant surprise. It was long and low-ceilinged with a wide, curved window cut through the solid rampart wall of the castle to give a view out over the bay. There was a long pinewood table (freshly scrubbed, like the rest of the kitchen, by Laura) and chairs, dressers and cupboards and rows and rows of crockery shelves. All the cooking was done on a large butane gas cooker – for which Laura brought up fresh fuel containers once a month. In addition there was a vast, wood-burning kitchen range and oven which were seldom used. The water came from a pump with a long handle that stood over a low stone sink. Smiler could only guess that the water came from a well down in the bowels of the castle's foundations or else from the lake. On the cushions of the window-seat was a black and white cat with a litter of kittens in an old wicker basket.

Smiler ferreted around the place and eventually found all the supplies for a light lunch. He fixed up the Laird's bread and cheese and beer on a tray and carried it up to him and set it on the corner of the long refectory table near his armchair.

The Laird said, "Where are you going to have your bite, lad?"

Smiler said, "In the kitchen, if you please, sir. It's nice looking out of the window down there."

The Laird nodded. "Aye, it is. There is no better place to eat in a house than the kitchen, close to the heart of things. Breakfast and lunch you can take where and when the fancy strikes you, but at night we eat together – in the kitchen when we're alone, and up here if we are lucky enough to have company which is not often."

So Smiler went back to the kitchen and had his lunch on the windowseat with the cat and her kittens. When he had finished he collected the Laird's tray and then washed up the crockery in the big stone sink.

After that he was a bit at a loss to know what he had to do so he spent some more time making himself familiar with the lower rooms of the house.

While he was doing this he suddenly heard the sound of a bell echoing and reverberating from the floor above.

He ran up to the main hallway to find the Laird standing at the foot of the grand stairway tugging away at the tufted end of a long rope which ran up through a hole in the ceiling to some invisible bell high in the top regions of the house.

When the Laird saw Smiler, he stopped ringing and said, "When the bell rings, work begins. But if it rings at night, you know the place is on fire or we're being attacked." He winked and went on, "Right, first to deal with old Laggy and then we'll introduce you to Mrs. Brown."

Surprised, Smiler said, "Mrs. Brown, sir?"

"The cow, lad. On account of her colour."

The Laird then led the way down into the bowels of the castle and through a maze of passages which Smiler had so far not discovered until they came finally to a small door that led out through the very bottom part of the rampart wall to the space set aside for the animal and bird pens. Beyond the pens and built against the wall was a long, low wooden hut with one big glass window in its front and three glass skylights on the roof. On the door was painted –

SURGERY: 24 HOUR SERVICE.

"That," said the Laird, "was painted on by my humorous minded son – himself a surgeon in the Navy. A man like your father, I imagine – only content when he's got good teak planking between himself and the sea. Now then, you get old Laggy and bring him along."

Smiler went off to Laggy's pen and brought him to the surgery. For the next half hour Smiler saw a different Sir Alec Elphinstone. The gander was placed on the bench in the spotless surgery and the Laird gave it an injection of some stuff with a name which Smiler could not remember. When the bird passed out, the Laird began to examine its broken wing. Smiler watched the gentleness and sureness of the man's hands with fascination. From the moment he began to deal with the bird it was as though the Laird had completely forgotten everything else in the world but the job before him. Although he talked to Smiler, explaining what he was doing and now and again asking him to pass things, his eyes never left the prostrate greylag. He located the break in the main wing bone, set it, and then splinted it up with light strips of thin wood which he taped into place. As Smiler helped him by holding and turning the goose, he bound the whole of the left wing against the bird's body with tape and bandages so that it could not move.

When the operation was over, the Laird said, "Right, Samuel M. – take him and put him in the pen hutch. When he comes round he's on soft mash for a few days. In a month the wing will be as good as new. When you've done that we'll visit Mrs. Brown."

Smiler went off carrying Laggy whose head and neck hung limply over his arm. It was a few minutes before he realized that the Laird had called him Samuel M. The strangeness of it almost made him stop in his tracks. That was what his father alone called him! And the Laird couldn't possibly have known that. What a funny thing. Then, suddenly, he felt very pleased and very proud about it.

A short while after this, the thought of being called Samuel M. by the Laird was gone completely from his head because he found himself alone in the small pasture dealing with Mrs. Brown.

Mrs. Brown was a small cow with her right horn a little twisted. She had large, gentle eyes, a shiny brown coat and a long swishing tail. The Laird led him across the pasture to the cow and took her by the small rope halter she wore round her head. He led her to a tall birch tree and fastened her to a short length of rope that hung from the tree.

"When she knows you – she'll stand for milking without the roping," the Laird explained. He sat down on a three-legged stool which they had brought from the surgery together with a large milk bucket, and gave Smiler his first and only lesson in milking. With the pail under Mrs. Brown's udder, he showed Smiler how to hold a teat in each hand and work with a gentle but firm pulling and squeezing action so that the warm, sweet-smelling milk squirted into the pail. "Easy as falling off a log," he explained. "Just work your way around the bell-pulls and strip her out evenly . . . until there's no more to come. You'll have no trouble with her."

He sat Smiler down on the stool and stood by to monitor Smiler's first attempts and to advise him. Then, after a few minutes, he said, "Aye, you're doing fine, Samuel M. In a few days you'll have the touch of a master." And with that he walked off and left Smiler with Mrs. Brown.

While the Laird had been with him Smiler had felt reasonably unworried. But the moment he was on his own a hot sweat broke out all over him, and his hands became awkward and somehow unwilling to do the motions which the Laird had shown him. In addition, Mrs. Brown's manner seemed to change with being left alone to a stranger's manipulations. With the Laird she had been the most biddable cow in the world, standing quietly and chewing the cud contentedly. But a few

moments after the Laird had gone her manner changed, and she started
to play tricks. As Smiler leaned his head against her flank as the Laird
had done, concentrating on the milking process, she suddenly switched
her long tail round and hit him a crack on the face with the tufted tip.
The blow was so unexpected that Smiler gave a sharp cry and fell
backwards off the stool. As he lay in the grass Mrs. Brown looked round
and stared at him in innocent surprise, as though she was wondering
what he was doing.

Smiler got back on the stool and turned his head this time so that if
she did flick him again it would not be on his face. Mrs. Brown did flick,
three times, and Smiler took the blows stoically and said aloud, "You
don't catch me like that again, old girl."

As though Mrs. Brown understood and wanted to show him what a
novice he was, she gave a low moo and, with a short, swift kick of her
nearside rear leg, knocked the milk bucket and stool over.

Smiler lay on his back with milk running around him and could have
cried with despair. All that milk gone! But he pulled himself up and got
back on the stool and said firmly to himself, "Serves you right, Samuel
M. You had the bucket on the ground and not held between your legs
like the Laird showed you."

This time he held the bucket firmly between his legs and began
milking again. As though she understood that the kicking trick was out
of the question, Mrs. Brown tried a tail flick or two. Smiler took the
knocks with fortitude. Then Mrs. Brown suddenly twisted her head and
long neck round, so that her muzzle was close to his face, and snorted a
fierce warm burst of sweet cud-breath at him.

"Please, Mrs. Brown!" cried Smiler.

Mrs. Brown gave him another breath snort and then abruptly moved
her rear quarters sideways two yards. Smiler was left sitting well away
from her with the bucket between his legs and the teats gone from his
hands. Sighing he dragged the stool and pail over to Mrs. Brown and
went back to milking, but by now he was so flummoxed and hot that he
could not remember which teats he had been working. In the next fifteen
minutes Mrs. Brown kept him on the alert with tail switches, breath
snorts, movings-away, and short, rear-leg kicks to try and get at the
bucket. Smiler managed to deal with them all. Finally, shaken, hot all
over, he had the cow stripped and the bucket half full of milk. He carried
the bucket well away from Mrs. Brown and then untied her from the
tree. Mrs. Brown gave a couple of bucking kicks with her back legs and
trotted off to the far end of the pastures.

Smiler went wearily back to the castle lower entrance to be met by the
Laird coming out carrying a pail of wet mash for Laggy's pen. He

looked down at the short measure of milk in the bucket, then at Smiler, and grinned.

"Kicked the first lot over, did she, lad?"

"Yes, sir – but it was my fault. I didn't have the bucket between my legs like you showed me."

"No matter. She'd have tried something else – like all women. Never been a new lad here that she didn't play up the first time. That idiot of a Willy McAufee she played up for a week. But she'll stand for you tomorrow. Just from the little bit of watching ye I could see you've got good hands. She'll know it, too, and give you no more trouble – unless the mood's on her for some mysterious feminine reason. Right, take the milk up to the dairy, and mind how you go on the stairs. They can be tricky too. Aye –" he grinned broadly "– there's no a stone stairway in the place that at some time or other hasn't claimed the broken neck of a servant or an Elphinstone in the past. And hurry back down. We're not a quarter done yet."

Smiler started up the long stone stairway thinking that after Mrs. Brown he felt as though he were completely done. He only hoped the Laird was right and that she would stand for him tomorrow. As for today, he wanted no more trouble.

But it was a wish not to be granted. Sitting at the top of the stairs, his back to Smiler, was Midas the golden labrador. Coming up behind him Smiler forgot all about the warning cough with the result that, as he came abreast of the dog, Midas turned and snapped at him.

Smiler jumped to one side to avoid being bitten and the milk pail hit the stone wall, tilted, and half the contents went slipping down the stairs before Smiler could steady the bucket. He groaned aloud as he watched the milky flood cascade over the grey worn stone steps. It was little consolation that Midas, in apology, came up and licked his milky wet hand on the bucket handle.

* * *

But within a fortnight Smiler was thoroughly at home in the castle and on the island. He knew his way around and never forgot to cough if he came up behind Midas. And with Mrs. Brown, after four or five days during which she tried her usual tricks on him, he became quite confident. Mrs. Brown, deciding that he had served his apprenticeship, now stood quietly for him and there was no need to tie her to the tree. With hands that grew more expert each time Smiler would strip her down. He loved the sound of the warm milk hissing into the bucket and the sweet odour of the beast's flank as he leaned his head against it.

Until he got used to them, and could work out his own system and
routine for dealing with them, his daily chores took him a long time. But
as he learnt his way around he found himself with more time on his
hands than he had expected. Because he liked the Laird so much and
was grateful to him he found himself doing something which wild
horses couldn't have dragged him to do had he been staying with his
Sister Ethel. He actually went around *looking for jobs!*

The main job was the state of the castle. He found dusters and
brooms, scrubbing brushes and scourers, and soap and polish, and attacked the place, starting first with the great main room and the wide
stairway. He polished and scrubbed and dusted and while he worked he
often sang one of his father's songs.

Once the Laird came and watched him and said, smiling, "Samuel
M., you'll soon have the place so tidy and spruce that it'll no be a fit
abode for a couple of bachelors like ourselves."

"But I like doing it, sir," said Smiler.

"You're sure, lad?"

"Yes, sir."

"That's good then. At first I thought you must be sickening for
something."

But although Smiler was happy from being able to please the Laird,
there were other things that made him happy before the first week was
over. One was the afternoon when he was trying to get the rust off the
suit of armour by the terrace door with some wire wool. As he worked
away one of the white fantails came sailing through the doorway and
perched on his shoulder. Smiler stopped working, delighted, but afraid
to move lest the bird take off. But the fantail gave a few slow coos and
settled down and slowly Smiler began to work again. After that the
other birds and animals began to take to him. Within no time at all he
was walking around the place almost as decorated with birds and
animals as the Laird himself — and always, wherever he went, Bacon
was with him showing no jealousy of the other animals.

But the part of the day that he liked best was after he and the Laird
had had their supper in the kitchen. They would wash up together and
then, since the evenings were light until very late, they would go down
to the beach where a small black and white rowing boat was pulled up
and the Laird would take him out on the loch.

He taught Smiler how to row and he taught Smiler how to fly-fish —
for the Laird was incapable of getting into a boat without taking a fly
rod with him. But this was different fishing from any Joe Ringer or his
father had done. The Laird fly-fished while Smiler at the oars kept the
boat on a steady drift across the mouth of the small bay. Smiler was

fascinated by the man's skill, watching the smooth bend of the rod and
the sweet curl of the line as the Laird cast, then let his team of flies sink a
little before he began to work them back to the boat. The Laird never
caught more than would meet their own and the animals' needs for food.
There were small red-and-yellow spotted brown trout and then the
larger finnoch, or young sea-trout, which were a steely blue with
blackish markings. While the Laird fished he talked and answered
Smiler's questions, explaining how the trout and the finnoch were really
the same family, only the finnoch had taken it into their heads to migrate
out to the sea estuaries each year and then came back to spawn in the
burns that ran into the loch. And after fishing, he often sat Smiler with
him at his small fly-tying desk in the study off the main hall. He showed
him how to dress the flies on the bare hooks, using feathers, coloured
silks, gold and silver tinsel wire, and little hackle feathers from the capes
of some of the cocks and hens that lived in the poultry run. He taught
him, too, the names of the flies, names that are a litany to any fly-
fisherman . . . Peter Ross, March Brown, Mallard and Claret, Alexan-
dra, Butcher, Grouse and Orange, Woodcock and Green, Watson's Fancy, Snipe and Purple, Waterhen Bloa . . . hundreds of them. One – the
Parmachene Belle – tied with a strip of white duck or swan wing with a
slip of red feather alongside it to make it look like a piece of streaky
bacon – was so fashioned because the old loggers in Canada and
America had used bacon for fishing but – when bacon ran short – they
had made flies to imitate it. Smiler's first efforts to tie flies were, as the
Laird said, "Enough to put the fear of the Lord into a finnoch and send
him off his food for a week." But Smiler, who had good hands, and
didn't like to be beaten, persevered and in the end began to tie a very
nice fly.

Sometimes while they were fishing, Dobby, the otter with a missing
foot that roamed free around the island now, would swim out and circle
the boat and get cursed for putting the fish down. But later, when Smiler
began to take the boat out by himself, he loved Dobby to come. He
would drop the large rock that served as anchor overboard, strip off, and
dive into the water and be delighted to see Dobby make circles around
him, a stream of silvery bubbles wobbling surfacewards from his
nostrils.

Lying in his bed at the end of the third week, curtains drawn to show
the light sky of the summer night, Smiler told himself, "Samuel M., if
you don't know how lucky you are to get a place like this then you ought
to be. You got a good job and you're getting to know things. Like
handlin' a boat, and fishing, and all those flies you can make, and the
animals and birds. Why it's kind of . . . well, perfect. Not a fly in the

ointment" he chuckled to himself— "– except ones you can fish with."

He lay back, feeling Bacon stir at the bottom of the bed, and the thought suddenly struck him. When he found his father in October and things were sorted out, maybe the Laird would let him bring his father up here for the rest of his leave. They could all be together. Gosh! That would be perfect.

*   *   *

The next morning early, as Smiler came back from doing his feeding and cleaning rounds, he looked up to see the flag of St. Andrew flying from one of the corner towers of the castle, lazily flipping its folds in a warm westerly breeze.

As he was making breakfast, keeping an eye on the frying trout and the toast under the grill, the Laird came into the kitchen.

Smiler gave him good morning and then said, "Sir, please, why is the flag flying today?"

"Because, lad," said the Laird, "we want some more supplies, and also I need my newspapers and mail. It's for Mistress Laura to come up."

"But she can't see it right down the other end of the loch, can she?"

"No, she can't. But someone on the hill or the loch will see it and pass the message. You think you're living up here lost like Robinson Crusoe, but ye're not, Samuel M. The hills, the braes and the glens are full of eyes. There's always a keeper, farmer or shepherd to spot the flag and pass the word. And remember this – if there's ever trouble up here all that needs to be done is to fly the flag at half-mast and there'll be someone along within the day."

After breakfast Smiler went down to release Laggy from his pen. The bird was recovering well and each day now he was let out so that he could graze on the grass of the meadow above the small bay, and swim in the water. The gander had got to know Smiler well. Wing still bandaged tightly to its side, Laggy would follow him down to the water and join the other wild fowl that were paddling about in the shallows.

Smiler, seeing the flag flying over the grey towers of the castle, found himself thinking about Laura. Not that he had much time for girls. But it was nice to know she was coming up. She was a bit bossy, of course, and a chatterbox. Still, if a chap, say, had to be cast away on an island with a girl then she'd be better than most. She wouldn't go all helpless and be a nuisance. If he had to choose between his Sister Ethel and Laura he knew which he would choose. Suddenly the thought of being cast away on a desert island with his sister made him go off into a fit of giggles. . . . She'd want everything spick and span, grumbling about footmarks on her nice sandy beach, sweeping around with big palm leaves, and forever scouring away at the tin cans they would use for cooking. Oh, couldn't he just see it! No, thank you. Give him someone like Laura any day.

Laura arrived an hour before noon the next day. Smiler was up in the wood at the back of the castle chopping down some young pine growths to make stakes for an enlargement to the wild-fowl enclosure that the Laird was planning. It was hard work. Not for the first time, he dropped his axe and, with Bacon at his heels, moved quietly to the edge of the rockface drop and lay looking down at the place where the big salmon had its lie behind the underwater boulder. He liked watching it. Mostly the fish rested almost motionless behind the boulder. But now and then, as though bored with its long wait for the autumn floods that would let it run the burn where it would find a spawning mate, it moved off majestically in a slow circle. Watching it, Smiler wondered what it would be like to have a fish that size on his line. In the Laird's study was a stuffed salmon weighing thirty pounds which the Laird had caught years and years before. . . . Thirty pounds, thought Smiler – the line would fair go whizzing out, burn your fingers if you let it. . . . He looked up, the sound of a motor coming to his ears. On the sun dazzle far down the loch he saw the black shape of a boat.

Forgetting his work, he jumped to his feet and began to run back to the castle to tell the Laird that Laura was coming.

The two of them, with an accompaniment of animals and birds, met her at the jetty steps. She was wearing her tam o'shanter and dressed as before. Smiler leaned over and took the bow rope and made it fast. The boat was more heavily loaded this time with sacks of stores and two butane gas containers. At her feet was a wickerwork hamper which she lifted out with her. After they had passed their greetings she explained that the hamper held a red-throated diver with a broken leg and a young cormorant whose plumage was covered in oil.

The Laird said, "Take them along to the surgery pen, lad. I'll deal with them after lunch."

When Smiler got back from putting the birds in the surgery pen, it was to find Laura in the kitchen getting the lunch trays. She grinned at him and said, "Well, Samuel Miles, I'll say this for you – you keep the kitchen a sight tidier than that daft Willy McAufee used to. And the Laird tells me you're a dab hand with the floor polish and the scrubbing brush. The next time I come up I'll bring you a pretty apron to tie around your waist."

"Don't you . . . well, don't you just dare," said Smiler embarrassed.

"There's no call to be upset," said Laura. "On a farm or a place like this there's no such thing as a man's or woman's work. Just work. You like it here?"

"Of course I do. It's the best job I've ever had," said Smiler.

"And how many jobs have you had in your long life?"

Smiler smiled, suddenly untouched by her teasing, and said, "More than you think."

"Well, here's another for you." She handed him a full tray. "Carry that through to the Laird and I'll bring ours."

They all had lunch in the sunshine on the terrace and during it Laura brought the Laird up to date with all the local news and gossip. For Smiler, listening, none of it made much sense because he knew none of the people or places mentioned. But he was content to sit and listen, feeling that he was beginning to belong to this place and that he would be safe here until October came when he could go to meet his father in Greenock.

After lunch the Laird went off to the surgery to deal with the new invalids and Smiler helped Laura to unship the rest of the stores and stuff from the boat and carry them into the castle. This done, he left Laura in the castle and went off to do his afternoon tasks and to milk Mrs. Brown. When he brought the milk back to the kitchen it was to find that Laura had lit the fire in the big old kitchen range. The kitchen was stifling with the heat although the wide window was open.

"What have you lit that for?" asked Smiler.

"What on earth do you think? That old gas thing may be good enough for two men on your own. But how would I bake a batch of bread on it, leave alone a proper dinner tonight? But it will be another couple of hours before it's ready so I'll take ye up to Cearciseanan and we'll have a swim."

"Keerk what?" asked Smiler.

"Cearciseanan – that's Gaelic for the Hen and Chickens."

"The Hen and Chickens. What are they?"

"You'll see. Come on."

Laura led Smiler down to her boat and a few moments later they were motoring farther up the long arm of the loch. Laura pointed ahead to the three islands in the middle of the loch, explaining that the big one was called the Hen and the two little ones the Chickens. As she ran the boat ashore on the small beach of the Hen, she reached into a locker under the stern seat and tossed a pair of swimming trunks across to Smiler.

"They're my brother's," she explained. "He's bigger than you, but you can draw them tight with the waist string."

They pulled the boat high on to the beach and then Laura began to undress, Smiler didn't know where to look or what to do as she stripped off sweater and shirt and then began to undo her jeans, but to his great relief he soon saw that she was wearing a two-piece bathing dress under her clothes. He looked quickly away from her sun-brown, firm body and then ran up the beach and undressed himself behind a rock. The swimming trunks were much too big for him but the cord through the waist held them firm. When he came out from behind the rock Laura was already in the water.

"Come on," she called. "We'll swim right round the islands."

Smiler waded into the water and joined her and they began to swim around the three islands. It was quite a long way and Smiler had to admit to himself that it wasn't something he would have set out to do himself. He was a fairly strong swimmer but he soon realized that Laura was a stronger one. Curiously enough, instead of feeling jealous about this, he found himself pleased about it. She was a girl who could look after herself and Smiler liked that. Most of the girls he had known in Bristol before they sent him off to approved school couldn't think about anything else but making up their faces or nattering all the time about clothes.

When they had made the circuit of the islands, they lay on the beach and let the sun dry them.

Laura said, "You really do like it up here with the Laird, don't you, Sammy?"

"Yes, I do," said Smiler. "I like him and I like the place and all the animals and birds. It's like . . ."

"Like what?"

For a moment Smiler didn't reply. His eyes were on the steep cliff face on the far side of the loch, on the purpling heather slopes of the hills above, the green tree-filled cleft of a glen, and the thin white scar of a waterfall marking the higher reaches of a burn. Below the tops was the slow movement of grazing sheep and on the tops now, although he couldn't see them, Smiler knew the red deer would be feeding, their calves hidden in the bracken and tall grasses and heather of the corries. High over the water a pair of buzzards circled and clear across the loch came the sweet, rippling call of sandpipers.

"Well . . ." said Smiler a bit embarrassed, ". . . sort of like . . . well, like paradise."

Laura rolled over and rested on one elbow and smiled at him. "So it might seem. But there's more than that to it. Aye, it's beautiful and it looks good. But there's other things not so good. There's the hoodies always ready to attack some injured creature, there's the golden eagles after a mountain hare for their young, the vixen hunting for her cubs, the

wild cat after the grouse and the otters after the fish. Also it's summer
now, but you should see it in winter when the hill is all snow and life is
hard for beast and man. You're like all summer tourists. All you see is a
nice picture postcard sort of place —"

"I'm no tourist!"

"Then what are you?"

"Well . . . I'm a . . . well, I'm a worker."

"Why up here — this isn't your country?"

Smiler said nothing. For the moment he felt very angry with her. Just
because this was her country didn't mean no one else could like it or understand it. He knew, too, that everything in nature had to hunt to live.
That was the way it was. And, of course, he knew things were hard in
winter.

Suddenly Laura laughed. "You should see your face! It's gone just
like my father's does when he's crossed. I was only teasing you." She
stood up, the wind taking her dark brown hair as she brushed sand from
her legs and arms.

Smiler, his anger suddenly gone, said before he could stop himself,
"You like doing that, don't you? Teasin' people."

Laura smiled and pushed her hair back over her neck. "Of course I do,
you daft loon — but only those I like. Come on." She turned and ran for
the boat.

Smiler stood looking after her and slowly a broad smile flushed across
his sun-tanned, freckled face and he had a feeling inside him as though
. . . well, as though he had drunk too much fizzy lemonade or
something and that he was gradually filling with bubbles that would
float him away.

*   *   *

As they made their way back to the castle in the boat, Laura and Smiler
were watched from the far southern shores of the loch.

High up on the side of the brae that flanked the burn which ran down
from the waterfall, a man was sitting in the shadow of a large boulder at
the side of a narrow track holding a pair of field glasses to his eyes. He
was a man of about forty, plumpish and heavily built. He wore a brown
corduroy jacket, dark breeches and stockings, and heavy walking boots.
A rucksack lay on the ground at his side. His face was running with
sweat and every now and then he brushed at the cloud of flies that
swarmed over his head which was bald with little tufty patches of fair
hair above his ears.

He watched Laura and Smiler motor back to the castle and tie the boat up at the jetty. When they disappeared into the castle, he swung the glasses and picked up the figure of the Laird who was digging a hole for one of the posts of the new extension to the wild-fowl enclosure. He watched the Laird for some time and then slowly swung the glasses to make a close survey of the beach and the meadow and the tree-clad rise behind the castle. Then he put the glasses down, rubbed his chin thoughtfully, and began to hum gently to himself as though he were well content. He had a pleasant, round jolly sort of face — except for his eyes which, instead of being jolly and friendly, were still, and coldlooking like marbles.

He fished in his rucksack, took out a can of beer and opened it. He drank from the can, finishing it in two long swallows. He threw the empty can away into the heather and then slowly said aloud to himself, "Billy Morgan, given the right timing, I think you might be on to a bit of all right here. Yes, Billy, something really good. Sweet and easy as kiss your hand."

Five minutes later he was making his way back along the track and a bend in the glenside soon hid him from the sight of the loch.

6

The Birthday Present

That evening was one of the nicest that Smiler could remember for a long time. They had dinner in the main hall and Smiler had to admit that, compared with Laura's, his cooking was very rough and ready. They began with smoked trout from the loch and then there was roast chicken – served by the Laird at the head of the table with a great flourishing of carving knife and fork – with roast potatoes and fresh green beans from the small garden patch on the slope above the castle. Afterwards there was blackberry pie (the berries preserved from the previous year's crop) and custard. By the time they were finished Smiler was so full he could hardly move. And, while they ate, the dogs and animals moved around them and a row of fantails and other birds sat on the terrace balustrade outside the open doors and watched them like an audience. Laura had prepared the meal in the two hours since they had come back from swimming.

But when she brought the dinner in Smiler saw, too, that she had found time to change. Her long, brown hair was tied back with a green silk strip and she wore a short red dress with green stripes, and thick-heeled black shoes that went *clack, clack* across the polished floor boards. Suddenly she seemed very grown up and different. So much so that Smiler couldn't keep his eyes off her as she carried the dish of chicken to the table – until she said, "And which, Sammy, would you be gawping at? Me or the chicken?"

It was during the dinner that Smiler learnt something of the history of the Elphinstones and their castle. While he and Laura drank milk and orange juice, the Laird was treating himself to a small bottle of wine. From the moment he had said grace, he kept up an easy flow of talk, telling stories and making them laugh. But the story that Smiler liked best, although it didn't make him laugh, was one about another Sir Alec Elphinstone – an ancestor of the Laird's – whose picture hung at the top of the great stairway. Smiler, who was very fond of history, listened fascinated because the man the Laird was talking about had once lived in this castle, had eaten at the very same table and had fished and swum in the loch outside.

When Charles Edward Stuart – Bonnie Prince Charlie – the grandson of James II, had come back to Scotland to make a bid for the throne of England in 1745, he had landed on the coast not far away and had called all the clansmen to him at Glenfinnan. This was the town to which the truck driver had given Smiler and Bacon a lift from Fort William. The Laird of those days had joined him. He had marched south with the clans to take part in the great victory of Prestonpans, and had soldiered and campaigned with the Prince as far south as Derby where the tide of fortune had turned against Bonnie Prince Charlie.

Finally, retreating into the Highlands, the Prince's forces had been defeated by the Duke of Cumberland, Butcher Cumberland, at Culloden Moor not far from Inverness. After many adventures Bonnie Prince Charlie had escaped the country never to return. With him had gone the Sir Alec Elphinstone of those days, after making a hurried visit to the castle to say goodbye to his wife and children.

The Laird said, "Aye, he went with his Prince. And, like him, never to return. From those days the House of Elphinstone has never recovered. The Butcher's men sacked the castle of every valuable except a few pieces of silver plate that Lady Elphinstone hid. But the one thing they wanted and didn't get was the Elphinstone jewels. Sir Alec took them with him, they say, to raise further funds for the Prince. We've been poor as cathedral mice ever since. When you go up to bed, Samuel M., you can see the jewels. Next to Sir Alec's picture at the top of the stairs is a painting of his wife. A grand lady and she is wearing some of the jewels."

"What would you do with them, if you had them now, sir?" asked Smiler.

"Do? Why, laddie, be sensible and sell the lot, and use the money to good purpose. Put the farms in order, plant the forest, break new land, and polish up this old ruin and leave a fine going concern for my son. But most of all – for there would be money to spare – I'd set up a fine wild life sanctuary at this end of the loch. Turn it over to the beasts and the birds. Aye, and have enough money still to pay for wardens to keep people's thieving hands off the beasts. The sea ospreys would come back and breed in peace from egg stealers, and so would the golden eagles, the peregrines, the merlins and hobbies, and that bonnie bird the hen harrier. When I was a boy there were always two pairs of ospreys breeding here. One on the Hen and the other pair on the far Chicken. And I'd have a surgery and hospital and maybe a wee experimental station for studying. We all have dreams, laddie, and that's mine. And dream it will stay." He looked at them both and slowly smiled. "Of course, I wouldn't forget my friends. I'd buy Mistress Laura here a good farm and leave her to find a fine, hard-working young man to go with it."

"And what would you buy Samuel?" asked Laura.

The Laird turned to Smiler. "What would I buy you, Samuel M.?"

Embarrassed for the moment, Smiler said, "I don't know, sir."

"Then you should do," said Laura. "You're old enough to begin thinking about the future. What about –" she grinned "– since you're so taken with cooking and housework – a hotel?"

"I don't want nothing to do with any hotel, thank you. I want to be outside with animals and things. Perhaps, well . . . perhaps I'd like to be a farmer, or someone like –"

"Like what?" asked the Laird.

"Well, like a vet. So I could look after animals like you do, sir. Only I'm not very good at learning. And I'd have to get exams and go to University and all that."

"University – that's a waste of time," said Laura. "All they do there is grow long hair and beards and want everything put on a plate before them. You should hear my father about it."

"Take no heed of Mistress Laura," said the Laird. "If you want to do a thing you can find ways. Maybe sometime –" he glanced at Laura slyly "– when we're not plagued with womenfolk – we'll have a chat about it."

"Well, that's aye put me in my place," said Laura. "However, while you're waiting to decide your future, you can help me carry these things back to the kitchen and we'll make the Laird some coffee."

Much later, after they had sat with the Laird having his coffee on the terrace and the birds had gone off to their roosts and purple and grey shadows had claimed the face of the loch and the night sky had turned to a wash of silver light with the stars studding it like gems, Smiler took his candlestick off the main hall table and went up to bed.

At the top of the stairs he held the candle up to throw light on the portraits of Sir Alec Elphinstone and his wife. Sir Alec he had studied before. He was the man holding a sword and buckler. But Lady Elphinstone Smiler had never properly looked at. She was sitting on a red velvet chair in the main hall. Behind her, through the open terrace door, could be seen the sun sparkle on the loch and the distant outline of the Hen and Chickens and the far hills. She wore a tall, white wig with elaborate ringlets falling to her bare shoulders. Her long dress was of grey silk with ruchings of blue ribbons at the neck, sleeves and skirt-hem. One of her hands rested on the head of a black greyhound. On her fingers were three rings set with great sparkling stones which Smiler imagined must be diamonds. About her throat and looping over her bosom was a long necklace of green stones which Smiler guessed could be emeralds. On the fingers of her other hand which grasped a tall, elaborately mounted shepherd's crook, were more rings. But the most splendid of all the jewellery she wore was on a black velvet band that ran across her high forehead and was caught back under her wig. It was shaped in an eight-pointed star. The centre of the star was an oval stone of a bluish colour, shot with purple and green fire, and each ray of the star was studded with diamonds and pearls. The whole thing, even in the dim candlelight, blazed in a great burst of rippling colours.

Gosh! thought Smiler. Just fancy what all that lot would have been worth! A fortune. And, although he could understand why the long dead Sir Alec had felt he wanted to go off and support his Prince, he couldn't help feeling, too, that it was a shame that the Laird didn't have the jewels now. Fighting and battles and putting people back on their thrones was important of course in those days. But today . . . well, the Laird could have done more good with the money they would fetch. Just fancy, if there were sea ospreys nesting on the Hen right now, coming down, wings up-folded, legs and talons thrust out to take the trout from the loch for their young.

From behind him, where she had come silently up the stairs, Laura said, making him jump, "How much longer are you going to stand there mooning at her?"

Smiler, recovering from his surprise, said, "I was really lookin' at the jewels. But she's very . . . well, beautiful, isn't she?"

"Aye," said Laura judiciously, "she is. Though she'd have had trouble doing the cooking and housework in that wig and fancy dress."

Used now to Laura's sharp comments, Smiler grinned and said, "Anyway, I bet you'd like to dress up like that if you could."

"Perhaps I would if I was going to a fancy dress ball."

As they climbed the stairways and threaded the stone corridors to their rooms, Smiler asked, "Is the Laird so very badly off?"

"Aye, by his lights he is, and that's what counts. But he's no so poor as any farmer or fisherman. Did you really mean that about wanting to be a vet?"

"I don't know," said Smiler. "I suppose so – but I got a lot to do first before I can think about it."

Laura paused at the door of her room. "Like what?" she asked.

"Well . . . things."

"You've told the Laird about these . . . things?"

"Yes."

"And you can't tell me?"

"Perhaps . . . sometime."

"I'd like you to, sometime. Goodnight, Sammy." She gave him a smile and went into her room.

*   *   *

Laura stayed the next day and night and then went back. The Laird and Smiler were on their own again. For Smiler the days went by like a dream. He worked hard, looking after the animals and clearing up the castle rooms as best he could. Even so, he found that he had a lot of spare time on his hands. By now he knew every bird and beast about the place and they all knew him. Wherever he went or worked there was always one or another of them with him as well as Bacon. But there were two animals which had taken a particular liking to him. One was Laggy who, by now, was growing fat with good and regular food. The greylag would waddle alongside of him, wing still bandaged to its side. In the evenings when he went out in the boat to fish it would swim behind. When he hooked a trout some of the excitement of the catch seemed to pass to it and it would raise its long neck skywards and cry *gag-gag-gag* as though applauding the catch. The other animal was the otter, Dobby. From the Laird Smiler knew now that the otter was so called from the Gaelic word for otter – Dobhran. Laggy would never follow Smiler beyond the limits of the small bay, but Dobby did not mind how far they went.

On the still evenings, when there was only the occasional breath of a breeze, Smiler liked to let the boat drift down the far side of the island towards the spot where the big salmon had its lie. There had been no rain for weeks now. The level of the loch was dropping fast and the water, though it always held a faint umber stain of peat, was as clear as glass. Smiler would hang over the side of the boat and drift right over the big fish's lie and the salmon would not move until the following shadow of the boat, cast by the westering sun, touched it. Then it would move off slowly. But sometimes it would see Dobby swimming underwater first. Then, with a great sweep of its noble tail, it would be gone leaving a puff of stirred-up sand and gravel rising like a small cloud from its lie. Dobby, Smiler noticed, liked this side of the island, where the water went down deep from the steep cliffs. It was a good place for trout and finnoch. Dobby would roll over lazily on the water and then go under and soon be out of sight. Sometimes he would be underwater for so long that Smiler would become anxious about him, but eventually the otter would surface with his catch and then lie on his back in the water and eat it or swim to a favourite rock at the foot of the cliff and eat there. Once or twice, however, he was down so long that Smiler was sure something had happened to him. On the second occasion he rowed back to the castle jetty almost in a panic to tell the Laird about it. But, as he got out of the boat, Dobby surfaced at the steps and came ashore.

Although he only rowed over twice to the far south shore of the loch, Smiler knew from the talks he had had with the Laird a great deal about the wild life over there, and sometimes the Laird would get out his maps and show Smiler the maze of lochs, burns and hills that stretched away southwards from the loch.

The days and weeks passed and August was running out. The purple of the heather was fading a little and when Smiler walked through it little clouds of pollen rose from it. Up on the hills the roe-deer and red-deer calves were growing fast. Soon it would be autumn and the red-deer would start their rutting, the echoes of the calling stags roaring and rolling through the tops. And soon, Smiler told himself, it would be October and he would be off to meet his father. When the moment came he knew he would be sad to go.

One evening after they had had their supper, the Laird rose to his feet and said, "Samuel M., we've both got a job to do before Mistress Laura comes up on Friday. I'll show you yours – which is not difficult. Though mine may not be possible unless we get some rain or a good stiff breeze on the water. Come with me."

He led the way to the foot of the great oak stairway. The big bottom post was decorated on top with a carved lion holding a shield between its forepaws. Puzzled, Smiler followed him.

"Take the beast's head," said the Laird, "and give it a good twist clockwise."

Smiler did as he was told. As the head turned he noticed that the carved collar about its neck hid the moving joint. There was a faint click and, lower down the big post, one of the small decorated panels flipped open on a spring. Behind the panel was a narrow cavity with a heavy, old-fashioned key in it.

The Laird took it out and shut the panel door. As he did so the lion's head turned back to its original position.

"Gosh, that's very dodgy, isn't it, sir?" said Smiler.

"Dodgy, my lad, is the word," said the Laird. "And dodgy in my ancestors' days they had to be. This castle is full of hiding places. Hiding places for men and women in trouble and for money and the good Lord knows what. This is the key of the antiquated safe in my study."

"Do you always keep the key there, sir?"

"No, Samuel M., I do not. It would not be prudent in a good Scot. I hide it where my fancy takes me."

The Laird led Smiler into his crowded little study where an old-fashioned safe sat on the floor in a corner. It was a big safe, taller than

Smiler. The Laird opened the safe and from it he drew out four bundles wrapped in green baize cloth.

He put the bundles on the table and unwrapped them. Smiler's eyes grew round with surprise. There was a pair of eight-branched silver candlesticks, two wide shallow silver bowls, their rims decorated with a running relief of birds and animals and their centres engraved with the arms of the Elphinstone family and two sets of condiment dishes. Reclining mermaids held the salt dishes and there were two leaping salmon with large perforations in their heads through which to shake rough ground pepper. The most magnificent of all was a long, narrow dish, which was supported at each corner by royally antlered red-deer stags rising up on their hind feet. All the silver was dull and tarnished, but the beauty of it made Smiler catch his breath.

As he set it out the Laird explained that the silver was all that was left of the Elphinstone treasure and that it had been a gift from Charles the First to one of his ancestors.

"Crikeys, sir," said Smiler. "It must be worth an awful lot of money."

"A fair bit, Samuel M. A fair bit, laddie. And many's the time I've thought of selling it. But it canna be done. 'Twas the personal gift of a king. Also, there's a saying that if it ever leaves the castle for good then the last of the Elphinstones goes with it. Personally, being a rational man, I doubt it, but like a good Elphinstone —" his bright blue eyes twinkled and he scratched at his beard "— I'm in no mind to take any chances. Anyway, there's your job. You have the key and you know where it lives and it has to be cleaned by this weekend. Aye, lad, it must shine so bright that your eyes will blink to see it. With this drought going and the loch like a sheet of glass you've got the easier job."

"What is your job, sir?"

"To fill the big dish there, lad. What good is it without a royal fish to grace it?"

"You mean a salmon, sir?"

The Laird gave Smiler a mock serious look and said, "Samuel M., learn one thing fast. When a good Scot or a good fisherman talks of a *fish*, only one thing is meant. A salmon. And for this occasion there never has been a fish lacking."

"But what is the occasion, sir?"

"Can ye not guess? The silver, the fish, Mistress Laura coming on Friday and the rest of her family and a few others on the Saturday. A real ceilidh — and one that happens only once a year."

"I know," said Smiler quickly, "it's your birthday, sir."

"Aye, it is, Samuel M."

Before he could stop himself Smiler said, "And will you be very old, sir?"

The Laird grinned and then said, "Old enough to want to do better, lad, and young enough to keep on trying – which makes me somewhere between one and one hundred. Now then, I'm away on my own to try for a fish before the light goes."

But when the Laird came back as the last light went he brought no salmon. The next morning, when his round of work was finished, Smiler took one of the silver candelabra into the kitchen and sat in the sunshine at the window and began his polishing. The cat and her kittens were on the long seat beside him. Bacon was curled up in a patch of sun on the floor and Midas was lying full stretch across the open doorway. The small yellow-brown bird which Smiler had first seen perching on the Laird's sporran came and sat on the window ledge. Smiler knew now that it was a siskin, which had suffered from a bad infection that the Laird had cured.

Smiler polished and polished as though his life depended on it. Because he liked the Laird so much he wanted the silver for this birthday to be brighter than it had ever been before. Also, as he worked, he considered the problem of money. He was a practical, straightforward thinker and he liked to have a problem to work on. He knew by now all the things the Laird would like to do on his estates and also for the animals and birds which he treated. If he were the Laird and wanted all that . . . well, he wondered what he would do about the silver? It was nice to have, of course – and it was a present from a king. But, gosh – it would sell for enough money to do some of the things. Still, it was a kind of family thing. Like the big silver watch his father always carried. That had belonged to his father's great-grandfather and, although it had long stopped going, he knew nothing would ever make his father part with it – and there had been hard times in the past when even a few pounds would have helped. It was a kind of good luck thing. And so was the silver, too. And you didn't sell your good luck.

When they were having their lunch on the terrace, the sun beating down on the still loch, making the Hen and Chickens dance gently in a heat haze across the water, he asked the Laird:

"You wouldn't ever sell the silver, sir, I know. But then – why did you say you would sell the jewels if you had them?"

"A good question, lad. A gift is one thing. But a handful of jewels bought by the family out of its wealth in the past – they're just possessions. And as a family's fortunes go up and down, so they buy or sell. Some of my land I've sold to put the money to good use on the estate. And the jewels I'd sell for the same reason. They came from and

belong to the Elphinstones and every head of the house has a right to
make his own decision about them. But it is also an idle question, lad.
The jewels have long ago departed. The big question now is – when am
I going to get a fish?"

That afternoon the Laird and Smiler took Laggy into the surgery.
The Laird had decided that the wing had had long enough to set. The
bandages were cut away and the splints removed. Laggy squatted
docilely in Smiler's hands while this was done. The Laird examined the
wing, his long, capable fingers probing and pressing carefully.

"As good as new," he said. "He'll be flying within the week. But first
he's got a lot of preening and oiling of the wing to do before he'll feel like
taking to the air."

Smiler carried Laggy outside and set him down. For a while the
gander just stood still, unused to the freedom of its left wing. Then it
gave itself a little shake and followed Smiler down to the water's edge.
Smiler watched it paddle out into the shallows. Floating in the slow
current drift Laggy began to preen and sort the long primaries and the
secondaries of its left wing flight-feathers. It gave Smiler a good feeling
to watch the gander. After all, if it hadn't been for himself and Bacon the
greylag wouldn't have been sitting on the water as right as rain again.
That was a good thing to see. Probably that's what a vet was nearly
always feeling. Feeling good because he had put some animal right. He
sighed, suddenly. Blimey, it was still a long way to October, and then
there would be everything to be sorted out by his Dad, and then . . .
How could he ever get to be a vet? He'd have to go back to school, or
something, again. And all that studying! And, anyway, his father
wouldn't be able to afford things like college and so on. He grinned to
himself suddenly – not even selling great-grandfather's ropey old silver
watch would help!

*   *   *

During the next three days the Laird fished early morning and late
evening for his birthday fish without any success. All day the sun was a
brazen orb in a cloudless sky, and the loch was a great sheet of tinted
glass with only now and then the breath mark of a feeble, fast-dying
zephyr to flaw it. From time to time during the day Smiler would see the
Laird straighten up from whatever work he was doing, raise his eyes to
the sky and say, "Oh Lord – if it's no great inconvenience to you, please
send a roistering south-westerly with rain in it!" But the good Lord
showed no signs of being willing to oblige.

Smiler's interest, apart from polishing the silver every day, which he did in order to keep it bright, was in Laggy. Watching the gander on the bay he would sometimes see the bird half-raise himself in the water and flap both of his wings. But he never did it with any great effort. It was almost, Smiler thought, as though the gander wasn't ready yet to trust the mended left wing for flying.

On the Friday morning Laura arrived just before lunch. The boat was heavily laden with supplies which Smiler helped her to carry up to the castle.

While they were having lunch together in the kitchen Laura said, "Of course you've thought up a birthday present for the Laird?" One look at Smiler's face told her that he hadn't. She raised her eyebrows in despair. "You men! You're all the same. My father, now, never remembers for my mother until the last minute and then he dashes into Mallaig or Fort William and pays a lot of money for something she doesn't want."

On the spur of the moment Smiler said, "Well, I did think I'd make up a special fly and tie it for him."

Laura tossed her hair back and said sharply, "And that's something you've just thought of, Sammy, and you know it. Anyway, if it's a fly that can catch a fish in these conditions, he should have it now or I can see him going without his birthday fish for the first time for years. You'd better put your thinking cap on and decide on something for him."

A little cross with her and himself, Smiler stood up and said, "You don't have to worry. I'll think of something."

He went off to do his early afternoon jobs, cleaning out pens, cutting more stakes for the wild-fowl enclosure, and milking Mrs. Brown. All the time he worked, he was wondering what he could give the Laird. What on earth could he give him? There weren't any shops around. He *could* have tied him a special fly if Laura hadn't been so scoffing about that. Often these days when the darkness drew in he would light the oil lamp in the Laird's study and sit at the bench tying a fly. He had become reasonably expert with the simpler ones. But salmon flies, he knew, were big, complicated affairs and very difficult to tie. One evening, working at the desk, he had remembered what the Laird had told him about the Parmachene Belle being fashioned after streaky bacon. Bacon was his dog. He had thought that if his dog, in a way, had a fly called after him, it would be nice if he had a fly called after himself. A Smiler fly. So he had set to and invented a Smiler fly, chuckling to himself as he had worked at it because he had used only colours that had something to do with himself. He had made the tail from a few wisps of fibre from a cock pheasant's tail — because the feather was sort of freckled like himself. The body had been easy. He just wound on yellow silk for his own fair hair. For the little throat hackle under the body of the fly he had used a

tiny scrap of jay's feather because it was blue like his eyes. For the wings
he had used two small slips from grey goose quill feathers – because it
was through Laggy that he had come to the castle. But although he had
used the fly once or twice he had never caught anything on it. Most likely, he felt, because the hook was a bit big for trout or finnoch to fancy in
such hot weather and low water conditions. Anyway, he couldn't tie a
special fly for the Laird now. Laura had made that impossible. There
were times, he told himself, when he could give that girl a good thump!
Would have done had she been a boy.

The thought of the present worried him all the afternoon. In the end
he decided that the best he could do was to make a birthday card for the
Laird. He was a fair hand at drawing and printing. He would get some
stuff from the study tonight and take it up to his room when he went to
bed and work on it quietly.

When he got back to the castle later that afternoon it was to be met by
Laura whose face was red and hot-looking. She said, "That kitchen's
roasting with the range on. I'll do the rest of the baking for the party
when it's cooler tonight. Let's go down to the Hen and have a swim."

So Smiler rowed them down to the Hen, beached the boat, and they
had a swim. Then they got back into the boat and Laura lazed in the
stern while Smiler sat up forward. There was no need for either of them
to row because the loch current set in a gentle drift westwards back to
Elphinstone castle. Smiler, who didn't like sitting and doing nothing,
picked up the fly rod which now – like the Laird – he always carried in
the boat. It was an old split cane rod which the Laird had handed to him
for his own special use, saying, "It's called a 'Knockabout', Samuel M.
But if I ever see you knock it about I'll put you on bread and water for a
week."

With Laura half asleep in the stern, Smiler flicked his line and cast out
ahead as they drifted. Then, as the Laird had taught him, he began to
work his flies back just fast enough to beat the drift of the boat. He was
using two flies, one on the tail of the nylon cast which sank quite deep
and another, a dropper, much higher up the cast. Smiler liked to work
the rod and line so that the dropper just came tripping and bobbing
along the water surface. Mostly, he had noticed, he got trout and finnoch
to the dropper more than to the tail fly.

From behind him as he began to fish, Laura said sleepily, "You dafty,
you'll never get a fish on a day like this. The trout have more sense than
to come up and risk sunburn. They're all tucked away, cool and easy, in
the shade at the bottom."

Smiler said nothing. All right, he might not get a fish – in fact was
pretty certain that he wouldn't – but he just liked the ritual of fishing.

He liked the sweet action of casting and seeing the two flies drop gently to the surface.

And, anyway, you never knew. If he was daft enough to be fishing, then there might be a fish daft enough to come to his fly. How often had he heard the Laird himself say, "Laddie, if there's one thing for certain about fishing it is that there is nothing certain about it." So sucks to Laura, thought Smiler.

The boat drifted down towards the castle. Behind Smiler, Laura went to sleep. As they neared the little bay, Smiler saw Laggy swimming in the shallows and he wondered when the gander would fly again. It had been so long since Laggy had flown that Smiler wondered if the bird had forgotten how to do it. What a stupid idea, he told himself. One day Laggy would take off.

Normally, when they were abreast of the bay, Smiler would have taken the oars and pulled in to the jetty, but today it was so much cooler on the water that he let the boat drift on into the shadow cast by the tall cliff face of the island. Looking at the rocks some twenty yards away on his right he could see how much the loch had dropped in the last weeks. He reckoned it was a good four feet already. The big boulder at the foot of the cliff which was Dobby's favourite place for eating fish was now high and dry.

As Smiler's eyes came back from Dobby's boulder, his right arm moved automatically sending the line and cast out ahead of him. The flies dropped gently to the smooth surface and he watched the slight ripple die as the tail fly sank. Gently he began to work the line in and lifted the tip of the rod to bring the dropper tripping on the surface. The fly had dapped along no more than a couple of feet when Smiler saw something which he had never seen before in his life.

A great head and a curving length of smooth, dark, steely back broke water like a porpoise surfacing. The whole action was so lazy and slow that it seemed to go on for ages; seemed in fact to Smiler that it wasn't happening, that he was imagining it, that it was all a warm, lazy daydream.

A few seconds later, though, he knew that it was no dream. The head and tailing fish sank out of sight. Almost immediately there was a hard tug as the dropper fly was taken, and line began to scream off Smiler's reel.

Smiler sat and held the curving rod and wondered what on earth he was supposed to do. His heart began to pound wildly with excitement. Then, when Smiler felt that all the line must be off the reel, the wild, first run of the fish stopped. The line went slack and the rod straightened.

It was at this moment that the boat rocked a little and Laura, her voice calm, spoke from behind him. "You're into a fish, Sammy. Wind in the slack quickly and get in touch with him – if he's still there."

Hardly knowing that he was obeying her, Smiler began to wind line back as fast as he could. He got about ten yards in when he felt the pressure of the fish on the line and the rod bent again.

Behind him Laura said quietly, "Easy now. Keep your head. Make *him* do the work. If he wants to run let him, but the moment he stops – get in touch again. And don't worry about him taking all your line. I'll see to that, or my name's not the same as my father's."

Deep down in the water, twenty yards from the boat, the fish tugged hard and then began to run again. This time Smiler, coming more to grips with the situation, let him have the line but held the rod tip up so that the fish had to work against its gentle but insistent power. Once, thinking to steady the fast run, Smiler put his hand down to try and brake the revolving face of the reel, but the spinning handle smacked his fingers sharply, drawing blood from them. From behind him Laura, now on the centre-thwart and unshipping the oars, yelled, "Don't do that, you loon. He'll break you!"

The fish took thirty yards of line and bored deep. Suddenly, the strain went off the rod and line. This time Smiler, beginning to be steadier now, reeled in until he made contact. But the moment he did he put no great pressure on the fish. He just held the rod so that he could feel the fish at the other end and the fish could feel him, and he said aloud, "Holy Crikeys! What am I going to do?"

Laura, the oars out now and gently paddling, looked over her shoulder and said, "You're going to do what I tell ye, Sammy, and if you do you'll have the finest birthday present the Laird could wish for. But if ye don't then ye'll have lost the first salmon you ever got into. What's the breaking strain of your cast?"

Now, from his father and Joe Ringer in the past, and from the Laird since he had been at the castle, Smiler knew all about the breaking strains of nylon – and he knew exactly what his was.

He said dismally, "It's only five pounds."

Very calmly Laura said, "That's aye fine for a big trout. But yon's a handsome fish. You've got to treat him like a baby, nice and easy. And don't think it's going to be a quick business – because it isn't. And sooner or later, when he jumps, and jump he will, lower your rod point fast or he may break you and –"

But Smiler didn't hear any more. The line began to sing from the reel again. The rod point bowed and there was no thought or feeling in Smiler except the deep, agonizing excitement that came from the almost magical contact between himself and the fighting fish.

From behind him Laura, no stranger to this situation, helped him. As the fish ran she rowed hard on the same course and called to Smiler that, whenever he could, he was to take up line, but without using any force that would put too much strain on the thin nylon cast.

So began for Smiler one of the most exhausting, demanding, and exciting thirty minutes of his life. The fish ran, and Smiler gave it line, and Laura rowed after it and they gained line back. The fish ran again and took them well out into the loch, away from the island. Then it lay still, deep down, and Smiler just kept in touch with it, realizing now that each time the fish ran it was tiring itself a bit more. And so far, except for the paralysing moment when the fish had head-and-tailed to take the fly, Smiler had seen no sign of it.

The sulking fish moved unexpectedly and, this time, headed straight back for the boat. The line went slack across the water. Laura, pulling the boat around and away from the line of the run which would have taken it under the keel, shouted instructions at Smiler. He swung the rod out clear from the bows of the boat and reeled in fast. To his relief, in a few seconds he felt the fish again. But no sooner did he feel it than the fish was off, away at an angle back towards the island, and this time it jumped.

Twenty yards from the boat the salmon came out of the water with a sudden explosion of surface spray. It soared upwards in a great flashing curve of silver flank and gleaming yellowy-white underbelly. For a moment or two it hung in the air as though fixed and carved in its power leap for all time.

"Rod tip!" shouted Laura.

But Smiler scarcely heard her. He just stared at the leaping fish, transfixed by the beauty and exciting splendour of the sight – and he forgot to lower his rod tip.

The great fish crashed back into the loch, spray spouting high in the air, a rain of water glinting in the sun, and then was gone from sight. The rod in Smiler's hand straightened and the line running from its tip went still and slack.

Behind him Laura shouted, "You loon – you've lost him!"

And Smiler was sure he had lost the fish. He began to reel in, yard after yard, and there was no sensation of contact at all on the line. A terrible wave of disappointment swamped him. "You fool, you fool, Samuel M.," he lectured himself. "You've lost the Laird's birthday present and the first salmon you've ever hooked!" He turned towards Laura and, long-faced, gave a despondent shrug of his shoulders. He was about to say something to her when the loose line coming back through the rings of the rod suddenly jerked, tautened, and twanged into life. The next moment line was running out faster than it had ever done before.

It was from this moment that Smiler really became a fisherman. He was trembling with excitement, and he had a lot to learn, but there was a resolute, fighting part of him now which kept saying, "Keep your head, Samuel M. Keep your head."

And as far as he could he did keep his head. When the fish ran, he let him go. Then, as Laura rowed after the fish, Smiler took in line and made gentle but firm contact with the salmon. Now and again he could feel the fish give savage tugs with its head to try and free itself from the fly. A few minutes later it jumped again. But this time Smiler was ready for it. He lowered the rod tip and, as he recovered line, felt the fish still on.

For ages, it seemed to Smiler, the fish took them up and down the loch. They went beyond the end of the castle island and then back almost as far as the Hen, and then back until they were off the small bay – and, with each passing minute, Smiler wondered how long he would be able to hold out. His arms and hands ached and under the hot sun he was running with sweat – and it didn't help that every time he made some small mistake Laura shouted a correction to him from her place at the oars and he wished she would shut up. But he had to admit to himself that she knew how to handle the boat, following the fish fast, swinging hard aside when the fish ran for them, and holding it gently in position when the fish halted and sulked far down in the deep water.

It was during one of these lulls in the battle that the fish slowly came up from the depths and rolled briefly on the surface, its belly flashing.

Laura said, "Aye, Sammy, that's the sign. The beast's tiring. Keep your head now and we've got him."

Eyes on the skirl of foam-flecked water where the fish had gone out of sight, Smiler said despairingly, "But how are we going to get him? There's only a small trout net in the boat. That's useless."

"You'll no need a net, Sammy. We'll take him into the bay and beach him. Just you do what I tell you."

So, under Laura's instructions, the operation began. She started to edge the boat beachwards while Smiler gave or took line as the fish followed or moved away. But, minute after minute, the fish was worked slowly towards the beach, and every little while the salmon came to the surface and rolled, showing gleaming flanks and pale belly, and then dived away into a fast but much shorter run.

Suddenly behind him Smiler heard the bows of the boat grate on the gravel of the beach.

Laura said, "Keep your eyes on him. Keep the pressure easy, and step out."

Holding the bending rod high, his eyes out on the water where the fish was, Smiler stepped overboard and almost up to his waist. He waded ashore and, from the corner of his eye, saw Laura jump out and pull the light boat up on to the beach clear of the water.

The next moment she was racing past him down the beach shouting, "Now bring him in below you and leave it to me. Don't force him. Just baby him. He'll come now."

Gently Smiler began to put strain on the fish. Not much, but enough to show the tired salmon who was master. Slowly the fish obeyed and Smiler won line.

From the beach below him, Laura called, "Watch him. When he sees me waiting he'll make a last run."

And, sure enough, as Smiler shortened line and slowly swung the great fish into the shallow water at the beach edge, the salmon saw Laura. The fish turned and ran and Smiler, in command and clear-headed now, let him go. But the run was short and he worked the fish back until it was held in six inches of water over the gravel slope of the beach. The fish rolled once or twice, struggled briefly, and then was still from exhaustion.

Laura went into the water and slowly around the fish so that it was between her and the shore. She bent down with an easy, confident movement and caught the wrist of the fish's great tail in one strong hand and – each action flowing sweetly into the next – she lifted the salmon high and walked up on to the beach.

Before Smiler could move she dropped the arching, struggling fish to the ground, picked up a large stone, and gave it two quick, expert taps on the head and killed it.

Smiler ran up and stopped, staring down at the fish. It was enormous. It lay there quivering gently, its spotted, steely, silver flanks and belly just touched with the coming rusty red of its spawning colours, long curving underjaw showing it to be a cock fish and – deep set in the scissors of its jaw – the tightly bedded fly which it had taken.

Suddenly a great surge of elation swept over Smiler and he did two things which, in his calmer moments, he would never have dreamt of doing. He tossed the rod to the ground in a way which would have got him bread and water for a week and then began to dance around the fish, shouting, "We've done it! We've done it!" And then, the second thing, he suddenly grabbed Laura and danced her around with him, hugging her to him and kissing her, and his excitement was so great that it was not until a long time afterwards that he remembered that she had hugged and kissed him back.

*   *   *

But all victories bring dark moments to the conquering spirit. The fish weighed eighteen pounds when the Laird — full of praise for Smiler — put it on the scales. And there was more jubilation when it was discovered that it had been caught on the Smiler fly. But there was an agony in Smiler during all the jubilation. The moment he could get free, he slipped out of the castle and raced with Bacon up through the woods to the cliff edge overlooking the spot where he had first hooked the salmon. Lying with his head thrust out over the cliff top, he looked down, knowing that, if the salmon he had so often watched was not there, then wild horses could never drag him to eat a mouthful of fish at the birthday party.

To his great relief, the fish was still there, a long dark shadow, lying in the lee of the boulder. Smiler got up, and with Bacon at his heels, went happily back to the castle.

7

The King of the Castle

The Laird's birthday party was the best party Smiler had ever known.

The next morning before lunch two large motor boats arrived from the far end of the loch bringing Laura's mother and father and her brother who worked on the farm, and six other people, neighbours and friends of the Laird. In a short while everywhere there was a great laughing and chattering, and joking and to-and-froing, and a climbing up to rooms and down again, and people being lost in the maze of corridors, and a stern warning coming from Laura and her mother that nobody, but nobody, would be welcomed in the kitchen.

The sun blazed down on the loch as though its thirst was so great and lasting that it meant to drain it dry and still not be satisfied. Bacon got excited with so much company and ran in and out of legs and got chased out of the kitchen. Midas lay in the sun across the terrace entrance and, as people passed unwarily, nipped and growled until he got tired with the whole process and went soundly to sleep. And the birds, the fantails and the whole coloured collection of jay, owl, magpie, siskin, sat around on the parapets and window cornices and wondered what was happening. But the wild fowl, a little upset by the confusion, kept well away at the far end of the beach, and Laggy paddled out into the bay and turned his back on the whole affair.

On the terrace Smiler and Laura had set up a long trestle table for lunch. One end was covered with glasses and bottles of beer and whisky and cider and jugs of milk and orange juice – and, while they were all drinking before lunch, Smiler's salmon, yet to be cooked, was brought in on the great silver dish and exhibited. Smiler and Laura had to tell the whole story of its catching and they were bombarded with questions. Smiler, who never meant to part with it as long as he lived, brought the Smiler fly from his pocket and it was handed around and discussed by the men and a note made of its dressing. Laura's father, Jock Mackay, a craggy man with warm brown eyes wreathed in weather wrinkles, declared, "Aye and it must be a bonnie flee that can bring a fish up with the loch as it is." Then he winked at Smiler and added, "And I've no doubt that Laura, here, badgered you with her shouts and instructions. Ye should have been warned that she's a good but noisy ghillie."

When Smiler fairly said, "She was fine, sir. I couldn't have done it without her," Mrs. Mackay, warm-skinned, dark-haired, a big-bodied, handsome woman, said, "There you are, Jock Mackay, there's a lesson in gallantry that all ye men could take to heart."

The Laird, who was wearing his best jacket and kilt and had banished the mice, grass snakes and other occupants from his clothes for the day, went from one to the other, joking and chatting and refusing to be drawn about his age — except to say that he would never see twenty-one again.

In the afternoon while Smiler was in his bedroom, there was a knock on the door and Laura came in carrying a parcel and put it on his bed.

"What's that?" asked Smiler.

"It's a present from my mother."

"A present? What sort of present?"

"If you open it you can see."

Smiler opened the parcel. Inside was a green and white striped shirt, a grey cardigan, a pair of brown trousers with a little white stripe in them, a pair of suede shoes and some green socks.

Before Smiler could say anything Laura went on, "For dinner tonight everyone dresses up. And knowing you had nothing . . . well, Mum thought . . ."

"But I can't . . . I mean, she oughtn't to do this. She doesn't know me."

"Don't be daft. Of course she knows you from me. And don't you tell her that she mustn't do something. That's the quickest way to get a piece of her tongue. Anyway —" she grinned teasingly "— you're the birthday hero. You've got to look your best."

She was gone before Smiler could think of anything to say. But as he looked down at the clothes he had a nice warm feeling about Mrs. Mackay.

When Smiler put on his new clothes and went down to the main hall that evening, he was glad that he had them for everyone had changed to their best clothes. The men were sitting around on the terrace, having their drinks before dinner. One of them was dressed in full Scottish piper's regalia and he was marching up and down the terrace playing on his pipes a selection of laments and marches that went wailing and rolling and skirling out over the quiet waters of the loch.

When dinner was served Laura came in bearing the great silver dish with the birthday fish on it, led by the piper who headed her twice round the table before the dish was set in place. Everyone clapped and cheered and then rose and was silent as the Laird said grace. Smiler couldn't stop looking at Laura, who was wearing a long white velvet dress with a wide sash of Mackay tartan looped over her shoulder and caught at her waist with a silver buckle that held a great cairngorm stone. Suddenly, remembering how he had kissed her on the beach, he lowered his head as he felt his cheeks burn. Gosh, what a thing to do!

But he soon forgot his embarrassment as the dinner got under way and the evening celebrations began. The flames from the candles in their silver holders rose still and golden in the warm night air. The noble fish was served and it melted in Smiler's mouth like cream and caviar. It was followed by a great saddle of lamb and dishes of steaming vegetables. The glasses were filled with wine and a glass was served to Smiler — but he didn't care for it much and soon changed to hard cider, telling himself to be careful for he knew from experience that it could be dangerous. At the end of the dinner Jock Mackay rose to his feet and proposed a birthday toast to the Laird, and the Laird replied, and then it seemed that everyone wanted to get up and propose a toast to someone or something. Everyone was laughing and talking and the babble of sound spread from the great room out over the terrace and echoed above the quiet waters of the loch.

But it was the part after dinner that Smiler liked. The old piano was dragged from the Laird's study and Mrs. Mackay played and the piper piped and songs were sung and dances danced. Smiler, who soon picked things up, found himself part of reels, jigs and strathspeys that — with the help of his cider — set his head spinning. Laura helped him to pick up the movements and told him the names of the dances which Smiler found fascinating. They had *Strip the Willow*, the Strathspey dance, *Jenny's Bawbee* (which was done by Laura and Smiler and Mr. and Mrs. Mackay), and then a host of others: *Ye're Welcome Charlie Stuart*, *Roxburgh Castle*, *Dashing White Sergeant*, *Highlandman Kissed His Mother*, and *My Love She's But a Lassie Yet*.

Then two swords were taken down from their place on the wall above the wide fireplace and Laura did a sword dance. With her hair, tartan sash and skirts flying, Smiler thought she looked wonderful and he clapped his hands and shouted with the rest of the company in applause. After that each man and woman had to sing a song or tell a story or riddle. Smiler sitting with a glass of cider in his hand, face flushed from dancing and singing, could see his turn coming. Quite suddenly it seemed that every story or song he had ever known had gone from his head and he dreaded the moment when his name would be called and all eyes would be on him.

When his turn came Laura called to him, "Song or story, Sammy?"

"A song, of course," said the Laird. "He's aye singing about the place like a bird."

From the piano Mrs. Mackay looked at Smiler and gave him a warm smile. Somehow her smile drove all the nervousness from him. He stood up and sang the first verse of the first song which came into his head and Mrs. Mackay soon picked up the melody on the piano.

> *Ye Mar'ners all, as you pass by,*
> *Call in and drink if you are dry.*
> *Come spend, my lads, your money brisk —*
> *And pop your nose in a jug of this!*

And here Smiler, remembering how his father used to do it and make him laugh, raised his cider glass and drank. Then he went through the whole song, and finished with the verse which his father always rounded off with a big wink and a swig at his glass.

> *Oh, when I'm in my grave and dead,*
> *And all my sorrows are past and fled,*
> *Transform me then into a fish,*
> *And let me swim in a jug of this!*

To his delight they made him sing the last verse again and they all joined in and raised their glasses on the final line.

After that the rest of the evening went by in a whirling and swirling of songs and games and buffoonery which set the great hall ringing. It was a great tidal wave of companionship and gaiety which finally swept Smiler away like flotsam on the flood and he found himself, exhausted but happy and his head reasonably clear, in his bedroom. The window was open and he rested his arms on the sill, looking out over the roofs and towers to the loch and the hills that framed it.

There was a movement behind him and Laura joined him, taking a place by his side at the window. They said nothing. They just leaned out, watching the night.

It was then that Smiler, not knowing what prompted him, began to tell Laura about himself. He told her the whole story of the approved school and his escape and about all the adventures which had finally brought him to Scotland so that he could meet his father in October. He finished by saying, "The Laird knows — and now you do. But I don't want anyone else to know. You'll keep it secret, won't you, Laura?"

Laura touched his arm with her hand and said quietly, "Aye, I will, Sammy. But I'm glad you told me — and I'm sure your father will settle things fast when he gets back."

Then, as though for their special benefit, Nature put the final crown to a wonderful evening.

Slowly in the north, the dark sky began to lighten. From high in the heavens it was as though some unseen hand was gently letting spill a great, pleated fold of silver, pink and grey silk. As the silk fell it spread wide at its base and was slowly lacquered with green, orange and pale purple washes of fire, all leaping upwards, flickering and shimmering about the swaying folds. Smiler watched spellbound. He'd never seen anything like it in his life before.

Beside him Laura said, "Yon's the Northern Lights."

As she spoke the tight gathering of fires at the apex of the curtain suddenly swiftly unfolded, flashing wide, and the whole sky was flooded with a blaze of silver and pink which swept round from the north encircling the entire heavens and then was gone.

*   *   *

All the visitors left on the Sunday evening. The following few days seemed very flat for Smiler. He polished up the silver and put it back in the safe, and he hid the key away in the staircase post. For the rest of the week the weather stayed hot and sultry except for two thunderstorms when the rain deluged down for about an hour. But the water from the storms did nothing to raise the level of the loch. Each day now it dropped a few more inches. By the end of the week Smiler had long recovered from feeling dull.

Between them, he and the Laird finished the extension to the wildfowl pen. But they were both worried about the greylag gander. Laggy paddled on the bay or grazed in the meadow with the other wild fowl, but he showed no signs of wanting to fly. Once or twice as the Laird and Smiler watched him on the water, he would raise himself up and flap his wings, as though airing and exercising them – but he never made any move to take off.

They took him into the surgery and the Laird made an inspection of the wing in case it had not set properly.

When he had finished, he said, "It's as good as it ever was, Samuel M."

"Then why won't he use it?" asked Smiler.

The Laird considered this for a moment and then said, "Well, I can only suggest one thing. Say now you'd been a bonnie long jumper and you broke your leg. When it was mended – if you were of a certain turn of mind – you might not be too keen on risking it for the long jump again."

"You mean Laggy's scared to try to fly?"

"It could be, lad. He's got all the food and comfort he needs here without risking a flight. But I don't think we need worry. Every creature in nature needs more than food and safety. When the time comes and he sees the other greylags flying over, away to their breeding grounds. . . . Well, then, the mating instinct will be too strong for him. The need of a wife will hit him like a bolt from the blue and he'll be up and away. Aye, old Mother Nature won't stand any nonsense from him, then."

So they put Laggy back with the other wild fowl and Smiler hoped that the Laird was right. But each evening when he took the boat out and Laggy followed him to the limit of the bay Smiler used to call to him, "Come on, you silly old Laggy — fly!"

However, Laggy's problem faded from Smiler's mind when that next weekend Laura arrived on the Saturday without the flag being flown for her. She brought up some supplies — but she had really come because a telegram had arrived at the farm for the Laird. It was from his married son in London to tell him that he was a grandfather. His son's wife had just given birth to a baby boy.

The Laird, who had been expecting the news, was very excited about this because it was his first grandchild. By now Smiler knew that the Laird had had two older sons but they had both been killed in the fighting long ago in Korea.

They all went into the great hall and they drank the health of the new baby and the Laird with a twinkle in his eye said, "Well, they've taken over long enough about it."

Laura, in her forthright way, said, "You ought to go down to London and see the baby, Laird."

"No, lass, I couldn't do that. There's too much here to do. Besides, I couldn't leave Samuel M. alone."

"Why not?" asked Smiler. "I could manage, and I wouldn't mind. I'm not afraid of being here alone."

"And, anyway," said Laura, "I could come up and keep him company for a few days later on. Why don't you go?"

"I'll give it some thought," said the Laird.

"If you give it too much thought, you'll never go," said Laura bluntly. "You could do with a holiday away from here."

The Laird considered this, and then he rubbed his beard and gave Smiler a look over the top of his wire-rimmed spectacles. "You really think you could manage, lad?"

"Of course I could, sir."

"It's a big old place to be in alone."

"It doesn't scare me. And anyway, sir — if anything went wrong I could always fly the flag at half-mast."

"Aye, that you could."

"And I'd be up in a flash," said Laura. "So that's settled then. You can come back in the boat with me tomorrow morn and my father will drive you to Fort William for the London train."

"That's right," said Smiler.

The Laird smiled. "Ye've got it all fixed between you it seems. Still . . ."

"You're going," said Laura firmly.

"Of course you are, sir," said Smiler. "You haven't seen your son for ages. And now there's the baby."

The Laird slowly shrugged his shoulders. "Well, it seems I am. But only for a few days. It wouldn't be right to leave you here on your own any longer, though I must say you'll have enough work to do to keep you out of mischief and to send you dead to sleep the moment your head touches the pillow at night."

The next morning the Laird, looking quite different dressed in a tweed suit and with his beard carefully brushed and combed, went off in the boat with Laura and Smiler was left on his own. He stood on the jetty and waved to them as they went out of the bay. Then, when they were gone, he turned round and looked up at the castle. A pair of jackdaws sailed over the high turrets and a pack of hunting swifts screeched as they flashed above the terrace, hawking for flies and midgies. Samuel M., Smiler thought, you're here all alone. You're the king of the castle! At this moment Bacon pushed his cold nose into his hand as though to remind him that he was not quite all alone.

Whistling to himself, Smiler walked off the jetty to begin his morning chores.

But Smiler would not have whistled so happily if he had known that at that moment he was being watched from the far southern shore of the loch. Hiding behind the boulder from which he had watched the castle before was Billy Morgan, field glasses to his eyes, and a can of beer on the ground at his side. He watched the boat with Laura and the Laird in it disappear into the heat haze down the loch and then came back to Smiler and followed him as he began to go about his morning work in the pens. Slowly he lowered the glasses, took a swig of his beer, and then rubbed his plump face thoughtfully. Being a man who had the habit of talking out loud to himself, he said, "Well now, Billy Morgan – what do you make of that, mate? The Laird away in his best suit with the girl, and that tow-headed lad left all on his own. Yes, Billy, what do you make of that after all your watchin' and plannin' and being eaten half to death by flies on this hillside? Has the moment come? Are you perched on the edge of riches? Are your Lucy Lockets at last going to ring with the sweet music of silver?" He took another swig of beer, and went on,

"Who knows? Maybe yes, and maybe no. I think I'll have to take the long walk back and have a chat with that squint-eyed Willy McAufee." He stood up and smiled contentedly – but for all the plump wrinkles on his face his grey marble eyes remained cold.

*   *   *

Because he had extra work to do Smiler finished later that day. He had his supper in the kitchen and then he took the boat out with Bacon in it and Dobby swimming alongside. He fished outside the bay, but caught nothing. There was no wind and the loch was dead flat. After a while he let the boat drift down the cliffside of the island and leaned over and watched the big salmon move away from its lie as he passed. Dobby disappeared underwater just off his eating rock and stayed down for a very long time. By now Smiler was used to this and did not worry about the otter. When he reached the end of the island he unshipped the oars and rowed right round it, coming into the bay from the other side. As he pulled into the jetty Dobby surfaced some way out and came flopping up the jetty steps, his pelt dripping with water. Smiler watched as the otter gave himself a quick shake, ridding himself of water so that his coat was sleek and shining and dry again.

In the gloaming Smiler went back into the castle and lit his bedtime candle. Dark shadows in the hall and on the stairway danced away before his candle as he went up to the top landing. From the oil paintings the long line of Elphinstone ancestors looked down at him, their faces and eyes seeming to come alive in the wavering candlelight. Smiler found it all very eerie. Suppose the castle *was* haunted and the Laird, out of kindness, had never told him? A shiver ran down his spine. Then, because he was a sensible boy, he told himself not to be silly. But he was glad to have Bacon at his heels and pleased too when they came across Midas in one of the corridors. Midas, as though feeling lonely himself, rose ponderously to his feet and joined them.

Smiler slept that night with Bacon on the foot of his bed and Midas curled on the carpet near its head. He lay in bed with the window wide open. Now and again, before he dropped off to sleep, he saw the black flickering of a bat's silhouette waver across the pale night sky and caught the sound from the castle wood of the pair of long-eared owls that lived there calling to one another.

However, after a couple of days on his own, Smiler became quite used to his solitary state. On the third day Laura arrived early in the morning, just for an hour, to tell him that she would come again that weekend and stay some days with him. She couldn't come before because – they were into September now – the whole farm was busy harvesting and her mother couldn't spare her.

The following day was one of the hottest that Smiler could remember since he had been on the loch. The animals were listless and scarcely moved from the shade and showed little interest in their food, and Mrs. Brown gave only half the milk she usually did. Smiler himself felt that all the marrow had gone from his bones. He worked stripped to the waist and the sweat ran off him. His body now was as brown as a ripe hazel nut and his muscles were hard and firm.

He was too hot and tired to cook himself any supper. He had a glass of milk and some biscuits and then went out in the boat, hoping to find it cooler on the water. Bacon and Dobby went with him. Laggy, still showing no desire to fly, paddled as far as the bay mouth and then turned back. Stripped off to the bathing trunks which Laura had left for him, Smiler let the boat drift, too tired even to bother with fishing.

Close to the foot of the cliff, off Dobby's eating rock, Smiler threw the stone anchor overboard and let the boat swing on the length of the mooring rope. Bacon curled up on the stern seat and Dobby slid over the side to do some fishing.

Smiler sprawled himself belly down across the centre thwart, his head over the boat side, and watched the antics of Dobby in the amber clear water below him. Although Dobby had lost a foot he was still a very strong swimmer. After a time Smiler lost sight of the otter and decided to take a swim himself. He stood on the thwart and dived into the water, the rocking of the boat behind him upsetting Bacon from the stern seat.

Smiler went down in a long, clean dive and then swam underwater towards the rock face. He held his breath for a long time, relishing the coolness of the water on his body. He came up close to Dobby's rock and hauled himself on to it. The top was covered with fish bones and tiny dried fish scales that glistened like pearls in the sunlight. After a time Dobby appeared, fishless, and climbed out on to the rock with Smiler. Finally Smiler lay back and went into a daydream, wondering where his father was at this moment. It would soon now be October. The *Kentucky Master* would be on her way home, steaming through the Atlantic. . . . And soon he, Smiler, would have to make his way to Greenock and get all the approved school mess cleared up. . . . And after that? Could he really ever become a vet? He'd learnt a lot from the Laird and had begun to read one of his books about veterinary surgery. But how could he do it? It all seemed a bit of a dream. October. Greenock. When he left here would he ever see the Laird again? Or Laura? Gosh, he hoped he would. Especially Laura.

At this moment Smiler heard Dobby stir. He sat up to see the otter sliding into the water. Feeling hot again Smiler dived into the water after the animal. As he went down, eyes open, close to the rock face of the cliff, he saw Dobby below and ahead of him. The otter swung back in a circle and flashed by him, the long, sleek form rolling and twisting, and headed for the underwater rock face. As Dobby neared the rock face and Smiler began to rise from want of breath, he saw a most extraordinary thing. Instead of Dobby turning away from the rock face and swimming along it, the otter suddenly seemed to go right through the rock and disappear.

Smiler came to the surface puffing and blowing to get his breath. He frowned, puzzled at what he had seen. How could an otter swim through rock? He waited to see if Dobby would surface. But after a few minutes there was no sign of the otter.

After treading water for a while, Smiler porpoise-dived and swam down the submerged rock face as close as he could get. The water under the cliff was, although clear, in deep shadow. Smiler swam to the spot where Dobby had disappeared and reached out for the dark rock face. But his hands touched nothing. What he had thought was rock was dark shadow. His breath going, he let himself rise slowly to the surface, his hands outstretched into the shadow. As his head came out of water he felt his still submerged hands touch rock. Smiler held on to the rock and slowly his feet came up behind him. He quickly puzzled out the situation. In the face of the rock was a tall, narrow entry which was bridged at its top. The top, to which Smiler was clinging, was only about six inches underwater. With the loch at its normal level it would have been four or five feet under. Curious and intrigued, Smiler took a deep breath and dived down again. He went right to the bottom of the loch and found one side of the entrance. He began to work his way to the surface again holding on to the smooth side of the tall narrow archway.

Smiler went right to the top of the archway again. Holding it he popped his head out for fresh breath. He went down once more and traced up the other side of the entrance with his hands while his eyes tried to probe the darkness ahead of him. He was half-way up when something bright flickered far in the darkness. Suddenly, from out of the deep gloom, Dobby shot past Smiler, holding a finnoch in his jaws, the fish's white belly gleaming.

A few seconds later Smiler was sitting on the eating rock where Dobby was crouched over his kill, chewing at the still body of the finnoch.

Smiler's face was very thoughtful. In his methodical, sensible way he began to figure things out.

Although he knew that otters could stay underwater for a long time, there was a limit. They just had to come up for breath. But sometimes

Dobby would be under for ages. Although Smiler used to keep his eyes watchfully on the glass-smooth, calm water around the cliff he had never seen as much as half a whisker of Dobby's muzzle appear above the surface. Sometimes the animal was down so long that Smiler had given him up and rowed back to the castle. What he was thinking now was that entrance could be to an underwater cave. The water level was only about six inches above the top of the archway. It couldn't be any higher inside the cave obviously. It might well be that, if he was brave enough to explore, he would find that above the level of the water in the cave there would be an air space. It could be quite a big space supplied with air from the cracks and crevices of the cliff in some way. And it was in there that Dobby sometimes went for fish and, when he had made a catch, he probably surfaced in the cave, climbed out, and had a leisurely meal. . . . While all the time, Samuel M., he told himself, you've been a-sittin' outside in the boat fussing about him.

Well, so it might be, thought Smiler. But one thing was for sure – he wasn't going to risk swimming underwater into a dark hole like that and end up getting stuck or running out of breath. Still, even as he decided he wasn't going to do it, his curiosity began to rise in him. The thing was a mystery and it was there right under his nose and it wasn't possible for him to ignore the challenge.

All the way back in the boat, and while he was getting ready for bed, Smiler kept thinking about the possibility of finding a secret underwater cave. Say there was a place inside where you could come to the surface and find all the air you wanted and rocks or a shelf to sit on? Just one clean dive in from the boat and, before half your breath was gone, up you would pop into another world. It was a pity that everything under the rock face was in such dark shadow. With a bit more light he might have risked it.

With a bit more light! He suddenly sat up in bed and smacked himself on the top of the head. You fool, Samuel M., he scolded himself. You fool! You could have all the light you wanted if you went at the right time! In the late evening the setting sun threw all the south side of the castle island cliffs in deep shadow – but at mid-day, when the sun was due south, it would be shining straight at the cliff, straight at the mouth of the underwater archway. He would be able to see a long way without even going through the archway if he didn't want to.

He lay back in bed knowing that when the sun was right the next day he would be around at the cliff face in the boat. Blimey! – a secret underwater cave! It might have stalactites hanging from the roof, if that was the word for the ones that hung and didn't rise from the floor. Or, less pleasant, there might be a skeleton in there of some old clansman

from years and years ago, or of a boy like himself, caught exploring. . . .
He pushed the thought from him. Anyway, even if it was only just a cave
with nothing in it, it would be fun to show it to Laura. He would scare
her first by just diving clean off the boat and through the entrance
without saying anything. . . . It took Smiler a long time to go to sleep
that night.

The next morning as he worked around the castle he kept looking up
at the sun and judging its position. Two or three times he went into the
great hall to check the time on the big grandfather clock at the foot of the
stairs.

All morning the sun seemed to dawdle up the cloudless sky like a heat-
weary laggard, but eventually the clock showed ten minutes to twelve.
Smiler ran down to the jetty where the rowing boat was moored and
pulled out of the bay and round to the cliff face. He dropped the stone
anchor some way up from the entrance and then, paying out the rope, let
the boat drift down until he judged it was just level with the underwater
archway.

Impatiently he jumped into the sunlit water under the cliff, took a
deep breath, and porpoise-dived down, swimming strongly. In the
blazing light of the sun the whole appearance of the place underwater
had changed. Smiler could see the rough, narrow-arched entrance clearly. He swam down as deep as he could and grabbed the side of the entrance and looked through. The water was green and blue shot and
adrift with little motes of light. He saw at once that the archway was
only about two feet thick. Beyond it he could see an underwater strip of
sandy loch floor sloping gently upwards.

Smiler went up, took another deep breath, and dived down again.
This time he swam to the inner edge of the archway and looked up.
Some way above him he could see the surface ripple of the water,
making weird patterns from the light reflected from the sandy bottom —
but he saw something else, too. Floating on the surface, proving to him
that it was the surface and not some trick of light, was a short length of
an old tree branch that had got sucked through the archway somehow.

Although he had plenty of breath left to get back to the outer water
and surface, Smiler gave himself a kick upwards towards the floating
branch.

His head broke water and the first thing he was aware of was the
echoing sound of water lapping against rocks where he had disturbed
it.

Smiler looked around. He was in a large cave the sides of which rose
up nearly twenty feet, converging to make a rough, dome-shaped roof.
The wall of the cave on the righthand side of the entrance rose in a sheer,

rugged sweep of rock. On the lefthand side the water washed gently over a smooth, flat layer of rock. The water was only about a foot deep. Beyond this, clear of the water, was a bank of small stones and broken rocks that sloped up to a small platform. The cave was lit by a shimmering, green light that came through the underwater entrance. But light came in, too, from another source. High up, almost in the domed roof and to one side of it, a thin, horizontal shaft of sunlight angled downwards to illuminate the small platform. Smiler guessed that this must come from some narrow slit in the rock face of the outside cliff.

Smiler swam to the bank of stones and boulders and climbed up on to the narrow platform of dry rock. The first things he saw were the dried-up bodies of two half eaten trout with a scattering of bones and fish scales around them. This was clearly Dobby's eating place when he came fishing in the cave.

Standing on the platform, water dripping from him, Smiler took a good look around. On the far cave wall he could clearly see the high-water mark of the loch. He reckoned that when the loch was at its fullest, the water would be a foot deep over the platform on which he stood. At the back of the platform, where the cave wall ran up in craggy steps and ridges, was a stretch of loose soil and sand and a line of old drift wood and leaves which had been left there as the water receded. He looked up to the crack through which the roof light came. It was too far up for him to climb and explore. Then, as his eyes travelled down the rough face of the rock, he saw that about two feet above his head was a hole in the rock. For a moment Smiler almost ignored it, but then something about it brought his attention back to it sharply.

It did not look like a natural hole. It was about a foot high and a foot wide and its sides were sharply and regularly cut. Smiler realized that the hole had been chiselled and cut out of the rock face.

Finding footholds, Smiler hoisted himself up to the level of the hole and looked in. It was dark inside and he could see nothing. Smiler got his right arm free and groped inside the hole, feeling around with his hand. The hole ran back into the rock about two feet and Smiler's fingers touched nothing but the bare, dusty sides until his hand reached the end of the hole. There, instead of feeling rough rock, his hand rested on something hard and dry which moved under his fingers. From the feel of it he knew that it was not a loose stone.

Panting with the effort of holding on to the rock face as he probed, Smiler got a grip on the object and pulled it towards him. Smiler got a firmer grip on the object, and then climbed down the few feet to the rock platform.

He sat down and rested the object between his legs. He stared at it, wondering what on earth it was. It was brown and roughly shaped like an outsized and pretty battered football. The whole thing was bound tightly with a criss-crossing of thin leather thongs. The knots holding them had dried up so firmly that they defied Smiler's attempts to undo them.

Smiler sat there like an inquisitive ape which had been presented with something it had never seen before. He raised the object, which was fairly heavy, and shook it. There was the faintest rattle from within. He smelt it and it had a faint smell of old leather. The only thing which Smiler didn't do, which an ape might have, was to take a bite at it to see what it tasted like. He did, however, try to work one of the knots free with his teeth, but the knot-turns were set hard and unmovable.

Well, Samuel M., he thought, whatever is inside you're going to need a knife to get at it. For a horrible moment he wondered if there were a skull inside and what he could hear rattling were the loose teeth. The thought made him feel suddenly lonely and a bit scared in the cave. For all he knew any moment now, just because he was here and disturbing things, the roof might come crashing down – Holy Crikeys!

Almost before he knew he was doing it, Smiler was on his feet. He grabbed the brown football thing to his chest and took a fast header off the platform. He cleared the little shelf below, went deep down, and streaked through the underwater exit with panicky, froglike jerks of his legs.

Ten minutes later Smiler was back in the castle sitting at the kitchen table with the sharpest knife he could find. He sawed away at the binding thongs and realized now that they were thin strips of hide. And the brown, stiff wrapping, he guessed, was probably some kind of deer skin. Here and there on it were a few wet patches of browny-red hair. When all the thongs were cut, Smiler began to unwrap the stiff, hard, hide covering. Inside this was another covering of faded red cloth. This came away easily and out on to the table tumbled a heap of all shapes and sizes of small parcels, all wrapped in torn off pieces of stained and rotten linen sheet.

When Smiler unwrapped the first and biggest of these, he knew exactly what he had found in the cave. He just sat and stared at it wide-eyed and whispered to himself, "Holy Jumping Jumpers!"

Lying on the well-scrubbed table top was the great eight-pointed diamond star brooch of the Lady Elphinstone whose portrait hung at the top of the grand staircase. And, as Smiler unwrapped the other parcels, more and more of the Elphinstone treasure came to light. There was far more of it than just the jewels, rings and necklace that Lady Elphinstone was wearing in the painting. The kitchen table was a-glitter and a-sparkle with the fire of jewels, pearls, and gold and silver.

Smiler just sat and gawped at it all. Although he was overcome by the richness of the treasure, the thought that slowly obsessed his mind – and gave him a very odd sort of feeling – was that the last person who had looked at this fabulous sight was Sir Alec Elphinstone in 1745. He was the first one since then who had ever seen it! Holy Crikeys!

He suddenly leaped up and began to do a war-dance around the kitchen, waving and flailing his arms and shouting at the top of his voice. Midas growled from the doorway in protest and Bacon, who thought it was some new game, began to bark and cavort around the room with him. Only the cat on the windowseat who, like all cats, had long ago given up trying to humour or understand human beings, went quietly on with her grooming.

8

The Skipper and the Chief Mate Come Aboard

Smiler was so excited that it took him a long time to go to sleep that night – and when he did it was to dream wildly. He found himself marching with the old Sir Alec Elphinstone in the victorious army of Bonnie Prince Charlie, riding a shaggy pony and carrying a claymore miles too big for him. And then, when victory turned to defeat and rout, he was escaping with Sir Alec across the high hills, hiding in the corries and glens while the King's men searched for them. After days of hard tramping, they came back at last to the castle where Sir Alec, sad-faced, thanked him for his services and sent him away to his hill farm home. At home, his family all gathered round to hear his adventures – and it was a mixed up sort of family. Although his father was his father, his mother was somehow Mrs. Mackay and interested in nothing of his doings except to ask him had he always had enough to eat. She plied him now with mountains of food which Laura, red-faced from the hot range, brought to the table. . . .

He woke the next morning feeling exhausted and was horrified to find that he had gone to bed and left all the jewels on the kitchen table. He bundled them up in their original wrappings and put the whole lot in the safe. As the long, hot day dragged by he was itching to tell someone about his discovery. He wondered if Laura would come up for a quick visit later in the afternoon – which she did sometimes. After he had milked Mrs. Brown that afternoon he found a job to do up in the wood behind the castle so that he could watch the loch westward for a sign of her boat. He had almost given up hope when he saw the boat coming, riding high on the silvery heat shine of the loch water. A few minutes later he heard the distant *put-put-put* of the motor.

He raced down to the jetty to meet her. When she stepped out of the boat carrying a large basket of fresh-baked bread and other provisions for him, he started to gabble away about his discovery and made no sense at all until Laura said firmly, "Stop rattling away like a loon, Sammy, or I'll think you've gone daft from loneliness up here. Now begin at the beginning."

So Smiler calmed himself down and began at the beginning and

Laura listened wide-eyed and, when Smiler had finished she said, sounding very like her mother, "You're no pulling my leg, are you?"

"Of course I'm not!" shouted Smiler. "Come on, I'll show you!" He grabbed her arm and began to pull her up to the castle so impetuously that her basket overturned. There was more delay while the bread and provisions were gathered up, except for one scone which Bacon grabbed and disappeared with.

In the castle, Smiler opened the safe. In a few moments all the jewels and treasure were laid out in front of Laura. Smiler watched her grow more wide-eyed at the sight of the sparkling, gleaming hoard, and he shifted impatiently from one foot to the other.

Laura slowly looked up at him and said, "Sammy . . . you're the boy wonder! The Laird will never know how to thank ye." Her eyes went back to the jewels. "Aye, look at the bonnie beauties."

Then to Smiler's surprise she picked up the eight-pointed star on its head band and slipped it on to her forehead. Grinning at Smiler, she asked, "How do I look?"

"Smashing," said Smiler. And she did, with her dark hair flowing to her shoulders and the diamonds of the great star blazing on her warm, brown forehead.

Taking the star off, she said, "Aye — yon Sir Alec of those days must have been a canny man. He knew the Prince's cause was lost forever. Like a good Scot he hid the lot away and said nothing to anyone. Not even to his good lady because he knew the Butcher's men had ways of making folk talk. He died within weeks, they say, of a fever, without a chance to say where the jewels were."

"And no one knew about the cave," said Smiler. "I reckon he found it as a boy when he was swimming and he said nothing. Just in case it came in handy sometime. And I'd never have found it if it hadn't been for old Dobby. Gosh! Just think — the Laird will be able to do all he wants now." He grinned. "You might get your farm."

Laura looked up at him and a slow smile spread across her face and she said, "Then all I'll need is a handsome and hard-working husband to go with it. Can you think of anyone of our acquaintance, Sammy, who would meet the bill?"

Suddenly Smiler found himself blushing. Quickly he leaned over the table and began to collect the jewels. "I'd better get these back in the safe," he said.

*   *   *

An hour later Laura left the castle. Hers had only been a flying visit to see that Smiler was all right and to bring his provisions. She explained

that she would not be up again for three or four days because things
were so busy on the farm at the moment. The Laird would certainly
have returned from London by then and she would bring him back.

When darkness began to fall Smiler went into the kitchen and made
himself some supper. He put it all on a tray and carried it up to the main
hall where he ate it. After supper he read more of the book on veterinary
surgery which the Laird had lent to him. It was pretty hard going and
there were lots of words that Smiler did not know. He went into the
study and brought back the Laird's dictionary. He kept at it for over an
hour. But his mind was not really on his task. He kept thinking about
the Elphinstone treasure and how pleased the Laird would be about its
recovery and how he would now be able to do all the things he wanted to
do. Finally he put the book down and curled up comfortably in the
Laird's big velvet, wing-backed chair and had a good think about
himself and his father and what they would do once all this approved
school business had been cleared up. Maybe he could get his father to
find a shore job. After all he was a good cook and there were plenty of
places he could get work. But he was doubtful about it. His father had
this thing about the sea. Smiler realized that if you had a thing about a
thing and it was kind of in your blood . . . well, there wasn't much you
could do about it. It was like himself now . . . he knew he never wanted
to live anywhere but in the country and to work always at something to
do with animals. His education hadn't been up to much so far, but he
was still young enough to do something about that. If he kept at it . . .
well, the old book on veterinary surgery would one day become child's
play to him. "Yes, Samuel M.," he said aloud, "you've got to get your
head down and work. That's what you've always got to do if you want
something what's really worth having."

He lay back in the chair and day-dreamed about being a vet. Maybe,
too, he could have a farm to sort of go with the business. Then he
remembered how Laura had sat at the great table, not so long ago,
wearing the eight-pointed Elphinstone star. She'd looked
smashing. . . . For sure the Laird would buy her a farm, and then all
she would need – he recalled her words now without any embarrassment because there were only Bacon and Midas to see him – would
be a handsome and hard-working husband to go with it. His eyes
flickering with sleepiness, he grinned and said aloud, "Well that
does for you, Samuel M. Hard work you could manage, but nobody
would call you handsome. . . ." And with that thought he drifted off
to sleep.

Long, long after midnight Smiler woke with a start to hear Bacon
barking. Even in half sleep Smiler knew that it was Bacon's half-

puzzled, half-enquiring bark. Bacon seldom used an angry bark. He was much too trusting a sort of dog.

Smiler opened his eyes and was immediately dazzled. The light of a strong torch was full on his face. Beyond its fierce glow he could see nothing. Startled, he started to move from the chair, but a hand moved out and pushed him firmly back.

A man's voice said, "Just you sit nice an' easy there, matey. We'll have some proper light going in a couple of ticks."

Still trying to puzzle things out, sleep not fully gone from him, Smiler stayed where he was. It was a calm, not unfriendly voice and had a Cockney accent.

"That's the ticket," said the man.

Farther down the great hall Smiler saw the beam of another torch break out and he watched as the person holding it moved around. Within a short while the person with the other torch had found the bedroom candles at the foot of the stairs and also the big oil lamp which stood on a small side table. The candles and lamp were lit and, as the great hallway was filled with their soft light, the torches were switched off.

Although he did not know his name, Smiler found himself looking up at the plump face of Billy Morgan. Billy Morgan was dressed in a green windbreaker, navy blue jersey and shabby old corduroy trousers. He gave Smiler a nod and a smile, but it was the kind of smile which never touched his eyes. Instinctively Smiler felt there was something wrong with the smile.

Smiler said, "Who are you . . . and what do you want here?"

Billy Morgan nodded approvingly. "Two sensible questions in the circs, lad. But, sorry to say – you ain't goin' to get an answer to the first one. Just sit tight and be a good lad, and nobody'll lay a finger on you. Just think of me as the Skipper and 'im down there –" he nodded to where the other man was putting the oil lamp on the far end of the table, "– as the Chief Mate. Though if either of us, matey, was daft enough to ship to sea to find a fortune then we'd need our Uncle Teds examined. The best pickings is on shore and for pickings we have come."

Smiler digested this and, because he was no fool, though he was pretty scared by now, he wasn't long in putting two and two together.

The man at the other end of the table was very small and thin and his shoulders were hunched up around his neck giving him a jockeyish look. He wore a flat cap, a muffler round his neck, a shabby jacket much too small for him, and a pair of flannel trousers so big that they flapped around his ankles as he moved. He had a narrow, pointed face, creased with wrinkles, and seemed pretty old to Smiler. As he moved about he kept up a thin, tuneless whistling to himself.

Screwing courage into himself Smiler said firmly, "You two better get out of here before I set the dogs on you. They'll . . . they'll tear you to pieces."

Billy Morgan gave his humourless laugh and said, "Good try, lad. Good try. But not good enough. Still – seven out of ten for guts. No, no . . . we been watchin' this little tickle for weeks waiting for the right moment and there ain't a thing we don't know, me and the Chief Mate. Them tikes of yours is just too friendly. 'Cepting Midas, of course. And 'im you got to step on before he turns nasty. Now, you just sit there nice and easy while we does our business." He called to the other man, "All right, Chiefy. No trouble this end. Get the key – and let's make it Uncle Dick."

The Chief Mate, whistling to himself, pulled a sheet of paper from his pocket, consulted it, and then moved to the side of the fireplace and began to fiddle with one of the carvings of the wainscoting. After a moment Smiler saw a small panel spring back. The man groped inside and then shook his head.

"Number One empty, Skipper," he reported.

"Get on with it, then. It's got to be in one of 'em according to reliable information received."

Glued to his chair, his eyes watching every movement, Smiler knew exactly what they were about. There were a lot of secret hiding places in the hall. The Laird had shown some of them to him from time to time. His own fear suddenly left him, driven right out of his mind as he realized fully what was happening – and just what it could mean to the Laird. These men were thieves and they were after the Laird's silver and – Holy Crikeys! There was more than just silver in the safe now!

Before he could help himself Smiler got up from the chair and shouted, "Just you two listen to me! There ain't nothing –"

Billy Morgan's big right hand shot out and pushed him roughly back into the chair.

"Easy, lad. There ain't a ting-a-ling you can do. So sit tight and keep yourself in one piece. Just think of it in a sensible way. The Laird's got plenty and he ain't goin' to miss a few bits of old silver. And what's it to you, anyway? You're just a workin' lad like ourselves, and workin' lads must eat. Nothin' you can do, anyways. Two to one. Nobody's going to say you could have done anything."

From down the hall where the Chief Mate had been fiddling with another hiding place under one of the windows, the whistling stopped, and he announced, "Number Two empty."

"Not to worry," said Billy Morgan easily. "Four more to go yet. Got to be in one of 'em. He moves it around, he does, the Laird. Cagey old cove. Likeable, though. Pity to do his silver, but there it is. There ain't no end to the class war."

He winked at Smiler, but Smiler only glowered back at him. For all his easy talk he could tell now that this man was a real villain. His eyes never smiled and he seemed very sure of himself. But Smiler was more concerned now with the Chief Mate. He had a list of hiding places around the hall and if the one in the stairway post was on the list Smiler knew that there was nothing he could do to save the silver – and the Elphinstone treasure which was in the safe with it. Anxiously he kept his eyes on the Chief Mate. But, as he watched him, his mind was busy on another problem. The man in front of him knew Midas' name, and they had this list, and they'd been watching the castle for a long time – but no amount of watching could have given them the hiding places. Somebody else must have done that. Smiler had an idea who that might have been. It wasn't a good thing to think about someone he had never met, but from what Laura had said about Willy McAufee. . . . Well, he didn't have a very good reputation, and it could have been him. Unseen by the Skipper, he crossed his fingers and hoped that the Laird had never shown Willy the present hiding place of the key.

Within ten minutes the Chief Mate had exhausted all the hiding places on his list. There was no sign of the key and he broke off his whistling to announce, "That's the lot, Skipper. No key." He sat on the end of the long table, floppy trouser legs swinging, and began to whistle to himself.

Billy Morgan screwed his face up in thought and began to pull at his chin with the fingers of one hand. Staring up into the shadowed recesses of the hall ceiling, he said to no one in particular, "No key. No silver. Well, well. . . . It's enough to make a man of poor spirit weep. But not you, Skipper, 'cos you knows there's silver here, and you knows it's in the safe, and all safes must have keys. And the Laird, being a canny Scot, is a hard-thinking, far-seeing man. Now then . . ."

He took a turn or two up and down in front of the fireplace in silence for a while. Smiler watched him while the Chief Mate swung his legs and whistled faintly and tunelessly.

After a moment or two Billy Morgan came back and stood in front of Smiler. Then, quite surprisingly, he said to Smiler, "And what would you do in my position, lad? Take the bad fall of the cards and pull out of the game to eat disappointment pie? Or, like a real sport, put on your best smile and ask Lady Luck for just another dance? Don't bother to answer, lad. We've got a real sticky tarbaby of a question. We must give it the best of our thought which can't be done on a dry gullet."

He went to the terrace door and came back with a large shabby rucksack from which he pulled a can of beer. He sat himself on a chair by the fire where he could watch Smiler and opened the can. He drank his beer, his eyes seldom leaving Smiler. His face wrinkled and creased itself with his passing thoughts so that he vaguely reminded Smiler of a fat rabbit munching on its food, the little wings of fair hair on either side of his head sticking up like small ears.

After a few minutes, during which he finished his beer, his face suddenly moved into a smile and he nodded his head approvingly, "Aye – that's the ticket. Never say die – even though you can hear the hearse at the door. On your plates of meat, lad."

Smiler said, "What do you mean?"

"I means stand up, lad. On your feet. We're going to deal with this problem real methodical and not to say logical or my name's not . . . well, whatever it is. Stand up!" The command was curt and sharp.

Smiler slowly stood up.

"Chiefy," said Billy Morgan, "Go through his Lucy Lockets."

The Chief Mate, without interrupting his whistling, came up the room and began to run his hands through Smiler's pockets, emptying all the contents on to the nearby table. Smiler made no protest. At the moment there was nothing he could do or say. They hadn't got the key and that was all that he cared about.

Billy Morgan went to the table and sorted through the small pile of belongings. None of it interested him, except a stout brown envelope in which Smiler kept the wages that the Laird had paid him weekly. Billy Morgan half-pulled the folded pile of notes from the envelope, riffled their edges with his thumb and said, "Not bad, not bad. A nice little pot of honey. Well, we'd better have it in case it's all we get." He put the envelope into his own pocket.

Unable to stop himself Smiler shouted, "You're a rotten old thief!"

Billy Morgan shrugged his shoulders and with a humourless smile said, "A tea-leaf, yes, lad. But not all that old. And far from rotten. Sound as a bell, in fact. But there's no need to apologize. I take no offence."

The Chief Mate stopped his whistling and said, "If that's all we're going to get, let's go, Skipper. There ain't goin' to be any more because there ain't no key. The Laird must have found a new hiding place since –"

Billy Morgan silenced him with a wave of his hand and said, "Don't give up, Chiefy. The boat's sound, the breeze is nothing and yours truly's at the helm. There's no key on the boy, that's true. And that's

what I wanted to know first. Step by step you climb to success. It could
'ave been on him. But it isn't. That's step one cleared. Now for step
two." He smiled at Smiler and asked, "You savvy what that is, lad?"

"If I did, I wouldn't tell you," said Smiler firmly.

"Ah, beginning to get a bit saucy, are we? Very nice. Like to see a boy
with spirit. Give me a lad with backbone any time." He reached out and
patted Smiler's shoulder, and then said suddenly, "You've seen the
silver, ain't you?" When Smiler did not reply, he said affably, "Oh, yes,
you 'ave. You was 'ere for the Laird's party. The 'ero of the hour with
your salmon and all – that you won't deny."

"I'm not telling you anything," said Smiler.

Unruffled, Billy Morgan said, "Then let me tell you something.
You've seen the silver 'cos you had the job of cleaning it. And the odds is
that you know where the key is because the Laird, bless his tartan socks,
is a nice old trusting cove when he likes someone. And like you he does is
the way the chorus of the song goes around these parts. So to save
yourself and us a lot of hubble-bubble why don't you just tell us where it
is?"

Suddenly angry, Smiler shouted, "Why don't you just push off?"

To Smiler's surprise the man beamed at him, and then said, "Very interesting. Oh, very – for them, like me, what can read between the
lines." He turned to the Chief Mate and said, "Take a lesson, Chiefy, in
how to be a success. In other words, you got to use your loaf if you
wants to eat cake. Now, when I asks our friend 'ere to tell us where the
key is – what does he say? He tells us to push off. *Not*, you will notice,
that he don't know where the key is, or that wild 'osses wouldn't make
him tell us anything. No, Chiefy, he just says to push off. A rudeness I
overlooks because it tells me what I want to know. He knows where the
key is. Don't you, lad?"

Smiler, lips pressed tight together, his face glowering with obstinacy,
said nothing.

"Very good," said Billy Morgan. "Oh, very good."

Suddenly he thrust out his right hand and pushed Smiler roughly
backwards so that he collapsed into the winged armchair.

"That," said the man, "is only a tiny taste to show you I can be rough
and very ready if the circs demand it. But for now, just sit there and
think things over, lad. I'm going to do the same with another beer. Stubborn I can see you are, and no fool, and it is ditto and doubled for your
humble 'ere. Very well then, we'll both do a little thinking. There's
always some way to loosen up a stiff tongue."

Billy Morgan went back to his chair and settled himself with another
can of beer. The Chief Mate, following a nod from Billy Morgan, went

and sat near the terrace doorway, a thin trickle of whistling coming from his pursed lips as he watched Smiler.

Smiler sat in his chair and also did some thinking. In a curious way, he was not frightened now. He was, in fact, very angry with himself. Samuel M., he thought, you didn't use your head. This Skipper man isn't a fool. You should never have let go and told him to push off.

He sat there, wondering and puzzling away at what he could do . . . or more importantly, what they would do. It was no good trying to make a dash to get down to the boat and row away. The Chief Mate's eyes were always on him and so were the Skipper's. The moment he made a move they would both be after him. Looking towards the terrace, too, he realized that he must have slept for a long time in his chair before the men had arrived. The sky was beginning to lighten very faintly with the coming of dawn. He screwed himself round in his chair and looked at the grandfather clock at the foot of the stairs. Its hands showed half past four.

Seeing his action, Billy Morgan smiled, nodded, and said, "Don't worry about the old tempus, lad. We got all the bird-lime in the world to think up something really tongue-loosening for you. And if we don't — well we can always beat the truth out of you. Not that I go for violence, mind you. Not, that is, unless the circs don't give me no option."

Smiler said, "You're wasting your time. Even if you beat me I couldn't tell you where the key is 'cos I don't know."

Billy Morgan shook his head. "Too late, me old cock sparrer. Oh, much too late to be anything like the genuine article."

Billy Morgan sat there, thinking, quite undisturbed by the thin whistling of the Chief Mate. Midas lay snoring at the fireside and Bacon was stretched out asleep under the table. Smiler huddled back in his chair, a dark scowl of thought and self-displeasure over his tanned and freckled face. Outside the sky grew paler and a brisk morning wind came sweeping down the loch from the east, raising a choppy ripple on the waters, and from the island shores the sandpipers and redshanks began to call. Distantly Smiler heard Mrs. Brown give a low moo to greet the coming morning. Nearer, on the roofs above the terrace, came the cooing of the fantails and other pigeons. A few moments later one of the fantails came hovering low over the terrace and then sailed through the open doors and perched on the back of Smiler's chair.

Billy Morgan eyed the bird and said, "The dove of peace, eh, matey? Or it could be, if you was to be sensible. A real little paradise is all this place. Bird and beast and man all trustin' one another. Just like it should be. And real grateful, too, I am to that old bird because it gives me a notion for openin' up that safe without trouble."

He stood up and approached Smiler.

"Stand up, lad. Smartish now." His face creased with its cold smile, and the red tip of his tongue ran around the edges of his lips.

Smiler stood up. Billy Morgan produced a long length of cord from his windbreaker pocket and said, "Turn round. Hands behind."

For a second or two Smiler contemplated making a dash for freedom but decided against it. He would get nowhere. He turned round and Billy Morgan lashed his hands firmly together, leaving a long length of cord trailing from them to act as a lead.

Billy Morgan said, "Right. Come along with me." He gave Smiler a push towards the terrace door and followed at his side, holding the length of cord. At the door he said to the Chief Mate, "Get down to the boat and bring me the troubled-Harold."

Then, with a jerk on Smiler's cord, he led the way along the terrace and down the steps at the far end to the garden and headed for the meadow and the water-fowl pens.

The Chief Mate disappeared in the direction of the jetty.

Smiler, puzzled now to know what the Skipper had in mind, and not having any idea what a troubled-Harold was, went obediently across the meadow to the wild-fowl pens and the strip of beach where he had landed his salmon. Twenty yards out Laggy and a motley collection of water fowl were swimming around feeding and making their morning toilet, flapping their wings and bobbing their heads and necks underwater. Far up the loch the faces of the hills were dark with shadows, but the sky above them was now a pale wash of faded colours as the dawn began to strengthen.

They halted at the water's edge. Billy Morgan stared around him, his eyes sweeping over the water-fowl pens and the ripple-streaked island bay.

"Nice," he said to himself. "Oh, very nice. A great and good work the Laird is a-doin'. The Laird and you, lad, real angels of mercy to any bird or beast in trouble. Jam-tarts full of love for 'em. Wouldn't 'arm a hair or a hide or a feather of a wing. Lovely to see. Highly recommendable, And you're a clever man, too, Skipper. Real clever. There's always a way if you use your loaf." He looked round to see the Chief Mate approaching. "Ah, here comes Chiefy with troubled-Harold."

Smiler turned and saw the Chief Mate coming along the beach. A cold shock of apprehension swept through him as the mystery of troubled-Harold was solved. The Chief Mate was carrying a double-barrelled shotgun.

Smiler turned to Billy Morgan and said, "What do you want that for? Look here –"

"Easy, lad," said Billy Morgan. "Easy. No need to lose your wool."

He took the gun from the Chief Mate and handed the lead rope to him to hold.

Billy Morgan took a couple of cartridges from his pocket and loaded the gun. Then he cocked an eye at Smiler and said, "You gettin' the idea, lad? No? Then I'll tell you. You knows where the key is – but you won't tell me. So, how do I find the right tongue-loosening oil for a stubborn lad? Easy. Always a way to deal with the most awkward of customers – if you knows their soft spot. And your soft spot is animals. Take old Laggy out there. Everyone round 'ere knows about Laggy and what you and the Laird 'ave done for him. Take all the other animals – and take 'em I will, one by one with this –" he smacked the stock of the shotgun smartly with the flat of his hand and went on, his voice cold and menacing "– unless you finds your tongue!"

"You wouldn't dare! You rotten devil, you wouldn't dare!" Smiler shouted.

"Oh, yes, I would, lad," snarled Billy Morgan. "I'd take Laggy and Dobby and Midas and your precious Bacon . . . the whole boiling lot one by one unless you talks. You don't believe me? Here, watch this for a beginning!"

He swung round, raised the shotgun, and took aim at Laggy swimming a few yards away on the water. Seeing the movement, Smiler gave a wild cry and flung himself at the man, kicking out at him as he fired. But Smiler never reached the Skipper for the Chief Mate, with surprising strength for such a small man, held the cord firmly and jerked him to a halt so roughly that Smiler spun round and nearly fell over.

The sound of the shot thundered in Smiler's ears and he saw the spread pattern of the shotgun pellets raise a white trail of foam on the water. As he saw the spouting water, he realized that his shout and lunge forward had put the Skipper off his aim. The shot had fallen just short of Laggy and the ducks. Then he saw something else, something that, for a moment, made him forget the savageness of the Skipper. The ducks, mallards, pintails, pochards, and shovellers went up in an explosion of flight, all taking off in a flurry of wings and webbed feet beating at the water. But the thing that held Smiler transfixed was that as they went, Laggy went with them. The greylag was so shocked and frightened that he forgot his fear of his well-mended wing. With a loud *gang-gang-gang* of alarm his great wings opened and his big feet thudded on the water, thrusting him forward. Neck outstretched, wing tips hammering at the ripples, he went forward in wild alarm and in a few seconds was air-borne.

Forgetting the two men, Smiler saw Laggy rise, swing up in a great curve, and then, high above the low-flying duck, turn and head westwards down the loch, wings beating strongly. Within a few moments the high-flying gander was hidden from sight by the tall towers of the castle.

Although Smiler was shaking all over with shock, there was a small part of him that sang with gladness for the greylag. Laggy was up and away and free, really free to join his own kind.

A hand fell on his shoulder and Billy Morgan spun him round. "Well, lad. That's just a taste. If you hadn't put me off, that there bird would 'ave been a goner. So what do you say?"

Recovering now, his face a stony, stubborn mask, Smiler looked at the Skipper. He would have liked to kill him. He was a dirty, rotten so-and-so. Even now, he had to hold himself in to stop his impulse to jump forward and kick and pummel the brute. But, for all his anger and contempt for the man, an icy cold part of Smiler's brain was sending clear and sensible signals. If he didn't tell where the key was then this man would carry out his threat. If the Laird were in his place now, he knew exactly what the Laird would do. The Laird, as he did, loved all living things. If Laggy *had been* killed, then not all the silver and precious stones in the world could have brought him back. Or Dobby, Midas, Bacon and Mrs. Brown and all the others.

Smiler said, "I'll get you the key."

"Aaaah!" Billy Morgan sighed with pleasure. "Now that makes sense. Good sense." Turning to the Chief Mate he said, "Untie him, Chiefy. He's learnt his lesson. We'll have no more hubble-bubble from 'im."

Smiler said nothing. He was beginning to understand the man's way of speaking, and he was thinking to himself that from now on he was really going to use his loaf — and if he could cause trouble he would.

As he turned away to walk back to the castle between the two men, the sun suddenly lipped the high crests of the hills and he felt Bacon press his cold muzzle into his hand.

9

The Distress Signal

With the coming of the sun the weather changed. The wind which for weeks had been light and from the east swung a hundred and eighty degrees through the north to the west. Big thunder-heads of cloud began to pile up over the seaward end of the loch. With its change the wind strengthened and the ripples on the water grew rapidly to long, deep wave troughs, scud and foam breaking from their crests. Within an hour the sun was hidden by a pall of dark grey clouds and fierce squalls raced up the loch from the west in hissing, grey veils.

Sitting at the big table in the hall watching the two men, Smiler could hear the skirl of leaves eddying along the terrace and the constant sough and sigh of the wind through the pines at the back of the castle. The changed weather matched his mood, dark and gloomy. Although he couldn't see what else he could have done, he kept blaming himself for what had happened. After all, he was in charge of the place and he had failed in his duties. If he had really used his wits he might have made the Skipper think that he had no idea where the key was. And now – he looked down the table. At the far end was the Laird's silver and the collection of stained linen packets that held the Elphinstone jewels.

When he had produced the key and the two men had emptied the safe they had soon found the jewels. Even the Chief Mate's wrinkled face had lightened with joy at the sight and his whistling had grown louder. The Skipper had been so elated that a shade of warmth had come into his eyes. He had said, gloating over the jewellery, "Look at it, Chiefy. The biggest haul of tom-foolery you could wish for!"

When he had asked Smiler where the jewels had come from, Smiler had really used his loaf. He had told the Skipper that the Laird, just before he had left for London, had found a secret cupboard in one of the tower rooms – for which he had been searching for years – and the jewels had been there. Smiler had done this deliberately because he was already planning to cause trouble.

The Chief Mate was now on guard at the terrace door, holding the shotgun. The Skipper was at the end of the table, methodically beginning to pack the silver and jewels into his big rucksack, making ready to leave. Coming back to the castle from the beach Smiler had seen down by the jetty the boat in which they had arrived. It was a sturdy craft with an outboard motor. Even with the bad weather which was now racing in from the sea, Smiler knew that they would have no trouble in getting away. He knew, too, that it would be hopeless to try and follow them in the Laird's small rowing boat. It would be swamped the moment he got outside the bay.

His mind teasing away at all sorts of schemes for outwitting the men, Smiler watched the Skipper packing the rucksack. Samuel M., he thought, you've got to find a way. There's got to be a way. Just think.

His freckled face was stubborn and set with thought. There just had to be a way. But how? Even if, when the rucksack was packed, say, he made a grab for it and ran . . . how could he ever get past the Chief Mate at the door? And if he *could* dodge the Chief Mate and make for their boat they would be peppering him with gunshot before he got it started. He needed time . . . time to get safely away. How on earth could he get safely past the Chief Mate? Come on, Samuel M., he scolded himself, think. There's got to be some way. He looked at the Chief Mate. Small and ancient looking he might be but he could be a fast mover and thinker. He had shown that when he had jerked Smiler back fiercely to keep him off the Skipper. Smiler's eyes moved away from him to look at the Skipper. As he did so, he saw the stairway post that had held the key and then. . . ! It suddenly came to him! What a fool!

Without any movement of expression to show his sudden excitement, he let his eyes travel up the stairs. Well, of course, you fool, he told himself. If you can't go out the front and you can't risk the back way through the kitchen – then you have to go some other way. These men might know a lot about the castle from, probably, Willy McAufee – but they couldn't know everything. And he, Smiler, knew his way around the castle now as well as the Laird.

Still keeping a stubborn, dejected look on his face, Smiler began to work it out. Once he had his hands on the rucksack, all he had to do was to sprint up the stairs and lose himself in the maze of corridors and tower steps. At the back of the castle there was one tower with a stairway which ran down to a little door that led out on to the battlement wall at the back. Because of the rising slope of the hill it was only a ten or twelve foot jump to the ground.

Excitement began to bubble inside Smiler. That's it, Samuel M. That's it. Once free of the castle he knew exactly what to do. . . .

From the end of the table as he packed away the last of the Elphinstone treasure and silver, Billy Morgan squinted up at him and said, "Well, lad, that's the lot. And as sweet and unexpected a tickle as a man could wish for." He looked out at the terrace and the distant view of the loch. "Dirty weather blowin' up. In another half-hour only a good boat could live out there. But for your own good, seein' as you've been so helpful and I wish you no harm, we'll take the oars from your boat so you can't try anything stupid like followin' us. Right then, let's be goin' with our load of honey."

He picked up the rucksack by its straps and walked up the room. Smiler sat where he was. Billy Morgan shook his head sadly. "You come with us as far as the jetty, lad. Not trusting you out of my sight till there's water between us. On your plates of meat and move."

Smiler rose from his chair and went to the head of the table which was only a couple of yards from the great stairway. As the man came up to him he knew that this was the only moment he was going to have. Once outside he wouldn't get two feet away without the gun peppering him around the legs.

He took a deep breath and told himself, "This is the moment, Samuel M. Work fast and keep your head."

Swinging the rucksack in his hand, Billy Morgan came up the length of the table. Outside the wind whistled with a sudden squall and a quick splattering of rain swept across the terrace. Smiler turned, as though to walk ahead of the man, but he hardly had his back to him when he swung back swiftly and punched Billy Morgan's plump stomach with the full force of his right fist. The result was gratifying. Smiler's muscles over the past months had grown hard and strong. The breath wheezed out of Billy Morgan and he doubled up, instinctively clutching at his injured midriff with both hands so that the rucksack fell to the polished boards.

Smiler was on the rucksack like a flash and leaping up the great stairway three steps at a time. He didn't look back to see what was happening, but he heard the Skipper shout and then the sound of feet thudding across the floor.

Holding firmly to the precious rucksack Smiler shot up the stairs. He swung round the landing post at the top, raced by the portraits of the elegant Lady Elphinstone and the warlike Sir Alec, and disappeared into a corridor like a hunted rabbit going into a warren. Behind him he heard an angry bellow from the Skipper. The whole plan of the castle clear in his mind, Smiler sprinted down the corridor, swung left, charged up a flight of stairs and began to work his way by a devious route towards the tower which would give him escape to the woods at the back of the castle. Behind him he could hear the noise of the following men. But as he reached the top of the stairs, he was aware of something which he knew could be more than awkward for him. He had forgotten Bacon who had been resting under the great hall table. And here now, hard on his heels, was Bacon, barking his head off and prancing ahead of him as though this was some splendid new game. He knew that, as long as Bacon was with him, the dog's barking would give the men a lead to his whereabouts.

He ran down another corridor. Then, thinking fast, he stopped by a bedroom door and opened it. He swung half in and Bacon, thoroughly enjoying the lark, dashed into the room past him. Smiler turned on his heels and jumped into the corridor, slamming the door. As he raced away he could hear Bacon barking in a frenzy behind the door.

For two or three minutes Smiler ran through the top corridors and pelted up and down stairs until the sounds of pursuit faded behind him. Satisfied that he had a good lead, he headed for the back tower.

He came darting out on to the low battlement top, hoisted himself up on to the parapet and jumped. He landed with a crash right in the heart of a large rhododendron bush and rolled in a tangle of leaves and branches to the ground. The next second he was on his feet and heading at top speed for the pine trees. When he was well in the pines he stopped and looked back, listening, his shoulders rising and falling as he fought for breath. There was no one in sight behind, but he could hear, very faintly, the sound of Bacon's barking. To make it easier for running he slipped the rucksack over his shoulders and raced away along a small path that led to the southern cliffside of the island. As he did so, he was not relishing the moment to come.

In a short while he was out of the trees on to the close turf of the cliffs. The wind coming up the loch, full of rasping rain squalls, smacked hard into his face. The whole loch as far as he could see was a wilderness of white-capped, rolling waves.

Smiler, head lowered against the wind, ran across the turf to a point on the cliffs immediately above the underwater entrance to the cave. He halted on the edge and shuddered. There was a rough jumble of loose boulders for about ten feet below him and then a sheer drop — into water that was beating against the base of the cliff in great, swinging rollers, leaden and sullen looking with spouting spume and froth marbling them.

Smiler looked back to the trees. There was no one in sight. Then he looked down at the water and his heart sank. Holy Crikeys, it was going to be like jumping off the top of a church tower! For a moment he thought it was too much, that he couldn't do it. . . . Then self-anger burst inside him and he shouted aloud into the wind, "You got to do it, Samuel M. You got to do it!"

The next minute he was scrambling down amongst the loose rocks and boulders to the point where he could make his jump. He looked down and saw Dobby's rock, the waves now crashing over the top of it. But it was only a brief look because he knew that the longer he looked the more likely he was not to jump.

As the rain and wind battered at his face, he took a deep breath, grabbed his nose tight with his right hand – and jumped.

It was the most extraordinary three or four seconds of Smiler's life. As he leaped out into space, the fierce wind took him and, from the resistance offered by the hump of the rucksack on his back, it swung him round in a slow spin like a lazy top. He went down to the water, feet first. One moment he was looking at rock face and the next at the loch. Trees, cliffs, loch, hills and scudding clouds and rain storms swept before his eyes in a slow swirl – and then he hit the water with an almighty bang. A great spout of foam shot skywards and then peeled off into a ragged, dying ring of wind-torn spray petals.

Smiler went under and down and down until he thought it would go on for ever. Then, slowly, the motion stopped and he began to kick for the surface, his nose and mouth full of water where his hand had been jerked away from his nostrils. He kicked upwards against the weight of the rucksack and, when he thought it would never happen and he would burst from holding his breath, he was on the surface. For a moment he rode there, swinging high and low on the wave troughs, panting and fighting for breath. From the corner of his eye he saw Dobby's rock. A quick glance upwards showed him that the cliff top held no watcher. He swam towards the cliff well to the right of the rock. He knew exactly where the underwater arch was in relation to the rock. It was hard work with the silver-weighted rucksack dragging at his back and the mad turmoil of water at the cliff foot tossing him here and there, but after a little while he judged that he was in the right position.

He trod water for a moment and took a deep breath. Then, with all the strength he could muster, he heaved himself up and porpoise-dived down, fighting with arms and legs to get low enough to go through the archway and saying to himself, Keep going, Samuel M. Keep going. . . .

Two minutes later Bacon arrived at the cliff top and began to run to and fro along its length, barking and whining. A little while after that Billy Morgan and the Chief Mate arrived. Billy Morgan, no fool, had heard Bacon barking in the room when they had lost Smiler in the castle. He had let the dog out and the two men had followed it through the castle maze and finally out on to the battlements at the back. Here Bacon had jumped down the wall and raced away through the pines after

Smiler. The two men had gone back through the castle and had followed up through the pines as fast as they could.

They stood now looking along the line of the cliffs and watching Bacon racing up and down and barking.

Through the wind the Chief Mate said, "What you think, Billy? Is he makin' a swim for it?"

Billy turned on him with a snarl. "You fool. Look at the water. No one would try that. Take a header down there and try to get across to the shore? What you think the boy is? Superman?"

"Then where is he?"

"Hidin' along these cliffs somewhere. He knows the place well. He's here somewhere and we're going to find 'im – and when we do I'll welt the skin off his rear end good and proper. He probably knows some cave or nooky place. We'll find it. But we ain't taking no chances. He might have doubled back and be trying for the boats."

"Well, he can't use ours," said the Chief Mate. "I got the spark plug in me pocket."

"Maybe – but he might be mad enough to try the other boat. He ain't wantin' in guts. You get back there and make sure he can't use it – and keep your eyes peeled. You see 'im – then give him a touch of lead around his legs. That'll bring him up short. I'll see what I can do with the tike."

The Chief Mate began to trot off along the cliff top towards the jetty with the gun under his arm. Billy Morgan started to search along the rocks and boulders that reached a little way down the cliffs. Bacon, who had lost the scent of his master, went with him, his barking now changed to a low, anxious whining.

Billy Morgan was a methodical man, especially when he wanted something badly. And right now he wanted Smiler and the silver and jewels. He made a careful examination of the cliff top as far as the westerly point, the wind buffeting at him and the rain squalls drenching him. Then he came back and worked the cliffs all the way up until the point where they began to slope down to the little promontory that sheltered the castle bay. Here he was met by the Chief Mate, who reported that he had fixed the boats so that Smiler couldn't use them.

"No sign of 'im?" he asked Billy Morgan.

"No. But the young devil's around somewhere."

"What we goin' to do, then?"

Billy Morgan rubbed his fat chin thoughtfully and then said, "I'm goin' back to where the dog was and do some serious thinkin'."

The Chief Mate's eyes widened. "What, in all this weather?"

"If it snowed enough to put out the fires of Dingley Dell, I wouldn't

leave this cliff while there's a scrap of daylight. That silver and tom-
foolery is ours and I mean to 'ave it. Now you get back to the castle
kitchen and fetch up some food. I'm going to find that lad. Nobody
hands Billy Morgan one in the Bread-basket and gets away with it."

*   *   *

In the underwater cave Smiler sat on the ledge below the niche in which
he had found the Elphinstone jewels. Although there was some light
coming in from the thin slit high up in the roof, it was darker in the cave
than he had known it before. It was also colder.

Three feet below his ledge the surface of the cave water, taking turbulence from the rollers outside, sloshed and slapped around sending little gouts of spray spurting up on to the ledge.

Smiler had come through the cave entrance all right, but the weight of
the heavy, water-sodden rucksack had held him down so that he had had
to fight his way to the surface. He flopped over now on his back,
exhausted. Trickles of water streamed away over the ledge from his wet
clothes and the water-logged rucksack.

For about five minutes Smiler lay flat out, getting his strength and his
breath back. Then he slowly sat up and began to take stock of his position. Above the noise of the water in the cave he could hear the whistle
of the wind through the crack high above him. He stood up and stripped
off his clothes and wrung all the water he could from them. Then he
spread them over the rock face so that they would dry out a bit. It was at
this moment that he realized that he was hungry. Remembering that the
Skipper had a supply of beer in his rucksack, he wondered if the man
had kept food there as well. He pulled out the silver and jewels and
stacked them neatly against the rock wall. At the bottom of the rucksack
were two cans of beer, a large unopened bar of chocolate, and a packet of
biscuits wrapped in cellophane through which the water had not
penetrated.

Smiler had a breakfast of a small piece of chocolate, three biscuits,
and a can of beer. He was careful about not eating too much food, but he
had no worry about getting thirsty because he could always drink the
loch water.

Sitting there, as naked as the day he was born, and finding the hard
rock unkind on his bare bottom, Smiler began to sort things out.

Thing Number One was that at the moment he was safe and he had
the silver and jewels. In two or three days, he knew, Laura and the Laird
would be up. All he had to do was to sit things out until then. . . . At
least, he thought that was all. But when he began to think about that,

then Thing Number Two came popping into his mind. In those two or three days the Skipper and the Chief Mate wouldn't be idle. They would be looking for him. They would guess he was hiding somewhere because they would know that he could never have swum from the island to the loch shore in this weather with a thumping heavy rucksack on his back. For certain they would make a thorough search of the island – and they wouldn't be the only searchers. The moment they let Bacon out of the bedroom (might already have done so), then Bacon would come looking for him. And Bacon had a good nose and would certainly lead them to the cliffs. Holy Crikeys, he thought – Bacon could spoil everything! First thing you'll know, Samuel M., he told himself, is that that old Bacon will be sniffing away at that cliff crack up there and then barking his head off if he gets a scent of you. . . . It mightn't happen right away but sooner or later it would. And when it did, all the Skipper and the Chief Mate would want would be a pickaxe and crowbar to break their way in from the top.

Sitting cross-legged, munching at his biscuits and sipping his beer, Smiler gave the situation very hard thought. Time, he decided, was not on his side. He had to get help as soon as he could. The moment the Skipper saw anyone coming up to the island he knew the man would run for it – and to bring help to the island while this weather lasted could only be done in one way. Laura would never come up unexpectedly on a friendly visit while the weather was bad. But, if he could somehow get back to the castle when it was dark and hoist the flag to half-mast, then early the next morning someone on the mainland would see it, and maybe see it long before the Skipper noticed it. In fact, the Skipper might never notice it. And then – suddenly Smiler felt more cheerful – it wouldn't just be Laura who came up. It would be her father and brother, all anxious to know what the trouble was.

That's it, Samuel M., Smiler told himself, that's it. You got to sneak out tonight and get that flag up to half-mast.

*   *   *

While Smiler was in his cave, sorting things out and planning his future movements, the Skipper and the Chief Mate were not idle. Billy Morgan, though he w⌐s a rogue and a villain, was far from being an un-intelligent man – and his intelligence was spurred now by the thought of losing the wonderful load of swag which he had found in the castle.

So, for the whole of that morning, he searched the cliffs methodically and to help him he had Bacon. He made a rough collar and lead with the cord with which he had bound Smiler's hands, and he worked Bacon slowly along the line of the cliffs and the rocks and boulders and gullies just below their crests before they fell away in sheer rock faces. It was hard work in the high wind and stinging rain but Billy Morgan kept at it until he had searched the whole cliff top again and again and again. Each time Billy Morgan and Bacon passed within a few feet of the cliff crack which let light into Smiler's cave. But the slit was hidden in the crevice of two horizontal overlapping rocks and not visible to any passer-by. If the weather had been clear and windless Bacon would almost certainly have caught the scent of Smiler coming from the cave. But this day there was no hope of doing so. The wind and rain tore along the brink of the cliffs sweeping all scent away.

In the end Billy Morgan realized that this was probably the reason for Bacon's lack of success. But, if the weather wasn't helping him in his search, he knew that so long as it lasted there was no hope of Smiler getting off the island. And the weather had become worse. The wind had strengthened to almost gale force and it was heavy with rain. Now and again from the surrounding hills there were long, rolling peals of thunder and vicious blue jabs of lightning.

Billy Morgan and the Chief Mate took turns for the rest of that day to stand watch on the length of cliff in case Smiler should come out of his hiding place. They wore old mackintoshes which they had found in the castle storeroom. While one was on watch the other ate, rested and got dry in the castle.

Down at the jetty the two boats had been made secure. The spark plug had been taken from the outboard motor and the oars of the Laird's boat had been carried up to the castle and hidden. In addition, the Chief Mate had found a length of chain and a padlock and key in the storeroom. He had passed the chain round the centre thwart of the Laird's boat and looped it around the centre thwart of their own boat, and then through an iron mooring ring in the jetty wall. Nobody could move the boats without unlocking the padlock or cutting the chain.

It was not until darkness fell that the two men gave up their shared vigil on the clifftop. They retired to the castle for the night where the peat fire in the great hall had been piled high so that they could dry off their wet clothes.

They made themselves comfortable with a glass of the Laird's whisky each before the fire.

The Chief Mate said, "How long we goin' to keep up this lark, Billy?"

Billy Morgan said, "Now don't you start fussin', Chiefy. So long as this weather lasts nobody's comin' up here. And as one what 'as done his time at sea I can tell you that it's set for a couple of days at least. That lad's a-hidin' somewhere with all our tom-foolery from the nicest tickle that ever was. I ain't givin' that up until I have to. That lad's only got a few biscuits and a piece of chocolate and growin' lads have got demandin' Auntie Nellies. If we can't find 'im with the dog – then he'll be out for food sooner than later. He won't come out for nothin' else – so we can both sleep in the kitchen tonight. That's where all the grub is. And we'll 'ave the dogs with us."

"But say we 'ave to give it up?" said the Chief Mate.

"Then we 'as to, Chiefy, and we'll 'ave worked for over a month for no more than this bit of chicken feed." As he spoke he pulled Smiler's money envelope from his pocket and slipped the notes out on to his knees.

"How much?" asked the Chief Mate.

Billy Morgan counted the notes and said, "Little more than a pony. . . . Hullo, what's this?" From among the notes Billy picked out a piece of folded paper. He spread it open and after a moment or two he said, "Well, well, who'd have believed it? 'Ere, take a dekko at this."

He handed the paper over to the Chief Mate and then leaned back in his chair. Staring at the ceiling he said aloud to himself, "Well, well . . . come the worse and you felt real nasty, Billy . . . then real nasty you could be. . . . Yes, real nasty. . . ." He slowly began to chuckle to himself and it was not a very pleasant sound.

*　　*　　*

Late that afternoon it had grown so cold in the cave that Smiler had put on his partly dried clothes. To keep himself warm he did some exercises but they did not seem to help much. However, they did make him hungry, and by the time darkness came all his chocolate was gone and half the biscuits.

Once the darkness came, the cave became a very eerie place. The sloshing and slapping of the water filled it with weird echoes and sounds and he could see nothing at all.

He lay down on the uncomfortable ledge and shut his eyes and set himself to wait. But the trouble was that he had no idea of how much time was passing. Smiler didn't like the situation at all. It was like being buried alive and he could understand how it would be very easy to let himself go and get panicky. Being a sensible sort, he decided that he must do something about it, so he started to think of all the things that had happened to him since he had run away from approved school . . . all the nice things and the bad things and all the nice people and the bad people – like the Skipper. With his eyes shut he went through the whole history and, to his surprise, he found that it helped him a lot. He thought about Laura and the Laird, and then his father and the *Kentucky Master* – the first of October wasn't far off now – and then of Laggy. Where was Laggy now, he wondered. And then it struck him that out of something bad, like the Skipper firing at the greylag, something good had come. That was a real tickler, good coming out of bad. . . .

So Smiler passed the time until he thought it was sufficiently late for him to make his foray. Stiff from lying on the ledge, he got up and stripped off all his clothes except his underpants. He had decided that once he was outside the cave he would swim westwards along the cliff. It was not so far that way before he could get ashore. To try and swim eastwards up the loch, along the line of cliffs and round the bay was much farther. Moreover, it would take him against the loch current.

Feeling his way cautiously, Smiler dropped over the ledge into the shallow water and then launched himself gently outwards. He swam by guesswork until his hands felt the wet rock above the cave entrance. Backing a little, he took a deep breath and dived down, hands and arms outstretched to find the side of the cliff opening. To his surprise as he went deep he saw the opening at once as a grey wavering outline lit by the faint light of the night outside. He swam through and surfaced without trouble. He trod water for a few moments. After the darkness of the cave, he was able to see quite easily the line of cliffs and the white crests of the breaking waves. But when he started to swim westwards he realized that it could not be done. Something had happened to the set of the loch current. Instead of running east to west along the cliffs, it was now setting strongly from west to east. Smiler turned and went with it on the longer, but now easier, haul up and round into the bay. As he swam he worked out that the bad weather from the west and the driving wind must have altered the loch current.

Once outside the cave and being taken easily along the cliffs, although the water was rough, Smiler felt much happier. He was a strong swimmer and the long rollers did not worry him, and it was nice to be doing something instead of stuck in that cave getting a sore bottom on the rocks.

Ten minutes later Smiler reached the steps of the jetty. He lay half in and half out of the water, looking at the two moored boats and then up to the dim silhouette of the castle against the dark, clouded night sky. The wind was still very strong, but for the time being there was no rain.

Smiler went up the steps and examined the boats. He saw at once the padlock and chain and made a face to himself. The Skipper was no fool. From the top of the jetty Smiler went away to the right, keeping just along the fringe of the beach, and then circled away to the flight of steps that led up on to the battlements at the righthand side of the castle where the flag-hoist was. The flag was always kept there, attached to the halyard and rolled-up ready to be broken free by its retaining lanyard. If the Skipper knew about the flag signals and had taken the flag away – then he was sunk.

But the flag was there. Smiler freed the halyard from its cleat and hauled the flag up the long face of the corner tower and then on to the tall flagpole that rose from the tower roof. Looking up it was difficult to see how far the rolled flag had gone. When he thought it was about far enough he broke it with a tug on the other halyard haul and at once he saw the whiteness of the Saint Andrew's cross stream pale and ghostly into the wind. The flag was too far up the pole so he lowered it to half-mast, fastened the halyards round the cleat, and slipped away down the battlement steps.

Deciding to make a wide half circle around the north side of the island to reach the westerly end of the cliffs, Smiler started across the meadow. He had only gone about fifty yards when a large shape loomed up through the darkness and Mrs. Brown gave a low call. She moved up to Smiler and, lowering her head, sniffed at his bare knees. It was then that Smiler realized that she had not been milked that day. For a moment he was tempted to leave the cow. But then he thought that she might not get milked for a couple of days more if chances went against him. Knowing this would distress the animal he decided to milk her. He went down on his knees and began to strip Mrs. Brown. The cow stood placidly in the gloom chewing the cud. The smell of warm milk going to waste on the grass made Smiler's mouth water, so – as he milked – he twisted first one teat and then another sideways and squirted the milk towards his mouth. But for as much as he managed to catch in his mouth, four times more just squirted against his face and ran down over his naked shoulders and chest. The thought of how funny he must look made Smiler giggle with the result that he swallowed milk the wrong way and had a choking fit which he had to stifle in case anyone should hear.

Half an hour after Smiler had finished milking Mrs. Brown he was back in his underwater cave. Somehow now the total darkness did not seem so unfriendly or frightening, nor did the cave feel so cold. He put on his damp clothes, made a pillow of the rucksack and lay down to sleep.

Five minutes later he sat up suddenly, the skin at the back of his head creeping with fright. A wet hand had passed across his face!

Frozen into immobility by fright Smiler sat bolt upright. To his left the water of the cave splashed and gurgled. Then distinctly near his feet he heard something move, first a scraping, scratching sound and then a quick *flap, flap.* The next minute something cold and wet slid along his bare leg.

Smiler let out a yelp and reached down with his hand to push it away. His fingers came into contact with wet fur and there was a little snuffle of pleasure as a whiskery nose was pushed into the palm of his hand.

Smiler almost collapsed with relief. It was Dobby. The animal must have scented him on the island and, unseen, had followed him into the water on his swim back to the cave.

Smiler lay back on his pillow, his heart still bumping from the shock. A little way away he could hear Dobby moving around. Then there was a steady crunching sound which told him that the otter had caught a finnoch or a trout and was eating it.

When Smiler woke the next morning, Dobby was gone. Daylight was angling through the roof crack and the cave water itself was shot with swirling gleams of light from outside. By Smiler's side were the bones and scales of the finnoch which Dobby had eaten. Alongside of it was another finnoch, quite a big one, from which a bite had been taken in one flank. Cheered by the light in the cave, Smiler looked at the finnoch and thought, Well, Samuel M., if it comes to it and you can't get any other food then you'll have to try raw fish. Then, standing up, he dived into the green cave pool and had his morning bath.

10

The Empty Boat

The reason that there was more light in Smiler's cave was because the sun was shining from a cloudless sky. But it was no friendly, warm sky. All around the sun was a pale halo of greyish-green light, and the westerly wind had moved a few points to the south and was blowing even harder than the day before. It was the kind of weather which at one glance would have made any fisherman decide that it was time to do a little net mending and stay in harbour.

The wind was blowing full gale force now and great waves were breaking over the westerly point of the island, thundering against the rocks and sending spouting cascades of water halfway up the cliffs. Driven in from the sea and circling over the eastern end of the loch were clouds of gulls, terns and other seabirds, wheeling and dipping in the wind. The cairns and rocky ledges of the Hen and Chickens were covered with the roosting birds, all squared round with their heads pointing down wind.

Billy Morgan and the Chief Mate were astir at first light. The Chief Mate made breakfast for them both and, because he was a somewhat more considerate man than his boss, he made up plates of scrap for Bacon and Midas.

After breakfast Billy Morgan and the Chief Mate made a thorough search of the island, beating through all the bushes and likely hiding places, and even examining the swaying, wind-tossed tops of the pines and ashes. They took Bacon with them on the lead, but Bacon showed no interest in their search until they reached the cliff top again. Then Bacon began to whine and bark and Billy Morgan let him off the lead. Bacon immediately ran to the point on the cliff from which Smiler had jumped into the water.

Watching him Billy Morgan said, "Either that tike is a damned fool or he knows something we don't know. There's nothing for it, Chiefy, but to give them there cliffs one more good going over."

"Goin' over," said the Chief Mate gloomily, "is just what will happen if you gets too near in this wind. I reckon we leaves it for a few hours. Maybe the wind'll drop as the sun gets higher."

"Blow harder more likely," said Billy Morgan. But since he no more relished being blown off the cliff top than the Chief Mate did, he agreed to wait for a few hours. They both went back to the castle, leaving Bacon racing up and down the cliff top in his own search for Smiler.

Two things so far neither of the men had noticed. One was the big white stain in the meadow grass where Mrs. Brown had been milked. And the other was the flag of Saint Andrew which streamed in the wind at half-mast.

During the morning Smiler finished the last of the biscuits and was down to drinking the loch water. From the fierce whistling of the wind across the cliff crack and the increased agitation of the water inside the cave he knew that the weather outside must be blowing very hard, harder in fact than the day before because the wind-note from the slit above him was much higher and fiercer. The waves on the loch outside would be far too big to risk a rowing boat, he knew. Even if, Samuel M., he told himself, there was a boat to be got. It would need a stout hacksaw to cut through the chain that secured the boats.

That day passed slowly for Smiler and for the two men. The wind blew fiercely all day and was far too strong for the two men to risk a close examination of the cliffs. Just after mid-day Bacon gave up his search and came back to the castle. But in the evening, a couple of hours before darkness, there was a sudden lull in the weather. The wind dropped completely and the flag of distress flopped limply against its pole so that there was even less chance of its being seen by the two men or anyone from the loch shore.

From the castle terrace Billy Morgan cast an eye at the sky and the racing waves of the loch outside the bay and said to the Chief Mate, "I ain't spent more years than I like to remember at sea to be fooled by this. I seen the weather play this kind of trick before. This 'ere lull might last an hour, might last six hours. But it'll blow again and next time harder than ever. Come on — we'll 'ave another look at them cliffs."

"What if we don't 'ave no luck, Billy?"

Billy Morgan pursed up his fat face and scratched the little wings of hair alongside his bald head. Then he shrugged his shoulders and said, "Then we must give the lad best and up sticks. We can't risk another day out here. It'll grieve me jam-tart for the rest of me life — but there it is. All that lovely silver and tom-foolery what could 'ave put us on easy street for the rest of our natural — whipped from under our noses. You go and get that dog. If there's any scent up there maybe he'll get it now the wind's gone. That lad's up there in some cave or cranny or my name ain't Billy Morgan."

So Bacon was fetched on the lead and in the windless lull the two men went to the cliff top and freed him. And Bacon found Smiler. With no strong wind to dissipate Smiler's body odour as it came out of the cliff crack when Bacon came to the two overlapping rocks he picked it up at once. He barked loudly and began to scrape at the rocks and at the loose soil around them. Billy Morgan climbed down to the rocks and leaned out over the top one and saw the long narrow line of the open slit.

Tugging Bacon back to the cliff top he stood in front of the Chief Mate and gave him a big wink.

"We got him," he said. "Dogs always knows. Come on. We got things to get. His scent's comin' out of a crack between two boulders. Could be a cave down there — not that he could 'ave got through the crack. Aye, that's it — must be some underwater entrance. He jumped over and dived in. 'Andy little blighter, ain't he? Yes . . . it's got to be like that or my name ain't Billy Morgan."

"You think so, Billy? Sounds a bit —"

"Course I thinks so — because this 'ere tike tells me so."

* * *

Sitting inside the cave Smiler was well aware that the wind had dropped. The water still rolled and splashed beneath the ledge, but there was no longer any whistling wind noise from the thin crack high above him. All his clothes had more or less dried out now and he was fully dressed.

The going of the wind gave Smiler hope. If the bad weather was going to pass then the heavy seas on the loch would drop within a few hours. Or, at least, drop enough to make it safe for a rowing boat.

"But how, Samuel M.," he asked himself, "do you get a rowing boat?"

He sat there tackling the problem. The oars had for sure been taken away and hidden, but that didn't worry him. Piled at the far end of the jetty were some lengths of timber and planking which had been delivered months before for the construction of new pen houses. With a short piece of planking for a paddle he knew that he would be able to manage the boat. He would go with the current up the loch and edge into the nearest shore. Once on the lochside he could take to the hills. If he had anything like a start, the two men would have no chance of catching him and taking the rucksack from him.

But how did he free the boat? There was a hacksaw in the castle workshop, but the chain was a good stout one. It would take a very long time to cut through it — and a hacksaw at work made quite a lot of noise . . . too much. One of the men, especially if there were no wind to drown the sound, would be bound to hear. How, he asked himself, could he free the boat from the chain? He sat there puzzling about it and then remembered something his father used to say when faced with a tricky problem — "There's more ways than one, Samuel M., of cracking a nut when there's no nut-crackers handy."

Well, thought Smiler, so there might be. You could take a hammer to it, and if you didn't have a hammer —

At this point he jerked upright and smacked himself on the forehead. "Of course! Of course, you fool, Samuel M.," he told himself out loud. He knew exactly how to do it and to do it fast and with the minimum of noise.

Just then over the wave sounds in the cave he heard a dog bark. He jerked his head up towards the cliff crack. The bark came again and with it this time there was a scrabbling, scraping sound. A small trickle of earth and fine shale cascaded thinly down the inside of the cave on to the ledge. The dog barked again and Smiler knew that it was Bacon. Bacon was up there on the cliffs and had scented him through the crack. Alarmed, he stood up and moved away out of the line of the crack. Pressed against the far wall of the ledge, where he could not be seen by anyone looking through the crack, he waited.

Bacon barked once more, and then the scrabbling sounds ceased. Smiler waited, and the minutes passed. No sounds came from the slit. Smiler waited on, but still nothing more was heard. Slowly Smiler relaxed. Maybe Bacon hadn't scented him. Maybe he was just hunting along the cliff and barked and scratched at the crack out of curiosity. His alarm passed from him and he went back along the ledge, elated by the bright idea he had had about the boat, and began to pack up the rucksack. As soon as it was dark enough he was going to leave.

As time passed the inside of the cave grew darker. The sun dropping to the west threw the outside water into dark shadows and the light from the crack was so faint now that he could hardly see it. Then suddenly Smiler heard Bacon barking once more. Almost immediately there was a heavy *clunk, clunk* over his head and then the sharp ring of metal striking stone. A cascade of loose roof debris and earth from around the inside of the crack spilled down the steep cave wall to the ledge. Clearly from outside he heard the sound of men's voices.

Smiler was swamped with a feeling of gloom. They'd found him – and Bacon had been the cause of it all! Pressed against the cave wall out of the sight line from the crack, Smiler heard the thumping and metallic sounds begin again. More thin spills of rubble began to fan down the cave side. He knew exactly what was happening up there. The Skipper and the Chief Mate were attacking the rocks with crowbar and pickaxe.

If he took to the water now they would see him and they would only have to get their boat and pick him up. But it was just a matter of time before they broke through the cave roof. How long? If it took them until dark then he might have a chance.

The digging noises stopped. There was silence except for the splashing of the cave water. Suddenly very clear and setting up weird echoes in the cave, a voice came down through the crack.

"All right, me old cock sparrer – we knows you're there. Just you stand well clear of this 'ere 'ole – otherwise you're likely to get a rock on your noggin."

It was the Skipper's voice. Smiler said nothing. They couldn't be sure he was here and he wasn't going to give them any hope.

"Don't feel like speaking, eh? Never mind – we knows you're there. Your old tike told us so."

At this moment a thin torchlight beam suddenly angled down from the crack. It hit the dusty resting ledge six feet away from Smiler, who was pressed back against the cave wall in such a position that no light from the crack could reach him. The light above moved a little, but it had a limited range because of the narrowness of the crack. As it moved Smiler's heart suddenly sank inside him. Shining brightly in the now steady beam was one of the beer cans resting on the ledge where he had been sitting!

The torch clicked off and the Skipper's voice came booming down. "Lost your tongue, 'ave you? Well, well, matey, I hopes as 'ow you enjoyed the beer. But by now your Auntie Nellie must be pretty empty!"

The sound of pickaxe and crowbar started again above Smiler. There was nothing he could do but wait – wait impatiently until it was dark enough for him to risk moving out of the cave. It was all a question now of how long it would take the two men to break into the cave from above. Huddled against the cave wall Smiler told himself that the moment they did, even if it was light still, he was going to take a header into the water for the cave entrance.

*　　*　　*

While Billy Morgan and the Chief Mate laboured on the clifftop in the fast fading light, sending rocks and boulders tumbling over the cliffside to make an entrance, Laura was working in the kitchen of the Mackay farm at the western end of the loch. She had the television on and was watching it while she did some ironing. She was all alone in the house. Her brother had gone off to spend the evening at his girl friend's house at Lochailort, and her mother and father had motored into Mallaig to visit friends for the evening.

The light in the kitchen was going but she did not switch on the lamps because there was enough glow from the television set to see to do the ironing. As she worked she was thinking about Smiler up at the castle and how he had discovered the Elphinstone jewels and of something that her father had said when she had told the family about it.

"The Laird will give the lad a good reward, that is for certain. Let's hope he makes something of it."

"And why should he not?" Laura had asked stoutly.

"Well, lass, I don't know. But I get the feeling that there's aye something a wee bit wrong with that lad. Turning up from nowhere and no sign of any kith or kin worrying about him. And don't give me that saucy stubborn look of yours just because you fancy the colour of his bonnie blue eyes." The whole family had laughed and Laura had been unable to stop her blushes. Just for a moment she had wished she could have told them the truth about Sammy. Well, one day they would know.

Just then the telephone rang. She went through to the hall to answer it. It was a keeper called Angus Bain who lived over in the next valley south of the loch.

"Is your father there, Laura?"

"No, he's away with Mother to Mallaig for the evening. There's only me here. Can I help ye?"

"Well, I thought ye ought to know. I was up on the tops a wee while back getting an old ewe of mine out of a peat hag she was stuck in. This'll make the third time in a month – the beast is for ever in some trouble. There's one spot up there I can just get a sight of the Laird's place so I took a look through my glasses. My, but there's a fair wave going on the loch just now –"

Suddenly apprehensive, Laura said sharply, "Angus Bain, what are you trying to say?"

"Well, I thought your father ought to know seein' as he acts for the Laird. Is he no away to London, did I hear? That's why I asked myself why should his flag be flying at the half-mast if he's no up there? So, I thought your father ought to know —"

"Thank you, Angus. I'll take care of it. Thank you." Laura cut him off and put down the telephone.

Her heart beating fast, she ran back into the kitchen, switched off the set and her iron, and then began to collect her oilskins. There had been no hesitation in her at all at what she must do. Sammy was up there all alone and the flag was at half-mast.

A few minutes later she was down on the farm quay wearing gum boots, oilskin coat and hat. Behind her in the house she had left a note for her father. She filled up the outboard motor tank with petrol and as she did so cast a look up the loch. The light was almost gone. There was no wind going, but the whole of the loch was seething with long curling rollers setting eastwards towards the castle island. Usually the trip took about an hour, but with the set of waves and the current now with her, she guessed she could do it faster this evening.

She spun the motor into life with the starting cord and swung away from the little stone quay. Once she was well out she realized that it was not going to be an easy trip. She had to regulate her speed so that the following rollers kept sweeping gently under the boat and not breaking over the stern. If she went too fast she took the crests of the rollers and plunged down into the troughs ahead, the bows dipping dangerously low and shipping water. More hurry, less speed, she told herself sensibly and settled down to navigate with care. But for all her care there were times when she could not avoid the boat taking water. Before she was far up the loch she had to have the baler out to keep the level of the water down. As she began to bale, the night came down and the wind returned.

There was still no cloud and she could see well enough. But it was as though all the elements were now conspiring to stop her from getting to the island. The wind which had been a little south of west when it had died away now came back stronger than ever – and from due south. It came up in a shrieking, buffeting mass. It surged up over the heights of the loch south shore and then, full of turbulence from the barrier of the hills, howled down on to the loch in a confusion of air currents that fought and tangled with one another. One moment the wind was ahead, then astern, and then it came sweeping across her starboard beam making the boat yaw away. Within five minutes the long, rolling eastward set of waves was gone and Laura found herself in a confused, heavy chop of waters that spouted high, now against the bows, now over the stern and then smashing into the sides of the boat.

Although she was frightened, she kept her head. She swung the boat over to the south side of the loch hoping to find calmer water there. If anything it was worse because there was more air turbulence right under the lee of the hills. She veered away to the north side of the loch and found the conditions there almost as bad. The force of the wind was so strong at times that it flattened the high tops of the angry waves and sometimes brought the boat up dead. Her left hand and arm stiff and sore from holding the tiller, Laura baled away at the water in the boat with her right hand. Since she knew there was a fair chance of the boat capsizing she kicked off her gum boots so that if she had to swim they would not hold her down.

The curious thing was that, while she was frightened for herself, working the boat and baling mechanically, her real thoughts were always on the flag at half-mast and there was a misery in her that something had happened to Sammy. Not once did it occur to her to run the boat ashore and seek the haven of the lochside for her own safety. But in the end she was forced to do this because the level of the water shipped aboard began to rise faster than she could bale it out. With the boat sitting heavily and dangerously low in the water she sensibly worked into the north shore. She ran the boat up on to a spur of sand and, although the waves beat at the stern and slewed the boat sideways, she stood up to her thighs in water and baled until it was safe enough for her to take to the loch again. In the next two hours she did this three times. The exhaustion and fatigue made her body ache all over, but not once did she think of giving up. Always she had before her the picture of Sammy in trouble at the castle, lying there maybe dangerously injured or ill. . . .

It was midnight when Laura at last rounded the point of the castle bay. The wind was still blowing strongly from the south but had dropped a little in the last ten minutes. She ran into the jetty and jumped out and tied up. There were no other boats at the jetty.

She raced up to the castle and was met by Bacon, who barked a furious welcome. In the great hall Midas was asleep by the fire and made no move. Shouting his name Laura hurried up the stairs to Smiler's room. The room was empty. She went all round the castle, in a fever of anxiety, looking for him. She searched all the castle with Bacon at her heels and then she took a torch from the kitchen and went through all the animal pens, the wild-fowl enclosure, and then through the woods behind the castle and finally out on to the cliff top. Here, Bacon suddenly raced ahead and led her to a great gaping hole in the side of the cliff where two heavy slabs of rock had been prised away.

Laura leaned over the edge of the hole and shone her torch downwards. She saw the narrow ledge below and the heaving pool of cave water and she knew that this must be the place where Sammy had found the Elphinstone jewels. But there was no sign of Smiler there. On the ledge an empty beer can winked in the beam of her light.

Exhausted and despairing Laura went wearily back to the castle and into the great hall. On the table where she had not noticed it before was a piece of red cloth which she at once recognized as the wrapping from the Elphinstone jewels.

She ran across to the Laird's study and looked in. Her heart sank as she saw the open door of the safe and knew that the silver and the jewels were no longer there.

She went back into the hall and collapsed into the wing-backed chair and oddly into her mind came her father's voice, saying, ". . . but I get the feeling that there's aye something a wee bit wrong with that lad." Almost immediately she was furious with herself for thinking, even for a moment, that Sammy might have taken the jewels on his own account.

Shivering and feeling sick with fatigue and apprehension, she dragged herself into the kitchen and made herself a cup of coffee. Before she had half drunk it she rested her head and arms on the kitchen table and sank into a deep sleep. Against the fatigue and strain of the loch journey, and her worry and fears for Sammy, and the shock of the missing silver and jewels, her mind and body had no defence except a relapse into sleep.

When Laura awoke it was still dark. Putting on her oilskins she went up to the great hall and out on to the terrace. The wind was still blowing a full gale from the south and with it now came solid sheets of rain. The terrace was awash and every spout and gutter of the castle was noisy with the rush of rain-water. Using her torch Laura made another inspection of the surroundings of the castle, but in her heart she knew that she was wasting her time. If Sammy had been on the island she was sure that she would have found him by now. Always at the back of her mind was the thought of the Laird's rowing boat which was missing from its jetty moorings.

She came back and searched the castle once more and then, as the dawn came up, though it brought no cessation of the gale and the rain, she made another inspection of the island. Coming back she saw that there was no food or water for the animals in their pens and one look at Mrs. Brown told her that the cow had not been milked for more than twenty-four hours. To give herself something to do which would take her mind off her thoughts, she watered and fed the animals and then milked Mrs. Brown. Wherever she went Bacon went with her, full of restlessness and whining to himself now and then.

When the daylight had strengthened more she went down through the driving rain and wind to make sure that her boat was still safely moored at the jetty. It was filling with water from the rain and the wave spray that burst over it. She went aboard and baled it out. As she did so she was wondering what she would do next. With the weather as it was she was in no mood to risk the boat trip back to the farm. Last night's experience had been enough for her. Anyway, her parents would know from her note where she had gone. Looking up she saw the castle flag still flapping stiffly in the wind at half-mast. When she went up she decided she would hoist it right up.

Her eyes coming back from the flag, she looked out across the bay towards the Hen and Chickens. She could only just make them out through the driving veils of rain. Now and again the thicker squalls blotted them out altogether. Then, just at the mouth of the bay, she saw something rising and falling sluggishly in the angry surging and rolling waves. A large roller suddenly took the object and swept it upwards and then burst right over it. In that moment of time Laura caught the flash of black and white paint.

She dropped the baler and snatched the canvas cover off the outboard motor. It took her some time to start the engine, but fifteen minutes later she was motoring across the choppy bay and ran alongside the object. It was the Laird's rowing boat, floating the right side up — but filled to the gunwales with water. The boat was empty and one side of the centre thwart had been smashed clean in half. She circled round it and then headed back for the jetty. As she went her eyes were blinded more by tears than rain and she was praying to herself that Sammy had never been fool enough — no matter what the reason — to risk putting off in the boat while the gale had been blowing. The moment he was outside the bay he would have been helpless.

*   *   *

But this was exactly what Smiler had done because he had been given no choice. He had clung to the security of the cave while the Skipper and the Chief Mate had worked at enlarging the hole in the roof. It had taken them a long time and while they had worked the darkness had fallen and the gale had come back, stronger than ever, from the south.

In the end Smiler had hoisted on the heavy rucksack and taken to the water. He had dived out through the entrance. Clinging as close as the breaking waves would allow him to the foot of the cliffs he had swum along them towards the bay, helped by the strong current that still set that way.

Ten minutes after he had gone, Billy Morgan had widened the hole in the cliff enough to allow him to get his head and shoulders through and shine the torch around the cave. It had been empty.

Billy Morgan and the Chief Mate had run up to the jetty to check the boats. They had found the rowing boat gone and the fastening loop of the chain hanging still intact over the side of their own boat.

It was at this moment that Smiler in the rowing boat, half a mile eastward down the loch, had run into disaster. The short plank length he was using for an oar was completely useless and he was drifting helplessly in the wild sea. A wave had taken the boat beam-side on, swung it high and capsized it. Smiler, heavy rucksack still on his back, had been thrown into the loch. The boat had rolled right over above him and the keel had struck him on the forehead. He had gone down conscious only of a blinding pain in his head.

Destination Still Unknown

The bad weather eased a bit as the morning wore on, and just after ten o'clock Laura's father and her brother arrived at the castle in a stout motor boat which they had borrowed from a neighbour. Both were very relieved to find Laura safe and sound. But that did not stop her from getting a scolding from her father for going off in the boat on her own in such bad weather. However, there was little edge to his scolding because he was so relieved to find her safe.

Laura told them all she knew and took them to see the hole in the cave top and then the Laird's rowing boat which had finally drifted ashore in the bay close to the wild-fowl pens.

The two men hauled the boat out on to the beach and tipped the water from it.

Jock Mackay examined the smashed centre thwart and said reflectively, "Something gave that an almighty crack. . . . Aye, a real smack that got. . . ."

Laura turned away. She couldn't stand the sight of the boat. She might have been happier if she could have known that it was Smiler who had cracked the thwart in half. He had done it with a large rock picked up from the beach in order to slip the chain loop free from the boat.

Jock Mackay turned, put his arm around his daughter, and said, "You'd better be coming back with us, lass. The Laird's due back tomorrow. He phoned late last night. There's nothing to be done up here now. If the lad went overboard in last night's weather then —"

Laura pulled away from him and ran up to the castle, her hands over her face.

As Jock made to move after her, his son stopped him, saying, "Leave her a while, Father . . ."

When they did go up to the castle, they found Laura in the great hall, and it was a Laura who had now recovered her self-composure.

She said, "You two go back and bring the Laird up tomorrow. I'm going to stay here. There's all the animals to be looked after and the place is a mess. And I can tell by looking round that there's been more than Sammy up here recently. The police should know about it as quick as possible."

"You don't think the lad went off on his own account with the silver and stuff?" asked her father.

"Of course I don't! Sammy's no thief! He must have gone off with it to keep it safe from whoever was here. Clearly someone else has been eating in that kitchen. And why would Sammy use a pickaxe and crowbar to open up the cliff top? The sooner you get back and tell the police about this the better. I'll be all right up here. And what's more, I don't think . . . well, I'm sure Sammy's all right somewhere. He's got to be." But although she said it stoutly there was a dark shadow of doubt hovering always at the back of her mind.

Laura's brother said, "Maybe, Father, before we go back we ought to motor round the Hen and Chickens. If the lad put out last night from the bay, the current would take him down that way. If he went overboard he might have made them."

So before the two men headed west down the loch, they took the boat up to the Hen and Chickens and motored round them all. The strong seas were smashing against their low rock sides and sweeping up their small beaches. Nothing grew on them except some small patches of heather, some sea-holly, and tufts of pink thrift. While his son managed the tiller Jock Mackay got out his field glasses and scanned each little island as they circled it. But he could see no sign of Smiler. The only life on the island were the roosting flocks of seabirds.

The two men went twice round all the islets and then turned away and made their way back down the loch.

*   *   *

But the two men, as men often do, were accepting something as fact on the basis of their own experience. Both knew the loch and they were sure that anyone going overboard in the previous night's weather would have had no chance. If they had gone ashore and searched each islet thoroughly they would have learned better, learned that there is always some odd quirk of fate to upset apparent facts and well-proven experience.

Smiler was on the Hen and alive. In the darkness it was a large underwater rock just off the small beach of the Hen that the craft had struck. Smiler had gone overboard and had been hit by the turning keel. The blow had dazed him so much that he did not know what he was doing or what was happening to him. He had gone down and then been sucked up by the maelstrom of waves and thrown towards the beach. When his hands had felt rocks and shingle he had instinctively grappled for a hold. Like some blind, unknowing animal he had crawled forward.

A wave had sucked him back from his hold and then another had thrown him forward to the beach. On his hands and knees, bowed down by the weight of the rucksack, he had struggled forward and finally had escaped the reach of the waves. Not knowing what he was doing he had crawled on, panting and sobbing, with nothing to guide him except his powerful instinct to get away from the water.

He lay now, exposed to the searing wind and rain squalls, in a small hollow at the top of the Hen, a hollow that was ringed with weather-worn and bird-marked rocks. On the rocks at this moment was roosting a small flock of black-headed gulls. The birds surrounded Smiler in a silent colony, heads facing the wind, their plumage tightly bedded down to take the air-slip over their bodies. Smiler lay on his face, the rucksack still on his back, and two gulls were perched on the rucksack. It was not surprising that Jock Mackay had not spotted him. From the loch all that could be seen was a flock of gulls sheltering on the rocks.

There was a large bruise on Smiler's right temple and a cut on his left cheek which had ceased bleeding though the rain still kept the wound open and raw. Smiler, after long hours of unconsciousness, was now sleeping and dreaming. In his dream he was out on a sunlit, cloud-shadowed autumn loch in a boat fishing while Laura lazed in the stern with her back to a silent outboard motor. He was playing a sea-trout, the taut line singing from the reel, when from behind him he heard the *thud, thud* of a heavy motor boat engine. He looked round but there was nothing behind him except Laura, her hair teased by the wind, her brown face smiling at him, and a wide stretch of empty water.

It was at this moment, as Jock Mackay's boat was two hundred yards away, heading down the loch, that Smiler opened his eyes and rolled over to his side and groaned. Immediately the flock of gulls went up and around him in a wild, white explosion, calling and screaming in fright.

Slowly Smiler sat up and blinked his eyes to clear them. Rain and wind swept into his face blinding him for a moment. Then the squall passed and he saw the dark shape of the motor boat on the heaving, steely waters moving fast away down the loch. To his ears came the regular *thud, thud* of the motor which he had known in his dream.

Smiler flexed his arms and became aware of the heavy rucksack on his back. Awkwardly he slipped it off, every muscle in his body stiff and sore, his head throbbing sharply each time he moved it. He looked down at himself and saw that he was wearing just shirt and trousers and was barefooted. A sudden shivering fit passed through him and his body trembled as though it would never stop until he clenched his teeth and flexed his muscles to halt it.

He gave another groan and then tried to remember what had

happened. Slowly it all came back to him. He had smashed the centre thwart to free the rowing boat and had gone out into the bay using his plank paddle. He had heard the Skipper and the Chief Mate shouting behind him. As he had reached the limit of the bay and the current and wild sea had taken him eastwards, he had seen a torch dancing on the jetty. Then it had moved, pitching and swaying, out towards him and he had known that the two men were after him. Beyond that he remembered nothing.

Long after Smiler's boat had capsized, the two men had continued their search for him – but the high seas and howling winds had eventually forced them to look to their own safety. Angry and frustrated they had run for the eastern end of the loch and beached their boat for Willy McAufee to take over. By morning they were miles away in the hills heading for Fort William.

With the gulls crying and circling above him Smiler now stood up unsteadily, swaying in the force of the wind. He knew that he was on the Hen. He looked towards the castle away over the angry waters and it was suddenly blotted from his sight by driving rain.

Smiler sat down. Samuel M., he thought, you can't just sit here. You've got to do something. The rain squall cleared and he saw the castle again. This time he noticed that the flag now flew from the top of the mast. That meant that someone had come up during the night. His body shook with a shivering fit again and his head throbbed. He had to do something, had to get off the Hen before he passed out again. The castle disappeared in the rain but the picture of the flag stayed in his mind. Somebody had answered his signal last night. "What you want now, Samuel M.," he said aloud, "is a signal too." He considered this for a while and then, stiffly and awkwardly, began to make his way down from the rock. He knew exactly what he was looking for.

Fifteen minutes later, Smiler was on the point of the Hen nearest the castle island. On the beach he had found a six-foot length of bare oak branch which had been washed ashore. He had fastened his shirt to it by the sleeves to make a rough flag. He sat now on the highest rock he could find, naked to the waist in the buffeting wind and rain, holding his flag aloft. Every now and then his body shook with a spasm of shivering. In the end, exhausted from holding the flag aloft against the tearing wind, Smiler searched around and found a crevice into which he could jam the end of the branch. He wedged rocks around it, too, to keep it in position. Then, feeling ill and completely done-in, he could not stop himself from lying down. In a few moments he was gone from the world in sleep.

If the gale had kept up for the rest of that day things might have gone very badly for Smiler. He was in no shape to pass another night on the

Hen. But, in mid-afternoon, the rain stopped and the wind eased down to a steady, firm blow. The shirt flag flew steadily above Smiler who lay sleeping, turning and groaning in his dreams.

On the castle island Laura, trying not to think about Smiler but not succeeding, went about her chores. She had fed and watered all the animals during the morning and then had spent some time tidying up in the castle. In the afternoon when the rain stopped and the gale eased she went into the meadow to milk Mrs. Brown.

As she came back she looked out over the loch towards the Hen and Chickens and caught sight of something fluttering. The next moment she had put down her milk pail and was running for the castle.

She got the Laird's field glasses from his study, focused them on the Hen, and saw the shirt flying from its crooked staff and something huddled under it.

With a great surge of hope welling in her heart, she ran for the jetty and her boat. She started the motor and cast off. Bacon came racing down the jetty and jumped into the boat with her, barking furiously.

As the boat swept out into the bay Laura said aloud, "Please God, let it be him. And if it is —" her jaw firmed angrily "— no matter if Jock Mackay is my father, he'll hear from me about not searching the Hen properly!"

* * *

When Smiler awoke he saw at once that Laura was in the room. She was sitting at the window, resting one elbow on the sill and looking out. Against the pale evening sky her profile was etched sharply, and a faint breeze through the half open window stirred her long hair. Although he felt weak and drained, he lay contentedly, just looking at her and feeling a warmth in himself grow because she was there. Never in his life had he been more thankful than when he had seen her boat come tossing towards the point of the Hen. When she had rushed up to him and hugged her arms around him he could do no more than just shiver and tremble against her and say her name over and over.

She had brought him back to the castle, seen him to bed, and had wedged him around with three hot water bottles. Then she had brought him hot milk and made him take some aspirins. When he had wanted to talk, she had shaken her head severely. He was asleep within seconds of finishing his milk.

Through the window now he could hear the call of pigeons and the cry of gulls. An early star showed in the pale oblong of sky and he knew that the wind and rain had gone, that the fierce gale was over. Putting his hand up to his cheek he realized that she had stuck a strip of plaster over his wound while he had slept. His head still ached a little and the bruise on his forehead had come up in a large bump. His body felt as though every muscle had been over-stretched on a rack.

Slowly, sensing that he was awake, Laura turned her head and smiled at him. She got up and came across to the bed. Without a word she knelt down and took his hand. With an instinctive, unthinking movement she leaned forward and rested her cheek against his. Smiler had never known a moment like it before in his life. He had the feeling that not only was he safe for ever, but that he could never be lonely or afraid in his life ever again.

Without a word they stayed like that for a while. Then Laura suddenly stood up and turned away from him so that he could not see her face.

Smiler said, "It's all right, Laura. And I'm all right too." Then, his voice rising, he went on, "And do you know – Laggy flew! When the Skipper fired his gun he just took off. Right across the bay, *flap, flap* and up and away down the loch. Holy Crikeys, it was really something to see!"

Laura turned back, her face composed now, and asked, "Who's the Skipper?"

"Oh, I forgot. 'Course you don't know about him. And the Chief Mate."

Laura said with unexpected primness, "There's a lot I don't know – and there's a lot I've got to know. But if you think you're going to tell me it now, Sammy, you've got another think coming. You don't do or say a thing until you've got some decent food into you."

Smiler gave her a grin and said, "You sound just like a nurse in a hospital."

"Aye, and that's how I mean to sound and be until you're your proper self again. Now, you just rest there until I get ye something."

"I'm starving," said Smiler. "What am I going to have?"

"Wait and see," said Laura as she went to the door.

"That's what my Sister Ethel always used to say."

Half an hour later Laura brought him a bowl of soup and three poached eggs on toast and a dish of tinned fruit.

While he was eating Smiler told her the story of his adventures. Laura sat on the end of the bed and listened with a severe expression on her face. Outside the night darkened and the flames of the four candles in the room wavered gently in the faint draught from the window.

When Smiler had finished Laura said, "I've no idea who the two men could be. They fit no one around these parts. And I'll doubt whether they're hanging around here now. They've taken to their heels. But I can tell ye, if that sly loon Willy McAufee had anything to do with this he's going to be sore sorry for himself."

In fairness Smiler said, "Well, I don't know that he did. Only that the men had a list of the hiding places where the Laird used to keep his key." He slowly grinned at her and said, "Do you know what an Auntie Nellie is?"

"No, I do not."

"Or a troubled-Harold?"

"Sammy Miles, is your mind wandering?"

"No. Auntie Nellie is your belly. And troubled-Harold is a double-barrelled shotgun. That's what the Skipper called them."

"You sound as though you liked the villain."

"No, I did not. But he had a funny way of speaking. He called the jewellery tom-foolery." Then, with a lack of bashfulness which surprised him even as he spoke, Smiler went on, "Can I ask you something very private, Laura?"

"How would I know until you've asked it?"

"Well, it's about the Elphinstone jewels. The Laird's going to be very pleased, isn't he?"

"Aye, he is. But that's no private matter."

"Well, it is in a way. You might get your farm, you know."

"Away with ye. That's just happy talk."

"And he might, when – well, when the bit of trouble I'm in is cleared up – arrange for me to study. You know, to be a vet."

"Aye, he might. But you're a long time getting to the private part."

"I'm coming to it now," said Smiler grinning and still surprised that he felt no awkwardness. "What I want to know is . . . well, when I'm really grown up and a vet . . . well, would you marry me?"

For a moment Laura's face showed her surprise, then she gave a little frown and said severely, "Sammy Miles, that bump on your head has made you lose your wits. You must be daft to think I'd answer a question like that."

Smiler lay back against his pillows and said, "You don't have to answer it now. But when I get to be a vet – well, you just watch out. I'm jolly well going to come and ask you. I never did meet anyone like you before and just think – if I was a vet and you had a farm –"

"And if pigs had wings they would fly and a fine old world that would be."

Tight-faced Laura came to the bed and took his tray, but as she moved away she turned and smiled back at him and said, "Mind you – if you did come and ask I'd no say that I wouldn't give it serious thought.

But for now, you get your head down on those pillows and go to sleep. I'll be up in a little while to snuff your candles."

When Laura had gone, Smiler lay back on his pillow and thought how pretty she looked. Not just when she smiled and laughed, but also when she tried to look stern and cross. She was a wonderful girl. Holy Crikeys, she was. Not like the rest. She could do things that would make most other girls turn and run. . . . Despite the low throbbing still in his head he grinned happily to himself and thought, Samuel M., the sooner you get to be a vet the better.

When Laura came up an hour later he was locked in sound sleep. She leaned over him and arranged the clothes around his shoulders and then slowly put out a finger and touched his sun-tanned, freckled cheek above the cut on his face.

The next morning to Smiler's surprise he found that he felt worse than he had done the previous night. Laura noticed it at once and she took his temperature and checked his pulse. But all she would say when Smiler asked her about them was, "They're aye fair enough. But what you've got is a . . . a sort of reaction. You'll not be getting out of that bed in a hurry, I can tell ye."

But Smiler had no wish to get out of the bed. He slept on and off during the morning and now and again found himself shivering and going cold all over. This was the beginning of a fever that didn't leave him until the following afternoon. During that period things became pretty mixed up for Smiler because he couldn't sort out whether he was dreaming them or whether they were actually happening. Sometimes he was being chased by the Skipper and the Chief Mate all around the island with Bacon barking at his heels. At other times the big four-poster bed seemed to be adrift on a dark, stormy sea. The little carvings on the supporting posts were alive, the flowers and leaves fluttering in the wind, the gnomish men and women clambering up and down, and the red velvet canopy cracking and booming as each gust took it. Once the room was full of deep calm and he saw the Laird and Laura leaning over him. The Laird's face looked grave and he slipped up the sleeve of Smiler's pyjamas and gave him an injection in the arm. As he turned away Smiler saw that he had the small brown owl sitting on his shoulder. The owl twisted its head right round, looked at Smiler, ruffled its feathers, and then gave him a wink from one amber-brown eye.

The curious thing was that when Smiler really did come round the Laird and Laura were standing at his bedside, and the owl was on the Laird's shoulder.

Smiler looked up at them and said, "Hullo."

The Laird smiled and said, "Hullo, Samuel M. How do you feel?"

Smiler said, his mind still a little fogged, "This is like the first time. The first time I came here. Did I get a drop of malt this time too?"

The Laird laughed. "No – ye got something that worked faster." He reached out and put his hand on Smiler's brow and after a moment nodded. "Twenty-four hours and you'll be your old self. Until then you're under Mistress Laura's orders."

Smiler looked at Laura and met her smile with his own. "She can be very strict, sir."

"Aye, maybe. But ye'll just have to put up with that. . . ." The Laird paused and then put out a hand and ruffled Smiler's fair hair. "This is no time for too much talk, Samuel M. But I'd have you know now that I'm much in your debt. You're a good, brave lad."

Left on his own, feeling weak but much better, Smiler stared at the cloud-flocked patch of blue sky through the window and wondered why it always pleased him so much when the Laird called him "Samuel M." Apart from his father he was the only other one to do so. He had a feeling that in some way it had to have a very special meaning . . . almost as though, while his father was away, the Laird had quite naturally taken his place. Then, thinking about his father, he lay and began to work out in his mind how long it was to the first of October and the return of the *Kentucky Master*. So far as he could make out without a calendar handy he thought it could not be more than just over a week. Well, he would be up and about long before then.

*   *   *

At that moment in the police station at Fort William, a sergeant was opening the morning's mail. At the top of the pile was a crumpled white envelope addressed in pencilled block letters and carrying an Edinburgh post-mark.

The sergeant opened it. Inside was a letter on a single sheet of lined writing paper and a newspaper clipping. The letter was written in pencilled block letters and one corner was stained with tea or coffee droppings.

The letter read:

THE LAD WHAT IS MENTIONED IN THE ENCLOSED IS WORKING NOW FOR SIR ALEC ELPHINSTONE AT ELPHINSTONE CASTLE. SENT IN THE NAME OF JUSTICE AND FAIR PLAY. A WELL-WISHER OF THE LAW.

The sergeant picked up the newspaper clipping and began to read it. The clipping, ringed around with red pencil, had been cut from an old number of *The Times*. Actually it had been cut out by Smiler after Sir Alec had shown it to him because he had wanted it to give to his father. He had kept it in his money envelope which Billy Morgan had taken from him.

The sergeant read it through, then read the letter again, and then screwed up his mouth as though he suddenly had a bad taste in it, and said, "A well-wisher of the law, I don't think."

*   *   *

That day, too, Smiler was allowed up for a couple of hours in the afternoon and he sat in the great hall and told Sir Alec all his adventures, and particularly about the way Laggy had flown off.

The day after that he felt so much better that he was allowed to get up in the morning on the understanding that he took a rest after lunch. During the morning the Laird brought out the Elphinstone jewels and he told Smiler some of their history and he made Laura, who was still at the castle, wear some of them.

As she stood before them with the glowing emeralds around her brown neck and the eight-pointed star on her brow, gleaming under her dark hair, the Laird said, "And don't either of ye think I'm not a man of my word. You'll both get your reward."

Smiler, his eyes on Laura, saw her suddenly blush, and then he knew that he was blushing too and all he wanted to do was to get up and go out on the terrace and hide his face. But before he could move, a familiar stubborn, stern look came over Laura's face. Taking off the jewels, she said primly, "Well, I've no time for fancy parading around all morning. There's work to be done in the kitchen."

When she had gone Smiler and the Laird went for a walk outside and the Laird was full of all the different things he would now be able to do to his properties and in setting up a wild-life sanctuary at this end of the loch.

"We'll have it properly guarded, lad, so no thieving nest robbers can get in. There were ospreys here this spring that had their eggs taken. With luck they'll be back next year and things will be different. And we must not be selfish . . . we'll fix it so that the public can come on certain days and enjoy it too. And you, Samuel M. . . . well, when your bit of trouble is settled, you can get your head down to some real hard work towards becoming a vet. But it will no be easy. You'll be starting late and you've a lot of lee-way to make up. But it can be done if you set your heart on it. Aye, it can be done. . . ."

As they made their tour of inspection, Smiler was full of questions about just how you went about being a vet and the Laird explained to him exactly what would have to be done; the subjects to be studied, the examinations to be taken, and the years of hard work ahead. The awful thought suddenly came to Smiler that if it was going to take all that while – not that he minded the hard work and so on – it might be that by the time he really was a qualified vet Laura might have become married to someone else . . . Holy Crikeys, what a terrible thing that would be!

The Laird, seeing his long face, said, "Are you all right, Samuel M.? You look as though you've lost a shilling and found a penny."

"Oh, I'm all right, sir. Thank you, sir," said Smiler. "I was just wonderin', sir, whether I could do all the studying somewhere here in Scotland? So, well, so that I could come sometimes and see you and . . . well, everyone else?"

The Laird considered this and then said, "Aye, it could be arranged – if your father's agreeable. When he's back and you've cleared up things we'll see about it."

Smiler's heart lifted.

After lunch that day Laura ordered Smiler up to his room to take his rest. With his shoes off he lay on the bed fully clothed, staring out of the window, thinking about the years of work ahead of him and of his father now soon due at Greenock. He was sure that his father would agree to his living in Scotland. Gradually he drifted off into sleep.

He woke an hour later. Although he had promised to stay in the room until Laura called him, he felt too restless to stay and decided to risk her anger. He put on his shoes and went quietly down through the castle and on to the wide landing above the great hall. A beam of sunlight struck through the great mullioned window and lit up the painting of Lady Elphinstone. She was a very grand lady, he thought, but by no means as beautiful as Laura. He turned from the painting and, leaning on the top balustrade, looked down into the hall.

It was at this moment that he realized that there were people in the great hall. Their voices came clearly up to him. He moved along the balustrade, almost to the top of the stairs and crooked his neck to look down.

The Laird was standing to one side of the stone fireplace. Near the long table, their backs to him, Smiler saw two men in uniform. They were policemen. Their hats with checked bands rested on the table. The taller of the two – who was an inspector – was speaking to the Laird, who held two pieces of paper in his hand and was frowning over them.

"They came through the post anonymously, Sir Alec. That kind of thing usually does. But I'm afraid, sir, we have to act on it just the same. I take it you knew this lad's history?"

An awful feeling of emptiness swept through Smiler. He saw the Laird approach the long table and put down the two pieces of paper. Even from where he was he recognized the crumpled newspaper cutting with a large red pencil circle around it.

The Laird said, "Aye, Inspector, I knew. But some things you know and then properly forget. You have your job to do, I know. But there is no doubt in my mind that the lad is innocent. More than that, he is absolutely convinced that when his father docks at Greenock on the *Kentucky Master* in a few days' time . . . well, then as a boy should, he's certain that his father can sort things out for him. And I've no doubt at all that he will."

The Inspector looked at the other policeman, hesitated, and then said, "Sir Alec – we've been some time getting around to this visit here. That's because we've been in touch with the English police authorities. When this lad went on the run again from Wiltshire, the English police felt that his father should be brought home to help deal with the situation. They got in touch with the shipping company who cabled the *Kentucky Master* on which this Mr. Miles was serving as a cook. Unfortunately the father was not on board. It seems that he failed to report back to the ship when it left Montevideo many weeks ago. Nobody knows what has happened to him. I'm afraid the lad has got to go back to the English police and the approved school. Maybe there'll be deeper enquiries into the theft affair in due course, but for the time being that's what must happen to him. I'm sorry, sir, but I must ask you to hand the lad over to us."

"Good God, this will break the lad up completely!" The Laird paced away towards the terrace, pulling hard at his beard.

But Smiler hardly saw him or heard any more of the talk. What could have happened to his father? A host of black fears invaded his mind.

Swamped with despair he turned blindly away from the balustrade and moved back past the painting of Lady Elphinstone, his head bowed, his shoulders shaking. It was then that he felt someone take his arm gently. He didn't have to look up to know it was Laura who must have come quietly up behind him and overheard the talk.

She put her arm round his shoulders and led him back up the stairs into his room. As she closed the door Smiler turned and she put her arms around him and held him while he fought to master his black sorrow. She held him tight and, shaking, he buried his face in her shoulder. Then, after a little while, he began to control himself. Through all his anguish he knew that he must take a grip on himself.

Suddenly he stepped away from Laura and looked full at her, his face tear-streaked, his mouth set obstinately.

"I'm not going with them! It's all wrong! I'm sure my father's all right. Nothing could have happened to him. And I never ever stole anything! I'm not going with them!" he shouted.

Laura said, "Oh, Sammy . . . Sammy . . . you can't do anything else . . ."

"Yes, I can. If . . . well, if there's no one else to help me, I can help myself. But I'm not going back to that school. Never!"

"Be sensible, Sammy. They'll come after you. They'll —"

"Let them. But they've got to catch me first. No, I'm not going with them."

He turned quickly and went to the wardrobe, pulling open the door. Before he could take out any clothes Laura was at his side. She slipped between him and the wardrobe.

"Sammy — one last time. Think. You've got to think and be sensible."

Bitterly Smiler said, "If my father's not coming back yet . . . well, then I got to do things for myself. But one thing I'm never going to do is go back to that school. I'm not staying there for something I never did." He put out an arm to ease her aside. "Let me get my things."

Laura held her ground. For a moment or two she looked him squarely in the eyes and then she said quietly, "You're wrong, Sammy. Aye, you're awful wrong. But I can see you must do what you must do. And since you must do it, I'm no the one to stand in your way. You're going to run for it again — is that it?"

"Yes."

"Then I can do no more than help you. Listen, you're supposed to be resting here another hour and the Laird will not let them disturb you until then. Now you go out the back way and meet me on the far side of the water-fowl pens. And don't worry about your things here. I'll see to them." She moved him away from the wardrobe.

"Oh, Laura, thanks. And I know what I'm doing is right."

Laura shook her head. "I doubt it fine. But there was never a woman could make a man see sense when he didn't want to. Now, out with you."

Heavy with a numbing grief, not even trusting himself to think any more of his father than that he was missing, pushing all the memories of them together from him, Smiler left the room and made his way quietly out through the back of the castle.

Fifteen minutes later, hiding in the shade of the trees the other side of the pens, Smiler saw the Laird's black and white row boat slide round a rocky bluff and glide into the shore. Laura was at the oars and there was Billy Morgan's old water-stained rucksack on the floor boards, packed with Smiler's clothes and few possessions.

Without a word Smiler got into the boat and Laura went down the side of the island to keep out of sight of the castle. At the end of the island, as she began to swing the boat out to cross to loch's north shore, Smiler looked back at the towers of the castle just showing over the tips of the pines. The thought of the Laird there and all the animals knifed through him in a sharp pain. He had planned one day to bring his father here. . . . Had known how his father, who was as mad about animals as he was, would love it. He fought to keep his tears back. He was on his own. He had to be tough. . . .

Laura said, "Bacon wanted to come, but I shut him in my room. You'd no get far with him around. There's most of your things in the rucksack and a bit of money. Where I'm going to land you there's a track up through the woods. At the top of the woods you'll hit an old road. Keep along it and you'll finally make the Fort William road. After that . . ."

Smiler looked across at her. He knew she thought he was doing wrong. But he couldn't help that. He just had to get away, right away, and when things were more settled he would have to work everything out for himself. He only had himself now. . . . Whatever could have happened to his father? Tears suddenly misted his eyes.

A little later the boat grounded on the shore at the foot of the woods. Laura jumped out and pulled the boat up on to the sand and Smiler followed her with the rucksack.

They stood together in the afternoon sunshine. High up in the blue a pair of golden eagles soared in lazy sweeping circles. Down the shore sandpipers called and a handful of redshanks flickered with white-barred wings over the water.

Smiler put down the rucksack and said brokenly, "Thank you. . . . Thanks, Laura. I hope . . . well, I hope you don't get into trouble over this —"

"Oh, Sammy!" Suddenly Laura put her arms round him and hugged him, kissing his cheek, and then for a moment their lips met. It was a moment Smiler would always remember, her lips against his, her loose hair in his face, and the slow shake of her shoulders under his hands.

The next moment he stepped away from her and picked up the rucksack. Two yards apart they looked at one another, each with tears in their eyes. Then Smiler said, "Goodbye, Laura. Don't worry, I'll be back sometime."

He saw Laura's face go slowly stubborn and set. The look was one he had often seen before, and she said firmly, "You'd better be back sometime, Sammy. You'd just better for I'm not forgetting you've made me a promise to ask a certain question one day. Now, away with you,

you daft loon, and keep your eyes skinned for the police – they'll be hoppin' mad about this. And let them be!"

* * *

Six hours later when the cars moving along the road had turned their sidelights on, Smiler stepped out of the cover of a clump of bushes at the roadside and raised a hand for a lift to a car coming up the road. He did it without much hope because many cars had passed, ignoring his signals.

But this car stopped a few yards past him. It was a very old four-seater touring car with a canvas hood which had been patched in a few places. The paintwork was shabby and the nearside back mudguard had a big dent in it. As Smiler came abreast of it, the driver leaned across and looked out of the near-side window. He was a large-faced, middle-aged man wearing a battered straw boater with a coloured ribbon around it. He had a black, thickly waxed sergeant-major's moustache that curled into sharp points at each end. In his mouth was a pipe with a piece of insulating tape around the broken stem. His dark eyes held a lazy, good humoured twinkle.

He said in a slow, easy voice, "Where you headin' for, me dear?"

Smiler said, "I dunno exactly."

The man chuckled, "Destination unknown. Good as any. Hop in."

Smiler opened the car door. As he did so the man said, "Mind Scampi. You'll have to nurse him on your lap. Dump your rucksack with the rest of the junk in the back."

In the half-light Smiler saw, curled up on the shabby leather seat, a very large Siamese cat. The man reached over and lifted the cat. Then, when Smiler was settled, he dumped the cat on to Smiler's lap. The cat opened one baleful eye at the disturbance and then settled to sleep on Smiler's knees.

As the man drove off, he said casually, "Don't be surprised if I make a smart detour now and then suddenlike – but just at the moment, me dear, I'm not anxious to meet any of the boys in blue. Little matter of an unpaid hotel bill at my last stop. Lovely night, ain't it? Lovely, indeed, after the weather we've had. Lovely night, quiet roads, destinations unknown – what more could a man ask for? Beautiful. Beautiful."

For the first time in many hours, almost the edge of a smile touched Smiler's lips.

* * *

POSTSCRIPT: *In Smiler's room at Elphinstone castle, Sir Alec was reading a note that had been left for him. It ran:*

Dear Sir Alec,

    Since my father wont be back yet there are things I got to do for myself. Im sorry leaving without saying good bye, but Laura will explain.

    I hope Bacon wont be much trouble till I can come for him.

Yours faithfully,
Samuel Miles

The Painted Tent

1

The Duchess Takes
a Look Ahead

Smiler surfaced slowly from a deep and dream-filled sleep. In the few moments before he opened his eyes Smiler had no idea where he was or what had happened to him. His arms and legs ached; there was a crick in his back, and a heavy weight on his lap.

He opened his eyes. Resting on his lap was a large Siamese cat with a torn left ear. Smiler found that he was sitting in the front of a small car. Through the windscreen he could see the slope of a heather-covered hill and a clump of red-berried rowan trees. Beside the road ran a small stream, swirling and cascading over sun-bathed grey boulders and flanked by tall bracken growths. A pair of hooded crows flew out of the trees and a yellow wagtail dipped and bowed on one of the stream boulders.

A shadow fell across the window at his side and a man's voice said cheerfully, "Wakey-wakey! Go dip your face in the burn, lad, and then there's a mug of coffee waiting."

Standing by the door was a large-faced, middle-aged man wearing a battered straw boater with a coloured ribbon around it. He had a black, thickly waxed sergeant-major's moustache that curled into sharp points at each end. His dark eyes held a lazy, good-humoured twinkle.

Memory coming slowly back to him, Smiler said politely, "Good morning, Mr. Jago."

"And a good morning to you, Samuel Miles." The man lifted the cat — which Smiler now remembered was called Scampi — from his lap, and went on, "Down to the burn with you."

Stiffly Smiler made his way to the stream, splashed water over his head and face, and then wiped himself on his handkerchief. The water was ice-cold. It brought the colour back to his cheeks, and drove away the fuzziness of the uncomfortable night. He realized now that he must have slept while Mr. Jago went on driving through the night. Mr. Jago, he thought, looked as fresh as a daisy. And Mr. Jimmy Jago, Smiler acknowledged, had been good to him for he had picked him up late on the Fort William road and had helped him to get well away from trouble.

Going back to the car Smiler said to himself — for Smiler was a great one for talking to himself in times of trouble or doubt – "You were lucky, Samuel M., that Mr. Jago came along." Although most people called him Smiler he didn't himself much care for the name. He preferred Samuel Miles, or better still, Samuel M., which was what his father called him. At the thought of his father a shadow passed across Smiler's thoughts.

At the back of the car, which was a very old four-seater tourer, were set out three small wooden boxes. On one of them was a camping-stove, roaring gently to itself while a saucepan of coffee simmered on top of it.

Mr. Jago, opening a tin of sardines for Scampi, looked up and said, "Sit yourself down, lad, and take some coffee. No food for us – we'll get breakfast later. But animals is different. If Scampi don't get his regularly, then he'll howl his head off until he does."

Smiler sat on his box, cradling a mug of hot coffee in his hands, and Mr. Jago sat on his box with his mug. Scampi crouched on the grass and ate his sardines from a small saucer. Scampi was far too great an aristocrat to eat anything straight from the can.

Mr. Jago sat there, eyeing Smiler, and saw nothing to turn him from an opinion he had formed very soon after he had picked him up the previous night. The lad was in trouble and, more than that, the lad was down in the dumps. Jimmy Jago had no difficulty in recognizing this because he had often been in trouble himself – though not so often down in the dumps. He was a good-looking, healthy, strong boy – somewhere around sixteen years old, Jimmy guessed. Yes, a likely-looking lad, tallish, fair-haired, well-built, with a friendly, heavily freckled, squarish face, and he had a pair of angelic blue eyes which, when he smiled, made him look as though butter wouldn't melt in his mouth. Not that he, Mr. Jago, was going to be fooled by that. Boys were boys and trouble clung to them like their shadows – and so it should be because that was what in the end made men of them, good, bad or indifferent.

Mr. Jago finished his coffee and, while Smiler was having a second mug, he lit his battered old pipe, tipped his boater back on his head and, giving Smiler a solemn look, suddenly offset by a slow wink, said, "Right, lad – catechism time."

Smiler, puzzled, said, "Catechism time?"

Mr. Jago grinned. "I was well educated, though there's times when I prefer it not to be obvious. Catechism, from the verb to catechise; meaning to instruct or inform by question and answer. I ask the questions – and you answer 'em if you're in the mood. As the Duchess would say, 'Trouble shared is trouble spared.' "

"Who's the Duchess, sir?"

"We'll come to her later – if necessary. All right, then – catechism.

You for it or against it?"

"Well, I . . . I don't know, sir."

"Let's try it then. Full name?"

"Samuel Miles, sir."

"Ever used any others?"

Smiler hesitated. Because he liked the man and was grateful to him and was naturally truthful anyway, unless it was vital to be otherwise, he said, "Now and again, sir."

"A fair answer. Would have had to say the same myself. Right, then — age? And don't keep calling me *sir*."

"Sixteen in October."

"Well, that's only a few days off. Place of birth?"

"Bristol."

"A noble city. Almost as good as Plymouth."

Smiler grinned. "Is that where you were born?"

"Thereabouts — so I'm told. But right or wrong, I'm a real Devon man." As he spoke, his voice was suddenly rich and ripe with a West-Country accent. He went on, "Parents?"

Smiler's face clouded. Slowly he said, "My mother's dead, sir. A long time ago."

"I see. And your father?" Mr. Jago saw Smiler's lips tighten and tremble a little, and with rare understanding said quietly, "Well, we can leave that one for now. Got any relations in Bristol still?"

Smiler said, "Oh, yes. My sister Ethel. She's married to Albert — he's an electrical engineer and plumber. But I don't want to go back to them. Not yet, anyway."

"Nobody suggested it, lad. Now then — what put you on the road, all your gear in a rucksack, flagging me down at nine o'clock of night on a lonely Highland road? Trouble, eh?"

"Yes, sir."

"Police or personal?"

"Well, a bit of both, really. But I'd rather not——"

"Of course. We'll skip it, but keep our eyes skinned for the police." Mr. Jago grinned. "Splendid body of men, as I should know from long experience. How are you fixed financially?"

"I'm all right. I was working and made some money."

"Like work?"

"Of course. If it's the right kind."

"Fair answer. Well then — that about clears it up. No need for the jury to retire to consider a verdict. It's as plain as the freckled nose on your face that you're a case for the Duchess, so we'd better make tracks for her. Take us a couple of days. Maybe a bit more."

"Who's the Duchess, sir?"

Mr. Jago leaned back and blew a cloud of smoke into the sunlit air. A big smile creased his face as he twirled one end of his fine moustache. "The Duchess, my lad? Well, now . . . how would I describe her? She's God's gift to anything in trouble. She's directly descended from Mother Ceres. She's got green fingers that could make a pencil sprout leaves if she put it in the ground. She can talk the human language and a lot of others. She's an angel — though she'd need a thirty-foot wing-span to lift her off the ground. She knows the past and the future and has a rare understanding of the present — and she's got a temper like a force nine gale if you get on the wrong side of her!"

"Crikeys!"

"Exactly, Samuel. Exactly. And she's what you need to straighten out whatever it is that's bothering you. So let's get going."

As Mr. Jago rose and began to pack up the car Smiler said, "Is she really a duchess?"

Mr. Jago nodded. "She is indeed, lad. The only one of her kind, but not the sort you're thinking of because, if she were, then, I suppose, I would be Lord Jimmy Jago — seeing that I'm her son."

*　　*　　*

So, in the company of Jimmy Jago and Scampi, Smiler began the long journey southwards down the length of the country. Sometimes they kept to the main roads and sometimes, when Jimmy obeyed some instinct peculiar to him, they worked their way along side lanes and made detours around the big cities. Sometimes they ate in small cafés or at pull-ups for truck drivers. Sometimes they bought their food and ate under the open sky at the edge of a field or wood, and always they slept out with Smiler on the front seat and Jimmy — because of his greater size — in the back, and Scampi — who liked the warmth of a human body — slept sometimes curled up with one, sometimes with the other.

As they went Smiler became more and more resigned to his parting from the good friends he had made in Scotland and the little world he had known there. But never for long could he forget his worry about his father, or still the natural fear he had that the police might find him and send him back to the approved school from which he had originally escaped — and to which he meant never to return if he could avoid it because he had been sent there in the first place for something he had never done.

Jimmy was amusing company but, for all their chat and the stories

Jimmy told as they travelled the roads in the ancient car, Smiler never came to know much about Jimmy himself. And he was far too polite to ask any direct questions. Jimmy suffered from no such inhibitions and during their journey he came to know a lot about Smiler – and guessed much more. It was the result of Jimmy's gleanings that brought a surprise for Smiler on the morning of their third day of travel. He was fast asleep in the passenger seat when he was awakened by the car being brought to a stop. Smiler saw that they were parked in a street of small neat suburban villas. Smiler recognized at once where he was. It was a Bristol street only a little way from the one in which his sister Ethel and her husband Albert lived.

As he stared puzzled at Jimmy he was greeted by one of the man's slow winks.

"That's right, lad. Bristol. I don't aim to have any near and dear ones worrying about what might have happened to you. Nip along and tell 'em you're all right and not to worry. I'll be waiting."

Five minutes later Smiler eased open the door of Albert's workshop at the back of the house in which he had always lived while his father was away at sea.

Albert looked around from his bench where he was turning a thread on a piece of piping and stared at Smiler. Then slowly he smiled broadly, nodded his head, and said, "Now, ain't that odd? I was only just thinkin' about you."

Smiler, who knew he was all right with Albert, that Albert was always on his side, said, "Where's Sister Ethel?"

"Don't worry about her. She's off to the super-market. Just gone."

Though he was very fond of his sister, Smiler had always been in her bad books, chiefly because – no matter how hard he tried not to – he messed up her neat little house and, according to her, was going to the dogs with the bad company he kept. Sister Ethel had a natural instinct for magnifying and exaggerating the smallest upset into a mountain of trouble and tragedy.

Smiler said, "That's all right then. But I haven't come back for good, Albert."

"Fair enough, Sammy, fair enough. Just a friendly call to say everything's all right, eh? You chose the right day. The police was here yesterday this time. But I'll have to tell Ethel about this . . . maybe this evening over supper cocoa. You all right for money and everything?"

"Yes, thanks. I worked in Scotland and had some good friends, and there's another waiting. He's going to fix me up . . ." Slowly Smiler's lower lip began to tremble and then he burst out, "Oh, Albert . . . did you . . . did you hear about Dad?"

"That I did. Police told us. Missed his boat in Montevideo and no sign of him since. But that ain't worryin' you, is it? Because if it is — don't let it. I've known your Dad since before you was born. Not the first time he's missed his ship. Not the first time he's disappeared into the blue. But he always turns up."

"But something bad could have happened to him, Albert."

"Think so? Not me. Nor should you. You're just like him. Your sister might worry about you, for instance, when you took off into the blue from that approved school. But did I? No. Like father, like son, I said. Never lost a wink of sleep. That's how you want to look at it, Sammy. Two of a kind, you are. Always land on your feet."

What Albert said suddenly struck Smiler as sensible. He hadn't thought about it that way before. Convinced of his own innocence he had run off from the approved school, kept out of the way of the police, found jobs, had adventures and made many friends — and had always been sure that in the end things would turn out right. Particularly the moment when his father got back to help him. *But — all the time people were worrying about him like he was worrying now about his father when there was no reason to worry.*

Albert grinned. "Sinks home, don't it? So, don't worry about your Dad. When you least expect it, he'll turn up. Always did, always will. When you least expect him he'll come marchin' in through the door, breezy as a west wind."

"You really believe that?"

"Yes. And if I was a bettin' man — which I was until I married your sister — I'd bet on it. Still, there's one thing — wherever you fetch up, just now and then drop us a line. Not to the house. Just to me care of the General Post Office, Bristol. I'd just like to be able to give a bit of news to Ethel now and then. Like that — if the police come askin' again, which they will, I can say truthfully, 'No, we ain't had no letter from him here.' Strict truth." He winked.

So Smiler promised that he would write sometimes, and then he left well before his sister was likely to be back.

In the car again with Jimmy, he slowly began to feel much happier. "Samuel M.," he told himself, "you've been making mountains out of molehills. Leave Scotland you had to because of the police. But worryin' about Dad . . . well, Albert's right. All seamen miss their boats now and then. Always fall on their feet, though. Like a cat with nine lives."

Scampi sitting on his lap purred as though he understood and approved.

*   *   *

From Bristol they went down through Somerset, taking their time and keeping to the side roads. In the mildness of early October, the light of the declining sun cast a pale golden wash over the country. They climbed the Quantocks and then on to the high stretches of Exmoor with the silver spread of the sea away to their right. They went down into small river valleys, through the white- and pink-washed huddles of old villages, and now and again far away to their left they got glimpses of the high tors of distant Dartmoor.

Jimmy, back in his own West Country, took great gulps of the mild, clear air, sucking it in as though he had been a fish out of water too long. And because he was a well-read, self-educated man and had no reason to disguise the fact at this moment, he told Smiler – who had an appetite for information and knowledge as big as any he ever carried to a well-filled table – many things about his land. He told him of the Monmouth Rebellion on the Somerset marshes, and the merciless Judge Jeffreys who had brought death and exile to the rebels; of the story of *Lorna Doone* and the wild Carver family who had terrorized the countryside; of *Westward Ho!* and Amyas Leigh; of real people like the great Drake; of Frobisher, Raleigh and of the sturdy, dour Cornish miners and their support for Bishop Trelawney. And Jimmy taught Smiler – who had a naturally good voice – songs about them, songs new and old . . . *Judge Jeffreys was a wicked man, he sent my father to Van Diemens land . . . And shall Trelawney die? Then twenty thousand Cornishmen shall know the reason why . . . There was a little man come from the West, he married a wife she was not of the best . . .*

For Smiler, it was almost as though he were with his father, for they were both great ones for singing together. Because of this and also of what Albert had said, Smiler felt happier than he had done for a long time (although it was only a few days) and his troubles lifted because in the young there is a natural good balance of the emotions, and dark thoughts like stones sink from sight in the sparkling pool of the present.

But there was one moment when Smiler realized that Mr. Jimmy Jago had his dark troubles, too. Once he stopped where they could get a good view of distant Dartmoor. When Smiler said that he would like to go there some day Jimmy, without looking at him, said in an almost angry voice, "Aye, lad, it's a wild, beautiful place – but there's many there now who could wish they'd never seen it, could wish they were a million miles away from it."

Smiler knew at once what he meant.

He said, "You mean the people in prison there? In Princetown jail?"

Jimmy turned and looked at him and said, "What else would I mean?"

When they drove on it was some time before Jimmy's good spirits came back. But back they did come. An hour later they dropped down into the valley of the River Taw, which had its source high up on distant Dartmoor and flowed to the sea at Barnstaple and out into the wide estuary to meet its sister river the Torridge.

They crossed the river by an ancient stone bridge and then the road began to twist and climb along the sides of a small valley through which ran a wide brook. The sides of the valley were patched with woodland and stubble fields and, high over a plantation of firs, Smiler saw three buzzards wheeling and soaring.

They climbed away from the valley, lost sight of it, and then came back to it down a steep hill. At the bottom of the hill was a long, low farmhouse, slate-roofed, with white-washed stone walls. To one side of it were stables, two large stone barns and, beyond them, green meadows and patches of woodland flanking the sides of the twisting brook.

Mr. Jago drove through the open farm gate into the wide gravel space before the house. As the car was pulled up Scampi jumped from Smiler's lap through the open car-door window and disappeared around the corner of the house.

Jimmy Jago grinned. "He's off to see his missus. Travellin' man is Scampi but he's always glad to get back."

As Smiler and Jimmy got out of the car the front door of the farm opened and a woman stepped out into the wide porchway. She was a tall, very plump woman of middle age. She came out to greet them like a galleon under full sail, moving for all her bulk as though her feet only just touched the ground. Her hair was red, a tight mop of close curls, and she wore dangling earrings made from silver coins. The ample folds of her long green dress flapped in the valley breeze. All over the dress was a close design of birds, animals, flowers, signs of the zodiac and other symbols. (During all the time Smiler was to be at the farm he was always discovering some new symbol or bird or animal on the dress. In fact, he sometimes had the feeling that the whole design changed every time she wore it.) Her plump face was jolly and creased with a smile and she had soft brown eyes dark as the waters of a woodland pool.

She cried, "Jimmy!" The next moment she had clamped her arms around him and – though he was a big man – it seemed to Smiler that he momentarily disappeared into the green, multi-patterned folds of her dress. She smacked two great kisses on his face and then released him.

Jimmy stepped back, straightened his boater, and said, "Surprised to see me, Ma?"

"And why should I be? The news was on the wind an hour ago. Yin got it first." Her voice like herself was large and jolly.

"Yin," said Jimmy to Smiler, "is Scampi's wife. And this lady, Sammy, is my mother." Then to his mother he said, "Meet Samuel Miles, Ma. He's a friend of mine." Then to Smiler he said, "Sammy – the Duchess."

Smiler held out his hand to the Duchess and said, "I'm very pleased to meet you, ma'am."

The Duchess took his hand, shook it warmly and vigorously and said, "Welcome to Bullaybrook Farm, boy." Then cocking her head to one side she eyed him closely and enquired, "Libra? Am I right?"

Smiler, puzzled, said, "Please, ma'am?"

"Your zodiac sign," said Jimmy. "When were you born?"

"October the tenth."

"Then it is Libra," declared the Duchess. "And this is a good day for you, boy. Yes, a good day. Mercury's not bothering your sign."

"I brought him along, Ma," said Jimmy, "because he's in trouble. Thought you could sort him out a bit – meantime he's got broad shoulders and good hands so he could be useful around the place."

"Why not? But remember, boy, for the next three days always go out of the house right foot first and come in left foot first." She gave him a wink and continued, "Come on then – into the house."

She turned and sailed before them and Smiler was careful – even though he felt that it was really a joke – to step over the threshold with his left foot first.

*　　*　　*

That night Smiler lay awake in bed for a long time sorting things out. He had been given a small room at the back of the house which looked across to the brook. There were four bedrooms and a bathroom on the first floor. Down below as you came through the porch door was a large hall, to one side of which was a dining-room and then a long farm kitchen, stone-flagged. On the other side was a large sitting-room with an open stone fireplace, the ceiling dark-raftered with oak beams. From there, now, Smiler could just catch the faint mumble of the voices of Jimmy and the Duchess as they talked. A picture of the room was clear in his mind.

Before the fire were a sofa and chintz-covered armchairs. A wide, circular table stood in the middle of the room and there was a big grandfather clock just inside the door. But what had interested Smiler most were the walls of the room. They were covered from floor to ceiling with pictures, framed photographs and old posters and prints, and every one of them had something to do with circuses or fairs. There were photographs of liberty horses, of tiger and lion acts, of performing elephants and seals, of high-wire and trampoline artistes, and trained dogs and pigeons. Some of the photographs were old and faded and some were quite new. The posters were past and present advertisements for travelling circuses, bold, garish colours flaming in the mellow light of the room. Over the fireplace itself was a large oil-painting showing the head and shoulders of a clown with a bulbous red nose, his face masked with traditional makeup, and on his head a battered old tophat. Even under the make-up a half-sad, half-comic expression showed through from the real man. At the foot of the picture was a little gold plaque with the words *The Duke* printed on it in black.

Smiler guessed – and later learned – that the Duke had been the Duchess's husband. A lot of things had become clear to Smiler before he went to bed. While they were having tea in front of the fire Scampi had come into the room followed by another Siamese cat. The two had settled on the hearth and the other cat had started to groom Scampi. The other cat was Yin, Scampi's wife, who was showing her pleasure at having him back from his travels with Jimmy.

Later, while the Duchess was getting the supper, Jimmy had taken Smiler up to his room and explained to him that the Duke had been dead for five years. The Duchess, who had travelled the circuses as a fortune teller, had retired to this farm where – apart from the normal farm work – she took care of a few retired or sick circus animals and boarded others when some circus acts were off the road. Her busiest time, Jimmy said, was just after Christmas when most circus acts took a rest before starting the Spring travels. At the moment there were very few animal boarders at the farm.

Jimmy said, "After you've had a chat with the Duchess tomorrow and if you want to stay and like animals there's a job here until you get yourself sorted out. And" – a distant look came into his eyes – "sorting things out sometimes takes a long time, as you'll learn as you grow older. Now, unpack your gear, and then you can take a stroll round the place before supper. There's over a hundred acres, mostly wood and hill pasture and over a mile of the Bullay brook. But don't go poking into any of the barns yet or the Ancients will take against you."

"The Ancients?"

"You'll meet 'em. I wouldn't spoil your pleasure."

Lying in bed now, seeing through his window the October sky stippled with bright stars, Smiler remembered how, coming back from his stroll around the brook meadows, he had walked into the farm kitchen and had found the Duchess and Jimmy talking to one another. But it was in a language that meant nothing to Smiler – though later he learned that it was Romany, for the Jago family were of true gypsy descent. Just for a moment, before they saw him, he had the feeling that an argument was going on between the two. The impression had been brief but the memory lingered with Smiler. He wondered now if the Duchess and Jimmy had their troubles just as he had.

Outside a little owl called to its mate and the sound of the brook over its stony bed came in a ceaseless murmur. Smiler began to drift off into sleep and, as he did so, he had a feeling of loneliness which could not be fought down. Behind him in Scotland he had left all his friends . . . the face of Laura, his girl friend, floated before him, cheeks sun-tanned, dark hair lifting in the loch breeze and her deep brown eyes alive with laughter. How long would it be before he saw her again, how long before he could get out of trouble and do all the things he longed to do? And then his father . . . He sniffed, then tightened his lips against the misery that threatened to claim him. Five minutes later, when the little owl called again, Smiler was deep in sleep.

*   *   *

The next morning Smiler had breakfast in the farm kitchen. He had porridge, two fried eggs and four rashers of bacon, three slices of toast and marmalade, and a large mug of milky coffee, all of which he polished off with ease.

The Duchess nodded approvingly and said, "That's the way I like to see a boy eat. Some folk treat their food as though it was going to bite them. Now then, come along with me and we'll get you settled."

She led the way out of the back door and across a yard to a little walled garden which lay behind one of the barns. There was a small green lawn in its centre and flower-beds all around. Standing on the lawn, almost covering it, was a tent. But it was no ordinary tent. Its shape reminded Smiler of illustrations he had seen in history books of the battlefield pavilions knights in armour had used. It was supported at its four corners by stout poles and its roof was domed, the canvas stretched over a cane framework. From a tall spiked flagpole on the top of the dome a red and white silk pennant flapped in the morning breeze. The tent canvas was striped in red, yellow and blue and over the half-open door was a wooden signboard inscribed:

THE DUCHESS OF MINTORO –
THE FUTURE AN OPEN BOOK
Patronised by Royalty

Seeing the look in Smiler's eyes, the Duchess said, "Beautiful, isn't it? I've spent more than half my life working in it. But not since the Duke died. Except for the odd friend now and then. Stands there all through the good weather."

She went into the tent and Smiler, a bit nervous, followed her. She sat down at a cloth-covered table and nodded to him to sit opposite her. She draped a small silk scarf over her red curls and said, "Give me your hands, boy."

Smiler held out his hands and the Duchess took first the left one and then the right one and studied their palms and after a while said, "Young hands, young heart and the future only just beginning to write itself there. But the lines are good, the signs are right. You'll have your share of troubles and your share of happiness. At your age – even though I could tell you more – there's no need to know more. But this I'll tell you – you'll never work inside four walls, but you'll work with your hands and your head in a way no countryman or farmer does."

"I want to be a vet.," said Smiler.

"Maybe. Wanting comes before doing and the future is first shaped by the past and the present and then tidied up and fixed by the Great One." The Duchess released his hands and after a smile and a chuckle added, "And I'm glad to see you keep your nails clean, boy. That's a good sign. Hands are the tools God gave us. We must respect His gift always. Now then, let's get down to the present troubles and see what we can see."

The Duchess reached out to a sidetable and lifted from it a small stand on which stood a crystal ball. It was covered by a silk cloth which she took off. She made Smiler put the palms of his hands about it for a few moments. Then she signalled to him to take his hands away, gave the crystal a quick wipe with the silk and began to stare in it, saying, "Keep quiet. Don't interrupt, and shut your eyes."

Obediently Smiler shut his eyes. Although he was not quite sure in his mind whether he really believed that the Duchess could read the future and the past, he decided that it would be bad manners to decide that she couldn't. So, he began to think about Laura in Scotland, and his father who had missed his ship at Montevideo, and about the day which seemed so long ago now when all his troubles had begun back in Bristol, of the afternoon when an old lady had been jostled off the pavement by a fair-haired boy and her handbag stolen. A policeman seeing the act had gone after the thief. Rounding a corner he had spotted the boy running down the pavement and had finally caught him, still holding the handbag.

The boy had been Smiler, but it was not Smiler who had taken the bag. He had been standing round the corner when a boy he knew – with fair hair like himself, one Johnny Pickering, and no friend of his – came rushing past him and had tossed him the handbag, shouting "Hide it!" Smiler had been caught running away because he was running after Johnny Pickering to make him take the handbag back. But in the juvenile court the parents of Johnny Pickering had sworn that their son had been at home all afternoon and that Samuel Miles was lying to save himself. Smiler had been sent to an approved school but had quickly run away, determined to keep his freedom until his father came back on his boat, the *Kentucky Master*, and could sort things out for him. But Smiler's father had failed to rejoin his boat at Montevideo and the police in Scotland had caught up with Smiler. He had had to go on the run again which was when he had met Jimmy Jago. . . .

Smiler heard the Duchess's voice coming to him, a dreamy far-away voice cutting into his thoughts.

"I see water . . . nothing but water. No . . . now there's a boat. A small boat and a girl in it. She's brown-haired and holding – drat, the boat's gone. . . . Now then, what's this? More water and another boat. But a big one this time and there's a lot of men all lying around in the sun on the deck and one of them's got something. . . . Oh, yes – it's a mouth organ, and he's playing to them——"

Smiler opened his eyes and said quickly, "That's my father. He plays the mouth organ. Is he all right?"

The Duchess said nothing; she just stared at the crystal ball. Her dark brown eyes were fixed as though she were hypnotised, and her big, jolly face was slack and expressionless.

Conscious that he had disobeyed her orders, Smiler closed his eyes and kept silent. After a moment or two the Duchess began to speak again and her voice, now sounding far, far away, gave Smiler an eerie feeling.

". . . Everything's whirling, like coloured snowflakes . . . Birds, animals, people. . . . Ah, there's a room, a big room, the ceiling so high it's lost in shadows, and a grand stairway . . . and oil paintings of fine ladies and noble gentlemen . . . and suits of armour. There are people there, and holly and mistletoe hanging. . . . The girl is there, and the man on the boat, and another man, tall and white-haired and bearded . . . And, yes, yes – you're there Samuel Miles . . . You're all together and there's happiness around you – Oh, no!" The duchess's voice suddenly broke off. Then, her voice quite different, she went on, "Blood . . . Oh, I don't want to see . . . suddenly such darkness over the bright morning sun . . . and there's a man running . . . running . . . running for his . . . No, no, I don't want to see it."

The Duchess gave a sudden groan and stopped speaking. Smiler, scared, opened his eyes. The Duchess was leaning back in her chair, her hands over her eyes, her shoulders shaking.

Not knowing what to do, Smiler reached out and touched her and said, "Are you all right, ma'am?"

The Duchess dropped her hands from her face, gave herself a little shake, and then suddenly smiled.

"I'm all right, boy. There's nothing to worry about. Sometimes the ball goes wild and mixes up the futures. You know the girl and the tall man with the beard?"

"Yes, ma'am."

"And the man with the mouth organ?"

"That's my father."

"Then you need have no worry. Time is going to bring you all together. Whatever happens between now and then, there's that happiness waiting for you."

Smiler considered this and, although he certainly hoped it was going to be true, he didn't see how anyone could ever really see into the future. He said, "You really know that from the crystal ball, ma'am?"

"Of course, boy."

"But . . . well . . . can there be a magic like that? I mean———"

"I know what you mean, boy. You can't understand how anyone can believe in magic?"

"Well, only in a sort of a way, ma'am."

The Duchess smiled. "Then you want to open your eyes, Samuel Miles, and see the magic right under everyone's noses every day of life. You live on a great ball called the earth that spins through space like a top and nobody falls off – that's magic. The sun rises and sets each day, and the seasons come and go – that's all magic. The swallows fly to Africa for the Winter and then back here in the Spring – that's magic. But the greatest magic is life itself. The fact that you and every other living thing is alive is the greatest magic of all. Nobody knows how or when it happened except the Great One. What's more, if we can remember the past and live the present, what's so odd about some of us being able to look into the future? It's just a gift, like other people can make music, write poetry, or invent machines that take others to the moon. Magic, Samuel Miles. Every breath we take is part of magic. And my magic is to be able to see a little farther ahead than most other people, and so far as you are concerned you've been told that one day you, your father, that girl, and the tall white-haired man will all be together. Does that chase your worries away?"

"Yes, ma'am, it does. But . . . well, what about the man that was running?"

The Duchess gave Smiler a steady look and then said evenly, "You don't have to worry about him. Just for a moment his future got crossed with yours. Just as telephone calls get mixed up sometimes."

The Duchess took the silk cloth and draped it over the crystal ball. With a warm smile she said, "Right, Samuel Miles – now I want to hear all about yourself and your troubles. Take your time and start from the beginning."

So Smiler told her everything about himself and of all his trouble; starting from the time when Johnny Pickering had come running around the corner and tossed the old lady's handbag to him, through all his adventures since he had run away from the approved school, right up to the moment that Jimmy Jago had picked him up on the road in Scotland.

When he had finished the Duchess said, "Well, you aren't the first that's come to this house with the police after them. Circus and Romany folk sometimes have to follow their own laws – and the police don't like that. But if you keep your fingers crossed and your eyes open you should have no trouble here. The local policeman is a friend of ours. You'd like to stay here, would you?"

"Yes, please, ma'am."

"Well, the wages are small, the work hard, and the food good. And since, if you're going to begin something, there's no time like the present, I'll take you over to the Ancients because you'll be working under them."

A bit diffidently, Smiler asked. "Who are the Ancients, ma'am? Are they men?"

"Of course they are."

"And are they very old?"

The Duchess chuckled, her fat chins bobbing and her curls shaking. "They're both old – that's why they're called the Ancients. Bill and Bob Old. That's their name. And a word of warning – never play cards with them for money."

2

The Starlight Men

The Duchess took Smiler across the yard to one of the stone barns where he met Bob and Bill Old. They were twin brothers in their early fifties, small, sturdy-looking men with weather-brown, wrinkled faces, bright, mischievous-looking eyes and the perky, cheeky air of a couple of jackdaws. So far as Smiler could see, there was no way of telling them apart except by the clothes they wore. Above his gum boots and corduroy trousers Bob wore a green sweater and on his head, cocked saucily over his iron-grey hair, was a green woollen bonnet with a white bob on the top. Bill's dress was the same, except that his sweater and bonnet were red. But after a few days Smiler realized that the clothes were no sure guide because they swopped clothes some days according to their fancy. They lived a bachelor life in a small cottage up the hill from the farm. Smiler never learned where they had come from or what they had done before they began to work for the Duchess, except that he could guess from their talk that they had both been travelling men and knew a great deal about circuses, fairs and gypsy life. This last he knew because when they didn't want him to know what they were saying they would talk in the Romany language that the Duchess and Jimmy sometimes used.

The Duchess said to them, "Samuel Miles – your new hand. He's a good lad; work him hard, and treat him fair. He's been in a spot of trouble, still is – so he's one of our kind." Then, with a look at Smiler, she nodded at the men in turn, saying, "That's Bob – and that's Bill. At least, I think it is." With a chuckle she ruffled Smiler's hair and swept regally out of the barn.

The two men looked at one another and then at Smiler. Then they walked slowly round him and, as they did so, Bill said, "Good shoulders."

Bob said, "Stands well."

Bill said, "Wind sound, I should think."

Bob said, "Let's see how he moves."

Bill said to Smiler, "Trot."

Smiler said, "Please?"

Bob said, "Trot. Once round the barn."

Suspecting that he was having his leg pulled Smiler gave a grin and solemnly trotted round the confined space of the barn.

Bill said, "Nice action."

Bob said, "Sprinter?"

Bill shook his head. "No, stayer."

Bob said, "He'll do then."

Bill said, "Welcome, Samuel Miles."

"Thank you," said Smiler.

Bob said, "You like playing cards?"

Smiler grinned, "Not for money."

Bill said sadly, "She's warned him."

"Pity," said Bob. "Only thing left is work. This way lad."

Bill gave Smiler a nod and a wink and went out of the barn, and Bob took Smiler in hand, explaining very solemnly what he would be expected to do. For Smiler it presented no problems because it was going to be much the same work that he had been doing in Scotland. There were animals to be fed, cages and pens to be mucked out, bedding to be carried, and corn sacks and hay bales to be humped, and then helping in all the hundred and one seasonal jobs that had to be done around the farm.

The barn they were in was used as a store and a garage for the tractor and other farm implements. The other barn, which was fitted out with cages and pens, held the boarders which were in residence at the moment. Outside in the large field which ran from the back of the farm down to the brook, there were at the moment two donkeys, a shetland pony, and the house cow. Between the two barns was a short run of stables for the horses that would be coming during the off season. At the moment they were empty. Bill explained that he and Bob, after they had left work and gone up to their cottage, had been taking it in turns to come down around ten o'clock at night to see that everything was all right in the barn which housed the birds and animals. Now, since Smiler was on hand in the farm, this was to be his duty. Before he went to bed he would make a last inspection and, if he heard a commotion at night, he would have to go out to attend to any trouble.

Smiler decided that he liked Bob and Bill, though he found it difficult to know when they were being serious or pulling his leg. Up in his room after work where he was getting cleaned up and changed for supper Smiler decided, too, that it had been a lucky moment that had brought Jimmy Jago along the road at the right time to pick him up. "You were lucky, Samuel M.," he told himself. "And let's hope the Duchess is right about what she saw in the crystal ball."

When Smiler went down to supper he was surprised to find that Jimmy Jago was not there, though he had seen him around during the day.

"Has Mr. Jago gone off again?" he asked the Duchess.

"Yes, he has, Samuel," said the Duchess. "Jimmy goes and comes like the wind. He's got restless feet and he doesn't like a roof over his head long. He's always on the go, buying a bit here and selling a bit there, and God knows what else, and never an answer to a straight question. You'll get used to it."

"But Scampi's not gone."

"No — " she grinned — "I expect Yin wouldn't let him. Now eat your supper and, while you're doing it, tell me all about this business of yours of wanting to be a vet."

So Smiler, between mouthfuls, told her all about his ambition to be a vet, and then to marry Laura Mackay, his girl friend, who was going to have a farm one day so they could combine the two things. When he had finished, the Duchess eyed him severely and said, "With the education you tell me you've had, you've set yourself an uphill struggle — but that's all to the good when you're young. Well, if it's education you're after we'll have to see what we can do about it once you're settled in. Meanwhile, when you go up to your room, take this with you."

She put something on the table between them. It was a small model in coloured clays of a boy with fair hair, whose shoulders were hunched forward slightly, supporting a small pebble which he was carrying like a rucksack.

"What's that for, ma'am?"

"It's for you — but isn't you, Samuel. It's that Johnny Pickering of yours."

"But — I don't understand?"

"It's more magic, Samuel. Not black magic, but good magic. He did you harm, he caused you all your trouble. He's got a bad conscience because no one can escape their conscience. I've put a spell on him. Not a bad one, but a naggling one." The Duchess tapped the tip of her large nose. "A niggling, naggling one. Keep it in your room and one day you'll find that pebble's come unstuck and tumbled off. That will be the day when things will begin to go right for you. You'll see."

"You really mean that, ma'am?"

"Of course. And you must really believe it, Samuel. Really believe it. You know why?"

"No, ma'am."

"Because the strongest part of all magic is belief. When that pebble falls . . . well, you'll see."

*   *   *

That night before he went to bed Smiler walked across to the second barn to see that the birds and animals were all right. (Later on he never bothered to go down through the house, but would step out of his bedroom window on to the roof of the kitchen extension and then jump down to the path. To get back he always kept a couple of boxes handy to step up on so that he could reach the roof.)

He unlocked the small door of the barn with the key which was hidden under the water-butt. Bob had already conducted him around the inmates of the barn and he knew most of their names and some of their histories. He switched on the overhead light and walked down the length of the barn.

Just now most of the large pens and cages were empty. In one was a chimpanzee called Freddie who was convalescing from a bad attack of bronchitis and had been left there by a circus which had been touring the West Country. Freddie, curled up in a bed of hay, looked up as Smiler came to his cage, wrinkled his mask at him in a friendly gesture, and then piled hay over his head as if to indicate that he wanted no more disturbance. In a cage a little farther down was a black poodle bitch recovering from a broken fore-leg. This was Mabel. Seeing Smiler she came out of her sleeping-box and walked across to him on her hind legs and thrust her muzzle between the bars and held out her plaster-bound foreleg for him to shake. Smiler fondled her muzzle, shook hands with her and sent her back to bed. In other pens and cages, all for some reason or other temporary lodgers, were animals from the menageries and children's zoos which travelled with the circuses; a barbary ram, a small honey bear, a porcupine and, in the end pen, a South American tapir which was stretched out on its side snoring like an old man.

On the other side of the barn were the bird cages. All of these were empty except for three. One held a griffon vulture, huddled on its perch like a dejected old lady with a shabby boa of feathers around her neck. Another held a pair of Indian mynah birds. As Smiler stood in front of their cage one of them opened a sleepy but bright eye, surveyed him, and then, giving a drowsy whistle, said, "Lord, look at the time! Look at the time!" whistled once more, and closed its eye. But of all the creatures in the barn, the bird in the third occupied cage was the one which interested Smiler most of all. It was a peregrine falcon.

Her name was Fria and Bob had told him that she had been taken from an eyrie in Wales – before she could properly fly – by a falconer who intended to train her. But the circumstances of his own life had changed after a while and he had given her to the Duchess. He had felt that this was the best thing to do because to have loosed her to freedom would only have meant her death. She had had no training in how to hunt for her food and her wings were stiff and incapable of long flight from lack of the exercise she would have had in the wild state.

Fria sat on her perch, eyes wide open, and watched Smiler. She was now over two years old and had long moulted into her adult plumage so that her whitish breast was streaked crosswise with grey, whereas before her breast had been buff-coloured and streaked vertically with brown. Her back was now a deep blue-black. There was little gloss or shine to her feathers and she looked a sorry sight. But for all this there was still a fierce dignity in the way she stared from fixed eyes at Smiler as though to prove that for all her captivity her spirit was still far from broken.

Smiler felt a lump rise in his throat as he eyed her. He didn't like to see animals in captivity at all, though he knew that it was inevitable that some had to be, especially those to whom freedom would mean death. But Fria moved him more than all the others. Of all creatures he loved birds because they seemed to carry the real meaning of freedom in their lives. In Scotland he had watched the high soaring of golden eagles and the lazy circling of buzzards, seen the strong, steady flight of geese and the wild aerobatics of green plovers, and before that, when he had first run away from approved school, watched the wing-trembling hover of kestrels over Salisbury Plain and the marauding swoop of sparrow-hawks along hedges and around trees as they chased their prey.

Now, watching Fria, he wondered if she could remember back to the days of her eyrie life, to the moment when her wings were growing strong enough almost to the point of lifting her into flight alongside her falcon mother and her tiercel father . . . to take her up into the freedom of the air where she would be taught to stoop and prey and slowly gain a mastery of the air which would have been her real life. It was something he didn't like to think about.

He moved away, switched off the light and locked up the barn. As he went to his bed, because all his recently passed troubles and adventures had, without his knowing it, begun to mature him, to change the boy of near sixteen to the beginning of manhood, he told himself that although Nature was full of death and cruelty it was savagery that was without real evil. But the cruelty of man towards animals came not from any natural law but from the stupidity and thoughtlessness of men. Before he slept he told himself, "Samuel M., things should be different, they really should. And they could be if people knew how to care." For a while he even wondered whether he could really bear to stay here where so many animals were cooped up and then decided that he could because, at least, he could look after them even if he could never give them freedom.

When he awoke in the morning, however, he didn't feel half so gloomy about things and, if he had, the work he had to do through the day would have given him little time for brooding.

*   *   *

Within a month Smiler was feeling very much at home at Bullaybrook Farm. He knew the routine for all the jobs he had to do, and he did them well, for he was a good worker. The Duchess was pleased with him and so were Bill and Bob for, although they laughed and joked and pulled his leg, when it came to work they would not tolerate a half-done, sloppy job. In his spare time and at the week-ends Smiler, too, had begun to discover the country around the farm. In the store barn was an old bicycle which had been bought in some deal by Jimmy Jago. Smiler put it in order and explored the surrounding lanes and the brook and river valley on it.

And in that month the shape and purpose of Smiler's life began to be defined. The Duchess had a talk with the local veterinary surgeon who came now and then to treat sick or ailing animals. After he had gone she explained to Smiler (though he knew some of this already) that he would have to study for the General Certificate of Education, first at the Ordinary level and then at the Advanced level – in which he would need two or three passes. When this was done he could apply for admission to one of the Universities which provided courses leading to degrees in veterinary science or veterinary medicine and surgery. Once he had a degree it would give him the right to be registered in the Register of Veterinary Surgeons and to membership of the Royal College of Veterinary Surgeons and the right to practise the profession in the United Kingdom. Apart from studying general subjects, Smiler would eventually have to tackle chemistry, physics and biology.

Listening to her, Smiler felt swamped by the prospect of the task ahead and his face showed it.

The Duchess chuckled and said, "Cheer up, Samuel. You can go a long way in small steps if you've plenty of time ahead of you – and you've got that. Fix your eye on the first mountain-top and forget the ones that lie beyond. Their turn will come."

Grinning ruefully, Smiler asked, "How am I goin' to get up the first mountain, ma'am? I never did much at school."

"That's your fault. But it's never too late."

To prove it the Duchess arranged with a friend of hers, a retired schoolmaster in a nearby village, to start giving Smiler lessons two evenings a week in general subjects. Twice a week Smiler cycled to the

village and was coached by the retired schoolmaster, a Mr. Samkin.
Every day thereafter Smiler had to find time, either before or after
supper, to work at a small table in his own room. Since the nights were
now drawing in as October passed he didn't mind so much, but he
wondered how he would stick it when the winter passed and spring and
summer came, and all the springs and summers of the years ahead when
the evenings were drawn out and full of invitation to go abroad into
fields and woods. The only answer he could find was to tell himself, "If
you want something bad, Samuel M., then you got to work for it. The
great thing is not to think about it too much, but take it step by step like
the Duchess says."

Smiler's birthday came and he was sixteen. Jimmy Jago was at home
for it and gave him a good second-hand watch. "Now you're a working
and studying man, my lad, you must value time. It's like water under a
bridge. Once gone you can't bring it back." The Duchess gave him a
thick sweater she had knitted herself, a stormproof jacket for the winter,
and a fountain pen for writing up his notes because Mr. Samkin was old-
fashioned enough to value good writing and turned up his nose at biros
and self-propelling nonsenses like that. And Bill and Bob – not without
design – gave him an old twelve-bore, single-barrelled shotgun,
promised to provide the cartridges for it, and to teach him how to use it,
so that from then on he could shoot the pigeons and rabbits around the
farm for the table and also for feeding Fria – and relieve them of the job.
When Smiler asked about having a licence for it, Bob looked at him (or it
might have been Bill), winked, and said, "We'll meet that fence when we
come to it. But remember – if we ever see you handle that gun anyway
different from what we're goin' to show you, then you get your backside
beaten and you'll be thrown in the Bullay brook."

But the best present of all was a letter from Laura Mackay which the
Duchess gave him when they were alone. Before he had opened it,
Smiler – blushing a bit – asked, "But how could she write to me . . . she
don't know my address?"

The Duchess shook her head, setting her red curls dancing, and said
severely, "Not 'don't know', boy. 'Doesn't know'. Mr. Samkin would
give you stick for that. And how your girl knows your address is my
business – there's not a county in the whole of this Kingdom where I
don't have friends. Now up to your room and read it before you start
work."

Smiler ran up to his room and sat by the window and read it.

Dear Sammy,
    An old gypsy man called by the other forenoon when Mum and Dad

were out. He made me swear some sort of secret daft rigmarole and then told me where you were. So I'm writing and no one will ever know unless you say so, and I wish I could come down to see you. And you can write to me because if Mum and Dad saw the letter they would never ask questions and anyway they would never give you away, not after everything. I hope you are keeping well as everyone here is, including the Laird and Bacon that is still with him. I miss you a lot, though I think you were a daft loon to go on the run again, but then you always thought you knew best. Look after yourself.

Yours,
Laura

P.S. Don't forget you promised to ask a certain question one day. XX

Smiler read it through twice and each time little shivers of pleasure ran through him. Then he took his new fountain pen and a sheet of paper eager to answer the letter right away – but the excitement was too much for him. He just couldn't keep his bottom still on the chair and his right hand shook. He wrote "Dear Laura" – and then was stuck. He'd never written a letter to a girl in his life. Then he remembered one of the first things Mr. Samkin had told him: "Before you put anything to paper, first of all think about it, then think about it again, get your mind settled about what you're going to say – and then write. Many a man has ruined himself by a few ill-considered scrawls of ink on a piece of paper."

Smiler got up, went out of the window, across the kitchen roof and into the far barn. He walked the length of the cages and pens and finished in front of Fria. This now had become a ritual with him. It was always with Fria that he finished up. As he stood there one of the mynah birds opened an eye, whistled, and called, "Oh, look at us! Look at us!" But Smiler scarcely heard the bird.

Fria, her dark-brown eyes wide open, watched Smiler. She sat there, her breast feathers slack and shabby, the slate-blue feathers of her wings loosely laid, lacking the taut, steely compactness which would have marked a healthy bird like a coat of mail. There was a dinginess to the dull yellow of the cere at the base of her beak and of her long-taloned feet. The only feeling of power and wildness in her came from the stance of her head, in the unflinching gaze of her eyes bracketed by the black cheek-marks curving downwards. She knew Smiler now. It was he who fed her with pigeons, rabbit pieces, and the bodies of the barn mice caught in the traps which were around the place. She knew him, too, because he moved always without any sudden movement. Since he had come he had changed the bathing-tray in her cage for a wider, shallower one which she preferred. Now she bathed each day whereas before she had known no regular desire for the cleanliness which all peregrines love.

Standing before her, touched as he always was at the sight of her, Smiler said softly, "Fria . . . Fria . . ." The falcon made no movement. "Fria, I've had a letter from Laura . . . all the way from Scotland. And one day I'm going to be a vet. and I'm going to marry her. I am. I promised to ask her. Not yet, of course. Not never — I mean, not ever — until I'm a real vet. And I'm going to be because everyone's helping me. That's good, isn't it? Maybe . . . well, perhaps I'll be able to think of something that . . . well, something that I can do for you, old girl."

Fria closed her eyes. She shut Smiler out. She shut everything out, closing out the world, drawing back into the limbo of her own un-fathomable nature.

Smiler went quietly out and switched off the light.

*　*　*

Bob and Bill gave Smiler lessons in shooting and he soon became a fairly competent shot and — after one or two lapses, when he did get his backside kicked but was not thrown into the brook — a very safe handler of a gun. Although he didn't like killing things he now shot rabbits and wood pigeons and justified it because he knew that they were for the pot and for the griffon and Fria. But everything else was safe from him.

One day as he was pushing his bicycle up the hill from the farm a white minicar with a police sign on it pulled up alongside him. A youngish-looking policeman with a red, plump face leaned out.

"Hello, there — you're Sammy, aren't you, the Duchess's nephew?"

For a moment Smiler didn't know what to say. Then remembering Mr. Samkin's edict, he thought for a moment or two, and said, "Yes, I'm Sammy."

The policeman smiled. "And I'm P.C. Grimble — not Grumble, though I do. Nice to meet you, Sammy, and a word of advice." He winked. "So long as you keep that twelve-bore on your own patch I don't know it's there and I don't want to know. But you step on the highway with it and . . . well, that's it." He winked again, and then drove off. And so Smiler began to learn that although the law is the law — as he well knew — there was in every country community a law within the law, but it was one which had to be strictly observed. That he was the Duchess's nephew was news to him but, since he now knew something of the way the Duchess could arrange things, he decided that there was no point in mentioning it to her.

So, through the autumn and into the winter, Smiler worked hard and studied hard. The leaves turned brown and gold and fell, leaving only the green plantations of fir and pine to stand black against the early sunset sky. The rains fell and the Bullay brook and the Taw were swollen with chocolate-brown spates from the run-offs and streams bringing down the rich red Devon soil. And, as the spates began to fall, so the salmon and the sea-trout ran high up the river and cleared the weirs to seek their spawning-grounds. Smiler, hedging in the meadows by the brook, would sometimes creep up and watch the hen salmon cutting at their gravelly redds in the spate-cleared water while the cock fish hovered close by, ready to fertilize the eggs with their cloudy milt. He grinned to himself when sometimes a cheeky little trout would dash in first – a boy trying, as Bob or Bill said, to do a man's work.

Now, by the time he had finished his work, it was dark so that it was only at the weekends he could get on his bicycle and explore the country around or go for long walks – which was what he preferred most to do. But, being young and not wedded to the habit of regular sleep, there were times when even after the day's labour there was an itch in his limbs for movement. Sometimes, after checking the creatures in the barn at night, he would delay going back to bed and in moonlight or clear starlight go off for a tramp for an hour or two. It only took a little while for his eyes to become accustomed to the dark and he moved quietly and unobtrusively and was well rewarded. He soon found where the nearest badgers had their sett, knew the fox earths, and the trees where the kestrels and buzzards roosted. He was no longer startled when a barn owl ghosted silently by him over the short field-stubble. His hair no longer stood on end almost when a little owl shrieked suddenly. The dogs on the neighbouring farms knew him and now, when they scented him, never bothered to bark, and there were dozens of places where the pheasants roosted and it would have been easy for him – had he been a poacher – to raise a hand and take one. But Smiler preferred just to be out, to be an inhabitant of a night-time world which few other people knew. He knew the track that came down the hill by the farm which the travelling otters used when they came over country to reach the brook and so to the Taw, and the places in the clumps of cotton-grass where the jack-snipe bedded down. But the place he liked to go to most at night, particularly if there were a moon, was Highford House.

Highford House was about a mile and a half from Bullaybrook Farm. To get to it Smiler would follow the brook up the valley for a while then cut up the valley side through rough pastures and woods, across a small lane, and through a long stretch of Forestry Commission land which overlooked the Taw valley. The house, which had been built in the latter part of the nineteenth century, stood on the top of a hill that flanked the west side of the river. Once it had been a splendid mansion standing in its own park and woodlands. Now it was derelict and only a broken shell of its former self. The roof had been stripped of its lead and tiles, the windows of the magnificent rooms were without glass, and all the grand oak staircases had been removed. The park had become pasture and the once well-kept gardens had been reclaimed by thorn, elderberry, and small saplings of beech and oak. No formal flowers remained but the primroses, cowslips and other spring flowers had come back, and in autumn it was a riot of willow-herb and balsam. Built of great greystone blocks, it straddled the hilltop with its back to the woods, stranded like the skeleton of some long-dead monster. The winding drive that led out to the road was overgrown and hard to pick out. The once carefully kept rides of rhododendrons and azaleas had become a jungle and a sanctuary for all sorts of birds and animals. The jackdaws, kestrels and owls knew its broken roof parapet and crumbling walls and nested among them. Badgers and foxes over the years had burrowed to the wide maze of cellars that lay under the falling rubble, and grass snakes and adders in summer sunned themselves on the fallen stone slabs. Just behind the house was a tall, redbrick tower, relic of some older house that had once crowned the hilltop. Parts of the stone stairway that twisted up the inside of the tower still remained. But after the first floor there were great gaps in it and anyone who moved inside was in danger of setting off falls of brick and stone from higher up the tower. It rose high above the old house and the wilderness of woods and derelict park and from its top miles of the curving valley of the Taw could be seen, a valley where road, river and railway kept company, parted, and moved companionably together again as they ran northwestwards to Barnstaple and the sea.

It was here one December night that Smiler, still restless after a day's work and an evening's study, made his way to what he called his "thinking-place". This was the wide parapet ledge of the roof at the back of the house. He reached it by climbing the stout stems of an old ivy and, once ensconced, he could look down into the rubble-filled shell of the house or across the wilderness that had been a formal garden to the redbrick tower. Though his eyes and ears were always wide awake for the movement of a night bird or animal, the squeak of a field mouse or the scrape of a rat or rabbit, he would let himself go off into a reverie, imagining the times when all his troubles would be over, his father back and he well on the way to being a vet. Sometimes, a shadow amongst the

other shadows of the old house, he would just sit and dream and later
hardly know what his dreams had been. Now and then he would even go
over in his mind all he was learning from Mr. Samkin – but not often.

He was sitting there this night, one of sharp frost, the fields already
hoared and the stars blinking sharply through the cold air, warm in his
sweater and storm jacket, when he heard a noise come from the inside of
the house which he had never heard before. From below him, but away
near one of the empty front windows of the ground floor, he heard the
sound of something metallic suddenly ring out. Just for a moment or
two he was startled and felt the quick prick of fear tingle his scalp.
Although there was always a friendly feeling about the place, despite its
ruined and lonely state, his mind leapt to the thought of ghosts and
strange spirits. But a moment later he forgot them because clearly to his
ears came a decidedly human grunt and a man's voice said crossly,
"Next time bring a bugle and blow it." Two men came into view,
picking their way across the rubble below, clearly lit by the wash of
starlight that flooded through the gaping roof. Moving quietly they
crossed to the front window and paused there, surveying the stretch of
wild pasture outside. The smaller of the two men carried a sack or a
workman's tool-bag slung over his shoulder and Smiler guessed that
something had probably fallen from this to make the noise he had heard.

The man with the tool-bag slipped through the window and was
gone. The other man remained, as though waiting to watch that the
other got unobtrusively away before he too left. One side of his face was
clear in the starshine and Smiler saw that it was Jimmy Jago. For a moment his instinct was to call out to him, but he checked himself. He knew
by now something of the ways of the Duchess and Jimmy and Bob and
Bill. They were circus and Romany people and their ways were secret,
even magic, and they lived by different rules than ordinary people.

At that moment Smiler was glad of Mr. Samkin who was making him
read Kipling and remembered some lines from the last poem they had
done –

If you wake at midnight, and hear a horse's feet,
Don't go drawing back the blind, or looking in the street,
Them that asks no questions isn't told a lie,
Watch the wall, my darling, while the Gentlemen go by!

So, Smiler sat where he was, a shadow in the angle of a ruined parapet
ledge. And below, Jimmy Jago waited like another shadow. Then, from
outside, there suddenly came the double note of a wintering curlew, or
so Smiler thought it was until he saw Jimmy move, drop something
among the rubble to the left of the window, and then slide out into the

night. He knew that it had been an all-clear signal from the other man, who, he felt, might easily from his appearance have been either Bob or Bill.

To be on the safe side, Smiler sat where he was for fifteen minutes by his birthday watch — hands luminous — the present of Jimmy. He wondered, though he knew it was none of his business, what Jimmy was doing up here when only that morning he had supposedly driven off in his shabby old car on a dealing trip for two or three days. One thing was clear: neither of the men was poaching for there was nothing in the house to poach.

When he thought the coast was clear Smiler climbed down and went into the house. He picked his way across the broken rubble and stones of the floor to the window. Lying on the ground to one side of it was the object Jimmy had dropped.

Smiler picked it up. He stared at it puzzled. It was a very small broom or besom made of bunched hazel twigs bound together with a couple of twists of binder twine. Although it had no long wooden hazel pole for a handle it was a miniature of the hazel besoms that he used sometimes to sweep the floor of the barns.

Smiler studied it, shook his head in bafflement, and then told himself, "Samuel M., Jimmy's business is Jimmy's business and he's your friend."

He put the besom back where he had found it. But all the way home — although he knew it was none of his business — he just kept wondering what on earth anyone should want a besom for in a ruined old mansion that it would have taken an army of men and builders to bring back to its former glory.

3

All Kinds of Monkey Business

It was three days before Jimmy Jago showed up at the farm again. He returned after supper. While Smiler was studying in his room he could hear him and the Duchess talking in the kitchen. It was not possible to hear what they said, but he had the impression that now and again some sort of argument was going on between them. However, Smiler, who knew what it was to be in trouble of his own, wisely decided that other people's affairs were nothing to do with him unless he were invited to share them. He sagely decided to say nothing and keep his own counsel – but this could not keep him from the use of his eyes.

Three times before Christmas arrived he sat on his parapet ledge at Highford House and saw the two men leave, always around the same time. Now, when he went up there – which was less often as winter gripped the valley – he always looked to see if the hazel besom lay by the window. If it did he was content to stay. But if the besom was not in its place, then he quietly made off.

He wrote Laura regularly now and took a great deal of trouble over his letters so that they should be grammatically correct. It annoyed him sometimes that Laura did not write as often as he did, but when he taxed her with it she wrote back and told him ". . . not to be a daft loon. Do you think I've got nothing else to do all day but sit and write letters? And anyway you only write to me so much because you want to show off your grammatics."

Smiler also wrote to Albert a couple of times without giving his address. He got Jimmy Jago to post the letters well away from Devon while he was on his travels.

Through all this, Smiler went twice a week to Mr. Samkin who lived in the village at the head of the brook valley. But, although Smiler studied hard, he was not as happy at Mr. Samkin's as he had been. Mr. Samkin had taken on another student for extra coaching. This was a sixteen-year-old girl from the village called Sandra Parsons whose father was the local postman. Sandra had fair hair, blue eyes, a nice but slightly hooky nose, and a funny sort of giggle of a laugh which Smiler found irritating. But the chief thing that annoyed him was that Sandra was too friendly towards him. She so often found excuses to cycle down to Bullaybrook Farm and talk to him, when he should have been working, that he took to hiding when he saw her coming. On a Sunday, with two or three other girls, she would walk down and they would hang about the small stone bridge over the brook and, when he went off for a walk, follow him, giggling and laughing. But he had to admit that while they were at Mr. Samkin's Sandra was entirely serious and attentive to the instruction being given. Once in a fit of pique when Sandra spoilt one of his walks by joining up with him he called her nose "a hooky beak". Instead of being put out she laughed and said, "Oh, Sammy – that just shows how uneducated you are. It's an aristocratic nose. All the Parsons are descended from the King of the Barnstaple Treacle Mines. I suppose you'll tell me next that you didn't know treacle comes from a mine?"

Smiler groaned inwardly. There was nothing he could do but tolerate her, avoid her as much as possible, and feel more determined than ever to stick to his vow not to go to her Christmas party which she began to talk about well in advance.

By the time Christmas arrived there were a few horses in the stable, a couple of rosin backs and a small black pony which, given encouragement by Bill and Bob when it was in the yard, would go up on to its back legs and waltz and pirouette across the cobbles.

Christmas came with the first light fall of snow and a frost that made the ground bone-hard and lapped the fringes of the Bullay brook with a rim of ice. Jimmy Jago was at home for Christmas and Bill and Bob came down to have Christmas dinner with them all. Afterwards they all sat around the fireplace and exchanged presents. Smiler one weekend had gone on the train to Barnstaple to buy his presents for people – and had been considerably hampered in the expedition because Sandra had got wind of it and turned up on the train with two other girls. It had seemed to him that every time he turned a street corner or went into a shop there they would be. The best Christmas present Smiler had was a quiet word from Jimmy Jago before Bill and Bob arrived.

Jimmy said, "Never mind how, but I got a mate of mine to ask at the shipping company about your Dad. Seems he missed his boat at Montevideo because he went up in the hills for a two-day trip and got fever at the hotel where he was staying. He was in hospital up there for a couple of days before they realized he was from a ship."

"But he's all right now, isn't he?"

"Of course he is. But that isn't the half of it. Montevideo wasn't his lucky place. Just as he was getting over the fever, he slips on the tiles of the hospital corridor and breaks his leg." Jimmy grinned. "Would you say your old man is accident-prone?"

"It's news to me," said Smiler.

"Well, not to worry. Everything's all right. The company have taken care of him. He's on another of their ships now. It picked him up on its way to Australia. My mate couldn't find out when it's due back in this country. He didn't like to be any nosier in case the company began to wonder what he was so interested for."

"Oh, gosh, Mr. Jimmy – I'm glad he's all right. I mean, I knew he had to be, but it's nice to know. Thank you very much."

And the worst present of a kind was a Christmas card from Sandra Parsons. Inside it was a formal invitation to Smiler to attend her party on the night after Boxing Day. When he groaned about it the Duchess, with a warm glint in her eyes, said, "You're growing up, Sammy. You've got to learn that there are a lot of things you have to do in life out of politeness which you don't want to do. But I'll let you into a secret. Most of them usually turn out to be very pleasant. You write a nice *thank you* and say you'll go." She winked. "But there's no need to tell Laura about it if you don't want to."

The Duchess was right, of course. When Smiler went to the party it took less than half an hour for his initial reticence and shyness to wear off. Then he began to enjoy himself. Mr. and Mrs. Parsons were warm-hearted, friendly people and soon made him welcome. And Sandra and her friends, now that he was amongst them and part of their accepted company, seemed less giggly and stupid than he had thought. They played games and danced to a record player and Smiler – who had not done much dancing in his life, but had a natural sense of rhythm – soon picked up the steps required of him. Although it was not part of his choosing, Smiler found that he danced with Sandra more than with the other girls and, in some mysterious way, when games were played he found himself partnered by her or on her side. This, without his knowing it, made Smiler an enemy – a big, well-built farmer's son of eighteen called Trevor Green who regarded Sandra as his girl friend. He was far from pleased at the way Sandra and a few of the other girls had taken to the fair-haired, freckle-faced Smiler. Trevor Green was not the kind who brought his grievances out into the open. Also, he had enough intelligence to realize that if he showed his jealousy of Smiler openly then it would do him no good with Sandra and might – in the way of many females – merely provoke her to a more galling display of her liking for Smiler.

Trevor Green, from the day of the party, worked secretly against Smiler. Sometimes in the darkness of early evening he would walk through the brook fields and leave gates open so that the cattle strayed. Another night he crept into the barnyards and punctured both tyres on

Smiler's bicycle with a fine bradawl so that Smiler would not suspect sabotage. He worked in the dark and in the way the country folk used to think the bad-tempered pixies worked when they wanted to make trouble and more work for those they disliked. He opened the hatch-gate of the disused leat which had once served the old Bullaybrook Mill. The brook was in spate and the water raced down the old leat, poured through a broken bank above the barns, and flooded the yards and the stables one night. Quietly and stealthily as the New Year came in and January wore away through wintry, roaring days of wind and rain, Trevor Green spaced his mischief and caused Smiler a great deal of extra work. But in the way of life, and without knowing it, he at last did something which, though it caused Smiler trouble and worry to begin with, in the end gave Smiler great pleasure and joy.

One night after Smiler had made his last inspection of the animals in the barn and had returned to his bedroom, Trevor Green crept up to the barn, took the key from under the water-butt, and let himself in. He closed the door and switched on the light. The only windows in the barn were at the far end and could not be seen from the house.

He went down the row of cages and pens and opened the doors of the Barbary ram's pen and that of Freddie the chimpanzee. On the other side of the barn he opened the cages of the griffon, the mynah birds and of Fria. None of the animals paid much attention to him. An eye was opened from sleep and then closed. Fria stared graven-faced at him, eyes unblinking. Within a few minutes he was gone, chuckling to himself, picturing the trouble Smiler would have in the morning when he arrived and found birds and animals loose in the barn.

It was a stupid trick, the product of a small, jealous mind — and it would have been a complete failure had it not been for Freddie. Most of the animals were so used to their captivity that they were content to stay where they were and go on sleeping. So was Freddie for a long time. He was warm and comfortable in his straw bed. He had cocked an un-curious eye at Trevor as he passed, yawned, and drifted away into sleep again.

But at four o'clock in the morning Freddie woke and sat up blinking. That the barn lights should be on was unusual, and the unusual now stirred Freddie's curiosity. He saw that the door of his cage was open and shambled over to it, long arms swinging, his knuckles brushing the ground, his large, old man's mouth working soundlessly as though in silent irritation at the break in barn routine. One of the mynah birds cocked an eye at him and, giving a sleepy whistle, said, "Lord, look at the time! Look at the time!" Freddie gave a pout of his thick lips at the bird, scratched his head and then dropped to the floor. Grunting to himself, he made a little tour up his side of the barn, absent-mindedly picked up a piece of wood from the floor and rattled it along the bars of the tapir's cage. At the far end of the building was a flight of wooden steps that led to a loft. Freddie went up the steps and sat on the top rung. The trap-door leading into the loft was closed. He banged on it as though it were a drum for a while and then dropped from the top steps to the ground in an easy movement. He enjoyed the exercise so much that he went up the steps and repeated the performance. He walked down the length of the bird-cages to the open door of the griffon's cage.

The griffon, head sunk between its shoulders, eyes half open, followed his movements, its great beak swinging slowly. Freddie raised his head to it, wrinkled his face, and chattered gently through clenched teeth. He banged his piece of wood to and fro across the open doorway. The griffon shook out its shabby plumage and sidled along its perch a few inches.

Freddie climbed up the bars of the cage and sat on top of it. Experimentally he reached down through the bars with his piece of wood and tried to touch the griffon.

Reluctantly the griffon flopped down from its perch to the cage floor like a disgruntled old woman and shuffled into a far corner. Freddie carried on a little chattering conversation to himself and then crossed over to the top of the mynah birds' cage. They turned their long beaks up to him defensively and half opened their wings to a threatening posture. One of the birds took off from its perch, swooped through the open door and flew up to the window ledge at the far end of the barn where it settled, whistled, and called, "Say it again! Say it again. . . . Oh, clever bird!"

Freddie, stirred now by his unusual liberty, chattered with excitement and sidled quickly along the top of the cages, moving in a sideways, hump-backed posture. He did a little jumping dance on top of the griffon's cage. Then he dropped to the floor, ran along the barn, climbed the loft steps on the rear side, swung from a rung with one foot and dropped to the floor. He landed outside Fria's cage.

Fria, wide awake now and disturbed by all the unusual movement, looked down at him and gaped silently through her strong hooked beak. Freddie rattled his stick against the open door. Fria, alarmed, edged along her perch to the side of the cage. Freddie, grunting, hauled himself up into the open doorway of the cage and walked in, keeping well away from Fria. He leaned over her shallow tin bath and took a drink of the water. Then, with a sudden movement, he seized the side of the bath and up-ended it. Water streamed all over the floor and the bath went half-rolling, half-sliding towards Fria. Freddie gave a sudden scream of excitement and leapt after it.

Fria moved with her characteristic swift peregrine shuffle across her perch. As Freddie came after her, waving his stick, she launched herself towards the open door. She flew awkwardly and weakly, losing height, and landed clumsily in a heap in the dust and straw alongside the ram's pen.

Freddie sat in the doorway of her cage and watched her. Fria straightened herself up, shook her wings into place, and stared at him.

Highly excited now, Freddie did a chattering dance in the doorway, dropped to the ground, and went after Fria. Alarmed, Fria ran along the ground, wings half open for flight. As Freddie came swiftly for her, she launched herself again. This time her wings beat more strongly as she strove to lift herself above the pursuing chimpanzee.

She made the top rung of the barn ladder, hitting it clumsily, and just managing to hold on with her talons. Freddie eyed her from the bottom of the ladder, grunting with pleasure at this new-found game. Then he went up after her.

Fria spread her dark slate-grey wings and flew awkwardly half the length of the barn, aiming for the top of the griffon's cage. She missed it, tried out of some dim instinct for the mechanics of flight to check herself with a braking of her wings, hit the side of the cage and fell to the floor. The mynah birds, now thoroughly astir, shrieked and whistled and Freddie came chattering after her.

Frightened, her heart beating with near-panic strength, Fria jumped into the air as Freddie neared her. Fear gave her enough strength to take her up and into a clumsy half-turn. She came out of it awkwardly and flew in slow wing-beats down the barn to the loft steps again. After her, delighted with the game, came Freddie.

It was Freddie's delight in his antics that benefited Fria. In her own cage she had never done more than exercise her wings now and then by flapping them as she sat on her perch, and using them to half-jump, half-fly to and from the cage floor. She had never known the pure wonder of a peregrine's real flight, knew nothing of the mastery of the air which is the supreme gift of the falcons, had never as an eyas stood ready for the first essay in flight on some eyrie lip with a deep drop below and the freedom of the skies above, nerving herself for the first launching into space to take her place alongside tiercel and falcon winging and wailing encouragement as they quartered the air a few feet out from the eyrie. Her wing muscles were stiff, unused, and untrained in co-ordination. When it came to flying she had almost everything to learn. With Freddie pursuing her now, she was forced into a series of panic lessons. For the next half-hour Freddie kept up his assaults and each time Fria was forced to make her escape, and each time she did some little of the stiffness and awkwardness of her wings dropped from her.

In the end whether from design, from the forced exercise of her natural wit, or from pure luck she escaped him by finding the ledge of an old bricked-up window high above the door which led into the barn, where Freddie, grumbling and chattering with frustration, could not reach her.

She sat there trembling with nervous and physical exhaustion while Freddie danced below her for a while. Then, as though tired of the taste of freedom, Freddie shambled off down the barn, jumped into his cage and bundled himself up in his straw bed and slept.

The mynahs which had escaped swooped down and into their cage. Fria sat on her ledge and slowly the fear she had known began to leave her. But as it died away, so did some part of the old Fria. For the first time in months she had known a kind of freedom and its unusual touch had stirred something in her spirit.

* * *

Smiler was the first into the barn the next morning. One glance told him that things were not right. The light was still on and, more obviously, Freddie was sitting on the lowest rung of the loft ladder placidly chewing at an onion – his favourite food – which he had taken from a string of these vegetables which was hung up over the grain-store bin beneath the far window.

Freddie looked up, gave Smiler a welcoming grunt, and then shambled across to him, holding the half-eaten onion in his mouth. Before Smiler could do anything Freddie shinned up him, clamped one long arm around his shoulders and nuzzled his face into Smiler's neck affectionately, almost choking him with the strong odour of onion.

Smiler took one look down the row of cages and saw the mischief that had been done. With Freddie in his arms he went down the barnside, shutting pen doors and cages. He prised Freddie from him and put him in his cage, where he retired happily to his straw bed to finish the onion.

Smiler crossed the barn and closed up the griffon's and the mynah birds' cages and then stood in front of Fria's cage. It was empty and the upturned bath lay across the damp boards at the back of the cage. Smiler, feeling angry at whoever had come into the barn to cause trouble, turned slowly round with a grim face. In the dim, early morning light from the far window he saw Fria sitting on her ledge about sixteen feet from the ground. Her eyes were open, watching him, but her head was sunk into her shoulders and her feathers had been shaken out so that she looked like some disreputable old owl.

Smiler stood there, not knowing what to do. He had left the barn door open and he knew that he would have to go back along the length of the barn to close it before he could attempt to catch Fria. Once the barn door was shut he could unhook the loft ladder and set it against the wall, take a sack and go up to Fria. With luck, he could throw it over her before she moved. Watching her out of the corner of his eye, he began to move slowly up the barn. Fria watched him unmoving.

With a feeling of relief Smiler reached the door and shut it. Trying to keep his movements easy and unalarming, he found a sack and then unhooked the loft ladder. Very slowly he raised it against the wall. As the top of the ladder came to rest a foot below her Fria suddenly half-flapped her wings and, lowering her head, bated at the ladder top below her. Smiler kept still and waited until she had calmed down. Then very slowly he began to climb the ladder. As far as Fria was concerned he would have gladly let her go to her freedom had she been able to fly properly and look after herself by killing, but he knew that once she was loose outside she would have only the slimmest chance of survival.

Smiler crept up the ladder, making a soft clicking sound at the back of his throat — something which for weeks now he had taken to doing when he fed Fria. It was a sound she understood. It meant food. Smiler prayed that she was hungry enough now to stay where she was in the hope of being fed.

When he was four rungs from the top of the ladder Smiler halted. Taking his weight on his feet, his knees pressed against a ladder-rung to give him a firm balance, he slowly got both hands to the sack and with an unhurried movement spread it wide so that he could swamp the falcon with it.

Slowly he began to raise the sack and Fria watched as it came level with her feet. Then, just as Smiler was poised to make his bid to capture her, from far down the barn Freddie, his onion finished, and greedy for another, suddenly began to chatter loudly and shake at the bars of his cage. The sound disturbed Fria. All her fears during the night chase had been associated with it. As Smiler made a lunge to cover her, she ran sideways along the ledge and launched herself downwards. Smiler, just saving himself from falling from the ladder, turned and saw her wing clumsily down the barn towards the far window. She rose awkwardly to the light coming through. Then, realizing it offered no escape, she made a scrabbling turn, so close to the glass that her left wing flight feathers swept away an accumulation of old spiders' webs. She lost a couple of feet on the turn and, the panic she had known during the night returning to her, she swept back up the barn. She was faced with an awkward turning maneuver to avoid the end wall of the barn. She made a mess of the turn, hit the wall lightly, and tried to cling to it. For a moment or two she hung, wings beating, her talons scrabbling against the surface for a hold, spread-eagled like some awkward bat. Then she fell away sideways, and flew straight for the barn door, half-dazed with fear and shock.

At that moment the door opened inwards. Bob Old stood on the threshold. Fria dived towards him, swerved slowly to one side, and flew out into the open as Smiler gave a far-too-late warning shout.

Outside a strong west wind, damp with the promise of rain to come, swept across the brook valley. For the first time Fria felt the living, pulsing power of moving air cushioned under her wings and was tossed up out of control like a vagrant sheet of newspaper. She met the force with panic and wild wing-beats, and her beating wings took her up almost vertically across the face of the barn wall.

Just under the roof of the barn, and protected by a little gable of its own, was the loft doorway. Projecting from the top of the doorway was a stout wooden rafter with a pulley wheel attached to its end. Unused now, this projecting pulley beam had formerly served for hauling sacks of corn from carts below for storage in the loft.

As she beat frantically upwards Fria saw the overhang of the small gable roof and the long length of the pulley beam. From instinct rather than design she flew into the shelter of the little roof, raised her wings and settled with a desperate, scrambling movement of legs and talons on the beam. Once there she squared around slowly to face the force of the blustery wind.

Down below Smiler and Bob stared up at her.

Bob said, "How did she get free?"

Angrily Smiler said, "Some stupid devil got in the barn last night and opened some of the cages."

Bob considered this, and then said, "That don't surprise me. There's one or two around her don't altogether take to us. Circus folk, gypsies, didikys they know we are – and because they don't understand our ways they take a delight in being awkward."

"But what are we going to do about Fria, Mr. Bob?"

"Go up and open that loft door and just leave her. Come food time, put some out for her in the loft. When she's hungry enough she'll go in and then we can put the ladder up from here and close the doors on her. No trouble then."

"But say she flies off or gets blown off? She doesn't know how to look after herself. She'll just die."

"Ay, she might, Sammy. But then again, she might not. Animals may not think like humans, but they've got their own kind of common-sense. She'll settle for herself what she wants to do – and my guess is that she'll come into the loft for food when she's hungry."

* * *

But Fria did not come into the loft, though Smiler did everything he could to get her back. That first day he opened the loft doors and put food and water on the broad sill of the hatch opening. When Fria saw him at the opening she shuffled along the pulley beam well out of reach, took a firm grip on the weather-worn wood and sleeked down her feathers to ease the wind resistance against her. Time and again, as Smiler worked, he came back to see her, but she scarcely moved her position on the beam all day.

That night the food and drink were left on the ledge and the loft doors open. A new and more secure hiding-place was found for the barn key. When Smiler made his night visit the food was untouched and the dark shape of Fria on her beam was silhouetted against the night sky.

For two days Fria did not move from her beam except to shuffle back under the protection of the small pent roof when it rained hard. She sat and watched the strangeness of the new world before her, like a medieval carving. There was nothing wrong with her physically except that her body, her flight muscles and her talents were unused and un-trained. Her eyes, which could take in the whole horizon without moving, except the little segment of the loft in her rear, were the wonder eyes of a falcon, nature's great gift to her kind. Her wide-ranging eyes had eight times the power of man's and a depth of focus that could show her the quick beat of a rook's wing miles away, the fall of a late leaf half-a-mile up the far valley side, and the movement of a foraging, long-tailed field-mouse through the winter grasses down by the brook.

Fria sat on her beam and watched this new world. She watched the movement of the cattle in the pasture, the quick flight of pigeons coming high over the valley woods, the movement of people and traffic now and then at the brook bridge, the rolling, changing shapes of the rain-clouds sweeping in from the distant sea, and the coming and going of Smiler and Bob and Bill and the Duchess about the farm. But there were two things she watched in those first days with special interest. At noon one day, when a scattering of sparrows were squabbling on the yard cobbles over a few handfuls of grain that had been spilled, a sparrow hawk came round the corner of the barn in a swift, low-flying, piratical swoop. As the sparrows rose in alarm, the hawk burst into their midst, did a half wing-roll and took one of the sparrows in its talons and flew on with it.

Something about the hawk and the maneuver wakened some ancestral memory in Fria. Three times a day for the first two days Fria saw this maneuver and each time a sparrow was taken. And another bird wakened a response in her. Now and again a kestrel came quartering up the valley and hung over the pasture by the brook. Fria eyed it the first time, watched the wing-tip tremor of its poised hover and saw, as plainly as the kestrel could see, the movement of a winter foraging vole in the brookside grasses. When the kestrel plummeted with upraised wings and made its kill, Fria shuffled restlessly on her beam. She lowered her head, trod impatiently with her feet and uttered a faint call, a thin wail — *wickoo, wickoo* — that was barely audible. Again and again Fria watched sparrow hawk and kestrel in their hunting and always an excitement stirred in her which sent a swift tremble through her wings or made her lower her head and wail gently.

And during those days Smiler watched and worried about Fria. But on the morning of the fourth day he felt happier. Sometime, either during the night or at first light, Fria had moved down from her beam to the loft edge. One of the mice Smiler had taken in a barn trap was gone. Late that afternoon when he checked he saw that she had been down again and had taken a piece of meat from the food laid out for her. He saw, too, that the small bowl of drinking water he had set out was tipped over and he guessed that Fria had tried to take a bath in it.

From then on Fria began to eat regularly and Smiler would find her castings lying on the ground below the beam. When she was used to feeding, Smiler began to move the food farther and farther back from the loft opening because he wanted to train Fria to go well back into the loft to eat, so that one day he and Bob would have a chance to set up the ladder and shut the doors on her before she could get back to her beam. But Fria was not to be tempted. When the food was set farther back into the loft she refused to eat for two days and Smiler put it back on the ledge of the loft opening.

He did this with a definite plan in mind. He explained it to the Duchess. "You see, I don't really want to catch her just to shut her up in her cage again. What good's that going to do her?"

"Well, she can't sit up on that pole for ever, Sammy."

"But that's it, ma'am. She won't. If I feed her regular——"

"Regularly."

". . . regularly, and she begins to get strong and . . . well, sort of more contented . . . Well, then maybe she'll fly. You know, take off on a little flight. But she'll always come back for her food, because she can't hunt for herself. Not, anyway, until she's a real good flyer. When she's like that — well, isn't there a chance she might start to hunt?"

"Well, I suppose there is. But not a strong one, surely?"

"Maybe not, but there is a chance and it's worth trying, ma'am. Gosh, I know if it was me and I could have the chance I'd take it. What kind of life is it just sitting in a cage?"

The Duchess eyed him silently for a moment, pursing her plump lips, and then said quietly, "Well, I'll tell you what, Sammy. Even though I'm an old circus hand and I'm used to animals in cages and being trained, I've got to admit that the older I get the less I like it. So from now on the responsibility is yours. You can have Fria. She's your property and you can decide what is best for her."

"Really, you mean that?"

"I do."

Smiler jumped up. "Oh, thank you, ma'am. Thank you." He moved to her, put his arms around her without thinking, and gave her a hug.

The Duchess chuckled. "Well, thank you, Sammy. It's a long time since any man did that to me. But remember, whatever you decide may be best for Fria, she may have ideas of her own. She's a woman. And women have minds of their own."

That night when Smiler made his late-night barn visit, he looked up at the dim shadow of Fria sitting on her beam and, since there was no one around to hear him, he said aloud, "All right, you old bird up there, you start doing something for yourself — and I'll help you all I can."

It was from that day that Smiler started to keep a diary. It was a secret diary which he began for a variety of reasons. He wanted to keep a record of all that might happen to Fria. He felt, too, that it would be a good exercise in improving his English.

His first entry read:

February 2nd. (I think). Started this diary at Bullaybrook Farm, N. Devon. Fria belongs to me. Though of course she really belongs to herself but I am going to help and also get some books from the travelling County Library about peregrine falcons which in a way will be like helping in my vet. studies. Windy night, some rain. The Duchess is OK. So is Dad. So is Laura. And in a way so is Sandra. Bob says he can guess who did the barn job, but he won't tell me.

4

Two Under Instruction

During the next few days Fria was content to stay on her beam except for the times when she flew down to the loft ledge to eat or drink. Jimmy Jago came back to the farm for a couple of days and when Smiler showed him the falcon, he said, "Well, as long as she stays there she's safe from any farmer's gun. If I were you, too, Sammy, I wouldn't say anything about her to anyone. Somebody around here doesn't like us, lad. They might take a crack at her."

"What I'm hoping," said Smiler, "is that she'll pluck up courage and learn to fly properly and look after herself."

Jimmy cocked an eye at him. "And then what? Find a mate and raise a brood? That's what she should do but there's no chance of that. The falcons are dying out. There might be the odd pair out on the cliffs around Baggy Point but the breed is going and human beings are responsible. She might be happier free — but she'd be much safer in a cage."

"If you had the chance, Mr. Jago, and could catch her — would you put her back in a cage?"

Jimmy chuckled. "Good question. And the answer is — no. How often have you seen me go into the barn?"

"Not often."

"That's because I don't like to see anything caged up. The Duchess and I never quarrel about anything but that — things shut up in cages. No, I'm with you — give her a chance and, if she takes it, good luck to her."

From the County Library van, Smiler got some books on birds and read all about the peregrine falcons and, his interest roused, he got other books and began to understand something of the way the wild creatures of his country had to fight for their existence against the sometimes deliberate and sometimes careless ways that men put their lives in jeopardy. And, because he was determined to be a vet. one day, through his reading he made himself understand the careless ways in which death came to many birds because of the poisonous chemicals used in pesticides which were eaten on dressed seeds or contaminated insects by the small birds, and passed on to the predators like the hawks, owls and peregrine falcons when they ate their prey. The poisons from chemicals like Dieldrin, Aldrin, Heptachlor and DDT built up through the whole food chain of insects, rodents, small birds, wood pigeons and the fish in the seas and finally killed the preying birds at the end of the chain. Although he sometimes talked about this with Mr. Samkin, and asked his advice about books, he never mentioned Fria to him or to Sandra. Not that he distrusted them but he knew now how a careless remark could spread and he wanted Fria left alone to take her chance of freedom if she chose to do so. So far she showed no sign of doing this.

Every morning when he went out to the barn Fria would be sitting on her beam, either far out to enjoy the winter sun or drawn back under the small pent roof if the weather was bad. She ate and drank regularly now, and often, clinging to her beam, would rise and beat her wings as though she longed to let go and launch herself but could not find the courage. But some differences Smiler did notice in Fria. She ate more and her plumage was coming back into a better condition. She was so used to him, too, that when he came to the loft entrance she would move only the minimum distance along her beam to be out of his reach. Sometimes Smiler would stand and watch her for quite a long time, and he would talk to her in a soothing voice, but as the days went by there were times when he got angry with her and scolded her for not taking off and trying her wings. As an experiment he withheld her drinking and bath water for two days, hoping she would fly down to the brook, but Fria stayed where she was. Smiler, unable to be cruel, restored her water.

Yet, in the end, it was water which made Fria leave her beam. For many days she had watched the world around the farm and was familiar with it and with the passage of human beings and the creatures of the ground and the air. So far few other animals had marked her presence on the beam. The starlings and sparrows and the odd jackdaw had seen her and recognized the menace which was written in her shape and stance. They kept away from the front of the barn now. If the cohorts of rooks that had taken to wild aerobatics over the valley wood as the time for repairing old nests crept on had seen her they might have been bold enough to come down in ragged company and mob her into moving. So far she had escaped their sight. Fria saw and knew them all.

Most of all, though, she watched, particularly if the morning were sunny and there was a touch of added warmth in the air, the movement of the water in the brook. At the end of the first farm field the brook bank had been carried away by flood and the stream spread back in a wide half-moon over a gravelly shallow only a couple of inches deep. A restlessness which had been slowly growing in her was always more marked when Fria watched the sunlight rippling over the shallows, for although the air is the peregrines' first love and true element they all have a love, too, of water, of bathing and cleanliness. Smiler had provided her with a bath but Fria, although she used it now and then, did not like it. Her feet slipped on the smooth metal of the tray and she found if difficult to bob and dip her head under and send the water rolling over her mantle in the way which instinct demanded of her.

One windless, sunny morning in mid-February, Fria sat surveying the brook and the shallows. Suddenly, when no one was watching, she launched herself from the beam, gave a few slow beats of her scimitar-pointed wings and glided the two hundred yards down to the brook. She settled a little clumsily between two patches of cotton grass at the edge of the pool, raised her head to the sky, and then walked into the shallow water. With the gravel firm under her feet and nothing to block off her wide area of vision, she took a bath. The first she had ever known in freedom.

She dipped and bobbed her head under, letting the water roll back over her neck and down her wings. She loosened her breast feathers and plucked and preened at them under water. For five minutes she made her toilet and through every second, although she seemed relaxed, she was aware of all the movement around her. Then she walked out of the shallows, shook herself, gave a half-hearted preen of her breast, slid her beak down a couple of the primaries of her right wing and jumped free of the ground and began to fly back to the barn. There was neither wind nor obstacle for her to negotiate. Her wing muscles had grown a little stronger and less stiff with the limited liberty from her cage so that she flew up at a long angle easily and unhurriedly. A wood pigeon coming high and fast down the valley saw her and dropped like a plummet into a clump of ash trees by the brook bridge. The hens in the run at the back of the farm kitchen saw her and they froze into a crouch and waited for her to pass. Fria saw them all and more. She saw Bob on a tractor far down the valley, the flick of a jay's wing in the hedge that bordered the hill-road beyond the farm, and the lithe movement of a black mink quartering along the rabbit-holed hedge below the rooks' wood. But they meant nothing to her in terms of food or preying. She swung up to her beam, misjudged it a little, high shooting it, then corrected her flight and dropped awkwardly on to her accustomed perch. She sat there for the next fifteen minutes preening and combing her plumage. Fria had made her first voluntary move away from captivity.

*   *   *

That night another – and very different – move was being made for
someone to escape captivity. The River Taw that flowed into the sea at
Barnstaple began life in a lonely area of boggy marshland, seamed with a
hundred small rivulets and streams, forty miles southwards on the high
slopes of Dartmoor. A man who knew the river could – except for now
and again making a quick road or rail crossing – pick his way easily from
the source down to the first mud banks of its tidal reaches without, particularly at night, much fear of being observed or questioned. Jimmy
Jago was such a man, and there were many others, river keepers,
fishermen, country people and poachers.

This night Jimmy was high up on the moor, almost to the top of Taw
Head, a wild expanse of mires and marshes where small streams and
water gullies had cut deep into the heather-peat soil, a place where a
man had to move carefully if he wanted to avoid going up to his waist in
the boggy, treacherous ground. Though it was dark, with only starlight
to guide him, Jimmy knew his way around from the reconnaissance he
had made in the last months. To his left the great bulk of Hangingstone
Hill lifted a long shoulder against the sky and then sloped gently
southwards to the scarp of Whitehorse Hill. This was the very heart of the
moor. Within a radius of two or three miles of this place rose many rivers,
some to flow south to the English Channel and some north to the Atlantic
. . . the Taw, the Okement, the Tavy, the Dart, the Teign and others.

Jimmy, with a heavy pack on his back, moved up the side of
Hangingstone Hill until he came to a small outcrop of rock, its crest
covered with whortleberry bushes. Underneath the overhang of the rock
the ground had been scooped back and trod bare by generations of sheep
that had used it for a refuge. There were three sheep in it now. They
scattered as Jimmy appeared.

He went under the overhang and slipped off the pack. From it he took
a sheet of thick polythene and wrapped the pack in it, binding the four
corners into a tight twist at the top and cording them securely so that all
dampness would be kept out. From his jacket pocket he took a small
trowel. Squatting on the ground, he began to dig away at the hoof-
packed earth. After an hour he had made a hole large enough to take the
pack and deep enough so that when he scraped back the loose soil there
was a good three-inch layer above it. The rest of the earth he scattered
over the ground, stamping it down with his feet. In a couple of days the
sheltering sheep would have packed it down even harder and no one – if
by any unlucky chance anyone should come that way at this time of the
year – would know the ground had been disturbed. Then he took the
trowel and rammed it hard into the earth wall a few inches below the underside of the overhanging boulder. He forced it in until only the small

circle of the top of the brown, work-worn handle showed like the knob of a root.

This done Jimmy backed out of the recess and looked around him. The night was far from silent. There was the incessant sound of water noises from the mires and small streams, the cough now and then of one of the sheep he had disturbed, the high call of a curlew and far away, from one of the lower valleys, the barking of a dog. But although Jimmy heard them it was without interest. There was only one concern in his mind at that moment, the demand of blood and kinship which in thought carried him eight miles farther south across the wild, unfriendly spread of the moor to the grim, grey jail at Princetown. He had done all he could. The clothes and provisions in the pack were there to be taken if the man for whom they were destined could ever reach them. Many men in their time had escaped from the prison working parties that laboured in the fields and quarries surrounding the jail, slipping off when the longed-for cover of heavy moorland mist suddenly descended. But to escape was one thing. A man then had to beat the moor, to find his way off it, avoiding all the roads because they were at once blocked with police patrols and barriers. The eight miles between Princetown and the spot where Jimmy now stood could for some men, particularly if they were city bred and the weather turned against them, just as well have been eight hundred.

Jimmy suddenly gave a little shiver of cold and apprehension and then turned away northwards and began to work his way back to the lower slopes where the Taw after a few miles would find its stripling strength and form and begin the long flow to the sea.

* * *

Mr. Samkin, although he was nearing his seventies, was an active man, both physically and mentally. He was very short and broad-shouldered and the way he walked reminded Smiler very much of a bulldog. When he asked a question, too, he had a habit of shooting his head forward which increased the resemblance. His motto was work hard and play hard – but he insisted that work should be done before play. Smiler liked him, since Mr. Samkin never treated him as a schoolboy, but as a young student with a brain and ideas of his own. Smiler soon took to speaking frankly about things and having decided opinions of his own, and Mr. Samkin encouraged this.

Once, for instance, Smiler grumbled about the dullness of some of the books which he had been set to read in his study of English literature. This applied particularly to Sir Walter Scott. In talking one evening after their tuition period was over and Sandra had gone, Smiler said, "I can't see, sir, why you should have to read something which doesn't interest you – like Sir Walter Scott. What good does it do you?"

"The good a thing does you, Samuel, isn't always apparent immediately. Anyway, why don't you like Sir Walter Scott?"

"I don't know, sir, but I don't."

With a humorous glint in his eye Mr. Samkin said, "That's not a good enough answer. All right, Samuel, this weekend you write me a five-hundred-word essay on your objections to reading Sir Walter Scott."

"Oh, sir . . ."

Mr. Samkin chuckled. "It won't kill you. And let me ask you this – have you ever read his *Marmion*?"

"That's a poem, isn't it, sir?"

"Yes."

"No, I haven't, sir. His books are bad enough."

"Well, perhaps you've missed something. Listen to this."

Mr. Samkin, with a sly twinkle in his eyes, recited:

We hold our greyhound in our hand,
    Our falcon on our glove;
But where should we find leash or band
    For dame that loves to rove?
Let the wild falcon soar her swing,
    She'll stoop when she has tired her wing.

Smiler, eyes wide, said impulsively, "Oh, I like that."

Mr. Samkin chuckled. "Of course you do. Because he's caught your special interest. So, I suggest you give Sir Walter Scott another chance – but you also do the essay. Good night, Samuel."

At the door Smiler turned and said, "You deliberately chose that bit, sir. About the falcon. Why?"

Mr. Samkin, beginning to pack tobacco into his pipe, said casually, "Oh, I keep my eyes open, Samuel. And – when my eyes aren't good enough – I use those."

He nodded to a side table where lay a pair of Zeiss binoculars of which Smiler had been aware almost from the first day he had started his tuition. He would have given anything for a pair like it.

Mr. Samkin went on, "Do me a good essay – and any day you want to borrow those you can have them."

"Oh, thanks ever so much, sir."

"I prefer 'Thank you very much'. And don't worry. I'm not a gossip."

Smiler went down the hill to the farm with Scott's words singing in his mind. *But where should we find leash or band for dame that loves to*

rove? Let the wild falcon soar her swing. . . . If only she would,
thought Smiler. If only she would and, while she was about it, learn to
hunt and look after herself. He had already seen Fria fly down to bathe
now and then. But that wasn't enough. Still . . . it was something.

*   *   *

But Fria, as February wore towards March and in the lee of sheltered
banks a stub-stemmed primrose or two began to blossom, showed no in-
clination to soar. Nevertheless she was changing.

Most days now she flew confidently down to the shallows and bathed.
Now and then, instead of pitching by the water, she would change her
mind and beat round with a quicker rhythm in her wings, circle, and go
back to her beam perch. Her wing muscles were stronger and a slow
confidence in her flight powers was building in her. Once, too, as she
stood in the cotton grass by the water, the movement of a beetle over the
ground a foot from her caught her eye. With a reflex that had nothing
almost to do with her, she jumped and snapped up the beetle in her beak.
But once there, she held it for a moment or two and then let it fall. She
was well fed, the beetle meant nothing to her in terms of hunger, so she
dropped it.

Now, too, when she took her short flights she was noticed, but not by
many humans. Mr. Samkin had seen her, it was true. So had the river
bailiff as he came up the Bullay brook one day checking the spawning
redds and keeping an eye open for dead salmon kelts. But the bailiff was
like Smiler — he loved all animals and he kept his own counsel.

The birds and animals knew her now and they kept clear of her,
crouching, hiding or going to cover if they were anywhere near her. Not
even the rooks were tempted to interfere and mob her. They were busy
with their nest-building and full of an exclusive excitement of their own
as they robbed sticks from one another and began their mating flights
and battles.

Only once did the rooks come near to approaching Fria. One mid-
morning she launched herself from her beam and began to glide down to
the water meadow. But the wind that morning was uncertain.
Boisterous gusts would suddenly sweep down from the head of the
valley towards the wood and, meeting it, would swirl in turbulence and
rise in a great roar over the tops of the trees. Then, with a suddenness
unheralded, the wind would drop altogether. As Fria was half-way
down to the meadow one of these sudden squalls came racing down the
valley. It caught Fria unawares. Thrusting up from beneath her, it
tipped her into a double wing-over before she knew what was

happening. For a second or two she was a panic-struck plaything of the wind which swept her across to the edge of the wood where for a few seconds, wings flicking hard against this new power that assaulted her, Fria was swung and tumbled out of control in the turbulence. The next moment the up-funnelling wind took her under her spread wings in a firm, steady cushion of power that lifted her up to the level of the rookery trees and then above them.

A few rooks saw her. They went up into the wind, rolled and dived untidily towards her, calling angrily to drive her away, knowing there was safety in their numbers, for if she attacked one there were others to confuse her with a blustery assault from an unseen quarter. But Fria was unconcerned with the rooks. Three or four unintentional flicks of her wings took her a hundred feet above the rooks and their wood. Then, as suddenly as it had come, the wind was gone. For a few seconds Fria hung high in the air, hovering on outstretched pinions, kestrel-fashion. In those few seconds a new world came into the scope of her wide-ranging eyes. She could see the Bullay brook running all the way down the valley and disappearing under a road bridge. Beyond that she caught a glimpse of the curving Taw and the hills, oak-and-pine-covered, on its far side. She saw houses, farms, hamlets, a train sliding up the valley line and the passage of cars and lorries along the Exeter–Barnstaple road. High above them all, she saw for the first time two broad-winged buzzards circling in the air, turning and wheeling with a slow mastery of the wind. The kestrels she knew and the sparrow-hawks, but these were the first buzzards she had seen. It could have been that she did it from panic, or from a half-understood sense of distant kinship with the hawks, but – for whatever reason – she suddenly uttered in her free state a harsh plaint of *kek-kek-kek*. Then she slid sideways, half-closed her wings and planed down towards her bathing-place. Before she realized it she was going at a speed she had never known before. She overshot the edge of the brook shallows and, instinctively, threw herself up and came out of her dive with wings braking hard against the momentum that still lived in her body. She hovered like a kestrel and then settled clumsily on the brook bank twelve yards from her usual place. It had been her first real experience of the powers of her flight. She sat on the bank for fifteen minutes before she took off in a lull of the wind and flew back to her beam. Nobody at the farm had seen her maneuver.

•   •   •

Mr. Samkin approved of Smiler's essay on Sir Walter Scott, though he did not agree with his findings. However, Smiler was given permission to borrow the Zeiss binoculars whenever he wished. His need for them was soon to come.

The next evening after Smiler had finished his supper and was rising to go up to his room to study, the Duchess said, "Sit where you are, lad. I want to talk to you for a moment."

"Yes, ma'am." Smiler ran quickly over in his mind all the things he had done at work that day but could think of nothing wrong. The Duchess had shown that she had a sharp eye for slovenly work, and on the few occasions when Smiler had day-dreamed and done a bad job she had told him about it.

The Duchess, guessing what was going through his mind, smiled and shook her head, setting her red curls bouncing (Smiler, prompted by a suggestion Sandra had once made, wondered whether the curls were only a wig) and said, "It's nothing you've done, Samuel. It's what other people have done and, for the sake of peace and quiet here, I want you to know something about it."

"Yes, of course, ma'am,"

"You know, lad, that Jimmy hasn't been here for more than a week. That's because I've told him to keep away from this place——"

"What, for good, ma'am?"

"No — until he comes to his senses. We've had a family quarrel, Samuel. I can see his point of view. There's fire in his blood and anger in his heart. Heeding them could cause him trouble. But that's nothing to saddle you with. All you have to know and say — if anyone asks for him — is that he's got a job travelling with a fair and you don't know which one or where and you don't know when he will be back."

"Yes, ma'am. But he will be back sometime, won't he?"

"I hope so."

Smiler frowned, and then, brightening, said, "Couldn't you look in your crystal ball and find out?"

The Duchess fondled the ears of the Siamese cat Scampi who was sitting in her lap. "One thing I've never done, Samuel, is to ask the crystal ball anything about the future of my kith and kin. It's bad luck."

Up in his room, although it was none of his business, Smiler wondered what the quarrel between the Duchess and Jimmy had been about. He had at the back of his mind a feeling that Jimmy's night excursions to Highford House could have something to do with it. He was pretty sure, however, that Jimmy no longer went there. The little switch broom of hazel twigs had disappeared and, for the last four times when Smiler had been there at night, he had seen no sign of Jimmy and the other man. However, the night before he noticed that the broom was gone, Smiler had discovered something new. No one else but a regular visitor like himself, and then someone with sharp eyes, would have seen it. Some old lengths of roof water piping, which normally lay half-hidden in the long grass, had been collected together and put back in place up the side of the house and fitted to a length of guttering which still remained on one of the lower roof projections. At the bottom of the pipe a disused old iron container from some long ruined wash-house had been dragged into place under the spout. On Smiler's next visit after this discovery the iron container was half full of water that had run down the pipe from the broad, stone roof parapet. Smiler was sure that the farmer who grazed his cattle on the surrounding paddocks and pastures had not fixed up the water supply because in the far corner of the pasture was a modern drinking-trough which was fed from a standpipe linked to the main water supply.

Sitting in his chair and staring at the little clay model of Johnny Pickering on the mantelshelf – the pebble still firmly on its back – Smiler puzzled over all this for a while. Then, with a shrug of his shoulders, he decided that it was no business of his. The Duchess and Jimmy had been good to him. It was not for him to go poking his nose into their quarrels or affairs.

When he went over later that night to make his rounds of the animals in the barn, he paused at the door and shone his torch beam up towards Fria. She was sitting huddled on her perch, well back under the little pent roof.

With an exasperated shake of his head Smiler called up to her, "You stupid old bird – you can't sit up there for the rest of your life."

No movement came from Fria.

*   *   *

March came in that year with an unexpected warmth and mild breezes from the west. Suddenly the hedgerows were starred with primrose clumps, there was a fresh, metallic greenness to the uncurling fronds of the hart's-tongue ferns, and fragile violets showed their blooms. The fat buds of ash began to swell and there was the smallest drift of green from the hawthorns. There was no rain for two weeks. The Bullay brook dropped to a trickle and the Taw ran low and crystal clear while the estuary at Barnstaple filled with returning salmon waiting for the first spate to let them run the river where even now the kelts from the previous year's spawning season drifted about the pools in which many of them would die before the spate could help take them down to the sea.

On one of these days Smiler spent a day with the local veterinary surgeon – an excursion which had been arranged by the Duchess. The vet.

picked him up in his car in the morning and he went round with him on his visits.

The vet. was a cheerful man who liked company especially when it was the kind which was happy to sit and listen to him talk. And talk he did to Smiler as he made his visits to farm and cottage and the small country towns and hamlets. If Smiler had been in any way faint-hearted about his ambition to become a vet. it was a day which would have probably made him change his mind. As it was, at the end of it, his mind was in a whirl but his ambition was still intact. He heard about and saw all sorts of animals and diseases. He learnt about pigs and their enteric complaints and bacterial infections and was told that the pig is basically a very clean animal; he was shown how to handle birds, hens, geese, turkeys and budgerigars; his ears sang with talk about diet deficiencies of proteins and vitamins; he was given the life history of the warble fly that attacks bullocks; he stood by, his eyes missing nothing, while lambs were injected for dysentery, and his head was made to spin with a litany of the diseases of animals – foot-rot, foot-and-mouth, Johne's disease, Scrapie, liver fluke, mange mite, dog fleas, lice, keds and maggot flies – and then surgical details of neutering and spaying cats and the delivery of calves by Caesarean operation. With a twinkle in his eyes and his pipe seldom from his mouth, the vet. inundated Smiler with theory and practical demonstrations all that day as though – rightly proud of his profession – he wanted to test Smiler, to make sure that he really knew what he wanted and knew exactly what it would entail. And Smiler stood up to it because hard work and often dirty work held no fears for him. He knew what he wanted. He wanted to be a vet. and – he was going to become one.

At the end of the day the vet. took him to the bar of the Fox and Hounds Hotel at Eggesford, not far from Bullaybrook Farm, and bought them both quarts of beer (though Smiler would have preferred cider). While they sat drinking it, the vet. said, "Well, Samuel – that's just one day. And not ended yet. There'll be more waiting for me at the surgery. Think you can take it?"

"Oh, I'm sure I can, sir."

The vet. eyed him over his tankard and said, "Ay, I think you can. You've got a good pair of hands and a strong stomach. You've a long way to go, but you've all the time in the world before you. If ever you want any help come and see me."

That evening Smiler wrote in his diary:

Spent the whole day with Mr. Rhodes. I think the Duchess must have told him to rub my nose in it – and didn't he by half! But it don't make no difference. Bother – any. I'm going to be a vet. The beer at the Fox and Hounds was good. I think I could get to like it as much as cider. Letter today from Laura. Only two mingy pages and most of that about somebody's funeral she went to. Fria just the same.

5

Some Hard Lessons to Learn

The mild weather hastened Spring to the Taw valley. While Smiler went on with his work at the farm and his studies with Mr. Samkin – who now had Smiler groaning because he was insisting that he should learn some Latin and was hinting that very soon Smiler would have to take a proper series of correspondence courses with some educational institution so that he could prepare for his first examinations – things were happening in other places which would eventually shape Smiler's destiny.

In Bristol Albert and Ethel had received a letter from Smiler's father by air mail from Australia. The relevant part of the letter which concerned Smiler read:

> I don't know what the police and the shipping company have been playing at in not letting me know what's been going on. They say they've sent me stuff but I never got it. Anyway, that's all water under the bridge, and I can't get back yet to do anything about it. There's a dock strike out here and we're stuck till the lads decide to unload us – and could you see the company flying me home? Not B. likely.
>
> But that don't worry me because I know my Samuel M. You just give him the letter what I'm enclosing and he'll know what he's got to do. But I don't want you or Ethel to do or say anything about this to anyone, mind, until Samuel M. gets the letter.

Ethel, who was sitting holding the sealed letter to Smiler while Albert read to her, made a sour face and said, "Just like him. Putting it all on to somebody else. Out of sight, out of mind."

Albert gave an inward sigh and said mildly, "Well, dear, it isn't quite like that. What else could he do? And my bet is that he's given Smiler some sound advice."

"That Smiler – the trouble he's caused."

"Not to us, dear. To the police, maybe — but then they're paid for it."

Ethel held up the letter gingerly by one corner as though it might contain poison and said, "Well – and what about this? We get letters from him – but no address and postmarked all over the place. How we goin' to get this to him?"

Albert sighed again, audibly this time, and said, "I don't know. But I'll find a way." He rose and took the letter from his wife. Looking round the prim front parlour where he was not allowed to smoke and always had to wear his carpet slippers, he went on, "I'll just go out to me workshop and think it over for an hour. Something'll come to me."

After half an hour contentedly smoking in his workshop, nothing had come to Albert. But he was not downhearted because Albert was a philosopher and he knew that most problems had a way – if you waited long enough – of solving themselves. He only hoped that this one would not be so long in coming that it would be too late for Smiler to take whatever advice his father was giving. He locked the letter away in his little workshop desk for safety. Ethel, he knew, had the curiosity of a jackdaw. She was well capable of steaming the letter open and reading it.

In Bristol, too, Johnny Pickering was becoming a little frightened and puzzled. He was getting letters recently from all over the place – Southampton, London, Manchester, Glasgow, Durham – and seldom a week passed without one dropping on to the front door-mat.

They were all printed in ink in the same hand without address or signature and there was never more than one sentence in them. The first six had read:

CONFESSION IS GOOD FOR THE SOUL
YOU DID IT AND THE INNOCENT SUFFERED
OWN UP AND AVOID BAD LUCK
NOTHING WILL GO RIGHT UNTIL YOU ARE RIGHT WITH YOURSELF
THE BLACK HAND IS OVER YOU AND THE GREEN EYES ARE WATCHING
ONLY THREE MORE WARNINGS BEFORE FATE STRIKES

At first Johnny Pickering had tried to take no notice of the letters. But he could not keep it up. Things suddenly *did* seem to have started to go wrong with him. He slipped on the pavement and badly twisted his ankle. His girl friend told him she wanted no more to do with him and found herself another boy. He began to get in trouble at work breaking things in the china shop where he was employed as a counter assistant.

He knew perfectly well what all the letters were about and he thought they came from Smiler. But he couldn't work out how Smiler could be dodging about all over England posting them. He said nothing to his parents, but his slowly changing manner, making him irritable and rude, often brought him a smart backhander from his father. There were times when he heartily wished he had never stolen the old lady's handbag and put the blame on Smiler.

And while Albert pondered what to do about Smiler's letter and Johnny Pickering swore, less and less convincingly, that he was never going to be daft enough to go and make a clean breast of things to the police, Smiler was facing his own problems; some minor – like the way Sandra still hung around and foisted her company on him whenever she could; and one major – his disquiet over Fria who still sat on her beam and did little more than fly down to the shallows most days to bathe and was quite content to take food from the loft ledge.

He talked his major problem over one day with Mr. Samkin who had become, in a way, more of a confidant for him than the Duchess who seemed to go about the farm now preoccupied and – Smiler guessed – clearly worrying about the rift with Jimmy.

Mr. Samkin said, "There's nothing you can do but have patience, Samuel. In the wild state Fria would have been taught everything by her parents. Animals have to be taught. But she was taken before all that could happen. Now, if she wants to live free, she's got to learn everything herself. Imagine if you woke up one day on a Pacific island beach – ten years old, and you couldn't speak, knew no language, had never climbed a tree or peeled a banana, couldn't swim. How would you feel?"

"Pretty lost."

"Well, that's Fria. She's pretty lost. But she's got food and water and shelter of a kind. No matter what kind of spirit she's got she's sensible enough to stay where she is. Would you take it on yourself to drive her away deliberately? To cut off her food supply?"

"I couldn't, sir."

Mr. Samkin smiled gently. "Of course not. But something might. Some accident. If on your desert island you slipped and fell into the sea you'd make an instinctive effort to swim. If it came off – you'd have survived. If you were hungry you'd find yourself picking some fruit or other and trying it. If you didn't like its taste you'd spit it out. If you liked it you'd eat it. Self-education forced on man or beast has only two ends – survival or death. Fria isn't going to move from the safety of her beam until something too powerful for her to resist makes her."

"And then she might die, sir."

Mr. Samkin nodded gravely. "The odds are she will, Samuel. There's
no sentiment in Mother Nature."

*   *   *

Two days later the mild weather broke. The westerly breezes died and
the wind moved round to the north-east. There was a night of bitter,
sharp frost and the next day the wind freshened and with it came a hard,
cold rain which swept down into the Taw valley in rolling, biting clouds
and came racing up the Bullay brook in veil after veil of stinging, blinding squalls. In no time at all the woods and fields ran with water and
the brook rose a foot before mid-day, swirling riverwards now in a
brown flood carrying winter debris and litter with it. Birds and beasts
hugged their shelters. The rooks clung to their wood and were tossed
and drenched on their nests, sitting close to the first eggs which had
been laid. In the fields the bullocks and sheep moved to sheltered corners
and turned their backs on the icy downpour. In the farm-yard the only
animals who enjoyed themselves were the few ducks the Duchess kept.
They puddled about over the flooded cobbles and shovelled and dabbled
their bills in the mud around the banks of the swollen shallows where
Fria bathed.

Fria had no temptation that day to bathe. She sat on her beam, well
back under the little pent roof, and faced the cold onslaught of rain. Had
she been an entirely wild peregrine she would have crept into the shelter
of some small cliff crevice or tree hole and hidden from the weather. She
sat there all day until just before the light began to go. There was a lull in
the cold rainstorms and she flew down to the loft ledge and ate, tearing
at a small rabbit which Smiler had left for her. Over the months she had
learned slowly and awkwardly now how to pluck and find the breasts of
the pigeons she was given and how to tear at the skin of rabbits and find
her way to the succulent flesh of flanks and hindquarters.

Her meal done, she flew back to her beam and watched the evening
darkness flood the valley while the renewed rain, heavier than before,
slashed down as though it meant to drown the world. The brook was so
swollen with the run-offs from the valley that it had come up four feet in
a fast storm spate, a coffee-coloured foam and scud-topped torrent that
beat high against the arch of the small stone road-bridge and was
already spreading over the lower parts of the pasture and, within an
hour, was to be over the road by the bridge.

When Smiler went out late that night to visit the barn, the rain
battered against his storm jacket and the yard water swilled around his
gum boots. He flicked his torch up to Fria and saw her huddled tight

back against the barn wall into which the beam was set. For a moment or two he was tempted to creep up quietly into the loft and make a grab for her and put her back into the shelter of her cage, but it was a thought that died almost before it was born. In the darkness and rain he was sure to make a muff of it and, anyway, he knew that Fria would not be sleeping. She would be alert to any noise or movement from the loft. He did his round of the barn, came back across the flooded yard to check the stable doors and then went off to bed.

He lay in bed, reading and listening to the rain beat at his window, and finally he slept.

Outside Fria knew no sleep. She knew only the darkness peopled by darker shapes and the noise of the rain and the higher, steadier noise of the spate-filled brook racing away towards the Taw.

An hour before first morning-light the weather changed. The steady downpour eased off, sometimes stopped for a few minutes, and then abruptly what wind there was backed to the north-west and began to strengthen. Within half an hour it was roaring straight in from the sea and the long reaches of the Atlantic, thundering over miles of countryside and howling down into the valley from the far slope in a full gale that stripped dead branches from trees, seized anything that was loose and tossed it into the air, plucked slates from roofs and tore great patches in the old thatch of cottages. It came now not in one long steady pulse of moving, turbulent air, but in great gusty spasms that would follow a lull, and sometimes – because of the vagaries of the land over which it poured – it would change direction suddenly.

Her body plumage tightened down against its force, her eyes half closed as she faced the wind, Fria clung to her beam and there was a strength now in her legs and talons that held her firm against the sudden vortices and vigorous updraughts that swirled against the little pent roof above her. Now from this side, now from that, now from above and now from below, the violent, invisible tide assaulted Fria, and she held her place and would have gone on holding her place had it not been for the unexpected.

The loft door which was open behind her was held in place by a small bar on its rear side which was hooked into a stout staple which had been driven into one of the cross-beams of the roof timbers that straddled the inside of the loft. The hook and staple were strong, but the wood of the cross-beam, though its heart was a solid core of oak, had an outer lay of ancient wood which had been bored and tunnelled by woodworm. Each time the wind roared into the loft and then was drawn back like a violently receding wave, the suction wrenched at the loft door, trying to draw it shut. And each time the door jerked under the vacuum pull of the wind the staple worked a little looser.

Finally, as the first grey light of dawn struggled through the curtains of wind-driven rain, the gale smashed against the face of the barn, shaking its roof and timbers, soared upwards, howled around the loft and then was drawn back in a fierce out-going eddy, violent with turbulence and power. The staple was pulled from its beam and the loft door was sucked back with a speed and savagery that would have killed anything which barred its path. The door crashed into its frame, shattering and bursting it outwards. Timbers and woodwork flew out into the air and the door, torn from its hinges, followed on the heels of an explosion of sound like a crack of thunder. The wind took the door, lifted it, and sent it slicing high through the air as though it were a sheet of paper. (It was found two days later by Bob and Bill in field of young wheat at the top of the hill road at the brow of the valley.)

And with the door went Fria.

The great crash of the door slamming into and through its frame six inches below and behind her was like the report of a cannon being fired close to her. She jumped with fear on her beam and half spread her wings in panic. The wind took her. Wings wide, her long tail-feathers spread, the wind sucked her up like a straw and she was whipped across the face of the barn and then swung round its corner. As though the gale were some living, malicious personality treating her like a new toy in its old, old game, it flung her skywards on a great updraught of eddying and coiling currents of air. She went up five hundred feet in a few seconds and, as she went, she was pitched and somersaulted out of control.

A fully mature and experienced peregrine with all its powers could have ridden the wind and would have known better than to fight the impossible. A fully mature and experienced peregrine would never voluntarily have put to flight in such a wind and – if caught in one – would have gone to ground, to eyrie or to shelter as quickly as it could along the line of least resistance, stooping with the wind's direction and flattening its line of dive long before sanctuary was too dangerously near.

Fria had no such wisdom. In a panic she fought the air with her wings, and the wind took the resistance she gave and flipped her over and upwards in a ragged series of back-somersaults. When Fria righted herself she was a thousand feet above ground, though she could see little of it in the pale morning light because of the scuds of driving rain that charged across the land in rolling onslaughts.

Fria wailed with panic, caught sight of the barn far below her, and automatically, since it represented shelter, half rolled, closed her wings and began to dive towards it as she had once come down from high above the rookery to her bathing-place. The maneuver did her no good at all. The power of the wind, rising almost vertically beneath her, held her where she was for a moment and then lifted her and rolled her over and over. She was swung up another five hundred feet, and the howling and roaring of the wind around her filled her mind with a greater panic.

For some seconds the gale threw her about the sky in its updraught and then spewed her out of its ascending vortex into the gale-force main stream of its south-easterly path. There, from luck, chance, or some dim ancestral bodily memory that informed her muscles and wings, she found herself doing the right thing. With three-quarter-closed wings, her tail feathers tight in a narrow wedge shape, her head lowered, she found herself going downwind fast and slowly losing height.

Her panic eased a little with the discovery, and she leaned on the back of the wind, increased her glide to a faster dive, and came down through the rain and saw the earth coming up to her fast. She saw trees, woods, fields, the dark shine of a flooded river and then, away to her right, the rain-darkened stonework of a building that reminded her of the barns and Bullaybrook Farm.

Full of fear, but calmer now that she was under some sort of control, Fria leaned across the wind and wore down the gale in a fast, curving arc and — because she wanted to do it — her natural flight powers obeyed her and she began to flatten her descent though she did not slacken it much. She flashed dangerously low across the tossing, waving tops of a wide expanse of fir plantation, dropped below its far edge into shelter from the gale, and found herself heading fast for the sprawling bulk of the grey stone building she had seen. She curved across the building ten feet above it and, now in some primitive control of herself, threw up sharply and then had to fight the upsurging momentum of her own body with rapid brake-beats of her wings. A few seconds later she landed clumsily in tall grasses fifty yards from the building. She sat, hidden in the wet grasses, the rain beating down on her. She sat, half crouched, her wings half spread, the rain striking down at them, and she wailed three or four times like a lonely, unhappy, lost child. But as with an untutored, immature child one emotion moves on erratic impulse rapidly to another Fria felt sudden anger in herself. Her wailing ceased. At this moment, since her eyes never missed any movement, she saw something stir in the tall grasses a couple of feet from her.

It was a little shrew that had been flooded out of its earth burrow. Fria jumped forward and angrily grabbed at it with her beak. Her powerful mandibles clamped across its tiny neck and killed it. For a moment Fria sat with it in her beak. Then with a toss of her head she jerked it from her.

● ● ●

Smiler was full of dismay when he discovered that Fria had gone. The manner of her going was no mystery to him or to Bob and Bill.

"That old door, Sammy, must have come out like a shell from a gun. But if she was up on the beam it wouldn't have hit her," said Bill. "Don't you worry. She'll be back when she gets hungry."

But Smiler was far from content with that. Fria was not a homing pigeon. The gale could have blown her miles away, and the gale was still blowing. She might, perhaps, have been injured, broken a wing or something, and be somewhere in the nearby woods and fields. He decided that he just had to try and find her. If she were uninjured and wanted to stay free . . . well, that was all right with him. But if she were injured . . . well, then he had a duty to try and find her.

That day was a Saturday and he finished work at mid-day. He ate a hurried lunch and then cycled up to Mr. Samkin and borrowed his binoculars. From then until the light went he spent his time cycling around the countryside and along the paths in the Forestry Commission plantations looking for Fria. The wind was still blowing hard, but the rain had now slackened to occasional fierce showers.

Smiler went to every high point he could think of and searched the sky and then the countryside for a sign of the falcon. But he had no luck. He went to Highford House. He sat there for half an hour, sweeping his glasses round and round. But there was no sign of Fria. At least no sign that he could recognize, though he passed one as he left the place by way of the overgrown garden. The limp, bedraggled mole-grey body of a dead shrew lay in the grass. And he would have been surprised – and delighted – if he could have known that Fria was watching him as he moved about the building and the garden.

Fria recognized him. But that was all. She was no familiar dog or cat to come to him, eager to make herself known. She sat where she was and watched him go. Neither hunger nor thirst had worried her yet, but there was a difference in her which now informed all her movements and emotions. She had ridden the gale. The memory of her panic had gone but not, probably, the memory of the way she had finally used the wind to achieve sanctuary of a kind. Like all creatures, once she had done something the repetition of the act presented no fears. She learned by doing; and the more often a thing was done the more adept a creature became at it. Nature is a rough teacher, but her lessons stick, or else. . . .

Smiler cycled back to the farm with a long face and it was made longer when the Duchess reminded him that Sandra was coming to dinner – a return invitation which the Duchess had insisted he make because he had been to Sandra's party. Smiler groaned, and groaned again when the Duchess said, "And what's more, you've only got half an hour to bath and change before she comes. And, of course – " she grinned and reached out and pulled his snub nose – "you'll walk her home in the dark afterwards like a perfect gentleman. And you needn't think you're being untrue to that Laura of yours. She's not sitting at home every night doing her knitting and mooning about you. Now get off with you – and don't fuss about that bird. God's hand is large and it casts a wide shadow over the world."

"Who said that?" asked Smiler.

"Well, I did of course. I just said it."

"Oh, I thought it was a quotation."

"Well, thank you, Sammy. But remember – there's no wisdom in any book which wasn't first spoken by someone."

Smiler paused at the door and with a grin said, "Do I really have to walk her home?" Then he ducked out of the doorway to avoid a cushion being thrown at him. The Duchess went off into the kitchen chuckling to herself. But once she was alone and the thought of Smiler's falcon came back to her, her face grew serious. She was remembering something Jimmy had said before she had told him not to stay at the farm any longer.

"If freedom is your right, then it's better to die than let any man take it from you. And, if needs be, it's better to be hunted all your life than live in a cage."

That evening was not the ordeal which Smiler had thought it might be. Sandra looked very nice in a blue dress which contrasted with her fair complexion and blonde hair. It was curious, Smiler decided, how once you got used to something you almost stopped noticing it, like the slight prominence of her aquiline nose. In fact, too, the word aquiline pleased him because he had only recently discovered it in his reading and – following Mr. Samkin's instructions never to pass a new word without looking it up in the dictionary – he knew that it came from the word *aquila* – the golden eagle. Hooked like an eagle's beak . . . "Well, be fair, Samuel M.," he told himself, "it wasn't really as bad as that."

Over dinner the Duchess told them tales of her circus life and how she had been born in a horsedrawn caravan in a field somewhere on the south side of Dartmoor. When she was old enough she had worked with her mother selling the wooden clothes-pegs her father and brothers made from door to door, and posies of spring and summer flowers, until the day had come when she was a young woman and had met her husband, the Duke. She had gone into the circus with him and started her career as a fortune teller. But after he had died her heart had turned from the circus and, with the money she had saved, she had bought Bullaybrook Farm and retired.

When dinner was over they played three-handed cards and put records on the player, though neither Sandra nor Smiler thought much of the records because they were donkey's years old. Then the old piano was opened up and Smiler, who in the past months had spent a lot of time on it and, having a good ear, had taught himself to play quite well, gave them some of the songs they knew and others that he had learnt from his father. While he played one of his father's favourites, *The Streams of Lovely Nancy*, he wondered where his father was at that moment and how long it would be before he saw him and between them they could get all his troubles sorted out so that he could go full steam ahead with his ambition to be a vet.

Walking Sandra back up the hill to her village afterwards it was very dark and half-way up the hill Sandra stumbled and took his arm to keep her balance. And then she kept her hand on his arm and, somehow, a little later Smiler found that she was holding his hand. He felt very embarrassed about it but clearly Sandra did not consider it anything strange.

She said, "If you're going to do all this studying why don't you try to be a doctor? After all that's a much better thing than spending your time with dirty old animals and birds."

Smiler said indignantly, "Animals and birds aren't dirty – not if people keep them properly. And, anyway, being a vet. is harder than being a doctor. After all, people can tell a doctor where they've got their pains and aches and, if he's done his stuff, well, he ought to know how to treat them. But animals can't speak. You've got to . . . well, sort of get into their minds for them and find out what's wrong sometimes."

Sandra said, "You've always got an answer, haven't you?" And then, going off at a tangent, she went on, "I had a good look tonight, and you know, I don't think that is a wig the Duchess wears. It's her own hair. But why does she wear it in those tight little curls?"

"If you're so interested – why didn't you ask her?"

At the front door of Sandra's house, she paused in the darkness before going in and said very politely, "Well, thank you very much, Sammy, for a very pleasant evening."

"Thank you for coming."

Sandra laughed and said, "And now, if you want to, you can kiss me goodnight."

Startled, Smiler blurted out, "Good Lord, I couldn't do that!"

Sandra giggled. "Why not?"

"Well . . . well, you don't. You don't kiss people unless you love them."

"And you don't love me?" asked Sandra teasingly.

"Of course I don't."

"Who do you love them?"

"That's none of your business."

"I don't care if it isn't. And, anyway, I kiss people because I like them and they've been nice to me. So — " She leaned forward and gave him a smacking great kiss on the cheek and nearly poked his left eye out with her nose.

Smiler turned and ran until he was out of the village. When he slowed up and began the walk back down the hill, he thought, "Gosh, girls . . . you have to be on your toes all the time with them, or you're in trouble."

Half-way down the hill he had further proof of this which he entered at the end of his diary that night.

The diary entry finished:

. . . but I'm sure Fria can't have gone very far. I'm going to spend all day tomorrow looking for her. If she's lodged up somewhere I could bring food to her.

Trouble tonight with that Sandra. I think she only does it to get me all muddled up. Which is what it does what with worrying about Fria and thinking about what Laura would say. Though you never know with her. She might just laugh her head off. And to make matters worse that boy friend of hers (Sandra's) must have been hanging around because he stopped me on the hill coming back and told me what he would do if I didn't keep away from Sandra. I told him he could keep his old Sandra. And then he got nasty so — him being bigger than me — I said to put his head in a bucket and ran for home.

Being a vet. is much more difficult than being a doctor.

I think it could have been Trevor Green that caused all the trouble in the barn and let Fria free. The pebble is still on Johnny P's shoulders. Can't see how it can ever fall off.

'And so to bed' — Samuel Pepys Miles!!

6

First Steps Towards Freedom

Smiler had an early breakfast the next morning, did his chores around the barns and the yard, and then spent the rest of the daylight hours searching for Fria. At times, when he met farm workers and the country people he had now come to know, it was a temptation to ask them if they had seen the falcon. But he held back from doing so because he knew how fast the news would travel round, and that would alert trigger-happy folk who just shot at anything that moved.

The gale had dropped now to a steady blow from the north-east, driving great banks of high cumulus clouds across a pale-blue sky. Now and again there would be a fierce, brief shower. The Taw and its tributary streams were running high and some of the valley fields were flooded with the spate.

Smiler cycled for miles to every vantage point he could think of and others that he picked off the one-inch-to-the-mile ordnance survey map he had bought of the district. He got wet and he got dry again, and he got tired and he got hungry. At lunchtime he called at the Fox and Hounds hotel bar and had a pint of cider and a plate of sandwiches. The barman was a jolly man with dark hair and long sideburns and wore a red waistcoat. As he served Smiler, he said, "The Duchess's nephew, ain't you?" When Smiler nodded, the barman grinned, thrust out his right hand, and said with a wink, "Here you are then, tell me fortune. Shall I win the football pools next week?"

Smiler laughed, but as he ate his lunch the idea came to him that if he didn't find Fria maybe the Duchess could look in her crystal ball and get some information – though he had to admit that it was a slim hope.

For the rest of the afternoon Smiler searched, using Mr. Samkin's binoculars and carefully putting them back in their case when he had finished each time. He saw plenty of birds. There were lapwings still flocking on the high fields, mallard, widgeon and teal flighting along the flooded meadows, and once a skein of geese moving high in a wavering line northwards against the wind. Buzzard pairs wheeled and soared over the dark pine woods, swans winged heavily up the river and kestrels hovered over the brown heather and dead bracken clumps in the forestry clearings. But Smiler saw no sign of Fria, although once, high, high up, two or three thousand feet, he guessed, he picked out to the north a small, dark crescent shape which was gone quickly into the blazing eye of the sun as a racing cloud-patch uncovered it briefly. It was a peregrine, Smiler was sure, but he couldn't believe that it was Fria, riding so high and so confidently. A few seconds' observation of the bird marked it as one that had been born to freedom and wore its liberty and powers untouched by any taint of captivity. Smiler was right, for the peregrine he briefly saw was a tiercel from the cliffs of Blackstone Point beyond Ilfracombe.

With his glasses Smiler scanned the edges of woods and the clumps of isolated elms and oaks, seeking for the still graven shape of Fria perched on some high branch or merged against some tree-trunk. All he saw was the movement of wood pigeons and ring-doves and the black scattering of rooks and crows. Knowing that Fria was used to barns and farm buildings, he searched around field barns and hay stores and the roofs of the farmhouses – all without success. It was this knowledge that Fria might have chosen some building for shelter that took him with only half an hour of daylight left to Highford House, debating in his mind whether if he did not find Fria today – a Sunday – he could dare ask the Duchess for the next day off to go on with his search and promise to work the following Sunday to make it up. If it had been Jimmy Jago he had had to ask he knew that permission would have been given. But there was no Jimmy around now, and the Duchess had a funny little streak about jobs being done when they should be done. And, anyway, in his heart he felt that the Duchess had already given Fria up as lost for good.

He went all over Highford House and the ruined buildings around it. He searched inside the red brick tower, climbing as high as he dared until he met a great gap in the spiralling stone stairway. There was no sign of Fria.

Despondently Smiler gave up the search and went back to where he had left his bicycle in the wild rhododendron shrubbery at the back of the house. He cycled away down the wet, gravelly, moss-patched old driveway. As he went a jay shrieked suddenly at him from a branch as though in derision.

* * *

Fria watched him go. She was lodged within a foot of the top of the red brick tower. Here, there had long ago been a fall of bricks from the curved side of the tower which had made a recess about two feet high and three feet wide. The recess ran back through the masonry to the inner wall of the tower, forming a shelf which was protected from the weather. Two bricks had fallen inwards from the rear wall making a hole through which one could look down into the well of the tower past a small section of stone stairway that still survived to the great gap that reached far below to the commencement of the stairs again. On the outside of the tower, ivy had grown up, rooted in the bricks twelve feet below. It covered one side of the recess and formed a leafy screen. Above the recess stonecrop had taken root and formed pale green pads along an ornamental ridge. From the tower-top — where the seed had years ago been excreted by a thrush — a trail of bramble, touched now with new leaf spurs, cascaded downwards in a ragged sweep.

From the ground it was almost impossible to see that the tower-top held Fria's recess. But Fria, although she sat well back, could see everything that moved below. She had seen Smiler come and now she watched him go and, because she associated him with food and she was hungry, there had been a moment before his going when she had almost wailed from the sudden sharpness of the association twisting physically inside her. Hunger she had, but not thirst. Twice that day she had taken off into the steady wind and flown to the tower-top where the rains had formed puddles in the warped and dented hollows of the old lead roof sheeting that still remained there. And twice that day she had moved off in a slow, circular flight, low down, skirting around Highford House itself, beating with steady wing-flicks across the bullock pasture and then coming back in a fast rising flight to the tower recess. Flight was not now the panic-maker it had been. The wind was firm, a steady blow which she mastered and used easily so long as she was not called upon to perform any unexpected or skilful maneuver. On her second, non-drinking flight, she had dropped to the grass where she had killed the shrew. Mice and shrews she had eaten before and hunger spurred her search for this shrew. The shrew had gone, its limp body long ago seen by a crow and carried away.

If Smiler had stayed another ten minutes he might have found Fria, for now, as he cycled down the drive a half a mile away, she suddenly wailed and moved forward to the edge of the recess. In the dying light she launched herself easily and flapped slowly across the abandoned, ruined gardens, moving more like an owl than a peregrine. She dropped her head and searched the ground beneath her. Even in the fading light, her great eyes — so big that if a man's were in the same proportion to his body size they would have been three inches wide — missed nothing. She saw a pale cinnamon moth climbing a dead willow-herb stalk, saw the slight heave of the ground where a mole worked unseen, and the slow draw of a dead leaf where a worm pulled it down into its tunnel. She was hungry, and hunger is the great dictator. A fieldmouse poked its nose from under a rain-flattened patch of long-dead wild geranium. Fria saw the fine tremble of its whiskers, and small skin-movement as it creased its snout and flicked its eyes from side to side. Because the mouse meant food to her and she wanted it she slid up into the air a few feet. Her muscles were schooled by the desire in her to hang above the rodent. She hung on poised wings, her long primaries just trembling, the narrow wedge of her tail suddenly spread wide as she hovered like a kestrel. She did what many of her wild kin often did from time to time. Sometimes, indeed, they hovered, sharing the same field or orchard with a kestrel for at certain times of the year there was a strange amity between the two species.

The mouse moved out from its shelter and ran in jerky, staccato movements between the tall grasses. Fria moved, following it, hovering still. Then, the excitement in her for food so strong, she raised her wings and dropped to the grass, thrusting out her legs, talons open to grasp the mouse. The mouse leapt away and scuttled to the safety of the root tangle of an old crab-apple tree. Fria, missing the mouse, hit the ground lightly but clumsily. She sat on the grass, folded her long wings over her tail, preened irritably at her slate-streaked pale breast and then wailed gently. After a few moments she jumped lightly into the air and began to quarter across the ground between the tower and the ruined house, hovering and watching the ground and then sliding a few yards to another vantage position. But nothing moved on the ground, and a steady rain shower, heavy, and pounding the ground with fat drops, blackened the sky and drove the last of the light from the day.

Fria winged over gently and beat up to her recess. She shook the water from her plumage and then walked to the back of the recess and began to dress and preen her feathers. The night settled around her, steady with the noise of creaking branches and the whisper of the ivy leaves that screened part of the recess opening. Fria slept, forgetting her hunger and her anger. An hour later a barn owl that lived in a dead oak a mile away came drifting over the abandoned garden and took the field mouse that Fria had missed.

*　*　*

The next morning in Bristol a letter arrived for Johnny Pickering before he went off to work. Inside was the familiar sheet of paper and on it was written: THERE IS ONLY ONE WAY TO AVOID THE DARK DAYS AHEAD.

His father, sitting across the table from him, saw the paper in his hand and said, "What's that, then?"

In surly tones Johnny Pickering said, "Never you mind. It's my business."

His father, bad-tempered and with a headache from too much beer the previous night, leaned across the table quickly and gave him a smack on the head which sent Johnny from his chair to the floor.

"Add that to it, then," said his father.

It was a good beginning to the week, thought Johnny as he cycled to work. But, anyway, he was used to taking the odd clout from his father and he certainly wasn't going to let the letters upset him. Yet, tell himself what he may, he *was* upset by them. Knowing what he did about Smiler he couldn't see them as being his style. Somebody else was doing it. Suddenly the alarming thought struck him that maybe the police suspected him and someone at the station was trying to frighten him into telling the truth. He was so absorbed by this thought that when a small van drew up rather sharply ahead of him, although he braked hard and in reasonable time, his front wheel hit the back of the van and was too much buckled for him to ride it. As he dragged his bicycle to the pavement he remembered the words in one of the letters: NOTHING WILL GO RIGHT UNTIL YOU ARE RIGHT WITH YOURSELF.

* * *

And at the breakfast table at Albert and Ethel's house, Ethel, in her dressing-gown and with her hair in curlers (a sight which Albert could not bear but had to), said "Well, have you decided yet what to do about that letter for Smiler?"

"No, I haven't."

"But you've got to. It's important."

"Well, what do you want me to do? Put an advert in all the papers all over the country? Have an S.O.S. broadcast on the radio? *Will Samuel Miles, wanted by the police, please contact his brother-in-law where he will hear of something to his advantage.* I don't think. Not with a copper waiting on the doorstep."

"Oh, sarky, aren't we, this morning," said Ethel.

"Sorry, luv," said Albert, who was really a nice-natured man. Monday morning was always bad for him because he was suffering from Sunday when he was made to go to chapel twice a day and tidy up and dig in the small garden which he hated and then no television in the evening because Ethel didn't hold with it on a Sunday.

"Well, something's got to be done," said Ethel practically. "Nobody's going to turn up out of the blue, ringing our doorbell to tell us where he's hidden himself."

"I suppose not," said Albert.

* * *

And on that Monday morning a prisoner at Princetown Gaol was marched out with a working party under the guard of warders to do quarrying on the moor close to the prison.

He was a tall, solidly built man in his forties. He had short, sandy hair, blue eyes, and a tanned craggy face creased with good-humoured lines. Cheerfulness was second nature to him and self-reliance went with it. Bitterness he had known once but it had been burned from him.

He looked up at the rain-washed sky and, because he had always lived an open-air life, sensed at once the quarter the wind was in, knew from the look of the day whether it would shift and what changes might come. On this morning he knew for sure that the likelihood of there being a sudden, cloaking Dartmoor mist was something he wouldn't bet a farthing on.

He walked along in the ranks of prisoners and watched the long slopes of the moor, caught the white-barred flick of a snipe's wings as it rose from a ditch, and half-whistled, half-hummed a tune to himself. The man at his side – one of the trusty few who knew his secret – winked at him and said from the side of his mouth, "No excursion ticket for sale today, Maxie."

Maxie winked back and grinned. Like was long, life was earnest, and patience was a good thing – but best of all, he told himself, was faith. His day would come. The mist would come and all he would need would be a hundred yards start, and he would be away towards the high tors he knew like the back of his hand, and streaking like a hare for freedom. And why shouldn't he? A man had to do what his heart and his nature told him was just. But justice was one thing and the law was another. He grinned to himself and then, seeing a wood pigeon in flight across the road ahead, he fell to thinking of the time when he had been a very young man and kept pigeons . . . brown and white and black and white West of England tumblers that fell through the sky in a madness of whirling wings and somersaults that cut the air with a sound like tearing calico . . . the beauties, the little beauties. . . .

* * *

And that morning Smiler sat at breakfast without much appetite. The

Duchess, with Scampi on her lap, eyed him over the table and knew exactly what his trouble was and, because she was a good-hearted woman, though easily severe when she felt it was wise, she said, "If you square it with Bob and Bill and work all day next Saturday, you can take today off to look for that blessed Fria of yours."

"Oh, thank you very much, ma'am. I would like to do that."

Smiler had no trouble arranging things with Bill and Bob because more than once he had done them good turns. So once more he set off on his bicycle with his map and his glasses, and as he rode along he settled his plan of campaign if he should be lucky enough to find Fria. He didn't want to capture her. All he wanted was to know where she was and then keep an eye on her. She was free now and he had a good idea that hunger would force her to find some kind of food for herself, even if she had to scavenge for it. All he wanted was to be on hand while she learnt to look after herself and – if it was a slow process – to be able to leave her a dead rabbit or wood pigeon now and then to keep her going. On no account, he told himself, was he going to take over full provisioning because that would be a mistaken kindness. Fate had set her free and now – if she still survived – she would have to learn the hard lessons of a life of liberty for herself. If she had been brought up naturally in her parents' eyrie, they would have done the teaching for her. He knew, for instance, from his reading, that the great skill of a peregrine stooping vertically from hundreds of feet on to its flying prey, slashing past it and killing it with the rear talons of one or both feet was something which had to be taught by the parents. Maybe, if Fria survived long enough, she would learn that great maneuver of speed and timing for herself.

As he rode through the countryside, stopping now and then to sweep the landscape with his glasses, Fria was already learning some lessons for herself. She woke at first light. In the grey dawn she flew up to the tower-roof and drank some water. The rains had gone, but the sky was overcast with low, heavy clouds that broke now and then to show patches of blue sky from which a watery sun briefly bathed the land in its light. Her thirst satisfied, Fria went back to her recess. Hunger was a tightening knot inside her. On the bricked face of the recess a brief movement caught her eye. It was a small spider which had crept to the mouth of a funnel-shaped web it had made in a crack between the bricks. Its movement brought a quick reflex action from Fria. She stabbed at it with her beak, caught, and swallowed it. She moved around the recess and found another spider which she caught and ate. The acts of catching and eating stimulated her. Within the next half hour she had taken four wood lice that had moved from under the dead ivy leaves which littered one corner

of the recess. The amount of food was negligible and the taste faintly dis-
agreeable. Having, for the moment, exhausted the insect life of her recess,
she walked to the edge and looked down into the garden. After a few
moments she flew down and settled in the damp, overgrown tangle of
grasses and dead bracken. She began to stalk slowly through this
miniature jungle, her eyes alert for any movement. She took a worm that
writhed, half-dead, at the edge of a puddle and ate it. She spent an hour
scavenging through the wild garden, took three more worms, four
spiders, and a fat dor-bettle. The knot of hunger in her slackened a
little, but not enough to come anywhere near satisfying her. Because she
was a bird of quick temperament the slow process of feeding irritated
her to the point where once or twice she gave an angry call ...
yek-yek-yek.

She launched herself and flew up twenty feet and began to quarter the
ground, hovering like a kestrel. Her move into the air sent a thrush that
was cracking a snail on a loose masonry slab by the old house flying fast
and low into the cover of a thicket of dead old man's beard which trailed
in a tangled mantle over a stunted hawthorn bush. Fria, alert and
reflexes working sharply, went after it like a sparrow-hawk. But she was
far too slow and the thrush found sanctuary easily. Fria soared up a little
at the end of her chase and hovered briefly over the hawthorn and its
creeper tangle. A pair of magpies coming over the roofless house saw
her, and recognized the menace of her shape and poise, sharp-tipped
wings flicking, tapping at the air as though they quivered in some fine
ecstasy. They dived for the cover of the dark labyrinths of the
overgrown rhododendrons by the old driveway.

Fria beat up to the top of the tower and settled there above her
recess. She sat there for ten minutes slowly bobbing her head up and
down irritably as though she were giving herself a good talking to. She
saw the movement of dozens of birds in the great arc of her vision,
caught the black and white fidgeting of a dipper on a post down by the
flooded river and, once, the streak of blue fire as a kingfisher went fast
downstream. She watched a handful of people waiting on the platform
at Eggesford Station and the movement of sparrows quarrelling on its
roof. Then, much nearer, in the rough pasture which had once been
well-kept parkland, she saw something move at the base of a large chestnut tree. Its lower trunk fanned out in sloping grey buttresses and the
ground around was bare and mud-trampled by the feet of sheltering cattle. Fria's eyes focussed sharply. A wood pigeon was sitting on one of
the exposed roots of the tree. Fria saw its eye colour, saw each feather
and the dull burnish of its breast and — though it meant nothing to her —
a dried red stain on its gorget, close to the lesser coverts of its right

wing. A farmer shooting the previous day had winged the pigeon and there were three or four pellets lodged in the shoulder girdle of its right wing. The bird could fly but only clumsily.

Fria recognized the bird. She knew the white patches either side of its neck and the white bars on its outer wing coverts as it flapped awkwardly from the root to the ground. She had been fed pigeons in the barn and she knew their flight from her beam-post above the loft. And she knew the succulence of their flesh. The hunger drive in her took her into the air. Maybe the ancestral memory of the peregrines' age-old craft operated independently in her. She slid away down wind in a half circle and then came back into the wind and with swift wing-beats rose and gained height. She flew fifty feet above the wood at the rear of Highford House. Down wind of her now, three hundred yards away, the pigeon moved slowly over the trampled ground close to the chestnut tree.

Fria gave three or four quick beats of her wings and went down wind fast in a long shallow stoop. A jay shrieked a warning to the world as she went over. A rabbit at the edge of the wood flattened to the ground. Fria knew nothing except the pulse of air against her as she gained speed and the figure of the pigeon growing in size as she neared it. She swept into the shadow of the tree and, although the pigeon saw her late and jumped clumsily into flight and there would have been no escape for it from an experienced peregrine, she made a complete mess of her first real attempt to take food for herself in flight. An experienced bird would have come down with its legs extended forward and tight up against its breast, the three front toes of each foot drawn up and the long rear toe daggering below, and an experienced bird would have swept close over the pigeon's back, and the deadly rear toes would have sliced into the bird. The peregrine's wings would have gone up at the moment of strike and the pigeon would have died of shock or its wound.

Fria, when she was within three yards of the pigeon, dropped her feet so that she could grab the bird with them. The movement slowed her flight and threw her off line. She grabbed at the bird as it went away below her, hit it clumsily on the wing with a harmless, already clenched foot, and tumbled it over on its side in the air.

They came to the ground together in an untidy, flapping whirl of wings. The pigeon jumped clear and, flying low and awkwardly with its damaged right wing, headed across the pasture towards the woods. Angrily Fria went after it, flying fast and easily overtaking the injured bird. She grabbed at it again and missed as the pigeon swerved in panic and tried to gain height. But its damaged wing had no power to take it up. It skittered across the grass, hit the ground and rolled over. Fria followed and, raising her wings like a kestrel, dropped on to it.

The pigeon flapped its wings and struggled. Fria sat on it, grasping it with her strong talons, and then, instinctively to still its movements, she stabbed at the bird's neck with her beak. More by luck than design, she got a hold on the pigeon's neck and, with an angry twist of her head, broke it and the pigeon died. Fria had made her first kill.

She ate it where she had killed it, out in the open so that she would have been aware of the approach of any danger. From the pigeons she had been given in captivity she had learned how to pluck and plume them, tearing out the breast feathers. Sometimes in the past she had plucked them properly and sometimes had only made a token show before tearing at the carcase meat. Today, impatient with hunger, she plucked and ate and then plucked again as the pigeon lay on its back and she held it steady with her feet. She ate for more than half an hour. When she had finished the pigeon lay on its back in the wet grass, its wings outspread and untouched. The flesh had gone from its breast and legs. Its back was untouched, and the flesh had been cleaned from the neck. It lay there cleared down almost to the framework of the bird it had been.

Gorged, Fria rose at last from her kill and flew heavily and leisurely back to her tower and then sat in her recess and cleaned and preened herself. The experiences, clumsy and fortunate, of her first kill passed into her memory and the small store of her natural knowledge was increased.

* * *

Smiler was lucky. His last place of call before going home was, as usual, Highford House. This time he went to it along the road that crossed the Taw by the old stone bridge at Eggesford and climbed the hill below whose crest lay Highford House. He pushed his bicycle along the lower drive that ran back from the hill road. Clear of the trees, the drive, grass-grown now, and almost vanished, crossed the pasture which had once been the park.

The light was going fast, but the patch of loose plucked feathers and the spread carcase of the pigeon stood out sharply a few yards to the right of the drive. Smiler crossed to it and knelt down. There was an immediate excitement in him. It was the first remains of a peregrine kill he had seen in the wild, but he had no difficulty in recognizing it because he had cleared such carcases away in the barn after he had fed Fria. He was delighted that Fria had to be around here somewhere and that she had – no matter how – managed to make a kill. From the way the bird had been stripped he knew that Fria must have been very hungry. In her greed she had even nipped out small pieces of the breast bone.

He gathered up the pigeon's remains and stuffed them down a rabbit hole. Left in the open, although it might have been scavenged by fox or rat, it might also be seen by a keeper. For the moment – if Fria was lodged in the vicinity – he was not keen that any keeper or farmer should find evidence of her presence.

He hurried to the old house, climbed to his vantage point and in the fading light swept his field-glasses around the close neighbourhood. He scanned the woods and the isolated tree clumps and found nothing. Most peregrines, he knew, were not keen on lodging in trees so he gave the top storeys of the old house and the red brick tower a careful survey, but he could find no sign of the falcon. Actually, he had his glasses on the ivy-screened, bramble overspill of the recess for a few seconds, but in the dim light the opening of the recess was no more than a broken patch of brickwork. Fria, bodily content, and well back in the recess, saw him as he crouched on the top parapet of the old house.

Smiler finally gave up his search as the light went. He returned to the farm, but he said nothing about finding the kill. He wanted to find Fria before he said anything to the Duchess or Bob and Bill. He could not get the next day off to search for her again. He would have to wait for the week-end. In his diary that night he confided a small doubt that had risen in his mind.

He wrote:

. . . of course, until I've actually spotted Fria up there I can't be sure. The kill might have been made by some other peregrine. Mr. Samkin tells me that there still are a pair or two out on the cliffs near Ilfracombe. But would they have come so far inland to make a kill. Hope not. So roll on Sunday when I can have another look for her. I'd go up at night with a torch but that might be seen by people.

After Mr. Samkin's tonight, that Trevor Green was waiting outside to take Sandra home. Her face! If looks could kill he'd have been a gonner.

* * *

During that week the education of Fria progressed. She caught her first field-mouse from a hovering pitch like a kestrel, her talons clamping on it through the grasses and killing it immediately. She took a starling which was running up and down the roof parapet of the old house prospecting for a nesting-site by launching herself downwards from the tower top. The starling saw her coming, panicked and, instead of diving for cover, flew upwards. Fria flicked her wings rapidly three or four times, increasing the power of her shallow stoop and then, with her momentum, threw up easily, rising almost vertically under the bird, and half-rolled and grabbed it from underneath with one foot. As she flew back to the tower she took its neck between her mandibles and broke it, the tooth in her upper mandible which fitted into a notch in the lower biting through to the vertebrae and snapping the bird's spinal cord. She was learning fast and every day discovering her latent powers. But she was still far from the perfection and smooth co-ordination of muscles, strength and deliberate intent which could take an adult peregrine at fifty or sixty miles an hour in level pursuit and at over a hundred miles an hour coming down in a vertical stoop from a height.

Fria was still hungry. Exercise and her freedom had given her an appetite bigger than she had known in captivity. Apart from the small prey, insects, mice, and the occasional small bird she might get, she needed at least the equivalent of one wood pigeon a day and, as she came back into condition, sometimes two a day. At the moment she was getting nothing like that. She was always famished and always looking for the chance to satisfy her hunger.

At first light now she was astir and spent a long time hovering over the jungled purlieus of gardens and wild shrubberies taking what she could find either from the air or by stalking on foot. As the light strengthened she would rise and fly to the woods that crested the hill and hang above them at fifty or a hundred feet feet watching the ground below. The birds knew her now and when she appeared over the trees they went silent and into cover.

That week she caught two more wood pigeons. The first she bungled but luck stayed with her. As she hung over the wood long after the alarm calls had died away a pigeon came flying back from the water-trough for cattle at the far end of the pasture. As it began to rise towards the first trees at the wood's edge Fria went down to cut it off. She tipped over into a slightly steeper dive, gave a flick or two of her sharp-pointed wings and angled swiftly towards the pigeon, the white flash of its wing bars showing every single covert feather in her vision, the wet gleam of its beak where it had been drinking a collection of silver reflections. Because she was above it the pigeon only saw her when she was fifty yards from it. The bird swung sideways and dipped for the cover of the shrubs at the foot of the wood's edge. Fria swung with it, curving and steepening her dive. The pigeon, knowing it would never reach cover, dropped to the ground and crashed into the base of a small gorse bush, smashing against the prickly barrier and scattering a thin shower of yellow blooms. Fria over-shot the bush. Hungry and angry, she threw up and rolled over. Seeing the dazed bird at the foot of the bush, she came down with wings raised high over her back and grabbed it with her outstretched talons. She killed it and ate it beneath the bush. It was a small bird, still with a winter thinness about it.

On the Friday she made her first clean kill. She knew now that the pigeons often used the water-trough for drinking. For two successive days she had tried for them and failed. They had seen her almost as soon as she had begun her dive and had wheeled away and found the sanctuary of the wood in good time.

Whether Fria reasoned out the cause of her failure or whether chance showed her the solution could be long debated without resolution for only she could know. But on the Friday a warm air current rose strongly from the wood below, smooth and without turbulence. She found herself circling easily at a much higher pitch, well over two hundred feet. When she saw a pigeon coming back from the trough she angled over and went into her dive with fast wing strokes. Her height and the position of the pigeon made her attack take a much steeper line. She found herself going down in a half-vertical stoop, faster than ever she had gone, except for a few times when the gale had whipped her away from the barn. And as she went she automatically, instinctively now, put her legs forward and close up to her breast, talons tightly clenched, to keep the air stream slipping smoothly past her body. With her wings almost closed she streaked downwards and the pigeon left this life without seeing her. As she hurled past it she dropped her legs to make a grabbing movement at the bird, but her speed was so fast that she hit it with clenched talons on the side of the neck. A puff of feathers exploded from the blow, and the pigeon, dead with a broken neck and shock, rolled over and tumbled to the ground in an untidy swirl of limp wings and legs and a following gentle parachuting of small feathers.

Fria opened her wings, braked against the speed of her dive, and, without gaining height, slewed round in a fast circle, low over the pasture, and came back to the pigeon. She settled on it, grasped it with her talons and flew low and clumsily with it in the direction of her tower. But the bird was heavy and as she reached Highford House she dropped down with it and settled on one of the broad parapet ledges where she ate it.

Late that afternoon she took a lapwing which was grub-hunting in the parkland grass. She did it from the same high pitch which gave her the element of surprise, but the kill was not made with the ripping blow of her rear toes as an experienced falcon would have made it. She hit it with clenched talons dropped. The blow killed the rising bird with its stunning force and she went down after it. This time she carried the lapwing easily to her tower and ate it on the roof above her recess.

7

Strangers in the Mist

On Sunday morning as soon as he had finished breakfast Smiler hurried off to Highford House. Since it was only a couple of miles from the farm, he went on foot and across country to it.

He reached the house just after nine o'clock and climbed to his favourite parapet lookout. He was determined to sit there all day and, if Fria was around, to find her. In the pocket of his storm-coat were a packet of sandwiches and a can of cider which the Duchess had given him.

It was a warm morning without wind, balmy, with a strong touch of Spring mildness. The sky was cloudless. Blue and long-tailed tits belled in the shrubberies and worked the slowly budding branches of trees and bushes for food. The wood was full of birdsong and far below him the river meadows were free of flood water. The river itself was beginning to clear in colour and the salmon and sea-trout were running. Through his glasses as he swept them round searching for Fria, Smiler saw two fish jump in the pool below Eggesford bridge. But he saw no sign of Fria. Half an hour before he had arrived Fria had killed one of a flock of black-headed gulls that had come inland, following the river. They had been foraging in the pasture of the old parkland. She had flown at them from her tower, dropping low and going very fast, not more than two feet above the ground, towards the flock. They had gone up as she was almost on them in a cloud of white and grey wings. She had swung up-wards under one of them, rolled on to her back and grabbed at the bird's breast and made the easiest kill she had ever known. She had carried the bird to the edge of the wood and eaten it, and then, full and contented, had flown up to the lower limb of an ancient oak, made her toilet, and now sat there in the sun. She was hidden from Smiler by a yew tree standing next to the oak, its glossy evergreen foilage screening the lower part of the oak tree.

After an hour's watching Smiler got restless and walked and scrambled around the parapet of the house. He found the carcase of the pigeon which Fria had eaten there and this gave him fresh hope. He found another viewpoint from a different part of the roof and sat down with his back against a stone slab, enjoying the sunshine. He had been working hard all week and was now doing an extra night's session with Mr. Samkin, and he had worked all day Saturday. Within half an hour he was asleep.

Ten minutes later Fria came flying back to her tower recess. She saw Smiler sleeping on the roof, swerved a little from her line, and landed on the tower. She dropped down to the recess, shuffled in, gave a little shake to settle her breast feathers and folded her long wings over her tail. She was well fed for the moment and she dozed.

Half an hour later Smiler woke up. He rolled over on the long parapet ledge and, resting his chin on his hands, stared idly through the small gap in the roof ledge which had been cut for the rain water to run off into a now non-existent gutter. He had a funnelled view of the woods and shrubberies that crowded close to the old garden.

A movement in the rhododendron bushes caught his eye, a quick, pinky-white flicker. He reached for his glasses and focussed on the spot. Clear in the lens was the face of Jimmy Jago. He was standing in the cover of the shrubs watching the tower and house.

Smiler was puzzled. For a moment his delight in seeing Jimmy almost made him move to stand up and wave to him. Then he remembered the other times when he had seen Jimmy here at night. He stayed still, watching. Something was wrong between Jimmy and the Duchess. He was sure, if their quarrel had been patched up, she would have told him and certainly have said if Jimmy were coming back to the farm. Smiler decided that it was wiser to stay hidden where he was. "Whatever's going on between those two, Samuel M.," he told himself, "it's private to them or they would have told you."

Jimmy kept his station at the fringe of the shrubbery for five minutes and then moved, taking advantage of every piece of cover, crouching now and then to keep his figure clear of any sky-line. He passed between the tower and the back of the house, and Smiler held him in his glasses. He seemed so near that Smiler felt he could put out a hand and touch him. He wore a battered felt hat, a shabby, green windbreaker and crumpled, brown corduroy trousers. But the thing that interested Smiler most was that in one hand he carried a small white envelope. Smiler could see it plainly.

As Jimmy passed out of his line of sight around the far corner of the house Smiler wondered what on earth he could be doing up here with a letter and − without doubt − not at all anxious to be seen by anyone.

Smiler stayed where he was, unmoving, but keeping his glasses trained on the place where Jimmy had gone out of his sight. After a few minutes Jimmy reappeared and went quickly and unobtrusively back to the woods beyond the tower. Smiler saw at once that he no longer carried the white envelope with him.

Puzzled and intrigued, Smiler watched Jimmy disappear. He sat there for fifteen minutes to make sure that Jimmy had really gone. His curiosity growing stronger each moment, he decided that it could not do any harm to go down and see if he could find out where Jimmy had put the letter. The whole thing was a mystery and – although it was none of his business – his curiosity was too strong to be denied. He was not going to take the letter if he found it. He just wanted to know what was going on – and then, since it involved Jimmy, keep his mouth shut.

Sure that Jimmy had now gone, he was on the point of rising when the whole affair was driven completely from his mind. Fria launched herself from her recess, dropped low over the garden for a moment, then rose and half-keeled over so that she swept the length of the house parapet, passing within two feet of Smiler. He watched transfixed. She was so close that he could see the nostril holes of her strong hooked beak and the brightness of her dark eyes framed in her brown-black mask lines. Her wings and back seemed a darker slate colour than he remembered. She held her legs up loosely towards her breast and the brightening yellow of their skin gleamed in the sun as from her half-canted position she suddenly rolled right over in flight and moved away.

"*Blimey Old Riley*," Smiler breathed to himself, "*she's super!*" His excitement was suddenly so strong that it sent a shiver through him and made the skin of his cheek-bones tingle and would have brought tears to his eyes if he had not sniffed hard. He raised his glasses and found her in them, watching every movement. There was no other thought in his head but of Fria.

Fria, having eaten well and had her doze, had moved from her recess in order to satisfy another want. Since she had left the barn beam the only bath she had taken was in a largish puddle that had formed on the tower leads after the heavy rain. But the feel of the lead beneath her feet was like the slippery tin of the old bath she had used in captivity and the puddle was only half an inch deep. Knowing what she wanted, knowing where she could find it, Fria was in no hurry.

Now that Smiler had found her – though he had not seen her come out of the recess on the tower – it was almost as though she wanted to go through her paces for him, to show him that she was well on the way to being able to look after herself and that her dawning new powers were giving her a confidence in herself which was half the battle of survival.

In actual fact Fria had no thought for Smiler at all. She had seen and marked him as she went by the roof, but as she beat up and over the far pasture woods she was obsessed with a spirit of playfulness which she had never known before.

Watched by Smiler, she ringed up leisurely over the woods, circling on an air current, and only now and then giving a quick flick of her wings to speed her climb. She went up five hundred feet and then hung at her station in a slow level swing that was a couple of hundred yards in diameter. She went idly round and round and every bird in the wood and beyond it was aware of her. But by some magic of communication they knew that she was no threat, or maybe it was that there was a subtle difference in the style of her flight that told them she hung high, not in menace, but in the enjoyment of the slow ecstasy of her own powers.

From her curving pitch Fria marked a solitary crow perched at the top of the chestnut tree in the old parkland. She rolled over, half closed her wings, and went down in a fast dive which was the extent of her stooping powers so far. Five seconds later she whipped over the top of the crow, two feet above him, and threw up. For the first time ever she went up vertically and let herself go until all the momentum had gone from her body. She levelled out and hovered, looking down at the crow who, in the moment of her pass at him, had thrown himself backwards, raising black beak to ward off danger and had then fallen clumsily into a tangle of twigs and branches where he was now croaking curses at her.

Glasses on her, Smiler laughed and fidgeted with delight, and for the next five minutes the world was forgotten as he watched Fria's first display of play, the need for which is instinctive in all peregrines.

She went fast along the edge of the wood, six feet from the ground and chased a green woodpecker which was coming in from the pasture in a lazy looping flight. Fria went up under the bird, rolled on her back, just brushed him with her talons clenched, and was gone; beating high on quick wings before the bird knew what had happened. On pitch again, and a little higher this time, she came down over the green length of a fir plantation and chased a passing wood pigeon, whose eyes – from experience – were all for danger from the ground below, not the sky above. She passed inches above him. The bird slewed downwards in a plummeting panic dive for the cover of the pines. She swung upwards in a tight circle, going over on her back, and came out at the bottom of the circle and overtook the pigeon six feet above the nearest pine-tip, flashing by him in play, crying to herself and exhilarated by the tight vertical loop she had made for the first time in her life.

Then, pressed by her real need, she came back fast towards Smiler. She passed with a hiss of wings between the tower and the old house and slanted down the valley-side to the river. Some way below Eggesford bridge the valley woods reached right down to the river and the overhanging trees on either bank made a tunnel through which the Taw raced over a rocky bed. She dipped low over the river and went fast down the tunnel.

The white flick of a dipper on a moss-topped rock in mid-stream caught her eye. Fria swerved and came down almost to water level and dropped one leg to pick the bird off as she passed. But the dipper, which had survived many a sparrow-hawk's similar corsair attack, dived under the water, running along the stony bed for a couple of yards before surfacing and flying into the cover of some dead nettles on the bank.

A few hundred yards down the river Fria found a pool left in a rock basin by the dropping river and she settled and took her bath.

On the roof of Highford House Smiler sat in a quiet trance. The last he had seen of Fria had been her plunge into the river tunnel. The glasses idle in his hands on his lap, he just sat and shook his head in wonderment. The ruffled, spiritless bird of the barn was gone. He knew that this was the beginning of a new Fria, and from what he had seen of her display he guessed that she had now found she was able to take food for herself. He had no more worry about that.

An hour later Fria came back. She had bathed and then made her toilet on the branch of an oak hanging over the river.

Smiler saw her coming up the valley side and put his glasses on her. In the talons of her right leg, dangling a little below her body, she held the body of a dipper which had not been so fortunate as the first one. She flew to the tower-top and settled. Holding the dipper with one claw, she began to plume and eat it. When she had finished she cleaned her beak, preened her breast feathers and then dropped down and settled on the ledge of the recess. For a moment she raised her wings, half-arching them above her back, flexing the muscles, and then shuffled into her quarters.

With the last of the light going from the sky Smiler made his way back to the farm, the joy and excitement which were still in him making him kick out at odd stones on his path and swing with a hazel stick he had picked up at the dead heads of last year's foxgloves and tansies.

*   *   *

Back at the farm while he was having supper Smiler suddenly remembered Jimmy Jago.

He said to the Duchess, "Have you heard at all from Mr. Jimmy, ma'am?"

"Not for two weeks. He was in Newcastle then. Did you have any luck with Fria?"

Smiler realized that she had changed the subject deliberately and he knew enough about grown-ups now to ask no more questions. He had his own evasions to practise, too. Fria was his, and the last thing he wanted was a lot of people knowing where she was. At some time or other he knew that someone must see her flying, but it was ten to one that they would think she was a falcon that had come inland from the far coast and would not be tempted to go searching for her. Since he had no good reason to ask the Duchess to keep the discovery a secret (and knowing, too, that she had many friends with whom she loved to gossip) he said diplomatically, "She's around Eggesford way by the look of it. I found a pigeon she's killed and eaten."

The Duchess smiled to herself. Though he had tried to cover it, she had noticed the excitement in Smiler when he had returned. In her own mind she was sure he had found Fria. Being an understanding woman, she had decided that if he did not want to be frank with her it must be for some good reason of his own.

For the rest of that week Smiler only managed to get very short glimpses of Fria. He had found that by eating his lunch quickly he had just time enough to run up to Highford House and spend a few minutes there before he had to get back to his afternoon work. If he missed this expedition there was just enough light now as the evenings lengthened with March's going to give him a short time up at the house before night fell. Mostly Fria was sitting on the tower-top or the recess ledge when he arrived, since she liked to hunt in the morning or late afternoon.

The following week-end he spent most of his time up there. While Fria was away from the tower he went inside and climbed the stairs as high as he dared go. There was a twenty-foot gap before the remains of the top flight began again. The narrow lancet windows of the tower were either boarded over or smothered in ivy growths so that it was dark inside. The darkness gave away the position of Fria's ledge, for the daylight angled into the tower through the small gap in the bricks at its rear. As Smiler stared up at the shaft of light it suddenly flickered and then was blotted out. He ran outside and, with his glasses, saw from his parapet that Fria had returned and gone into the recess.

That Fria was getting enough food now he had no doubt. Often, as he explored through the woods around the hill, he came on the remains of her kills and could easily identify them. There were more wood pigeons than anything else, but Smiler also came across black-headed gulls, lapwings and partridges – and once, where the railway passed over the river above Eggesford, the remains of a tufted duck lying on the gangers' track at the side of the line.

Since he could not always be borrowing Mr. Samkin's binoculars,

Smiler took all his savings from his wages and the little money he had
brought to Devon with him and bought himself a pair of second-hand
glasses in Barnstaple one week-end. They were not as good as Mr.
Samkin's but they were good enough to satisfy Smiler.

Mr. Samkin said to him one night after Sandra had left, "You never
want my field-glasses now."

Rather wooden-faced, Smiler said, "No, sir. Thank you." For some
reason which he found it hard to explain to himself he did not want to
say a word about his discovery of Fria and her progress in adapting
herself to her new life.

Mr. Samkin gave a little smile. He could read Smiler like a book and
he could have explained to him his reasons for wanting to say nothing
about Fria.

He said, "I'm not going to put you in the witness-box, Samuel, and
grill you. Field-glasses are as personal a possession to a sensitive man as
his watch, his fountain pen, or his trout or salmon rod . . . even if he has
to fit himself out with secondhand ones to begin with. And don't worry
too much about people around here. Most of them never lift their eyes
above the horizontal. They only know the sun is shining because they
feel the heat on the top of their heads. But there are some whose eyes
miss nothing. Nine out of ten of them give thanks for what they may see
and keep their own counsel. The tenth is a scoundrel, and damned be his
name, for profit is his god."

Before he could stop himself, Smiler blurted out, "I know where she
is, sir. But I don't want to say, even to you, please, sir."

Mr. Samkin, with a twinkle in his eyes, said, "You don't have to tell
me anything, Samuel. I go for long walks. I have eyes in my head."

April came and, as was the custom each year, Bob and Bill brought
out the painted tent from the barn store and set it up on the small lawn.
On fine afternoons the Duchess would sit in its doorways, with Scampi in
attendance, and knit or just enjoy the sun and her own thoughts. Now
and again someone would come for a consultation and the Duchess
would oblige them.

The hawthorns were in half leaf and the ashes began to show green.
Spring was stirring and the early blackbirds and thrushes had already
laid their eggs, though not so soon as the sparrows and the starlings
which haunted the barns and the farm buildings.

Fria was used to hunting for herself now, though she was still far from
possessing all the skills of an experienced peregrine. Her condition had
improved; the yellow skin of her legs was now almost buttercup-
coloured and the slack, half-hardened quills of her primary, secondary
and tail feathers had firmed up. She flew with a compact, powerful

rhythm. She fed well, sometimes taking two wood pigeons or their equivalent each day. But she never killed without hunger. She killed only to eat, and death came swiftly as her hooked beak bit into a bird's neck, jerked, and snapped through the neck column.

But, now, for some reason beyond her understanding, she found herself impelled to strange moods, mostly at first light. She would fly to the tower-top or sometimes to the tall crest of a near-by oak and sit wailing softly to herself or shuffling to and fro, croaking and talking to herself, and then suddenly raise her wings and beat them in quick spasms without taking to the air. Only after she had killed did the mood leave her.

* * *

In the first week in April Johnny Pickering got another letter. It read: LEAVE IT TOO LATE AND YOU KNOW YOUR FATE.

Worse still, as he went out of his house to go to work, he found a police car parked on the opposite side of the road. As he bicycled away the car started and slowly began to follow him. Before he could help himself he began to ride quickly, touched with panic, and his heart almost stopped as the car passed him. He waited to see whether it would draw in ahead. But the car went on and swung down a side turning. The two policemen in the car were completely uninterested in him. They had merely stopped in the road to send a message over the radio on a matter which in no way concerned Johnny Pickering. But Johnny Pickering had had a nasty moment and was far from recovered from it when he reached work.

In that first week of April Smiler had a letter, too. It was one which sent him out to his morning work whistling his head off. Laura had written to say that there was a good chance that at the end of April or the begining of May – by dint of much badgering of her parents – she would be coming down for a short holiday to Devon and could Smiler find her rooms or a lodging somewhere near him? "But I can't give you the proper dates yet because it depends how the work goes here on the farm. And my father's not whole-hearted convinced about me going yet (though he will be) because to hear him carry on you'd think I was a bairn in arms still and Devon as far away as Australia. Parents! (Though Mother's all on my side I fancy). The latest from himself is that – if he lets me go – I'll have to pay my own railway fare, but he'll have to reckon with Mother over that."

So Smiler went whistling about his work as though, Bob said, he had swallowed a canary.

And on the Friday morning of that first week in April, the mist for which Maxie had been praying for weeks and weeks without the weather obliging, came to the moor.

*   *   *

It came down at three o'clock in the afternoon. The sky was overcast with low, barely moving clouds, and there was the faintest fret of a drizzle in the air. Slowly the distant tors and stretches of the moor were lost in what seemed a thickening of the air. Then, suddenly, the drizzle fined and became a veiling of mist which changed rapidly into a grey-white blanket that cut all visibility down to a hundred yards and still closed in.

In the quarry where Maxie was working, watched by the warder guards, a whistle blew and was followed by shouts from the warders for the prisoners to cease work and to assemble on the quarry bed to be marshalled for the march back to Princetown Gaol.

Maxie dropped the sledge hammer with which he had been breaking up stones and began to walk towards the assembly point. As he went, the mist thickened and the warders' calls became harsh and demanding. Maxie knew that his moment was coming. He walked slowly, judging the quick thickening of the mist and the dwindling distance between himself and the men and warders beginning to congregate in the quarry.

He was fifteen yards from the group when a heavy pall of mist swirled across the quarry and the group was lost for a moment. Maxie dropped to his knees behind a quarried block of stone, rolled over, and let himself fall off the small track into the cushion of heather and tall grasses below a small bank. He rose and stooping low began to run away from the group, following a small water gully that sloped upwards to the low crest of the quarry.

Maxie was a strong, fit man and he had not allowed prison life to soften him. He went as fast as he could now, knowing that every yard he made before his absence was discovered would be precious, and he knew exactly which course to take. For months he had studied the quarry area and the wide sweeps of the moors around it. The knowledge was a vivid map in his mind which he followed unerringly. He had the true countryman's gift of a feeling for his surroundings, of carrying in his mind small and large patterns of the twists and turns of streams and tracks, and of sensing his direction from the drift of the mist and the wind-angled lean of bushes and isolated trees.

Behind him, suddenly, there was the shout of alarmed voices and then the blowing of whistles. He knew exactly what had happened. He had been missed. As he ran he could picture the scene. The men would be marshalled in a tight file, a couple of warders would be checking the roll-call again while another warder would already be on his radio link alerting the prison authorities in Princetown. He knew, too, that in this mist none of the warders would come after him. They had the other prisoners to keep safe and they knew that if the mist for the moment was Maxie's friend it could also in a few hours become his enemy. To make a breakaway was one thing – and many men had tried it – but to keep going through the mist, knowingly and unerringly following a line to safety, was a task few men could accomplish successfully. Within half an hour there would be blocks formed on all the moor roads. The moment the mist lifted, search parties would begin to comb the moor, and with daylight there would be a helicopter or two to help them.

But for the moment Maxie was safe and he was away. Within half an hour, too, rumour would run through the prison itself.

"There's one away."

"Who?"

"Maxie Martin – the Gypo."

"Good luck to 'im."

Five minutes later, swinging slowly round in a circle to bring him on a north- instead of the south-bearing line of his escape, Maxie crossed the main Princetown–Tavistock road. He jumped the far ditch, found the remembered stone wall of a small field and headed along it. At the top of the field he climbed the upper wall and dropped down to the heather and short sheep-bitten turf of the moor.

At the meeting-point of the field's side and top stone walls, he took his line from their right angle. Loping at an easy pace he began to head steadily through the mist, the daylight fading, and prayed, but without any panic, that within the next half-mile he would hit the broad mark which would be his true route to that night's sanctuary. After a while, although he was going steadily uphill, the ground began to fall away to his right, plugs of grey stone breaking its face and then, muted but unmistakable through the mist, came the sound of running water.

He went caterways down the slope and found his mark, a small stream, cascading and rippling down the bottom of a boggy-floored combe. Maxie, keeping just clear of the miry ground, began to work his way up the stream. His confidence rose for it was far from the first time in his life that he had used this route. There had been a time when he and Jimmy Jago, blood brothers, had caught the small, hungry trout in the stream, had poached the odd lamb from the moor flocks and – but less often – had cut out some foal from the herds of moor ponies to take away to be sold or used for caravan work eventually. He smiled to himself as he remembered the odd times when some snorting, angry

moor stallion had come charging at them to protect its progeny —
though at the time it had been no laughing matter. And it was no
laughing matter now. He was away and he was going to stay away.
Princetown was never going to see him again. . . . He'd sooner die
first, for wasn't that better for a real man than being shut up like a rat in
a cage for years and years and the heart's truth sounding clear as a bell
that the law was one thing, but justice another?

After an hour of slow progress the ground grew marshier. He had to
stop now and then to pick up the sound of the water to his right. He
came out finally on to a wide, sedgy, peat-bogged plateau from which
the stream rose. He circled the bog to the west and picked up through
the mist a broken stone wall, studded here and there with twisted thorn.
In its lee was a narrow track. He followed this, scaring small parties of
sheep that now and then loomed out of the mist, hearing the thud of
their feet as they went away into the gloom, until the wall ended. Then
he swung left-handed, well above the stream's boggy source.

He began to climb now, edging his way up the long easy slope of a
moorland tor. But he had to go slowly for the darkness had come and,
although his eyes had made some adjustment to the misty gloom, he
knew that one rash step, a trip over a rock outcrop, could twist an ankle
or break a leg and take all chance of freedom from him. He reached the
top of the tor after an hour, recognizing it, knowing where he was from
times past. There was a small ring of stones enclosing a bare arena from
which he heard the sound of sheep scattering as he entered it. He sat
down with his back against a rock and rested. From a small flat tin
which every day for months he had fixed with adhesive tape under his
left armpit and worn whenever he went out on a working party, he took
a small section of chocolate and ate it slowly. Then he took one of the
five cigarettes the tin held and lit it with one of the red-tipped matches
in the tin, striking the match against the face of the rock. He smoked
contentedly, knowing himself safe from pursuit while the mist lasted,
knowing, too, that he was safely on his proper route. Another two hours
would take him to the cache at the bottom of Hangingstone Hill where
Jimmy Jago had promised to leave provisions and a change of clothes for
him.

As he sat there he sensed that the mist was beginning to thin a little
and there was the faintest suggestion of a breeze stirring. That did not
surprise him. It was April and late for any heavy, prolonged mist. But
the mist had given him all he needed now. Once he reached the cache
and could get rid of his prison clothes he knew that he could make the
rest of his journey, the first stage to freedom. He sat there, high above
the moor, alone, and content with his isolation.

But Maxie Martin was not alone. Fifty feet from him, across the other side of the small circle, sat another stranger in the mist whose ears had heard his approach; whose eyes had caught the small flare of the match; who sat, now, perched twelve feet up on a granite outcrop and, as the wind thinned or parted the slow veils of mist, could see the shadowed figure of Maxie sitting with his back to his rock.

It was a peregrine tiercel, a full adult in its third season. It sat there, humped against the mist and darkness, looking like a spur of the rock on which it sat.

It was a tiercel born in a Welsh eyrie. Its falcon and tiercel parents had been one of a few pairs of Welsh peregrines which, out of lingering atavistic compulsion, made the passage from their birth-place far south to the high passes and lonely peaks of the Spanish Pyrenees to winter. Adult now, the tiercel had long lost all contact with its parents. The previous year it had mated and, out of a clutch of four eggs, only one had hatched to give the world an eyas falcon which had been shot by a Welsh chicken farmer long before the time had come for it to make its passage to Spain. The brood falcon had started her passage four days before the tiercel and had been trapped in the chestnut woods above Canterets by flying into a fine nylon net hung between two trees as she dived after a pigeon. She had been sold to a Spanish falconer.

The tiercel that sat on the rock close to Maxie now was in passage back to his Welsh hills. He had rested the previous night on the cliffs of Belle Ile off Quiberon in the Bay of Biscay. In the morning he had beat up three thousand feet and, aided by a mild southerly wind, had crossed the Brittany peninsula, meeting the coast at St. Brieuc. He had winged his way north without urgency over the Channel Islands and hit the English coast at Start Point in Devon. On the southern slopes of Dartmoor he had dropped to a small river and had drunk and bathed and rested.

Late in the afternoon he had taken off and, hungry, had moved up the moor, two thousand feet high, his eyes watching the vast spread of ground below him. The migrant birds were arriving. He marked the small movement of whinchat, stonechat and warblers and, once, the hawk shape of a cuckoo quick-flighting along a shallow moorland combe. Far below the skylarks hovering and sang and he saw a covey of partridges break cover near the Princetown–Tavistock road. The tiercel watched the movement of cars along the road, saw clearly the shine on the swinging points of pickaxes being used in the small quarry by the prisoners, and the network of small streams, gathering to become rivers, that flowered from the high reaches of the moor. Over a moorland farm, the lichens and moss on its slate roof clear to him, he saw the flight movement of three pigeons, flying high and in formation. They were a kit of three flying tipplers – a breed of domestic pigeons trained, not as homers for long-distance flying, but for endurance in the air. Flown in competition by their trainers they could circuit, sometimes as high as two thousand feet, for as long as twenty hours in the air before being called or forced down from exhaustion.

The tipplers were fifteen hundred feet below the tiercel and flying in an inverted V formation. The tiercel winged over, dropped his head and stooped, picking up speed with a few rapid, sharp-cutting beats of his wings. He came down the sky almost vertically, wings closed, legs thrust forward and close up to his breast, talons clenched, his speed increasing with each second. He struck the leading tippler at eighty miles an hour, dropping his right leg and ripping into the base of the bird's neck with an extended rear talon. With the pigeon's feathers exploding about him, the tiercel threw up into a tight vertical circle as the two other pigeons dropped, zig-zagging and panic-flighting, for the farmhouse roof a half a mile away. The tiercel, wind singing against his half-opened wings, went down after the tumbling, dead bird. He grasped it out of the air a hundred feet above ground and flew heavily with it on a long slant that took him to the top of the tor where he now was perched.

There he had eaten it, preened himself, rested a while, and then the mist had come down cloaking him suddenly with dampness and gloom. The tiercel hated flying in thick rain, thunder clouds, or in mist. He stayed where he was, restless at first, making small cries now and then to himself, and later quietening as the night slowly joined the mist and darkness closed in.

He sat now watching the red glow of Maxie's cigarette-end pulse and wane as the man smoked. Only the thick mist, which would cloak and confuse him if he took flight, kept the tiercel there.

Two hours later the tiercel still sat on the granite rock spur. The mist was thinning slowly. He would sit now until first light. Five miles away Maxie had found the cache and the trowel which Jimmy Jago had hidden. He sat on the ground and dug the waterproofed haversack free. Inside were clothes, a pack of food, a small flask of brandy, a pencil-slim torch, cigarettes and a lighter, and an envelope with ten one-pound notes in it. These notes he knew were only a reserve in case he was forced to abandon his journey towards the sanctuary which had been prepared for him at Highford House.

He stripped himself completely of all his prison clothes and of his socks and boots. When he was dressed in the outfit which Jimmy had provided, he buried all his old clothing in the cache hole and covered it with earth.

The mist was thin now and the wind had freshened. Maxie occasionally caught glimpses of the sky and the stars above him. He dropped down the torside and flanked the edges of the mire which was part of the spongy womb from which the stripling Taw found life. When he reached the little combe through which the Taw first began to run with any strength and definition he stopped. Flask in hand he knelt beside it, leaned over and sucked at the water to drink. Then he took a swig from the brandy flask. Before he stood up he reached his hand into the water and splashed it over his face and the back of his neck, talking to himself in the language which the Duchess and Jimmy used between them. The libation was not done for the sake of coolness. It was a ritual thanksgiving born of sentiment and an acknowledgment of the magic which from the dawn of time all water had carried for primitive man and his descendants. And for this particular water Maxie had a special reverence for he had been born within sight and sound of it in a caravan in a field on the river bank below the village of Brushford Barton.

Just before first light Maxie left the growing river and made a detour around the village of Sticklepath which lay on the main road between Okehampton and Exeter, a road which was the northern boundary of the moor, every yard of which in daylight would hold danger for him. He crossed it with the last of the mist and rejoined the river a mile farther north.

And, with the first light, back on the moor the tiercel shook his body and head, splaying and shuffling his feathers free of mist drops and the discomfort of the night. He dropped from his rock, flew across the small tor-top arena and then rose leisurely into the air, climbing up on the breast of a mild northerly wind, leaving behind him the early soaring and singing larks, moving up and up until he should be satisfied with a pitch from which he could, a speck in the sky lost to the world below, move on towards the eyrie of his birth.

8

Spring Courtship

That morning — which was a Saturday — Smiler told the Duchess over breakfast about Laura's letter and asked her if she knew anyone in the district who would be able to give her lodgings.

"She's coming sometime at the end of the month, or the beginning of May, ma'am."

The Duchess eyed him quizzically across the table and said, "With her parents' approval, I hope?"

"Oh, yes, of course. Her father's being a bit difficult right now, but Laura and her mother will see to him."

The Duchess chuckled. "I don't doubt it. What chance would one man have against two females? Well now, let's see. Lodgings. Mr. Samkin has a room that he lets sometimes if specially asked."

"Oh, I wouldn't want Laura to be up there. I mean, Mr. Samkin's nice and all that . . . but well, he teaches me and it could be a bit difficult of an evening if I was up there studying. . . ."

The Duchess chuckled. "You mean your mind wouldn't be on your work with Laura in the house? Well, then, what about the Parsons? They take in visitors during the summer. They'd have a room. And Sandra would be company for her while you're working — unless you were thinking of asking for the week off?"

"I hadn't exactly thought of that, ma'am. But I don't fancy Sandra and Laura together."

The Duchess laughed. "No — and I don't fancy that they would fancy it."

Smiler said after a moment's pause, "I was wondering . . ."

"Yes?"

Embarrassed, Smiler said quickly, "No, I couldn't."

"You couldn't what?"

Smiler shook his head. "No, it doesn't matter. I'll ask Bob and Bill. They'll know some place."

"You won't ask them anything, Sammy. And I can't think why you're making such a bowl of porridge about the whole thing. You know perfectly well what you've got in mind. There's another spare room here. You'd like her to stay here, wouldn't you?"

"Oh, ma'am – could she? She could help about the house and farm and she's a good cook———"

"And what sort of holiday would that be? No, the matter's settled. She can stay here and she doesn't have to pay a penny or do a hand's turn unless the fancy takes her. Maybe, too, we might arrange it that you have a week's holiday while she's here. But not if I don't get an extra special good report on your work from Mr. Samkin. He's not particularly pleased with your Latin at the moment."

"I know. I don't seem to get on with it very well."

"Well, you'd better get on with it if you want a week's holiday. But no matter what –Laura stays here."

"That's super, ma'am. You're very good to me, ma'am."

The Duchess grinned. "Now you're buttering me up. But don't think because I've got a soft spot for you that I'll give you a week's holiday just at a flicker of those blue eyes of yours. Latin will get you that."

Smiler went out to work whistling. From the kitchen where she was washing up the Duchess heard him. With a shake of her head at Scampi, sunning himself on the windowsill, and a grin, she said, "Men."

She reached out and turned on the radio for the regional news. The first item she heard was an account of the escape of a Princetown prisoner, Maxie Martin. Her face showed no surprise. The weather report the previous night had mentioned the mist over Dartmoor. The two went together and, for weeks now, she had known that one day they would. Her mind went back, as it had often done, to the morning she had taken Smiler into the painted tent and the crystal ball had shown her the figure of a blood-spattered running man and would have shown her more had she not closed her eyes against it. She switched off the radio.

As she did so, some twenty miles to the south of Bullaybrook Farm Maxie had gone to ground for the day. Following the river in daylight was a risk he would not take, a risk he did not have to take because the one commodity he possessed in abundance was time. He had climbed the slope of a rough pasture on the river-bank into a broad stand of dark firs. Some way in the wood was a small clearing where trees had been felled. One quick look around showed him that nobody had been working in the clearing for days. At the side of the clearing was a large pile of green-needled branches and slim fir tops that had been trimmed off the felled trees. Maxie burrowed into the pile, made himself a rough but not uncomfortable couch and then pulled loose branches over the opening, forming a screen thick enough to hide him but through which he could watch the clearing. He opened a tin of sardines and ate them

with some biscuits from his store. Then he lay watching the clearing as
the daylight strengthened. Around him the birds' dawn chorus gathered
strength. For the first time that year he heard the chiff-chaff, the tolling
of a cuckoo, and the lyrical, rippling notes of a willow warbler with its
dying fall down the scale. A dog fox came to the edge of the clearing,
sunlight gleaming briefly on its chestnut flanks, scented him and turned
back into the firs. Maxie lay there content with his freedom, confident in
his own skills and the loyalty of friends to preserve it for him.

*   *   *

The tiercel was in no hurry. He soared above the lightening land at three
thousand feet and then, finding an air current, went lazily up on it into
the fire-streaked glory of a cloudless, dawn sky. He went so high that no
human eye from below could have followed him and then he side-slipped
free of the rising column of air and winged northwards slowly.

The whole horizon was his except for the narrow wedge of view that
flared away behind him in a broadening segment from his tail. He
rocked now and then and below him the land tipped and swung like a
coloured compass-card on its gimbals. He saw the white foam of water
over the weirs of the Taw miles away, the smoke and dawn haze over
distant Barnstaple and Bideford, and the pewter spread of the estuary
and sea slowly being burnished by the rising sun. He loitered, idle and
wandering, sometimes swinging out to the west and then curving in a
great circle following the invisible coil of an air current that up-
cushioned his almost fixed wings. The sun rose clear of the eastern
reaches of the land and burned in an orange-ball through the faint morning haze. The sky brightened, waking the pink and cream colours of
farmhouse and cottage walls, silvering the slates of narrow church
steeples and burdening the movement of bullock, cows and sheep at
graze with long black shadows.

A thousand feet below, a flock of sandpipers flew northwards, making
the quick passage from the South Devon coast to the Bristol Channel
and beyond in their migratory flight back from Africa. Their sharp,
musical trilling voices came up to him clearly as they chattered on the
wing. He watched the quick flick of their white-barred wings, the play of
light over their bronze backs and, on a sudden impulse, he tipped over
and went down after them. He gave eight quick wing strokes in two
seconds to speed his stoop, closed his wings, the long primaries folding
slightly over his tail, and dropped like a dark spearhead. Within seconds
he was stooping at well over eighty miles an hour and the ravished air

hissed away from his body with a thin, tearing sound. But there was no hunger in him.

He marked the leading bird and shot past it a couple of inches from its tail. As the flock scattered in confusion, their panic cries filling the air, the tiercel threw up fifty feet below them and soared upwards, bursting through their ragged ranks. Then he rolled over, rocked on his wings, and watched them streaming earthwards, seeking the cover of the woods and river-bank below. He called *krek-krek-krek* after them and then drifted away to the north, watching the line of the river below and the worming movement of a train coming along the tracks between main road and river.

A little later he was over the church of Eggesford above the left bank of the Taw. Then, directly below him were the ruined house and tower of Highford. Over a thousand feet below he saw the figure of Fria sitting on the tower-top. He recognized at once the larger shape and size of a falcon. He flew on, and had the sharp-curving wriggle of the Bullay brook below him. He marked Smiler driving a tractor loaded with hurdles across one of the brook fields, saw Bob leading one of the horses across the yard, and the Duchess's white line of washing fluttering in the strengthening morning breeze.

Suddenly he turned, edged round in a half-circle and with quick wing-beats flew back along his course until he was over Highford House again. He circled at a thousand feet, watching Fria below, and wailed gently.

Fria made no movement. But she had seen the tiercel. She had seen him the first time he had flown over, and she watched him now. He swung round in a great circle and then came back, sliding lower down the sky and calling again. Watching him, Fria shuffled her feet a little and bobbed her head out of the excitement suddenly in her of seeing one of her own kind. The tiercel dropped lower in a short stoop, rolled twice in display and, flattening out, swung round the large chestnut in the old parkland. He came back to the ruined house and passed a hundred feet over Fria with a slow rocking movement of his wings.

The tiercel flew over her three times, wailing gently now and again. Fria followed his movements bobbing her head and shuffling her feet.

The tiercel came back and settled on the roof parapet of the old house. He sat there, shook his feathers into place, and stared fiercely across at Fria. Both birds sat for five minutes without stirring and then, suddenly, the tiercel flew across to the tower and settled on the far side of the leads from Fria. She turned and faced him across the tower top.

The tiercel, like all males, was only about a third of the size of the falcon. His back was a darker slate-colour than Fria's, and his breast, grey-barred, was creamier. But though smaller there was a strength and compactness about his bearing which Fria still lacked. His feet were as golden as Devon butter from good living and there were bright amber glints in his brown eyes. They sat facing one another for a while and suddenly Fria bobbed her head quickly three or four times. The tiercel shuffled his feet, flicked his wings and, lowering his head, neck outstretched, wailed softly.

For half an hour they sat watching one another and Fria made no sound. Then the tiercel abruptly launched himself from the tower and flew out across the parkland towards the edge of the woods. He climbed quickly into the sky and disappeared over the crest of the trees out of Fria's sight. With his going she wailed loudly and shifted around on her station restlessly, but she did not move from the tower. With a slightly raised head she watched the sky.

Ten minutes later the tiercel came back. Fria saw him at once. He hung a thousand feet above her and held something in his talons. He called to her, not wailing, but in a commanding *krak-krak-krak*. He flew directly over Fria holding a magpie he had taken from the far side of the wood. As he passed he dropped the bird.

Fria watched it fall in an untidy tumble of sprawling black and white plumage. It dropped into the rhododendron shrubberies a hundred yards from her. Fria made no movement and her immobility seemed to enrage the tiercel. He dropped from his pitch and dived at her, wailing and chattering to himself. He passed three feet above her, the wind of his passage ruffling her feathers, and then swung up, climbed high, and disappeared over the woods again.

Some minutes later the tiercel came back to his high station, holding a turtle dove. He dropped it for Fria and she ignored it as it fell through the gaping roof of the ruined house into the rubble below.

The tiercel dived, wailing plaintively at her again, and then disappeared down the long wooded slopes to the river.

He was gone for half an hour. Fria sat in the strengthening morning brightness. Flies buzzed in the ivy foliage below and an early bumblebee climbed awkwardly over the patches of stone-crop on the tower-roof. After a time Fria began to bob her head, shuffle her feet and wail softly to herself. She shook and aired her wings like a cormorant and then stabbed at a fly which settled on one of the bricks at her feet. For ten minutes she sat still and carven but her head was cocked slightly and her eyes watched the great segment of her vision for any sign of the tiercel.

She saw him when he was a mile away, flying high and coming down the river line from the opposite direction to the one which he had taken in leaving.

Fria wailed, bobbed her head and then flew off the tower. She beat up swiftly on a line to meet the tiercel. He saw her coming, swung away and began to ring up higher and higher above her. Fria followed him to a thousand feet and hung there. The tiercel was over another thousand feet above her. He circled easily, sitting over her, wailing and croaking to himself. Then the tiercel made a short stoop half-way down to Fria. As he flattened out at the bottom instead of throwing up, he dropped something from his right foot.

It was a sandpiper — one of the flock which the tiercel had disturbed earlier on and which he had taken two miles up the river. The dead sandpiper dropped lightly, the breeze against its loose wings and tail swinging and eddying it.

Fria watched it fall towards her. It passed twenty yards from her. As it dropped away below her she turned over and went down after it in a dive more than a sharp stoop. She turned under it, half rolled on her back and grabbed clumsily at it with both feet. She took it in her right foot, swung slowly on to an even keel and then began to fly down to the parapet of the ruined house. As she did so the tiercel wailed and called above her.

Fria settled on a stone slab and began to feed on the sandpiper, taking no notice of the tiercel above. After a few moments the tiercel came down and settled on a parapet block ten yards from her. He sat silently watching her as she fed. The courtship had begun.

*   *   *

When Smiler went up to Highford House that Saturday afternoon there was no sign of Fria. On the roof he found the remains of the sandpiper and knew it had been a fresh kill. He waited for an hour, hoping that Fria would return, and then went down the hill to the river and worked his way through the leafy tunnel in search of her, thinking she might be perched somewhere after taking a bath.

Two hours later he went back to Bullaybrook Farm by way of Highford House and was delighted to see Fria sitting on the tower-top. He went happily back to the farm.

Fria was alone and the tiercel had gone. An hour before Smiler had first arrived the tiercel had taken wing, circled over the ruins, and called to Fria. She had gone up to him, and the tiercel had led the way, climbing high and heading for the coast, the call of his birth eyrie working in him. But as they had passed high over the coastline at Morte Point, unused to the wide vista of sea that opened under her, Fria had turned back. The tiercel had followed her and, after circling her for a while, had led the way northwards again. Fria had followed and then half-a-mile out at sea had baulked and returned south. The maneuver was repeated three times, and on the last occasion Fria had resolutely headed south for Highford House. The tiercel had watched her go and then turned northwards by himself, flying high between white banks of cumulus clouds.

Fria now sat alone on her tower while Smiler made his way back to the farm. He was half-way down the hill when he saw the white police mini-van pull away from the front gate. It came up the hill and stopped alongside him.

Grimble, the cheerful-faced policeman, leaned out and gave him a nod and a smile, saying, "Hullo, Samuel — been setting some rabbit snares?" Smiler grinned back and said, "They're not worth poaching with all the mixy about."

"You'd rather have a nice bit of red hake, eh?"

Smiler knew by now that "red hake" was the country term for salmon that had been illegally netted or gaffed from the river. He said, "I wouldn't know how to go about it."

"Pull the other one. Jimmy Jago wouldn't be backward in teaching his own kin how to poach a salmon."

"Well, he never has."

Something about the man's manner put Smiler on the alert.

The policeman said, "Where is Jimmy these days, then?"

"I don't know. Somewhere up north with a fair, I think."

"So you haven't seen him for some time, then?" The man's voice was casual, but Smiler sensed that there was some real intent behind it.

Keeping to the strict truth — though if pushed his loyalty to Jimmy would have made him forsake that — Smiler said, "He hasn't been around the farm for weeks. Why do you ask?"

The policeman chuckled and said, "Because the parson isn't the only one who takes an interest in his parishioners. Very fond of Jimmy, I am. Always like to know how he's getting on and where he's to be found — if I should fancy a piece of nice red hake."

He winked at Smiler and drove on. But Smiler, who, in the last year had developed an ear for insincerity, and could see through a deliberate casualness, was not deceived. The police wanted Jimmy Jago. He wondered why. Then he told himself, "No business of yours, Samuel M. Forget it."

After supper he went up to his room and opened his Latin dictionary, but before he began to force himself to study he decided that he would much rather be learning the Romany gypsy language which the Duchess and Jimmy spoke together. No hope of that. Meanwhile there was the Latin waiting and, unless he made a good showing in the next few weeks, he knew the Duchess well enough to realize that he would get no holiday during Laura's visit. Gosh, that would be terrible.

He shut the thought from his mind and began to do the translation Mr. Samkin had set him . . . *Abhinc annos tres* . . . *Three years ago* . . . His mind wandered. "Three years ago, Samuel M.," he told himself, "you were thirteen and kicking around the streets of Bristol, pinching milk bottles off doorsteps and comics from shops and not a blind idea in your head of what was going to happen to you or what you wanted to do." He bit the end of his pen and stared out of the window at the night sky and wondered what he would be doing three years from now and then, on the point of sliding into daydreams, he jerked himself back and, groaning, got down to his Latin again.

* * *

At ten o'clock that night Maxie came out of his pine-bough hide. He stretched and did some toe-touching to take the stiffness from him. Then, pack on back, he went through the darkness down to the river. There was hardly a length of the river from this point to the sea where, either on one bank or another, trout and salmon fishermen had not made a pathway to move from one pool or fishing-beat to the next. Maxie drank from the river which had dropped now to almost normal level and was clear of all spate colouring. Maxie moved quietly, a dark shadow following the river. He had twenty miles to go and all the night before him. There were a few high clouds but plenty of starlight to help him, and his eyes rapidly accustomed themselves to the gloom, and memory of past forays along the river served him well. He knew each bridge, each weir, each small road-crossing and he recalled the places where the railway hugged the river and the road the railway. So far as he could he kept on the left bank to avoid both. He rested once, sitting below the steep river-bank to smoke a cigarette and take a few sips from his brandy flask.

Sunrise he knew was somewhere around half-past six. At half-past five he reached Eggesford bridge and crossed the road a hundred yards back from the river, knowing that there would be a man on duty in the high-perched signal box at the level crossing by the station. Ten minutes later he was climbing the hill and reached the Highford House parkland. He knew Highford House and its tower well, though it had been ten years since he had seen them.

He climbed through the empty window which Jimmy Jago had

always used to leave the house, picked his way over the rubble and down a broken flight of steps to the old cellars under the house. His feet left prints in the thick dust on the steps. Grinning to himself he took his cap off and reached back and dusted the marks away behind him. It had taken Jimmy six months to pass information to him, principally by leaving notes around the fields and quarries where the prison parties worked, notes that were read and then swallowed at once. Jimmy, when he planned something, was always thorough.

Maxie, now safe from observation below ground, switched on his pencil torch and went along the passage which was littered with broken masonry blocks – some conveniently arranged long ago by Jimmy – so that he could use them as stepping-stones to avoid leaving traces. The passage took a rightangle turn and opened into what had once been a wine vault. Brick-arched bin recesses were cut into three sides of the vault. Maxie flicked his torch along them from left to right and counted. His light stopped on the fifth recess. The floor was covered with some broken planks and the section of an old door. Maxie lifted aside the door section. Underneath was a round manhole.

He raised the hinged manhole lid and shone his torch down a short run of iron ladder-way which led to the main sewer system. He climbed down the ladder and lowered the manhole cover, against which he had leaned the door section. The cover closed and the door section dropped with it and masked it.

At the foot of the ladder there was an open space, shaped like an inverted bowl, its sides and roof brick-lined. Regularly spaced around it were four entrance and exit tunnels about two feet high which in the years long past had conducted the house drainage and storm water away. The place now was dry and well ventilated by the tunnels that breathed air through broken manholes and ventilation shafts set in the outside walls.

In the domed chamber itself was a nondescript chair and a low canvas safari folding-bed with a pile of blankets and a pillow on it, and there were three boxes stacked against one of the walls close to a niche which held three candlesticks already fitted with new candles.

Maxie crossed to the candlesticks, lit them, and, leaving one in the niche, set the others on the boxes. At the back of the niche a plain white envelope was propped.

As the light from the candles grew stronger from a few minutes' burning. Maxie dropped his haversack on the chair and then took the envelope.

Sitting on the bed he opened the letter. Inside was a large single sheet of paper covered back and front with typescript. At the sight of the typescript Maxie smiled. Jimmy was a careful man. He would never have risked using his own handwriting. Maxie was sure that the typewriter he had used would have long ago been destroyed or sunk in some bog or river. One glance at the typing showed that it had been an old, well-worn machine. He knew, too, that nothing in this chamber could ever be traced to Jimmy. Oh, Jimmy was a loyal man and a careful one and when the fire burned in him trouble for a blood brother meant nothing . . . they had shared enough in their time.

Maxie sat and read the letter. It was long and full of instructions and cautions. Maxie read it all carefully, and to some paragraphs gave particular attention.

Nobody comes up here much, except the farm blokes and later maybe weekend picnic parties so you must stay fixed until after sunset. Can't say how long things will take once I know you're away from the moor, but will make short as poss and let you know next move which I'm already working on. . . .

. . . you've got food for over a month, water outside from roof, you'll see. Not likely to have a drought this time of year so no worry. . . .

If anything goes wrong and you have to run for it you must take a chance on you-know-who – and the climate isn't healthy there at the moment but I don't see you being turned away.

When he had finished reading the letter Maxie burnt it, and then set about making himself comfortable. He unpacked the stores from the boxes and sorted them and he blew out two of the candles. He might be a long time here and the light from one was enough for him. He whistled softly to himself as he moved around. The first stage was over. Everything now depended on Jimmy. The thought of having to live in the chamber for weeks and weeks gave him no qualms. After prison life it meant nothing. He would be free to leave it between sunset and sunrise. There were plenty of animals who lived a nocturnal life – now he had joined them.

* * *

Just after sunrise the next morning, as Fria was sitting on the tower-top, the tiercel returned. He flew high above her, circling and calling. Fria looked up, bobbed her head and did a little shuffling dance on the tower bricks, but she made no sound. The tiercel stooped and threw up ten feet above her head. As he shot skyward Fria called *kek-kek-kek*. The tiercel swung away down river and passed out of sight. Fria waited immobile on the tower and at ease, as though she knew he would be back, as though she knew that the desire in him to return to his old eyrie was weaker than the blood drive in him to find a mate.

She saw him as he came back, two thousand feet up. She launched herself from the tower and flew easily up to meet him. When she was five hundred feet below him he dropped a bird for her. It was a golden plover. As it passed by her Fria went down after it, caught it, and flew with it to a lower, thick branch of an oak on the edge of the wood, settled, and began to eat it.

The tiercel came down and sat two yards away from her on the outer end of the branch. He watched her eat. When she had finished Fria sat facing the tiercel. They watched one another, still as carved figures, while the Spring morning grew around them. After half an hour the tiercel suddenly wailed, stretched his wings high over his back and then flew off to the ruined house. Fria sat on the oak branch and watched him. He moved about the parapets and ruined roof of the house, exploring the niches and ledges, a restlessness driving him on. Often he was lost to Fria's sight. Sometimes he flew half-way back to her, wailed or called softly as though to entice her, and then turned back to the house again. He flew to the tower and worked his way over the leads and then dropped down to the recess ledge and shuffled inside. Fria made no move, but something of his restlessness and excitement was slowly communicated to her, though she gave no outward show of it.

Smiler came up to Highford House after lunch. There was no sign of Fria on the tower-roof. He climbed up to his favourite observation spot on the roof of the ruined house and began to search the surrounding countryside with his field-glasses.

Then, lying on his back and scanning the sky, he found Fria, and with her the tiercel. For a moment he could not believe his eyes and his hands trembled so much that the glasses shook and he lost both birds. Steadying himself by leaning backwards against a parapet stone, he picked them up again and a long sigh of pleasure broke from him as he realized that the thing he had longed for might have happened. "Samuel M.," he told himself, "don't be too sure, but . . . oh, let it be."

The tiercel was flying high above Fria, but Smiler could see that it had to be a tiercel. It was much smaller than Fria and much faster. Above him both birds had long seen Smiler but were unconcerned with him.

As he watched now, Smiler was treated to one of the rare sights of Nature. The tiercel was giving a courting display of his powers to Fria. He stooped vertically and plunged a thousand feet down to Fria in less than seven seconds, threw up alongside her and soared high again in an angled, elongated figure of eight and rolled out of the bottom of the figure to dive at her again with rapid wing-beats and swing about her in a tight circle. For five minutes the tiercel cut and winged and dived and stooped, knifing his way into and out of figures and maneuvers with a terrifying mastery of flight. Fria circled on a steady pitch and gave no sign that the aerobatics meant anything to her. But down below Smiler held his breath in an agony of delight at the display, the sound of the tiercel's occasional wailing and calling and the air-hiss of his stoops coming faintly down to him. At the end of the display the tiercel winged up and, as though drawn after him by some irresistible pull, Fria rose too. In a few seconds both birds were gone, lost behind a slow-moving bank of clouds.

Smiler waited for the rest of the afternoon for them to return. He saw no sign of them, but he was not unhappy. He had a strong feeling that they would be back – but even if they did not come back he knew that he would still be happy because Fria with a mate would have found the life which was her true destiny. He climbed down from the roof and went back to the farm with a light step, singing to himself.

Just before sunset the peregrines came back, flying in from the south together, and landed on the recess ledge a yard apart to roost for the night.

When darkness was full, and the last of the Sunday traffic on the main road in the valley had thinned to an occasional car, headlights dusting the night with stiff, golden probes, Maxie came out from the house, drank from the water tank and filled a plastic container to take back down to the chamber with him. He stretched his arms and breathed the night air and then moved quietly away towards the shrubberies. Under the pale starlight, from their tower-top, the two peregrines saw him and watched unmoving. They were soon to know him and accept him as part of the night movement and sounds around them, Fria without concern, for she was used to human beings at close quarters, but the tiercel always with a sense of unease for the shape of man to him was the shape of danger.

* * *

In his diary that night Smiler wrote an account of the tiercel's coming, and finished:

. . . and if he stays and they really mate they might make an eyrie on Fria's ledge and I could get to see the young ones. I might even be able to get up inside the tower sometime and see them through the brick gap, though I wouldn't want to do nothing – bother, anything – what would scare them away.

Anyway, I'm glad for Fria she's got a husband. Crikeys! I'll have to find a name for him.

Saw Sandra and that Trevor as I came down the hill tonight. She made some daft remark and rolled her eyes at me – just to annoy Trevor really. Perhaps she'll stop all that nonsense after Laura's been. . . . Laura – hooray, hooray and three cheers.

9

Family and Other Affairs

The April days lengthened and for Smiler – who had now heard from Laura that she was definitely coming at the end of the month – often seemed unreasonably laggard in their passing. He worked hard on the farm and hard too at his studies – particularly Latin – because he was determined to get a week's holiday for Laura's visit.

Spring took the valley in days of boisterous winds and slashing rainstorms, and then changed mood to clear the skies and summon up balmy southerly breezes that made the hedgerows and meadows and woods alive with the spring fever of wild life and the spring thrust of growth. The adders and grass snakes found warm rock slabs on which to sun themselves, and the little green lizards scuttled in the stone rubble of Highford House. Primroses padded the lane-sides, violets and milkmaids made purple and lilac patterns in the fresh green of new grass, and the trees were hazed with leaf, except for the tardy oak. The dippers, kingfishers and the yellow and grey wagtails were nesting along the river, and with each fair rise of water the salmon and sea trout moved upstream. The larches were suddenly decked with the pale glow of new growth, and the voles, shrews and field mice built their nests and burrows and brought off their naked pink litters of shut-eyed young. The early wild daffodils already showed brown seeding-heads, and tulips flamed precociously in cottage gardens.

The Duchess sat in the entrance of her painted tent on fine afternoons but the silk cloth remained over her crystal ball. She had no desire to look into the future. She knew that Maxie must be at Highford House and, although she knew, too, that Smiler often went there, she had enough knowledge of Maxie to realize that he would never show himself to anyone. But, nevertheless, she could have wished that Smiler would not got there.

In Bristol Ethel nagged regularly about the letter Albert had for Smiler; and Albert could find no answer for her except that something would turn up.

The police all over the country, but particularly in Devon, were still keeping an eye open for Maxie.

And in more than one creature, human and otherwise, the restless drive of April was forcing new patterns of behaviour, not all of them sensible.

Trevor Green asked Sandra Parsons if, when his father bought him a farm of his own in a few years' time, she would marry him. Sandra refused to commit herself – not because she did not like him or thought the prospect unpleasant but because for the moment she had no intention of giving up one shred of her liberty to live each day as it came while she could. She said tantalizingly, "Anyway – who knows what can happen in three years? You're not the only pebble on the beach by a long chalk. A farmer's one thing, but I rather fancy I'd like to marry a doctor – or, perhaps, a vet. They've got more class." She knew perfectly well that Trevor Green had learnt that Smiler hoped to be a vet. one day.

Trevor Green, had he been a well-balanced young man, would have understood her teasing mood, but the idea was fixed in his head that Smiler was his rival, Smiler, who, he knew, was studying to be a vet., Smiler, too, a person who knew where he was going and was pretty sure to get there. Trevor Green wished Smiler in Timbuctoo, but since that couldn't be arranged, he just wished him ill and waited for a chance to promote it, large or small.

Up at Highford Manor, Maxie found himself – to his surprise – strangely restless in his new captivity. In simple terms it was not the captivity that irked him but the lack of work to feed his mind and body. In Princetown there had always been work and always – no matter how limited – company. And Maxie, who loved company, also had little time for idleness. The lack of these began to work on him, and there were days when he sometimes took the risk — out of sheer boredom – of leaving his safe chamber for a few minutes out in the sunshine and fresh air. It was from this need that he discovered the peregrines and found a great lift in his spirits from watching them now and then. He did this during the first hour of light on some fine mornings.

*   *   *

For the first two days after his return the tiercel hunted with Fria and, particularly when there was a good movement in the wind, would give his courtship displays. At other times he continued to creep into crevices of the roof structure of the ruined house and around the broken places in the brickwork of the tower, searching for a nesting-place and croaking and wailing at Fria to follow him.

Fria remained uninterested. But as the days went by two things happened to her. The first was that by hunting with him she learned to make her stoops steeper and faster and, either from chance or imitation as she watched his killing, learned to extend her rear talons and strike a bird cleanly and quickly to death. As far as flying ability was concerned, although she improved her skills vastly, she never reached the high degree of mastery which the tiercel had, never quite seemed to have the effortless and exuberant mastery of the air which was his, especially when there was a strong wind blowing. The second thing was that the tiercel's persistent, almost fussing, excitement around the tower and the house searching for a nesting-site eventually passed to her. She joined him, and the two of them spent long periods creeping and probing and testing likely places. Because these were few, there were times when the tiercel would fly off, perhaps hoping that Fria would follow him, to search for other places in the district. Fria showed no true interest, sliding away from him and turning back to Highford House after a while. She was tied to it, in memory possibly, as her true birthplace, her natural eyrie area, because it was here that she had become completely free and had made her first kills.

Always the tiercel came back to her and, eventually, his excitement shared fully by her now, Fria picked her spot – which was the recess that for so long had been her refuge. She fussed around it, scratching at the brick dust and eroding brick faces of its floor, lowering her breast to the ground and working a slight hollow which it would fit. Now and again she would rest in the hollow in a brooding position. After a couple of days, the tiercel seemed to accept that this was her chosen spot. He gave up his search and would sit on the tower or the ruined house or sometimes on the top branch of the big oak on the wood's edge and wail and croak to her. One morning, early, and seen only by Maxie, Fria came out of the recess and flew to the rooftop and there the two birds mated as they would do daily afterwards until there were eggs in the tower recess.

Smiler missed their earlier matings but he saw later ones. The daylight was spreading further into the evenings now and on the days when he did not have to go to Mr. Samkin he walked up to Highford for an hour before settling to his studies in his room. He was well used to seeing the tiercel now and slowly the tiercel was getting used to seeing him. But the peregrine never sat on the tower-roof when Smiler was in his place on the housetop opposite. He would fly off to the great oak or ring up into the air and disappear. Fria would seldom follow him. Mostly she sat in the recess hollow and Smiler could just see the top of her head through his glasses.

One week-end towards the end of April Smiler carried a work-bag up to Highford with a kit of tools. In the close-grown fir plantation behind the shrubberies he found a fallen fir tree with a sound trunk. He stripped the branches from it with a billhook and saw, and then cut regularly spaced notches along its length. Into these he fitted split lengths of branches, screwed home firmly with three-inch screws to form ladder rungs along the spine of the trunk. Waiting for a time when both peregrines were away from the tower, he carried the ladder inside and maneuvered it up the staircase until he came to the gap. He wedged the butt end into a corner of the stairs and then lowered the top of the ladder across the gap and against the beginning of the higher flight of stone steps. By angling the ladder over the gap diagonally he managed to wedge it securely and then climbed up. He had no intention of trusting himself to the upper portion of the stairs whose broken base projected out over the gap. He found, however, that from the second rung from the top of the ladder he could stand up, using his hands against the inner tower wall for support, and just look through the hole in the bricks into the recess. He stood there the first time, legs trembling, balancing himself and hoping that nothing would slip.

The recess was far bigger inside than he had guessed it might be. The hollow that Fria had scooped for herself was clear to see. It was about two inches deep and completely bare. Scattered over the ground were a few dead twigs, a pigeon's iron-grey tail feather which Fria had carried up and idly dropped, and the bleached, frail bones of the skeletal frame of a small bird which had been one of Fria's very early kills.

Knowing now that with caution and by choosing his times he could observe the eyrie, Smiler started down the ladder. He was three feet down when its butt-hold gave way. The ladder slipped around a hundred and eighty degrees without losing its original slanting position. Smiler was spun round, his feet slipped from their rung and he just managed to hold on with his hands, hanging and swinging over a drop of thirty feet to the stone steps near the bottom of the tower. The moment of shock gone, he held tight with his hands and then found the strength in his back muscles and legs to draw his feet up under him and hook them over the nearest rung. He rested like that for a moment or two, the panic and fright easing from him, and then went slowly down the underside of the ladder, from rung to rung, dangling like a great sloth out for a leisurely excursion.

He reached safety and stood breathing hard. "Let that, Samuel M.," he told himself, "be a sharp lesson to you. The next time you come up you bring a cold chisel and hammer and make a hole in the stonework for a proper footing for the ladder."

He carried the ladder out of the tower and hid it in the shrubbery among clumps of dead bracken.

That evening while he was having supper the Duchess told him that she had met Mr. Samkin who had told her that there had been a vast improvement in his Latin. He could, she said, consider his holiday as good as a certainty. In addition Mr. Samkin would also let him off his study visits that week.

Then, before Smiler could thank her, she went on, "And when your Laura's gone you've got some serious thinking and deciding to do."

"I have, ma'am?"

"Yes, you have, Sammy."

"I don't understand you, ma'am."

For a moment she eyed him severely, fondling the ears of Scampi who sat in her lap. Then she said, "Oh, yes, you do, Sammy. Have you forgotten that so far as they're concerned you're in trouble with the police? Have you forgotten that somewhere off on the high seas you've got a father who most certainly would like to know what you're up to? You tell me you write to your sister and her husband, but they don't know where you are or much about what you're doing. I think you ought to tell them – in confidence. They won't let you down and they can write to your father——"

"You don't know my sister Ethel, ma'am, she——"

"I think it more likely that you don't know her. You approach her like a man and she'll treat you like one. You're not a small boy now whose ears she boxed for dirty hands and a runny nose and untidy habits." She grinned suddenly, and went running on, "Now don't start to fidget. I'm going to say what I'm going to say. You've got to do some straight thinking for yourself. You've got yourself nicely placed here, we all like you, you're working hard at your studies so you can get to take examinations, and you've got Laura coming, and if you can get a spare hour or so you're off to Highford House after that blessed falcon of yours."

"Well, ma'am, I don't see anything wrong in that."

"And there isn't – except that it's not enough because you've got a shadow over you. And let me tell you, Sammy, that a lot of people in this world have shadows over them and really can't do anything about them. But you can."

"You mean about the police and all that?"

"That's what I mean."

"But I can't do anything about that." Smiler paused and eyed her closely. "I'm waiting for that pebble to drop. You told me, ma'am, that——"

"Whatever I told you didn't mean that you could sit on your bottom, do nothing and wait for it to drop. It'll drop when you do the right thing."

"Which is what, ma'am?"

The Duchess shook her head, her red curls bouncing. "You're sixteen and a half. That's old enough, Sammy, to figure out almost any problem for yourself. Let me say this, innocence is a light in the eyes which reasonable people can always recognize."

Smiler understood her perfectly, but he said despairingly, "But I couldn't give myself up to the police now. Besides . . . it might get you into trouble for having me."

The Duchess chuckled. "You freckle-faced, blue-eyed devil – you don't twist me like that. You let me handle any troubles that might come to me. I'll give you until Laura has gone to think it over. Now off with you and get your nose in your books – and begin to think about what I've said."

But after Smiler had gone the Duchess sat on and knew in her heart that she had been motivated by more than Smiler's interests. She wanted him away from Highford House. Every time he went up to the place there was the risk of danger, of the odd turn of Fate's dice which could alter the lives of many people.

*   *   *

In his diary that night, Smiler wrote:

At supper tonight the Duchess gave me a blowing up about things. I can see why in a way. Fact, I suppose she's right, but I'm darned if I'm going to think about it until Laura's gone. Might ask her about it. Blimey – walking into the police and giving myself up! Funny about the Duchess. I think she's missing Jimmy a lot or got something on her mind.

Nearly killed myself on the tower ladder today. Saved by a Tarzan act. Me Tarzan – you Laura. Ha-ha!

*   *   *

On the Monday of the last week in April the falcon Fria laid her first egg. Its shell was a dull white marked with reddy-brown and some violet blotches. The next day she laid another, and a third on the following day. After that she laid no more and started to brood and, at first, she was content to share some of this task with the tiercel. By this time, too, Smiler had made his ladder fastening secure. When he managed to slip up to Highford on the Tuesday for half an hour before supper he put the ladder in position while the two peregrines were away from the tower.

When he saw the eggs he nearly fell off the ladder again with delighted surprise. But as he put the ladder away amongst the bracken he decided firmly that he would not use it again for fear of disturbing Fria or the tiercel until there were young birds in the nest. He knew from his reading that once the full clutch was laid and the falcon began to brood in earnest it would take twenty-eight or a few more days for the incubatory period to be completed. So the ladder lay in the bracken and the new growths raised their green crozier heads around it.

A week before Laura arrived Fria was sitting steadily. At first the tiercel had shared some of the brooding with her so that she could go off and hunt, but as the days went by Fria sat more and more tight on the eggs. The tiercel began to kill for her. Twice a day, in the early morning and late evening, he would come back from his forays and, hanging high over the great oak at the wood's edge, would call to her. Fria would come out and catch the kill which he dropped. Sometimes she would eat it on the oak branch but more often as the days went by would take it to the tower-top where, standing on the leads, she could eat without being seen because she was hidden by the brickwork of the crenellated parapet that decorated the summit of the tower. At first, too, she would sometimes fly down to the river to drink and bathe. But later she was content to fly down to the edge of Maxie's water-tank and drink from that, and her bathing became very rare.

With Fria sitting steadily, the tiercel often left her for long periods after he had fed her. In time he knew the river valley and its surroundings for miles north and south of Eggesford. And quite a few people came to know him. The water bailiff, standing quietly and hidden under the overhang of some trees, saw him come down one day over a stretch of reed and iris-thick swamp and take a mallard drake as it was planing down to the marsh. The tiercel carried it to a gravel spit in the middle of a fast, shallow run of the river not twenty yards from him. He stood like a statue for half an hour watching the peregrine feed. A few visitors to the Fox and Hounds Hotel saw the tiercel flying high but a lot of them failed to recognize his breed. But some of them did and most of them kept quiet about what they had seen. But the presence of the peregrines inevitably became more remarked and the rumour of their whereabouts began to spread slowly . . . a little trickle of news and speculation amongst local people and visitors, a trickle which, blocked here, would seep along some new channel.

Away from Eggesford the tiercel was shot at twice. Once by a young man from Barnstaple – who had driven out for a day's poaching with an unlicensed shotgun – as the tiercel swooped round a corner of a wood chasing a pigeon; and another time by a farmer, walking gun in hand along the edge of a field of young corn. The tiercel who had been feeding at the foot of the hedge flew up as the man crested the rounded swell of the field and came into view. Instinctively he had brought up the gun and fired. A few pellets from the outer spread of the shot pattern rattled against the tiercel's left wing harmlessly. The farmer, who was not by nature an intolerant man, watched the tiercel fly away, recognized the bird late for what it was, and was thankful that he had missed it.

Luckily, so far, no one had discovered that there was a pair of peregrines in the district and that their eyrie was in the red brick tower at Highford House.

* * *

Laura arrived on the late afternoon train from Exeter at Eggesford Station. Smiler had been waiting for half an hour. Not because the train was late but because he had arrived early. With his own money he had hired a car from a local garage, and the garage proprietor sat in it now outside the station, grinning to himself at the excitement which Smiler – whom he knew – had been unable to suppress. Jerking up and down on his seat as though t'were full of pins, he thought. Must be a girl. Can't be nothin' else but a girl.

Inside the station Smiler walked up and down the platform restlessly. He wore a new pair of trousers, a freshly ironed blue shirt with a bold red tie, and a slightly over-sized green and blue-checked jacket which Bob – who did a little second-hand trading on the side – had sold him at a bargain price, pointing out, "Never mind the fit, lad, you'll grow to it in a month. Look at the material. Genuine West of England cloth and a bargain at a quid." His fair hair was bound down close to his scalp with a liberal anointment of some violet-smelling hair lotion which had been left behind by Jimmy Jago. "From the days," had said the Duchess, "when he found it in his fancy to do a little serious courting but soon thought better of it."

The sparrows and starlings quarrelled on the station roof as Smiler paced up and down. Across the tracks below the bank a man was fly-fishing in the pool under the bridge. Smiler watched him, relishing the smooth parabolas of the line's movement, and remembered the one and only time that he had caught a salmon on a fly and how he would never have landed it but for Laura's advice.

He heard the rattle of the train when it was a quarter of a mile away and then the challenging, bugle-like notes as it hooted for the level crossing and the station. As the train rolled to a stop along the platform Smiler stood rooted to the spot with a sudden trembling in his legs and a hard dry lump in his throat, watching the few passengers descend.

Dismay swept over him as they all disembarked and moved towards the station exit. Laura was not with them. Loose brown hair, brown eyes and a sun-tanned skin. . . . Gosh, he thought perhaps after all this time I've forgotten what she looks like. Panic rose slowly in him.

A voice from behind him said, "Well, you dafty, aren't you going to give me welcome?"

Smiler turned. Standing beside him, case in hand, was a tallish young woman, her long brown hair tied in a pony-tail, wearing a red trouser suit that fitted her slim body as though it were another skin, a flash of white silk scarf at her throat, white, wedge-heeled shoes on her feet, and a smile on her lips which were made up with dark red lipstick.

"Laura! Gosh, I didn't recognize you!" He grabbed at her hand and began to work it like a pump handle.

"Well, thanks, Sammy. That's aye a gay welcome to Devon. And did you think, you loon, that I'd come wearing my farm or boat clothes? And when you've finished with my hand I'll have it back and you can give me a kiss. It's all right– don't fret – the stuff's kiss-proof." Her eyes shining, she leaned forward and Smiler kissed her, his head swimming so much that for a moment Laura put up a hand to stop him pushing her backwards.

"Oh, Laura," cried Smiler, "you look super! You're so grown up!"

"It's a thing that happens– but you don't have to shout it to the whole world. And you've not done so bad yourself. You've filled out and you're taller. And, my goodness, laddie, have you become a smart dresser. Where did you get all this gear?" She fingered the loose sleeve of his jacket.

"From one of the Ancients."

Laura laughed, leaned forward and kissed his cheek, saying, "That doesn't surprise me. Never mind, things will seem different when we get into jeans." Then, spontaneously, she hugged his arm and went on, "Oh, it's good to see you, Sammy!"

"And me, you, too. Here, give me that." He grabbed her case and, hurrying her along the platform, went on, "I've got a car waiting, hired it myself, and the driver's the garageman, and he says he grows the most marvellous dahlias and he's got a cat that keeps biting out its own fur and eating it so I said I'd look it up in one of my vet. books and see what I could do about it, and – Crikeys! I forgot to ask. Are your mother and father well?"

"Aye, they send their love. And my father's a few pounds poorer by

way of my rail fare and so's my mother because of this." Laura fingered
her red suit.

And the car driver, seeing them coming, hopped out of the car quickly
to take the case and stow it away, and said to himself that although he
had known it must be a girl, *this* was a girl that could make both a man's
eyes pop out on first meeting unless he blinked fast to keep them in.

Driving them back to the farm, the garageman eyed them in his
mirror as they sat in the back holding hands and, because a silence had
descended on them that he thought might freeze them up forever,
grinned and said to Laura, "You're the best-looking number, miss, that
I've ever picked up from Eggesford and there've been one or two movie
stars among them." Then with a wink, he went on, "Sammy here didn't
tell me he had such a good-looking sister!" At that they all laughed and,
somehow from that moment, the strangeness was gone from the two
and they were Laura and Smiler and the months of separation dissolved
like a river mist under the first warm rays of the sun.

From that moment began the happiest week that Smiler could
remember for years and years – which was not strictly true, but un-
derstandable, for the memories of the young are short.

The Duchess took to Laura as though she were one of her own
daughters, and a favourite one at that. And Laura took to the Duchess
and knew at once that the red curls were no wig, and she helped with the
cooking and in the kitchen as though she had lived in the house for
years. The whole building was a babble of chatter and laughter and happiness which – when the two were away from the place – the Duchess
would sit back and think about, sighing to herself with a mixture of
quiet joy and nostalgia.

The Ancients, because they wanted to and also because they knew it
teased Smiler, brought Laura a posy every morning when they came to
work – not a posy between them, but one each. They mock-quarrelled
with one another as to which was the best, making Laura give a decision
which she did, meticulously keeping the score even but wondering what
she would do on her last day which would be an odd one. She need not
have worried because the Ancients – as it turned out – knew better than
to embarrass a lady. On the last day they brought a double-sized one
between them. And, from the depths of the stone barn, they hauled out a
girl's bicycle which Jimmy was – or had been – hoping to refurbish and
sell one day. They put it in order and Laura was free to roam the countryside with Smiler on his bicycle, both of them in working denims and
shirts and Smiler's haversack loaded with a lunch provided by the
Duchess.

One lunchtime Smiler took Laura into the bar of the Fox and Hounds and, while she drank cider, he had a glass of beer because he felt it was a more manly, grown-up thing to do when Laura was with him. But the gesture was spoiled when she said, "You don't have to make such a face drinking it and from what I remember of you, you had a giddy enough head from a drop of cider without taking to beer." When Smiler protested and they quarrelled happily, the barman, Harry, came over. Winking at Laura, he said, "If he's giving you trouble, miss, just say the word and I'll throw him out."

But there were to be serious moments between the two during that week. The first came when Smiler took Laura up to show her his room and tell her all about his studies and about the peregrines up at Highford House, and a dozen other things. As he was talking Laura touched the little clay model of Johnny Pickering and said, "What's this, Sammy?"

Smiler told her, and her face grew serious.

She said, "Coming from where I do, I won't say that kind of magic doesn't work, but there's times when a body has no call to depend too much on it."

"What can you mean?"

Laura smiled. "I'll tell you when I have the mind. Right now you can walk me down this Bullay brook of yours. There's daylight for an hour yet."

They walked down the brook for a mile, and sat on the edge of a deep pool where, as the dusk thickened, a sea trout jumped and the small brook trout dimpled the water film as they fed from a drifting hatch of stone flies. The pipistrelle bats cut the darkening sky above them with fast and erratic wing-beats. Because their ears were young, they could catch the thin high notes of the bats talking to one another. After a while the talk between them ceased. Smiler held Laura's hand and, a little later, Laura laid her head against his shoulder. They rested there in the slow vibrant bliss of their reunion while the world darkened softly around them. Suddenly from the thickets on the other side of the brook a nightingale began to sing – which was no surprise because for the right people nightingales have a wonderful sense of timing.

That night Smiler wrote in his diary:

Laura's here, and gosh I don't know whether I'm on my head or my heels. She's more lovely than what I remembered her like – and just as cheeky and bossy which is super. Super. Super Laura. The peregrines tomorrow. (I am going to get a box with a key and lock this diary up from now on.)

* * *

The next morning as the first light touched the high wood crest behind Highford House, Maxie who had been stretching his legs with a walk came back to the house. He was reluctant to go down to his chamber and stood for a moment in the shadowed angle of a buttress by his water tank. The dawn chorus was in full song and the thickets and shrubberies were alive with bird movement. He watched a kestrel come across the field from the big chestnut and hover over the old garden below the tower. Maxie smiled to himself as the tiercel — who had passed the night on the tower-top — suddenly launched himself downwards and chased the kestrel away, racing and swerving after it with rapid wing-beats. The kestrel dived into the top branches of an old crab-apple tree by the wood and screamed at the tiercel as it went by.

Keep off my patch, thought Maxie. As the tiercel came back and settled on the tower Maxie nodded upwards to the bird. Good for you old man, he thought. You look after what's yours. A missus and soon you'll have kids. You're lucky. Oh, yes, lucky.

He turned away and climbed through an empty window into the house and made his way to his vaulted chamber, memory plaguing him, and impatience growing in him because he had waited long now and had had no word from Jimmy Jago.

Two hours later Smiler and Laura arrived at Highford. Smiler helped Laura to climb to the roof and they sat on the parapet together watching the tower. The tiercel was nowhere to be seen. Through the glasses they could just see the top of Fria's head as she brooded her eggs in the recess. After about fifteen minutes, from high overhead, came a long drawn call of *wickoo-wickoo*. A thousand feet up the tiercel circled.

"He's brought her food. You just watch," said Smiler. As he spoke Fria shuffled out to the lip of the ledge, raised her head, shook her loose feathers into trim and flew off, rising with a slow flapping movement until she was well above the old oak. From high above her the tiercel dropped the jackdaw which he had taken as it flighted between two clumps of fir plantations. The bird fell slowly and Fria with quickening wing-beats flew up and under it, rolled over as it passed her, and came down in a short stoop and seized it.

She dropped down and flew under the green canopy of the old oak and settled on her feeding-branch. The tiercel circled for a while and then, half closing his wings, came down fast to the tower. He pulled out of his dive, wings open, hanging for a moment above the recess ledge and then settled on the lip. He shook his plumage firm and sat on guard until Fria should have finished her meal.

Laura watched him through the field-glasses. He sat full in the light of the morning sun which caught the bright yellow cere at the base of his

strong blue-black beak, a bold glare in his eyes. His dark-crowned head
and the darker streaks of his cheek and moustache stripes and the steely
shine of his back and wings were like the armoured accoutrements of
some arrogant, feudal knight.

She said with a touch of awe in her voice, "Oh, Sammy, isn't he the
bonny bird? He looks like some noble prince in armour ready to fight to
the death for his lady."

From that moment for both of them, the tiercel was named and
became the Prince, Twenty minutes later Fria came back from her meal
and the tiercel Prince dropped from the tower and beat away fast and
low down the slopes of the parkland to disappear near the river.

Smiler said, "He's away to the river for his morning bath."

They climbed down from the house and Smiler showed Laura the
ladder he had made, explaining that he was not going to use it again until he was sure that the eggs had hatched.

They went back to their bicycles and rode off to go to Barnstaple.
Laura wanted to do some shopping for presents to take back to her
father and mother and friends, having said that morning to Smiler, "I
know you don't want to waste time shopping in a town but it's got to be
done — so we might as well get it over and then you won't be fussing
about it for the rest of the week."

It rained hard that afternoon. To escape it they went to a cinema and
sat at the back, holding hands, and Smiler when he came to write up his
diary that night could not remember even the name of the film they had
seen.

He wrote:

> The tiercel is the Prince. Laura named him after one look, bang on
> the nose. Had to take some eggs up to the village after supper from the
> D. to Mr. Samkin. Laura stayed behind nattering to the D. Glad she
> did, really. Not very keen about Sandra seeing us because you never
> know what she's going to say just out of devilment. Come to think of
> it both Sandra and Laura like doing that. Mr. Samkin asked about
> Fria and I told him about Prince. I got a feeling that he already knew
> there was a tiercel up there. Shouldn't be surprised if he is already
> paying a visit now and then to Highford. He's a quiet one, but he's all
> right. I wish the teachers at my stinking old school had of been like
> him.

What Smiler did not write in his diary was that coming away from
Mr. Samkin's he had run into Sandra who had said, "I hear tell that
you've got your girl-friend staying at the farm for a week."

"Don't be silly," Smiler had said indignantly. "She's not my girl-friend. She's just some relation of Jimmy Jago's and I'll be glad when she's gone so she isn't tagging along all the time."

Sandra tossed her fair hair and grinned.

"The only time I saw her tagging along you had a grin on your face like a Cheshire cat that had taken all the dairy cream."

"If you think that, you ought to get your eyes tested."

As he cycled back down the hill Smiler thought, with a moment's crossness, that it was a funny thing that some people couldn't keep their noses out of other people's business. But by the time he got to the bottom of the hill he was saying to himself, "Samuel M., you didn't handle that right. You should have just told the straight truth. Maybe that would have put her off for good."

10

The Moment of Decision

If the time of waiting for Laura's arrival had passed snail-slow for Smiler, the days of her week in Devon appeared to race by. High pleasure seemed, like a glutton, to bolt and swallow the hours voraciously. They visited Highford at least once every day. Laura was disappointed that she would not be there when the young arrived, but she made Smiler promise to write and give her all the news of them when they showed. They cycled for miles around the countryside, fished for trout in the Bullay brook, went now and again for a lunchtime drink at the Fox and Hounds, and explored the river for miles up and downstream — and, by skilful manoeuvring, Smiler managed to keep Laura away from the village and Sandra.

The morning of the day before Laura was due to go back, they walked the Bullay brook to the point where it ran into the Taw. They sat on a high bank overlooking the main river. A hundred yards downstream a heron stood in the shallows, fishing. A black mink ran along the far bank, scented them, raised its head, gave them a beady stare, and then turned back along its tracks and disappeared. A salmon jumped in the pool above them, bored with the long wait ahead until spawning time. A solitary early Mayfly hatched from the water. It drifted away on the film with raised wings to take the risk of a few moments' peril from lurking trout before it could lift itself into the air to its all too brief freedom.

Lying on his back in the grass, Smiler said, "I can't believe you're going tomorrow. Where's all the time gone?"

Laura was silent for a while, and then she said, "Sammy, I got something to tell you."

Smiler rolled over on his elbow and looked at her. A small, serious frown creased her suntanned brow.

"Well, what?"

"Well, before I left home my mother told me there was something I had to do."

"What was that?"

"Well, she knew from me that although you were writing to your sister and her husband that you hadn't told them where you were —

except in Devon somewhere. And she felt that was all wrong. And . . . well, since I knew where they lived in Bristol from you, she said I had to go and see them on the way down and tell them where you were."

Smiler sat up quickly. "You did that?"

"Yes. I stopped off in Bristol. And it's a good thing I did. They're both very nice and I like them."

"Albert's all right. But my sister Ethel – you don't know her. If she takes a mind to its she'll be off to the police and – oh, Laura, why did you do it?"

"Stop panicking like a loon. Your sister won't do anything of the kind. They both promised me that before I exactly told them. And then . . . well, they gave me this for you."

Laura took an envelope from the pocket and handed it to Smiler.

Smiler recognized the writing on the envelope at once. It was his father's.

"It's from Dad."

"Yes, I know. Your Albert said you had to have it urgently, but he'd no way of sending it to you."

Smiler turned the letter over. "You know what's in it?"

"Of course not. I don't open people's letters. But from what Albert told me your father had written to him I do know that it's some good advice. And that's something that some folk – not a hundred miles from here – don't take to too gladly. Why don't you open it and see?"

Smiler opened the letter. It was a long letter in which his father explained what had happened to him to cause him to miss his ship, and how things had gone from then on, and a lot of chatty stuff about his doings. Reading it Smiler had a vivid picture of his father and his memory rioted with all the good things they had done together in the past – but all that was washed from his mind as he read the last paragraph:

. . . Well now – to the real thing, Samuel M. I know from Albert and the police reports that the company sent me about most of your goings on. But the thing is – no matter how you've been able to look after yourself (and I'm really proud about that) – you've got the wrong end of the stick. O.K. so you didn't pinch the old girl's bag and you ran away from that place they sent you. But that wasn't the thing to do and it no more is the thing to keep on doing. I don't know when I'll be back, but that makes no difference cos I should only make you do what you really ought to have done – if you'd used your noddle – long ago, and that's walk up to the nearest copper and give yourself up. The police aren't fools. The fact you run away tells them something was wrong, and the fact of giving yourself up will just make it more so. I'm not going to start sparking off and giving you orders. I know my Samuel M. All I know is that you got my advice – not orders – and I'll know you'll do the right thing. O.K?

Yours from the bottom of the world, but hoping to be home soon – lots of love, Dad.

P.S. They tell me you want to be a vet. That's fine – but you can't really settle to that until everything is cleared up, can you? Chin up.
Love again, Dad.

Silently Smiler handed the letter to Laura. As she read it he looked around him, at the sunlit river, and the green fields and the wood-sweeps of the valley-side. Above the high crest of the firs that hid the Highford hilltop from him he saw a handful of rooks sporting in the air, and far above them a pair of buzzards circling slowly on their broad wings. Fria and Prince were up there somewhere, Fria for certain would be sitting on her three eggs and in a couple of weeks they might be hatched. . . . All this and his work with Mr. Samkin and his pleasant billet with the Duchess to be thrown away, to be walked away from, perhaps for good, just because his father . . . A lump rose in his throat and he screwed his face muscles up to stop unwelcome tears seeping into his eyes.

Laura handed the letter back to him. "Your father's a fine and sensible man. Wronged you've been, but you've done nothing for yourself by running away. Oh, Sammy – I've told you that before."

Stubbornly Smiler said, "I never robbed that old lady – and I'm not giving myself up to the police."

Laura eyed him silently for a while and then she smiled and said, "You've got the letter. You know what your father thinks. I'm saying no more. It's no place of mine to tell you what to do. A man must make his own decisions. So, Sammy, I'm saying no more about it."

"But it means leaving the Duchess, and the peregrines, and all my studying and ——"

"No, Sammy," Laura interrupted him and stood up. "I don't want to hear anything about it. I know what you'll do. Now come on, let's walk up the river and have a bar snack at the Fox and Hounds and I can say goodbye to Harry."

And so it was that the subject was not mentioned between them again until a few moments before Laura got into the train at Eggesford to begin her journey home.

Smiler gave her a kiss and a hug and then took from his pocket a sealed envelope and handed it to her.

"Don't open it now, Laura. In the train. It's for you. It's a kind of present. Well, two presents." He grinned suddenly. "You brought me a letter – now you got one to take back with you."

The porter came by them and, winking, said, "Come on now, miss. Can't hold the train up. Parting is such sweet sorrow – but there's always another time and nothing stops the grass growing."

The train pulled out of the station and Laura waved from the carriage window until the curve of the line hid her. Smiler waved back, and two thousand feet above Fria's tower the tiercel caught the red flick of his bandana handkerchief and soared higher to chase a solitary buzzard, teasing it with short, playful, mock stoops.

In the carriage by herself Laura opened the envelope. Inside was a letter and a small silver chain necklace with a little silver fish hanging from it.

The letter read:

I got it in Barnstaple that day for you to wear and remember our promise for one day. I hope you like it.

I hope you'll like the second present too what is that I've made up my mind to do it.

					Lots of love for ever, S.

Laura fixed the chain round her neck with tears in her eyes. Back at the station Smiler went out to the hired car. The garage man opened the door so that Smiler could sit alongside him. Seeing his long face, he grinned and said, "It ain't the end of the world, you know. But if it is, we can go back over Kersham bridge. I'll pull up so you can jump into the river and end it all. Knew a chap who did that once. Sumertime it was, though, and the river dead low. Broke his leg on a rock."

*　　*　　*

Two days later Smiler finished work early and went up to Highford House. He sat for an hour on the roof. Fria was sitting tight on her eggs. The tiercel, Prince, was nowhere to be seen until five minutes before Smiler left. Suddenly he came down from the high blue sky in a vertical stoop over the tower. Fifty feet above it he threw up in a great figure of eight, the sound of his stoop and maneuver making the air sing. Then he rolled over and dived at the roof of the house. He passed two feet above Smiler – as though, Smiler thought, he knew it was goodbye and this was his way of saying it – and then landed with a quick back flicking of wings on the tower-top. Smiler saw the movement of Fria's head in the recess and heard her call quietly to the tiercel.

He climbed down from his roof perch and made his way back through the woods, looking at his wrist-watch to check the time because he knew exactly when the little police patrol car would be coming up Bullay brook hill.

As he loitered down the hill the car came over the brook bridge, passed the farm and began to climb the hill. Smiler raised a hand and the car pulled in by him.

With a broad smile on his red face Grimble, the policeman, said, "Hullo, Samuel. Your girl-friend's gone, I hear."

"Yes," said Smiler glumly. For a moment or two he felt his courage ebbing from him and he had a sudden desire to turn and run away. Then he thought of his father and of Laura and the whole of his future and he suddenly stammered out, "I got to tell you something. . . . You see . . . well, I want to be a police . . . I mean ———"

The policeman grinned. "If you want to be a policeman, you'll have to wait. You're not old enough yet."

"No, no, I don't mean that. I mean, I'm wanted by the police."

For a moment there was silence between them and then the man said, "Say that again."

"I'm wanted by the police. I'm a sort of . . . well . . . criminal, and I want to give myself up and get it over to really prove I didn't do it, and than I can be clear with my father and Laura and . . . well, and then get on with my studies. So you'd better take me back with you."

The policeman considered this and then said calmly, "Well, now – this all sounds very sudden and serious. A criminal, eh? Sort of on the run, you mean?"

"That's right." It was funny, Smiler thought, but he was feeling easier now as though for days he had been all stuffed up with . . . well, like with overeating, and now suddenly he was back to normal and really feeling good. He went on, "You see I escaped from approved school way back early last year and I got this place working on a farm in Wiltshire and then things went wrong there and then I went to the Laird in Scotland and then again things went wrong and ———"

"Now, hang on." The policeman smiled. "This sounds as though it's going to be a long story. I think we ought to go down to the farm and go into all this with the Duchess." Then, with a twinkle in his eyes, he said, "You wouldn't describe yourself as a dangerous criminal, would you?"

"No, of course not."

"Good. Then I won't put the handcuffs on you. Come on, hop in – and let's see if we can get this cleared up."

So they went down to Bullaybrook Farm and in to the Duchess who, the moment she saw them together, had a shrewd idea of what might have happened because Laura — in strict confidence — had mentioned Smiler's father's letter, and it had been clear that Smiler had something on his mind for the last few days. The Duchess produced cider and biscuits for the policeman, Mr. Grimble. His wife had had her fortune told more than once by the Duchess who had — the last time — accurately foretold that their fourth expected child would be a girl — which it was to Mrs. Grimble's delight. All the others were boys, "little hellions", she called them.

Smiler told the policeman his story, sticking only to the main facts. When he had finished, P.C. Grimble stroked his plump chin, took a sip of his cider, looked from Smiler to the Duchess and then, as though producing a great pearl of wisdom, said, "Interesting. Very interesting."

Smiler said, "If you're going to take me away, can I have a little while to pack some things?"

P.C. Grimble nibbled at a biscuit and then said, "Well, now, let's think about that. There's a lot of things I'll have to go into with my Super, and then we'll have to get on to the Bristol police and so on. All takes a little time and it's half-past seven now and my supper's waiting at home. Then, too, you *have* given yourself up so you *aren't* likely to change you mind about it — I hope?"

"No, sir."

"Well then, what I'm going to do is put you in the charge of the Dutch — I mean, Mrs. Jago, here, until I get proper instructions, maybe tomorrow. So what I suggest now, Sammy, is that you go on up to your room and get on with a little studying, so that Mrs. Jago and me can have a quiet talk."

With a smile the Duchess, giving the nape of Smiler's neck an affectionate squeeze, pushed him gently and said, "Off with you."

When they were left along together P.C. Grimble said, "He's got guts."

"He's got more than that."

"Seems to me pretty certain he didn't do it. But that won't stop the trouble. I mean, you've had him here, harbouring as they say, and you knew all about him, and you put it around he was a nephew or something."

"Yes, I did — and I'd do it again. And so would a lot of other people who've also helped him, knowing all about him. Don't you worry about me. All my life trouble has risen with the sun for me most days. It's like an old friend now. I'd miss it."

"Well, yes. . . . Anyway, I don't suppose they'll make much of it. We're reasonable people, you know. Jimmy brought him from Scotland — that right?"

"Yes."

"Where is Jimmy these days?"

The Duchess shrugged her shoulders. "I doubt if I looked into my crystal I could find out. He goes with the wind. The family wanderlust runs hard in him."

"Like it does in Maxie Martin."

"What would you expect?"

"Seems like Maxie's got clear away."

"I suppose so."

"Mistake putting him in Princetown. He knows the moor and all this country like the back of his hand." Mr. Grimble shook his head, drained his cider and, rising, said, "But he'll never make it. They never do, you know. He'll get picked up one day. The boy's got the right idea finally. You can't go on running away from your rightful troubles. Face 'em."

"You preach a good sermon, and I agree with you."

The policeman grinned, reaching for his peaked cap, and said, "And there's plenty of things you could tell me – without looking into any old crystal ball. But you know me, I do my job but I don't go around bullying my neighbours about their business unless they ask for it. Well, I'll let you know about the boy soon's I hear."

*　　*　　*

Upstairs in his room Smiler sat at his work-table, an English grammar book open and neglected before him. On the mantelshelf the little clay figure of Johnny Pickering stood, shoulders bowed with the burden of the pebble on them. Through the window he saw the quick lightning-blue streak of a kingfisher flash down the brook. A pied fly-catcher flirted from the top of a laburnum tree in the garden and took an early moth. One of the few horses left at keep, rolled in the meadow on its back then righted itself and shook its black mane. A kestrel hovered on the far side of the stream, wing-tips lightly pulsing as it watched the movement of a field mouse foraging in the long grass.

Suddenly Smiler gave a deep sigh and pulled his diary out of the table drawer.

He wrote:

I've done it. And right afterwards I felt good about it. But gosh, now I feel awful.

More than those few lines he had not the heart and spirit to write. At the moment his world was upside down. At the moment, too, in a seaport in Wales Mr. Jimmy Jago, sitting in his car, was penning his last threatening message to Johnny Pickering. It read – THE SANDS OF TIME ARE RUNNING OUT AND YOU KNOW WHAT YOU HAVE TO DO. At that moment, too, in his hiding-vault at Highford House Maxie Martin– worried that something might have happened to Jimmy Jago – made a decision that unless he had news from him within the next fortnight he would have to take action on his own.

At supper that evening Smiler said to the Duchess after a long silence, "I had to do it, ma'am, because of the letter from my father. But I'm sorry to make trouble for you, ma'am."

"What trouble, Sammy?"

"Well, about me being your nephew and you having me here knowing everything."

"Don't give it another thought, Sammy. The police won't bother about any of that." She smiled. "If they did they'd have too many people on their hands collecting everyone who has known about or helped you since you went on the run."

After supper Smiler went to the barns because he felt that if the police came for him the next day he ought to pay a farewell visit to the animals. Actually, except for the farm creatures, there were very few boarding or circus animals left. The chimpanzee was there but he was going in a week, but the griffon and the mynah birds were gone and so was the bar-bary ram, the honey bear, and the tapir. The Duchess, Smiler had the feeling, had slowly turned against having caged animals, and she and the Ancients were now concentrating more on ordinary farming. They still took the horses, but that was different, Smiler thought, because they weren't caged up like the others. Freddie, the chimpanzee, shuffled to the front of his cage. Smiler scratched his head and then wandered round the few other cages that held boarders, his heart heavy. In a few days now he could be back in that approved school and all his freedom over the past year would have meant nothing. . . . Then he checked himself. "No," he told himself, "you got it wrong, Samuel M. Without all that you'd never have met Laura, Laura above all, and all the other people you've made friends with. And you wouldn't have known you wanted to be a vet."

He slept badly that night, waking on and off and lying in the dark, listening to the sound of the running brook, the occasional screech of a little owl – and twice the eerie churring notes of a nightjar.

The next day dawned with a change in the weather. The sky was full of low cloud and driving rain and Smiler went about his farm work waiting for the call from the Duchess that the police had arrived for him. But there was no visit or word from them that day.

But the following day P.C. Grimble called and said that the Bristol police were making enquiries. In the meantime they had passed a strict order that Samuel Miles was not to leave Bullaybrook Farm.

The next day, as Smiler was helping Bob to cut grass for silage in one of the lower valley meadows, Bill came into the field and said that Smiler was wanted at the farm right away.

Smiler said, "Is it them?"

Bob and Bill, who knew all about his trouble by now, looked at one another and then Bill said, "We'll there's a big black car in the drive."

Smiler said, "It's bound to be the police. I'd better say goodbye."

Bob shook his head. "Don't rush your fences, Sammy. It could be a lawyer to tell you your rich uncle's died in Australia and left you a fortune."

Smiler grinned. "Some hope."

But as he went up to the house the grin went from his face. There was a police driver sitting behind the wheel of the car.

In the big main room of the farm were the Duchess and a police inspector. He was a broad-shouldered man with a pleasant, square face with deep lines weathered into it as though time, trouble and the battering of the world's darker trials had marked it hard. He had grey hair and steady brown eyes and, Smiler thought, did not look the kind of man anyone would fool about with. He sat at the table. In front of him was a plate of biscuits and an untouched glass of the Duchess's cider.

The Duchess put a motherly hand on Smiler's shoulder and said, "Sammy, this is Police-Inspector Johnson from Bristol."

Smiler said nervously, "How do you do, sir?" and held out his hand.

The Inspector smiled and shook hands and then said, "I'm very well, thank you, Samuel Miles. Now sit down over there, lad, and we'll have a little chat."

As Smiler sat down, the Duchess said, "I'll leave you two alone."

When she was gone from the room, the Inspector gave Smiler a long, steady look, cleared his throat and said, "Well, you've led us a merry old dance, haven't you? And done it very well, I'd say, considering half the police in the country have been looking for you. With that fair hair, blue eyes, and freckles you stand out like a bright penny amongst a bunch of dull old coppers." He chuckled suddenly and added, "That's a joke, lad. Dull coppers."

Smiler said, "I know, sir, but . . ."

"But you weren't sure whether it was in order to laugh, eh?"

"Yes, sir. Am I going back to that approved school, sir?"

"Don't let's rush things, lad. There's some details and questions first. And — " the Inspector's voice hardened — "I want straight answers. Right?"

"Yes, sir."

"Good. You say this Johnny Pickering stole the old lady's handbag and tossed it to you as he ran away?"

"Yes, sir."

"He was not a friend of yours?"

"No, sir. I knew him, but he wasn't a friend. I didn't like him and he didn't like me."

"I see." The Inspector put his hand in his pocket and pulled out a piece of writing paper and put it in front of Smiler. "Have you ever seen that before?"

Smiler looked down at the paper. On it was written in capital letters: THE SANDS OF TIME ARE RUNNING OUT AND YOU KNOW WHAT YOU HAVE TO DO OR ELSE.

Smiler shook his head. "Never in my life, sir. What is it?"

"I ask the questions, lad. You give the answers. That note was sent to Johnny Pickering and quite a few others like it. You any idea who could have written them?"

"No, sir."

"Recognize the writing?"

"No, sir."

"How long is it since you saw Mr. Jimmy Jago?"

Puzzled, Smiler said, "Not for weeks and weeks, sir. No more's the Duchess."

The Inspector grinned. "I didn't ask you whether Mrs. Jago had seen him lately. Just answer the question straight. Have you ever heard of Maxie Martin?"

"No, sir. Who's he? Oh, I'm sorry, sir."

"Ever heard his name mentioned?"

"No, sir."

"Have there ever been any strangers visiting here? Someone perhaps you might have been told to forget you'd ever seen?"

"No sir."

"You're sure?" The Inspector's voice was suddenly severe, a little frightening.

"Yes, sir. I'm sure, sir. And please, sir – what's this got to do with me giving meself up?"

The Inspector's face slowly creased into a smile, and he said, "Nothing. That's clear. Well, that's about all, I think. There's just a few small details to get settled. Until your father gets back, do you want to stay here or go back to live with your sister and her husband in Bristol?"

For a moment or two Smiler looked blankly at the Inspector. Then, puzzled, he said, "But how can I do either, sir? I've got to go back to the approved school."

"Approved school? Oh, that." The Inspector grinned and shook his head. "That won't be necessary. Somebody else is going instead. More or less volunteered to."

"Sir?"

"Johnny Pickering, lad. We went along yesterday morning early to ask him a few questions about all this. Sitting at breakfast he was. Eating eggs and bacon and reading his morning post. He had that letter in his hand." He nodded at the paper on the table. "He took one look at my men, jumped almost out of his skin with fright and made a clean breast of things——"

"Oh, no sir," Smiler almost shouted. "He couldn't have done because the pebble hasn't dropped and——"

"I don't know anything about pebbles, lad. But the penny certainly dropped for him." He stood and gave Smiler a warm smile, and then said gravely, "Samuel Miles, it is my duty to inform you that you are a free man. You were unjustly convicted and, no doubt, in due time some form of compensation will be made to you. In the meantime – where do you want to be? Here or with your sister in Bristol?"

For a moment Smiler stared at him open-mouthed, a whirl of emotion almost making him giddy. He couldn't believe it! He couldn't believe it!

"Here – take some of this. Can't stand the stuff myself." The Inspector handed Smiler the untouched glass of cider.

Like an automaton Smiler took it and drank unthinkingly, draining the glass.

The Inspector chuckled. "You're a good Devonshire cider man, I see. Perhaps you should stay here."

"Oh, yes, sir! Yes, sir – please."

"That's it, then."

"Oh, thank you very much, sir."

"Don't thank me. Thank whoever wrote this." He picked up the letter and put it in his pocket. "Now, pop off with you. I want a last word with Mrs. Jago before I go. And, Samuel Miles, remember this always. No matter what trouble you get into, rightly or wrongly, there's only one way of dealing with it. Face up to it. Don't run away from it."

"Oh, yes, sir . . . I know that now. But still . . ." Smiler paused.

"But still what?"

"Well, sir – to be honest, although it's been a worry at times I wouldn't have missed the last year for anything, because you see, sir, I would never have known about wanting to be a vet., and Fria and the Prince, and . . . Oh, gosh!"

The Inspector cocked one eyebrow at Smiler and said, "Perhaps you'd better go and lie down. All the excitement and then the cider have been a bit too much for you."

Up in his room Smiler threw himself on his bed and kicked his legs in the air and it was all he could do not to shout his joy aloud. He was out of trouble! He could stay here! He didn't have to go back to Ethel and Albert. Better still. No approved school. Completely cleared, he was. An innocent man. Gosh, that Johnny Pickering! Blimey Old Reilly, he'd like to have seen his face when the police walked in. Bet he never finished his eggs and bacon and——"

He jumped off the bed suddenly. Johnny Pickering and the pebble. He looked at the mantelshelf, at the small clay model. There was Johnny Pickering, shoulders bowed but — miraculously — the pebble was no longer on his back. It had slipped free from his shoulders and lay on the shelf at his side. Smiler stared at it in awe. Crikeys, the Duchess had been right! (Much later the thought occurred to him that maybe the Inspector had told her everything before he had been called to the farmhouse and, while he was being questioned, she had slipped up and taken the pebble off. Then he pushed it loyally from his mind. Not the Duchess. Oh, no. She would never do a thing like that.)

That evening at supper— which was a very happy affair — Smiler said to the Duchess, "Who do you think wrote all those letters to Johnny Pickering?"

"Well, who do you think?"

"I don't know. It wasn't you, was it, ma'am?"

"No. But it was a good friend of yours." The Duchess smiled, one hand stroking Scampi who sat in his usual place on her lap. "Someone, too, who travels around a bit."

Smiler cried, "Mr. Jimmy! Is that it?"

"I'd guess so, Sammy. That's the thing about Jimmy. No trouble's too much for a friend."

"Gosh, that was pretty clever of him. Sending those things and sort of preying on Johnny Pickering's mind and then when the police walked in — Whow! No wonder he blurted it all out."

"That was in Jimmy's mind all right."

Smiler was silent for a moment or two and then he said quietly, "Why was the Inspector so interested in Mr. Jimmy and all that? And he asked me, too, if I'd heard of anyone called Maxie Martin or seen any suspicious strangers around here. I didn't get that at all. Did he ask you that, ma'am?"

"More or less."

"And do you know anything about Maxie Martin?"

Pursing her lips a little, the Duchess eyed Smiler across the table and then said quietly, "Yes, I know someone called Maxie Martin. And I think it's time you did, too. He's a man who was in Princetown prison and escaped nearly two months ago. The police are still looking for him. The reason they're interested in us is that Maxie Martin is Mr. Jimmy's half-brother."

Eyes wide, Smiler said, "An escaped convict! And he's Mr. Jimmy's half-brother. . . . Oh, I see. The police must think that Mr. Jimmy helped him."

"They certainly do."

Smiler let this sink in for a moment or two, and then he said, "I suppose I'd better not ask you if he did help Maxie Martin?"

The Duchess smiled. "You're growing up, Sammy. You couldn't have put it more diplomatically. No, I don't think you'd better ask me."

"Anyway, I don't care if he did help him. He helped me, too. He must have had a good reason. What's a half-brother?"

The Duchess shook her head, her curls bobbing gently and said, "Not anything, really. It's what they liked to think they were. The Duke and I . . . well, when Jimmy was about ten years old, we more or less adopted Maxie. His mother and father were travelling people and they both got killed in an accident on the road. So we took Maxie, and he and Jimmy became like twins. Always in one another's pockets, always in mischief and so on together."

"I see. But why did Maxie go to prison?"

"Because of his wife. She was a Romany, a lovely girl, and Maxie loved her. He thought the sun rose in her eyes in the morning and the moon floated there at night. He worshipped her. But she was a wild thing and one day she ran off with another man, after telling Maxie that she didn't love him any more. Maxie had to take it, and he did. But after about a year the other man . . . well, he treated her badly, knocked her about, and eventually he left her ill and without money and . . . well, she killed herself. So Maxie went after the man and killed him."

"Crikeys!"

"There was no way the law could punish the man, so Maxie made his own law – and he went to Princetown."

"But Mr. Jimmy stood by him and helped him to escape and even now he's——"

"That's another story, Sammy, and you can tell it any way you like to yourself. So far as I'm concerned Maxie Martin was like a second son. But, as you know, the law of the land is the law. You can't go round making your own laws."

"Oh, yes, I know that, ma'am. But I can see why Mr. Jimmy . . . well, if someone's like your own flesh and blood, you've got to stand by them, haven't you?"

The Duchess got up from her chair and looked down at him. She said solemnly. "It's a good question and as old as time, but as far as I know nobody yet has ever found a true answer to it."

That night as Smiler lay in bed in the dark, he suddenly sat up with a jerk, remembering something which had long gone from his mind. Highford House and Mr. Jimmy Jago and the little hazel besom and . . . and . . .

11

The Dangerous Days

The days of May came and went, and each fresh day put on some new brilliance and colouring to garb itself with the high panoply of summer. The nests held fledglings, hungry ever, gaping great orange-skinned throats upwards for their food. The growing young cuckoos, strangers in hedge-sparrow and reed-bunting nests, had long hoisted the legitimate fledglings into the hollow of their backs and tipped them out of the nests to die. Summer is birth and death and joy and despair. The may trees bloomed in a cloudburst of white. Dragon- and damsel-fly nymphs climbed the river-weed stalks to the surface and shucked their grotesque disguises to hatch and fly winged in blue and silver, copper and green-bronzed ephemeral glory under the sun. Gorse and bloom misted the meadows and river-banks with their Midas touch. The Spring lambs had grown leggy and awkward, forsaking the grace and joy of their young games. The rhododendrons around Highford House made a patchwork of red and purple against the dark green of firs, and the white and red candles of the chestnuts were in full blaze. It was a time of hunting and being hunted, a time of hard labour and danger for every creature that had young to feed and foster. For them this was no holiday time. Nature had opened her summer school and there was never a second chance if a single of her lessons went unheeded.

Before June was in, Smiler paid a visit to Albert and Sister Ethel in Bristol and his sister never once grumbled at him, not even when he up-set a cup of tea on the new carpet of her front parlour. He told them all his adventures and left with them a letter to be sent to his father. And he learnt that his father would soon be back home. But although he had quite enjoyed visiting them, he was happy to return to Devon.

Long before this, of course, he had written to Laura and given her all the news, and the letter which she had sent back was so private and precious that he decided that he would keep it all his life and never let anyone see it. In the letter was a photograph of Laura which he put in a frame and it now stood on the mantelshelf in his bedroom, alongside the clay figure of Johnny Pickering, pebble at his feet, which he had not been able to bring himself to throw away because he felt that it was part of his good luck and had to be kept.

He went regularly to Mr. Samkin and one evening, when Sandra was not there, he told him all about himself and his adventures. He was the only one in the neighbourhood that he told except, of course, P.C. Grimble, who now always stopped and had a chat with him when they met.

Sandra Parsons had become more of a problem to him because she was forever hanging around or asking him to tea, or to Barnstaple to go to the cinema. It was as though she knew that he had no thoughts for anyone but Laura and cheerfully and saucily took this as a challenge, enjoying his embarrassment which was considerably increased now, because whenever other people were around she would refer to him as "Sammy, my darling" – and this particularly if Trevor Green was present.

And, as often as he could, Smiler went up to Highford to visit the peregrines.

Just over four weeks after Fria's last egg had been laid the first peregrine was hatched, breaking out of its shell with the help of the rough egg-tooth on the end of its beak. Four days later there were three nestlings in the recess and Fria brooded them now, feeling their living stir beneath her body. For almost a week Fria refused to leave the eyrie, even to catch the food the tiercel would have dropped to her. The tiercel brought the food to the lip of the recess and Fria would feed there. Prince would stand by, watching her eat, and now and then they would talk to one another in harsh croakings and low whickering noises.

The first time that Smiler saw Prince bring food to the ledge he guessed that the eggs must have hatched and his hands shook as he watched the pair through his field-glasses. He decided that he would come up daily and the first time that he saw Fria and the tiercel off the eyrie together he would put up his ladder and have a look at the recess.

At Highford Maxie Martin was still living in his underground vault and was getting worried because he had not heard from Jimmy Jago and his food was beginning to run short. But until his food was gone he had no intention of leaving the place. Jimmy would come. He had all the faith in the world in Jimmy. But life he knew was full of the unexpected and if, by some stroke of Fate, Jimmy did not come – then he would have to look after himself. In the meantime he took his exercise at night and before going down at first light he would stand and watch the tower and the peregrines.

He knew before Smiler that the eggs had hatched because one morning after the first egg's hatching, he picked up from the foot of the tower part of the broken shell which Fria had cleared from the recess.

The following morning there was more shell on the ground. As the light crept over the hill Maxie would stand and watch the dark silhouette of the tiercel perched on the tower-top take slow colour from the sky, revealing sleek slate-dark wings and tail, the pale chest-mantle with its bold streaks and the face-markings growing plainer each moment. He waited always until the tiercel with a soft *kak-kak-kak* to his mate would launch himself into the air and start the first hunting sortie of the day. When that happened Maxie knew that it was time for him to go to ground.

Two weeks after the last peregrine was born Smiler saw the young. It was a Saturday afternoon and from the house roof he saw Fria come to the edge of the recess, shake her plumage and fly off to join the tiercel who was hanging a thousand feet up above the wood.

Smiler climbed down, got his ladder and set it up inside the tower. He climbed up to the back of the recess and looked in. It was a moment he was never to forget. The three peregrines were huddled together not more than a foot from him. Their eyes were now open and their bodies were covered with a greyish-white, fluffy down. One, a falcon, larger than the others, was propped up on its bottom, its back resting against the other two, and its feet were pushed out in front to keep it in position. Three of them . . . Fria's babies . . . Smiler had a moment of intense pride. Fria had come from captivity and into the wild state which should always have been hers. She had learned to look after herself, had been joined by a mate and now had young. Although he knew that it really had little to do with him, he felt as though he had been of some help . . . that, maybe, if he hadn't been around it would never have happened.

As he balanced on the ladder watching the young there was a call from outside the tower and the three peregrines suddenly stirred into activity, thin necks raised, heads wobbling and their beaks open. A shadow darkened the outside of the recess and Fria was on the ledge holding a pigeon.

Smiler stood transfixed, hidden by the inner gloom of the tower, and for the first time in his life – though he was to see it again – he saw a falcon feed her young. She plumed the dead bird and, tearing off small scraps of flesh, held them in the edges of her beak and presented them to the young who grabbed them from her, snatching and fighting feebly for their food. Now, really close to Fria, Smiler saw the change in her, the glossiness of her plumage, the gold boldness of her cere and legs, the intense, vital light of her eyes and the imperious regality of her masked face. Fria she was, Fria free and now Fria a queen in her own domain, nobility marked in her every movement.

He wrote to Laura that night and told her all about it. His diary for
that day read:

There are three peregrines. Eyases they really should be called.
They're funny things. In a way like little, feeble old men. One is much
bigger than the others so I think Fria must have brought off a falcon
and two tiercels. She flew off after feeding them and I didn't stay to
watch longer in case she spotted me.

Trevor Green came up the hill as I was coming back. He hooted
and swerved his car towards me a bit. A pretty poor sort of joke I
thought. He's got a mean face and I don't like him – but since I'm
pretty sure now he let Fria loose in the barn I suppose I should be
thankful to him.

*   *   *

As often as he could, Smiler got away to watch Fria and Prince. But
now, with June half done, there was a lot of work on the farm. In the
evenings when he was not with Mr. Samkin he worked on his own, so
that except for a quick visit during the week it was usually on Saturday
or Sunday that he made his real trips to Highford.

One weekend he climbed his ladder when the parent birds were away
from the eyrie. He was surprised at the change in the peregrines.
Already the signs of feathering showed in their down and they were active, if not entirely steady, on their feet. While he watched, two of them
fought together over the clean stripped carcase of a small bird. The
other, eyes alert, pecked at the occasional fly or bluebottle that had taken
up quarters in the recess to scavenge on the remains of the kills which
lay on the ledge. This time, as he watched, the tiercel came to the recess
with a small, collared dove. But within a few seconds of landing he
must have sensed Smiler's presence or seen some slight movement he
had made. He gave a sudden cry and flew off, leaving the young birds to
harry and worry around the dead dove, clamouring in frustration.

It was that weekend that Trevor Green – already once the instrument
of fate in Fria's life – discovered the peregrine's eyrie. On the Friday
evening he asked Sandra Parsons if she would go to a dance with him in
a near-by village on the following night. Sandra said that she couldn't
because she was going out with somebody else. This was not the truth.
She had neglected her work with Mr. Samkin recently and Mr. Samkin
had made it clear that she had better do something about it. She had
decided that she would work at her studies each evening over the
week-end but she was not going to tell Trevor Green that.

He said, "What are you doing then?"

"That's my business."

"Who are you going out with and where?"

"Wouldn't you like to know."

"I can guess. It's that Sammy Miles."

"Maybe, and then maybe not." Although basically she liked Trevor, there was an imp of mischief in her which prompted her always to tease him. One day she probably would marry him, but there was no call to let him think that he already owned her.

Sourly, Trevor Green said, "I can't see what you see in him. All those freckles and that snub nose."

"Listen to who's talking. Take a look at yourself in the mirror. You're no oil-painting. Anyway, I didn't say I was going with him. As a matter of fact – " it was fiction, and sparked in her by the glum look on Trevor's face and the exciting feeling of the power she had over him – "I'm not going out with him. It's a boy I met in Barnstaple. A doctor's son. He's tall and dark and an absolute dream – and that's all I'm going to tell you."

But Trevor Green did not believe her. He knew Sandra, knew that often she would say the first thing that came into her mind. She was going off with Sammy Miles, he was sure of that. Mooning about in the woods or talking about poetry and books.

He decided to watch the farm at Bullay brook the next evening and make sure for himself. So it was that at half-past seven when Smiler came out from an early supper and set off to pay a visit to Highford, Trevor Green was watching him from the hazel copse just above the stone bridge over the brook.

He began to follow Smiler, working up through the fields at the side of the hill road, and he was certain in his mind that he was off to meet Sandra somewhere in the woods.

Half an hour later Trevor Green, somewhat puzzled, stood hidden in the rhododendron bushes beyond Highford House and saw Smiler climb on to the roof of the ruined building and sit down behind the parapet. He decided that this must be a secret meeting-place which Sandra and Smiler used, so he settled down to wait.

A few minutes later Trevor Green saw the tiercel. Prince came back over the woods from the north, flying high and holding a greenshank which he had taken over the first tidal stretch of the Taw miles downstream.

The tiercel stooped from a thousand feet in a steep dive, whistled down over the far flank of the wood and then flattened out twenty feet above the rough pasture at the far end of the old parkland. The bird streaked across the grassland, swung sideways in a half roll to clear the ruined house and then rose to the top of the tower. Without stopping, the tiercel — which had grown more and more cautious as the young birds grew — slid by the opening of the recess, checked momentarily, dropped the greenshank on to the recess lip and was gone, winging out of sight down the slope to the river.

From the moment the tiercel had streaked across the parkland, Trevor Green had watched the whole maneuver. He was a countryman and, recently, he had heard rumours that some people had said they had seen a pair of peregrines around the district. He was quick-witted enough, too, to wonder if one of them could have been the falcon which he had set free in the barn. He remained where he was, watching the tower and Smiler.

Half an hour later Fria came out of the eyrie, her young fed, and launched herself into the air. She flew up lazily towards the big chestnut in the centre of the parkland. Trevor watched her rise higher and higher on quick wing-beats. When she was far up in the air, the tiercel came down from the heights above her, stooped past her playfully and called. Fria turned over and chased after him and for the next few minutes the peregrines played and wheeled, dived and stooped in the pale violet light of the thickening dusk.

Smiler watched them through his glasses, standing up on the roof in full sight of Trevor Green. And Trevor Green watched them, too. In the one was a surge of joyful delight at the heart-stopping aerobatics of the two birds, and in the other delight, too, but of a dark and revengeful kind. Wounded by Sandra's treatment of him, the farmer's son sought now only the satisfaction of wounding someone else in his turn. He moved away, back into the woods, knowing exactly what he would do. He would shoot both the birds. That would take the smile off Sammy Miles's face.

*　　*　　*

On the Sunday morning Smiler had an early breakfast and was away to Highford just as the dawn was beginning to break. He was early because he had promised Mr. Samkin — who in conversation with him had learned that Smiler had only been to church about four times in his life — that he would go to church with him in the village. Smiler wasn't over keen about it, but since it would please Mr. Samkin he felt he had to do it. All those dreary hymns and things, he thought to himself as he walked along, and someone spouting away about saving your soul. . . .

On this Sunday morning, too, Trevor Green was up early and making his way by a different route to Highford. Under his arm he carried his father's twelve-bore double-barrelled shotgun. The tower was only about thirty yards away from the roof-top. It was a good bet, he felt, that the peregrines had young. He'd shoot the male bird as it came with food, first barrel, and then, second barrel, blast a shot into the recess and finish the rest off. If he knew Sammy Miles, that would break his heart. Anyway, the birds were a pest, taking partridges, pheasants and young chicks. Good riddance to bad rubbish, and if anyone asked him about it he'd just keep a straight face and say he knew nothing.

On this Sunday morning, too, Maxie Martin was more reluctant than ever to return to his vault as the dawn began to break. Four days previously Jimmy Jago had turned up, climbing down into the vault just as darkness had set in. He'd arranged for Maxie to be taken aboard a small coaster that plied between Bideford and Ireland. Maxie was to be aboard before first light on the Monday morning – no questions asked. His only risk was reaching Bideford across country during Sunday night. Tonight, thought Maxie. Tonight he would walk out into the darkness and the vault would never see him again. . . .

He lingered just inside an empty window-space of the house and looked across at the tower. The light was coming fast. There was no dawn chorus now to greet the day with song. Daybreak signalled the resumption of food finding for the young. The silhouette of the tiercel stood carved against the paling sky. Maxie watched as the light strengthened and brought the bird's plumage to life. As he did so a movement away to his right caught his eye. It was Trevor Green coming out of the side of the woods with his gun under his arm. Maxie watched him for a second or two, saw the gun, knew him to be a countryman from his clothes, and guessed it was someone out for a rabbit or pigeon for the pot. He turned away into the house and made for his vault.

Trevor Green crossed to the ruined house and climbed up to the parapet. As he did so the tiercel saw and heard him. The bird dropped over the side of the tower and ghosted away down the hill to the river. On slow-flapping wings, a mode of flight that was awkward and cumbersome, disguising from some birds any warning signal that said peregrine, Prince flew down the river under the overhang of tall trees. The peal were in the river now, the young sea-trout which had wintered in the estuary of the Taw and the Torridge. One jumped twelve feet below the tiercel and his keen eyes marked it as it streaked away under water and lodged beneath a boulder. A dipper bobbed on a rock. Prince ignored it. He flew over and under the hanging branches, flapping along like a tired crow. Fifty yards ahead of him a stir of life at the edge of a bank of tall nettles and willow herb that overhung the river caught his

eye. A mallard duck edged out into the stream followed by four
ducklings. The tiercel changed from awkwardness into a flashing, steely
bolt of destruction. With quick wing-beats he dropped almost to water
level and closed in on the wild duck family. The duck saw him and
screamed in alarm as she beat forward. Her wings and feet slapped at
the water as she strove to gain height. The ducklings scattered into the
bank growths as the tiercel swept over the duck, dropped a taloned leg
and clutched her by the back, the long, pointed daggers of his toes
needling deep into her side and reaching her heart. She was dead before
he dropped to a gravel spit fifty yards farther on.

He stood on the gravel and began to pluck and plume his kill and then
spent half-an-hour eating leisurely. He bathed, made his morning toilet,
dressing and fussing and grooming his plumage, and finally flew off to
hunt for his family. Behind him a mink slid through the water and took
one of the ducklings. Before the day was out they were all to be dead.

Up at Highford House, Trevor Green was settled on the parapet, his
shotgun resting in a small embrasure through which he could cover the
top of the tower. He waited patiently for the return of the tiercel. The
old man first, he thought, and then Mum and the young ones. He
watched the recess opening on the tower, and now and then caught the
stir of Fria's head and neck as she brooded the young peregrines who
now moved restlessly under her, hunger beginning to coil in them.

Half-an-hour later Smiler came down the old shrubbery path. He
appeared around the side of the tower and began to cross to the ruined
house. Trevor Green saw him at once and anger spurted in him, but he
lay where he was unmoving and hidden, hoping that Smiler would not
come up to the roof. But it soon became clear that that was Smiler's intention. He crossed to the house, scrambled through the window-space
and reached up with his hands to begin his climb.

Trevor Green was on the point of showing himself and holding the
gun on Smiler to keep him from coming up, when low over the far end of
the wood he saw the tiercel coming back. All right, he thought, he'd deal
with the peregrines first and then let Sammy Miles make of it what he
would. He watched the tiercel slide over the edge of the wood and wing
downwards towards the tower-top. In a few seconds the bird would be
at the eyrie. Behind him Trevor Green could hear Smiler grunting to
himself and the scrape of his boots as he started the stiff climb to the
roof. Trevor Green eased his gun into position covering the recess
mouth. Whether the bird landed there or swung by in a slow roll to
throw in the prey he had brought did not matter. He would get him.
Whatever else he might not be, he was a good shot and had won many
prizes for clay-pigeon shooting.

Smiler came on to the broad roof parapet twenty yards away from Trevor Green. He pulled himself to his feet and, as he stood gathering his breath, he saw the whole scene. To him it seemed that everything was suddenly clamped into a cold, hostile immobility, freezing all movement in himself and in the world around him.

He saw the tiercel, tree-top high, Trevor Green lying prone sighting along his gun barrel, the sun-touched lip of the recess with Fria's head just showing . . . everything frozen solid as though the whole world and all life in it would never wake to action again. A wild rage rose in him and then burst from him in an angry shout. The noise magically broke the spell of stillness. The tiercel came in leisurely to the tower-top, checked, and raised long curved wing-tips to drop on the lip and present Fria with the dead pigeon he carried. At the same moment, Smiler leapt forward and threw himself on to Trevor Green's back as the farmer's son squeezed the trigger for the first barrel.

The shot blasted into the morning air, echoing against woods and walls. But the gun barrel had been slewed sideways as Smiler landed, and the shot went wide of the tower. The tiercel flew up in panic. Fria came out of the recess, wild with alarm, and flew straight across the roof of the ruined house, seeing below her as she passed the frantic movement of Smiler and Trevor Green as they rolled and fought with one another on the parapet, the gun held between them as Smiler struggled to tear it away. Fria beat up and five hundred feet above her the tiercel hung, wailing and calling, circling and waiting for her. Below him he saw, too, the fighting movement on the roof parapet. The gun roared again and the tiercel saw the two bodies separate and one fall over the inside edge of the parapet, thirty feet to the rubble- and stone-filled foundations of the house.

Circling and wailing together now, the peregrines, hanging high above their tower eyrie, saw a figure on the roof top, gun in hand, climb rapidly down. It bent over the body which had fallen, and then turned and jumped out of the window and raced away to disappear into the woods. This was Trevor Green, scared out of his wits, lost in an emergency, giving way for the moment to the simple primitive desire to put as much distance as he could between himself and a situation which he had no idea how to handle.

Smiler lay in a trough between two piles of rubble and stones, broken woodwork and shattered pieces of glass from long-broken window-panes. His body was lying on its side and his right leg was twisted grotesquely under him. Blood streamed from a long cut down one side of his face and spurted too from the inside of his left wrist where the main artery had been slashed by a jagged piece of glass in the rubble as he landed.

For a moment or two he came out of shock and semi-unconsciousness and shouted as loud as he could, instinctively and urgently, "Help! Help!" Then in front of his eyes, the sky and the ruined walls of the old house wheeled and dipped and spun round dizzily. He lapsed into unconsciousness.

Below ground in his vault, Maxie Martin had heard first of all the sound of the two shots then, in the following silence, the call for help from Smiler. But for one simple expedient which he had resorted to he might never have heard a sound. With Summer's coming, despite the underground channels leading off the vault, it was hot and stuffy in the chamber and he had taken to wedging a piece of wood under his manhole cover, leaving a gap of an inch or two for the hot, stuffy air to escape upwards.

A few seconds later, though moving warily and alert for trouble, Maxie stood over Smiler. He recognized him at once, for Jimmy Jago on his brief visit had told him something about Smiler. Maxie, although an impulsive, emotional man, was also a practical man. He had been in more than one emergency in his life. One look at Smiler told him that his right leg was almost certainly broken, that he was unconscious and could possibly have internal injuries, but more than that — he was bleeding to death from the blood that pumped away from his cut artery.

Maxie knelt beside him, ripped off his own shirt and began tearing it in lengths. Then he found a stone to bind into the temporary tourniquet which he must make to hold the pressure point on the inside of Smiler's left elbow. He worked swiftly and urgently, but expertly, and by the time he was finished his hands, arms and bare torso were covered with blood. Easing Smiler into a more natural position but not touching his leg, he went outside and brought water in an old can from his little tank and poured it over Smiler's face.

The cold water brought Smiler slowly round. He saw a face swimming above him and heard a man's voice saying, "Don't try to move. Do you understand? Whatever you do — don't move. I'm going to get help. You understand?"

Smiler had just enough strength to nod feebly and then he drifted off into darkness.

Maxie climbed out of the house and began to run for the shrubberies. He ran as he had never run before, half naked and smeared in blood. There was no power in his mind or his body that could have stopped him. He was running for help, running from danger into danger, into the end of a dream which he had cherished for weeks in his vault. And he ran, too, because there was a virtue in him which could not be denied.

Twenty minutes later he was in Bullaybrook Farm explaining what had happened to the Duchess. She heard him out calmly and then went to the telephone and put in an emergency call for an ambulance. When she had finished she came back and stood over him.

Maxie said, "I'll go back and stay with him till they come."

The Duchess said, "No. Bob's in the yard. He will go." She reached out and put her hand on his head, and went on, "What are you going to do?"

Maxie took her hand. "What can I do? I must take my chance — you've got to tell them something. Jimmy's got it all fixed for tonight. Jimmy would lie for me. But I won't lay that on you. Tell them the truth and I'll take my chance. All I ask for is a wash and a shirt."

The Duchess said, "Sitting in the painted tent, all I saw in the crystal for you was a man running, half-naked, covered in blood. No more." She moved towards the door then turned and went on, "I'm going to tell Bob. When I get back you must be gone. You know where everything is. I don't know the justice of things. There's only One who knows that. But there's always prayers — and mine are for you."

She went to find Bob, and when she came back Maxie was gone.

12

Envoi

Smiler was taken to the hospital. His right leg and two ribs were broken. The rough tourniquet on his arm had saved his life. It was almost the end of August before he was fit to move about normally again and his father was home and living in lodgings in Barnstaple to be near him.

Smiler said nothing about Trevor Green and his attempt to shoot the peregrines which had led to his fall. He said that it had been an accident, but after a week Trevor Green found his courage, made a clean breast of the whole affair, and discovered a new self-respect.

The Duchess told the police about Maxie Martin— though not of the vault at Highford since they did not ask — and the search for him was renewed, but he still eluded them, though the Duchess learned through Jimmy that Maxie had never joined the coaster which was to have taken him to Ireland.

Mr. Samkin visited Smiler regularly in hospital and afterwards and, when he was fit enough, Smiler went on with his studies, determined to start taking his examinations the following year.

Laura came down from Scotland for a few days, and they wrote to one another regularly and they both looked forward to Christmas when Sir Alex Elphinstone had invited Smiler and his father to spend the holiday with him in his castle on the loch.

At the end of August Smiler's father went off on a two-month trip. He was a working man and could not afford to stay idle, and Smiler — after a farewell visit to the Duchess, Jimmy Jago and the peregrines, went to live with his sister Ethel and Albert in Bristol, which to his surprise he found far from unpleasant.

On his last visit to the peregrines, the young birds were flying, two tiercels and a falcon. A few local people had quietly formed a protection society to look after them. In those few hours while Smiler lingered near the tower, watching the family in the air, the young peregrines learning their flying skills from Fria and Prince, he was filled with a quiet joy at the sense of freedom and purpose that they seemed to communicate to him. He had had a tiny hand in it. Nothing could ever take that from him.

●　　●　　●